12-

THE RAMAYANA

THE
RAMAYANA

Ramesh Menon

NORTH POINT PRESS

A division of Farrar, Straus and Giroux

New York

North Point Press
A division of Farrar, Straus and Giroux
19 Union Square West, New York 10003

Copyright © 2001 by Ramesh Menon
Introduction copyright © 2003 by Ramesh Menon
Distributed in Canada by Douglas & McIntyre Ltd.
Printed in the United States of America
Originally published in 2001 by Writers Club Press, Lincoln, Nebraska, as
The Ramayana: A Modern Translation
First North Point Press edition, 2003

Library of Congress Cataloging-in-Publication Data
Valmiki.
    [Ramayana. English]
    The Ramayana / Ramesh Menon.
      p. cm.
    Originally published: Lincoln, Nebraska : Writers Club Press, 2001.
    ISBN 0-86547-660-8 (hc. : alk. paper)
    I. Ramesh Menon.   II. Title.

BL1139.22 .E54 2003
294.5'92204521—dc21

2002027896

Designed by Jonathan D. Lippincott

www.fsgbooks.com

1 3 5 7 9 10 8 6 4 2

FOR

JANAKI AMMA AND REKHA JANAKI

CONTENTS

INTRODUCTION

The Ramayana is an epic tale set in the forested India of prehistorical times. One of India's most beloved and enduring legends, it represents historical fact to millions, who worship Rama, prince of Ayodhya, as an incarnation of the God Vishnu. Regardless of their religious orientation, Indians see it as a great work of literature, the story of a war between good and evil, and as a document prescribing a code of conduct that is still widely regarded. Rama is the hero of the legend, and the *ayana* is his journey, both physical and spiritual.

The plot is fairly simple, but the path that the main characters have to follow to fulfill their missions and attain grace is arduous. Prince Rama is about to be crowned *yuvaraja*, the heir apparent, by his father King Dasaratha, who wants to hand his kingdom down to his adored eldest son. Instead, a palace intrigue involving one of the king's wives ends in Rama's banishment to the forest for fourteen years. His wife Sita, whom he has just married, and his brother Lakshmana accompany him.

Wandering in exile, the three encounter several sages, or *rishis*, living austere lives in *asramas*, hermitages, and meditating in the wilds. From them the travelers hear many wondrous legends of bygone ages, the beginnings of the world. The *kshatriyas*, the warrior princes Rama and Lakshmana, also rid the jungles of countless *rakshasas*, demons that prey on the hermits who, by their constant worship, are the very holders of the earth.

When Ravana, Emperor of the *rakshasas*, hears that thousands of them have been slain, and when he is told of Sita's peerless beauty, he abducts her to his island home of Lanka (the Sri Lanka of today). Rama and Lakshmana immediately set out to rescue the princess. A race of monkeys with extraordinary powers, called *vanaras*, help them find her. A *vanara* army, which includes Hanuman, who is the son of the wind and worshipped as a God in India, goes with the brothers to fight Ravana and his awesome demon legions and to rescue Sita.

As a reward for years of penance, the God Siva has granted Ravana a boon of invincibility from death at the hands of any of the greater races of divine and demonic beings. Ravana has quickly become undisputed monarch of the world, "the greatest of all the created beings of his time." Though he is a matchless warrior, a powerful king, and an unequaled scholar, he is the epitome of evil, and his bloodthirsty demons have overrun the earth to tyrannize and corrupt helpless humankind. However, Ravana had not asked Siva for invincibility against mortal men, believing them too puny to harm him. Thus Vishnu, the Blue Savior in the Indian Trinity, is born as a human prince, Rama, to rid the world of the Demon. As an Avatara, a divine incarnation, Rama has the qualities of a human being but the weaponry and the strength of a God. Rama comes to kill the *rakshasas*, break the bonds of darkness, and restore *dharma* to creation. The notion of *dharma* is as old as the Indian tradition; its meaning encompasses such broad concepts as duty, work, righteousness, morality, justice, cosmic law and harmony, and eternal truth.

The themes of the Ramayana are timeless and universal. Goodness and love figure in significant ways—a father's love for his son, a son's love for his father, four brothers' love for one another, a husband's love for his wife and a wife's for her husband, and, not least, the love of friends for each other—as do avarice, evil, deceit and treachery, nobility of character, and selflessness and devotion. In short, all the experiences and values of the human spirit are woven throughout the legend, though they are rendered in titanic proportions.

Rama himself is the *Maryada Purushottaman*: the man of perfect honor; the perfect man. He is perfect because he is God incarnate. Yet, because of who he is and because his mission is in essence to save humankind, he must suffer more than any other man. In this sense, the epic certainly invites comparison to that other great ancient work, the Bible. The spirit of the extraordinary prince Rama permeates the epic, even as the spirit of Jesus of Nazareth does the New Testament. Both suffer and each one is crucified in his way, to save humankind. Both finally triumph.

More than anything else, reading the Ramayana brings the reader close to the noble, holy, and living spirit of Rama. Regardless of which religion one professes, or if one is an agnostic or an atheist, the touch of Rama's spirit is a profound, healing contact. This is the essential aim of the epic, for, like Christ, the prince of Ayodhya is an embodiment of goodness and gentleness, of sacrifice, and, above all, of love.

The Ramayana is also infused with the spirit of Rama's wife Sita. Hindus believe that she was an incarnation of the God Vishnu's consort, the Goddess Lakshmi. To this day Sita remains the archetypal image of chaste Indian womanhood. The Ramayana says that Ravana of Lanka was so powerful that even more than Rama's prowess, it was Sita's chastity and courage that ultimately were needed to vanquish the Demon. Ravana, whom no woman, no queen or princess of any race of heaven, earth, or the netherworlds had ever resisted, finds Sita proof against his every temptation, blandishment, and threat. This undermines and finally breaks his spirit before Rama actually kills him.

If Rama is the perfect man, Sita is no less the perfect woman. She suffers at least as much as he does, perhaps more. In the end she proves herself even Rama's superior. The image of the faithful Sita and her immaculate love and devotion for her husband have flowed down the ages to become unfading symbols of the ideal woman and wife.

The classical Indian artistic tradition is a devotional one, whether in music, literature, dance, painting, sculpture, or architecture. The sole object of art is worship, to give praise and to invoke *bhakti*, religious adoration and ecstasy, both in the artist and in those that experience his or her work. The purpose of the Ramayana was never less than to awaken the reader spiritually and set him on the great journey that finally, if after many lives, leads to the last goal of all existence—to *moksha*, *nirvana*, the truth that frees, to God. Without exception, the masters of old have said that listening to the Ramayana or reading it serves to exorcise one's sins, from this life and others, and to purify one's soul.

At the same time, the Ramayana is an expression of a liberal and earthy tradition, one that deals with the realities of greed, lust and power, war and kingship, nobility, tolerance, heroism, and suffering, and with the magnificent, joyful, and tragic inevitability of fate—the human condition. In this sense, the legend has all the hallmarks that distinguish an immortal classic of literature: it enshrines the deepest, most timeless values of humankind, while also being an incomparably enchanting tale. Above all, the Ramayana is a love story, written more than a thousand years before romantic love became one of the defining themes of Western literature.

The Ramayana is based on some of the oldest surviving legends in the world, though its exact age remains indeterminate. Modern scholars say it is more than two thousand years old, and place its approximate date of composition somewhere around 300 B.C. The devout Hindu believes it was composed several hundred millennia ago, in the *treta yuga*. The epic was called the Adi Kavya, the first poem of the world. A *kavya* is the work of a *kavi*, "one who sees"—a seer-poet, a visionary. It is said that the poet Valmiki was first inspired to tell the story of Rama by the God Brahma, the Creator himself. Valmiki composed the legend as an epic poem, in twenty-four thousand *slokas*, couplets, in high Sanskrit, in a complex meter called the *anushtup*. The *slokas* were grouped into *sargas*, chapters, which formed seven *kandas*, or sections.

The epic has come to us through countless generations of *gurus* and *sishyas*, masters and disciples, transmitted through the ages in the ancient oral tradition. Since its original composition there have been many interpolations and embellishments by numerous, now nameless, raconteurs—from saints and bards to grandmothers passing the story on to their grandchildren during long summer nights—in many languages and traditions.

Since it was first composed, the Ramayana has remained an essential component of the arts. Portions of it have been rendered as song and dance, in the classical and folk traditions of the many regions, languages, and dialects of India. In Kerala, the southernmost state, episodes from the Ramayana are performed in the heavily stylized Kathakali dance form. The dancers wear exaggerated, padded costumes and lofty wooden crowns and paint their faces in bright vegetable dyes to portray the mythic characters. A short episode from the epic is performed over several hours, traditionally in the courtyard of a temple. The Kathakali begins at dusk and extends into the small hours by the light of oil lamps.

In northern India, during the *Deepawali*, the season of lamps, the Ramayana is performed in full as open-air theater, usually at a large fairground. These nightlong performances are called *Ramleelas*—literally, the play or romance of Rama—and people from every walk of life throng to them, wrapped in thick blankets and warm shawls to keep the cold at bay.

Scenes from the Ramayana have been carved in stone on the walls of temples across India and beyond. The legend of Rama, most wise and loving, powerful and self-effacing prince and deliverer, has spread throughout Southeast Asia, to Sri Lanka, Nepal, Bangladesh, Malaysia, Laos, Vietnam, Thailand, Cambodia, and Indonesia, where it is read, told, sung, and danced in a dazzling array of native forms and idioms.

At least four retellings of the Ramayana into other Indian vernacular languages are literary classics in their own right: the *Iramavatara*, the Tamil Ramayana by the poet Kampan (twelfth century); the Bengali Ramayana of Krittibas Ojha (late fourteenth century); Tulsidas's *Ramacharitmanas* in Hindi (sixteenth century); and Ezhutthachan's *Aadhyatma* (or spiritual) *Ramayanam* in Malayalam (also sixteenth century).

There is a brief and relatively recent tradition of English translations and retellings of the Ramayana by Indian and Western writers. A number of these are far too short to capture the magnitude and grandeur of the original; others are rather too secular in presenting what is also basically scripture. In India, Chakravarti Rajagopalachari's Ramayana, first published in 1951, R. K. Narayan's slender 1972 volume, and Kamala Subramaniam's, published in 1981, are retellings by writers of generations before my own. They have all been very popular, each going into several editions. With the exception of Subramaniam's book, they are too short to be anywhere near epical. Also, all three either use "Victorian" or "Shakespearean" English or are very matter-of-fact in style. A more recent English Ramayana, contemporary in tone, was written by Arshia Sattar, whose rendering is elegant and knowledgeable but is also a secular and scholarly one.

For their times, these English versions of the Ramayana were pathbreaking. When they were written, the Ramayana was being progressively lost to young Indians who had been educated in schools where English was the medium of instruction and the system of education itself had become "modern," westward-looking, and irretrievably secular. By the twentieth century, it was Shakespeare who was revered by the colonized Indian, rather than Valmiki or Vyasa, author of the Mahabharata. During colonial times and after Indian independence in 1948, the spiritual tradition of the Ramayana and the Mahabharata was sidelined, even actively suppressed, in favor of analytical Western thought and attitudes, especially socialist ones.

Among the retellings by foreigners, the best known recently have been ones by the late William Buck and by the Briton Kenneth Anderson, who calls himself Krishna Dharma because he belongs to the Hare Krishna movement in England. Mr. Buck's translation is a short, chatty one, which takes a great deal of liberty with the actual story. Mr. Anderson's is longer, more "epical."

One must not ignore the actual translations of the epic, of which there are a few, including the three-volume edition by Hari Prasad Shastri. They are full-length, line-by-line endeavors, often with the Sanskrit text included, usually done by an Indian Sanskrit scholar or a member of a Hindu religious order. These have another sort of drawback: the English the translators use tends to be even more archaic than that of the few Indians who sought to retell rather than translate. The Sanskrit scholars' language is literal rather than literary, and hardly reflects either the poetry or the mystery of the Ramayana. I should also note the ongoing project at the University of California, Berkeley, to translate and annotate the entire text, which will consist of seven volumes and total more than two thousand pages when completed.

Though I have taken few liberties with the story or its sequence as it has come down in India, my Ramayana is not a scholar's translation, but a novelist's re-creation of the legend. The book is not based on a Sanskrit text, but on other English versions. The task I set myself, for which there did seem to exist a genuine place in our world of books, was to write an impassioned English Ramayana that is true to the spirit and story of the original. I felt I needed to write it well enough so that a reader of the early twenty-first century would want to read it for pleasure. I must further try to preserve some of the simple lyricism of the Ramayana, in what definitely has to be a prose rendition if anyone at all is to read it. My book must be not so short that it trivializes an epic, nor so voluminous as to be forbidding. It must be, first and last, a work of worship, but it must also be entirely modern and exciting without ever turning into kitsch. As I worked on it for the last ten years, I regarded the completion of this book as an act of faith, an offering to Rama.

Now that my work is finished, I have come to believe that any enterprise such as this one is always severely tested, but finally rewarded. Looking back, I see that along every step of the journey, whether I was aware of it or not at the time, there was help given me, and strength. And I hope that I might even have succeeded, in some measure, in what I set out to do.

Three hundred sixty-five human years make one year of the Devas and Pitrs, the Gods and the manes.

Four are the ages in the land of Bharata—the krita, the treta, the dwapara, and the kali. The krita yuga lasts 4,800 divine years, the treta 3,600, the dwapara 2,400, and the kali 1,200; and then another krita yuga begins.

The krita or satya yuga is the age of purity; it is sinless. Dharma, righteousness, is perfect and walks on four feet in the krita. But in the treta yuga, adharma, evil, enters the world and the very fabric of time begins to decay. Finally, the kali yuga, the fourth age, is almost entirely corrupt, with dharma barely surviving, hobbling on one foot.

A chaturyuga, a cycle of four ages, is twelve thousand divine years, or 365 times 12,000 human years long. Seventy-one chaturyugas make a manvantara; fourteen manvantaras, a kalpa. A kalpa of a thousand chaturyugas, twelve million divine years, is one day of Brahma, the Creator.

Eight thousand Brahma years make one Brahma yuga; a thousand Brahma yugas make a savana; and Brahma's life is 3,003 savanas long.

One day of Mahavishnu is the lifetime of Brahma.

THE DEMON'S BOONS

The Rakshasa sat in penance on the Himalaya, amidst five fires. Four he lit around himself to heat the blazing rock he sat upon; the fifth was the pitiless sun above. Ravana was the son of the Rishi Visravas, who was Brahma's own grandson. Ten-headed, magnificent Ravana sat worshipping the God Siva. But even after he had sat for a thousand years, Siva did not appear before him.

Growing impatient one day, the Demon picked up his sword, cut off one of his ten heads, and, chanting Siva's name, fed it to the fire. Still the Lord did not come to him. Another thousand years passed; Ravana severed another head and fed that into the fire. But even now, Siva did not come.

Ravana did not flinch. In nine thousand years, the Rakshasa cut off nine of his heads and fed them to the agni. But there was no sign of Siva. When ten thousand years of perfect worship had passed, Ravana reached for his sword again: to hew off his tenth and final head, and make an end of himself. Then his eyes were blinded with light such as they had never seen before. At the heart of the luster stood Siva, the God of Gods, smiling at his fierce devotee.

Raising his hand in a blessing over the Rakshasa, Siva said, "Ask for any boon you want."

Ravana asked for strength that no other creature in the universe possessed. After the offering of nine heads, Siva could not refuse him. He restored the Rakshasa's heads and gave him strength that would make him master of the earth one day.

But Ravana was not satisfied with one boon. He resumed his fervid penance, now in the name of his own great-grandsire: Brahma, the Creator. In a hundred years, Brahma also stood, four-faced and iridescent, before the Demon. "What boon do you want, Ravana? Ask me for anything."

Ravana's tapasya had been so remarkable he could have asked for moksha, enlightenment. But being a rakshasa, he said, "Siva has already given me boundless strength. Pitama, you make me immortal!"

Brahma replied, "Immortality I cannot give, not to any of the created. Ask for another boon."

Ravana thought for a moment. Then he said shrewdly, "Then bless me that I never find death at the hands of a Deva, Danava, Daitya, Asura, rakshasa, gandharva, kinnara, charana, siddha, or any of the divine and demonic beings of heaven and earth."

With a sigh, knowing what the consequences of this boon would be, Brahma said, "So be it," and vanished.

Ravana's triumphant roar echoed through the world. The Himalaya trembled; the sea rose in hilly waves and dashed against the shores of Bharatavarsha. Of course, the Rakshasa had thought it beneath his dignity to ask for invincibility against the puny race of men. For which mortal man could hope to threaten awesome Ravana's life? He was certain that now he was immortal.

And quickly, with his two boons, the Demon became sovereign of all he surveyed. For long ages he ruled, and darkness spread . . .

Hanuman could see into the little cloister from his leafy perch. He saw Sita shiver, when she knew the Lord of Lanka had arrived. Quickly she covered her body with her hands. Like frightened birds, her eyes flew this way and that, avoiding Ravana's smoldering gaze as he came and stood, tall and ominous, before her.

He drank deeply of the sight of her. He did not appear to notice how disheveled she was, or the dirt that streaked her tear-stained face. Before him, Ravana, master of the earth, saw his hopes, his life, his heaven and hell; and, if he had known it, his death as well. She stared dully at the bare ground on which she sat. She was like a branch, blossom-laden, but cut away from her mother tree and sorrowing on the ground.

Ravana fetched a sigh. In his voice like sleepy thunder he said, "Whenever I come here, you try to hide your beauty with your hands. But for me, any part of you I see is absolutely beautiful. Honor my love, Sita, and you will discover how deep and true it is. My life began when I first saw you and yet you are so cruel to me."

She said nothing, never looked up at him. Hanuman, little monkey in his tree, sat riveted by what he saw and heard. Ravana's eyes roved over her slender form, and they blazed. He whispered, "Sita, give yourself to me! I will love you as women only dream of being loved. Rule my heart, rule me, and be queen of all the earth. We will walk hand in hand in this asokavana, just we two, and you will know what happiness is."

But again she set a long blade of grass between herself and him, like a sword. She said, "I am another man's wife, Rakshasa. How can you even think of me as becoming yours, when I am already given? Not just for this lifetime, but forever, for all the lives that have been, and all those to come. I have always belonged to Rama and always will. You have so many women in your harem. Don't you hide them from the lustful gazes of other men? How is it, then, you cannot conceive that I would be true to my Rama? That it is natural for me, because I love him."

He looked away from her. Not that he saw anything except her face, even when he did; but he could not bear what she said, which was so savage and so true. He had never encountered such chastity, and to believe in it would mean denying everything he had lived for. Ravana turned his gaze away from her and a smile curved his dark lips.

Undaunted, Sita continued, "You court doom for yourself and your kingdom. Have you no wise men in your court to advise you against your folly?"

He laughed. "They all know I am a law unto myself. They know I am invincible."

"You have violated dharma; punishment will come to you more swiftly than you think. You don't know Rama. He is not what you imagine him to be. You speak of this sea being an obstacle between him and me. But I say to you, Ravana, even if the ocean of stars lay between us my Rama would come to find me."

BOOK ONE

BALA KANDA

{The beginning}

1. On the banks of the river Tamasa

"Holy One, I wonder if any man born into the world was blessed with every virtue by your Father in heaven."

Long ago, the sage Valmiki sat meditating in his hermitage on the banks of the Tamasa. The river murmured along beside the dark, gaunt rishi, whose hair hung down to his shoulders in thick dreadlocks. But otherwise the secluded place was silent; not even birds sang, lest they disturb Valmiki's dhyana.

Suddenly the silence was shattered; the air came alive with the abandoned plucking of a vina. A clear voice sang of the Blue God who lies on his serpent bed, upon eternal waters. Valmiki's eyes flew open. Though he had never seen him before, he had a good idea who his visitor was.

Narada, the wanderer, was Brahma's son, born from his pristine thought in time out of mind. A curse had been laid on Narada before the earth was made: that he would roam the worlds without rest. Once he sent his brother Daksha's sons, who wanted to create the first races of men, on an impossible quest. He had asked them how they could become creators unless they first saw the ends of the universe. And Daksha cursed Narada to wander forever homeless and restless himself, for the endless wandering he sent those children on.

A fine aura enveloped Narada. Valmiki's disciples stood gaping at him, until their master called briskly to them. Then they ran to fetch arghya, milk and honey, for the guest, who accepted their offering graciously.

Valmiki folded his hands. "Be seated, Maharishi."

Valmiki sat beside the hermit from heaven, by the languid Tamasa. As if he sought something, Narada stared up and down the river's course, while Valmiki sat absorbed.

Narada strummed a fluid phrase on his vina. "A blessing, dear Valmiki, for your thoughts!"

Valmiki laughed. "Muni, you are as subtle as Vayu the Wind. You can enter men's minds and read their thoughts; and surely mine as well." He paused, then declared, "Holy One, I wonder if any man born into the world was blessed with all the virtues by your Father in heaven."

"Tell me what the virtues are, and I will tell you the man who has them."

Valmiki began in his inward way, enunciating each attribute carefully: "Integrity, bravery, righteousness, gratitude, dedication to his beliefs, a flawless character, compassion for all the living, learning, skill, beauty, courage beyond bravery, radiance, control over his anger and his desires, serenity, a lack of envy, and valor to awe Indra's Devas." As Narada's eyes grew wistful, Valmiki continued. "I know I am asking for perfection in a mere mortal. But I wondered if a man of this world could have all these, which not even the Gods possess." The sage was convinced his perfect man could only be the figment of a romantic imagination.

Narada still gazed out over the river's crisp currents, as if the water on which the noon sun sparkled could conjure the image of Valmiki's paragon. At last he said softly, "In these very times such a man was born into the world. His name is Rama."

Narada beckoned to Valmiki's disciples to come closer as he began his story, as if it was a secret that not the jungle behind them nor their thatched huts on its hem should share, so precious was it. Weaving his tale into the river's drift, Narada began the legend of Rama, prince of Ayodhya, who was as noble as the sea is deep, as powerful as Mahavishnu, whose Avatara he was when the treta yuga was upon the world, as steadfast as the Himalaya, handsome as Soma the Moon God, patient as the Earth, generous as Kubera, just as Dharma; but his rage if roused like the fire at the end of time. His audience sat entranced, as heedless of the time that passed as they were of the flowing river. Valmiki sat in the lotus posture with his eyes shut, to listen to the tale of a human prince who was as immaculate as the stars.

The Tamasa turned dark with dusk, but the disciples sat entranced. Never before had they heard such a story. Twilight turned to night; the moon rose over the river. Narada's legend was of a living man. But he did not speak about Ramarajya, when a perfect kshatriya ruled Ayodhya as the world's heart, but of a time before Rama became king, the bitter time of his exile. It was those years in the wilderness that left such an indelible impression upon the memory of the race of men.

Moonlight turned to darkness, and darkness to scarlet dawn on the susurrant eddies of the Tamasa, when Narada finished his epic of Rama. There was not a dry eye among his listeners at what finally befell the exquisite Sita. Valmiki's disciples saw even their master wept.

Narada broke his trance; he stretched his ageless body and rose. With an airy wave, he was off again, plucking on his vina. Yawning, the disciples set about their daily tasks: fetching water and kindling the morning fires. But Valmiki stood a long time staring after Narada.

2. A curse

Long after Narada's visit to his asrama, the story of Rama haunted Valmiki. Months after he heard the legend he saw images of Rama's life before his eyes, whenever he shut them to meditate.

One morning, Valmiki walked along the banks of the Tamasa with his youngest disciple. Spring was in the air, abundant and heady. The sage saw the river was sparklingly clear, and decided to bathe in it. He sat dipping his feet in the jeweled flow and a fine languor stole over him. He said to his boy of sixteen summers, "Look, child, the water is like the heart of a rishi."

The serene youth handed his master the valkala, the tree bark with which to scrub himself. Above them, a kadamba spread its awning, and in the living branches they heard the sweetest song: two krauncha birds were mating there, abandoned to spring's fever. The male danced around his mate, fluttering his wings dizzily when he hopped onto her back. A smile on his lips, Valmiki leaned back to watch the ritual of love. On and off his mate the male krauncha danced, his joyful song setting the leaves alight; and she sang her ecstasy.

Suddenly, the air was riven by a vicious whistling. An arrow flew savagely to its mark. With a scream, the male krauncha fell off his mate's back and down to the ground below. His breast was a mess of blood and broken feathers; the arrow still stuck in him like a monstrous curse. For a few moments his little body heaved in agony; then he was gone. The shocked silence of the woodland was broken by the screams of the she bird.

Valmiki sprang to his feet, trembling. He saw a pale-eyed hunter stalk into the clearing. The she bird screamed her grief at him. The jungle man squinted up at her and grinned at Valmiki, showing stained teeth like fangs. A curse erupted from the rishi:

Ma Nisada pratishtam tvamagamah shasvatih samah,
Yatkrauncha mithunade kamavadhih kamamohitam!

Glaring the shifty fellow down, Valmiki strode from that glade. Part of him wondered at the strange expression of his anger; it had such a lilt to it, though the doom it pronounced on the hunter was final: because he had killed the bird at love, he would not live the full span of his life.

All day, those words returned to the sage's mind and echoed there in cadence. Valmiki thought: Because I spoke in such a rage of sorrow my curse welled from me in rhythm and meter. Later, as night fell, his disciples sat around their meditating guru. Under rushlights hung on the mud walls of the hermitage, they studied sacred scriptures inscribed on palm leaves.

Valmiki himself could not forget the morning. Again and again he heard the rapturous song of the birds; the evil hum of the arrow; the cry of the male krauncha and the soft sound of his small body striking the ground. And then the she bird's frantic screams. He saw the hunter's pale eyes, slanted like a cat's in his face, and he heard his own voice pronouncing judgment on the man in perfect meter.

Valmiki heard a gasp from his disciples. He opened his eyes, and it seemed as if a piece of the sun had fallen among them: Brahma had come to the asrama, dazzling the night.

Valmiki prostrated himself before the Creator. The padadhuli, the spirit dust from the God's holy feet, washed into him in golden waves. Brahma blessed the rishi and his sishyas, enfolding them in his pulsing aura, which surely removed their sins of a hundred lives. They stood before him with their eyes cast down because they could not look directly at his splendor.

In his voice of ages, Brahma said, "Valmiki, I put the sloka on your tongue with which you cursed the hunter. I sent Narada to you, so you could hear the legend of the perfect man from him. I want you to compose the life of Rama in the meter of the curse. You will see clearly not only into the prince's life, but into his heart; and Lakshmana's, Sita's, and Ravana's. No secret will be kept from you and not a false word will enter your epic. It shall be known as the Adi Kavya, the first poem of the earth. As long as Rama is remembered in the world of men, so shall you be. The epic you are going to compose will make you immortal."

His hand raised in a blessing, Brahma faded from their midst. The dazed Valmiki found himself helplessly murmuring his curse again, *"Ma Nisada pratishtam tvamagamah,"* in the meter called anushtup.

3. The Ramayana

On the banks of the Tamasa, Valmiki composed the epic of Rama. He sat facing east on a seat of darbha grass. His mind was as still as the Manasa lake upon the northern mountain, so the images of Narada's inspiration played on it like sunbeams. Noble words sprang in a crystal stream from his heart, as his disciples sat around him, listening breathlessly.

In a week, Valmiki composed twenty-four thousand verses. The legend came to him as if he was just an instrument and the real poet was another, far greater than himself. He divided the vast poem into six books* and five hundred cantos. When he had completed his work of genius, he called it the Ramayana.

When Valmiki had finished the Ramayana, two young men appeared in his asrama. They were as handsome and alike as the Aswini twins of heaven, and had voices like gandharva minstrels. The rishi knew they had been sent by providence. He taught them his poem. Lava and Kusa learned the Ramayana even as they heard it from the poet's lips, and they sang it as Valmiki himself could not. Valmiki knew Brahma had chosen them to take his Adi Kavya through the sacred land.

When they had Valmiki's epic by heart, Lava and Kusa prostrated themselves before him. With his blessing, they went from asrama to asrama in those holy times. Clad in tree bark and deerskin, Lava and Kusa came with their lambent song. Their voices matched as one, the Ramayana flowed from them like another Ganga. Rishis who heard them were enchanted and blessed the beautiful youths.

---

*The seventh book, the Uttara Kanda, and also large portions of the Bala Kanda are not usually ascribed to Valmiki, but are said to be later interpolations.

One day, Lava and Kusa came to a military camp on the edge of a great forest. There a king of the earth had undertaken an aswamedha yagna, a horse sacrifice. The twins went into his presence and, in an assembly of the greatest rishis, sang the Ramayana. The king climbed down from his throne and came to sit on the ground among the common people. He sat spellbound, and tears ran down his dark and sealike face. But Lava and Kusa did not know the epic they sang was about this very man, to whom inscrutable destiny had brought them.

He was Rama himself and he was their father.

4. Ayodhya

This is a story, sang the twins, to the rhythmical plucking of their vinas, of the ancient line of kshatriyas descended from Manu, made immortal by his son Ikshvaku, and later by Sagara and his sons. It is the tale of a perfect man, the greatest in his noble line.

The kingdom of Kosala was cradled by the river Sarayu. Kosala was ruled by kings of the race of Brahma's son Manu, descended from Surya, the Sun God. Down the deep streams of time, the House of Ikshvaku was renowned for the justice and valor of its kings. Kosala was a blessed country, verdant and fertile; ages ago at its heart, Manu the lawmaker created a city to be his capital and called it Ayodhya.

The turrets of Ayodhya reached for the stars and her fame as a focus of dharma on earth was known in Devaloka, the realm of the Gods. As glorious as Indra's Amravati above was Ayodhya in the world. Ancient trees lined her wide streets, washed with scented water at dawn and dusk so the city of truth was always swathed in fragrance.

Great Dasaratha ruled Ayodhya with bhakti as his scepter. His people were free from green envy, that insidious corrupter of nations: their king's virtue flowed among them like a river of fortune, and their hearts were wise and serene. The mean and ugly of spirit were never born in Ayodhya; why, it seemed a race of Gods had been incarnated in the mortal world to people this greatest of cities.

King Dasaratha had eight ministers, brilliant and dedicated men: Jayanta, Sumantra, Dhriti, Vijaya, Siddharta, Arthasadaka, Mantrapala, and Asoka. Then there were the rishis who advised him, among them his kulaguru, his family preceptor: the immortal Vasishta. The lamps to the Gods in the temples of Ayodhya never burned low, nor did the faith in the hearts of Dasaratha's subjects. With heaven's grace, the king's granary and his treasury were always full; quiet and measureless goodness was upon his kingdom.

But even such a rajarishi, a royal sage, was not perfectly happy. Dasaratha had no heir, no son to light up the autumn of his life and succeed him when he died. As the king grew older, his despair grew with him and it began to feed on his spirit. Not a day passed without Dasaratha's priests offering a prayer to the Gods to bless him with a son. But it seemed they fell on deaf ears in heaven.

One day, the king thought he should perform an aswamedha yagna. He called Vasishta, Vamadeva, and his ministers, and asked for their counsel.

His charioteer, Sumantra, said, "My lord, have you heard of Rishyashringa?* He is a simpleton in the world, but a prodigy of the spirit. Once the Devas cursed the kingdom of Anga and a famine fell on it. Your friend King Romapada sought Rishyashringa's intervention. No sooner did Romapada lure the muni into his kingdom, by giving him his daughter's hand, than it began to rain and the famine ended. Sire, I have heard Sanatkumara has foretold that four sons shall be born to you, when you perform an aswamedha yagna with Rishyashringa as your priest."

Dasaratha went to Anga and persuaded Romapada to send his flamelike son-in-law to conduct the aswamedha in Ayodhya. Messengers rode home before Dasaratha and his guest, and the city was decked out in arches, flowers, and banners to welcome the rishi.

As soon as Rishyashringa arrived, a horse of the noblest bloodline was chosen for the sacrifice, and he blessed it.

The prayers continued for weeks, and then a magic spring came to Kosala. The trees were full of soft new leaves, the Sarayu with sweet water, and Dasaratha went to the innocent sage and said, "Muni, the time has come."

Rishyashringa replied, "Send your horse across the plains of Bharatavarsha. Let the yagna begin."

After a year, the kshatriyas of all the kingdoms through which Dasaratha's white horse had flown like a storm came to Kosala. They came to the yagnashala on the northern bank of the Sarayu, under the

---

*Old temple murals always show this sage as having antlers growing on his head; most often, his face is also that of a deer, though he has a man's body.

sun and the stars. The horse came home unchecked and it was spring again, with the flowering trees all in bud.

5. The need for an Avatara

Toward the end of the aswamedha, Dasaratha fell at Rishyashringa's feet and cried, "Rishi, make my yagna fruitful."

Rishyashringa began to perform the intricate putrakama ritual at the holy fire, exactly as it is prescribed in the secret passages of the Atharva Veda. The Devas gathered above that fire for their share of the havis: these offerings are ambrosial to them, like sipping the sweetest currents of the human heart.

What the sacrificers of Kosala and their priest did not know was that the Devas came straight from a transcendent mandala, where they had taken a petition to Brahma.

Indra, the king of the Devas, knelt before Brahma and cried, "Father, we cannot bear Ravana's tyranny any more. His evil pervades the earth and men's hearts are corrupted from afar. They deny their Gods, and lie more easily than speak the truth. They are full of violence and seduce their brothers' wives. Ravana's demons swarm in the jungles of the earth; they desecrate the rishis' sacrifices and devour the holy ones.

"The Sun and the Moon go in fear of Ravana. The planets spin into sinister orbits at his will, and all the world has become a dangerous place. The yakshas and gandharvas live in terror. No sage dares pronounce a curse on the Lord of Lanka, because he is such an awesome sorcerer himself. Vayu the Wind blows softly, lest he ruffle Ravana's hair. Surya the Sun doesn't change his place over Lanka, be it summer or winter, lest he annoy Ravana and the Demon pluck him from the sky and extinguish him. And now Ravana threatens to invade Amravati if I am not servile to him. I cannot stand it, Pitama! My throne in heaven is worthless, as long as Ravana lives. And because of your boon to him, none of us can kill the Rakshasa."

Brahma said, "Ravana does have a boon from me that no immortal can kill him. But in his arrogance, he did not ask for a boon to protect him against the mortal race of men. He shall die by a man's hand. Be comforted: it is not long to the birth of that man into the world."

As Brahma spoke, a blinding splendor shone on them from the sky.

They saw Mahavishnu, the Savior, mounted on his golden eagle. He wore robes glowing like the sun against his sea-blue skin. He carried the Sudarshana chakra, the Panchajanya, and the Kaumodaki. Brahma and the Devas worshipped him with folded hands.

Across winds of light that Garuda's wings stirred, Brahma cried to Vishnu, "Lord, be born as a man to rid the earth of Ravana of Lanka. Or the Rakshasa will plunge the world into hell, long before the kali yuga begins. Only you can kill him; for evil though he is, he is greater than any creature in heaven or earth."

Vishnu spoke to Brahma and the Devas in his voice as deep as time: "I will be born as Dasaratha of Ayodhya's son, and I will kill Ravana. I will rule the earth for eleven thousand years, before I return to Vaikunta."

He vanished from above them. How they yearned for him to appear again, but the Blue One was gone.

On earth, on the northern bank of the Sarayu, Dasaratha's putrakama yagna was almost complete. Rishyashringa chanted the final mantras from the Atharva Veda. The fire leaped up, tall as trees, and the flames licked themselves into a dark figure: a divine messenger, his hair a lion's mane around his livid face. He wore burning ornaments studded with great jewels and a chandrahara, a moon-sliver, on his chest.

He stepped out of the fire, and flames were his body as he stood solemnly before Dasaratha and Rishyashringa. He carried a crystal chalice in his hands, with a silvery payasa brimming in it. He looked as Dhanvantari must have, when he emerged from the Kshirasagara with the amrita.

Said that being, in an ancient tongue of fire and earth: "I come from Brahma, Grandsire of worlds. He sends this payasa to your queens so they will bear you the sons you long for."

He held the chalice out to Dasaratha. The king stepped forward and took it. At once the messenger vanished. Like a man bearing the greatest treasure he could ever have, Dasaratha brought the chalice to his queens.

He came to Kausalya, his first wife, and said to her, "Look, the Gods have answered our prayers. You shall bear me a son to be my heir."

With his own hands, he made her drink half the payasa. Then he went to his second wife, Sumitra, and fed her half of what was left. He went to his youngest queen, Kaikeyi, and gave her half of what remained. Finally he went back to give Sumitra the rest.

And they heard the people of Ayodhya crying, *"Jaya! Jaya!"* as they broke into song.

Hope against Ravana of Lanka kindled in their hearts, the Devas came down from the sky to receive their share of the havis. Taking the burnt offerings in shining hands, they vanished back into their subtle realms. Dasaratha and his people returned to Ayodhya, with joy come among them like another god.

After being rewarded lavishly by the euphoric king, Rishyashringa and the other brahmanas went back to their homes.

6. King Dasaratha's sons

Dasaratha was as happy as a boy, as if only now the Gods had blessed him with manhood. He felt as strong as a Deva. The first few nights after the aswamedha yagna he went to his queens by turns; he made love as he had when he had just married them.

In some months, they announced in joy, Kausalya first, then Sumitra and Kaikeyi, that they were all pregnant. Celebrations broke out in Ayodhya: the Gods had not betrayed Dasaratha and his people. That year flew by for the king in cosseting his wives. He fed them with delicacies that stroked their palates or their fancy. He clothed them in finery that not even queens had worn before. Ayodhya was festive all year long, in breathless anticipation.

The ice on the Himalaya began to melt as the sun drifted north again and spring returned to Bharatavarsha. This was no common spring, but wore rainbow-hued lotuses in its hair, flowers that bloomed once in a thousand years. A hush of expectation lay over Kosala's capital. The clear pools were covered with lilies. The flowering trees that lined the streets of Ayodhya drooped to the ground; they were heavy with new leaves in every shade of green and untimely, extravagant flowers. A malaya breeze blew across the kingdom, carrying the scents of the spring through the city and up into the apartments of Dasaratha's queens; most of all, into Kausalya's.

All the earth seemed to strain, with senses of breeze and night, moonbeam and sunray, into the gracious Kausalya's chambers: Vishnu was to be born from her bright womb as a man! Then it was the month of Chaitra. Great rishis had arrived in Ayodhya, and, with occult sight, they saw Devas in the sky above the city.

The moon was waxing. It was the ninth day after amavasya. Rare and auspicious syzygies were strewn across the firmament. Five planets were in their signs of exaltation that night. The nakshatra was Punarvasu and the moon rose in his own house, with lofty Jupiter in the lagna Karkataka, cardinal sign of the Crab. Kausalya was as radiant as Aditi had been in Devaloka when she bore Indra. That night, Dasaratha's first queen gave birth to one greater than the king of the Devas. She brought Vishnu into the world, for its deliverance from Ravana of Lanka.

Kausalya felt no pain at all, just bliss, as Rama was born from her. He was as serene as the Manasa lake upon the mountain. He did not cry at being born into this sad and fleeting world. He only smiled, his eyes wide open and so knowing on his dark, dark face. A shower of barely tangible flowers fell out of the air around Kausalya's bed. Apsaras danced on clouds when little Rama sighed in his throat, blue as the lotus that blooms on satin pools hidden in the hearts of jungles.

When in a day, the moon had moved into the nakshatra Pushyami, the youngest queen Kaikeyi went into labor, and Bharata was born.

After another twenty hours, when the moon was in Aslesha, twins were born to Sumitra, who had drunk twice from the cup of payasa: Lakshmana, who would follow his brother Rama to the ends of the earth, and Shatrughna, bane of his enemies.

Ayodhya was more festive than Devaloka on high. The Devas were jubilant at the thought that Ravana would die as soon as Dasaratha's eldest son was a man: in just some human years, which for the Gods are but a few days. But the people of Kosala celebrated because now they would have another great kshatriya to rule them as wisely as Dasaratha had done.

In Ayodhya the singing and dancing went on through the night. The streets were choked with thousands of revelers, at midday and twilight, midnight and dawn. The lines outside the palace gates were interminable, when the queens brought their sons out onto their terraces. The people stood patiently for hours to catch a glimpse of the infants' faces.

Dasaratha gave them gold by the sack, and cows by the herd to the brahmanas. If through deep time there was ever a mortal king whose cup of joy was full, he was Dasaratha of Ayodhya. The feasting continued for eleven days, and then Vasishta was called to name the four boys and perform their jatakarma.

The next sixteen years were like a waking dream for Dasaratha. He watched his sons grow around him and outstrip every hope he may have had for them. They studied the Vedas and the other sacred lore with Vasishta, and were quick to learn whatever he had to teach. No matter how profound or complex the subject, how strange or new, they absorbed it at the first instruction.

Like the moon waxing day by day, the four princes grew: a young pride of lions. They learned the arts of war, as all kshatriyas must; and their skills were astonishing when they were barely ten. In their earliest teens they rode elephant, horse, and chariot like masters, soon competing just with one another. For there was no one else in the land, including their gurus, who could match them. Led by Rama, their archery was no less extraordinary. Their masters said that not even the Gods could equal the princes at the longbow, the mace, or the double-edged sword.

Now, usually, twins are exceptionally close. But in the palace of Ayodhya, nature was subverted by a higher order of attachment. From the beginning, the fair, shy Lakshmana was like his dark brother Rama's shadow; and Shatrughna was as attached to Kaikeyi's son Bharata. Rama and Lakshmana were inseparable. Since they were babies, Rama would not eat a morsel, or sleep a wink, unless Lakshmana was at his side, being fed from the same platter or lying in the same bed. Later, Rama would not hunt without Lakshmana carrying his quiver, or the older, the younger brother's. Dasaratha basked in the prodigious talents and the love of his sons. Arrogance laid no hand upon them; they grew up as humble and respectful as they were gifted.

And what can be said about Rama, his father's favorite? Dasaratha lived Rama, he breathed Rama, his every waking moment was Rama; and if one looked closely enough, his dreams as well. He loved his son perhaps more than any man should. It was devotion, obsessive and a little dangerous.

Rama seemed to live for his father's sake as well, indulging his every wish, anticipating his least whim as if he read the old king's thoughts; at times, even before they appeared in Dasaratha's mind! Those were perfect years, and Dasaratha's pride in his sons grew apace. Then so quickly, the princes were almost sixteen and of an age when they should take wives. Their father began to make delicate inquiries. But of course he was very particular about the girls his boys would marry.

7. Viswamitra

One day Dasaratha sat in his palace with his ministers and the rishis who lived in Ayodhya. He spoke to them about finding a bride for Rama. When he thought of his sons, he thought first, and at times only, of Rama. Then they heard a commotion outside. A tall rishi, with a great and stern face, arrived at Dasaratha's gates. He could have as easily been a kshatriya warrior as a hermit. Though he seemed a man of fifty or so, in fact he was older than you could imagine.

He came like a storm. In a voice more a king's than a hermit's, he commanded the guards at the gates to announce him to the court. "Tell Dasaratha of Ayodhya," said the stranger with eyes like live coals, "that Viswamitra wants to see him."

And he stood tapping a foot, impatiently; for he was in a hurry. The guards knew who he was. After paying quick homage to him, they ran into the sabha to tell Dasaratha about the visitor, who was a legend not only on earth but in Devaloka. Viswamitra had once been a kshatriya king, who, after an unequaled tapasya, had become a brahmarishi.

Dasaratha came out of his palace to welcome the great one. The stranger with the tangled jata and the burning eyes seemed pleased. After laying a long palm on Dasaratha's head in blessing, he went into the palace with the king, into the court agog at his arrival. The visitor did not speak, only looked around him with the regard of one who had seen many palaces in his time. Even when he was seated, Viswamitra, friend of the universe, was silent, as if to remind Dasaratha of his duty as a host: to praise his guest.

Dasaratha said in a clear voice, "Viswamitra, your coming here is a Godsend to me: like nectar to a mortal, rain to the famined, the birth of a son to the childless, like a treasure to a poor man!" Not imagining he might be held to his word sooner than he thought, he continued, "My lord, is there anything a humble kshatriya can offer a great brahmarishi? I have a kingdom I can lay at your feet."

With the faintest smile now, Viswamitra said briskly, "Spoken like a true son of the House of Ikshvaku. I know your offer is not a hollow one, Dasaratha. Indeed, today I have come to ask you for a favor. I have taken a vow for a yagna. But I find I cannot complete it, because two rakshasas of the jungle desecrate my sacrifice. They are mayavis and come invisibly. They rain rotten flesh, blood, and feces on my sacred fire at times when I have just begun, and at others when I have almost finished. I am forbidden anger and I may not stop them with a curse. I have come to seek the protection of a kshatriya king."

Dasaratha was eager to rush to Viswamitra's help. "Tell me how I can help you, Muni, and consider my help given."

Viswamitra said softly, "Send your son Rama with me to kill the rakshasas."

It was as if he had struck Dasaratha with a mace. The king crumpled in his throne. When he was revived with water sprinkled on his face, his mind was a storm of demons. "Rama is not yet sixteen," he cried. "His eyes are as tender as lotuses. If I don't see my son for an hour, I feel I am dying. Rama is my life. If you must take him, let me also come with my soldiers."

In his heart, he knew his word was given in honor and he could not break it. Viswamitra said kindly, "Only Rama can kill these rakshasas. Have no fear, I will protect him. Besides, if he comes with me your son will tread a lofty path of fame, and his deeds will become a legend. Your prince is born for fame, don't cling to him. His way lies with me, because the boy you know as your son . . ."

But Dasaratha cried in anguish, "Who are these rakshasas? How are they so powerful?"

Viswamitra said calmly, "In the line of the Rishi Pulastya, there is a rakshasa of matchless strength and intelligence called Ravana. He worshipped Brahma with a great tapasya and Brahma blessed him with a boon. But then he turned into an evil sovereign upon the earth.

"Ravana has gathered all the forces of darkness under his power. The two rakshasas Maricha and Subahu, who ruin my sacrifice, serve him. Ravana tolerates no yagnas anywhere; he knows they are a threat to him. He believes himself immortal and seeks to extend his sway over all the earth, with himself as supreme monarch in Lanka.

"But Dasaratha, why are you afraid? Don't you know who your son is? Ask Vasishta; ask any of your rishis here; they will tell you who Rama is."

But Dasaratha said, "I will lose my tender boy to feral rakshasas. I have heard not even the Devas and gandharvas can resist Ravana of Lanka. And you want to take my sweet prince to fight that monster's forces? I have heard the valor of those whom Ravana's servants kill is absorbed by the Rakshasa, while their spirits languish darkly. Have mercy on me, Muni, my child is not yet sixteen. He is the scion of my race, the heir to the Ikshvaku throne."

Then Dasaratha cried desperately, "No, Viswamitra! I will not send Rama with you. Maricha and Subahu are not adversaries for a sixteen-year-old. I will come to fight them myself, but I won't send my child."

Viswamitra's tremendous brows bristled and the sabha fell hushed. That rishi, whose curse could extinguish a galaxy, cried in a voice like doom, "You received me with such flattery; you made such promises to me. But now you go back on your word and bring shame on the noble line of Raghu. I will return from where I came, and you can live in your fool's paradise; until Ravana arrives at your gates one day. But I say to you, Dasaratha, if you want to tread the path of destiny written in the stars, send Rama with me!"

The rishi's voice echoed through the court. Suddenly Viswamitra seemed to have grown before their eyes, and his presence dominated the sabha like an omen. Still, Dasaratha was silent; blind with a father's love, he hardly knew what he did.

But now Vasishta, his guru, said to him, "A king of the House of Ikshvaku is meant to be an embodiment of dharma. Don't darken your ancestors' honor with this weakness. To break his word is unforgivable for the meanest kshatriya, let alone a king like you. You must send Rama with Viswamitra. The rishi will protect him as the wheel of fire does the chalice of nectar.

"You don't know who your son is, or you would not dream that two common rakshasas of the forest could harm him. And do you really think a brahmarishi cannot stop these demons himself? They would be like straws in a gale before his power. Viswamitra is a trikalagyani; he sees through the three times. He has some other purpose in asking Rama to go with him.

"Dasaratha, your son belongs not just to you, but to the very earth. The time has come for him to embark on his destiny. Give up this insane putrasneha; send him with the muni."

Light of reason dawned on Dasaratha. He knelt before Viswamitra. "Forgive me! I was blinded by my love for my child. I am happy to send Rama with you. But my son has never been alone yet, because his brother Lakshmana is like his shadow. I beg you, take them both to the jungle."

Meanwhile, Kausalya heard about Viswamitra's mission and quickly prepared the princes to go with the rishi. They took their three mothers' blessing, they made no distinction between them, and came to their father's court. They were taller by half a head than even the kshatriyas of those times, who were at least a head taller than the tallest man of today. And they were magnificent: Rama was dark as a blue lotus and Lakshmana fair as a moonbeam. Both princes wore their hair down to their shoulders. Regal, powerful, handsome, poised, and so humble, they prostrated themselves before Dasaratha. Then they stood before him with folded hands, like two young Gods.

Dasaratha said, "Brahmarishi Viswamitra has come to take you to the jungle, to help him complete his yagna. Go with him, my sons, and obey him in all things as you would obey me."

The princes bowed to their father and, without a word, crossed to Viswamitra's side. They stood quietly awaiting his command. The muni rose and led them out into the sun. When Rama and Lakshmana left Ayodhya with Viswamitra, a scented breeze blew through that city. The flights of birds, and every other natural omen, were auspicious all around them. As the king and his ministers stood at the palace door, waving to the strange company of princes and hermit, the sky filled with ethereal music and there was a soft rain of petals of light.

Vasishta looked at Dasaratha, and smiled.

8. Kamasrama

Viswamitra walked in front, his long strides leading quickly into the distance and out of sight of Ayodhya. Not once did the princes turn to look back, but followed the rishi, their quivers strapped to powerful shoulders, their swords bound to lean waists and their bows in their hands. Rama walked five paces behind Viswamitra, and Lakshmana five paces behind his brother.

The hermit did not say a word, and the princes, too, kept his silence like a sacred thing between them. Just as it was evening, they arrived at the southern bank of the Sarayu. Twilight birds filled the trees in armfuls, like leaves ablaze with song.

For all his fierce appearance, Viswamitra said gently, "Rama, take up water in your palms, and I will teach you the bala and atibala mantras. Then not hunger, thirst, nor tiredness will touch you on our way." When Rama approached, the muni laid a hand on the dark youth's head. "These mantras are Brahma's daughters. I know of no one in the three worlds more worthy of receiving them!"

He stared wistfully at Rama for a moment. Then the chant of the mantras spiraled from him like a flight of birds. It seemed to Lakshmana they flew down Rama's throat, as the heir to Ayodhya repeated the arcane words after the sage. The other birds of dusk fell silent, to hear the syllables of wonder.

After that initiation, Rama's body rippled with new resonance. Viswamitra taught Lakshmana also the mantras, and the brothers worshipped him as their guru now.

They prepared to sleep beside the whispering river, for night had fallen. As if it was a long-standing habit, they spread tall grasses into elegant mats for the muni and for themselves. When the hermit lay down, the princes also lay close to each other, for the first time in their lives on such beds. They fell quickly into tranquil dreams under the stars, as the moon crept above the trees and lit the river with silver light.

The next morning, Viswamitra was up before the sun. For a while, he stood gazing at the sleeping Rama by the magic light of dawn. Dew still lay on the ground and the river seemed hardly awake herself.

Viswamitra called softly to the sleepers, "Rama, awake, the first sandhya is here. Rouse yourself, Lakshmana."

The princes awoke. Rested and smiling, they waded into the fragrant river. Standing waist deep in the flow, they worshipped the rising sun with Suryanamaskara. They came out of the water and prostrated themselves at Viswamitra's feet. When he had blessed them, they resumed their journey. When they had gone until noon they came to a place where, shielding their eyes against the sun, now climbed to his zenith, they saw an enchanting sight below them: the dark Sarayu flowed in soft thunder into the Ganga, which fell from the stars!

How the two rivers sparkled at each other's touch. Viswamitra allowed himself a rare smile. They saw that the asramas of myriad rishis, all seekers after truth, dotted the banks of the rivers at the sacred confluence. It was one great hermitage, made up of a score of small ones.

Moved, Rama asked, "Whose asrama is this? Even from here I can feel how ancient and holy it is."

Viswamitra said, "Deep ages have passed since this asrama was founded. But once Siva himself sat in dhyana in this tapovana, and Parvati, the mountain's daughter, attended him. Those were the times when Kamadeva, who is formless now, had a body and a face. Kama came to this place and aimed his flower arrows at Siva. For a moment, Siva came under Kama's spell and reached for Parvati. Then, realizing what he did, he turned to see who dared pierce him with such subtle shafts of lust. Seeing Kama in the bushes, Siva glared open his third eye and made ashes of the Deva of love.

"The wind scattered Kama's ashes across the kingdom of Anga. Anga got its name because Kama, who was bodiless now, was called Ananga. The rishis you see are Sivabhaktas, and the asrama is called Kamasrama. Let us go down to the munis. Many of them see through time as other men see the world, and they have been expecting us. Look how they come to welcome us. They are overjoyed at the advent of Rama of Ayodhya."

They had a welcome fit for the Gods from the rishis of Kamasrama. Those sages knew, better than Rama himself, who he was and why he had been born. Viswamitra and the princes decided to stay with them beside the two rivers. The brahmarishi, and the others as well, regaled the young kshatriyas with stories of times out of mind: of the bygone millennia of krita and treta, especially legends of fathomless Siva. Slowly, evening deepened into night. Stars like cosmic lanterns appeared above them. They seemed to traverse the sky ever so slowly, for their keenness to eavesdrop on the shining tales of those mystic hermits.

9. The cursed forest

They had half a night of sleep after Viswamitra called an end to the stories under the stars. At dawn they bade farewell to the hermits of Kamasrama and set out again. The rishis gave them a boat of reeds in which to cross the rivers that flowed as one to the sea from their confluence.

As they rowed, with spray flying in their faces, they heard a turbulent rumbling as if the rivers were hollow in the place they forded. Rama, who was more at ease now with Viswamitra, cried above the water's roar, "What is this noise?"

The rishi replied, "The Sarayu springs in the high mountains, from the Manasa lake that Brahma made with a thought. The Ganga, which fell from the stars, you know about. This place of the echo is where the Sarayu flows into the golden Ganga. Worship the rivers; they are Goddesses and will bless you."

With folded hands the princes prayed to the swirling currents. It seemed to them that, in the bank of morning mist poised over the water, they saw two great and lovely faces. For just a moment, the faces shimmered in the air, their lips mouthing a blessing. But when Rama and Lakshmana glanced at Viswamitra to confirm the vision, he was already peering at the far shore as if he had seen nothing himself.

They gained that shore and walked away from the river, which was so wide they could not see the rishis who stood across it, waving to them still. Now they entered a jungle that grew, thick and forbidding, not a hundred paces from the water. Viswamitra walked unhesitatingly into the vana, as if he saw an invisible trail leading into it. The princes followed him.

Dark, dense, and damp was that forest. No light or wind entered it, to dry the rain and dew that lay upon the leaves and grass, or blow away an evil air that hung heavily. All was still, the silence deep and uncanny under the canopy of branches. An aura of stagnant age lay upon this jungle. There were no paths and it was plain that no men ventured in here. They heard snakes on the ground, bees in the air, and birds in the trees, all eerily loud. They heard their own breaths and heartbeats so clearly.

Rama said, "Surely this is a perfect forest for rishis to have their asramas; but it is deserted. Even the songs of birds seem to grate in their throats from anxiety. Are there no flowers, streams, or pools here? Why is this jungle such an ominous place?"

Viswamitra said, "Once there was no jungle here at all, but the kingdoms of Malada and Karusha, fertile and populous. When Indra slew the brahmana Asura, Vritra, he was guilty of brahmahatya. The rishis of Devaloka washed his sin from him with water from the rivers of heaven. This was the place where that water fell, with the sin. Indra cried out to Bhumi Devi in gratitude, 'I bless this country to be as fecund as the fields of Devaloka!'

"Malada and Karusha were the most luxuriant kingdoms in the world, renowned even among the stars. But then a scourge in the shape of a rakshasi came to this place. Her name is Tataka and hers is a twisted tale: for she was not born a rakshasi but the child of a yaksha called Suketu.

"Suketu had no children; he performed a tapasya to Brahma, to bless him with a son. Brahma did not give Suketu a son but a daughter, as strong as the yaksha could have wished any child of his to be. When Tataka was a ravishing young woman, Suketu gave her to Jarjara's son, Sunanda, a handsome young yaksha.

"In time, Tataka gave birth to a boy she named Maricha, whose death will bring you fame one day, Rama." The prince looked startled at the prediction. Viswamitra continued: "Sunanda died soon after his son was born and Tataka was unhinged with grief. Her hair hanging loose, drunk on forest brew, she went to Agastya's asrama. With her infant on her hip, she made advances to the great rishi. Agastya, bright as flames, cursed her, 'Shameless woman! Be a rakshasi as monstrous as your heart is full of darkness. Your beauty will be a thing of the past. You will feed on flesh, and all the creatures of the earth will hate you.'

"As soon as the curse was pronounced, Tataka's lissom body was transformed into demon flesh. She fled screaming from Agastya's asrama. She came to a jungle stream, her heart on fire with weird and unfamiliar lusts. When she looked into the water the face she saw reflected there, glowering back at her, was not her own but a face of terror. It was the face of Tataka the rakshasi, for fear of whom no man and few beasts enter this forest any more.

"She lives a yojana and a half from here, and drinks the blood of any creature that ventures into this jungle. Her son has grown up and left her. She lives alone, in torment under these trees, baying the moon through chinks in the awning of leaves, and waiting for her savior to come to deliver her.

"Rama, the prophesy is that you will free Tataka from her curse. Don't balk at killing her because she is a woman. She is wretched and evil, and you must rid this jungle of her."

Rama bowed before Viswamitra and, smiling sweetly, said, "When my father sent us out with you, he told us, 'Go with him, and obey him in all things as you would obey me.' Muni, I never disobey my father."

Rama flung back his handsome head, black locks brushing his

shoulders; raising his bow, he pulled on its string so that the jungle echoed with the virile twanging. A short way before them was a small hillock that thrust itself out from the surrounding entwinement of trees; from here, Viswamitra and the princes heard a puzzled roar. Tataka was amazed that anyone dared enter her forest and announce themselves so foolishly.

"*Aaaaoough?*" she roared like a surprised tigress, only louder. She loomed over the hill to see who the fool was. Her face was masked in mud, slime, dried blood, and worse. Her crimson eyes were glazed, her lips drawn back from her fangs in a snarl. Her hair was caked into braids of filth; her hands were raised in threatening claws. Her savage features blotted out a good piece of the sky, and she was not much smaller herself than the hillock she straddled.

When she saw them, she roared louder. She spoke no words any more, not even to herself, but only made vile noises. She clawed up fistfuls of earth and stones, and flung them down at Viswamitra and the princes. She did a demented dance on her hill, hoping to frighten them into running from her, so she could have the pleasure of chasing them before she caught and ate them. They were just three puny men; that much she could see, even with her faded vision.

But the oldest of the three raised his hands and chanted a mantra that pierced her black heart like an astra of fire. She roared louder still, and hefted a man-sized boulder to hurl down on them. But then the young one who was dark as a blue lotus raised his bow. With an arrow fiercer than a rishi's curse, he cut her arm off at the elbow. The boulder fell on her own feet and how she screamed, her great body shuddering. The other fair young warrior strung his bow. Playfully, he cut off her nose and her ears, so black blood spurted from her face. Howling like a storm, she vanished before they could hurt her any more. She had made herself invisible with maya.

They still heard her raging beyond the crest of the hill, and more rocks and stones came raining down on them as they climbed the slope. But as if she knew her time had come, the fight had gone out of Tataka. Rama and Lakshmana paused halfway up the hillock. They pulled at their bowstrings again, so the rakshasi's screams were drowned and the earth below them shook. Suddenly Tataka's screams stopped. She was stricken with a terror she had not felt for an age. She had fainted with that fear and with the pain of her severed parts. Her sorcery grew weak and they saw her again.

23

But up she leaped. Hadn't she drunk the blood of a hundred young fools like these? She pulled up a tree with her good hand and came lumbering over the hilltop. She loomed over them, screeching raw abuse. But Rama waited with an arrow fitted to his bow and the string drawn to his ear. As she plunged at them, he dropped onto a knee and shot her through her heart. With a sigh, she fell; like a strange avalanche, she rolled down the hill until she came to rest at Viswamitra's feet. They saw her rakshasi's form had changed in death. She was beautiful again and had a smile of pure release upon her face.

There was a flash of light throughout that forest when Tataka died: a light of the Devas. An unearthly voice, an asariri, spoke to Viswamitra. "We bless you, Brahmarishi, for bringing Dasaratha's brilliant sons to make this place clean again. Fare you well on your journey. And fare you well on all your journeys, Rama, for there are many before you."

The light was gone. Viswamitra said quietly, "Indra."

The rishi saw the youths had knelt at his feet for his blessing. He raised them up gently and, now, proudly as well. Though he had always known who these princes were, where was the proof of their stunning valor before they killed Tataka? In some satisfaction, Viswamitra settled for the night in the heart of that jungle, with Rama and Lakshmana beside him. As they slept they felt an uncommon breeze flow in sweet currents through the trees above them, as if those ancients were being awakened from a long nightmare. The princes drifted off along the river of dreams, and they fancied they felt the hearts of the old trees respond to that fresh draft in a thousand springs they had suppressed from Tataka's overweening evil.

When they awoke, to the joyful songs of birds in the trees above them, they saw their dream had been just a shade of the truth. All around them was the gushing outflow of a long-withheld spring! A riot of flowers of ten vasanthas hung from the trees in every imaginable color: champaka, asoka, punnaga, and delicate mallika blossomed overnight at Tataka's death. The air was no longer dank and purulent, but crisp and sweet with a thousand ineffable scents.

Birds gave excited throat to their deliverance. Deer walked shyly up to the princes and the rishi, and nuzzled their faces in their hands. They saw the canopy above was, in fact, far from opaque; today fingers of sunlight reached down to the floor of the forest. While the rakshasi was alive, even the sun had avoided her lair. The mango trees, palasas, and palms were heavy with fruit, ripened in a night, in supernatural abundance. The jungle celebrated more than the death of Tataka. It was ecstatic at the advent of Rama, who had slept under its branches.

As the princes went on their way, they saw the vana was strewn with a richness of clear pools and forest streams chatting through curving aisles of trees, and jungle paths revealed. Life had returned to the province of death, and celebration was everywhere. Even Viswamitra seemed moved. His eyes strayed from Rama's face to the miracle in the jungle around them, and then back to the prince's dark features. Abruptly, he raised a hand for them to stop. He said, "I am so pleased, I must give you a gift today."

Rama said, "But you have already blessed us; what gift could be greater than that?"

Viswamitra replied, "For two young kshatriyas on the threshold of life, the gift of devastras. They will help you someday against enemies far greater than Tataka. These are weapons only the restrained should have, and you, Rama, are born so. Now I am sure of who you are; no one else could have killed Tataka. Come, sit here with me."

When Rama sat, facing the east, Viswamitra taught him the mantras to summon the occult weapons. The rishi himself had the astras from Siva, long ago, when he was still a king and had need of them. When Rama spoke the secret mantras, the lords of the astras appeared before him. They were neither in this world nor yet in the next: they stood between realms, their bodies of pristine light. The eyes of some were turquoise flames; others had locks of green tongues of fire.

They said to Rama, "Now we are your slaves; we will do your bidding, whenever you want."

Rama said to them, "Dwell in my mind, until I have need of you."

They melted into him, and he glowed more than ever. Viswamitra said to Rama, "To teach what you have learned is to learn it twice over. Even if your brother had none of the greatness he bears so humbly, he would deserve to have the astras just for his love of you. Devotion like his is not of this world. Rama, share what I have taught you with Lakshmana."

Rama taught his brother the mantras, and the Gods of the weapons appeared before Lakshmana as well. He, too, had them enter his spirit in splendid forms.

10. The legend of Vamana

After they had walked for a day and some hours, Rama pointed ahead. "I see a green wood under the mountain. Deer herds, dark as clouds, move across the foothills and songs brim from thousands of birds. What forest are we approaching, Muni? My heart grows so glad at its very sight."

Viswamitra smiled to himself and said, "Once Lord Vishnu came as a Dwarf to quell the Asura Mahabali. He did tapasya in this place, before he asked Bali for three paces of land."

Rama's eyes misted over, as if mention of that legend stirred some deep memory in him. "Tell us about Vamana and Mahabali, Swami."

Viswamitra said, "Mahabali was the greatest king the world ever knew. He was an Asura; but his bhakti and his dharma were immaculate. He vanquished all the other Danava monarchs of the earth and the sky. He conquered the Maruts and Indra himself, and announced that he would hold a yagna to have himself crowned emperor of Swarga, Bhumi, and Patala.

"Led by Agni, the Fire God, the Devas came abjectly to Vishnu. He sat in tapasya in the asrama you see before you. Agni cried to Mahavishnu, 'You must stop Bali before he becomes emperor. Indra is in exile and all his Devas with him. In their places, Bali has made his demons lords of the elements, the luminaries, and the planets. They rule time now.'

"The Rishi Kashyapa said to Vishnu, 'Lord, my wife Aditi grieves for her sons, whom the Asura has cast out from Devaloka. Wipe her tears, Narayana: be born as our child to end the sorrow of your people. Be born in this very place, and let it be known as Siddhasrama.'

"Vishnu has always favored the Devas, in their endless wars against the Asuras. He said, 'So be it.'

"He was born from the mother of the Devas, Aditi, and Brahma's saintly son, Kashyapa Prajapati, in Siddhasrama. The Lord was a brahmana, perfect in every limb and feature. But he was small, as if he belonged to another, finer race: a mankind in miniature. In that first human incarnation, he was called Vamana or Upendra. Straightaway, shining like gold, he went to Mahabali's yagna.

"Seeing the exquisite young brahmana, Mahabali rose. He was as much a king of the spirit as of the world. The Asura gazed in joy at the illustrious Dwarf, and said, 'Welcome, young one; I am honored you have come to my sacrifice. You are as bright as a God and my heart insists that, though you have a human form, you are not of this earth. Ask me for anything and I will give it to you. For my very soul is anxious to please you!'

"The Dwarf smiled so brilliantly at Virochana's son that already Bali's life went out to the Vamana. The diminutive brahmana said in a ringing voice, 'Noble Mahabali, I would expect no less of you. These past months, the world speaks of nothing but your yagna. So I thought I would come and ask if I could have a small gift from you.'

" 'Anything, wonderful one.'

"But the Vamana held up a hand in caution, 'I will ask for but little, Bali. But be sure you give me what I ask.'

"The king smiled indulgently at the boy he thought was just a fabulous child. 'It is my great fortune that you have come to ask me for a gift. Whoever you are, I feel my life is complete only now that I have seen you. Ask me for anything. Be it my treasury or granary, my army or my very kingdom: just ask and it shall be yours.'

"The dazzling smile played on the boy's lips again. He said sweetly, 'I have no use for your treasury or your granary, your army or your kingdom, for mine is a life of tapasya. My only need is for a piece of earth to sit upon in prayer. Give me three strides of land, Bali, that I can cover with these legs of mine.'

"Mahabali was amused. He said in kindly patronage, 'Of course. You shall have them now.'

"Bali reached for the sacred water that sanctifies the gift, the giver, and the receiver. But Sukracharya, his guru, said, 'Bali, this is no child. He is the Truth that not even Brahma, the Devas, or the yogis can fathom. This is Narayana who has come to your yagna. If you give him what he asks, you will die.'

"But Bali would not listen, for Vamana had come to deliver him to a far greater kingdom than any in the world. An unearthly light shone upon the Asura's face also, and he said to Sukra, 'If he is Narayana, my yagna will succeed beyond my dreams.'

"Bali's queen poured the water into his palms, and he solemnly gave away the three paces of land the Dwarf had asked for. But the instant the holy water touched Vamana's hands, the tiny brahmana began to grow. He grew into his Viswarupa, his cosmic form. With his first stride, Rama, he crossed the earth; with his next, he covered the heavens. Then he stood refulgent before Mahabali and said, 'Where shall I set my third stride, Bali? My foot is raised.'

"The Asura was a great bhakta. Tears streaming down his face, Mahabali bent his head and cried to the Vamana, 'Set your third stride upon my head, Lord.'

"The Vamana set his foot on Mahabali's head. With the ecstasy of redemption, he thrust the Asura, who would have been emperor of the worlds, down into Patala; down to eternal kingdom and peace."

Viswamitra paused for a moment. They had drawn near the asrama. He pointed. "In that tapovana to which your hearts thrill, Vishnu set Mahabali free. And there is my asrama. It is this immortal place the rakshasas desecrate with their filth."

With the princes at his side, Viswamitra strode into the asrama of vibrant peace. They were like the moon flanked by the Punarvasu stars, risen into a clear night. The other rishis of the hermitage gathered around their master and the saviors he had brought to deliver them from Maricha and Subahu.

The princes of Ayodhya rested only briefly after their long journey. Then they came to Viswamitra, and Rama said quietly, "Resume your yagna, Muni; you will not be interrupted."

The same night, Viswamitra took diksha again. Rama and Lakshmana slept peacefully through that first night. The next morning, they rose before the sun, as dawn clutched at the horizon for a fingerhold. They bathed and came before the brahmarishi. He sat quiescent on a seat of darbha grass, after he had worshipped Agni Deva, who conveys burnt offerings to all the other Gods.

11. A yagna completed

Viswamitra had taken mowna, a vow of silence, for six days. Rama and Lakshmana stood watch over Siddhasrama. After their encounter with Tataka, they were eager for the rakshasas to appear. Day and night they stood in vigil, their bows in their hands, fitted loosely with arrows so the demons would not take them unawares. They guarded the asrama as eyelids do the eyes.

Five days went by, and Viswamitra's rishis said to the kshatriyas, "Today they will come. It is the last day and these rakshasas know the yagna well."

The fire in the yagnashala burned high. As he sat before the flames, Viswamitra's chiseled face seemed to be made of stone. The other rishis sat around Viswamitra. The chanting of the Vedas rose like smoke from the fire. August and sonorous, it spread through the world on subtle frequencies. Those timeless mantras brought a powerful healing upon the earth.

It was almost evening of the last day of the yagna. Suddenly, a lewd clap of sound shattered the sacral silence. A pungent darkness fell on the yagnashala, an unclean night of the elements and the spirit. Chilling shrieks and wild laughter rent the air. The two rakshasas had arrived with their bizarre clan. Maricha and Subahu were used to meeting no opposition when they came to Siddhasrama, and they had not bothered to make themselves invisible. They came as they were: devils of the forest, ugly as sin. They came in a swath of putrescence and a rain of excrement, rotting meat, and stinking blood. They came, the flesh of some of them obscenely bared, to violate the soul of the sacrifice.

Rama and Lakshmana had waited five days. Rama invoked the manavastra he had recently acquired, and shot an arrow into Maricha's chest, crying, "Let me never see you again or you die!" The arrow lifted the shocked rakshasa off his feet. It carried him through the air, aflame, screaming. It carried him past the wind for a hundred yojanas and doused him in the distant sea. But it did not kill him.

In the silence that followed you could hear, again, just the deep chanting of the Veda. Maricha's rakshasas and lean, tree-tall Subahu stood open-mouthed, their long fangs plain. The heathen screams had died in their throats; their rain of filth had ceased around them. But the prince of Ayodhya, the guardian of Viswamitra's yagna, did not wait for the stunned demons to recover. Like blue lightning, Rama invoked an agneyastra and, in a wink, made a heap of ashes of lanky Subahu. Quicker than thinking, he undid the mortal elements of the rest of the horde with a vayavyastra of Vayu, the Wind God. The weapon blew them apart as a gale would a dust heap in its path.

Shouldering his bow, Rama said, "Did you see, Lakshmana, the first astra was a compassionate one. The manavastra did not kill Maricha; it only punished him with fire and water. It has purified him."

Lakshmana wondered that his brother saw to the very sea just briefly, for no miracle was beyond his Rama. The sacrifice at Siddhasrama was completed. In joy, Viswamitra called Rama.

Embracing him, the rishi cried, "Rama of Ayodhya, your name shall be immortal! Men will remember you as long as the world exists. From yuga to yuga, your fame will be sung. The yagna you have helped me complete, in the teeth of evil, will bless the earth long ages after you and I are no more in it. Prince of light, today you have won a greater battle than you yourself yet know."

Viswamitra saw into the past and the future, as if they were plain before his eyes. The brahmarishi thought, "Not even Ravana of Lanka, who is evil incarnate, shall prevail against you, Rama. But I fear your way is long and fraught with sorrow, before you rid the earth of that rakshasa."

Viswamitra said nothing of these thoughts to the happy prince. He only joined the other rishis in crying, *"Jaya vijayi bhava!"* May you always be victorious.

At the end of the day, Viswamitra said to Rama and Lakshmana, "In the city of Mithila, King Janaka is performing another kind of yagna. We are going to Janaka's sacrifice and I want you to come with us. There is something there that should interest young warriors like yourselves. The bow of Siva lies in Mithila, like an arc of the sun. It lies in Janaka's palace, worshipped with flowers, incense, and prayers." He paused, then mused, "You know, no Deva or gandharva, no Asura or the mightiest kshatriya could ever lift Siva's bow. Many tried, from heaven and earth; none of them moved that weapon by a hair's width. Rama, you must see Siva's bow in Mithila, it is a wonder upon the earth. We will set out tomorrow; Janaka's yagna has already begun."

12. *By the golden Sona*

The next day, there was an unusual leave-taking at Siddhasrama. Before they left the asrama, blessed forever by Viswamitra's sacrifice, some extraordinary beings gathered in it to see them off. Many of them appeared out of thin air: colorful woodland spirits, lovely dryads and forest gods, vana devatas who were the guardians of the tapovana. Their bodies seemed to be made of leaves, bark, and green shoots, the glimmer of forest streams at twilight and living flesh of brown earth.

They wore shining feathers or coats of butterfly wings and wildflowers, which grew from them as if from tree or ground; and some were clad just in the breeze. They had forms of light, shifting sky-dreams and shards of rainbows, and they came in a motley throng, singing old songs, dancing to rhythms as old as the forest. They came with their untamed hearts full of blessings for the princes who had released them from the tyranny of the rakshasas. That terror had taken root in their bright limbs, enslaving these delicate ones in torment, making all the forest an evil place. Now they were free once more, and they came singing and dancing, and some even crying for joy.

The animals of the jungle had also gathered to see the travelers off. Tigers came with herds of wide-eyed deer; in this charmed place they lived in peace, beyond the hunt. And other beasts came as well, small and great: elephants wise as mountains, vivid swarms of songbirds full of mellifluous delight, and swans and friendly geese from the jungle rivers and lakes. Some of the more frequent visitors to the asrama, who were like the rishis' friends, had to be cajoled with many a promise that the munis would return soon. For they would set out, those innocent, wild creatures, as if they also meant to go with the journeying party. Even when the hermits and princes were well on their way, high above them they saw flights of familiar thrushes and swallows who would not be left behind. The paths of the air are freer than those of the earth!

Viswamitra walked around the asrama thrice in pradakshina. Then he strode off into the brilliant day with long strides, while the others followed, smiling among themselves at the pace he set. Of course, nobody ever grew tired: the brahmarishi had long since taught them the bala and the atibala mantras. When the sun was low in the western sky, they came to the banks of the golden Sona, and Viswamitra called a halt for the night.

The rishis bathed in the river, shot with saffron shafts of the setting sun. Standing in velvet water, they said their sandhya prayers. Then they gathered ripe fruit, mainly mangoes sweet as amrita, and lay on the green riverbank, chatting. They were full of quiet satisfaction that the sacrifice had been completed. It was a more profound achievement than any but the initiate could know. The munis were grateful the Lord of evil on earth had sent no fiercer force to disrupt such a powerful yagna as Viswamitra had undertaken. What few of his rishis knew was that Viswamitra had brought Rama and Lakshmana to his yagna not only to quell Maricha and Subahu, but to bless those princes themselves: so one day they would rid the earth of the Master of darkness himself, Ravana on his sinister throne.

By now Rama and Lakshmana had grown so attached to Viswamitra they were never far from his side. Beside the river, Rama said quietly to the brahmarishi, "This is a rich country, Muni. Wherever they turn, my eyes see every shade of green. Tell me, whose kingdom is this?"

With a glint in his eye, Viswamitra turned to face the prince. "Brahma had a son called Kusa, who was a rishi born from the Creator's thought. He was a yogin, and he married a mortal king's daughter, the princess of Videha, to ennoble the races of the earth. Four sons were born to them: Kusamba, Kusanabha, Adhurtarajas, and Vasu. Kusa told his sons to be kshatriyas on earth, and to rule.

"Those half-human and half-divine sovereigns founded separate cities, and they had great lands around them they ruled over. This green country, Rama, is called Vasumati. Kusa's youngest son, Vasu, ruled over this land and Girivraja was his capital."

The river whispered along beside them, as if it heard every word. The moon was rising in the east, and already his slanted rays set her currents alight. Viswamitra went on slowly while his rishis and the princes listened absorbed; he spoke with such quiet passion.

"Five mountains grace the kingdom of Vasumati, and the river that springs in Magadha flows between them like a garland of pearls flung across the earth. Kusa's eldest son, Kusanabha, had a hundred daughters by his seed, which was in part the seed of Brahma. He gave his daughters to the Rishi Brahmadatta to be his wives. Then he wanted a son, so he performed a yagna. During that ritual his father Kusa appeared before him and said, 'You will have a son, and his fame will resound through the world!'

"Kusanabha's son, who became the mightiest of the olden kings of the earth, was Gadhi, the great."

Now Viswamitra spoke as softly as the silver river flowed. When Rama and Lakshmana looked into his face in the moonlight, they saw his eyes had brimmed over. He wiped them briefly with the back of his hand. He said with a wistful smile, "Rama, Gadhi was my father." He paused, then continued, "I had an older sister called Satyavati. I loved her more than anyone in the world. She was my first friend, and my first guru. From her earliest years, she was wiser than any other child. She gave me something of her soul, which was my first instruction of heaven.

"My father gave her to be the rishi Richaka's wife. But she was so pure, and always with the Lord's name on her lips and his love in her heart, that she was not meant to live in this world for long. She gained Swarga in her human body. And from her love, she flowed upon the earth as a river: the Kaushiki of the Himalaya. It is on the banks of the Kaushiki that I sit in tapasya. Rama, how can I describe the peace that comes to me when I am there? It is as if my sister held me in her arms, as she used to when I was a child.

"But then, I was called south from my home beside the river in the mountains. I was to perform a sacrifice to stem a tide of evil risen in the world. I came down to Siddhasrama, as my masters of the spirit told me to. And you came to help me; otherwise I could never have completed my yagna.

"You asked whose kingdom this is. It was mine once, Rama, when I was a king as you shall be one day. But all that is past now.

"Look how high the moon has risen; half the night is over. The river and the trees, the birds in the branches and the beasts of the woods are all asleep, wrapped in covers of darkness. Only bhutas, pretas, and pisachas, for whom night is day and moonlight their sunshine, are abroad under the sky of a thousand eyes. Sleep now, my friends, and you also, children of Ayodhya. Sleep securely, for we are protected, and we must be on our way at crack of dawn."

He stretched his long limbs by the river, which scarcely gave a murmur now, and, turning on his side, fell quickly asleep. Yawning, Lakshmana and the other rishis lay down as well. They found they were exhausted after the day's long march and only the fascination of Viswamitra's story had kept them awake.

Rama sat alone for another hour, gazing at the moon reflected clear in the river, which was still as a lake now. He sat pondering the strange fates of men and his own long way ahead of him. It was opaque, yet mysteriously attractive; quite like a river, on which the days and years were slow ripples, gliding endlessly, with the moon splayed across them. But there are treacherous whirlpools along every river's course, and Rama wondered idly when they would spin into his life.

Soon, he also lay down beside his brother and slumber stole over him.

13. Ganga

The birds of day were full of song, a hundred wild symphonies in the branches, and the river was awake under the risen sun, when Viswamitra shook the sleeping princes awake. "Come, we have a long way to go."

When they had washed, Rama pointed upstream and said, "There are islands of sand in the water. Where shall we cross the river?"

But Viswamitra was already striding off in another direction. "Since the beginning, rishis have walked this way. We will follow their path."

So they marched north after the tall sage. The princes kept up with him easily, but some of the other hermits struggled. They lagged with rueful smiles and Viswamitra never turned to look back, as if he was content to have only those who could keep his pace arrive in Mithila. Rama and Lakshmana helped the others on the long way, carrying their spare-enough bundles for them, lending them an arm of support.

It was midday when they arrived on the banks of the Ganga. She lay before them like an inland sea; shading their eyes, they could barely discern her far shore. Swans and lotuses floated upon her in equal profusion, and so deep was her attraction they decided to spend the rest of the day beside her murmuring currents.

They bathed in her water and sat beside her, some dozing, others staring out across the enchanted flow; and they saw luminous daydreams, as they had not even during their dhyana in the mountains. Surely, she was awesome, she was magical, and her nearness made the body feel so light it seemed the soul could soar out and be free. In the late afternoon, the desire took the princes and the rishis alike and they waded once more into the calm, warm water. When they had bathed they felt cleansed: not just bodily but in spirit.

As the day was dying, they sat around Viswamitra. While a small fire they lit blazed up full of sparks, Rama said, "I want to hear the legend of Ganga from you. I can feel her enchantment upon me; tell us how she is tripathaga, the river of three paths."

Viswamitra's eyes were full of times that were no longer in the world, except as shadows upon the earth and the wide water. He gazed across the great river, and began quietly, "There is a mountain called Himavan, the Emperor of all mountains. That ancient spirit, who is not younger than the earth herself, had two daughters by his wife Mena. They were called Ganga and Uma, and their beauty was legend.

"Ganga was the older one, and Indra's Devas approached Himavan: they wanted his daughter for themselves, to make Devaloka more perfect than it already was. Himavan gave Ganga to the Devas; she flowed in heaven as a river of light and purified anything she touched. She flowed through the galaxies as Akasa Ganga, Mandakini, river of the firmament, with suns in her hair.

"Himavan's second child was called Parvati, mountain daughter. She sat in tapasya and won Siva for her husband. Their son was Karttikeya and he killed Tarakasura, the invincible demon of old.

"Later, there was an ancestor of yours, Rama, in the line of Ikshvaku, named Sagara. For many years Sagara had no children from his two wives: Vidarbha's daughter Kesini, and Kashyapa's daughter, the ravishing Sumati. Sagara went to the Himalaya with his queens and sat in penance for a hundred years. Men in those times were greater in every way than the men of today, and longer-lived as well. And men in the ages to follow this one shall live short and wretched lives. That is the nature of the yugas.

"When Sagara and his wives had sat in dhyana for a hundred years, the Maharishi Bhrigu came to them like a fire on the mountain, and said, 'Let your tapasya be fruitful, Sagara. One of your wives will bear you a son to continue the Ikshvaku line. The other will bear you sixty thousand princes of matchless strength and courage; but they shall not be kings.'

"Sagara's queens were radiant.

" 'Who will have sixty thousand sons?' cried Sumati, the younger.

" 'Who will have the one son?' cried Kesini.

"Bhrigu smiled, 'The choice is yours, and you seem to have made it already.'

"That rishi blessed them and Sagara and his wives returned to their kingdom. In those days, when the world was young, heaven and earth were hardly apart from each other as they are now. The earth was peopled, equally, with the children of the Gods and men. Sumati bore her husband Sagara sixty thousand sons. She did not bear them as children are born today, but by the miraculous motherhood of light and by the grace of the Devas, most of all, the grace of Brahma. Sumati's boys were handsome and brave, virile and arrogant.

"In time, Kesini also bore Sagara a son, the one who would become his heir. But to Sagara's despair, this boy, Asamanja, was an evil prince. In his childhood he would dismember insects, tearing off their delicate arms and legs when he found the little creatures wandering on the palace floor. Sagara thought it was just an infantile affliction and had elaborate pujas performed for the boy. But some years later, as he grew, Asamanja entertained himself by secretly slaughtering calves and ponies in the royal dairies and stables.

"Still, the king hoped his prince would mend. But when he reached his youth, Asamanja was caught drowning small children of the city in the Sarayu. He stood fondling himself as he watched their desperate struggles. Sagara saw his son was evil. Yet he waited, hoping against hope the boy would mend. Finally, his people came to petition Sagara against the prince. The king banished Asamanja from the kingdom, though it broke his heart.

"But there was some consolation for Sagara. Asamanja's son Anshuman was a noble, gentle child, and devoted to his grandfather. When Anshuman was a young man, Sagara undertook an aswamedha yagna. For his yagnashala, he chose the plains between the Himalaya and the Vindhya mountains, which glower at each other across the sacred land like mortal enemies. He sent a white horse across the country, with his grandson Anshuman riding with it: daring any king to arrest its careen, and claiming fealty from those whose kingdoms the horse crossed unchallenged.

"But there is always one king who obstructs the aswamedha yagnas of the rulers of the earth. Indra spirited away that horse. The brahmanas who had charge of the yagna said to Sagara, 'If the horse is not found and the yagna not completed, calamity will visit the House of Ikshvaku.'

"Sagara called his sixty thousand sons by Sumati, of whom their mother was so proud, and said to them, 'Go and find the horse, wherever it may be.'

"Like the wind, like fire, air, and tameless water, they swept away in quest of the horse, those ferocious, elemental Sagaraputras. They excavated the earth, they razed whole forests, to discover where the animal was hidden. They brought terror wherever they went, among men and beasts, great old plants, and even the rakshasas of the jungles. They came with such violence.

"They could not find the horse by land or by sea, though they searched for it with the powers of sorcery they inherited from their celestial ancestors. They burrowed into the nether worlds, the deep Patalas, where pale and grave Asuras and emerald nagas with resplendent jewels in their heads dwell in darkness and peace. They saw the elephants of legend, the Diggajas that bear the earth upon their heads. But they saw no horse of their father's aswamedha.

"They went deeper, down the spiraling paths of the twilight realms. They came to a dark cavern and, from within it, heard the whinny of a horse in tether. In they plunged and saw, seated in padmasana, the posture of the lotus, the Maharishi Kapila Vasudeva, his eyes shut, absorbed in the Brahman. Beyond the rishi in dhyana was their father's white horse, tied to a tree.

" 'Thief!' they roared, and rushed at Kapila with their weapons raised. The muni's eyes flew open to see who dared disturb his samadhi, and instantly those sixty thousand sons of Sagara were made ashes; for they all plunged into that unequal encounter in brash, foolhardy waves. When all of them were ashed, Kapila shut his eyes again with a sigh, as if nothing of any moment had happened. He went back to his meditation.

"Sagara waited a long time for his host of sons to return to him with the sacrificial horse. But when no sign or word of them came, he sent Anshuman after them into the Patalas. Anshuman followed the trail of mayhem his uncles had left and arrived at the mouth of Kapila's cave. He saw the glow from the rishi's body, and went in very quietly. The horse was tethered beside the muni, who sat lost to the world, his aura illumining the darkness. Anshuman waited patiently for Kapila to emerge from his trance.

"For a long time Anshuman stood motionless; at last, Kapila opened his eyes and looked gently at the prince. Anshuman prostrated himself at the rishi's feet. He said, 'Holy one, I am King Sagara's grandson Anshuman. I have come in search of my grandfather's sacrificial horse.'

"Kapila smiled at the noble youth. 'Your horse is with me, child. Indra left him here.' He pointed at the ashes strewn across the cave's floor. 'Your uncles came here in violence,' he said, 'and I was forced to burn them.'

"Anshuman grieved for his uncles. He wanted to offer tarpana for them, so their souls could rise into heaven. But he could find no water in Patala. As he ranged those dark labyrinths in quest of water, he heard a sound of vast wings. Garuda, who was Sumati's brother, flew down to him.

"Garuda said to the distraught Anshuman, 'No common water will wash the sins of your uncles. They violated Bhumidevi and outraged the spirits who are her guardians. Only the waters of Himalaya's daughter who flows through the stars can purify their souls. You must bring the Ganga down to wash their ashes; only then will they find deliverance.'

"Anshuman stood in awe of Garuda, and terrified by the task he himself had inherited. The eagle-winged one said to him, 'But it is not yet time for the sacred river to flow on earth. Take your horse home to your grandfather. He waits anxiously for you, and the aswamedha must be completed.'

"Anshuman did as Garuda asked, and Sagara was able to finish his yagna. But the king was a broken man after he learned of the death of his sons. He left his kingdom to Anshuman, as soon as the prince was old enough, and went away to the mountains with his wives. He went to perform tapasya, to purify himself before he left his body and was gathered to his fathers.

"Anshuman was a just king. But ruling his kingdom absorbed him entirely, and he found no time to undertake a penance that would bring the Ganga down to the earth, and to Patala below, where his uncles' ashes lay whispering in grief that their souls languished in a limbo.

"Anshuman's son Dilipa was a great kshatriya, as well. But not even he could bring the Ganga down to redeem his ancestors. The destiny of the Ikshvaku line was impeded by the unresolved sins of the sons of Sumati, and the ruling kings were hard-pressed to keep evil from the kingdom. For by now, the curse was into their very blood."

Viswamitra's story held princes and rishis in thrall. He bore them back to primeval times, dim and magnificent, when sovereigns of unearthly lineage ruled the kingdoms of the earth. Whenever he paused, the others sat with bated breath, lest they disturb his flow of inspiration beside the holy river.

"Dilipa had a son called Bhagiratha," resumed the brahmarishi, master of the ancient lore. "Like his father Anshuman, Dilipa ruled Sagara's kingdom until age and debility overtook him. He ruled for thirty thousand years, and that was how long men lived in those times if they were not killed in battle. But he did not rule as long as his fathers before him, for the curse grew stronger every day. Dilipa left his kingdom to his son Bhagiratha, and passed on from the world.

"By now, the curse on the Ikshvaku line told not just on the royal family but on the common people. Bhagiratha was the first of his line to realize that there was no hope in ruling, as best he could, and keeping darkness at bay, as well as he might. The curse already afflicted him grievously: he could not father a son. It was as if the sons of Sumati cried out in his blood for the expiation of their sin. Bhagiratha knew he had to exorcise the curse at its root. He knew he must spend his life in tapasya, if need be, to bring the Ganga down into the world to wash his ancestors' ashes.

"Bhagiratha left his kingdom in the hands of some trusted ministers. He went to the mountains and sat in an excruciating penance. At last, one day, at the end of a thousand years spent on the icy Himalaya, Brahma appeared before the king. The Grandsire of the worlds said, 'Ask for anything you want.'

"Bhagiratha's eyes swam with tears. His voice was long unused, since he had taken a vow of silence; besides, to whom would he speak in that blizzard-swept fastness, where not even mountain rakshasas ventured? Choking, Bhagiratha said, 'Father of worlds, grant that I may perform the niravapanjali for my ancestors with the waters of the Ganga; and that they attain Swarga. Brahma, grant also that I have a son to continue the line of Ikshvaku.'

"Unable to refuse this king of tapasya anything, Brahma said, 'You will have a noble son, to be king after you. But just think, if the Ganga comes down into the world, who will break her fall? The very earth will be shattered. If you want her to flow here, you must petition Siva to bear her fall.'

"Bhagiratha turned in bhakti to the Lord Siva, who is easily moved. When he had fasted in Siva's name, living on just air for a year, the God of Gods appeared before the Ikshvaku king.

"Siva said, 'You should not have to sit in tapasya for a cause as just as yours. I am pleased with your devotion to your ancestors. I will break Ganga's fall, and her pride as well.'

"After ages of flattery, verging on worship, by the Devas of the sky who adored her, Ganga had grown vain. When Brahma told her to flow down in the world, she scoffed at him. 'The earth will perish from this madness. For there is no one who can bear my descent!'

"But she could not refuse to do as Brahma asked. On the appointed night, the Devas gathered in the sky in their ethereal chariots, like a flotilla of full moons; while below, on a plateau of the Himalaya in the icebound north, Bhagiratha stood with his gaze trained on the heavens. There was no sign of Siva.

"Suddenly a deafening roar shook the firmament. High above him, beyond the chariots of the Devas which they flew out of harm's way, Bhagiratha saw her coming: she was a sheet of silver, filling the night sky. He shut his eyes with a prayer. He was sure this was the end of the world; for who indeed could support the fall of that ocean? Like a cosmic flash flood she came, hurtling down the Milky Way, and laughing as she did: she was amused that Brahma had not cared to heed her warning.

"But then, another figure loomed beside Bhagiratha. He appeared out of the very air. He was the Lord of night, Sarvaripati Siva, and his face was loftier than the moon and the Devas' vimanas. The Devas began to sing his praises when they saw him like that. But Ganga swept on, and only Siva knew what was in her arrogant heart. Exhilarated by her plunge down the constellations, she thought to herself, 'I will show Siva who I am. I will thrust him down into Patala!'

"Siva, who knows all things, stood smiling, his head exposed to her mad descent. With a crash like thunder in the galaxy, Ganga fell straight down upon Siva's hallowed head. Bhagiratha shut his eyes, certain this was the end. Even the Devas above fell silent; they, too, did not believe anyone could survive that crystal cataract.

"A hush fell on earth and sky. But not a drop of water, let alone a deluge, fell on the terrified Bhagiratha. Siva was not crushed under Ganga's tidal fall. He still stood smiling, lustrous in the moonlight. But she, endless river, had vanished: she was lost in Siva's jata. And struggle as she would, she could find no way out from where she was absorbed like a water drop. One drop in the ocean that was He.

"She roared and she screamed. She rose in dreadful floods and spun in whirlpools deep as the orbits of the planets. But there was no escape for her. At his inexorable will, she was a lake at the root of one strand of his hair; she trembled when he laughed. His time for prayer not yet over, Bhagiratha lay on his face before the Lord. For fear that Siva might never set Ganga free he worshipped Mahadeva, for the sake of his ancestors.

"At last Siva released Ganga along the hair of his head at the root of which he had held her. Drop by drop, he wrung her down onto the earth. High on the Himalayan tableland a pool formed, gleaming in the rising sun: the Bindusaras, made of droplets of the chastened river of heaven. Ganga, humbled, was called Alakananda.

"As Bhagiratha and the Devas watched, entranced, the pool grew into a lake, and the lake flowed into seven streams. Three of these flowed west and three east, down the Himalaya. The seventh stream followed Bhagiratha's chariot south, onto the plains of the sacred continent. She followed him playfully and in wonder at being in this new world which was once, in dim memory, her home.

"Her foam was white as milk as she flowed after the Ikshvaku king's chariot, which he rode like the free wind in his fervor to fulfill his task of such long standing. Ganga followed that chariot. At times she would flow straight and quick as an arrow, keeping easy pace with the horses; but at others, she meandered, coy and difficult, or undulated sinuous as a serpent. She who had washed the starry feet of Mahavishnu and had plunged through the zone of the moon, she who was purified for the third time when she fell on Siva's head, had come down the mandalas to liberate some ashes that lay on a subterranean cave floor.

"Tapasvin king and shining river finally arrived at the place where Bhagiratha's haughty ancestors, Sumati's sons, had entered the underworlds. The earth yawned open. Ganga swirled down into Patala and fell in a cascade into the cave where Kapila once sat in dhyana. Bhagiratha saw the baptismal waters flow into the cave mouth. He stood there, hardly daring to breathe. Then he saw his ancestors rise from the ashes in sudden spirit fire, their astral bodies purified, their long ordeal ended. Blessing him in sixty thousand ringing voices, they rose into heaven. The curse on the Ikshvaku line had ended.

"Brahma appeared, coruscant as suns, and said to Bhagiratha, 'Noble child, you have done the impossible! From this day, whenever any man prevails against the most difficult odds of fate, his effort shall be called a Bhagiratha prayatna. As long as the ocean has water in it, your ancestors will live in heaven. And the Ganga will be your daughter in the eyes of the Gods. I name her Bhagirathi.' "

Such mysteries filled Viswamitra's eyes as he ended his legend of times when the seas were still nameless, when kings of the earth were hardly mortal, but like Gods. When he had finished, his audience of kshatriyas and munis sat on in silence, claimed by the past. They sat unmoving by the mystic river that once fell from the sky, and the whispering of her currents bore them far from themselves.

Viswamitra said softly, "Ganga is called tripathaga because she who flowed in Swarga, flowed also on Bhumi and in Patala. The three paths."

He grew silent, and stared out at the silver expanse before them, stretching away to the horizon where the moon had risen and hung low: the same moon which had, once, witnessed Bhagiratha's incredible prayatna. Breaking his spell, Viswamitra stretched himself. Some of his hermits rose and went to walk beside the river, and the princes of Ayodhya went with them.

But later that night, after all the others were asleep and the fire had burned down, Rama lay awake beside his brother and hearkened to the Ganga. She spoke to him secretly of strange and marvelous ages, and he was amazed that he could understand what she said. Like lucid dreams, pristine legends played themselves out before his mind's eye and the river was his guru under the moon.

14. Rishi Gautama's asrama

The next day, Viswamitra's party crossed the wide water in a fisherman's coracle and the river blessed them on their way. On the northern bank of the Ganga, they came to the gates of Vishala. The city was built where Diti, mother of the Daityas, once sat chanting noxious mantras taught her by Kashyapa. She prayed for a boy who would kill her sister Aditi's son, Indra.

Diti became pregnant by Kashyapa's seed. But the vow she had sworn was exacting: a thousand years of perfect purity, even during her pregnancy. One day, after she had bathed, Diti fell asleep with her head on her knees and the tips of her hair brushing her feet. Indra had waited like a serpent for this moment's lapse. He flashed into her womb through her nostril, and cut her child in seven pieces with his diamond thunderbolt. But he could not extinguish life within those pieces. The seven pieces began to wail aloud inside their sleeping mother. Indra cut each of the seven pieces in seven again. But they still howled. In despair, the Deva hissed at them, *"Maa Ruda! Maa Ruda!"* "Don't cry! Don't cry!"

Diti awoke, shaking, and she knew what had happened. Indra said to her, "Your vow protected your children; even my vajra could not kill them. Here, take them, they are forty-nine now."

But Diti realized that now her sons could never kill the Deva king. She said to Indra, "Fate has decided that evil won't befall you. You take these sons of mine and let them be your brothers."

Indra took those splendid children among the Devas and they became companions to Vayu of the air. For what Indra whispered to them in their mother's womb, they were called the Maruts.

In Vishala, where once Diti kept an imperfect vow, King Sumathi of one branch of the Ikshvaku line ruled. He came out from his palace to welcome Viswamitra and his party. They stayed a night in that city and set out the next morning for Mithila. But when Sumathi visited them, Viswamitra's rishis told him how Rama came to Siddhasrama, and how he killed the rakshasas. It was from Vishala that Rama's fame first spread, with the story of how Maricha was carried a hundred yojanas to the sea by the manavastra.

They came to the outskirts of Mithila, grander than Vishala. Glowing silver and gold, jewels embedded in her walls, the city's towers and ramparts stroked the sky. Kshatriyas and rishis were full of wonder. At the edge of the city, Rama pointed to a grove of fruit trees with an auspicious air. At its heart was an asrama, in seclusion.

"What asrama is this where no one lives," asked the prince, drawn strangely to the place, "though it is so beautiful and built on the hem of a great city?"

A light in his eye, Viswamitra said, "If you think the asrama is beautiful now, you should have seen it when Maharishi Gautama sat in dhyana under its trees. Rama, this place was like a bit of heaven fallen into the earth.

"Gautama's tapasya was so profound that Brahma created a woman called Ahalya, of unequaled beauty, and gave her to Gautama to be his wife. For years they lived happily together. But one day, Indra saw Ahalya and was smitten by her. When Gautama went to the river for his evening bath, the Deva assumed the rishi's form and came to Ahalya. She knew him at once; but that lovely woman was flattered that the Deva desired her. She allowed Indra to make love to her on the very floor of the asrama where she slept nightly with her husband.

"When passion was slaked, Ahalya became sensible of the danger they were in. She cried to Indra, 'Go quickly, before my husband returns.'

"But in his arrogance and languor, he laughed, 'He will not finish his worship so soon.' He began to make love to her again, and Ahalya could not resist his caresses.

"The brief time of love is a long while. When they were satisfied, and Indra himself realized he should leave, it was too late. Just as the Deva prepared to go out with a last embrace, Gautama stood at the door, staring in amazement at someone who looked exactly like himself, holding Ahalya in his arms. But he knew at once who it was. Indra, king of Devaloka, stood revealed before the rishi. But Gautama was not moved.

"In a terrible voice, he cursed the Deva. 'Your vanity, that no woman can resist your charms, made you commit this crime. Let your charms be seen by all the world from today, a thousandfold. Let your body be adorned with a thousand phalluses, so everyone knows your real nature.'

"Reeling from the curse, the Deva fled. Already he felt the thousand appendages of his shame pushing their lewd way out through his skin. Thus, the Deva king was called Satakratu. For a thousand divine years, each of which is three hundred and sixty-five human years long, Indra sat in a fervid penance. Only then, Brahma softened the curse of Gautama: he changed Indra's thousand phalluses into a thousand eyes.

"But that evening after Indra fled, the heartbroken Gautama cursed Ahalya in their hut, 'Unfaithful woman, you have betrayed your womanhood. Be as dust on the ground!'

"She cried out in anguish. Tears in his eyes, the maharishi looked at his wife and knew he could not curse either her or himself forever. He said, 'In the treta yuga, Vishnu will be born as a prince of this earth. When his holy feet touch the dust you now become, you will be forgiven.'

"Before his eyes, she turned into dust on the floor of the asrama where she had betrayed him. Gautama vanished from this place and was never seen here again."

Now they stood on the threshold of the asrama. Viswamitra pushed the door and it creaked open. With his hands, he cleared the cobwebs that hung from ceiling and wall in thick lattices. He let in the light of

tant parts. They soon fell asleep. Only Rama and Lakshmana were still awake. They watched the moon rise near midnight, and were lost in a reverie of Viswamitra's astonishing life.*

16. Siva's bow

With the early sun, Janaka came back to Viswamitra and his party. The king said, "Through the night, I thought about your presence in my city at this auspicious time. I feel more certain than ever that you have come with a blessing for me. Command me, my lord; how may I serve you?"

Viswamitra replied, "Perhaps you are right, Janaka, and I have come to you with a blessing. But these princes of Ayodhya, who are master archers, have come to look at Siva's bow. Let the ayudha be fetched out. It may be that your fortune, like your ancestors', is still bound to it."

Janaka sat down with them. He said, "Before we look at Siva's bow, let me tell you how I came to have it. My House is called Videha, and Nimi was a great kshatriya in our line. After Nimi, the sixth king in olden times was Devaratha. It was to Devaratha that the bow was first given, and he was told to keep it safely.

"It happened in the days when Siva's father-in-law, Daksha, held his infamous yagna, to which he did not invite either his daughter Sati or Siva. But Sati went anyway. She did not want to be Daksha's daughter any more, and raising the inner fire of yoga in her body, she made ashes of herself. The Devas watched in terror; for in their vanity they had all come to Daksha's sacrifice.

"Siva arrived at that yagna with his army of ganas. He came with his bow in his hand to kill Daksha and the Devas. He said, 'Sati burned herself while you watched. I will part your jeweled heads from your bodies!'

"But they fell at his feet, and Mahadeva is easily pacified, for his heart is kind. He forgave the Devas, and gave Daksha a goat's head in place of the one Virabhadra had hewn from his neck. It was at that time, as if he did not trust himself in his terrible grief, that Siva gave his bow for safekeeping to my ancestor Devaratha. Ever since, the

*See "The Story of Viswamitra" in the Appendix.

bow has been with us and we have guarded it as our most precious treasure, the root of our fortune."

Now he paused, and glanced at Viswamitra. The rishi, who knew the best part of the king's story was yet to be told, smiled to encourage him. Janaka brightened as if a hope he held dear had been confirmed. He resumed slowly: he had arrived at the heart of his tale.

The king of Mithila said, "Some years ago, I was turning the earth for another yagna. Suddenly before my golden plow I saw a child lying on the ground, like a piece of the moon. She lay smiling at me, and my heart would not be still until I had brought her to my wife. We decided to raise her as our daughter."

Janaka's face lit up. "We called her Sita because we had found her in a furrow at the head of the plow, and we soon realized she was no ordinary child. Her devotion to her parents, her uncanny knowledge of people, her compassion, her gentleness and grace, and not least, Muni, her beauty, are scarcely of this mortal world."

He stopped again, and for an instant stared straight at Rama. That prince's heart was on strange, fine fire that he had never known before in his young life. He looked away in mild confusion, while Viswamitra hid a smile.

Now in the tone of sharing a secret, Janaka continued, "To tell you honestly, my friends, in Mithila we think of Sita as an Avatara of the Devi Lakshmi. Never before has this kingdom known such prosperity as we have since we found her."

They saw his eyes grow moist as he spoke of Sita. "I decided she would only marry a prince who was worthy of her. And we prayed that such a man might come for her someday. Meanwhile, so many kshatriyas came to Mithila, wanting to marry Sita. But I refused them all. One angry king cried at me, 'To whom then, Janaka, will you give your daughter?'

"Without thinking, I replied, 'To the man who can lift Siva's bow and string it!'

"A hundred kshatriyas came. But none of them could move the bow from where it lay, let alone pick it up. Once an alliance of kings brought a great army and surrounded my city. How could I withstand such a force on my own? I prayed to the Devas and they sent a host from heaven, because I was the guardian of Siva's bow. How swiftly that battle was concluded: the kshatriyas fled from the astras of the Gods. Yes, quite a tale hangs by the bow of Siva."

He rose and took Rama and Lakshmana by the hand. "Come to my palace and I will have Siva's bow fetched for you to see."

Just within the palace gates, the bow was displayed so that all who passed could look at it. It was kept in an iron casket and worshipped with incense, flowers, and mantras during the three sandhyas of the day.

Janaka led them to the palace arena, festive with flags, garlands, and banners for the yagna. Already, thousands of people had streamed into it, from far and near, for the sacrifice. When his most recently arrived guests were seated with honor, Janaka clapped his hands to his guards to bring the bow.

In its great casket, Siva's bow was wheeled in. It lay on a low golden cart, glimmering with jewels. A hundred strong men pulled on the massive ropes that dragged the cart of eight wheels. This was Siva's bow with which he had threatened the Devas. The crowd rose. A vast murmur of *AUM Namah Sivayah!* was heard, like an ocean wave in that stadium.

Janaka went to Viswamitra and bowed to him, to show that the rishi was the most revered person present. The king said aloud, "Brahmarishi Viswamitra, here lies the bow of Mahadeva, which has broken the pride of many a kshatriya. No Deva, gandharva, kimpurusha, kinnara, Asura, or great naga has been able to lift this bow; not through all the ages, since Siva gave it to my ancestor."

The guards flung back the casket's cover. The jewels on that weapon shot livid shafts of color through the day and the crowd gasped. Viswamitra turned to Rama at his side; the prince was as tense as a bowstring himself. Softly, the rishi said, "Rama, my child, go and look at Siva's bow."

A hush fell on the crowd when Rama rose. He was radiant; he was unworldly blue. He crossed gracefully to the casket. For a moment, he stood gazing at the bow. Then a smile lit his face. He said, "Muni, may I touch the bow?"

Janaka cried, "Of course! What else have you come for?"

Viswamitra nodded to Rama. The prince leaned forward and stroked the great weapon with his fingertips. Viswamitra whispered to Janaka, "Ask him if he can lift it."

Janaka shot the rishi a doubtful glance: he was afraid lest this prince could *not* lift Siva's bow. For suddenly, his heart was set on giving his precious Sita to Rama and no one else. But Viswamitra insisted, bristling his brows at the king.

Then Rama himself turned and said in a clear voice, "I think I can lift the bow and string it. May I try?"

A great intuition of destiny swept the people. The crowd was on its feet, ready for a miracle.

"You may!" cried king and sage together.

Effortlessly, as if it was his own weapon that he carried at his back every day, Rama picked up Siva's bow from its casket. The crowd sighed. Calmly, the prince bent the bow and strung it. A thunderflash exploded in his hands. The earth shook and most of the people fell down stunned: Siva's awesome bow had snapped in two. Smiling faintly, Rama placed the pieces back in the casket.

Janaka ran forward and embraced him, again and again. Then he hugged Lakshmana and, with tears in his eyes, he bowed over and over to Viswamitra, who had brought Rama to Mithila. Janaka cried to the dazed crowd, "The prince of Ayodhya has done what no other kshatriya could! I am delighted to give my daughter Sita to him. There is no warrior in heaven or earth like Rama." He turned to Viswamitra. "My lord, may I send messengers to Dasaratha? To ask him to come to Mithila, so Rama and Sita can be married as soon as possible."

Viswamitra glanced at Rama. He saw joy brimming on the prince's face, and he said, "Do so, Janaka. Let the news fly to Ayodhya." Within the hour, the king's messengers set out on the swiftest horses in Mithila's royal stables.

From her room, high up in Janaka's palace, Sita had seen Rama when he came and she had prayed he would string the bow. She had lost her heart the moment she set eyes on him: it was this prince she had always dreamed of and waited for. She knew him from long ago, from countless lives before. They had belonged together since time began.

17. Dasaratha goes to Mithila

Like the wind, Janaka's messengers rode for three days, until they saw the turrets of Ayodhya. Shouting to one another, they flashed up to Dasaratha's gates.

"Take us to your king!" they cried to the guards. "We come with joyful news from King Janaka and Rishi Viswamitra."

Dasaratha welcomed them eagerly into his sabha. The messengers' leader announced, "Great Dasaratha! Janaka of Mithila sends his greetings. He inquires after your majesty's health and the welfare of your kingdom."

Dasaratha waved impatiently to the man that he should deliver the news he brought. As the sabha in Ayodhya sat hushed, the messenger said, "Janaka wants you to hear a petition from him of which Brahmarishi Viswamitra approves. My master says: 'I have a daughter called Sita. I swore that the man who marries her must first string the bow of Siva, which the Lord gave my ancestor. Countless kshatriyas tried, and failed even to move the bow. But, Dasaratha, your Rama, watched by a crowd of kings, rishis, and my people, strung Siva's bow as if it were a toy. I want Sita to become your son's wife. My lord, accept my gift more precious to me than life. I beg you, come quickly to Mithila to bless the young couple.' Janaka awaits your reply."

Dasaratha rose and cried, "The children are in Videha with Viswamitra, and you all hear what my Rama has done!" He turned to Vasishta, Vamadeva, and his other ministers. "Janaka wants to have the wedding as soon as he can. If none of you has any objection, let us go to Mithila straightaway."

The rishis gave their assent happily, for Sita's fame had spread long ago to Ayodhya. It was decided they would leave the next morning. After their journey, the messengers from Mithila slept soundly; but the king of Kosala hardly slept that night, because he was as excited as a boy at the thought of seeing Rama again. It seemed like a lifetime since his child had gone away with that knowing Viswamitra.

The next day, the chariots and palanquins to carry Ayodhya's royal family gleamed in the dawn outside the palace. Night long, preparations had been under way in the queens' apartments and in the treasury. This was no ordinary visit by one king to another. This was the occasion of Rama's wedding, and cartloads of gold and priceless jewelry would travel with the party from Ayodhya.

It was customary for them to go ahead, and the king's rishis, Vasishta, and the others were the first to leave. When the sun was halfway to his zenith, Dasaratha himself emerged from the palace. He was greeted with a roar from his people, thronging to see him off to the wedding of their beloved Rama.

They took five days to reach Mithila, and Janaka rode out from his city to welcome Dasaratha and his company. With his relatives, his ministers, and Sadananda, Janaka came to meet Dasaratha. He saw Rama's father, and, eschewing formality, rode forward and embraced Dasaratha emotionally. The people saw that both kings had tears in their eyes.

Now Janaka welcomed his royal guest formally, saying, "My lord, I thank you for coming to Mithila. You honor me by accepting my hospitality. I am already thrice blessed that the great Vasishta has come to my city, and Vamadeva and Markandeya with him.

"But more than anything else, Dasaratha, your son has realized my most cherished dream for me. If he had not come, I would have been forced to break my oath that Sita would marry only the man who strung Siva's bow. My yagna is almost complete. As its culmination, you must allow me to have Rama and Sita married."

Dasaratha bowed and said happily, "It is not my place to tell a king like you when the wedding should take place. Your brahmanas must know that better than I."

Janaka took Dasaratha's arm and they entered Mithila together. Here also, the people milled in the streets to welcome the king from Ayodhya. Dasaratha and his party were lodged in a palace prepared for their stay. Viswamitra waited for them there. Overwhelmed when he saw the rishi, Dasaratha prostrated himself at his feet.

Viswamitra raised him up gently, murmuring, "Dasaratha, I hope you don't regret having sent your sons with me. The ways of fate are mysterious and I have lived longer than you to know them."

He led the king inside with an arm around his shoulders. Then Dasaratha's face lit up as if a sun had risen in his heart: Rama waited there, with Lakshmana beside him. Janaka and Viswamitra left the father and his sons together, and withdrew to the yagnashala where the Vedas were being chanted without pause.

Evening was upon them when the princes were left alone with Dasaratha, who embraced them repeatedly, tears flowing down his face. He made them sit close beside him, while he lay down to rest after his journey. He made them repeat all their adventures, beginning when they left Ayodhya with Viswamitra and ending with how Rama strung Siva's bow. At least ten times he heard the story from both Rama and Lakshmana, as if it was food, drink, and air to him. And he held Rama's hand tightly, as happy an old man as could be found on earth.

Rama and Lakshmana spent all night with their father, while Janaka and the rishis were at the yagnashala, where the sacrifice was nearing its end. Early the next morning, the ritviks collected around the vedika and the final rites were completed without blemish.

Janaka said to Sadananda, "I want to share my joy with my brother Kusadhvaja."

Sadananda sent messengers to Kusadhvaja, who was the king of Samkashya beside the limpid Ikshumati. When his brother arrived, Janaka, his ministers, his gurus, and his family gathered in the royal sabha.

Janaka said to his chief minister, Sudama, "My lord, fetch Dasaratha and his sons to our sabha."

The king of Ayodhya and his princes came, and they were resplendent. Janaka and Kusadhvaja went to Dasaratha with folded hands, and brought him, Rama, and Lakshmana to golden thrones set apart for them.

Dasaratha said solemnly, "Janaka, my friend, my guru Vasishta will recall the ancestry of the young man who is to marry your daughter."

Vasishta rose and traced the line of Manu. He told of the greatness of Ikshvaku, who was the first mortal king to rule Ayodhya. He told of Trishanku, Yuvanashva of renown, and his son Mandhata, who was called the jewel of the krita yuga. Of Sagara he spoke, of Anshuman and Bhagiratha, of Kakushta and Raghu, and of Aja, whose son was Dasaratha himself. He ended formally, Brahma's son, the kulaguru of Ikshvaku, the royal House of the Sun: "Now you know the antecedents of Rama. Be pleased to give your daughter Sita, who is a rare treasure among women, to Dasaratha's son."

Janaka bowed to Vasishta. He rose from his throne and said, "My lords, I too will tell you about my ancestors. Nimi was the first of our line, and after his son Mithi our city was called Mithila." He began the account of his illustrious line. Each king was named, down the august generations, and his fame recited, until he came to Svarnaroma, who was his own father.

Then Janaka said, "I ask you humbly to accept my daughter Sita to be your son Rama's wife. I have another daughter Urmila. She, also, is a lovely child, and I would be delighted if you take her to be the magnificent Lakshmana's bride."

He bowed to Dasaratha, who smiled and said, "It is our privilege to have your daughters for our sons' wives."

Viswamitra stood up suddenly and said, "Your brother Kusadhvaja has two daughters. I propose that they be married to Bharata and Shatrughna. Let your two ancient houses be bound together inextricably."

A murmur of approval hummed through the court, and Kusadhvaja rose and endorsed Viswamitra's proposal. Embracing Dasaratha, Janaka said, "My friend, let your sons purify themselves with the proper rituals. Three days from today, under the auspicious Uttara Phalguni nakshatra, we will solemnize the weddings."

The kings returned to their apartments.

18. Rama kalyana

In the sabha of Mithila, purified with mantras and incense, flowers and sacred yantras, Dasaratha waited with his sons and Vasishta, the chief priest. The princes of Ayodhya had also purified themselves with a three days' homa.

Vasishta said ritually to Janaka, "My lord, the princes wear the sacred kankanas on their wrists. They await the kanyadana, which blesses the giver and the receiver."

Now Janaka fetched his daughter. Sita was like the Goddess Lakshmi risen in her primordial lotus. The sabha fell hushed to see such loveliness upon the earth. She was as bright as a streak of lightning. Her eyes were as long as lotus petals, set wide, and she kept her gaze turned down to the ground. Her tresses, night-black and hanging below her waist, were braided with jasmine and stranded with strings of pearls. She wore a tawny silk sari, edged with gold threads and woven with crimson swans. She was entirely beautiful.

Rama's heart was given the moment he saw her. He also thought he knew her from long ago, another place and time. She walked slowly beside her father, like a princess of a higher world fallen into this one. Those who had come to attend the wedding broke spontaneously into praise. They rose and blessed her.

Janaka brought her to Rama, and he said, "This is my daughter Sita. From now, she will be yours and follow you on the path of dharma. Take her hand, Kshatriya, and my blessings be upon you both. Rama, she is a pativrata; she will be like your shadow."

Janaka poured holy water over Rama's hands, and sanctified the gift of his daughter. As the water fell into Rama's palms, they clearly heard music from Devaloka, as if it was being played in that sabha. It was music first created before the earth ever spun through darkness and light, and it made the spirit take wing. Out of the air, divine voices sang at Rama's wedding and Sita's. Lucent flowers fell out of heaven to bless them: flowers that melted away in a moment, and all Mithila was fragrant with immortality when Rama took Sita's hand in his, forever.

Janaka brought Urmila and gave her to Lakshmana. "Here is my daughter Urmila. Take her hand, Lakshmana, and let her be yours always."

Lakshmana did. Kusadhvaja brought in his two daughters, Mandavi and Srutakirti, and gave them to Bharata and Shatrughna. Seven times the four princes of Ayodhya led their brides round the fire. All of them exquisite, the girls followed a pace behind their young men. And there was no eye in that sabha, but it was tear-laden.

The kshatriyas, bright as Devas, and their brides lovelier than apsaras, came out into the open street to drummers' ecstatic rhythms. The common people sang out their blessings and showered vivid petal storms over the young couples, shouting their names and *"Jaya! Jaya!"* And now it fairly poured sweet, subtle blooms from the sky. The heartstopping songs of gandharvas wove teasingly through the melodies of Mithila's musicians: so heaven above and the earth below seemed to have become one realm, when Rama married Sita.

That city was festive and colorful as a rainbow all day long. At night, the celebrations began in earnest: the drinking, the wildest music and the dancing in the streets, in which the princes and their brides joined. These went on until the sun rose, gold and saffron.

Viswamitra came early to the young couples to bless them. He embraced Rama, as if he were his own son, and more. For a moment, it seemed the stern rishi's eyes shone with tears. He said, "My part is done. I must return to the mountains." He blessed them somberly. And then, with his rare smile, he was off, striding away toward the horizon. As they stood gazing after him, Viswamitra went back north to the Himavan and the banks of the Kaushiki. She was his sister, who waited for him.

19. Bhargava

After Viswamitra had gone, Dasaratha came to take his leave of Janaka. The two kings embraced, and when the time came to bid farewell to Sita, Janaka was overwhelmed. He clasped her to him, and then turned away quickly as if it would break his heart to look at her again. He blessed Rama and his brothers, Urmila, and his nieces.

Janaka rode out of Mithila to the place where he had come to receive Dasaratha, four momentous days ago. There he stood in his chariot, waving after the travelers until they dwindled in the distance. And still that king stood on, waving to his daughter, as her husband bore her away to another life. Sita rode in Rama's chariot, and once she had parted from her father, she did not turn back to look at him.

They had ridden for a day through friendly lands, when the riders out in the van of the company saw a plume of darkness ahead, curling into the clouds. Birds cried in alarm and wheeled panic-stricken. Beasts of the wild dashed across their path: terrified deer herds, elephant, and even a tiger. The darkness whirled toward them, swallowing the sun and quickly all the sky, until they were plunged in an unnatural night. Their horses reared in fright, whinnying; many unseated their riders. A pall of dust blew at them so they could hardly breathe.

The black wind whistled shrilly. Dasaratha cried, "I see evil omens all around. What dreadful spirit is upon us?"

Vasishta strained his eyes against the spinning darkness. Above the scream of the wind, which blew their armor off the soldiers' backs, he shouted, "Something terrible approaches! But the beasts of the earth run around us in pradakshina; whatever it is will pass."

But dread gripped the party from Ayodhya. The storm raged fiercer, as the eye of it drew near. Women swooned and strong men too. Soldiers were seized by that fear and fell from their horses in the dizzy night. Soon, few of the company were still conscious: only Rama and his brothers, Dasaratha, Vasishta, and some of the other rishis. Striding at them out of the freakish storm, they saw a tremendous figure illumining the darkness around him.

He wore the bare garb of a hermit. His unkempt jata, half of it piled high on his great head, also hung to his shoulders in thick locks. He lit the night he brought with the fire that puts out the planets when time ends. Those who had not fainted stood dazzled by him, shading their eyes. The blade of the battle-ax he carried on his shoulder glinted at them. In his other hand he carried a bow: a weapon as old and mighty as the one Rama had strung in Mithila. His eyes burned like molten drops of the sun.

Like Mahadeva come to consume the Tripura, Parasurama Bhargava, Vishnu's Avatara, brahmana warrior, bane of the kshatriyas, stood glowering at them. Vasishta and the other rishis folded their hands to the Bhargava. But inwardly they trembled that the kshatriya slaughterer was among the princes of Ayodhya. They had heard Parasurama had kept the oath he swore in his dead father's name: he had offered Jamadagni tarpana in blood. They had heard he was satisfied with the river of royal blood he had let flow, in revenge, and to quell the hubris of the kings of the earth. Yet it seemed wrath sat on his brow like thunder today, and he came swirled about in a furious night.

They offered Parasurama arghya and he took it from them. But all the while he shook with some powerful emotion. Then he had done with nicety. He seized the bridle of Rama's horse and cried in a voice full of sneering challenge, "I have heard about your archery, princeling; the people of the earth speak of nothing else. I have heard you broke Siva's bow in Mithila and I have brought another bow to test you with. For I don't believe what I have heard."

And he stood glaring at Rama, locked with him eye to eye. But now Rama shone in that gloom as brightly as Parasurama himself. A faint smile played on the prince's lips, though he said nothing yet, only held the Bhargava's gaze easily; while the other frowned at him, and growled at him, trying to shake his composure and make him look away.

Abruptly Parasurama thrust out the magnificent bow he had with him. "This belonged to my father, Jamadagni. If you are who they say, boy, let me see you string this bow and shoot an arrow from it. If you can, I will consider you a worthy adversary, and we shall fight a duel. But if you are afraid, only admit it. Accept that I am your master and I will leave you in peace."

Dasaratha gave a moan. His face was white. With folded hands, he cried to Parasurama, "I heard you had put out the fire of your anger with the blood of a thousand kings." Fear gripped his very soul; but out of love for Rama he confronted the Bhargava. Kneeling, he petitioned the apparition of wrath. "You swore to Indra you would lay down your weapons. You went to Mount Mahendra to sit in tapasya.

Then why are you here now to challenge my child? If you kill my son, it will be the end of me and of my house."

But Parasurama's glare did not move from where it was fixed on Rama's face. He ignored the king at his feet as if he were not there. He said just to Rama, "Viswakarman made two bows in the eldest days. They are the ancestors of all weapons and a legend across the three worlds. They are infused with the power of the first days of creation, and no mere mortal can bear them. Viswakarman gave one bow to Siva and the other to Vishnu. I am told you broke Sankara's bow, but I do not believe what I hear, because I know these weapons. If you did break a bow, it must have been another. Here in my hand is no replica, princeling: this is the bow of the Blue God who lies upon Anantasesha. This is Vishnu's bow, with which he broke a sliver from Siva's weapon, so the Three-Eyed One was shaken. Then they fought again and the Devas had to stop them, lest the stars be put out and the darkness of the void consumed. Yes, this is that bow.

"Siva gave his bow to the Janaka's ancestors, and Vishnu gave his to the Maharishi Richaka. And Richaka gave it to his son Jamadagni, my father. In his vanity, Kartaviryarjuna killed Jamadagni. And with this bow, Rama of Ayodhya, I spilled the blood of a generation of arrogant kshatriyas. And I, Parasurama, ruled the world for an age. When I had offered tarpana in blood to my father, I sat in penance to expiate my sin of killing a host of anointed kings. The earth I left to Kashyapa."

He paused, and his eyes were full of savage memories. His gaze was still fused with Rama's; neither wavered. The Bhargava said in his voice deep with a thousand slayings, "I have heard not only men but the Devas extol you, princeling. If you are truly who they say you are, string this bow and I will concede that we may fight."

Bhargava thrust the bow forward again. Calmly, Rama climbed down from his chariot; he raised his father up from the ground. Then he went up to Parasurama.

"You need not repeat yourself, Bhargava, I hear you clearly," said Rama quietly. "I am happy to accept your challenge, because you insult me by thinking I am afraid of you."

Quicker than the eye sees, Rama took Vishnu's bow from Parasurama. One moment, the Bhargava stood thrusting the great weapon at the prince; the next, Rama had taken the bow from him, strung it with an arrow like a streak of lightning, drawn the bowstring to his ear, and aimed the shaft at the astounded Parasurama's heart.

"Bhargava," said Rama softly, "Viswamitra is my guru and I honor him as I do my father. The brahmarishi was devoted to his sister Satyavati, and she was Jamadagni's mother. You are Viswamitra's kinsman, and you are a brahmana. Otherwise, this arrow would have already cloven your heart. Now tell me, Bhargava, what do you offer my arrow in place of your life?"

In a moment, the power of an age ebbed out of Parasurama's body. His hands shook; his spirit quailed. For the first time in his life, he knew that the kshatriya who stood before him was greater than himself. Brahma and the Devas had gathered in the sky, invisibly, to watch this encounter. They smiled when they saw Parasurama falter before Rama.

The fire was gone from the Ax-bearer; weakly he said, "You are my master, Rama of Ayodhya. I will turn back to Mahendra and never come down again, because I know that he who has come in my place is here. I know who you are, and it does not wound my pride to accept defeat from you. Rama, all my tapasya is yours."

Rama turned his bow to the sky and shot the arrow of Vishnu flaming into the darkness with which Parasurama had enveloped them. That shaft of infinite trajectory still flies through the deepest galaxies; some say the earth will end on the day Rama's arrow returns. The darkness vanished like the soul from a body at death, and the sun shone on them again. Parasurama made a pradakshina around Rama, then walked away toward the mountain of his penance, never to return to the world of men. An ancient mantle, which the Bhargava had worn for an age, passed on to the one who came after him.

Now Varuna, Lord of the ocean, appeared there in light. Rama gave Vishnu's bow to him, for the power of that weapon belonged to another time, another incarnation. If he kept it, he would forsake his destiny as a mortal man.

In place of the cosmic ayudha, Varuna gave Rama and Lakshmana each a bow. And these were great weapons as well, if not as awesome as Siva's or Vishnu's. The Deva of ocean also gave them each a magic, inexhaustible quiver, two swords in jeweled sheaths, and sets of armor, light as wishes, impenetrable. Then the God of the deeps vanished like a mist.

Once the bow of Narayana was gone, Rama's soaring anger seemed to leave him. No more did he burn like the fire that consumes the stars when time ends. He was the gentle prince of Ayodhya again, and his father's son. Rama said gently to Dasaratha, "Come, my lord, let us go home now."

Dasaratha embraced his son. But for the first time, he saw who Rama really was and he felt almost ashamed that he had ever presumed the prince belonged to him at all.

Such a welcome awaited them in Ayodhya. For a month there was music and dancing in the streets. And the people swore their Rama, who the rishis said was Vishnu incarnate, had surely found his Lakshmi. She was as gentle and humble as he was, and they truly were the perfect couple. The light of their love shone through Ayodhya and the people were full of joy, knowing their future was secure in the hands of a great and noble kshatriya.

But fate had other designs on the lives of the young couple, lost in each other's tender love. Time had a sinister way to lead them down. Far away on a jade island, a monster lived, whose path was to cross theirs in evil.

BOOK TWO

AYODHYA KANDA

{In Ayodhya}

1. Rama

Kaikeyi was Dasaratha's third and youngest queen, after Kausalya and Sumitra. She was his favorite and she was Bharata's mother. Her father, King Asvapati of Kekaya, was growing old, and Dasaratha sent Bharata to visit his grandfather. Sumitra's son, Shatrughna, went with Bharata. Asvapati was as happy as could be, as he lavished his love and hospitality on the princes.

In Ayodhya, not the sun above was the light of that city and its aging king, but Rama. The Devas knew who Rama was. But he himself was not aware of his divinity save on rare occasions, as when he faced Parasurama and someone from deep inside him rose to meet the Bhargava's challenge. Siva's bow and Vishnu's had been light in his hands; but he was hardly conscious of being Narayana himself, or he would not have suffered as he did during his life, as every mortal man must.

In fact, Rama was not aware of being special at all, and he gave freely and generously of his affection. However, the world saw qualities in him that were more than merely human. For instance, his appearance was so arresting that wherever the prince went every gaze turned to his dark face and his magnificent form. They said in Ayodhya that looking at Rama's face was like seeing a bit of heaven.

He was brave; he was strong and charming. He was imperturbable, as Vasishta and his father saw when Parasurama confronted him; until he strung Vishnu's bow, and then he was more fearsome than the Bhargava. But no man can live in the constant knowledge that his own son is an Avatara. Dasaratha quickly reverted to his simple and boundless father's love for his prince. He seldom thought either of Siva's bow or of Vishnu's. The old man knew nothing of Ravana of Lanka and the strange and perilous path his son must tread.

Rama was the soft sun at Dasaratha's side in the autumn of his days. The prince was kind and courteous, wonderfully intelligent and thoughtful of everyone; whether they were kings or commoners, he made no distinction. He saw unerringly into men's hearts, regardless

63

of whether they were kshatriyas or servants, and had the rarer gift of compassion.

If someone was harsh to him, from envy or sorrow, he never retorted in kind but tried to fathom the cause. Many who had come to the prince with their hearts set against him left praising him. It was easy to love Rama; indeed, it was impossible to resist him. His charm was a profound thing, not quite of this world.

Consider his nature. He never seemed to remember any good he did, and this he did daily because he was in a position to as his father's favorite son. But he never forgot a favor he received, however slight. They said in Ayodhya that he never forgot a smile.

But Rama was no fool, if he was kind. He read men's minds with the sureness of someone much older than he was; he saw through you with the first word or glance. You had the uncanny feeling he knew you better than you did yourself, and loved you no matter who you were. He might forgive you any malice at all, but you could never deceive Rama. Yet you never felt he judged you.

He loved the old and always had time for them. He said he learned so much from the elderly, about the world they had lived in for longer than he had. He went freely among his people, like a commoner himself, never with any guards. He said the people were his life, and they in return adored him.

Rama had just one obsession: he would never tell a lie; not under any circumstances, however expedient it was or apparently harmless. It was as if his life depended on the truth. His people marveled at this quality in such a powerful kshatriya. They said that of all the illustrious line of Ikshvaku, Rama was surely the jewel.

Rama had a deep and subtle mind, and was the joy of his gurus Vasishta, Markandeya, and Vamadeva. His knowledge of the Vedas and the other scriptures was exhaustive. But he was also original in his exposition of the sanatana dharma: he was luminously relevant. He could translate the oldest proverb or syllogism into startling everyday pertinence. This gift took even Vasishta unawares, with its simple brilliance. Often the rishi wondered if this prince learned from him, or the other way around. At times, when Rama illumined a great truth from the Vedas with a vibrant metaphor from the streets of Ayodhya, Vasishta wondered if he was not hearing the timeless wisdom for the first time. Rama's expositions verged on revelation.

Yet Rama never spoke out of turn; he had been born with the gift

64

of keeping his own counsel. With the discrimination of a Brihaspati, he knew unerringly who his friends were and who his enemies. It is perhaps absurd to try to enumerate the qualities of a prince whose perfections we know were, very likely, numberless.

He was an artist of merit. He played on the vina and the flute with talent; though neither with the same wild genius as he was to play one of them, an age later, near the end of the dwapara yuga, when he came again as another, altogether more flamboyant prince of the earth.

He was a master, as every kshatriya should be, of horse and elephant, and of the vyuhas of war. He drove a chariot like the fleeting wind. The Devas knew his archery was unrivaled not just in this world, but all the realms.

He was a master of his anger, and he had no knowledge of envy. As Narada said to Valmiki: in this prince of Ayodhya all the virtues that Brahma ever created were gathered as the galaxies are within the universe. Rama was an embodiment of grace. But most of all he was human; and like any man, he could suffer.

Not just his father, his mothers, his exquisite wife, and his adoring people loved Rama; the knowing earth wanted him to be her sovereign. After all, it was what he was born for.

2. A yuvaraja for Ayodhya

As he grew older, Dasaratha's world was fuller than ever of his eldest son. The father saw the greatness of the young man: with his three mothers, between whom he made no distinction; with his wife and his brothers; with the rishis and the ministers in the palace; and outside the palace, with the people of Ayodhya. And the aging king wanted to crown Rama yuvaraja, the heir apparent. He longed to see his son stand before him in the royal sabha, dripping with the waters of the abhisheka.

"My Rama will be a greater king than I ever was," he knew. "He is as strong as Indra and as wise as Brihaspati. Once I have made him yuvaraja, I can leave this world in peace."

But then he began to see evil omens in the air and on the land, and the water that flowed ran queerly. The king thought these were signs of his end. He called his ministers and told them he wanted to crown Rama yuvaraja. Dasaratha asked for the rural people of Kosala, and the neighboring kings and chieftains, to be called immediately to Ayodhya for the ceremony. He was in a hurry; the omens disturbed him.

It would take too long for him to invite Janaka; that king would rejoice, whenever he heard the news. The guests began to arrive. Dasaratha welcomed them according to their status and his own. There was a regal congregation in the king's sabha, and the common people thronged the palace yard and the street outside. Like the sea when the tide is in, the crowd surged.

Dasaratha entered, flanked by his gurus. He climbed up to his throne, that king who was a father to his people. When the cheering died down and he had their silence, his great voice resounded like a blessing among them.

"You all know that since the golden krita yuga the kings of my line have ruled your ancestors, since the days of Ikshvaku himself. I, too, have ruled to the best of my abilities. I have never strayed knowingly from dharma and I have loved you all like my own children. But now, this body of mine is old and it cannot bear the burden of kingship for much longer. The weakness of age is advanced in me. It is time, before I err as your king, that I give the reins of power to younger hands. I seek the consent of the wise, who have guided me through the years; I seek all your blessings. I want to crown my son Rama yuvaraja and be at some ease in my last years."

There was a swelling murmur of approval from the crowd. Dasaratha raised his hand to indicate he had not finished.

"You all know that Rama has every royal quality, and each one in more abundance than I ever did. No man was ever more suited than my son to be a king."

There was a roar of assent from the crowd. Again, Dasaratha raised his hand for them to be quiet.

"But I would only make Rama the yuvaraja for now, until he grows used to the burden he must shoulder. If you do not approve of my choice, you must tell me; and also whom you would rather have as your king than Rama."

But now there was no controlling them. They began to shout for Rama until Ayodhya reverberated with the syllables of his name.

"We will see Rama soaked with the waters of the abhisheka and his head under the white parasol!" cried someone, and the crowd roared for Rama to be king.

Dasaratha held up his hand again. Though his heart was full of joy, he said, "I thought you were happy with my reign. Why this unseemly delight at the very thought of Rama being crowned?"

But there was a twinkle in his eye. His people shouted their replies.

"Because he is Rama!" yelled someone, simply.

"We love him," cried another.

"He has more truth in him than the Devas," said a woman.

"He is the greatest of the Ikshvakus."

"He is brilliant."

"The strongest kshatriya of all."

"Wise beyond his years."

"He is one of us."

"He cries when we do."

"Even the earth wants Rama for her king. She told me in a dream."

"He is as blue as a night lotus."

"He is Vishnu's Avatara."

"He is beautiful, in his body and his soul."

His face wreathed in a smile, Dasaratha cried to Vasishta above the din, "My lord, let us prepare to crown Rama yuvaraja."

Vasishta ordered the city of Ayodhya to be got ready for the coronation. "Let there be flowers everywhere, from the palace arches to the streets, as though they sprouted for joy at this news. Let the royal road along which Rama rides his elephant be perfumed like the gardens of Amravati. Let there be music and dance. I, Vasishta, say to you that gandharvas will sing in the sky when Rama is crowned, and apsaras will dance on clouds."

Dasaratha called Sumantra and said, "Bring my son to me."

Today, Rama had gone out from the city: he should not be present when the king told the people he meant to make him yuvaraja. Sumantra went like the very yearning in the old king's heart, and Dasaratha climbed the marble stairs to the terrace of his palace to watch his son ride home. He stood there, his eyes searching the horizon, until a small cloud of dust appeared on it. He saw Rama's chariot with the Kovidara banner, as he flew home at his father's summons.

With fond eyes, the king watched his prince ride up the highway into Ayodhya. His lank hair flew behind him; his horses were in thrall to the one who drove them. Again Dasaratha remarked how long his son's arms were. The one at his side hung down to his knee. A thought of the Eternal One, who lies upon primal waters, dreaming the universe, flitted into the king's mind. But he did not care to think who else his son was apart from just his precious Rama. Just Rama was enough and more for him.

He watched his prince climb down from the chariot at the palace door. He watched him wade through the crowd that reached out to touch him. He saw him take the steps, two at a time, hurrying to his father whom he loved as he loved his life. Then Rama was with him on the commanding terrace. Dasaratha clasped his son in his arms and made him sit next to him on a golden chair.

His eyes mellow with the light of age, Dasaratha said solemnly so the crowd below heard him, "Rama, you are my eldest son and dear to me as my life. These good people want me to make you their yuvaraja. And I mean to crown you when the moon is full in the Pushyami nakshatra."

The people roared their approval again, like the very ocean, shouting Rama's name and "*Jaya!*" But Rama said nothing, only gazed for a moment into his father's face; then he prostrated himself at Dasaratha's feet for his blessing.

Her servants came running to Kausalya with the news, and she gave them silks and ornaments. Slowly the crowd began to thin, as the people drifted home. But Ayodhya was alive with the announcement, and soon singing and dancing broke out in the streets.

But Rama distanced himself from the celebrations. He sat alone in his own palace, lost in thought. He knew he should feel much happier than he did. But then, he was a wise prince and realized that kingship was always more a burden than a privilege. But he had been raised to be a king since he was born, and it was not only this thought that now worried him. Another, deeper anxiety stirred in his heart, for no reason he could name.

Something malignant seemed to mock him, from far away, but quite clearly.

3. *The joyful news*

When Dasaratha was alone, he realized he had been carried away by the crowd's excitement. He had made an impulsive commitment to his people, that he would crown Rama on Pushyami. Sumantra came to him and said, "Your Majesty, the moon enters Pushyami tomorrow."

Dasaratha came down into his private chambers. "Bring Rama to me now," he said to Sumantra.

Sumantra went to Rama's palace, which was a short way from his father's. He asked to be announced to the prince. Rama came out to the sarathy, who was like his own uncle, and, taking his hand, led him inside.

"You have come in a hurry, Sumantra. Sit down and refresh yourself."

But Sumantra said, "Not now, my prince. Your father wants to see you at once."

"But I have just come from him. What has happened since then?"

Sumantra did not know. Rama felt the serpent of anxiety unfurl its hood again and hiss at him. He felt two opposing currents of fate pull against each other for the right to bear his life along. A little confused, he came out into the sunlight with Sumantra. He climbed into his chariot and drove to his father again.

Dasaratha embraced Rama with some emotion. "I have been a good king, my son. I have kept the lamps to the Gods lit in my kingdom and in my heart. But of late I have seen evil omens. In a dream, I saw a great torch fall on the ground and be extinguished. I am told that, by gochara, the sun, Rahu, and Angaraka all afflict my janma nakshatra. The omens of the sky and of sleep never lie, and I fear not just for my life but for my sanity. Rama, you must be crowned yuvaraja before some calamity strikes me down.

"Impulsively, I promised the people that you would be crowned when the moon is in Pushyami. I did not realize tomorrow is Pushyami. But I am determined you will be crowned tomorrow. You must keep a fast with Sita tonight, and sleep on the floor, on a bed of darbha grass."

The old king paused; he studied his son's noble face. Slowly, he said, "Rama, great fortune provokes great envy. Bharata is not here and now is the time for you to be crowned. I know you will say he is devoted to you. But in my long years, there is one truth I have learned: that even the hearts of those who live in dharma are seldom pleased at the good fortune of others. Man's mind is like the wind and wild horses, my son: capricious and full of treachery. I feel sad to say this, but I am glad Bharata is away."

Rama stood before him and did not utter a word. When Dasaratha had finished, he touched his father's feet and left his presence.

69

Sita had come to the king's palace now, and Rama went with her to meet his mother Kausalya. They found her in the prayer room. Her eyes shut, she sat before an idol of Lakshmi, Goddess of fortune. She had heard her son was to be crowned yuvaraja. Sumitra and Lakshmana were there, as well, waiting for her since they heard the news. And they had waited for quite some time, while she prayed.

When Kausalya opened her eyes, Rama and Sita prostrated themselves before her. Rama said, "My father told me I am to become the yuvaraja tomorrow. I came for your blessing."

Her gracious face lit up. Laying her mother's hands on his head, she blessed him. Raising him up, Kausalya said, "Live long, my child, and may your enemies perish. Narayana heard all my prayers when I was childless, that I have a son like you. Great gifts are not given easily and I waited years before I had you. Bless you, Rama, and you, Sita. May you both always be a joy to your mothers." Sumitra blessed Rama and Sita as they lay at her feet.

Rising with a smile, Rama put his arm around Lakshmana and said, "Rule the world with me, Lakshmana; you shall be yuvaraja as much as I."

But then, it was not to be so simple.

4. Preparations for a crowning

When Rama had left his presence, Dasaratha called his guru Vasishta, and said, "You must see that Rama and Sita take diksha tonight, and keep a fast. So my son will have wealth, fame, and prosperity."

Vasishta was a trikalagyani; he saw into the dim future and the deep past. But he said nothing of what he saw. He went out and climbed into the chariot that waited to take him to Rama's palace.

Rama received his kulaguru, and they sat in an airy courtyard on silk-covered chairs. Vasishta called Sita and initiated the young couple into the fast for the next day's coronation. He sat with them awhile, then left them. The people milled outside to see Rama, and the prince's friends and many others of importance in Ayodhya waited for him.

Vasishta moved through the festive crowds in the streets. The city was in flower with blooms of every color. The main roads, the streets and alleys, the arches, erected hastily and festooned, the houses, the towers and ramparts, the terraces and great pillars had all burst into a heady spring of garlands. Joy, that Rama would be yuvaraja, burned through Ayodhya like soft fire.

Rama stood briefly on his terrace. He waved to the people and they sang out his name and Sita's in a million voices. It was dusk by now, and the sky grew dark as the sun sank in the west. It was time he went in and performed the Narayana puja.

Later, Rama and Sita lay side by side on an ascetic bed of darbha grass. Until they fell asleep, they gazed into each other's eyes by the moonlight flowing through the window. They were not allowed even to touch tonight, and they did not break that vow. Outside, the festivities continued through the night.

Well before dawn, Rama and Sita were roused by the sutas chanting the vabdya magadha. Rama rose and bathed. Facing east, he recited the Gayatri mantra. He put on white silks and worshipped his gurus.

Outside, when the first rays of the sun sprang above the horizon, the songs took up again. The singers had rested for just an hour before sunrise so they could be fresh for the morning of moment.

But in Dasaratha's palace, all was not well.

5. A queen's mind is poisoned

She stood like an old vulture on the terrace of the king's palace. She was Kaikeyi's maid, born with more than just her back bent almost in two. Manthara's spirit was twisted. She stood glowering down at the celebrations below: the flower-strewn streets of Ayodhya, bursting with music and dancing at the news that Rama was to become yuvaraja tomorrow. Her tiny eyes smoldered.

She seldom came up here onto the marble terrace, white as moonbeams. But this evening either the singing below or the quieter and more persuasive voice of fate made her labor painfully up the stairs. Nobody had bothered to tell Manthara what the celebrations were about; no one thought it would interest her. She was such a lone creature, and had no love for anybody. No one spoke much to Manthara. She had a foul temper, a worse tongue, and you could never tell what would set both off.

But now, she saw a young maid she knew skimming by with some flowers in a silver vase, singing to herself. Manthara called to the girl and asked, as sweetly as she could, in her croak of a voice, "What are the celebrations for, my dear? No one tells an old woman anything these days."

The young thing replied, "Haven't you heard? Rama is to be crowned yuvaraja tomorrow."

And she was away, humming a snatch of the song wafted up from the street, walking on air like the rest of Ayodhya. The girl quite missed the spasm of hatred that convulsed Manthara's coarse features. The hunchback stood on the terrace for a long time, and her cold mind plotted treachery.

Finally she hobbled down the smooth steps with remarkable alacrity, and sped ungainly through the corridors she knew so well: passages she had haunted like some ghastly specter since Dasaratha had first brought his third wife to his palace. She came to Kaikeyi's apartment. The old fiend had been with the queen since she was a little princess in her father's house. Without knocking, she burst into the room, where the lovely Kaikeyi lay on her bed of down, covered by a silken sheet. She lay languidly between sleep and waking, soft dreams in her eyes.

"Get up, foolish woman!" cried Manthara. "Only you could be asleep when doom is so near you. Blind queen arise, or you are lost."

Kaikeyi, who knew the crooked hag well, sighed in annoyance at being disturbed. But Manthara raged on, "The love of kings, dear imbecile, is like a summer stream: *short-lived.*"

Lazily, Kaikeyi propped herself up on a long, smooth arm. She asked, "What is it, Manthara? Who has wronged you now? Or are you ill? Your face is blanched; have you a fever?"

"No, I am not ill. But your husband means to crown Rama yuvaraja tomorrow. You are a simple woman, Kaikeyi, and innocent as a child. The king deceives you with honeyed words, while he saves the gifts of his deeds for Kausalya. Ah, he is a serpent. Look how cunningly he sent Bharata away to your father, so Rama's investiture would find no opposition. Wake up, Kaikeyi! Save yourself before it is too late; save your son's future. Dasaratha means to destroy you both."

But to Manthara's disgust, Kaikeyi did not hear anything beyond "your husband means to crown Rama yuvaraja." Dasaratha's third queen loved Rama like her own son, and she undid the necklace at her throat and pressed it into Manthara's hands.

Kaikeyi cried, "What wonderful news you of all people have brought me today! My son will become the yuvaraja tomorrow."

Manthara flung the priceless thing from her with a growl. She breathed, "Only a fool will rejoice at her husband's love for another woman. Don't you see it is Kausalya he has always loved? While you he keeps to indulge his old body. Oh, what would I tell your mother if I stood before her today? At least think of your son, woman. Think that Bharata will spend the rest of his life as Rama's slave."

But Kaikeyi said steadily, "Rama is a prince of dharma. Why, he loves me more than he does Kausalya. And he loves his brothers so much, that Ayodhya shall belong to all four princes when Rama is king. He is Dasaratha's eldest son; when he has ruled for a hundred years, he will crown Bharata king."

Choking with frustration, Manthara said, "A sea of sorrow has risen to drown you, Kaikeyi, and you don't even see it. After Rama, his son will rule Ayodhya. Bharata will be an underling, a servant: because his mother loves another woman's prince more than her own."

She shook her ugly head that anyone could be so stupid. "I bring you news of Kausalya's triumph and you reward me with a necklace! But I have lived many years more than you, young Kaikeyi. I saw you when you were born and love you as the daughter I never had. I love your son as if he were my grandchild."

She hissed her next words like an aged serpent: "I tell you, once Rama sits on the throne he will either banish Bharata or seek his death. That has been the way of kings with their brothers through the ages. Rama will keep Lakshmana close to him, because he is no threat to him; but not Bharata. Kaikeyi, send word to your son never to return to Ayodhya. For Ayodhya is no longer a safe place for him."

Manthara waited a moment. Seeing she had Kaikeyi's attention, she came out with what she had saved for the end of her tirade.

"All these years you were the king's favorite and you ignored Kausalya. Because your head was swollen, you insulted her time and again. And she bore it all patiently, biding her time. But think of the revenge she will have when she is the queen mother tomorrow. She will destroy what is most precious to you: she will have Bharata's life."

Kaikeyi's eyes grew round and Manthara saw that at last her poison had pierced the queen's heart. Kaikeyi's face was flushed; little gasps of outrage came from her at what she heard from her crooked maid. Her delicate body quivered with suspicion, and at last she whispered, "You are right and I thank you for opening my eyes. But if I have my way, it is Rama who will be banished and Bharata who will be crowned. But how, Manthara, how? Think, old woman, think hard! Or everything is lost."

Manthara smiled grimly: Kaikeyi was won; the rest would be easy. The hunchback said slowly, "I thank the Gods for opening your eyes to the danger that threatens you. But listen, I know how you can have Bharata crowned and Rama exiled. There is something you have forgotten, which I remember: once, many years ago, the king granted you two boons because you saved his life."

Spoiled, impulsive Kaikeyi, who had by now inexorably chosen the path of evil for herself, remembered. It was a war between Deva and Asura, between Indra and Sambara, the great Demon of those times. Indra was embattled and asked Dasaratha to come to fight at his side. A young man then, Dasaratha had gone at once. It was soon after he married his third and most beautiful wife, Kaikeyi. He could not bear to be apart from her, nor she from him; he had taken her with him.

But no dharma bound the Asuras. They attacked Dasaratha's camp in stealth one night and killed most of his guard. Dasaratha faced them single-handedly and took great toll of the demons. But he was outnumbered and, sorely wounded with dark arrows, fell unconscious. Kaikeyi ran out from her tent; with strength more than a woman has, she lifted her husband in her arms and carried him from the battle while Asura barbs whistled around her ears. Then the Devas arrived and the demons were driven away.

Kaikeyi nursed Dasaratha back to health. When he was well and knew what had happened, he said to her, "I grant you two boons, my love, whatever you want. Even my life, because you have saved it."

But Kaikeyi, so much in love, had laughed, "That you are alive is my greatest boon and that will do for me just now. But perhaps one day, when I am in need, I will remind you of your promise."

From that day, she had been Dasaratha's favorite queen. When they came home from war, Kaikeyi told her twisted maid, lightheartedly, how she saved Dasaratha's life and what he had promised her. Manthara had also laughed with her then; but she carefully stored what she heard in her black heart. Knowing life, and how long it is, she knew the two boons could prove useful one day. Kaikeyi had forgotten all about them; until now, when Manthara reminded her.

The queen's eyes flashed, and Manthara wheezed gleefully, "One boon will send Rama into the jungle and the other will see Bharata crowned."

Kaikeyi embraced the old monster, crying, "What would I do without you?"

Manthara said, "Make haste now. The king will come shortly to give you his great news. Enter the chamber of sorrow. Put on soiled clothes, stain your face with tears, and let him find you crying on the ground. Don't speak to him at first, but show him your woman's anger. He loves you, Kaikeyi, and you must take advantage of that tonight if Bharata is to be king. This will be a trial by fire. Pass through the flames and your victory will be long and sweet; falter, and you and your son shall be lost forever. Remember, Bharata's life depends on what you do tonight.

"Dasaratha will try to win you over with sweet words of love, and with gifts. Do not be moved, Kaikeyi. Be silent until he promises you anything you ask for. Then remind him of the boons. Call his word as a kshatriya to stand before you in dharma, and tell him what you want: that Rama be banished and Bharata crowned yuvaraja.

"You must not weaken, child; this night is for strength. Let your heart be made of stone tonight, and let your purpose govern what you say and do."

Kaikeyi nodded when Manthara had finished. Evil had taken hold of her completely, and it was doubly sad because it was well known in Ayodhya how this queen adored Rama.* But now cunning fate darkened her mind, so she hardly knew what she did. And Manthara, evil's agent or fate's, ruled her weakness.

Kaikeyi hugged the hunchback again. "My beautiful Manthara, no one loves me as you do. Your body is bent, but your heart is full of light. I will always remember this. When my Bharata is king I will adorn your hump with golden ornaments."

Manthara hissed, "There is no time for all that now. The task is at hand."

Kaikeyi went into the krodhagraha, the chamber of anger. She tore

---

*Indeed, she loved him so much that the Devas asked the Goddess of speech, Saraswathi, to sit on Manthara's tongue that day, so Kaikeyi's mind would be poisoned and destiny could take its course.

the silks from her lissom body. She ripped the flowers from her hair, the jewelry from her throat and her arms, in a frenzy, and flung them from her. She wept at will and black kohl ran down her fair cheeks.

She threw herself on the floor and cried to her deformed woman, "There is no question of faltering, Manthara. If Rama does not go to the forest and if Bharata is not crowned, I will kill myself."

Kaikeyi lay sobbing. She was like a lovely kinnara woman, her punya exhausted, who had been cast down into the mortal world.

6. The long night

It was late when he finished looking over the preparations for Rama's coronation. Then Dasaratha came to Kaikeyi's apartment; it was with her that he spent most of his nights. Tonight he came with news that he was sure would fill her with joy, because Dasaratha knew how much Kaikeyi loved Rama.

Usually she would be waiting for him. But tonight the guard said, "The queen is in the krodhagraha."

It was the first time Kaikeyi had ever entered the chamber of anger. Dasaratha rushed to her. He threw open the door; the darkened room was lit by two oil lamps. He saw his lovely queen askew on the floor. She wore a gown made of coarse cloth; her long hair was loose and disheveled. Her ornaments and flowers lay where they had been flung, glimmering in the lamplight. And she lay with her face in a pool of tears, her kohl smeared across her cheeks. She crooned to herself, tracing patterns in her tears with a finger like a mad woman.

Dasaratha took her hand. "Kaikeyi, what happened? Are you ill?"

She pulled her hand away and gnashed her teeth. She did not speak.

"Who has hurt you, my love? I'll have his head! I cannot bear to see you like this. My life is made of your smiles and you know it. Kaikeyi, please talk to me."

She lay where she was. Her eyes blazed briefly, when Dasaratha knelt on the floor beside her. "Anything you want from me you can have," he cried. "Only tell me what it is."

Now she spoke slowly, and her words were clear and full of a woman's wrath. She never turned her face to him, but said quietly, in a dangerous voice, "No one has hurt me, my lord. But there is something I do want like my very life, and only you can give it to me."

The king smiled in relief; he would give her anything. "I love you more than I do anyone except Rama. I swear on Rama's life that I will give you whatever you want. Just ask me quickly, and put an end to this torment. Ask, Kaikeyi, ask me now!"

She uncoiled herself from the floor like a cobra. Dasaratha saw madness in her eyes and such evil that he recoiled from her. Like a serpent she spoke to him, in a terrible voice he did not know. "Let Indra and the Devas be my witnesses. Let the Sun and the Moon be my witnesses. You have sworn on your precious Rama's life that you will give me whatever I want."

She drew a rasping breath and whispered, "Dasaratha, cast your mind back many years to when Indra called you and you went to war against Sambara. Do you remember the night you fell wounded with demons' arrows and I saved your life? That night you said to me that you gave me two boons, whatever I wanted. Do you remember?"

She raised herself and brought her face close to his. Sick to his heart that she was so distraught, Dasaratha nodded. He was anxious for this ordeal to be over. He saw she suffered, and he suffered with her. She paused to stare at him. She moistened her lips with the tip of her tongue. Still in her fell new voice, she said, "I said then there was nothing I wanted. But I would remember the boons and avail of them in a time of need. Dasaratha, tonight is the time of my need; tonight I want my two boons."

With no inkling of what she might ask, the king nodded again. He would honor his word, let her ask him quickly. But she wanted to be sure. "If you break your word to me tonight, I will take my life."

"I have said you can have whatever you want, Kaikeyi! Have I ever broken my word to you, or to anyone?"

She took a deep breath and said softly, "Listen then, my lord, to what I want. You have prepared Ayodhya for a coronation tomorrow, to crown Rama yuvaraja. The two boons I ask for are that Bharata be crowned in Rama's place, and that Rama be banished to the Dandaka vana for fourteen years."

He saw the reflection of the oil lamps dancing in her dilated pupils. At first, he did not seem to realize what she had asked. She said,

"Dasaratha, your dharma is a legend. Don't break your word to me and disgrace your ancestors and the House of Ikshvaku."

Then it dawned on him. Dasaratha keeled over where he knelt.

When he regained his senses, he passed his hands over his eyes to see if he was dreaming. Kaikeyi made no move to help him up. She crouched in the lamplight, a beast of darkness, her eyes alight with the mania of her purpose.

The king whispered, "Am I dreaming or have I lost my mind? Is this a memory from another life, which has escaped into this one? What demon has entered my heart and makes me imagine I hear abominations from my Kaikeyi, things she cannot have said?"

He got up and stood bemused, looking down at his wife in disbelief. When he saw how balefully she glared back at him, he knew she meant every word she had said. His legs were weak and could not carry him; he sat down. Then he lay on the floor and merciful unconsciousness took him again.

She rose and stood coldly over him, waiting, her heart set on what she wanted, while the lamps burned down. Dasaratha awoke again, now in more anger than sorrow. He said to her, "You are the cruelest woman in the world. I did not know you at all during the years of love I lavished on you. You are evil, and you are determined to destroy me.

"Serpent, tell me how Rama has wronged you. He treats you as much like his mother as he does Kausalya. Then why do you hate him? Just a month ago, you said to me, 'Rama is not only your first son, he is mine as well.' What happened to that love? Who poisoned your mind, Kaikeyi, so you now speak of sending your son into the forest for fourteen years?

"Why do you want to snatch my life from me, when not many years are left of it anyway? Perhaps your mind is afflicted with some passing madness tonight. Look Kaikeyi, I fall at your feet: think again of what you ask."

He laid his head at her feet pale as lilies. She drew away in contempt and said, "For long years you have deceived me with honeyed talk. But tonight I hold you to your sacred word. You come from a line of which it was said of old that the ocean honored the bounds of his shores for the dharma of the Ikshvaku kings. Dasaratha, how will you tell your people that you granted me two boons for saving your life, only to break your word as soon as I asked you to keep it?"

Dasaratha wept like a child. But she raged on, "I know that once Rama is crowned you will go back to Kausalya's arms. But be warned: I will not live through this night if you refuse me what I ask. Here is the poison I will drink and end myself, in despair that my husband was a liar."

She showed him a darkling vial. Dasaratha mumbled Rama's name over and over to himself, like some mantra.

He cried desperately, "You are not my Kaikeyi. You are a fiend that has possessed my innocent queen. Why else would you want Rama banished? But I tell you, whoever you are, Bharata will not accept the kingdom. He will not stand by and see his brother exiled."

He moaned like a wounded animal and a sweat of shock shone on his face. "Just this morning, before all the people, I said I would crown Rama yuvaraja. What will I tell them he has done, that I now banish him to the forest instead? What will I tell Kausalya, whom I have neglected for so many years from my love for you? And Sita? What will I say to the flowerlike Sita?

"Monster, you mean to be the ruin of us all; and when we are dead, you can rule Ayodhya with your son. Ah, these are the sins of past lives being visited on me; I have not sinned in this one to deserve such punishment. You speak to me of killing yourself? Listen to me, Demon. The sun may not shine any more; Indra may not moisten the earth with rain, and still the world may continue. But Dasaratha's life will leave his body the moment Rama leaves for the forest."

Again he fell at her feet. "Relent, Kaikeyi. It isn't you who wants this dreadful fate for us all. Know your own heart and relent, while there is still time."

But she would not.

All night, Dasaratha hovered between a swoon of insupportable anguish and ravaged waking. He begged her, repeatedly, to relent. Again and again, she replied that she would see Bharata crowned and Rama exiled.

Unhinged, at times Dasaratha called out to the Gods never to let this terrible night end; for only at dawn could Rama be banished. But at others, he begged the sun to rise at once, in mercy, because he could not bear the company of this she-devil. He was tempted to seek out Kausalya and Sumitra to share his burden with them. But he said to himself, "No, tonight I will bear this grief alone. Let those who love me and love Rama sleep in peace for the last time."

Finally, sobbing Rama's name, the wretched king fell into a long faint. Kaikeyi sat watching him, as a beast watches her prey. The lamps in the room burned out, and the night wore on in darkness.

7. At the palace

At crack of dawn, the sutas began to sing outside the door to wake the king. But the sky was overcast and the people of Ayodhya wondered that the morning Rama was to be crowned should be so forbidding. It seemed an evil omen on this auspicious day. Soon a gray drizzle began.

Kaikeyi prodded the king awake that morning of fate. He hoped to wake from his nightmare to find that was all it had been, and last night a dream. But ugly greed in her eye, his queen said to him, "Don't bring shame on yourself, Dasaratha, by breaking your sacred word."

He groaned; he awoke trembling. His eyes darted around the room now filling with wan light. Dasaratha whispered, "Let Rama be prepared to perform tarpana for me with the water meant for the abhisheka."

He looked imploringly at Kaikeyi. She wore finery once more; ornaments glittered on her body. She shook him roughly, and cried, "Enough! Day has dawned. Send for Bharata and have him crowned; let Rama leave for the forest."

Meanwhile, Vasishta and his sishyas arrived in the palace for the coronation. Despite the drizzle, the streets of Ayodhya were filled to bursting. The people sang and chanted Rama's name. Vasishta said to Sumantra, "Go and tell Dasaratha the fire is kindled and the muhurta is near."

Humming under his breath, Sumantra arrived in Kaikeyi's chambers. He said to Dasaratha, "My lord, everything is ready for Rama's investiture and the people await you."

Dasaratha turned to face his sarathy. Sumantra was startled to see Dasaratha's eyes were red and swollen. In a voice that had aged years in a night, the king said, "You make my tears flow, Sumantra."

Kaikeyi turned imperiously to the charioteer. "The king wishes to speak privately to Rama before the coronation. There is nothing to worry about; just that my husband spent a sleepless night. Go and fetch Rama here."

Pleased to believe her rather than what his eyes saw on his master's face, Sumantra went to fetch Rama. Karkataka, the great Crab, would soon rise on the horizon, and the moon was already in Pushyami. Sumantra hurried on his way. People in the streets, the crowd that eddied around the palace like a muted sea, cried to him:

"Where is the king, why hasn't he come out yet?"

"It is almost time for the coronation."

"Is he asleep on this great day?"

As he parted their tide with his chariot, Sumantra cried back to them, "Dasaratha wants to see Rama alone before the crowning. But I will tell him of your impatience."

He was a popular figure, and waving to them, he came to Rama's palace. The tusker Shatrunjaya, beautifully caparisoned, raised his trunk to greet Sumantra within the flower-decked gates. Sumantra smiled to himself at the thought of Rama on the elephant's back, ambling through the ecstatic crowd to be crowned.

Sumantra was shown into Rama's presence. The prince sat in a finely carved chair, wearing white silk. Enchanting Sita sat beside him with a chamara whisk in her hand. Sumantra bowed deeply and said, "Rama, the king summons you to the Queen Kaikeyi's chambers."

Rama said to Sita, "Mother Kaikeyi wants to bless me. You wait here, Sita, I will return shortly."

She said nothing, but went with him to the door and watched him leave. Her lips moving soundlessly, she prayed, "Indra, Yama, Varuna, Kubera: O Lokapalas, watch over my husband on this day of his fortune."

How the crowd roared his name when Rama came out into the streets. For the first time, the sun broke through from behind the clouds in broad golden shafts. The people allowed the chariot to pass, but slowly. They all wanted to see their prince clearly, and those that could reached out to touch him. The women of Ayodhya, wearing their best clothes and jewelry, sang out his name from their terraces. They threw armfuls of flowers down on the chariot as it made its way to Dasaratha's palace.

At last Sumantra cried to the people, "Time is short. We will miss the muhurta if you don't let us through." They parted like an ocean at a prophet's command. The chariot passed through them and came to the king's palace.

8. The boons of Kaikeyi

Lakshmana stood waiting at the lofty palace doors. Rama linked arms with his brother and they hurried along to Kaikeyi's apartment. The princes were announced. Eager as he was to prostrate himself before his father and have his blessing, Rama checked himself when he sensed the tension in that silent chamber. He gasped when he saw Dasaratha's face. Kaikeyi stood beside him like an evil spirit. Her lips were set in a thin line and her eyes shone insanely.

Rama went forward, fell at his father's feet, and clasped them; then at Kaikeyi's, but she moved away. The king sat where he was, slumped in a chair. He spoke no word of blessing, nor did he stir. His eyes remained shut, as if he did not want to see the world any more. But he spoke his son's name in a broken voice, and tears escaped his eyelids clamped together in some great pain.

Rama was confused. He said to Kaikeyi, "Have I done something to annoy my father? Or is he unwell? Is there bad news of Bharata and Shatrughna? I should not ask this, but have you quarreled?"

He heard her speak in a strange, distant voice, which was scarcely her own. "You haven't annoyed him, nor is there bad news from your brothers. Your father has something to tell you, but the words don't leave his lips. But I will tell you what he dare not say. Once this king granted me two boons for saving his life, whatever I chose. Last night I asked him to keep his word; but he would rather break it now."

Rama wondered at the harshness of her. There was such malice in her tone. "But you, Rama, can keep your father's oath. If you say you will, I will tell you what I asked him for."

Dasaratha sat turned to stone; only the tears leaked on from his eyes. Rama cried, "You don't have to ask me, mother. I would gladly kill myself to keep my father's word. I think you know that."

Kaikeyi said without emotion, "I want Bharata to be crowned in your place; and for you to spend nine years and five more in the Dandaka vana, wearing tree bark and deerskin like a rishi." Her lip curling, she asked, "Would you do this to keep your father's honor? For he, I think, will never ask you himself?"

Dasaratha groaned feebly, but Rama's eyes did not so much as flicker. Without a moment's hesitation, he said, "Of course I will go to the forest if you want me to. Why is there such conflict over this? Or that Bharata is to be crowned? It only pains me that my father thought he would hurt me with this happy news. Let us send messengers at once to Kekaya to fetch my brother home."

Kaikeyi said coldly, "You can leave the sending of messengers to me. You need not be in Ayodhya when Bharata returns. The king is so grief-stricken that one son of his shall be crowned and not the other, that as long as you are here he will not make Bharata yuvaraja. The sooner you leave for the forest the better."

Rama whispered, *"Shantam paapam!"*

Dasaratha swooned in his chair and Rama sprang to him. Now Rama's eyes were full, as he turned to Kaikeyi and said quietly, "Mother, you have not understood me. I am not anxious to have the kingdom. I never was. Didn't you believe that if you asked me yourself, I would gladly have gone away for your sake? It pains me that you doubted my love for you.

"I will go at once; and have no fear, I will not come back for fourteen years. But I must see my mother Kausalya and convince her that this is no tragedy but God's way for me, and a blessing for one as fond of the wild places of the earth as I am."

Dasaratha wept again. Rama fell at his father's feet once more, and touched his lips and his head to them. Then he touched Kaikeyi's feet and, rising quickly, walked out of the room. Behind him, he heard his father break down, calling his name, sobbing like a child.

Lakshmana came out with his brother. But his face twitched in rage and hot tears had sprung in his eyes. Rama linked his arm in Lakshmana's. When he thought of seeing Kausalya and breaking this news to her, even Rama felt weak. He steadied himself, and his face showed no sorrow but was as radiant as ever. They walked through the sabha of the coronation, past the giant urns filled with water from the sacred rivers of Bharatavarsha for the abhisheka.

Rama's pang for his mother passed. He did not so much as glance at the urns, nor at the white parasol beside the throne, nor the long whisks of silk thread at the doors, but came straight to Kausalya's apartment. His mind was calm and had just one thought: how he would soften the blow for her. Rama was accosted by some that he knew along the way. He spoke amiably to them, and carried on. Beside his brother, Lakshmana controlled himself.

But word had leaked from Kaikeyi's apartment already, at Manthara's shrewd instigation, and spread like fire through the palace. As they neared Kausalya's chambers, the princes heard cries of shock from the women of the harem.

"Rama banished? For what?"

"It's just an evil rumor."

"Has Dasaratha taken leave of his senses?"

"Rama banished to the forest? Today is Rama's coronation."

Through the walls, along the winding passages, they heard cries of dismay, as the news caught and burned along. But they arrived before the news at Kausalya's apartment. Rama was as unmoved by what he heard around him as an aswattha tree is by the cries of the birds in its branches.

The old guard at his mother's door sprang up. He came toward the princes, crying, *"Jaya vijayi bhava!"*

Rama smiled at him and moved on into his mother's rooms. Kausalya had spent the night in prayer. She sat before Narayana's image, pouring libations onto the fire for her son's fortune. Rama stood watching her offering arghya. As always, she wore thin silk. Her face glowed from the flames before her, her gracious features chiseled by the sorrows of the years. Rama looked at his gentle mother and he knew that in her life he was the single light. He knew it was years since her husband had seen her at all; so lost had he been in Kaikeyi's charms. But his mother had never said a word to Rama against Kaikeyi or his father.

Kausalya became aware of Rama and her face lit up with the same joy he saw on it whenever he visited her. She rose and came to him. He stood before her with his hands folded and his heart faltering. He knelt at her feet, as much to delay what he must tell her as for her blessing. She blessed him, laying both her soft palms on his head. Then she raised him up, and her eyes were moist.

"My noble child, may all heaven's blessings be upon you. Today your father will crown you yuvaraja, and I know you will prove a worthy heir to the Ikshvaku throne. May the Gods help you be as great a king as all your ancestors. Always be loyal and kind to your father, even after you are crowned. He loves you more than his life."

She clasped him to her; she felt him tremble. With a cry, she held him at arm's length. "My son, you are shaking. Are you ill?"

At once Rama grew calm. Yet when he spoke to her, his eyes avoided hers and sought the floor at his feet. But his voice was steady as he said softly, "Mother, I must leave you to go away to the Dandaka vana. For fourteen years I must live in the forest, to honor my father's boon to Kaikeyi. But still rejoice, because your son Bharata is to be crowned yuvaraja."

At first, she did not seem to know what he had said. He saw the shock in her eyes only when he had finished, and he leaned forward and caught her as she fell. He picked her up in his arms, easily as he might a child, and set her down in a jeweled chair. He sprinkled some water that Lakshmana fetched on her face, and she stirred again. As he knelt beside her, Rama could hardly look into her eyes.

"How will I bear this?" cried Kausalya. "Once my only sorrow was that I was a barren woman, whom her husband did not love. Oh, I would gladly exchange that sorrow for this one.

"Your father never loved me. His younger queens had their way with him and I was neglected. But when you were born, I thought the Gods had finally blessed me. I could bear anything then, even the snickering of Kaikeyi and her women. You are the light of my days, Rama. I cannot live without seeing your face, my son.

"I have always kept my vratas and worshipped the Gods unfailingly. But my prayers have been in vain, that this must happen to me now. I was born under an evil star and not all the prayers in the world can change my fate. I must have been a terrible sinner in my past lives; and my heart is made of stone in this one that it has not yet broken in a thousand pieces with everything I have endured.

"And now this? Oh no, Rama, this I cannot bear. I will come with you into the Dandaka vana. Yes, I have to!"

She buried her face in her hands, and her frail form shook with sobs.

9. Lakshmana's anger

Then Lakshmana could not stand it any more, and cried, "Our father has lost his reason! His love for Kaikeyi blinds him. But why should Rama sacrifice the throne for the whim of a greedy woman? For what crime is my blemishless brother banished to the Dandaka vana? A king should think of what is best for his kingdom, and not what suits his favorite wife.

"I will not allow this. Our father walks the way of sin. As God is my witness, I will kill him and his Kaikeyi, and the world will forgive my parricide."

The distraught Kausalya cried, "You hear your brother, Rama. He has my blessing! I speak as your mother who has as much right to your obedience as your father does. I order you not to go to the forest, leaving me at the mercy of the younger queens. If you do, count yourself guilty of the sin of the lord of the rivers: of matrihatya. For I will die if you go."

Rama remained silent. He let them vent their grief, knowing it was sorrow that spoke as anger and threat. He touched his mother's feet. Quietly, he said, "I cannot break my word to my father: that is how the ancient rishis have laid down the law for us. Think how Parasurama cut off his mother's head because his father asked him to. The dharma taught in the Shastras cannot be false. The Shastras say that a son who does not obey his father has no place in heaven.

"Lakshmana, you have sat at our guru's feet and learned dharma. You know about vairagya. You know a man should accept his destiny with equanimity, be it fortune or misfortune. I know you love me more than anyone else; but love does not turn to violent means for its satisfaction. Violence is never dharma and you must not give in to your anger. I must go to the forest; my fate lies there. I must keep my sacred pledge to my father and mother Kaikeyi."

He touched Kausalya's feet again. "Say the mantras of fortune over me; let me go to the vana. I will return to you as soon as my exile is served. Put away your grief and bless me. It is the way of dharma I go on, and in this world there is no other path to salvation."

Kausalya stared at her son. She saw he was perfectly calm and determined. For a long moment she stared, then she said slowly, "Rama, dharma clearly says that a man's mother is as sacred to him as his father. Both are equal gurus. I command you to stay here by my side." But then she broke down and began to sob. "Oh, my son, I cannot live without you. Even if I see you for just an hour, it is enough for me, and I can bear the burden of my life."

Lakshmana cried again, "I will kill the king and his Kaikeyi! You shall not go to the forest."

Rama turned to him and said sharply, "You add your anger again to my mother's grief. You do not help me, Lakshmana."

10. The way of dharma

Rama said, "Mother, the path I mean to tread leads straight to heaven, and any other to ruin. I must go to the forest. Bless me now; let me go in some peace."

He paused thoughtfully, then said with a smile, "Just yesterday, my father wanted to crown me, and today he must banish me to keep his word. If this is not the hand of fate, then I am much mistaken. Until yesterday Kaikeyi never made any distinction between Bharata and me; why, you could say I was her favorite son. Today she spoke words that struck me like knives and even her voice was not her own. If this wasn't fate speaking through her, for a more mysterious end than any of us yet know, I am much mistaken."

When he thought of Kaikeyi, there was anguish on his face. He said, "She would not have spoken to me as she did, and before her husband, unless I was paying for some sin of a past life. For in this one I have never hurt her before; nor she me. I tell you, Lakshmana, all this is fate working toward her own inscrutable ends. Not even the rishis who are masters of their senses are beyond fate; even they fall prey to the passions of destiny. Then how can we escape her? It is not that mother Kaikeyi is evil, or that she hates me; only that destiny uses her, even against her own nature. Do you think she feels no pain at what she does? No, she is the most wounded of all."

But Lakshmana fumed, "Rama, it is folly to attribute what a common, greedy woman does to fate. There is cunning and design in her. How is it that only now, when you are to be crowned, she asks for her boons? She planned this all along, biding her time, pretending to love you, and made long fools of us all. Only a weakling accepts such a fate. If you let me take arms against this fate, I will show you which is more powerful: what you call providence or my arrows!

"Listen to me, Rama. No one, not the people, not the kings of the earth, not even the Devas will oppose your being crowned today. By force, if need be."

But Rama smiled at him and ruffled his hair as one does to a child. He said patiently, "The way of the soul is longer than fourteen years in a forest. You want me to sacrifice immortality for a paltry fourteen years? No, Lakshmana, you are wrong. Calm yourself. Think with your intellect, not your burning heart, and you will see what I must do."

Kausalya knew her son's mind was made up; nothing would persuade him to abandon what he saw as being dharma and obedience to his father. In a low voice she said, "I see you will go to the vana no matter what. Rama, take me with you."

Rama looked at her and said gently, "How will my father bear my exile if you aren't at his side? You must not abandon him now. He needs you, mother, and your place is here with him. That is your dharma."

She was silent. At last she sighed, "I will stay in Ayodhya. May Narayana give me the strength to bear this as well."

Rama smiled at his mother. "Take strength in Bharata. He is also your son; he will look after you. Now bless me and let me go: the sooner I leave the sooner I will return to you."

Kausalya said, "When fate is ranged against me, what else can I do? Go with my blessing and may your exile be more joyful to you than kingship. May Indra's Devas and Viswamitra's astras protect you in the jungle. May your path always be clear, my noble son, and your valor tameless. Come back to me the day your exile is over. I will wait for you each moment of the cruel years."

She poured libation on the fire again, and prayed, "May the blessing that Indra had from his mother Aditi, when he went to kill Vritrasura, be upon you, Rama. May the blessing Garuda had from his mother Vinata, when he went after the amrita, be upon you. May the blessing Vamana bore, when he came to Mahabali's yagna, be upon you. May the jungle be a haven to you and a kingdom of joy."

She grew calm with these incantations. She marked a tilaka on Rama's brow and tied a raksha of protection around his wrist. Her anxiety had left her, now that she recognized her own dharma. She embraced her son. Her weakness had passed, and she said, "I know you will return after fourteen years. I, who have waited so long, will wait a little longer. And I will see you in your rightful place, on the throne of your ancestors. Now go while I am strong, before my heart fails me again."

Rama lay one last time at her feet. Taking the padadhuli from them, he went out without looking back again.

11. Sita

The news had not yet filtered past the palace doors into the streets of Ayodhya. Rama gained his own palace quickly, by crying to the crowd that time was short. He did not say for what. But the smile that he managed to keep along the way vanished as soon as he passed his doors. His mind was a whirl and he had broken out in a sweat when he came to Sita.

She saw his face and ran to him with a cry. "What happened, Rama?"

For a moment, he stood staring mutely at her. Then he slumped into a chair and buried his head in his hands. He took her hands in his, kissed them feverishly, and said, "Sita, my father has banished me to the Dandaka vana for fourteen years. He once granted Kaikeyi two boons for saving his life. Last night, she asked that Bharata be crowned yuvaraja and that I be exiled to the jungle."

She began to speak, but he raised a hand for her to be quiet. "Listen to me, Sita, my time is short. My father is bound in honor to keep his word. It is his dharma, and mine to uphold it. But I want you to be careful in Ayodhya. I want you to remember, always, that no man who sits upon a throne likes to hear another man being praised. Never praise me in Bharata's presence or show how much you miss me. Don't speak of me at all before him."

He smiled wanly and stroked her face. "Which does not mean that you forget me! Pray for me, Sita, keep your vows. I don't know how my mother and my father will bear this; be loving to them. But remember, no matter what has happened today, Sumitra and Kaikeyi are also my mothers. Bharata and Shatrughna will look after you; love them as your own brothers. But remember, Bharata will be king, and a king will abandon even his own child if it does not obey him. So tread carefully with Bharata: from today you are not his older brother's wife but his subject."

Sita's eyes did not fill with tears, as he expected; they flashed in anger. She cried accusingly, "Rama, what have I done to deserve such cruelty from you? The dharma I learned in my father's house was perhaps different from what you did here. But I have been taught that for better or for worse, a wife's dharma is to share her husband's fate.

"If you have been banished to the Dandaka vana, then so have I. I will go with you, Rama; my place is at your side. With you, I would walk down the paths of hell. The jungle will be like heaven for me. I must disobey you in this, my love; forget my disobedience, as you do the water you leave behind in a glass after drinking.

"I want to come to green riverbanks with you, and to hidden lakes. I want to see deer and tigers, great elephants, and all there is to see in the wild. Can't Rama who killed the rakshasas protect his wife? I swear I will never complain as long as you are with me. I will be content to gaze at lotuses on crystal pools and watch swans glide on silver water. Why fourteen, Rama? Let us spend a hundred years in the forest together."

But he said, "Sita, this is not the time to try me with frivolous arguments. I know you will miss me, but we are young and time is on our side: fourteen years will pass quickly. You must not make this parting harder than it is for both of us. You must obey me; that is your dharma.

"You are naive to think that life in the vana is sniffing flowers or watching gentle birds and animals. You don't know the terror of the jungle. Every waking moment is a nightmare for fear of savage beasts. You dream of green riverbanks; but the rivers are full of crocodiles. There are no paths and deadly serpents slither through the grass. And how will a princess like you sleep on a rough bed of leaves every night? Clad not in silk but tree bark.

"At times, we may not find water to drink for days; at others, no food for weeks, even roots or fruit. And how, my love, will your tender body bear the ferocity of the seasons? Burning summer, icy winter, and rain that soaks you to the bone.

"Be reasonable, precious Sita, and my exile will be over sooner than you imagine."

Now, for the first time since he knew her, he saw her eyes fill with tears, like lotuses with dew. They spilled over her lids, drop by drop. She made no move to wipe them and he could not bear the sight.

She said softly, her voice unchanged, "All that will only add excitement to our lives. And I just remembered something. When I was ten, some rishis who read the stars came to my father's palace. Even then, they told me I would spend many years with my husband in the forest. Rama, if you leave me behind I will take my life: either with poison, or fire, or I will drown myself.

"You are my world. I will be your wife not just in this life, but the next one, and the one after that, and forever. When even a moment without you is so painful for me, how will I survive a year, then another three and another ten after those?"

She spoke so calmly and reasonably that Rama was a little frightened by her. Not even his mother or his father, he realized, loved him as Sita did. He rose and clasped her to him, "You were born to come even into the jungle with me. I was only testing you. You are the rarest woman on earth, and I will take you with me wherever I go. That is our destiny: to be together. Let us feed the poor, give alms to our brahmanas, and all our possessions to our servants. Let us go lightly into the jungle."

Her face lit up like the sun emerging from behind dark clouds.

12. Lakshmana

At the door, Lakshmana heard all this, and he could not stand it. He burst into the room, fell at Rama's feet, and cried, "I will walk before you both in the jungle! You spoke of Shatrughna and Bharata remaining in Ayodhya, but not of me. Which means I will go with you."

He looked pleadingly at his brother, then at Sita. Rama raised him up and said, "Of you I need not speak, because you are part of me. But if you come to the forest, who will protect our mothers from Kaikeyi? Our father is a broken man and she rules his will. Who will look after Urmila, if you come with us?"

But Lakshmana said, "I don't doubt Bharata. He will look after our mothers better than his own, and his wife will look after Urmila. And if he does not, Rama, it won't take me long to come back and kill him.

"You must take me with you. I will carry your weapons and clear your path before you. I will gather fruit and hunt for you, while Sita and you walk together on mountain slopes. How else will you both eat? Think about it, Rama: you cannot leave her alone every time you go to hunt."

Suddenly Rama laughed. He embraced his brother and cried, "You will come with us, Lakshmana. I always meant to take you with me, because I could not live without you either. Go to our Acharya Sudhanva and ask him for our weapons. I thank God, Kaikeyi has not said we must go unarmed into exile. We will take the two bows Varuna gave us, the sets of armor light as sun rays and the magic quivers. Tell our master we need Varuna's swords, as well. Hurry back, Lakshmana; our time is short."

Like a delighted child Lakshmana hugged Rama, and ran to their acharya's armory. He was back in no time, his arms full of the glittering weapons the Lord of the sea had given them. Lakshmana was excited; gone were the tears and the rage, forgotten the animosity against Kaikeyi and their father.

His eyes shining, he laid the unearthly weapons at Rama's feet and cried, "What else, my brother? Our time is short you know."

Rama said, "I want to give away all our possessions as alms; for possessions possess one even from afar. Then we can leave in peace. Go and fetch Vasishta's son Suyagna, and his disciples. Let us take their blessings before we leave."

13. Rama and Dasaratha

They gave away everything they owned to their servants and to some deserving brahmanas. Rama, Lakshmana, and Sita came out into the sun. The princes carried Varuna's bows and the people were dazzled by those weapons. By now, they had heard of the tragedy that had struck Ayodhya like dark lightning. They cried out Rama's name in lament. They had filled the streets to watch him ride the elephant to his coronation, his face under the white parasol. Instead they saw him barefoot, going to bid farewell to his father.

"How can Dasaratha send Rama to the forest?" they cried.

"And the tender Sita with him?"

"Let us follow them to the vana."

"Let Kaikeyi rule over an empty city."

Rama walked silently through that eddying sea of sorrow, unmoved by what they shouted. He kept his eyes turned from their angry faces and passed on to the king's palace. His head bowed, Sumantra waited at Dasaratha's gates. But Rama smiled at the old sarathy and said gently, "Sumantra, announce us to the king."

Sumantra came in to Dasaratha. "My lord, Rama, Sita, and Lakshmana are here."

The king sighed and said in a clear voice now, "Fetch my wives and the others who are close to us by blood and by service. I want to see Rama with all of them one last time."

Kausalya came, Sumitra, and Kaikeyi also. Dasaratha nodded to Sumantra, and he showed Rama in, with Sita and Lakshmana. Rama entered, his hands folded. Dasaratha jumped up with a cry and tried to run to his son. But he slumped senseless to the floor. Rama and Lakshmana carried him to his throne.

When the king's eyes fluttered open, Rama stood before him and said, "Lord of the earth, I have come to take leave of you. Sita and Lakshmana will go with me. Give us your blessing."

In wonder, the father stared at his son, who was as calm as ever and no less radiant. He beckoned to Rama to come nearer, and whispered to him, "Kaikeyi has betrayed me. I am bound by my oath to her, but you are not. The people want you for their king. Disobey me today, Rama, and make an old man happy: take the throne that is yours by force!"

But Rama stopped his father's lips with his hand. "I cannot break your word. Besides, you must rule Ayodhya for many years still. Nine years and five will pass quickly, and I will come back to your feet and clasp them in my hands."

Dasaratha sighed once more. With all the courage he could find he said slowly, "Then go, noble child, and may this deed of yours be a legend through the world forever. You are the jewel of our line, the fulfillment of all the Ikshvakus. Yet I have a small wish you must grant me. Don't go today; spend one last night with your mother and me, and leave tomorrow."

Rama said, "If I stay tonight, tomorrow you will ask me to stay another day. But I have already gone, for my spirit is on its way. Abandon your grief, my lord. Don't let your great heart be burdened: I will be happy in the forest. Besides, Sita and Lakshmana are going with me; the years will pass swiftly, and swiftly I will come back to you. Now give me your blessing and your leave."

Dasaratha embraced Rama and wept. There was no dry eye in his court, save Kaikeyi's. She stood apart, her face a mask. The king said to Sumantra, "Order my army to go to the forest with Rama. Let chariots be laden with silks, gold, and ornaments for my children. Let Rama's palace be emptied and all his household go with him into the wilderness. Let our best hunters go with him and the finest cooks."

Kaikeyi stamped her foot and said shrilly, "You want to leave empty coffers and deserted streets for Bharata to rule! Remember your oath, Dasaratha. Nothing goes with Rama; he goes clad in bark."

With a wild cry, Dasaratha turned on her. "Wretched enemy, is there no limit to the torment you will inflict on me? Woman, your boons were only that Bharata be crowned and Rama exiled. There was nothing about my wealth or my people, and what I do with them; and nothing about me, or my life. You are a serpent I have nurtured at my breast. I will also go into the forest with Rama, and you can rule Ayodhya with your son."

But Rama said to his father, "All I need are some clothes made of valkala, as rishis wear."

Before Rama had finished, Kaikeyi ran out of the sabha. She came back, panting, with three rough robes made of strands of bark woven together. She came defiantly to Rama and thrust one bundle of coarse cloth into his arms. Her glittering eyes met his calm gaze, and a mad smile curved her lips. Rama donned the robe of bark she gave him, and Lakshmana put on another.

Dasaratha watched helplessly, almost beyond grief now. One valkala robe remained in Kaikeyi's hands, and she held it out to Sita. Sita took the strange garment from Kaikeyi. But try as she would, she could not put it on properly: she did not know how. She stood in that court, with some of the robe around her head and some still in her hands, tangled. She turned shyly to Rama and he quickly wrapped the rest of it around her waist, over the pale silk she wore.

Their hearts breaking, the women of the royal harem cried, "Sita hasn't been banished. Leave her with us."

"Take Lakshmana, but not the tender princess."

"How will she live in the jungle?"

When he saw Sita wearing valkala, Vasishta flashed at Kaikeyi in rare anger, "You will stop at nothing, will you? You have banished Rama. Let Sita rule from his throne if you want to be forgiven at least part of your sin. Or we will all follow Rama to the forest and build another city there. He will rule us and the forest will be Ayodhya.

"Fallen queen, your ambition has blinded you to one thing: Bharata will never accept this kingdom you have won for him with treachery. Shatrughna and he will follow Rama to the jungle. Take my word for it; I know these princes better than you do."

Dasaratha seemed to gain courage from Vasishta's anger. He said, "Stop this madness, Kaikeyi. Sita shall not wear valkala."

Kaikeyi fumed, but Sita could put aside her crude cassock.

Rama said to the king, "My mother Kausalya isn't young

any more. She will not be able to bear this sorrow unless you help her. If you don't share her burden, she will give up hope and her life with it."

Dasaratha sobbed bitterly. He said, "In my past lives I must have separated many children from their parents, that I am cursed like this now. And I can't even die of grief, as I gladly would to be rid of this agony. Because one evil woman wants to own this kingdom, this barren patch of dirt, all our people must suffer."

He shook his head in despair; he looked imploringly at Kaikeyi. But that queen's heart was set in stone.

Vanquished, Dasaratha said to Sumantra, "Yoke my best horses to my chariot and bring it to the door. Take my noble son to the edge of the forest and leave him there. I know now that no matter how a man follows dharma, the sins of his past lives overtake him inexorably. That is why I, Dasaratha, who was once a powerful king, can only watch helplessly while my innocent child is banished. And who banishes him? I, his father, who love him as I do my life, and his youngest mother, who did so until today."

14. Rama leaves Ayodhya

When the king's sarathy returned to the royal presence, the time had come for Rama to leave. Suddenly Dasaratha seemed to grow stronger. His voice was firm, and he said, "Sumantra, bring silks, and ornaments from the treasury to last Sita fourteen years."

Kaikeyi opened her mouth to speak. Then she saw the look in her husband's eye, and thought better of it. Sita was draped in finery by Kausalya and the other women of the harem, who paused from time to time to wipe their tears. It was as if they wrapped her not just in silk but in their love and blessings. They attired her ritually, like a bride, in that sabha of sorrow, and she was an embodiment of grace. Kaikeyi's lips throbbed, her face twitched; but Sita was enthroned in the hearts of the people.

Then Kausalya said loudly, so everyone heard her, "My child, women usually serve their husbands as long as they prosper. How many will share their husbands' sorrow and misfortune? But you are ready to follow Rama even into exile, and your sweet face shows no trace of regret. I bless you, Sita, purest of women."

Sita said softly, "Don't worry about your son, mother. He is my light and I will look after him."

Rama came to Kausalya and walked around her in pradakshina. Taking her hand, he said, "Don't grieve too much. This hour of parting is the hardest; the years will pass before you know they have come and gone. They will pass as night does in sleep, and I will return to you."

He went to Sumitra and Kaikeyi, and took the padadhuli from their feet. Kaikeyi flinched from his touch. "If I have ever offended you, forgive me, my mothers, I meant no harm. Give me your blessings; I will need them during my exile."

You could hear sobbing in the sabha as the women of the palace wept, and strong men could not contain their grief. Sita and Lakshmana sought their mothers' blessings; seeing his brother fall at Sumitra's feet, Rama's eyes were full.

Sumitra said to her son, "Serve Rama as you would your father. Lakshmana, my child, there is no sin in what you have decided to do. And I know that, with Rama, the jungle for you will be Ayodhya."

Rama walked around his father in pradakshina. As grief struck him again, he came back to Kausalya and fell at her feet once more. With Lakshmana and Sita at his side, he stood silently before Dasaratha, with his head bowed. He knelt at his father's feet and clasped them. Sita and Lakshmana took the king's blessing.

At last, Sumantra said, "Rama, the chariot is here."

Rama turned away from his parents and went out into the sun. In the teeming streets, the people wore finery to celebrate the crowning of a yuvaraja. The women began to wail when Sita, Rama, and Lakshmana climbed into Sumantra's chariot. In a tide, the crowd swept toward the chariot that bore their prince away from them. They reached out hands of grief to him; they stood in the horses' path. They cried to Sumantra, "Drive so slowly that fourteen years pass on your journey through these streets."

Some lay in front of the chariot wheels and had to be lifted out of the way by the king's soldiers.

But others cried, "Death to Kaikeyi! Death to Dasaratha!"

"We want Rama for our king today!"

"He belongs to the people. We will not let him go to the forest."

Rama also cried now. He knew all of them by their names. He had eaten in their homes and shared their joys and their hopes. He knew who their children were and which child belonged to whom. Parting from his parents he had borne resolutely; but now the tears came and he could not stop them. Sita wept beside him, and Lakshmana sobbed. This was a sea of love they plowed through, their chariot a ship of sorrow. This love was what Rama could hardly bear to be parted from. He cried to the sarathy, "Fly Sumantra, before my heart breaks."

Dasaratha ran out of his palace. For the first time in years, he ran out onto the street to pursue the chariot that bore his son away from him. But a few steps and he fell, and the people had to lift their king from the ground. Then Kausalya, who had controlled herself until now, tried to follow the chariot. Faintly Rama heard her voice above the crowd, screaming his name.

He heard the king crying, "Stop the chariot. Sumantra, I command you, stop!"

But Rama whispered to Sumantra, "Fly, Sumantra. Say later that you didn't hear him for the crowd."

He stood up in the chariot, dark and handsome, wearing valkala, and more luminous than ever. With his fine hands and his soft voice, he asked for passage from the swirling crowd. His people, who could refuse him nothing, parted, and he rode along the path they cleared. As Dasaratha stood benumbed on his palace steps, the banner on his son's chariot vanished from view. But the old king stood on for an hour with some of the sad crowd below him, lest Rama change his mind and return.

At last, Kausalya laid a hand on Dasaratha's arm in mercy, and, leaning on her after many years, he turned back into his palace. The people also began to disperse.

15. Grief

Dasaratha had crossed the threshold into the palace when it struck him like a blow that his son had really gone. The king's legs gave way under him. Kausalya could not bear his weight and Kaikeyi ran to his side. But when she took his hand, Dasaratha's eyes flew open. He snatched away his hand and cried, "Don't touch me! I never want to see your face again. And if Bharata is loyal to you, I will not look at him either."

He allowed only Kausalya to support him. Dasaratha pointed through the great palace doors and said sadly, "Look at the trail of dust that takes my Rama away from me. Dressed like two tapasvins, my sons have gone to sleep on beds of branches and leaves; and that flower of a girl with them. How will she endure the thorns that pierce her feet? How will Sita bear the terror of the beasts of the jungle? Kaikeyi, I hope you are satisfied with what you have done. I will die soon now, and then you and your son can rule Ayodhya over my ashes."

He looked around him by the last light of day streaming through the doors. The palace was dead without Rama: a body out of which the soul had gone.

Dasaratha said to Kausalya, "You are my Rama's mother. Forgive me for all the pain I have caused you. Take me with you to your apartment, Kausalya; let me seek my peace in you."

The palace guards carried him to her apartment and set him down on a couch. Kausalya sat beside him. After the sun set, the king and his first queen spent all night speaking together of their son: how noble he was and how true. Dasaratha did not stop crying.

Once, raising his arms above his head, he said, "Rama, you have left me and gone. Fortunate shall they be who live to see you return; but not I, my son, not I. My hours are numbered now. I feel death near me, as if he comes to fill the void you have left."

Kausalya wept. Her husband reached for her in the darkness. "Touch me with your tender hands I have not felt for so many years. I did not tell you earlier, but the vision of my eyes followed Rama's chariot and has not returned to me. I cannot see any more. But hold me now and let us share our grief."

Kausalya came to him. They sat with their arms around each other and found some solace. They whispered to each other about Rama: about how he looked now, and what he was like when he was ten, and five; how everyone loved him, and how he had broken Siva's bow. They spoke of nothing but Rama while they held each other and the night's living darkness swept like a cold wind through the fissures in their hearts.

Sumitra sat in the next room and realized that, instead of giving Dasaratha her strength, Kausalya was plunging him into deeper despair. Sumitra called the older queen, and said firmly in that solid night of sorrow, "Calm yourself, Kausalya. Rama is so pure that no harm will come to our children. The sun will not burn them, the breeze will blow gently around them and the vana devatas will all protect them. At night, the moon will wrap them in his light like a father. And which animal that dares attack them will escape with its life? Have you forgotten the devastras our sons command? Or the rakshasas they killed, when they went with Viswamitra?"

Kausalya grew quiet. Sumitra stroked her face. Lakshmana's mother said, "It is your strength Dasaratha needs tonight, not your tears. Fourteen years will flit by before you realize they have gone, and Rama will come back to you."

Kausalya was ashamed. Sumitra had also sent a son to the forest today, though he had not been banished.

16. The people of Ayodhya

Like a sea leaving its shores and seeking a new bed to lie in, the people of Ayodhya followed Rama's chariot beyond the city gates. Though he begged them to return, they followed him far beyond the limits of the city. Finally, he had Sumantra stop the chariot and spoke to them.

"If you love me, you must listen to what I say. I am going away to keep my father's dharma. I beg you, give this love to my brother Bharata. You know him well: he is a fine man, older than his years, kind and strong. He will rule Ayodhya as ably as Dasaratha. Welcome Bharata to the throne; he will be a good king to you."

But they began to shout him down. "We want you for our king!"

"You were born to be king; aren't you the eldest?"

"Stop the horses, Sumantra!" they cried.

"You cannot take our king from us."

The old and the infirm were in that crowd, and they shouted as loudly as the young. Rama climbed down from the chariot and went among them. One old man, who had no teeth left in his head, unfurled a battered old umbrella over him. "I will shield you from the sun, my prince. Your Sita wilts in the heat; let her get down and walk under my umbrella. It is a royal parasol, Rama, because it is held over you in love!"

"Come back with us, Rama, or we will all go into the jungle with you," said another old one.

A brahmana priest, who was also old but obviously as fit as any youngster in the crowd, said, "Look Rama, I have brought my sacred fire with me. I mean to stay with you for fourteen years."

Rama only smiled. He shook his head and walked faster to try to leave them behind. But they followed him, old and young, men and women. Then, as if nature herself wanted to bar the prince's way, the Tamasa lay ahead of them, rippling velvet in the dusk. Sumantra unyoked his horses and led them to drink.

Rama stood staring at the river, after its winding course. He turned to Sita and Lakshmana. "The first day of our exile ends. Let us sleep here tonight, beside the Tamasa."

The sky was burnished gold, fading quickly. They could hear the twilight noises of birds and daylight creatures returning to their roosts, their holes and hides.

Rama said to Sita, "Can you hear the wild folk coming home for the night?" Then he was somber. "But in Ayodhya, Dasaratha will not sleep tonight: he mourns his sons who have left him. My only consolation is that Bharata will be home soon." He put his arm around his brother. "Lakshmana, I am so glad you came with us. You shall be our protector, Sita's and mine."

Lakshmana had made beds for the three of them with leaves and grass, even as he used to when the princes had gone with Viswamitra. Rama lay down with a sigh. He asked Sumantra, "Have the horses grazed, Sumantra? Have you eaten anything? As for me, I won't eat tonight; there is no hunger in me."

Sita lay down beside him, Lakshmana on the other side, and they fell asleep, in calm, while a breeze played on their faces. All the people also lay down around them and slept, strangely refreshed by their adventure. The moon rose over the unusual spectacle, and the river whispered about it all the way to the sea.

Two hours before dawn, when the moon had set and no one stirred, not even the breeze any more, or the little creatures of night, Rama shook Sita and Lakshmana. He held a finger to his lips and whispered, "We must be on our way."

They woke Sumantra. Without a sound—the horses were well trained—they crossed the sleepy, murmurous Tamasa. On the other bank, Rama said to Sumantra, "Cross the river again and ride for a time toward Ayodhya. Then fly back to us on your tracks, before the sun rises and the people wake up. They must think we have turned back to the city. Otherwise, they will either follow us into exile or take us back to Ayodhya; and neither course is the way of dharma."

Sumantra was back within the hour. Rama briefly turned his face north; then he, Sita, and Lakshmana climbed into the chariot, just as the false dawn that comes before sunrise flushed at the horizon. Like the wind, they swept away toward the Dandaka vana.

17. The hunter king

Yoked to the swiftest horses in Ayodhya, the fine chariot carried Rama farther and farther from home. Through town and village they flew without stopping, across emerald plains, fording frothy streams, plunging through scented woods and swaying fields. For the night, they stopped beneath a large pipal tree out in the open, leagues from any habitation. They lay under portentous stars, which had shone down on the earth through the chasmal vaults of the universe ever since the earth was made. Starlight entered them as subtle destiny; but they lay asleep knowing nothing of its powerful mysteries.

With dawn the next day, they pressed on and came to the southern lands of Kosala. Here Rama asked Sumantra to hold his horses. Climbing down from the chariot, he stood gazing across fallow fields and sown in the light of the lonely morning, as the wildflowers around his ankles opened just for him and the birds in the trees sang the rising sun. But when he saw some farmers and their women come out of their simple dwellings, he climbed into the chariot again and told Sumantra to ride hard.

They came to the cool Vedasruti, whose waters were known for their sweetness. They forded the river and gained the far bank. On they drove and after half a day they came to the sacred Gomati. They crossed that river also, comfortably for the water was still low, and rode on.

Rama said wistfully to Sita, "These are the lands that Manu gave his son Ikshvaku in the krita yuga."

He told them about every land they passed. He knew each one's history intimately and spoke as if they were all precious parts of himself. They had come to the Syandika and forded her when, suddenly, grief seized Rama. He said in anguish, "Sumantra, when will I hunt with you again in the forests of the Sarayu? When will I see my father and mother again?"

But seeing tears spring in the old sarathy's eyes, he controlled himself. Now they had reached the southern limit of Kosala. Rama stopped the chariot. He climbed down and turned his face north, from where they had come. He folded his hands and said softly, "Land of my ancestors, let me leave you now. Gods of Kosala, bless me that I return to my mother and my father when my exile is over."

He raised his eyes to heaven and cried, "My people who love me, I go for the sake of dharma, the timeless wealth. Give me your blessing and I will come back to you in fourteen years, which is less than a day for the Devas."

Rama lay on his face upon the earth and kissed it; Lakshmana and Sita did the same. They climbed back into Sumantra's chariot and he bore them away toward the inscrutable future.

Kosala, land of the sons of Manu, faded into the horizon behind them. They came to the banks of the Ganga, tripathaga of the three streams that flowed through Swarga, Bhumi, and Patala. She lay like a sea before them, she who washed the sins of men: Ganga, whom the rishis adored because she was a Goddess; Jahnavi, in whose magical waters the Devas, Asuras, gandharvas, and apsaras came to bathe, and other beings who were not of humankind.

Her currents lapped at her banks. Her waves crested with silver foam, she bore placid streams and spinning whirlpools upon her, side by side. She was alive and, in their present mood, they were intensely sensible of her attraction. Rama gazed out across the wide water. Sighing, he said, "Let us spend the night under this tree."

They sat in silence by the river, watching the sun set in the west. His gold was scattered on the mystic flow that caressed the exiles, soothed them with wonderful whisperings. Peace was upon them, easing the harshness and grief of the past days.

They had chosen to spend the night near the city of Shringiberapura, which was ruled by an old friend of Rama's: Guha, the fierce king of hunters. Soon enough, curious rishis and other bathers in the holy Ganga learned of Rama's arrival and word reached Guha. He came excitedly out of his city to welcome his friend.

Guha came laden with mattresses of swan's down and a sumptuous feast. He shouted in joy when he saw Rama; the hunter king ran forward to embrace the dark prince. Guha said, "Stay with me and rule my city for as long as you like. Noble Rama, the honor will be mine!"

Rama embraced him warmly, but he said, "My kind friend, I am moved by your love. But I cannot accept any of your generosity today, only your affection: I am bound by an oath to live like a tapasvin for fourteen years. But not these horses, and I will be grateful if they can be fed."

When he heard what had happened in Ayodhya, Guha hung his head. Then he said, "Rama, allow me to watch over you myself tonight."

The hunter king spent the night with them. Rama waded into the river for his evening worship. Standing with the twilight current around his waist, he offered a prayer to Surya, God of day. When he came out Lakshmana washed his brother's feet and wiped them. He pressed them as he had every day in Ayodhya, since they were boys.

With a smile, Rama lay down beside Sita, on the bed of leaves that Lakshmana had become so expert at making. They both fell asleep almost at once. Sumantra, Lakshmana, and Guha stood watch, with their weapons.

As the moon rose and rode serenely on the Ganga, Guha said to Lakshmana, "You must be tired. Why don't you sleep? Have no fear for your safety tonight: Guha and his people stand guard over you."

But Lakshmana replied sadly, "How can I sleep when Rama and Sita lie on beds of leaves? O Guha, I am thinking of my father, that he will not survive this night. If I feel so sad despite being here with Rama, what must Dasaratha's grief be in Ayodhya? We will never see him alive again. And if he dies, how long will Kausalya and Sumitra survive in Kaikeyi's court? No, they will die as well."

Lakshmana spoke so earnestly Guha could see the funeral pyres of Dasaratha and his queens before his eyes. That rough hunter also wept with Lakshmana beside the Ganga, and the river carried their grief out to the distant sea, like sacrament. The night passed slowly; the very darkness was heavy with sorrow.

18. Across the Ganga

Rama was awakened by the dissonant cries of peacocks calling at the rising sun. *Viaon!* they screamed, *Viaon!* all along the riverbank, and set off a chorus of thrush and koyal, pigeon and tiny warbler. Soon every bird in the crowded trees was alight with song. Rama and Lakshmana waded into the transparent river to perform Suryanamaskara.

Rama said to Guha, "Can you give us a boat to cross the Ganga? We must press on, and send Sumantra back to Ayodhya as soon as we can."

Guha clapped his hands to call one of his men, and cried in his musical tongue, "A royal boat for the princes and princess. Be sure it is one of my own, and have our best oarsmen take them across."

A brightly painted boat from the harem of Shringiberapura was towed to the river for Rama's crossing. The kshatriyas strapped their bows and quivers to their backs and their swords to their waists. Guha bowed to Rama. "Last night, I learned the greatest lesson of my life from you: that dharma is the only path worth walking. Rama, I thank you."

The forester had tears in his eyes. He embraced the prince of Ayodhya, and then fell at his feet for his blessing. Rama raised Guha up and hugged him. He said, "You have been a true friend in my need, and that is dharma indeed."

They came to the river where the colorful boat floated. Rama turned to Sumantra; the sarathy's eyes were red from crying. He stood before his prince, but spoke no word, only gazed into his face. Rama laid a hand on his shoulder and said simply, "Go back to my father now, Sumantra."

Sumantra broke down and cried, "This has never happened before in the history of the House of Ikshvaku: that a crown prince, his wife, and his brother are banished into exile. I know now that chanting the Vedas and worshipping the Devas is of no use, if a prince like you must suffer this."

And he sobbed. Then, growing quiet again, he said ruefully, "Blessed are those that dwell in the Dandaka vana; our loss shall be their gain. All of us born in Ayodhya must have been great sinners in past lives: to have known you as we have, to have watched you grow to manhood, and to lose you now for a demented woman's greed. We are damned, Rama; not you, but those you leave behind." He embraced the prince and kissed his hands again and again, wetting them with his tears.

Rama held him close, then said, "Tell the king we are happy in exile. Tell him we will return to him in fourteen years, to take the dust from his feet. Give our love to Kausalya, Sumitra, Kaikeyi, and all our mothers of the palace. Tell my father that once he crowns Bharata yuvaraja, his sorrow, which is half for Ayodhya, will ebb from him. When he finds how able my brother is.

"Tell Bharata to look after all his mothers equally. Tell him he should care specially for Kausalya and Sumitra; they have been separated from their sons. Give him my blessing, tell him I said, 'Rule Ayodhya with dharma and earn a lofty place for yourself in the world to come.' "

Sumantra was still disconsolate. "Ayodhya will be like a woman who has lost her child. When I take this chariot through the city gates, there will be such a lament, as if I am a messenger with the most evil tidings, that I did not bring you back home. Why, these horses won't draw the chariot without you. I beg you, Rama, let me come with you. I will serve you well in the vana."

Rama touched the sarathy's face with his fingers. "I have to send you back. Otherwise, Kaikeyi will not know you have taken me to the jungle and she will torment my father. You don't have to prove your love to me, Sumantra; I know it well. But your place is beside your king in his dark time. Go, good sarathy. Give me your blessing and go in peace."

He turned to Guha. "I must wear my hair in jata. Can your men fetch me some sap of the nyagrodha?"

When the sticky milk of the pipal tree was brought, Rama and Lakshmana rubbed it into their hair. Soon their locks were thick and tangled, and they coiled them in jata like rishis of the forest. Sumantra cried again to see his princes transformed. The river beckoned now. Lakshmana held the boat steady while Rama and Sita climbed into it, and he climbed in after them. At last, the blue prince raised his hand in farewell and the oarsmen of the hunting people cast off.

Sumantra and Guha stood on the riverbank, waving after the boat. The currents were mild in the morning, and they went along rapidly. The figures on the bank dwindled. In midstream, Sita raised her voice in prayer to the Ganga: "Devi, Queen of the ocean! Grant that in fourteen years we cross your waters again, and seek your blessing on our way home to Ayodhya."

Rama and Lakshmana touched the clear flow and scooped up some water in their palms for achamana. They reached the southern bank, thanked the boatmen, and alighted from the reed craft. The Dandaka vana loomed before them. When the oarsmen cast off again, Rama waved once more to Sumantra and Guha, whom they could still see across the river.

Rama said to Lakshmana, "Now is our time for wariness. You walk ahead, my brother. Sita, you walk behind Lakshmana and I will bring up the rear. The jungle is not a place for carelessness. Out of your love you have come with me; but the paths and the years ahead are fraught with danger."

Thus they went into the towering Dandaka vana: Lakshmana in the lead with his bow in his hand, Sita behind him, and Rama last of all. When Sumantra saw them enter the jungle, he heaved a sigh. He wiped his tears and turned back to Guha and to the long, sad journey back to Ayodhya.

19. Into the deep vana

At first the forest turned their minds to sorrow; that was the effect it had on them. It was a twilight place, and so quiet they heard their own thoughts too clearly, especially their anxieties. They walked on wordlessly, as if they dared not disturb the vast silence. Just strange bird cries echoed, now and again; or they heard rustling in the undergrowth where unknown beasts made their way through the half-dark of day. A feeling of great eeriness was upon them. Their senses were sharp as arrows, their bows were strung, and between them was Sita, a little frightened and very brave. The brothers walked resolutely on.

Once they stopped to pick some luscious mangoes and made a sweet, if somber, meal of them. They avoided speaking as if it were forbidden: such was the initial spell of that awesome forest. And its creatures, if they watched the intruders from leafy hiding, did not show themselves yet, in mistrust and conspiracy. Having eaten and rested, the princes and Sita walked on. There were few paths in here and their progress was mostly through dense, trackless jungle. At times, when he could find no other way, Lakshmana drew his sword and cut one for them to squeeze along. The sun glinted like rare gold through the heavy canopy overhead, and they went south by his position.

Evening was upon them when they came to a small clearing. In its midst stood a spreading nyagrodha tree. Rama called a halt for the day. They sat beneath the patriarch of the forest, who grew at some distance from his fellows. By his size, he was older than any of the other trees: he was a giant of the earth, countless summers and winters he had seen. Lakshmana fidgeted uneasily and his face was dark after their long walk.

Rama laid a hand on his arm. "We must be calm in this place. The more agitated we are the more vulnerable we shall be." As soon as he spoke, a weight seemed to lift away from them; as if all this while the forest had strained to hear one of their voices, to discover what kind of men these were. Lakshmana's face lost its frown and now they reclined against the knotty roots of the nyagrodha, tired but speaking together, of this and that, to keep the silence at bay as the sun set. Sita said little but sat close to Rama, listening to them and to the immense jungle around.

With nightfall, Rama's mind turned back ineluctably to Ayodhya and sorrow took him again. He sighed, "Dasaratha, how sad you must be tonight and how gleeful Kaikeyi. Fear lays hold of me, Lakshmana: once Bharata is crowned and her purpose is secure, how long will Kaikeyi spare our father? She has no love for your mother or mine. If the king dies, she will hardly spare them. I think you should go back to Ayodhya, my brother."

He sat smoldering like a fire that has no more flames, or a sea that waves no more but has grown awfully still. Lakshmana laid a gentle hand on Rama and said to him, "You must not grieve like this; or who will comfort Sita and me? One thing is certain: I will not leave you and go back. I have no wish to see my father, or my mother even. I would not go into Devaloka if its gates were open, unless you were with me. Besides, I think you give Bharata less credit than he deserves. He will look after our father, and our two mothers as well."

The spasm of anxiety was smoothed from Rama's face. "What would we do without you?" he cried. "We would not survive a night in the forest, let alone fourteen years."

They gathered dry branches and twigs, and kindled a fire in a ring around themselves. In turns, making sure the flames never died, the brothers kept watch while Sita slept. Often during the night, at the periphery of the clearing, they saw animal eyes that glowed red, green, and yellow at them, in curiosity or in hunger. They heard ominous growling and snuffling; but no wild creature dared come near the fire, which crackled merrily through the night. They had gathered a good store of fuel before darkness fell, and it lasted until dawn.

Sita discovered that sleep in the forest was a deeper thing than it was in the city. She slept without fear, and dreamed lustrous dreams.

20. Rishi Bharadvaja's asrama

The next morning, the feeling of strangeness had left them. Passing a restful night in the jungle gave them a sense of being accepted, if not yet one of being quite welcome. The forebodings of the dark were forgotten as the sun climbed over the horizon. Day and night were so clearly divided in the wild, like different realms, each with its separate laws. Every day was a new beginning.

They chanted the Gayatri. When their morning worship was over, they walked south again, charting their course by the sun. Such sights greeted their eyes today: as if the forest had read their minds and their hearts while they slept, and now made them welcome. To their surprise, the deeper they went into that jungle the more trails they found, both fresh and worn. Then there were the animals of the vana: nilgai, chital and sambur, steaming bison, and a leopard with eyes like flames, stretched languid on a tree. Troops of merry, chattering langurs swung along with them for krosas in the leafy awning above. Once they heard a tiger roar a short way from the path on which they walked.

After a watchful day, the denizens of the forest knew the weapons the kshatriyas carried were not for cruel sport, and the jungle opened its heart to them. In innocence and wonder, the wild creatures came out to stare. Sita was enchanted. They came to pools full of dark lotuses in astonishing colors they had never seen, unless in forgotten dreams. Filigree creepers, entwined around knotted old tree trunks, created wild veils through which they passed between zone and zone of the jungle. Subtly, the forest entered them and they its ancient soul.

Quickly they learned that there were birds in the forest whose incredible beauty no poet had described, and whose songs were haunting legends of the jungle's living soul. They came to hidden lakes and streams, and saw swans gliding on them, haughty and utterly beautiful. As unfamiliar and captivating as the sights and sounds of the mysterious vana were its fragrances. These were exuded by flowers, dull and bright, which grew in profusion everywhere. Wafted on breezes, they blended in the air as if in a vast natural perfumery and were blown through the aisles of the forest, heady and delectable.

Rama, Sita, and Lakshmana made their way under the great trees, pausing occasionally when Sita wanted one of the princes to pluck a particularly exotic flower for her hair. They walked toward the Sangama, where the golden Ganga and the deep blue Yamuna flow together. Lakshmana pointed into the sky and they saw a plume of smoke rising in the distance. Rama held his hand up for them to be still; and then they thought they heard it faintly: the dim roar of the two rivers hurtling into ecstatic confluence.

Rama said in excitement, "Prayaga! And an asrama of rishis, probably Bharadvaja's."

Memories of Viswamitra and their journey with him came flooding back. The sun had climbed high over their heads and blazed down on the boiling world. But at the thought of Bharadvaja's asrama, they hurried on as quickly as Sita could walk. All day they went over uneven terrain: sometimes through flat, dense jungle and at others over steep hillocks that loomed abruptly in their path. Only when the sun was sinking in the west did they stand at the edge of an escarpment and see the two rivers below them, with an asrama tucked cozily between.

As they drew near, they saw many rishis about, preparing for their evening worship. Tame deer roamed among the munis' huts. When they saw the strangers they stood stock-still, quivering. Rama, Lakshmana, and Sita had not yet acquired the familiar scent of forest dwellers. The wild creatures still smelled the city on them and were wary.

The princes and Sita presented themselves before the profound Bharadvaja. When they prostrated at his feet, Rama said, "I am Dasaratha's son Rama. These are my brother Lakshmana and my wife, Sita. Bless us, Muni: we have been exiled to the Dandaka vana for fourteen years."

Bharadvaja's eyes took light. "I know about you, Rama of Ayodhya. I know, with such insight as God has given me, that you have been exiled for no fault of yours. Stay here with us for fourteen years. We will be more than happy to have you."

For just a moment, Rama was tempted. Then he said, "I thank you for your kindness, but we are still not deep enough into the jungle. If the people of Ayodhya discover that I am here, they will come often to visit us. I must find a more secret and lonely place."

Though disappointment flickered in his eyes, Bharadvaja nodded in agreement. He said, "Ten krosas from here is Chitrakuta. Rishis live on the mountain, and monkeys. It is a beautiful and auspicious place."

Bharadvaja insisted the brothers and Sita spend the night with him. He knew who Rama was and thought it a blessing that the prince had come to his hermitage. Late into the night they sat talking; many a time, overwhelmed by Rama's presence, the rishi implored him to stay on. Each time the prince refused graciously.

They were fed by the hermits and given a hut to sleep in. Tired as they were, sleep came swift and deeply. The next morning they went to bid farewell to Bharadvaja.

Bright as Agni from his tapasya, that rishi said, "When you reach the Sangama, follow the Yamuna east and you will find a well-worn path that runs for a krosa. After a krosa, cross the river and you will see the path continues on the other side. Walk that way until you come to a nyagrodha, a solitary ancient of the jungle. That sacred tree is called Shyama. Let Sita worship him, as siddhas have done through the ages, for he is a guardian of Chitrakuta. You can rest among his roots or go on, as you choose.

"Another krosa ahead is a softer forest: the Yamunavana of palasa, badri, and yamala trees. The trail through that vana is full of charming sights. You will see lakes, streams, and lofty falls. I have walked that way many times; the jungle is thick with bamboo, but the path will not hurt your feet. For there is gentleness upon it, and it leads straight on to Chitrakuta."

Bharadvaja came to the riverbank with the kshatriyas. He blessed them and went back to his asrama, his heart beating with Rama, his mind full of the dark prince. Without turning back, the brothers and Sita walked away beside the swift river. They walked a while before they found the path that skirted the water. A krosa from there they saw the ford where the river was slow.

The princes cut down bamboo stems and jungle vines, and lashed them together to make a raft; on it, they crossed the midnight-blue water. Sita worshiped the river in midstream, just as she had the Ganga a day ago. She prayed to the Goddess Yamuna to bless them.

South of the river, they took the jungle trail through the Yamuna-vana and came to a great nyagrodha, growing far from his fellows, like a lonely tower in the wilderness. With pradakshina, Sita worshiped that spirit and prayed aloud, "Ancestor of the jungle, bless us that we return safely to Ayodhya after fourteen years."

Rama said, "Let us press on; I am impatient to arrive."

The forest grew ever stranger and more vivid, as they went deeper into its spaces of mystery. Birds and flowers were more brilliantly plumed and petaled. Their songs were unfamiliar and their scents piquant. The path snaked through the Yamunavana, at times following the breathy river close to its bank, at others leading them far from the water, always climbing. The air was cooler here and, as Bharadvaja promised, they saw shining lakes and glittering waterfalls. The land was fresh and unspoiled, and they felt the earth received them like favored children.

They decided to spend the night beside the Yamuna. They were tired, and thought they would make their way to Chitrakuta early the next day. Peacocks screamed around them as they settled down, and a lively troop of langurs was full of gossip in the trees above. They no longer felt threatened by the forest, but welcome and elated. Friendly breezes toyed with their hair. They slept contentedly that night and no thoughts of Ayodhya disturbed them.

21. Chitrakuta

With a thousand birds singing, the jungle woke them at dawn. The feathered ones sang the sun in rapture, blessing another day in the world as they have done since there were first birds in its trees to give praise. It had been dark when they settled here the previous night. Now they stood astonished by the loveliness of the place in which they found themselves. Forgotten were yesterday's insoluble sorrows: this was their new life, of vibrant hill-green and deep river-blue. The flowers here were like pieces of a rainbow broken across the forest, and vivacious monkeys followed them again through the trees. They spied on herds of deer and came upon lakes tranquil as rishis' hearts.

The leaves had fallen off the palasa trees and scarlet flowers blazed on their branches like countless flames. From other trees, beehives hung heavy as little boats. When they ate the fruit of these forests, they knew they had never tasted anything to rival them. Tiny, nondescript songbirds, throats full of musical fire, sang down to incandescent peacocks. Those beautiful and tone-deaf fowl screeched back plaintively.

Rama, Sita, and Lakshmana walked on until a mountain rose before them out of the foothills. They saw herds of elephant, bison, and deer moving on its shoulder streaked silver with shimmering cascades. The echo of the falls drifted across the silence of the valleys, as if borne on the wings of birds. Slowly they made their way up, and searched for a place to live in. They came to Valmiki's asrama, and that rishi welcomed them. They took his blessing and climbed on. Then, in a flat clearing within a circle of eucalyptus and early pine, Rama stopped still. He felt certain that this was the place for them; as if here many paths of grace, laid on the earth in invisible arteries, converged, and imbued it with exceptional power and auspiciousness.

Nearby, the Mandakini, which flows into the Yamuna, gushed over her rocky bed. Rama and Lakshmana collected logs of wood with which they could build a kutila. But Lakshmana told Rama to stand aside, and with wonderful skill began to lash together their first home in the wilderness. He took two days before it was ready: a cozy log cottage on the hillside, thatched with grass and straw.

Outside, and a few yards from the little dwelling, was a shelter for worship. The construction was clean and strong, and Rama hugged his brother, crying jovially, "You couldn't have built it better if I had helped you! But we must offer a sacrifice of deer's flesh to the gods of the jungle, so they keep evil away from our asrama for fourteen years."

Expert hunter that he was, Lakshmana went off to stalk a herd of chital he had seen earlier beside the Mandakini. An hour later he came back, grinning, with a skinned carcass draped over his shoulders. They roasted the stag on a spit. Rama chanted the mantras for vaastu shanti and offered the meat to the Devas of light, to Rudra and Narayana, the vana devatas and the Gods who rule men's fates.

Rama bathed and entered the log cottage for the first time. Lakshmana and Sita went in after him. Contentment was upon them, since they could not have wished for better company or a more beautiful place in which to live.

Thus Rama, Sita, and Lakshmana arrived on Chitrakuta, and settled there. The sorrow of Ayodhya left them alone, save very rarely.

22. Sumantra returns

For a long time after Rama crossed the Ganga, Guha and Sumantra stood on the bank of the river. The old sarathy stood gazing after his princes and Sita like one who watched a bad dream: bemused, expecting to awaken from it at any moment. Gently Guha led Sumantra back into his city. He kept the old man with him for a day and a night, until news came back from the jungle that the exiles had reached Bharadvaja's asrama.

Near noon the next day, Sumantra bid farewell to Guha, yoked his horses, and rode back to Ayodhya. Three days and nights rode Dasaratha's sarathy, like Vayu, his heart full of sorrow. The fourth evening, when the sun had set, he arrived at the gates of Kosala's capital. Nothing stirred in the city. No music was in the air; no games of chess were being played on the street corners. No contests of wrestling or marksmanship did Sumantra see in the alleyways. No butter lamps lit Ayodhya; no women strolled out on their husbands' arms. Silence hung over the city.

At the clatter of Sumantra's wheels, the people flung open their doors and came out to see if Rama had returned. They crowded the chariot and cried, "Where is Rama? Where is our yuvaraja, Sumantra?"

The old sarathy hung his head and replied in a whisper, "I left him on the banks of the Ganga. He ordered me back to Ayodhya."

Before the word spread, and he was mobbed, Sumantra snapped his reins and drove on to Dasaratha's palace. The women of the harem saw him coming, and when they saw he came alone, hope went from them. They turned back to their apartments in despair, crying. Sumantra came to Dasaratha in Kausalya's chambers and knelt before his king. Dasaratha questioned him mutely with blind eyes.

Sumantra said, "We drove south for three days and I left him on the banks of the Ganga. I watched him cross the river. After waving to me, he walked into the forest with Lakshmana and Sita. And I saw them no more. The king of hunters, Guha of Shringiberapura, had news from his trackers that three days ago the princes and Sita arrived in Bharadvaja's asrama."

As he spoke, Sumantra's gaze roved anxiously over his master. Dasaratha had aged a life in the week since the sarathy had seen him. He had grown so thin, he might not have eaten at all since Rama left. Pale skin hung loosely on his face; tears leaked from his weary eyes like his life. He sighed with every word he heard, and shivered as if with some great terror. Now when he spoke, his voice, which once rang like thunder through his sabha, was barely audible. Sumantra had to move closer to hear what he said.

"Tell me more, so my pain grows a little less. Though there is no cure for me. Tell me how he walked into the jungle; tell me how he slept while you were with him. Did he send a message for me? What did Sita and Lakshmana say? Tell me everything, Sumantra: give me some peace."

"They wept, my lord, before they left me. Your sons rubbed their hair with the juice of the nyagrodha and twisted locks of jata on their heads."

Dasaratha listened to this in silence, and he seemed to become absorbed in the images of Rama that rose into his mind. But abruptly he sat erect and tried to get up from his couch. He could not, and cried, "Take me to him, Sumantra. I cannot live without my child. Yoke your horses; take me to him now!"

At his sides, Kausalya and Sumitra stroked his arms and tried to quiet him, though they also cried. Sumantra stood before them in anguish. The king clasped Kausalya's hands. He said to her, "Forgive me, Kausalya, forgive me. Don't be angry; ah, I could not bear that. Though I betrayed your love, you have always been kind to me. And now look what I have done. Forgive me, oh forgive me, Kausalya."

He sobbed like a heartbroken child. Kausalya cradled Dasaratha's head against her. She caressed his face, saying, "There is nothing to forgive, my lord. If I have spoken harshly to you these past days, it is only from my own sorrow. We will share this grief and conquer it, and Rama will come back to us."

But Dasaratha had fallen asleep from exhaustion. For a while, she held him quietly. Suddenly his eyes flew open as if a demon had visited his swoon. They darted here and there, as if searching blindly for something. Then he sighed and shut them once more.

Thus, with Kausalya's leave, Sumantra left Dasaratha. He bowed low to the king he had served for so many glorious years, and backed out of that chamber.

23. A forgotten curse

It was past midnight when Dasaratha awoke from a restless slumber. Kausalya and Sumitra sat beside him. Night was always a lucid time for the king. His mind seemed to clear when darkness fell, and so did his speech. Tonight he put his arms around Kausalya so she would hear what he had to say. Without Rama, he had no desire left to live in the bitter present; the past called him irresistibly. He thought he could see Kausalya dimly. He saw her as she had been many years ago: young and beautiful.

Slowly but clearly, he said to her, "Whatever a man does, good or evil, comes back to him someday. And he pays for everything. Once when I was young and a keen hunter, I had a strange adventure. I was expert at shabdavedi, by which one kills an animal from hiding, aiming blind at just the sound it makes. I was proud of my skill.

"It was a summer's end, I remember. I can see the parched earth thirstily drinking the first showers of the monsoon. The sky was heavy with storm clouds and the frogs on the swollen pools were giving throat all together to welcome the rain. I remember that day so clearly: as if it has returned to me and I have set out again to hunt beside the Sarayu, under the green mountain. The river had risen and everything had been lashed clean by the torrents of the past day.

"I stood very still, hidden in some thickets. I waited beside a pool on the river that was a favorite water hole for the animals of the jungle. For half an hour, I stood motionless and there was no sound save the songs of birds in the trees. Then I heard it, like music to my ears: the long gurgling noise that elephants make as they drink through their trunks. Never looking out from my hide, lest I give myself away, I eased my arrow through an opening in the thicket. Tracking the sound with only my hearing, I drew back my bowstring and shot a fierce arrow at where I judged the elephant's heart to be.

"Instead of the shrill trumpeting of a wounded beast, I heard a scream that froze my heart. It was the scream of a man. Then a voice was raised in agony: 'Who has shot me like an animal? I am a rishi; why am I hunted with arrows? Who are you, sinner? Come out; let me see you before I die.'

"I scrambled out in shock and saw a young sannyasi before me, fallen over on his side. My arrow had pierced him right through and protruded evilly from his chest. Its feathers were stained with his blood, which gushed from him and fell on the white sand. Beside him lay his water pot, from which all the water had spilled. A legend of pain was in his eyes, and anger.

"When he saw me he cried through lips that frothed blood, 'A kshatriya! What have I done to deserve your savage barb? I came to the river to fetch water for my old parents who are both blind. Now they will die without me, and thinking that I abandoned them.'

"His breath came in a tortured wheeze; more blood bubbled from his mouth. I fell sobbing at his feet. I told him how I came to shoot him with my arrow. I begged him not to curse me, to believe it had been a mistake. I held him in my arms, and between painful gasps he said, 'Fill the water pot and take it back to my father. You will find him a way down this trail. Tell him what happened; pacify him and try to prevent him from cursing you. As for me, I know you did not mean to kill me and I forgive you.'

"The effort of speaking drained him and he lay quiet for a while. But I saw his eyes glaze over, as death came for him. His face contorted in another spasm of agony, and he cried to me, 'Draw the arrow from me, Kshatriya, and let my life follow it. This pain is unbearable and I am dying too slowly.'

"He smiled wanly at me, and his thin face was so radiant and beautiful. I grasped the shaft of the arrow and, with a heave, pulled it dripping from him. With one last scream that echoed through those woods, frightening the birds in the trees into flight, his eyes rolled up and he was dead in my arms. Now there was peace on his face; his lips softened into a smile.

"For a long time, I stood stricken beside him. Then I picked up his water pot and filled it from the river. Summoning all my courage, and on heavy feet that wanted to turn and run back to the comfort of the palace, I made my slow way along that dreadful path through the forest, toward his father's asrama. The father heard me before I saw him, and thinking I was his son returning with water, hailed me.

"They sat at the door to their hut: two blind old people bent with age and poverty. Their eyes gazed sightlessly at me and I stood silent before them. The old muni said with some asperity, 'Why are you standing there so quietly? Your mother is thirsty; give her the water. This is not the time to be playful.'

"I took a deep breath and gave the water into the old woman's hands. Then I said, 'I am not your son. My name is Dasaratha, and I am a prince of the House of Ikshvaku.' I paused and moistened my lips, which were dry as deserts. They craned their heads to my voice. Somehow, I went on, 'I have caused you both great grief. What I have done is unforgivable. But I did not do it wantonly and I beg you to forgive me.'

"The blind father asked, 'What have you done, Kshatriya?'

"I told them as best as I could: how the water pot being filled had sounded like an elephant drinking, and how I shot my arrow without looking. The rishi and his wife received my news with grave calm. They were obviously master and mistress of their emotions.

"Slowly, the old man said, 'If you had not come here with such courage, my curse would have burst your head from afar like a melon. Take us to our son. We want to touch him one last time with our fingers, which for us are our eyes.'

"In misery, I led them by their wizened hands down the path of sorrow. Kneeling in the wet sand, the father stroked his son's face and wept. Then the mother knelt beside him. When her fingers felt her child's cold body and the wound in his side, she screamed and fell over.

"Grimly the old rishi performed the last rites for his son. He asked me to gather dry twigs and branches for the cremation. He piled them over his dead youth, chanting hymns from the Veda. At last, he offered water as tarpana to the departed soul, for his journey in death. Then he lit that fire with a touch of his hands.

"As it blazed up, his wife clutched his hand. The rishi turned to me. 'You cannot imagine how I suffer at being parted so brutally from my child. I curse you that in your old age you will also die of the grief of being separated from your son. Before you die, like us you will lose the sight of your eyes.'

"Before I could stop them, they walked into the fire and were made ashes with their son."

Dasaratha sighed. Kausalya held his hands tightly in hers and the tears she shed onto them burned him. She said, "You never told me about the brahmana's curse before."

"Only now I thought of him, when my sight left me and I was as blind as he was. Kausalya, hold me, and forgive me for everything I have done. My senses grow weak and I feel as if I am in a dark cave. I will not live long, my queen; the brahmana's curse will soon be fulfilled. Rama, I see your face before me, but you are so far away when I need you most. Oh, Kaikeyi has been the death of me."

He lapsed into incoherence. Kausalya held him close in the darkness, and Sumitra covered them both with a shawl. Dasaratha fell into an uneasy sleep. Only at times he would grow restless and whimper Rama's name.

24. The death of a king

The sun crept over the rim of the world, and the morning vandhis and magadhis came to Dasaratha's door, singing his praises. The women of the harem brought water and unguents for his bath. During the early hours, Kausalya had left her husband in a deep sleep and gone to her own bed for a short time. The women who slept in the queen's quarters came that morning, as they did every day, to awaken the king.

They stripped the sheets from his bed and saw them damp with sweat. Dasaratha did not stir, and his face was set in a serene smile. Growing anxious now, they shook his arms and then his body. But he slept on. It was the women's screams that woke Kausalya and Sumitra, and they came running. But their husband had left them forever in his sleep.

A cry went forth through the palace, and soon through all Ayodhya. The king was dead. Just five nights he had lived after Rama left; the sixth had killed him. It was as if he had only waited, that warrior, keeping death's messengers at bay in his final battle, until Sumantra came and gave him news of Rama. He had waited in desperate hope that his prince would change his mind and return to him.

Now he lay conquered, the smile of death's peace curving his lips. His face was miraculously unwrinkled again; all the conflict was gone from it. Dasaratha, great kshatriya, a father to his people, Indra's friend who had fought beside the king of Devaloka, the one Narayana had chosen to be his own father in the world, was dead because of a woman's weakness. He died of a broken heart, for what he had done to his son. He lay beyond caring, his hands folded across his chest, while his wives and the other women of the palace cried around his bed.

With hollow words of comfort, some of the women led Kausalya away. She wailed that now both her son and her husband were gone, what had she to live for? She would lie with Dasaratha on his pyre.

The people of Ayodhya were dazed: first Rama had been banished, now the king was dead. Insecurity, not untinged with guilt for having judged Dasaratha harshly in his last days, spread among them like a demon. It was the old terror of a people who were suddenly without a ruler. There was silence in the thronged streets; no other crowd so vast could have been so quiet.

Dasaratha had been blessed with four splendid sons; he had died with none of them at his side. Vasishta and the ministers of the court looked outside the palace and saw the crowd swollen there, on the edge of madness. They saw the people were so shocked they did not even cry. There was no telling what they might do in such a mood. Certainly, Kaikeyi's life was in danger. Vasishta decided Bharata must be sent for at once; until he arrived to perform the last rites for his father, the king's body should be preserved with oils.

This was announced to the people, and like sleepwalkers they returned to their homes. There were some murmurs about Kaikeyi, but mainly the people appeared to be too grief-stricken to think of any violence. Few slept that night. They sat up into the small hours, speaking of Dasaratha's magnificent reign, just as they had sat talking about Rama some days ago. Tonight no one mentioned the final tragedy that ruined the king's good name. Caught between sorrow and panic, the citizens of Ayodhya stayed awake.

All night they rode like time, the messengers whom Vasishta had dispatched to Rajagriha, the capital of Kekaya, where Bharata stayed in his grandfather Asvapati's palace. They carried this message to the prince: "Return at once to Ayodhya. A matter of life and death calls you home."

The messengers bore the customary gifts of silks and jewels that came from one king to another, and stern instructions from Vasishta not to breathe a word of either Rama's exile or Dasaratha's death. Across the river Malini, they rode like a gale. They thundered past Hastinapura, crossed the Ganga by dark, and turned west. They left Panchala behind and came to the Ikshumati. They forded her without dismounting and pressed on as if they rode for their lives.

All day and night, those men rode without rest. At dawn they came to Rajagriha, like a storm spent, but bearing the lightning of their message from Ayodhya.

As the messengers rode as if death rode behind them, while Ayodhya stayed awake mourning, Bharata had no inkling of the momentous events at home. He lay asleep in Rajagriha and was visited by nightmares such as come to a man but once or twice in his life.

He dreamed his father was perched on a precipice, his clothes soiled and rent, his hair flying in an eerie wind. Bharata watched Dasaratha fall from that cliff, down, down into a pit of excrement.

Then he saw the king again, covered in filth, drinking black oil out of cupped palms.

His dream shifted in evil. He saw all the oceans of the earth dried up, and a broken moon fallen into the seabed where numberless fish lay marooned and gasping. His dream turned dark again, and in that darkness a great white elephant crashed trumpeting through a field of cruel spikes planted in the ground, trying blindly to find his way home.

Dasaratha reappeared in his son's nightmare. His hair hung to his shoulders, pure white, and his face was calm and toothless. He rode in a cart pulled by mules and wore a garland of wildflowers around his neck.

Bharata awoke with a cry, his bed drenched with the sweat of fear. Shatrughna was at his side, shaking him. "Bharata, wake up! You are having a bad dream."

Bharata sat bolt upright in his bed, clutching his brother's hand. His eyes were wild; he panted like a hunted animal.

"I had such a nightmare, Shatrughna! I saw our father ride in a cart drawn by mules. You know what they say about dreaming of a mule cart."

Shatrughna shook his head. Bharata's breathing had grown easier now. He said, "That smoke from the pyre of the one riding in the cart will quickly grace the sky. Something terrible has happened in Ayodhya. I fear for the king, and for Rama and Lakshmana. My body feels as if it is on fire and my eyes burn. Shatrughna, I hate myself strangely and I don't know why."

The new day was just dawning when they heard the sound of horses' hooves in the courtyard below. Bharata jumped up and ran to the window. He saw his dream had been vindicated, and cried, "Messengers from Ayodhya!"

The exhausted messengers were received in Asvapati's sabha. Through Bharata, they presented the gifts they had brought. That prince was impatient to question the riders and hurried through the formalities.

Then he cried, "Is my father well? And my brothers and mothers? Have you come with bad news?"

The leader of those messengers gave a start; but he said with a quick smile, "Why do you expect bad news, my prince? All is well in

Ayodhya. But your guru Vasishta sends urgently for you, saying you must return at once."

"What has happened?" cried Bharata.

"We may not tell. But be sure Devi Lakshmi smiles on you."

Bharata turned to Asvapati, "Pitama, my guru calls me and I must go. But send for me at any time and I will gladly come again."

The old man's face grew sad. He rose from his throne and embraced Bharata. "Kaikeyi is fortunate to have a son like you. Bless you, my child. Take my blessings to your mother and your brothers, and my warm greetings to your noble father and your great guru."

Asvapati ordered Bharata's chariot to be laden with gifts, and a train to follow his grandson to Ayodhya. But Bharata was so preoccupied he scarcely noticed the elephants and horses his grandfather sent, or the piles of silks and the treasures of jewels and golden ornaments.

The prince mounted his chariot and cried, "Fly, sarathy. My heart is full of fear; leave the others and fly ahead!"

25. Bharata

Past elegant and splendid cities, through virescent plains and violet valleys Bharata rode. But his eyes saw little of the lands he crossed; his thought remained drawn inward, because dread would not leave him. Four days they rode, before they came to the borders of Kosala. After another day, by the thin light of the rising sun they saw the golden turrets of Ayodhya.

Bharata's face lit up. Shatrughna stood up in the chariot and roared, "Home! How I have missed you, Ayodhya."

But as they drew near the city the fear in Bharata's heart was stronger than ever. He clutched Shatrughna's arm. "Listen. I don't hear a sound. What happened to all the musicians, the dancers and the chess players? Where are the markets and the hawkers, and the gypsies? No scent of women's perfume hangs on the air. The streets are deserted, as if everyone in Ayodhya is dead."

They came to the inner gate, the carved and painted one called Vaijayanta. Dry garlands hung from the triumphal arches overhead. And though the guards rose and cried as they always did, *"Jaya vijayi bhava!"* the welcome was far from warm.

Bharata saw the people begin to emerge from their homes and line the streets. It seemed to him they were all in mourning and looked at him coldly. His heart pounding, he came to the king's palace. He leaped down from the chariot, took the steps three at a time, and ran to his father's chambers, while the guards in the corridors stared strangely at him. His father was not in his rooms.

Bharata ran to his mother's apartment; he thought he would find the king there. Kaikeyi came out when she heard his step in the passage. When he saw his mother, he knelt at her feet; she raised him up and embraced him fiercely. He felt her tremble.

Kaikeyi asked in an even voice, "How are my father and my brother?"

"Well, mother. And they send their love and blessings to you. But what has happened here? Where is my father? Why was I sent for?"

Kaikeyi said, "Your father, the noble Dasaratha, a father to his people, has attained the condition that all the living find one day."

Bharata's eyes rolled up and he fell. When he came to his senses, he sobbed, "There is nothing left to live for. Since I was a boy, whenever I came in here I saw my father on that couch. Now it is empty forever. My life is over. Oh, bring me to Rama; I need my brother."

For a time, Kaikeyi stood watching while her maids ministered to him. They gave him water to drink and pressed wet cloths on his forehead, which he pushed away impatiently. Now Bharata's mother came to him. Running long fingers through his hair, she said, "Come, come, my son, it is unmanly to give in to grief like this."

Like a wounded animal, Bharata cried, "What happened to him, mother? I thought I was perhaps coming home to Rama being crowned yuvaraja. And instead, I find this." Slowly he rose and sat on the floor near Dasaratha's couch, stroking it as if his father's feet were there. He asked, "What were my father's last words to me?"

Without blushing, Kaikeyi replied, "He sobbed like a child when death drew near. But he cried only 'Rama,' 'Sita,' and 'Lakshmana.' I did not hear him say your name once. His last words were, 'Fortunate shall they be who live to see Rama return to Ayodhya with Sita and Lakshmana.' "

"Where were Rama and Lakshmana when my father died? Where is Rama now?"

Casually Kaikeyi said, "Rama has gone to the Dandaka vana with Lakshmana and Sita. Your father banished him."

Her son cried out as if she had stabbed him. He shut his ears with his hands. "My father banished Rama to the forest? Why? Did he kill someone? Did he steal or seduce another man's wife? Tell me!"

Bharata held his mother by her arms and shook her like a doll. Kaikeyi cried to him to let her go. Then, embers of evil smoldering in her pale eyes, she hissed, "Listen to me, Bharata."

Something in her tone stopped him still. He waited for her to speak. Kaikeyi drew a breath, and said, "Rama committed none of those sins. But when the king planned to crown him yuvaraja, I reminded him of the boons he had given me when I saved his life. I told him I wanted Rama banished for fourteen years and you crowned yuvaraja."

She went nearer him. And so far from herself had Kaikeyi come, she did not notice her son recoil from her in horror. She caressed his face; her nails were long and painted like a queen mother's, rather than plain and clipped like a widow's. Clasping him to her, she said, "Your father loved Rama too much and he died when his son went away. But all that is the past. Bharata, the future of Ayodhya is in your hands. Set aside your boyishness; you must rule a kingdom now. From this moment, you must be a man and a king."

Her eyes blazed. Now he saw the madness in them, the power lust, and he pushed her from him so she fell on Dasaratha's couch. He stood menacingly over her, his eyes glittering, and she cowered from him. His voice was calm when he spoke. All the sorrow was gone, and cold rage had taken its place.

"Monster, how will I live with myself knowing that I am your son? Why didn't you drink poison or hang yourself, before you had Rama banished? Why didn't you drown yourself or set yourself on fire?"

His hand strayed to his sword, "But never fear: if you cannot kill yourself, I will gladly do it for you." But he paused when his weapon was half drawn from its sheath. He thrust it back, and sighed, "Rama would never look at me again if I killed you. Be thankful for the one you banished, evil woman; he stands guarantee for your life. Or I swear by my dead father, my sword would be buried in your treacherous breast."

Kaikeyi backed away from him. Bharata said to her, "How have I wronged you that you decided to ruin my life?"

"I am your mother. I have your interest at heart, even if you do not know what is good for you. Put away this childishness. This is not your frivolous youth any more, but reality. Be a man, and take the throne I have won for you with such suffering."

"Suffering! My father is dead, Rama sent away like some thief to the jungle and you speak of your suffering. Madwoman, devil, don't you realize you have ruined the House of Ikshvaku? Oh mother, how did you do this to Rama? Until the other day, you loved him so much I was sure you loved him more than me. I cannot believe the same woman has banished him. Tell me, who put you up to this? How could you think, even for a moment, that I would take the throne that belongs to my brother?"

He choked again. "Foolish woman, I would rather die. Never once in all the generations of Ikshvaku kings has a younger brother usurped his older brother's throne. Always the younger sons have served the older, and even so our line has flourished.

"Mother—my tongue turns to ashes to call you that—your ancestry is faultless, and that gives me some hope for myself. Otherwise, I should kill myself for being your son. Your father and your uncle are noble, and perhaps by a lifetime of penance I can expiate even your sin. As for your precious throne, for which you have caused all this misery, hear me clearly, serpent: I will leave immediately for the Dandaka vana and bring Rama back. For the rest of my life, I will be like a slave to my brother so your sin may be forgiven."

Again his hand crept to his sword, as if the temptation to kill her was too much to resist. He moaned, "Don't you see what you have done to all of us? To Kausalya and Sumitra, to my brothers and to me. This is no ordinary sin you have committed. You have murdered your husband and banished your son for the sake of a worthless throne! In every age in this holy land, your name will be spat upon, and I fear mine as well for being your blood. Have you seen the way the people look at me? Bharata the usurper, they say in their hearts, those who once loved me second only to Rama.

"For this life and another you will suffer, wretched Kaikeyi, just for the grief you have caused Kausalya. But why do I stay here, wasting my time on a fiend while my real mothers languish and my Rama is in the jungle? I must go and fetch him home. Ayodhya must have a king."

Red-eyed, with equal parts of grief and rage, Bharata stalked out of Kaikeyi's apartment. She stood staring after him, bemused.

Grimly, Bharata entered the king's sabha, followed by a shaken, tearful Shatrughna, who had heard the news by now. Vasishta and the other rishis and ministers awaited Bharata, wondering anxiously what he would do. Bharata strode in and stood as far from the throne as he could. He looked around at the worried faces that surrounded him and declared crisply, "I knew nothing of Kaikeyi's plotting and I do not want the throne. I have nothing further to do with her; I do not think of her as my mother any more. I will go to the forest and bring Rama back. But now, please tell the people what I have said and give me your leave. For I must go to my mother Kausalya."

Sumitra had gone to Kausalya and informed her of Bharata's return. Rama's mother came out of her apartment to meet Kaikeyi's son. They met in a passage and, with a cry, Bharata ran to embrace her. But she stepped back from him and said coldly, "How easy your way to the throne has been, my clever prince. You are fortunate to have a mother as capable as yours. As for me, now nothing holds me back in Ayodhya. Sumitra and I will leave for the Dandaka vana tomorrow. Enjoy the kingdom and its wealth with your mother. But remember, it is over your father's dead body and your brother's exile that you have climbed to this height. And one day, you will pay for your sin."

Bharata fell at Kausalya's feet and cried, "You must not think this of me! Rama is my God; I worship him. I knew nothing of Kaikeyi's scheming or none of this would have happened. May the sins of all mankind be upon my head alone, if what you think of me is true. Oh, I must have sinned horribly in lives gone by that you speak to me like this today. Rama, my brother, save me from this sea of sorrow I am drowning in!"

Clutching her feet as if they were his last hope, Bharata sobbed piteously. With a cry, Kausalya raised him up and embraced him. She kissed him and, wiping his tears, said, "Forgive me, Bharata; a hundred times over, forgive me for what I said. I meant no part of it. I am unhinged and it was only my sorrow speaking as anger. Don't cry, my son, or my burden will grow heavier. You are a noble prince and there will be a special place for you in heaven."

She led him into her apartment. Sumitra, who had never doubted Bharata, embraced him. Shatrughna came there as well and all night the four of them sat together, speaking of the dead king and of Rama,

Sita, and Lakshmana. The grace of compassion was upon them as they grieved together. It made their sorrow bearable.

27. Last rites

At dawn there came a soft knock at Kausalya's door. When Shatrughna opened it, he saw Vasishta standing outside. The son of Brahma had come to see Bharata. The rishi said, "Your father's body will begin to decay if you do not perform the last rites for him."

Wordlessly, Bharata rose. He followed his guru into the embalming chamber, where Dasaratha's body lay in state, preserved in oils on a bed of darbha grass. Bharata saw the yellowed skin, the smile of surrender on his father's face. He wept again, brokenhearted.

He said, "Dasaratha, why have you left me with such a cruel burden? How could you have banished Rama? I am afraid, father; bring my brother back to me."

Vasishta put an arm around him. "Compose yourself, my child. Sorrow weakens the mind, and you need your strength more than ever now. You must perform the rituals calmly, with courage. The people must not see you like this or they will panic."

Bharata stopped crying. A sudden numbness was upon him. The priests carried Dasaratha's body into the sabha, where the ritviks had assembled. The brahmanas performed the last rites with the sacred fire that Dasaratha kept kindled in his palace, the fire he had worshipped every day. Oblations were thrown onto it, while Bharata and Shatrughna stood by, solemn and silent.

Then a palanquin was brought in, covered with silk, embellished with flowers, and the body lifted onto it. Bharata and Shatrughna walked at the head of the procession. They came out into the dazzling sun. All Ayodhya had gathered in the streets to pay its last respects. In the end, Dasaratha had redeemed himself with the only sacrifice that could have appeased his people after Rama was banished.

In the royal cremation ground, the pyre was piled high with fragrant wood. The remains of so many illustrious kings had been made ashes here. With chandana and sarasa, padmaka and devadaru, Dasaratha's pyre had been built. In their palanquins the queens followed the procession through the sorrowing streets.

The ritviks intoned the Sama Veda. Dasaratha was lifted from his litter and placed ceremonially upon the pile of logs. Tears streamed down Bharata's face again and he touched his father's pyre alight with a burning branch. It caught, blazed, and soon a great sovereign of the earth was made ashes.

Kaikeyi dared not attend the cremation.

The princes bathed in the Sarayu and came home to the palace, where they and the queens spent the night lying on bare ground. On the twelfth day the sraddha was performed, and on the thirteenth the poor were fed and gifts distributed among them. Cows, horses, clothes, and land for the landless Bharata gave as alms, bountifully like his father.

But before the almsgiving, at dawn of the thirteenth day, the prince went to the cremation ground to collect Dasaratha's ashes and bones. In the cold morning, as he reached down to pick up those mortal remains with the golden tongs Vasishta had handed him, Bharata broke down once more.

"Father, is this all you are today, a handful of ashes and bones? Where are you now, mighty Dasaratha; where are all your regal and loving parts? These gray flakes of ash and a few cold pieces of bone? I should kill myself today if this is all that life finally is."

Vasishta took him by the arm. His guru said sternly, "The women who must cry already do so. You are a kshatriya; behave like one. You should comfort your people, and instead you stand here sobbing like a lost child."

It was a tone of voice his guru seldom used, and it brought Bharata up sharply. The prince looked into his master's eyes and saw such compassion there. He wiped his tears and controlled himself. With some semblance of calm, he collected his father's remains, to float them down the river to the sea.

With Shatrughna at his side, he offered anjali to the dead king at the cold pyre, and came back to the palace. That evening, Bharata and Shatrughna sat together in their apartment, trying to pick up the pieces of their broken lives.

Shatrughna said thoughtfully, "I wonder why Lakshmana did nothing to prevent this. He is my twin and we think alike." He touched his sword meaningfully. "I know what I would have done if I had been here. Yet my brother did nothing. I wonder what stopped him?"

With a wry smile, Bharata said, "Rama must have."

Suddenly they saw a grotesque sight in the doorway: Manthara stood there wearing garish finery. Her arms were red with sandal paste; her humped body glittered with ornaments. She wore a golden girdle round her waist, studded with diamonds and rubies. She stood smiling at the brothers, a smile as crooked as her back, and warded off the evil eye from them by cracking her knuckles against her temples.

With a growl, the faithful old doorkeeper pushed her into the room and said, "This is the demon who poisoned your mother's mind. She had Rama exiled and caused your father's death. She is sure that this is your moment of triumph, and wants you to know she contrived it."

Shatrughna gave a hiss of anger. Before Bharata could stop him he sprang at Manthara and struck her down. He seized her hair and began to drag her around the apartment, and then out into the passage so everyone saw, all the women and the servants. But no one came forward to help Manthara; they all hated her. Her screams and shrill abuse echoed through the harem. Shatrughna hauled her along; from time to time, he kicked her savagely, roaring, "I will reward you for what you have done!"

Scattered along that passage in the palace of Ayodhya, Manthara's ornaments were like stars strewn across the autumn sky. She bled from her nose and mouth, and there was a crimson trail where the wrathful prince dragged her. No one moved to stop Shatrughna and it seemed he meant to kill her.

Then Kaikeyi arrived. She ran to Bharata and begged him, "She has been with me since I was a child. Spare her life for my sake!"

Bharata looked coldly at his mother. "For your sake?"

Seeing her mistress, Manthara screamed louder. Kaikeyi shouted an order at the palace guards to restrain Shatrughna; none of them stirred to obey her. Roaring still, Shatrughna dragged the hunchback, pausing only to kick her.

Then Kaikeyi screamed at Bharata, "What would Rama say if he saw this?"

Bharata held up his hand and said, "Enough, Shatrughna."

Reluctantly, Shatrughna let Manthara go. She lay howling on the floor in a wretched heap. Kaikeyi ran forward to kneel beside her, and called her maids to bring cloths and ointments to stanch the hag's wounds. Shatrughna stood smoldering still, sorely tempted to finish what he had begun.

Now Bharata said clearly, so everyone heard him, "Shatrughna, except for Rama, my sword would be buried in Kaikeyi's heart. But it is not dharma to kill a woman, my brother."

He put an arm around Shatrughna and led him away. What Bharata said spread like light through Ayodhya.

28. To the vana

The next morning, when the brothers had finished their ablutions and had performed Suryanamaskara, Ayodhya's council of ministers filed into Bharata's chambers. Sumantra said, "Kosala cannot be without a ruler. The days of mourning are over. The people are waiting for you to be crowned; it is time you were king."

Bharata only stared at the old sarathy, and made no reply. Sumantra went on, "If you are doubtful, come and see how many of the noble are waiting for you in the sabha. They will all support you. The people know you were not involved with Rama being exiled, or your father's death. They are anxious to see you become their king."

They went out to the sabha, where Bharata saw the white parasol unfurled and forlorn. He saw the hundred urns of holy water in their neat rows; he saw the chamaras for his coronation. He walked silently around the urns, then leaped up onto the platform that had been raised for the investiture. The nobility of Ayodhya had packed the sabha, and through the great main doors Bharata saw the streets were full.

When the people saw Bharata on the dais, they shouted his name warmly and cried out for him to be their king. Bharata was silent for a moment; then he raised his hands for quiet and spoke to them.

"My brothers and sisters in sorrow, it is not dharma that you ask me to take the throne that belongs to Rama."

The people cried out his name and Rama's together. When they were quiet again, Bharata said, "I will go to the forest and bring my brother back. And I will serve his exile for him."

The commotion at this was deafening. Bharata smiled for the first time since he had come home from Rajagriha. He cried to them, "Gather my army; collect everything we need for a coronation. I swear to you I will crown Rama in the vana."

He jumped down from the dais to loud cheers and more shouting of his name and Rama's. By refusing the crown his mother had won for him by treachery, Bharata set alight the people's hearts with hope.

The next day, the vandhis and magadhis came to his door singing his praises as if he was already king. Bharata flew out at them, threatening to kill them if they came singing like that while Rama lived. Shatrughna had to restrain his brother, or he would have done those singers injury.

Back in his apartment, Bharata wept again. "Look how cruel they are, Shatrughna, that they rub salt in my wounds. How I wish I could still my anger with Kaikeyi's blood. She hasn't left me a shred of honor."

The ministers came again to summon Bharata to the sabha. They said Vasishta wanted to speak to him today. Brahma's son, Ayodhya's kulaguru, had been significantly absent from the court the previous day. Today, for the first time after Dasaratha's death, Vasishta sat in his customary place: as if to declare that all was well again in the kingdom. After the last day's events, he was convinced of Bharata's innocence.

Bharata saw this on the rishi's face and, bowing to his master, sat down beside him. Vasishta said gravely, "Before he died, your father left the Ikshvaku throne to you. Dharma demands you become king in Ayodhya."

Bharata said, "That isn't the dharma you taught me, unless I should change my dharma to suit circumstances. Rama is our king and I bow to him from here."

The crowded sabha was hushed. Bharata went on, "I am going to the Dandaka vana today. If I can, I will bring Rama back to Ayodhya. If I cannot, I will stay with him as Lakshmana does, until his exile is over. The roads are already being cleared; we leave with our army to crown Rama in the jungle."

Sumantra entered the sabha. He bowed to Bharata and said, "Everything is ready for the journey."

Bharata touched his guru's feet, and how proud of his pupil Vasishta was. His faith had been vindicated, and his boast to Kaikeyi: "Foolish woman, Bharata will never accept the throne that belongs to Rama." His eyes moist, he embraced the prince and said, "Noble Bharata, no one has learned my lessons in dharma better than you."

And so Bharata set off with a splendid train, with Kausalya, Sumitra, and Kaikeyi as well in her palanquin, aloof and bitter. The army followed him as he rode in his chariot at the head of that majestic force, with Shatrughna beside him. All Ayodhya was out again in the streets and the people wore smiles on their faces for the first time since Rama left. They cheered Bharata lustily. A good many of them journeyed to the forest with the army, to see Rama again.

29. A night in an asrama

Like a slow and great river itself, flowing across the earth for the first time, Bharata's army crossed the Tamasa. It was a magnificent force, with elephant, horse, and chariot, and numberless foot soldiers; the common people of Ayodhya walked with these. Sumantra drove Bharata's chariot. He knew the way he had taken Rama, and followed that trail as if it led to the soul of them all.

Their progress beyond the Tamasa was slower. After a week they came to the Ganga and Guha's city, Shringiberapura. Bharata called the same halt beside the golden river, full of the rumor still that Rama had gone this way. From his ramparts Guha saw the legions that flew the Kovidara flag, and said to his hunters, "Alert our warriors; I think Bharata comes to kill Rama. Blockade the river fords. He shall cross the Ganga over our dead bodies, if he comes with evil in his heart."

Guha rode out from his gates with a small company, carrying the gifts that a vassal king brings his emperor. Sumantra saw him coming, and said, "Here comes Guha, king of these lands, who loves Rama. He can show us the way to him. His hunters know the forest like the palms of their hands."

Guha bowed ceremoniously to Bharata, but his jungle eyes watched the prince guardedly. He saw the faithful Sumantra and was relieved. He scrutinized Bharata's face again, and saw no evil there. At last, he said, "My land is the garden of your kingdom. Be my guest for the night. But tell me, Kshatriya, why do you come to the forest with an army?"

Bharata flinched. He lowered his gaze and said sadly, "I see that my name is sullied even as far from home as this. Rama is dearer to me than my life, Guha; how can I think of harming him? I have come to take my brother home. After my father's death, Rama is the king of Kosala. Kings do not travel abroad without their armies."

Guha saw the sincerity in Bharata's eyes; he heard the love in his voice. A smile breaking out on his black face, the hunter embraced him. "You are of the same noble seed as Rama! As long as men speak of selflessness in the world, they will cite the name of Bharata of Ayodhya. How many men would refuse a throne, and all the power and wealth that come with it, for love of their brother?"

Guha saw tears spring to Bharata's eyes at the very mention of Rama's name. The prince did not sleep most of that night, for eagerness to be up early and across the river. The king of the hunting people stayed awake with him, as he had with Lakshmana. They spent the night speaking together of many things, while the army slept.

In the vast silence that bore the sea of breathing around them and the silken rustling of the river, Guha said, "Ten days ago, Lakshmana stood watch over Rama and would not sleep, though I begged him to. I said to him, 'I love Rama like my own brother. Sleep in peace; I will guard him even as you will.'

"Lakshmana replied, 'It isn't that I do not have faith in you, Guha. But how can I sleep when I see my Rama and his wife lying on the ground?' "

Late into the night, Guha told Bharata about the night Rama had spent beside the Ganga. And how the next day, when the brothers had rubbed their hair with the sap of the nyagrodha, they crossed the river; and how, finally, they walked into the forest, looking like two rishis, with Sita between them.

Shatrughna sat beside Bharata. The fire they had lit shone in their eyes. They listened to Guha tell how Rama had refused the food he had brought him, and the mattresses of down. Lakshmana had made a bed of grass and leaves for his brother. The hunter showed them the tree under which Rama and Sita had slept. Bharata picked up a handful of darbha grass and held it fervently to his eyes.

Guha said, "If someone had told me that four brothers were as devoted to one another as you princes of Ayodhya, I would not have believed him. I would have wondered what love could be so great that it exceeded the love for kingdom and wealth; especially when you are born from different mothers. But I know Rama, and I know how much I love him myself though he is no kin of mine. Bharata, now that I know your heart let me tell you this: earlier this evening, I was prepared to kill you if you had come to harm Rama."

Bharata sighed, "Guha, I have no rest until I see my brother before me."

A few hours before dawn the prince lay on the ground, and some semblance of sleep stole over him. But his dreams were dark, and he tossed and turned beside Shatrughna, who also slept poorly at his side.

They were up before the sun the next day, and Guha came to them and said, "My oarsmen will ferry you across the river with your people."

The princes, the queens—Kaikeyi had come because her safety could not be guaranteed in Ayodhya—Vasishta, and his rishis were taken across in a great riverboat called Swastika. Now they had Guha's hunters for guides, and went surely through the forest along the same trail Rama had taken. They spent one night very near where he had slept, and pressed on the next day, until, from a promontory, they saw Bharadvaja's asrama near the confluence of the Ganga and the Yamuna.

Bharata left his army a krosa from the hermitage. With Shatrughna and some ministers beside him, and Vasishta going before him, he climbed down the slope. When he neared the asrama he left the knot of ministers behind and walked in, taking only Vasishta with him.

Bharadvaja welcomed them with every show of affection; he made them sit by his side. When the ritual greetings were over between himself and Vasishta, he turned to Bharata. "You are king of Ayodhya now. What brings you to the forest? I would have thought you would be happy on the throne your mother won for you."

Bharata said ruefully to Vasishta, "Look, Master. All the world, even the wisest in it, is convinced of my guilt." To Bharadvaja he said, "You should not judge me like this, holy one; I am innocent. Rama is my brother. If you are so sad at his exile that you can hurt me without knowing the truth, how much greater my sorrow must be that my brother lives in the jungle. If you will direct me to him, I have come to crown Rama our king."

Bharadvaja gazed at Bharata for a long moment, and then at Vasishta, who inclined his head to affirm what the prince said. Bharadvaja took Bharata's hands. "You have earned an exalted place for yourself in heaven. As for Rama, he has gone to Chitrakuta with Sita and Lakshmana. I will show you the way there tomorrow. But tonight, you, your great guru, and the rest of your party must stay with me."

Bharata began to protest. But, his eyes twinkling, the rishi said,

"My son, there was no need for you to have left your army so far away. Send someone to fetch your soldiers and your people. I want to entertain you all tonight."

When the army and the people of Ayodhya arrived, Bharadvaja touched some sacred water with his fingers and invoked Viswakarman. At once a light appeared between earth and sky, illumining that hermitage. Within it stood the divine artisan. Bharadvaja said, "My lord, I want to entertain the people of Ayodhya tonight."

As the sun set slowly, it seemed the asrama and everyone in it slipped through a twilight crack and came by Viswakarman's power into an unearthly realm. Many-colored lamps lit the darkening sky; these floated everywhere, and transformed the hermitage into a precinct of dreams.

The air was fragrant, and uncanny bliss swept the people of Ayodhya when they heard celestial music around them. They saw tall gandharvas playing on instruments more softly resonant and complex than any they had heard. The great elves sang in voices that brought visions to their enraptured listeners' eyes. Then there were unworldly apsaras, their beauty ineffable, who served Bharadvaja's guests and danced for them. And the wine and the food? One cannot begin to describe the divine fare that passed the mortal lips of the people of Ayodhya that night. Into the early hours, the feast continued, the singing, the dancing, and the joy.

At dawn, Bharata came to Bharadvaja and said, "My lord, as long as they live my people will remember your hospitality. But now we must press on and find my brother. I am afraid that not even the company of gandharvas and apsaras can long assuage Ayodhya's grief at being parted from Rama."

The rishi described the way to Chitrakuta, exactly as he had done for Rama. He said, "I have heard he has built an asrama near the Mandakini."

Dasaratha's queens came before the rishi for his blessing. They walked around him in pradakshina and stood without speaking, their heads bent and their hands folded.

Bharadvaja said, "Bharata, tell me which queen is which prince's mother."

Bharata went to Kausalya and put his arm around her. "This is my mother Kausalya, who bore the noblest man ever born into the world.

And this is mother Sumitra, who bore the mighty twins Lakshmana and Shatrughna."

He did not go near Kaikeyi; he did not look at her. He said stiffly, "My father, Dasaratha, died because of a woman he loved like his very life. Out of her greed, she parted him from his eldest son. Oh, she is gentle and feminine to behold; but she is a devil. The third one, whose eyes are dry, who has not shed a tear these past days for her dead husband, is my mother Kaikeyi."

And the prince heaved a sigh. Bharadvaja laid a hand on Bharata's arm. "The ways of fate are inscrutable, my son. Do not judge your mother so harshly. I can see far into time and I tell you there is a deep purpose behind Rama's exile. The Devas, the rishis, all the hosts of heaven and the races of the earth will profit from it one day. And the clutch of evil shall be loosened for an age. Yet great suffering must go before any great deed, and your mother is only an unwitting instrument of destiny. The way ahead is long; don't be hasty with your judgment."

The army took a while to prepare itself for the march ahead; the people were still intoxicated with the night's magic. But once they thought of Rama, they were soon on their way. Through darkling forests and over fragrant hills they marched, following the Yamuna and fording other jungle streams. Bharata sensed his brother ahead of him; he saw Rama's trail clearly with his heart: a golden path.

On they marched, and the denizens of the wild were alarmed by the invasion of their privacy. Such a force had never come into this jungle before. Herds of deer scampered up steep hills, calling in alarm. Elephants stopped their lazy feeding to stare and then lumbered away, crashing through bamboo thickets. And overhead, another legion followed the army of Ayodhya, chattering down its displeasure: the langur tribes.

When they had marched some krosas along the southern bank of the midnight-blue Yamuna, when they had left the lone nyagrodha, Shyama, behind them, they came to the edge of a forest more dense than any they had seen yet, and dark as a thundercloud. Out of its heart there loomed a green massif. Its slopes were mantled with wildflowers, fallen like vivid rain from the trees; its rock faces were gashed with silver falls. A scented breeze blew down from that mountain and caressed them as if in welcome.

Bharata breathed, "Chitrakuta!"

A smile lit his face and Shatrughna's when they heard the Mandakini gushing downhill in the distance. They knew that in a few hours, all their torment would be redressed them: for they would see their brother Rama.

Shatrughna cried, "Send our best trackers ahead to find his asrama quickly!"

30. A reunion of brothers

Rama, Sita, and Lakshmana sat on the banks of the Mandakini. Sita dangled her feet in the water, while, near them and quite unafraid, a herd of deer drank from a pool in the river. The day was wearing on. They had grown used to the peace of Chitrakuta and the sorrow of exile did not weigh on their minds any more. The mountain surroundings of their little asrama were so picturesque it was impossible to be unhappy for long in that place.

But this afternoon, they heard alarmed trumpeting and heavy bodies crashing through the jungle. It was a herd of wild elephants trying to gain the higher reaches of Chitrakuta, as if they fled from some implacable enemy. Trampling down banks of bamboo, toppling small trees and crashing clumsily into bigger ones, the herd scrambled up the mountain. The great beasts splashed across the river, downstream from where the princes and Sita sat, and lumbered like a passing earthquake into the thick forest beyond.

Sita and the princes saw flocks of birds rise screaming out of the forest below them and wheel in the sky. They heard the incensed chattering of langur troops. The deer, which drank peacefully at their side, now cocked their heads and listened tensely to the cries of the other jungle folk. Calling sharply, they, too, fled up the mountain.

Rama said to Lakshmana, "Can you see what all the panic is about? I think a king must have come to hunt in the forest."

Lakshmana shinned up a tall sala tree. When he looked east, he saw the army of Ayodhya below him. He saw the banner of Kosala, flown by Bharata's vanguard, flapping in the mountain breeze. He cried down from the tree, "Sita, hide! Rama, put out the asrama fire. Put on your armor; pick up your bow: danger is here!"

He clambered down feverishly and stood panting. Rama smiled

at him and asked, "Who is coming, Lakshmana, that you are so alarmed?"

"The one who had you banished. Bharata has come with an army to make his throne secure. My astras are sad with disuse, Rama; they long to be buried in that traitor's heart. The scavengers of our jungle will feast for a year on the carcasses of his men."

Rama said, "So now you would have me kill my brother for the throne of Ayodhya. I know you speak out of love for me; but you should not abandon your good sense. You think Bharata comes to kill us. But he has convinced our father that the kingdom belongs to me. He comes to offer me the crown and take me back to Ayodhya. Wouldn't you have done the same thing in his place? Why do you think he loves me less than you do? Do you believe Bharata would betray me for a mere kingdom? Don't doubt him like this; it hurts me."

He paused; but anger was on him, and he said softly, "Perhaps the truth is that you want the kingdom yourself? I will tell Bharata to give it to you and to stay with me in the forest. You will see how readily he agrees. How can you be so suspicious, Lakshmana? This is our brother of whom you speak."

For a moment Lakshmana stood stricken; then, in the manner of a child, he changed the subject. "It must be our father coming to visit us, Rama."

Rama stood up to examine the approaching force. "Perhaps you are right. I see his favorite horses, and there is Shatrunjaya. But I cannot see the king's white parasol. Let us go back to the asrama. It is time for sandhya, and they are still an hour's climb away."

Even as they peered down at it, the army paused under the trees. Bharata had called the halt in deference to Rama's privacy. His trackers had come back to him in excitement. They pointed to a slope above them, and a strip of level ground upon it.

"There, my lord," said their leader. "If you look carefully you will see smoke rising into the sky. It could be the asrama of some tapasvins; but I think we have found Rama."

Bharata ordered his commanders, "Stay here until you hear from me. Sumantra and Guha, come with us, and a few trackers."

Shatrughna was already off up the slope and Bharata had to run to catch up with him. Guha went another way with some of his men. When he had gone a krosa, Bharata climbed a lofty sala. He saw the asrama, with the thrill of a sailor who spots land from his crow's nest.

He sent word back to Kausalya and Sumitra to follow carefully in their wake. With Guha, Shatrughna, and Sumantra, keen as anyone else to see Rama again, Bharata climbed on as quickly as he could. In the more level places, they ran up the mountain beside the cool Mandakini, until they arrived in a clearing in which there stood a cozy wooden cottage made of sala and asvakarna logs, thatched with leaves, with darbha grass spread at its door in welcome.

Through the window, Bharata saw Rama and Lakshmana's bows, inlaid with gold—Varuna's weapons—and beside them, quivers in which arrows shone like treasure. Across from the cottage was a raised platform where a fire burned. From here, the smoke they had seen rose into a clear sky. Before that fire, his eyes shut and his face tranquil, Rama sat at sandhya prayer with Sita beside him. Lakshmana stood by, with his back to Bharata's party and his arms crossed over his chest.

For a long moment, Bharata stood staring at the extraordinary sight of Rama, bare of his ornaments, wearing valkala, his hair coiled in jata, and sitting on darbha grass: at worship, like Brahma. Then his eyes swam, and with a cry, stumbling and falling on the way, he ran headlong to his brother.

"Rama!" Shatrughna also fell at Rama's feet. Rama raised them up tenderly and embraced them over and over again. Then Lakshmana was among them. Now he saw his brother before him, as he was and not as he had imagined him in his anger; and he remembered how much he loved Bharata. Rama made Bharata sit close to him, and welcomed Guha and Sumantra warmly, embracing them too.

Then he asked, "Bharata, why are you in the jungle, wearing valkala and jata? You should not have left our father alone. Tell me how he is, and how are our mothers? How is Guru Vasishta? And Sudhanva? I have thought of him often lately."

Bharata stared at Rama, drinking in the sight of his dark face. He turned away after a moment, and said only, "It has never been the way of the Ikshvakus that a younger brother rules the kingdom while his older brother lives. Come back to orphaned Ayodhya, Rama; it languishes without a king."

"But child, Dasaratha still rules Ayodhya. Why do you speak of a future that has not yet come to pass?"

Bharata turned his eyes to his brother in anguish, and cried,

"Dasaratha no longer rules Ayodhya. Dasaratha died of a broken heart."

Rama keeled over. Sita ran to fetch water, and Bharata and Lakshmana sprinkled it on Rama's face. But for a long time, he lay where he had fallen.

When he awoke, he sobbed helplessly. "I thought I would return to Ayodhya when fourteen years had passed, and take the dust from my father's feet. Now you tell me he is dead. And I was not there even to offer tarpana for him. Bharata, I will never come back to Ayodhya. Whose voice will I hear calling my name as Dasaratha used to, with such love? Whose arms will enfold me, as his always did?"

Rama lost control of himself. He turned to Sita and cried, "Did you hear what Bharata said? The king is dead. Lakshmana, you have lost your father!" And he sobbed and sobbed.

At last, Bharata said, "Rama, you must offer tarpana for him. Shatrughna and I performed the anjali in Ayodhya. But I know his soul will not find rest until you offer him holy water."

Rama grew calm; he wiped his eyes. In a moment, he said quietly to Lakshmana, "Bring me a cloth to cover my body; fetch me some ingudi. I will offer tarpana to my father."

When the cloth and the humble cake of dry fruit were brought, Rama said, "Sita, you walk in front. Lakshmana, you go behind her and I will follow. Let us go to the river."

From over the crest of the mountain the last rays of the sun fell, scarlet and golden, on the quiet Mandakini. Restraining his grief, Rama stood solemnly, waist deep in the water. Facing south, he raised his arms above his head. He said aloud, "Father, you have been gathered to our ancestors in Pitriloka. Quench your journey's thirst with this water."

He came out of the river and made the offering of pinda. He broke the ingudi cake, ground it with the flesh of a badari fruit, and set the pinda down on a seat of darbha grass that Lakshmana prepared. He said, "A man's Gods should accept the food he eats. We now eat this fruit in the name of our father, Dasaratha of Ikshvaku. Gods in heaven, be gracious and accept our offering."

The four brothers ate the fruit and embraced one another. Then, with their arms linked, the princes of Ayodhya returned to the asrama as night fell.

Shortly after the princes left the banks of the Mandakini, Vasishta arrived there with the two elder widows of Ayodhya. Kaikeyi had stayed far behind in the forest, her mind a sad fire. By the light of torches that the trackers held above their heads, they saw a faint trail at their feet. Kausalya said, "Look, Sumitra. It is the path Lakshmana has made when he carries water to the asrama."

They saw the simple pinda Rama had offered to the spirit of his dead father. Kausalya stifled a sob, "Look where the eldest son offered pinda to his father. Dasaratha, who lived like a God on earth, must now be content with a pinda of ingudi and badari."

Wiping her eyes, Sumitra said quietly, "And he shall be content for the one who offered it."

They followed Lakshmana's trail, and arrived at the asrama. Rama and Lakshmana came out to meet their mothers. Kausalya clasped Sita in her arms and fondled her as if she were her own daughter. Like Indra greeting Brihaspati, Rama knelt at Vasishta's feet; the rishi raised him up and embraced him.

Their grief binding them closer than ever, they sat together around a fire Lakshmana lit outside the log cottage. Like four flames of another fire sat the princes of Ayodhya around their guru. The other rishis and the ministers waited in a circle around the inner ring of Vasishta, the queens, and the brothers. Save for the cheery crackling of the branches Lakshmana had laid on, silence was upon them: the deep silence of the mountain, the sky above, in which fateful stars hung low, and the forest.

Rama said to Bharata, "I want to know why you have come here dressed like a rishi, when your place is on the throne of Ayodhya."

Bharata stood up and folded his hands to his brother. He said, "In his last days, our father strayed from dharma. He was separated from you and he died brokenhearted. He ruined his taintless life for the sake of an evil woman, my mother Kaikeyi, who has lost everything now. She does not have what she wanted; and Dasaratha, who loved her like his breath, is gone. Her fate is too horrible even to think of. She is destined for the worst hell of all.

"But I am not here to speak of the past. Come back to Ayodhya, my brother. Be crowned king, as the people want. Let the clouds of despair vanish from our sky, and the sun and the moon shine on us again. You are the jewel of the Ikshvakus, Rama. Return to us."

He spoke slowly; often, his voice choked with the strain of everything he had endured since he had been called back from Rajagriha. Rama rose and took Bharata in his arms. By now, most of the common people had arrived in that hermitage. Rama spoke loudly, so everyone heard him. He spoke with his arm around Bharata.

"How could anyone have thought for a moment that you wanted the throne for yourself? Noble child, you have more of the divine ancestry of Ikshvaku in you than the merely human. And you are a master of yourself. But as for my returning to Ayodhya, it is out of the question.

"There was never any error in what has happened, Bharata. It was the will of not just one but two of my parents that I spend fourteen years in the wilderness. And here I am. Our father died having made his wishes clear. I believe that one day you will realize what once seemed to be the obscure path was the way of dharma. Dasaratha died for that righteous way; though perhaps even to him the will of fate appeared cruel. Bharata, there are deeper forces at work in our lives than we know. There are greater tasks to be accomplished than we yet understand.

"So, my brother, as my father and my mother Kaikeyi wanted, I will rule the Dandaka vana for fourteen years. And you will rule Ayodhya."

Bharata began to speak, but Rama held up his hand and said, "It is late now, and our mothers have had a long journey. It is not right that we keep them awake any longer."

While the queens slept in the cottage, the rest of the people and the army of Ayodhya slept under the stars, most of them thinking how happily they could live here in the wilds as long as they were near Rama. His serenity and strength were like balm to their troubled hearts, and they slept soundly for the first time since he had left Ayodhya.

With sunrise, they gathered again around the ashes of the night's fire.

Bharata began, "Rama, I will grant everything you said last night. I will admit that our father was in perfect possession of his reason when he gave the kingdom to me. Ayodhya is mine, I grant you that. But I

141

have a great desire to lay what is mine at your feet. Take it from me. Ayodhya is a broken dream. Only you can put its pieces together again and heal our kingdom. Accept my offering; it is for the good of everyone. The task is beyond me, and not what I was born for. Help me, Rama: come back home."

Rama replied, "It is not that I don't understand you, or feel sympathy for you. But fate has ordained that my path lead through the jungle, and yours to the throne of Ayodhya. I grant that common sense might cry out otherwise; but fate is beyond mere common sense. Once I came out into the wilderness, I sensed fate clearly in my heart: the forest calls me more urgently than Ayodhya. For me Ayodhya is far away. I will surely return to it one day; but not yet.

"Think of time, Bharata: how she carries us along, helpless, on her mysterious currents. Her ways and her purposes are always secret, and just hers to know. What is gathered today is scattered without warning tomorrow. Think of our father. He led such a great life; just look at his end.

"Nothing except change is permanent in our lives, and nothing but death is final in this world. Death walks at our side on every trail; he wrinkles our skin and turns our hair white. We delight in each sunrise and sunset, and forget that our lives are shortened by every one. The seasons come, each with its own allurements; but they take great slices of our lives with them.

"The relations of men are like ships passing each other on the ocean; whether with fathers, mothers, wives, or children. We meet and are briefly together, only to part inevitably: if not in life, then surely in death. We must not make too much of our sorrow; it is nature's way. And who are we to question the wisdom of fate?

"Bharata, put away this petty grief. Accept your lot as our father left it to you, as his last dictate. Think of the Lord, who alone is beyond change, and walk the way of dharma without flinching. Go back to Ayodhya; take up the reins of kingdom in your able hands. I know you will be a great king. And our father knew this also, or he would not have left his body.

"Bharata, it is no use trying to swerve me from my path. It is written for me that I live in the jungle for fourteen years, and nothing you can say will change my mind. I can feel my destiny here; now that our father is dead, I can feel it more plainly than ever."

Rama fell thoughtful. But Bharata was not to be convinced so easily. He let the silence drift for a while, then said, "I flatter myself that I know you better than most, Rama. You are not moved by life's vicissitudes or trials, which shake other men. Leave off your stubbornness in this thing; whether it is the Dandaka vana or Ayodhya makes little difference to you. Come home, if only to save my mother and me from her sin. Let us have at least partial expiation by your return.

"Come home, Rama, out of your love for me if nothing else. Save me from the crime of sitting on your throne. Protect me from the world's censure, as an older brother should, for a sin I have no wish to commit. Everyone knows that when a man nears his end he loses his reason; that is what happened to our father. Your place is in the palace of Ayodhya, on its ancient throne. Only in the twilight of your years must you even think of the forest."

Bharata paused. When Rama was silent, he thought his brother had relented. He pressed on, "I have brought everything with me for the coronation. We will crown you here and take you back with us in triumph. Every nation must have the best man in it as its king. I am not your equal: the world, you and I, we all know that. Give up your obstinacy; the people have come to see you being crowned. They have come for the joy you robbed them of in Ayodhya.

"If you do not return, I will stay here with you."

Rama said, "You are a worthy scion of Ikshvaku, and the noble son of a noble father. But there is something you do not know, something not even Kaikeyi knows, which once our father told me. When Kaikeyi was given to Dasaratha, the kanya sulka promised to your grandfather Asvapati was that his grandson would be crowned king of Ayodhya one day."

A gasp went up from the army and the people. Even Bharata was visibly startled. Rama said, "Dasaratha could not in conscience forget his oath, any more than he could the boons he had granted your mother. It was as if Kaikeyi remembered her boons to remind him of the kanya sulka he had pledged to Asvapati.

"Bharata, it was against his will that he agreed to what Kaikeyi asked. He died of grief for what he had to do. How can you say he had lost his reason? Our father hated what he did for the sake of dharma; but he knew it had to be done. And now, as soon as he is dead, you expect me to break the solemn oath for which he gave his life?"

Bharata had no answer to this.

But now Vasishta said, "Rama, a man has three gurus: his mother, his father, and his master who initiates him into the way of the spirit. Of the three, the third is the most revered because he shows the way to eternal life. As your guru I say to you, for the sake of the House of Ikshvaku, for the sake of this sea of souls gathered here, who depend on you, for your mothers' sake, for Bharata's sake, and to honor what I say: come back to Ayodhya and be crowned. I, Vasishta, tell you that your dharma will not be tarnished even a little."

Rama grew sad to hear his guru, who loved him. But he said, "From my earliest childhood, my parents have been gurus to me. My debt to them is eternal. The love and generosity with which they brought me up has made me whatever I am today. I cannot break the sacred word I gave my father."

Bharata could not bear it. He said to Sumantra, "Spread darbha grass on the ground for me, Sumantra. Until my brother agrees to come back to Ayodhya and be crowned, I will fast—to death, if need be!"

But taking his brother by the arm, Rama laughed. "Bharata, this means of persuasion is not for a kshatriya! Only a brahmana may sit fruitfully in prayopavesha. Don't compel me like this. I will not go back and you will just add to my sorrow."

Bharata cried to the people of Ayodhya, "Why do you stand so quietly? Why don't you force him to return?" But the people replied only with an uneasy silence. Having heard what he had to say, they seemed to agree with Rama about the way of dharma. Or else they saw he could not be moved.

But Bharata cried, "If Rama insists that one of us spend fourteen years in the jungle, let me be the one who stays here. And let him return to Ayodhya and rule from the throne he was born to."

Rama replied, "When my exile is served I will come home. And then I will sit upon the throne of Ikshvaku, if you still want me to. But now, your place is on that throne and mine is here in the wilderness. It was our father's last wish and you should honor it."

The rishis murmured among themselves how fortunate Dasaratha was to have sons like these. Finally, Vasishta conceded, "Bharata, child, I am afraid Rama is right. For whatever reason, it was your father's last wish that you rule during the fourteen years of your brother's exile. You are bound in honor to obey your father. Let his death not be in vain."

Rama's face lit up.

32. *Parting*

When Vasishta spoke on Rama's part, Bharata, forsaken by his last ally, knelt in sorrow at his brother's feet. He said, "How hard you expect me to be that I must sit on Ayodhya's throne while you live in the jungle."

Rama raised him up. "Don't tell me you are not capable of ruling Ayodhya, for that is not true. You know as well as I do that you can rule the whole world if you set your mind to it. It won't be as hard as you imagine, Bharata. Our father's ministers are all with you, and you will learn quickly."

Bharata knew his battle was lost. He knew he would have to return to Ayodhya without Rama. He wiped his tears, and said with dignity, "Rama, now that Dasaratha is dead, you have the place of my father. I will do what you tell me to. Only don't ask me to take the kingdom for myself; that would be too cruel."

He had come prepared for this final exigency. Rummaging among the things he had brought with him for Rama's jungle coronation, he fetched out a pair of wooden padukas. He had brought these for Rama to wear when he was crowned in the forest. He laid them at Rama's feet, while his brother stood bemused.

Bharata said, "Step on these for a moment."

Smiling, Rama put on the padukas. When he stepped off, Bharata prostrated himself before the heavy sandals!

Bharata said, "Touched by Rama's feet, these padukas shall rule Ayodhya. And I, like my brother, will live for fourteen years wearing valkala, and my hair in jata. I will live on wild roots and fruit, and Rama's spirit will rule Kosala through Bharata. And the day fourteen years are over, be sure I see you before me; or I swear I will kill myself. Keep that in mind, Rama."

Rama said quietly, "I will." He embraced Bharata and Shatrughna, again and again. "Don't be harsh to Kaikeyi; remember she was only fate's instrument. She must already suffer terribly. I want you to swear, in my name and in Sita's, to be kind to her."

Bharata hesitated a moment before he nodded. He put the padukas on his head and walked around his brother thrice in pradakshina. Then he stood before him with folded hands. Rama went among the people. They cried for him; they reached out and touched him. They blessed him and he cried with them. At last, he came to Kausalya,

Sumitra, and the old and fond sarathy Sumantra. They did not speak, but only clasped one another. Bharata embraced Rama and Lakshmana, and touched Sita's feet. With a last, lingering look at Rama's face, with great destiny written so plainly upon it, Bharata led the people of Ayodhya back down the mountain, homeward.

Rama stood gazing after them until the last one had disappeared into the jungle below. He went back into the cottage and sat on the floor. He buried his head in his hands and sobbed long and disconsolately.

33. *Nandigrama*

With his brother's padukas beside him in his chariot, Bharata turned home. He was at some peace, that now he would rule not for himself but in Rama's name. He met Bharadvaja on his way back. After describing all that had happened on Chitrakuta, he sought the rishi's blessing. Beyond the Ganga, Guha embraced Bharata and went back to Shringiberapura, his heart full.

At last, Bharata rode into Ayodhya and passed under the arched gateway. He entered the forsaken palace with Rama's padukas in his hands. Tears rolled down his face when he saw the great sabha, empty and miserable as a durdina—a sunless day the Gods have cursed.

Bharata saw his mothers back to their apartments. Kausalya and Sumitra were tired but reassured at having seen their sons on Chitrakuta, and that the issue had been resolved of who would rule Ayodhya. Kaikeyi came home plunged in silence, her eyes faraway and blank: as if she did not know the world at all any more, or herself.

Bharata called a council in the king's court, of the old and the powerful of the kingdom. He addressed that council: "I will not live in luxury while my brother lives in the forest. Until Rama returns, I mean to move this sabha to the village of Nandigrama. Rama's padukas shall adorn the throne of Kosala and they will rule till he comes home."

Vasishta murmured, "And may your fame live long in this holy land, for you are the noblest of men."

Bharata bid farewell to his mothers. If Rama was deprived of their company and their love, so would he be. He climbed into his chariot with Rama's padukas. The court of Ayodhya went with him and the prince followed Vasishta, who had gone before him to Nandigrama. The people of Ayodhya went with Bharata: they would not miss the crowning of the sandals!

At Bharata's instruction, the white parasol was unfurled above the padukas, which were placed on a footstool below the king's throne, as if Rama sat there wearing them. And the crown was set above them. Bharata invoked the Devas: "Ones of light, bless me that the sight of these padukas, which are my brother's feet, guide me whenever I discharge the king's dharma. Bless me that I never swerve from the way of truth, while I rule in Rama's name."

Thus he who ruled Ayodhya lived in Nandigrama like an ascetic; and every day, he would spend at least an hour talking to his brother's padukas. But those who might have wondered if Bharata's extreme devotion had not a touch of madness about it, were soon convinced the young kshatriya was as sound as he needed to be. His reign was a just one, strong and mature. The people felt as if Dasaratha was still alive and sat upon Ayodhya's throne.

Far away, on an emerald island, an awesome and sinister sovereign grew unaccountably disturbed, and he could not fathom why. The evil that possessed Kaikeyi, in some mysterious way, had its source in his terrible soul. Ravana of Lanka slept poorly when that evil was frustrated by the love the princes of Ayodhya felt for one another. But the battle between darkness and truth had hardly been joined. Ravana knew nothing yet of Rama, or that his own empire of fear on earth would soon be threatened by the blue prince, who was an incarnation of grace.

BOOK THREE

ARANYA KANDA

{In the forest}

1. Leaving Chitrakuta

After Bharata returned to Ayodhya, the first few days in Chitrakuta were somber. Rama saw his brother's tearful face in his mind, and it would not go away.

Around them, the mountain was dotted with rishis' asramas. The princes often saw some of these hermits on the mountain paths or at the river, where they came to draw water and bathe; and they exchanged greetings and spoke to them. One day, the munis waved cursorily to Lakshmana from across the Mandakini; but they did not come to talk to him, as they usually did, where the river was narrow.

That evening he mentioned this to Rama. The next day, Rama saw that rishis from all the different asramas on Chitrakuta had congregated on the riverbank. They sat in urgent and secretive conclave, glancing over their shoulders time and again, as if they were fearful of being overheard. They saw him, but did not so much as wave, only whispered on among themselves. Rama crossed the river and went up to them.

He asked, "Munis, why do you turn away from me today? Have Lakshmana or I shown you any disrespect? Or perhaps Sita, unwittingly, when you came to our asrama? You are ill at ease when you see us. What have we done?"

The old kulapati of the largest band of rishis took the prince's hand. "Oh no, Rama, there is no grievance against you or yours. A graver matter concerns us: a fiend called Khara has come to Janasthana in these forests. He is the cousin of a great rakshasa of the south, a king whose very name we speak only in whispers. For he is an incarnation of evil." The old sage looked around nervously, and then breathed, "Ravana of Lanka.

"Khara performs bloody rituals in the jungle and offers human flesh to the powers of darkness. Recently, he has been sacrificing our brother rishis of Janasthana. He is a desecrator of yagnas, a cannibal, and we fear him. He has never been vanquished in battle and he is proof even against our magical siddhis. It seems he has heard of your valor, and means to try himself against you."

The old hermit sighed, "That is not all. Khara and his rakshasas are masters of sorcery. They put out our sacred fires with sudden gusts of wind. The vessels with our offerings vanish before our eyes, or we find them full of excrement. We don't know when the rakshasas will attack us. It is a matter of a day or two. We have decided to leave this place and go to the banks of the Malini, where the Rishi Kanva has his asrama.

"Come with us, Rama. Chitrakuta has become dangerous for Sita and yourselves."

Later, at noon, Rama walked a way through the jungle with the rishis, to see them on their way.

The princes and Sita stayed in Chitrakuta for a week after the sages left; but sorrow was with them constantly. One day Rama said, "This is where we received Bharata and our mothers, and heard their tragic news. I cannot wipe their faces from my mind, and my heart wants me to leave this mountain."

Before he had finished, Lakshmana cried, "Mine as well. This place is full of ghosts. Everywhere I turn, I see Bharata's face, gazing sadly at me that I ever doubted him. Rama, let us leave today."

Sita said quietly, "The asrama does not feel auspicious any more, as it did when we first came."

The same day, they collected their belongings. Rama and Lakshmana strapped on their quivers and swords and picked up their bows, and they climbed down the mountain with Sita between them. They left with little regret. The days since Bharata had come and gone had been anxious ones, when the peace they had found on Chitrakuta abandoned them, and their minds turned back to dark thoughts of Ayodhya.

2. Anasuya

Down through the fragrant pine forests of the mountain into flat country and denser jungles journeyed Rama, Sita, and Lakshmana. They returned to the vicinity of the true Dandaka, and, still skirting the vana, walked away from Chitrakuta for half a day. They saw the huts and fires of an asrama before them, where deer grazed tame as cattle.

The travelers came humbly before the radiant Atri, whose hermitage that was. The towering old man with the wonderful smile welcomed them with a profusion of blessings. He knew who they were and, though he was weak with age, rose to embrace Rama and Lakshmana with such love that they were reminded of their father. He set sweet fruit before them in wooden bowls, and urged, "Eat, my children, before we speak. You have come a long way from Chitrakuta."

Later, the princes, Sita, and Atri sat talking together. The great muni said, "Sita, child, why don't you go into the asrama and find my Anasuya? She will be so happy to see you."

Sita went gladly. Who had not heard of Anasuya, whose legendary tapasya had brought the first fruit into a world that a terrible drought had plunged in hunger? Anasuya's penance swelled the Ganga over her banks and ended the famine.

Inside the asrama, Sita found not an awesome, powerful woman but a wizened yogini with a shining face, huge eyes, and a smile to warm the heart. The skin hung loose and wrinkled on her shrunken frame, and she shook with age. But as Sita touched Anasuya's feet, she felt a current of love flow from that frail body and enfold her.

In a surprisingly strong voice, the yogini said, "It is fortunate you are a child of dharma. Or you would find it impossible to live in the wilds after being raised in a palace. Such an unusual girl you are, that you followed Rama into the jungle. Oh, I am so happy to see you."

Then, as if speaking exhausted her, she fell silent. But she reached out and stroked Sita's head. Sita felt entirely comfortable with the extraordinary old woman. The princess said, "Mother, with a husband like mine, it was impossible for me not to come with him. He means everything to me: he is my life, my God."

They sat together in a loving silence for a while, the old woman stroking Sita's head with her ancient hands that were still so fine. Suddenly Anasuya said, "I have a fair store of tapasya and I can give you any boon you want. Tell me, what would you have from me?"

But Sita replied shyly, "I have Rama; what else could I want?"

"Noble child! But wait, I have something from long ago such as you will not find in the world today." Taking Sita's arm for support,

Anasuya rose and went into her tiny dwelling. She returned with a square bundle, neatly wrapped in cloth, and gave it to Sita. "This was once mine, but now it is for you. Go inside and put on what you find in it."

Sita found precious silks inside the bundle and ornaments no craftsman of this world had made, but surely smiths of Devaloka. And there was a small bottle of perfume, so exquisite that a mere whiff of it calmed the mind. Carefully Sita donned Anasuya's silks, and emerged lovely as Lakshmi herself: a light of fortune in that wild place.

Anasuya was delighted. She walked around the princess, admiring her from every side, laughing like a girl. She made Sita sit beside her, and said, "Now I want to hear everything about you, from the day your father found you to the day Rama came and broke Siva's bow. I want to hear it all from your own lips."

Sita smiled in affection and she began at the beginning. Janaka of Mithila was plowing the earth to turn it for a yagna he planned, when at the base of his plow, in a cleft in the ground, he found a brilliant baby girl. Sita spoke about her early life, about her sisters and her friends in Mithila; but with no trace of nostalgia. Then she came to Rama's arrival in her city. Even before she saw him or her father told her about him, she knew her destiny had come for her.

Sita described how Rama broke Siva's bow while she watched him from her window. She spoke of Dasaratha's arrival and her wedding. She described the advent of terrible Parasurama, and the joy of returning to Ayodhya. But she said nothing about Kaikeyi, nor their exile, as if these were not worth speaking about. Anasuya smiled and smiled as she listened to the younger woman's melodious voice.

When Sita had finished, the yogini hugged her. "How soft and lovely your voice is. I wanted to hear about your wedding, and now I have heard about it from you."

Night was falling over the forest and Atri's rishis were returning from the river with their kamandalus in their hands. The fires which lit that hermitage were like the flames on a dove's breast; but all around them, the brooding jungle was absolutely dark. The tame deer had fallen asleep beside the munis' huts, and some even within them. The stars in the sky shone like God's ornaments.

Anasuya said to Sita, "Go to your husband now. He will be pleased to see you as you are."

Like Lakshmi, Sita went to Rama, bashfully; and how his eyes shone when he saw her wearing Anasuya's silks and fragrant with her unworldly perfume. Rama knew Anasuya had blessed Sita.

They spent that night in Atri's asrama, and early the next morning they came before the great sage. Touching his feet, they took their leave of him. Some of the other rishis brought them to the edge of the jungle, to a trail that wandered into it.

They warned, "Always be on your guard, Kshatriyas. The jungle is full of rakshasas who love nothing better than human flesh. Keep your bows in your hands and don't stray from the path of the munis."

Those hermits also blessed them. Then, as the sun does a bank of dark clouds, Rama entered the Dandaka vana.

3. Deeper into the jungle

The Dandaka vana was another, primeval world. Everywhere they saw rishis' asramas. Darbha grass grew profusely, as if just for the hermits, and fruit and flowers that munis love. All the forest, at least beside the rishis' path, was alive with a sacred aura. As they made their way, they heard the chanting of the Vedas around them: as if it was the very air of this place.

Often a sparkling rillet would gush across the path, and they would cross it by stepping on the large stones in the flow. Now and again they would come upon a clearing with a charmed pool or lake with reverberant lotuses on its water, and its banks tangled with plants that belonged to a more primitive time of the earth. Purple and scarlet, violet and golden, they thrust elaborate tendrils and phallic stamens from feminine cups and leaves. It was an enchanted dimension, the heart of the jungle, and it grew stranger as they penetrated deep into it along the hermits' trail.

Sometimes, herds of deer stood staring at them, fragile and quivering. The princes walked on in wonder, through some zones of the vana where rishis' asramas were not far from the trail, and others devoid of any sign of men save the path at their feet. They walked until evening, when they arrived at the edge of a clearing and saw a sprawling asrama. As the kshatriyas stood unstringing their bows, the very oldest rishi of the Dandaka vana came forward to greet them.

"Welcome, prince of dharma. Rama of Ayodhya, your fame travels before you."

That hermit and his fellows gathered round to stare at the blue prince. The eldest muni seemed satisfied with what he saw, and cried, "Welcome, Protector of the world, who are worthy of our worship!"

They fed the wayfarers with dark roots that were like none they had tasted, and uncommon maroon and crimson fruit, which weren't any they knew, but their flesh was succulent and delicious. They spent the night with the rishis and discovered that these hermits were children of the forest who hardly belonged to the world of men. All night they kept their fires burning. Around them wolves howled, and once or twice a prowling tiger shattered the numinous silence with his roar.

The next day the princes rose early and went on, for some power seemed to call them deeper into the jungle. To take with them, the forest rishis gave them sweet, dark jungle honey from black bees, so thick that it was nearly solid.

On they pressed and the jungle grew stranger and stranger around them; it was another domain of time. The path still snaked on ahead, interminably. The trees were unfamiliar, with brooding presences. Creepers entwined them like parasitic lovers and climbed a hundred hands above, reaching for the sun. The birds in the branches were unknown; though their plumage was often breathtakingly colorful, they screeched weirdly rather than sang. All this jungle was an oppressive place, so unlike Chitrakuta.

Suddenly a great fear, a thing of sheer instinct, lanced through them. Lakshmana, who led the way, stopped still and pulled an arrow from his quiver. Sita cried out softly and clung to Rama. Rama also drew a shaft and set it loosely to his bowstring.

A rank purulence hung on the air and a deafening silence engulfed them. As they stood motionless, they heard stertorous breathing ahead; next moment, a dreadful being appeared before them, blocking the path. A tigerskin was wrapped loosely around his waist. Slanted crimson eyes glittered in his slavering face; a blood drinker's fangs showed in his lipless mouth. He held a crude trisula in his hand on which the remains of his last three hunts were impaled, putrefied and flyblown. He was a rakshasa, twenty feet tall.

Before they could recover from the shock of seeing him, with a giant stride he was on them. He snatched Sita up and held her close, hissing like a monstrous lizard. In a reptile's voice, but in a tongue of men, he cried, "Fate has decided you will have short lives. For I am Viradha, king of this jungle."

He peered at them shortsightedly. "You are oddly familiar, but I don't know who you are. You are dressed like rishis, and you must be depraved munis to be in the jungle with a luscious woman. A disgrace to the valkala you wear. But I will drink your blood now, and make your woman my wife. You can see she will be happy with me!"

He fondled himself obscenely. Sita trembled in the devil's clutch and Rama dared not move because the rakshasa held her. But Lakshmana said defiantly, "Evil one, you are foolish to have crossed our path. You don't know who we are; but you will die at our hands today."

Viradha cried, "Tell me who you are! What are you doing in the heart of the Dandaka vana?"

Softly Rama said, "We are kshatriyas from the House of Ikshvaku. But tell us more about yourself, magnificent one."

The rakshasa laughed, a shrill, feminine sound; and Sita shut her eyes in terror. Viradha said smugly, "I am the son of Jaya and Satahrada. With Brahma's boon, I am invincible to every weapon in heaven and earth. Your puny arrows and your little swords cannot kill me, my strange princes. And I will slake my thirst with your blue blood today."

Quick as thoughts, Rama shot him with seven arrows, eagle-feathered and tipped with gold. Those shafts burned like fire. They pierced the rakshasa's hide and he screamed. But instead of killing him, the arrows fell out of him like burned twigs, smoking. With a tree-shaking roar, Viradha dropped Sita. Rushing at Rama and Lakshmana, he seized them up like babies in his massive arms and ran roaring into the heavy jungle.

Sita wailed, "Don't leave me!"

Lakshmana drew his sword and hewed off Viradha's left arm, and Rama the right; the monster's screams were like those of an army being slaughtered. Black blood spouting from him, he dropped them and fell on the ground. They struck him deep with their swords. But he only screamed and cursed them; he would not die.

Rama cried, "Weapons cannot kill him. Strangle him instead."

They held Viradha down together and fastened four hands around his thick throat. The rakshasa twisted this way and that. But the kshatriyas were strong, and slowly the demon's eyes rolled up in their sockets. As he died, his forked tongue lolled out of his black mouth.

As soon as life left his immense body, there was a flash of light and a splendid gandharva stood before the princes. His hands folded, and dazzling the trees with his luster, he said in an exquisite voice, "You are Kausalya's son Rama, the savior. And your brother is the noble Lakshmana. My name is Tumburu and, as you see, I am a gandharva. Many years ago, my lord Kubera, guardian of the nine treasures, cursed me to be born a rakshasa. I begged him to take back his curse, but he said, 'Dasaratha's son Rama will kill you one day, and then you will be free of your fiend's body and return to Devaloka.'

"For centuries I have waited for you to come. I have waited so long, I forgot who I was and believed myself to be just Viradha."

Again the marvelous being bowed to Rama. He said, "A yojana and a half from here is the Rishi Sharabhanga's asrama. Go to him, Kshatriyas, and seek his blessing. As for my rakshasa's body, I cannot touch it myself. But if you bury it under the ground it will molder in peace and be earth again. And I can return to my home in the sky."

Now Sita came flying there, sobbing and frantic. She saw Rama and Lakshmana alive and safe, and ran to them. Then she saw the gandharva and he bowed to her. They dug a pit deep enough to contain the swollen corpse of Viradha. They threw his arms in after his body, and his trident, and covered it all with earth and stamped on it. Bowing for the last time, Tumburu vanished in a blur of light. He went whistling like a tree full of birds, for the gandharva elves are the minstrels of Devaloka.

Rama, Sita, and Lakshmana set off in the direction Tumburu had indicated, toward Sharabhanga's asrama. They came to a clear stream, in which the princes washed Viradha's blood from themselves. They ate some of the invigorating honey the wild rishis had given them, and pressed on. They had no wish to spend the night alone in this jungle, at the mercy of its more dangerous denizens.

4. Sharabhanga

The sun was sinking in the west when they saw a clearing in the thick jungle ahead of them, and at its heart the wood fires of Sharabhanga's asrama. Just behind the last line of trees, Lakshmana stopped abruptly. Rama and Sita came up beside him and they gasped. Out of the sky a shining chariot flew down, drawn by unearthly horses whose manes were blue flames.

Noiselessly it landed in the clearing; not even the horses' hooves or the chariot wheels ever touched the ground. From that chariot stepped a king whose lambency rivaled the setting sun's. He was tall and wore ornaments that seemed made of blinding starlight. His silks were of colors beyond the rainbow's and flapped fluorescent in the evening breeze. Regally he stepped out of his amazing craft and his feet did not touch the ground!

As the princes and Sita watched from hiding, he paused in his stride for a moment, as if he sensed he was being observed. Then he went briskly into Sharabhanga's asrama, followed by the others who had come with him, all of them resplendent.

Rama breathed, "Indra!"

They stood staring at the unearthly chariot. The horses seemed to be made more of green light than flesh and blood. Then Rama could not bear it any more. He said to Lakshmana, "Wait here for me, I will be back in a moment."

But before he could step out from the trees, Indra and his Devas emerged from the asrama, crossed to their chariot, and flashed up into the sky at a speed that defied imagining. Rama stood rooted, gazing after the trail the chariot left, as it dwindled in a moment and vanished. The prince's cry, hailing great Indra, froze in his throat. Neither did he hear the Deva king say to his companions, "That was Rama of Ayodhya. But we must not meet until the purpose of his birth is fulfilled."

Something deep stirred in Rama and he smiled wryly at Sita and Lakshmana, as they also came out into the clearing to watch the chariot's trail dissolve into the sunset.

They walked into Sharabhanga's asrama. To their surprise, they found they were already expected and a welcome awaited them. Sharabhanga came to embrace the kshatriyas. Rama asked him, "My lord, who was he who just left your asrama?"

That ancient one smiled as he led them to where fine darbhasanas had been set out for his guests. Holding Rama's hand lovingly in his gnarled ones, Sharabhanga said, "That was Indra come to take me to Brahmaloka, for my tapasya is ripe and moksha near." He paused, his eyes twinkling. He squeezed Rama's hand and continued, "But I heard you had come to the Dandaka vana. I said to Indra, 'I must see Rama before I go with you to Brahmaloka.' And I will go happily, now that I have seen you, touched you, and spoken to you."

He laughed delightedly, putting his arms around the prince and hugging him. His manner was so lively he might have been a man of Rama's own age; Rama felt quite overwhelmed with affection. When they sat on the grass thrones Sharabhanga had laid out for them, suddenly the sage leaned forward and said earnestly, "Rama, I have a lifetime's tapasya. Take it from me as a gift."

But Rama laughed, "I will have to earn your tapasya then, Maharishi, and I don't know if I can. Besides, I do not seek other worlds just now, only a home in the Dandaka vana where Sita, Lakshmana, and I can live."

The old one could not take his eyes off the dark kshatriya. He laughed happily at Rama's reply. "Not far from here is Sutheekshna's asrama. He will find a place for you to live in. Go west along the pathway of the rishis and you will come to the Mandakini. Walk on against her flow, and you will arrive in a gentle land fed by a score of streams. A colorful forest grows on the river's bank, and you will see boats upon the water, laden with flowers. Cross the river and you will reach Sutheekshna's asrama."

He stared and stared, as if his eyes could never see enough of Rama's face. Only that rishi knew whom he saw in the prince's face; and light there that had shone before the world was made. Sharabhanga sat rapt and silent for a long time, gazing. Except for a great love, Rama himself knew little else of what the rishi's fascination meant. That sage smiled again, and he sighed with the contentment of one whose very soul was full. He clasped Rama's hand again and kissed it fervently.

He said, "One favor from you, my gracious prince! I know who you are, and, somehow, I think, better than you yourself do yet. And that is the way of the Avataras. But now, Rama, watch me with your loving eyes and let that be my final blessing as I shed this body of mine as a snake does its old skin."

Before Rama could protest, Sharabhanga, excited as a boy, had his disciples build him a pyre. He poured oblations on to it, chanting resonant mantras. Then, his eyes never leaving Rama's face, his palms folded to him, that rishi walked into the flames. Sita gave a small scream. But he was so calm, as if the fire did not burn him at all. As they watched, the fire licked Sharabhanga's body to ashes.

They stood spellbound: Rama at strange, rich peace, for reasons he understood only dimly. When the fire died down, Sharabhanga rose from its ashes, youthful again. His limbs were coruscant and the same smile was on his lips. He bowed deeply to Rama; then, borne on a spirit wind, he rose straight into eternal Brahmaloka. Petal rain fell out of the realm of the Gods at Sharabhanga's ascension.

The other rishis gathered around Rama. One of the eldest of them, their spokesman, said, "Rama, we live in this forest in terror. The rakshasas hunt us for food and for sport; and with each day, their evil grows apace."

They led Rama to a grotesque memorial to the fear that stalked their lives. At the heart of the asrama, they had heaped a pale mound as tall as five men. The rishi said grimly, "These are the bones of our brothers who have been killed and devoured. Not the asramas on the banks of the Pampa, not those by the Mandakini, nor yet the ones built on the slopes of Chitrakuta are safe. We heard you had come to the Dandaka vana. We heard you are the savior and we thought our long prayers had been answered. Fear haunts us, Rama. We are not free from it asleep or awake, not even in dhyana. Will you help us? You are our only hope."

Rama said quietly, "I give you my word, Lakshmana and I will do our best to rid your forest of its rakshasas. We shall be your hunters."

The rishis blessed them. They spent the night there, and the next day some of the hermits came out to show them the way to Sutheekshna's asrama. When the munis turned back, the exiles walked for a way through dense jungle, until they found themselves on the banks of their old friend the Mandakini. They tracked the river upstream, pausing now and then to gaze at a crystal pool full of black lotuses or at some other vivid flower that grew shyly in the deepest thicket, as if being seen by the eyes of strangers would wither its beauty.

The jungle was exotic, full of trees that exuded the most unusual auras and stood laden with blooms of extraordinary shapes and pungent and heady scents. There were spear blossoms and those that looked uncannily like men's heads. There were crimson plants, with perfectly formed sivalingas outthrust from yonic leaf cups.

The farther they went, the brighter and more unfamiliar were the birds in the branches. The monkeys no longer swung above them in troops but were lone and colorful, with faces like painted masks. Once a glimmering leopard stared down at them from a branch that overhung the path.

Lakshmana raised his bow, but Rama touched his arm and said, "This is his home; we are the visitors here. Look how handsome he is!" Green eyes flashing, a snarl on his lips, the leopard vanished without rustling the leaves.

They came to a valley of flowers that took their breath away. The trees were magenta and yellow, pink and white, purple and orange, as far as the eye could see, in a candescent blessing upon the earth. Scents from dreams hung in the air in this wonderland, and they saw boats moored on the Mandakini, brimming with flowers.

Ahead of them a mountain loomed, dark as twilight, and the valley of flowers lay in its shadow. Now some rishis stepped out of the trees on the far bank and hailed them across the river: "We hid because we thought you were rakshasas. We will bring a boat across for you."

Sutheekshna's friendly sannyasis ferried Rama's party across the Mandakini, and they arrived in that legendary muni's asrama.

5. A matter of dharma

Rama prostrated himself before the short, cheerful rishi whose cheeks were as bright as the blooms on the trees that flowered so extravagantly in his valley, because his tapasya was so profound.

Rama said, "Lord Sutheekshna, I am Rama. I have come to take your blessing."

Sutheekshna rose and embraced the princes. Laying his palm on her head, he blessed Sita. He cried in the most friendly, lively voice, "Rama, I am so happy you have come! You were on Chitrakuta when I last had news of you. You may not know it, but since your birth we rishis have kept a close watch on you. We have waited for you; and who knows, except that I heard you were coming I may have left this body of mine. A year ago, Indra came to me in a dream and said I had won all the lokas with my tapasya, even Brahma's." The rishi smiled; he was testing Rama gently. He said, "Take all the heavens from me, sweet prince, as my gift to you."

Rama also smiled, and replied, "I must win them for myself, my lord. But Sharabhanga sent me to you. Before he left his body, he said you would find me a home in the jungle."

The smile never left Sutheekshna's face; his eyes were alight to see Rama. He cried, "Stay here with us. There are roots and fruit aplenty to feed you. You have seen the flowers of my valley; I think they will please your Sita's heart. The river sings for us and you can take a boat on her at any time. Herds of deer come to visit; they are our friends, and speak to us in their own way. Stay here, Rama: you will be happy among us."

Rama listened attentively. But then he said, "I fear my kshatriya blood may get the better of me. I may kill a deer and desecrate this holy place. But for tonight I accept your gracious hospitality. Tomorrow, when we are less tired, we will decide on our next course."

With fruit even more juicy and unusual than they had eaten the last two nights, with honey even sweeter, and roots that tasted like venison, Sutheekshna entertained his visitors. They had wine brewed from some scarlet berries, which made their spirits soar. Late into the night, they sang songs in praise of the Gods above; and Sita bewitched them all when she joined in. Then she sang by herself in her strong, clear voice, with her eyes cast down or fixed on Rama's face.

They slept in peace that night. Sutheekshna's valley was protected by his tapasya, and no evil had yet crossed the river.

The next morning, Rama, Lakshmana, and Sita were up early. Rama bathed in the night-chilled Mandakini, redolent with lotuses.

He came to Sutheekshna, and said, "I think we should go on a pilgrimage to all the asramas in the Dandaka vana. We want to befriend every rishi who lives here. Bless us on our way, my lord."

Sutheekshna said, "May your journey be safe and joyful. Come back to me when you have met all the munis in our jungle."

Sita strapped their quivers on for the princes. Bowing to the sage and merry hermit, they set off, heading still deeper into the forest.

As they went, Sita lagged nearer her husband. She kept glancing back at him, until he walked beside her and asked, "What is troubling you, my love?"

She bit her lip and hesitated. Then very softly she said, "Dharma is a subtle thing. One can be true to it only if one's mind is entirely without desire."

She looked up at him, smiling as if she had transgressed her bounds already. Rama took her hand and urged her, "Go on."

She gave a shy laugh. "Three sins must be avoided if one is to live perfectly in dharma. You, Rama, are certainly free of the first two. You have never told a lie and never will. You have never and shall never, I think, even look at another woman with desire. But it is the third crime against the truth that worries me, ever since you swore to Sharabhanga's rishis that you would rid the jungle of its rakshasas. But the jungle is the rakshasas' home. They have not harmed you in any way, yet you have sworn to kill them. I am against our going further into the forest.

"Having given your word, Rama, the moment you see a rakshasa you will want to kill him. And for you, to think is to act. I have heard the very touch of a weapon is like fire. Varuna's bow in your hand is fire to your spirit. But you must never string it unprovoked; you must not kill even a rakshasa unless he attacks you first.

"Rama, you wear the valkala of a tapasvin; you must honor what you wear. My love, dharma is, most of all, peace."

Rama smiled and said solemnly, "I swear by our love that I will never kill anyone, even a rakshasa, unless I am provoked. But you must consider what provocation is. It is my kshatriya dharma to help those who seek my protection, as the rishis have done. The forces of darkness and light are always at war in the world. The earth prospers, humankind thrives, because of the prayers of these holy ones who dwell in the forest. Their penance is for the weal of all men.

"The rakshasas who feed on their flesh are minions of evil. It is my dharma to save the world from them. Just think of the rishis' plight: that for fear of the rakshasas, they cannot still their minds in peace and draw heaven's grace down for the earth's nurture. Sita, the world will fall into anarchy without the tapasya of these saintly men. I should have offered to protect them without their asking; their worship is more vital to the earth than the throne of Ayodhya. My love, they are the sacred support of the people, of us all. They are the holders of the world.

"We may lose our lives fighting the forces of evil; but fight them we must, as we are able. It is the very reason why fate has brought us into the Dandaka vana."

Sita was quiet. Rama put his arm around her and continued: "Your concern moves me; don't ever think I am not aware of it. And to watch over my dharma is your concern, whose else's? But I realize with each day in the jungle, in every fiber in my body, that I have been born for a purpose beyond just being a prince of Ayodhya. A powerful destiny seems to call me, Sita, one that I do not yet understand."

Sita looked into her husband's youthful face and saw how its lines were firming into manhood. Not just a world, but an eternity seemed to separate them from Ayodhya now. And Sita was a little frightened.

6. Ten years

Rama spoke to Lakshmana and they lengthened their stride through the jungle. They walked past rivulets and through some light thickets; they passed more than one mountain. They saw more enchanted pools, heavy with lotuses in rare colors. All day they walked, stopping only to pluck familiar fruit from the trees and eat them. They came to a lake full of sweet water with herds of deer on its banks. Wild pig came to drink, and they saw flocks of sarasa and chakravaka, goose and migrant teal, scarlet ibis and pelican, crane and painted stork.

The sun was sinking in the west when they arrived in a zone of asramas. There was a clutch of them built into a wide depression in the earth, none far from the others. Their rishis welcomed their royal guests with memorable warmth: wherever Rama encountered a hermit, he was unfailingly worshipped!

This was, at last, the deepest place in the Dandaka vana, its inmost heart. If they went on from here, they would be leaving the jungle again. Among these rishis, Rama, Lakshmana, and Sita spent ten years. They were peaceful years, save for frequent encounters with the rakshasas, who came in search of human flesh and human blood. Instead they found swift death at the hands of the blue kshatriya of Ayodhya and his brother; and it was violent deliverance for them. In ten years, the race of rakshasas dwindled in that jungle.

From asrama to asrama went Rama, Sita, and Lakshmana. In some they stayed a month, in others a year; everywhere they had the same welcome and hospitality. Slowly Rama grew used to being treated like an Avatara, though he neither encouraged it nor shrank from it. He accepted it as he did the sunrise or the moon in the sky, and it did not make him arrogant or change him in any way. And in the heart of the forest, his spirit was opened to him: a secret, mystic bloom, thousand-petaled.

Ten years went by, and Sita and the princes scarcely knew how. They became part of the jungle: like the deer, the elephants, and the mighty bison, the langurs and baboons on the trees, the lotuses upon the pools, and even the rakshasas. The jungle was now their home.

Lakshmana could fluently imitate the voices of the birds and beasts. He could call up a koyal or a tigress in season, convincingly mimicking the songs or roars of their mates. They went for long walks. They went bathing in the charmed streams and pools, and ten years passed like a dream: especially for Rama, who, more than any-thing, reveled in the company of every rishi he met. Individually, they were so unlike one another, and most of them were far from perfect. They had their petty bickering and jealousies, their lovable idiosyn-crasies and their shifting hierarchies within each asrama. Some were bhaktas of Siva, and others worshipped Vishnu. But to Rama, they were all fascinating without exception, and enviable. He could spend days listening to their conversation, ever passionate, if at times eccen-tric: always about great and holy God.

Ten years flew by, between asrama and asrama. Then Rama re-membered his promise to Sutheekshna that he would return to that rishi's sanctuary, when he had roamed the other hermitages of the Dandaka vana to his heart's content. So one day, some rishis beside the Mandakini heard themselves being hailed from across the river by three travelers who looked much more like jungle folk than they had ten years ago, when they last passed through the valley of flowers.

Sutheekshna was overjoyed to see Rama. Over and over again he hugged the prince, as though he was his very life restored to him. And he cried, "You have spent so much time in the other asramas. What is wrong with mine that you stayed just a day with me?"

Rama spent ten months with that jovial muni. Then one morning he remembered something that had tugged at his heart for a long time. He went to Sutheekshna and said, "I heard that Agastya Muni lives in the Dandaka vana. But the paths of the forest are so difficult that I hesitated to try to find his asrama."

Sutheekshna gave a delighted laugh. "Last night, just as sleep came over me, I thought to myself I must tell Rama to go and seek Agastya's blessing. But with morning, I had forgotten again. This has been happening quite often; perhaps until now it was not time for you to visit the incomparable one.

"Take the rishis' path south from here, and four yojanas away you will find Agastya's brother's asrama. You can spend your night there in safety, and I am sure the muni will direct you to his brother."

South went the princes and Sita. The southern forest was quite a different place. It was less dense, but strewn with open glades, with fruit and flowering trees. More streams and rivers flowed through it than to the north or the east. Most of the way, they walked under the warm sun and were glad of it. They did not have to go in single file as they did through the thicker jungle, and Rama asked Lakshmana, "Do you know the story of Agastya Muni?"

Being used to listening to his brother's stories since they were children, Lakshmana was eager to hear it; so was Sita, though she smiled at the younger prince's keenness.

Rama began: "Once there were two rakshasas who lived here in the southern Dandaka. They were brothers called Ilvala and Vatapi, and their fierceness and cruelty were legend. Their favorite diet was the flesh of brahmanas, and the manner in which they snared the unsuspecting munis was passing strange.

"Ilvala, who had powers of maya, would himself assume the form of a brahmana and wait on this very path. When a real brahmana came along, he would accost him tearfully. He would cry in the most priestly language that his father had just died and he would be honored if the traveling muni would attend the srarddha.

"Meanwhile, Vatapi, who was an even abler sorcerer than his brother, became a sacrificial goat. When the guest arrived, the goat was killed and a meal cooked with its flesh. When the guest had been fed, so he was past eating another morsel, Ilvala, his expression as bland as it had been all morning, would shout, 'Vatapi, come out!'

"Vatapi the goat would come bursting out of the visitor's stomach, spilling his entrails. Laughing between themselves, the two brothers would tear at the brahmana and devour him. Not even the Devas could kill Vatapi and Ilvala, because their maya was so powerful. Finally, the rishis of the jungle went to Agastya and begged him to help them.

"One day, as Ilvala waited on the rishis' trail, he saw a bearded muni coming along. He thought what a succulent meal the good sage would make. He accosted Agastya worshipfully. In chaste language, he begged him to come to his father's sraddha. He said the dead man's soul would be thrice blessed by the presence of such an illustrious guest.

"Agastya went with Ilvala to his asrama, where Vatapi was tethered with a rope. Ilvala cut the goat's throat and cooked its flesh. And Agastya made an enormous meal of him. With a grin, Ilvala called, 'Vatapi, come out!'

"But no goat tore its way out of Agastya's stomach. The rishi belched softly; he licked his fingers, smiling at his host. Ilvala called again, 'Vatapi, come out now!'

"Nothing stirred. Agastya began to laugh. He said, 'Your brother has been well digested. I don't think he will come out any more.'

"Ilvala howled, and before Agastya's eyes, he was a demon again: fanged and clawed, his eyes blazing. He flew roaring at the muni. But with just a look, Agastya made that rakshasa ashes."

It was evening when they arrived at Agastya's brother's asrama. He welcomed them excitedly; he also knew who Rama was. Indeed he seemed to know all about the brothers and Sita, and everything that had happened to them. They spent the night with him, and the next day Rama said, "We want to seek Agastya's blessing. Will you show us the way to his asrama?"

"Follow the rishis' path," said the slight sage. "My brother lives a yojana from here; you cannot miss his asrama if you stay on the trail."

They bowed to him and went on. Though the forest was less dense along this southern branch of the rishis' trail, there was such a wealth of wild creatures here that they walked in some absorption. This was elephant country, and bison moved through the tall grass in herds. There were many more lush clearings here than in the eastern jungle, as well as long stretches of tall bamboo thickets. Dense flocks of birds, migrated from distant lands, roosted, various and colorful, among the spreading trees. There was a deeper feeling of ancience about this forest than any they had yet experienced.

Rama walked briskly in anticipation of meeting Agastya. When they had gone a yojana, they saw that the trees were tended to, the deer were tame, and even the birds flew fearlessly down to them, much to Sita's delight. Then Lakshmana cried, "Look!"

Ahead they saw an asrama. Its rishis were hanging out their valkala to dry in the sun. Rama said reverently, "Do you know the Vindhya mountain stopped growing at Agastya's command? Not just men but even the Devas worship Agastya Muni. Lakshmana, I will wait here with Sita. You go into the asrama and tell him we have come to seek his blessing."

7. Agastya Muni

Lakshmana went into the asrama and found a young acolyte there. He said, "I am King Dasaratha's son; my name is Lakshmana. My brother Rama and his wife Sita are waiting outside. Please tell Agastya Muni we want to take the dust from his feet."

The sishya went into the agnihotrashala, where the fire of worship burned. Agastya stood unmoving before it, his arms crossed over his chest, a flame himself. The disciple waited silently, until his master opened his eyes and asked, "What is it?"

"Two sons of Dasaratha have come to visit you, the older one with his wife. They seek your blessing."

A smile breaking on his deep face, Agastya said, "For so long now, I have been wishing Rama here. At last he has come. Bring them to me with honor. You should not have made them wait; don't you know who Rama is?"

Never had that sishya seen his reclusive guru so excited to receive a visitor. He hurried back to Lakshmana, and cried with new respect in his voice, "Call your brother! Come quickly, the master is anxious to meet you."

Rama entered the asrama with Sita, and Agastya came out to welcome him. Rama lay at the rishi's feet, then Sita and Lakshmana did. Blessing them, raising them up affectionately, the great sage led them into the agnihotrashala and made them sit round the fire. First of all, he insisted they should eat something. Then he said to Rama, "I have heard you are the very image of dharma. Stay with me for a while; you shall be more than welcome."

He studied the prince's face intently, as if to satisfy himself that he was truly who they said. Rama met his gaze humbly, but unwaveringly, and at last the rishi rose and went into his kutila. He returned shortly, and his arms were full of resplendent weapons! He laid them before the brothers. "These are for you."

A magnificent bow sparkled with diamonds, emeralds, and rubies. An uncanny sense of familiarity overcame Rama and he reached out to stroke that weapon.

Agastya said, "The Brahmadatta was made by Viswakarman and was Brahma's gift to Mahavishnu. Here are two quivers Indra gave me, and this sword in its silver sheath; and not even astras can pierce this armor.

"This is the bow Narayana used against the Asuras in the war that was fought in Devaloka. It is yours now, Rama. When the time comes, you will need a chariot to face the Lord of Evil; Indra's sarathy Matali will fly down to you from Devaloka, with Indra's own ratha."

Bowing, Rama received the weapons. A thrill coursed through him and an urgent sense of destiny was upon him again—of some great task to be accomplished, and an implacable enemy who waited for him beyond the sunset.

They spent that day and night in Agastya's asrama. It was a moonless night and the silence was deep. Before they fell asleep, they sat around the fire watching the white owls like spirits in the trees.

The next morning, Agastya said, "Did you sleep well, Rama? Were you comfortable?"

Rama said warmly, "We felt we were back in our father's home in Ayodhya: so lovingly did your sishyas look after us."

They sat before the awesome rishi, and he said, "Rama, your exile draws to an end. You will return to Ayodhya with glory. How fortunate Dasaratha is to have a son like you to bring him honor."

Rama said softly, "My lord, I have been happy in the Dandaka vana. My exile has not been an ordeal, but a joy. How else would I have met all the holy men I have during these years, and learned what I have from them? But I don't think my father owes any honor he has to me. He earned his place in heaven with a virtuous life."

As he thought of Dasaratha, Rama's face was briefly clouded by sorrow. But he put aside those sad reflections and said, "We seek a quiet place to live in, these last years we have left in the jungle. Can you help us, Muni?"

Agastya thought a moment, then said brightly, "Do you know the true story of this jungle called the Dandaka? In ancient times, Dandaka was your own ancestor; he was Ikshvaku's brother. He abandoned this land of his because Sukracharya, the Asura guru, cursed it.

It was no forest then and such blight came to this kingdom that for five hundred yojanas, even down to the Vindhya mountains, it was a desolation.

"In the days when man and beast had fled the cursed land, a jungle sprang up here by dark sorcery: though no clouds would gather in the sky or even the wind blow through this place. No rishi dared build his asrama here because this forest was a home of evil, where only rakshasas lived. No Devas or gandharvas came here for fear.

"One day, I wandered down from the Himalaya and fate brought me to this place. I was the first man to enter the Dandaka vana in an age, and the rain followed me and the wind, unleashed; we had a storm like the deluge. Bolts of lightning fell from the sky, immolating many of the rakshasas, and it rained for ten days without let. How the parched earth welcomed my coming.

"Fell diseases, Yama's messengers, thrived in this forest. But I stilled them with mantras, and I burned the flesh-eating plants that grew at night's heart with fire from my mind. I had carried blessed seeds from Himavan with me; I scattered them through the endless darkness. Noble trees sprang up here, and bore flowers and fruit. At my tapasya, the rivers of the earth flowed back through the Dandaka vana; lakes and pools formed, with lotuses floating on their waters again, and swans.

"When they heard the old forest was transformed, the rishis came back. But the curse of Sukra had not been exorcised entirely. Parts of the jungle were still fastnesses of evil and not all the rakshasas had gone away. For many years, they were quiet. But Rama, since the day you arrived on Chitrakuta, a madness seems to grip them. By sun and moon, they come out of their lairs to hunt our people. As if the devils know their time is short and want to indulge themselves while they are still alive.

"Sukra's curse on this place was removed when your eyes first fell upon it. I have heard that in the east, where you lived for ten years, there are no rakshasas left. But rid us also of the demons in the south. Fate has sent you to us for this."

Rama inclined his head gravely, to say he would do as the muni asked. Now Agastya looked at Sita, and said warmly, "What a rare woman your wife is. Poets speak of women's natures as being as fickle as lightning: when their men are favored by fortune they are happy to be their wives. But as soon as their husbands fall on hard times, they abandon them. But not so this jewel of Mithila. Care for her always, Kshatriya; she is a pativrata, a goddess among women."

Sita blushed; her eyes filled with proud tears.

Rama said, "We are moved by your love, my lord. If you will tell us of a place beside a river where we can live, I will clear the jungle of its rakshasas. Sita will be happiest if we are also near some flowering trees."

For just a moment Agastya paused to think, before he said, "Two yojanas from here, near the Godavari, is Panchavati. It has a wealth of fruit trees and savory roots; it has herds of gentle deer. I would love nothing better than to have you spend the rest of your exile with me. But it is not to be. Great events have been conceived in time's womb and wait to be born into the world. To Panchavati you must go, Rama; your destiny awaits you there."

Agastya's lofty brow was knit at what he saw lay in store for the prince. He shook his head to clear it of that vision, and said somberly, "Yes, Panchavati is truly beautiful and quiet; just the place for you to build an asrama. Do you see that wood of madhuka trees, which stretches almost to the horizon? Pass through it and you will come to a lofty nyagrodha. From the nyagrodha, you must climb north. Panchavati is not far. Spend the rest of your exile there."

Rama rose and touched Agastya's feet; and Lakshmana and Sita after him. They made a pradakshina around the shining weapons he had given them. Then, picking them up and taking the rishi's blessing with them, they walked away in the direction he had indicated.

8. A friend in the wilderness

Through the interminable wood of madhuka trees walked Rama, Lakshmana, and Sita. At last, coming out from under its green ceiling, they found themselves at the foot of a hill. Between themselves and its gradual slope grew an immense nyagrodha, its branches falling in screens of aerial roots around its stupendous trunk. It was old and knotted, perhaps even a survivor of Sukra's curse. Few leaves adorned its branches in this season, and the princes saw a gigantic eagle perched on the tree, preening himself.

Drawing an arrow, Lakshmana whispered, "A rakshasa waiting for us. What a surprise he is going to get."

But Rama restrained him, and cried up to the bird in a friendly voice, "Who are you, great one?"

The eagle peered down at them, then he looked away; and then he looked at them again. Abruptly, giving throat to excited cries, he broke into a little dance on his branch, until he said in perfect human speech, "Children of Ayodhya, I am a friend of your father's!"

Rama sat down under the tree. To Lakshmana's dismay, he undid his sword and quiver and laid them on the ground. The great bird flapped down majestically and settled near Rama; Lakshmana stood tense, his bow strung and ready. The eagle was as tall as Rama. He was old, and descended from the pristine race of Garuda. Rama sat smiling and admiring him: his golden plumage, his snow-white cap feathers, his beak curved like a scimitar and talons like daggers. His expression was haughty as he looked askance at Lakshmana out of flashing green eyes, as if to say, "Fool! Am I not too noble to be a rakshasa?"

Rama said respectfully, "Mighty one, tell me about yourself."

The splendid bird said in his uncannily human voice, "Brahma's grandson Kashyapa Prajapati had many daughters. One of them was Shyeni. Vinata had two sons, eagles of light. One is Aruna, the sun's sarathy, and the other is Garuda, on whom Vishnu rides. Incandescent Aruna married Shyeni, and two sons were born to them: Sampati the older and Jatayu the younger. I, Rama of Ayodhya, am Jatayu.

"My prince, the forest you are going toward is an evil place. If you allow me, I will stay with you and be your guardian. When you go out to hunt with Lakshmana, I will watch over Sita."

The bird glanced at Lakshmana, who had not yet returned his arrow to its quiver. Jatayu said dryly, "With my life if need be."

Rama embraced Jatayu. "My father often spoke of you: how you and he hunted together and fought the war against the Asuras. I am so happy to meet you, noble Jatayu. I accept your offer gratefully; I am flattered you will be our companion."

When he heard that Dasaratha had spoken of Jatayu before, Lakshmana thrust his arrow back into its quiver. He folded his hands to the eagle, who inclined his head imperiously at him. They set off together and Rama wondered if, when he sent them this way, Agastya had known Jatayu would be waiting for them at the nyagrodha. The eagle flew along above them and they followed, on a course he seemed to know well.

Rama said to Lakshmana, "Our father used to tell me that Jatayu is a great warrior. He always spoke warmly of him, like a brother; as I hardly heard him speak of anyone else."

When they had climbed a way, and the air was cooler, Jatayu glided down to the ground. The Godavari flowed near this sylvan place, and it was rich with apple, peach, and pear trees, and darbha grass grew everywhere. They found a natural clearing, fringed with pine, with an auspicious feeling about it, and decided to build their asrama there. A small stream, a tributary of the river, flowed through this clearing and a fine breeze carried the scent of the lotuses that floated upon its water. Away on the shoulder of the mountain, they saw herds of deer; nearer them, peacocks strutted with their tails unfurled in nitid emerald and turquoise. Sita pointed and there was a herd of elephant, etched in stolid gray against the verdure of the slope.

Lakshmana, the expert woodsman, built them a kutila. He bathed in the Godavari and fetched lotuses from the river. He offered the flowers to the gods of the jungle and chanted the mantras for keeping evil away. Some hours later, he came to Rama and Sita and said the dwelling was ready. Rama admired the sturdy and elegant workmanship. Suddenly, he was so moved by the little hut of logs that Rama was in tears.

Hugging Lakshmana, he said, "You do so much for me and all I can reward you with is an embrace. My father may be dead, but his spirit is always before me: in you, my brother, who look after me like a father!"

Lakshmana blushed crimson, and Jatayu and Sita smiled to see him.

They lived happily in that asrama for some moons. Sita quickly made friends with all the birds, rabbits, and deer for yojanas around. She would talk to them just as if they were human friends; and they seemed to know exactly what she said. After she whispered to them, the deer would run off to the river and bring back lotuses in their teeth: flowers that were just the shade of blue she wanted for her worship, or for a wildflower garland to drape around Rama. All kinds of birds came and perched on her window, warbling to her in their lively tongues, bringing news from the corners of the forest. Or so she said, and Rama had no reason to doubt her.

Once during hemanta, autumn, the brothers went early in the morning to bathe in the cold waters of the Godavari. Braced and shivering, Lakshmana said, "Bharata must be bathing in the Sarayu and thinking of us." He grew wistful. "Such a noble brother we have, Rama: dark like you, selfless like you. Men are meant to take after their mothers. But not Bharata. He doesn't have anything of that evil . . ."

Rama laid his fingers across Lakshmana's lips. "Speak no evil of anyone at this hour, least of all our mother. As for Bharata, how often I think of him, and how much he loves me. I still see his face before my eyes: my padukas on his head, tears streaming down his face. How I long to be back in Ayodhya with my mothers and my brothers."

On their way back from the river, they spoke about the old days, about Dasaratha, and the four of them when they were children. The time they spent in Panchavati was contented and peaceful. But fate stalked them nearer with each moment that passed, and evil lurked round the corner of the bright days.

9. A battle at Panchavati

The princes and Sita fell into a pleasant routine. They would wake up early each morning, go to the river, bathe, and worship the rising sun. Rama and Sita would walk back, hand in hand, while Lakshmana followed with the water pot. They wandered through the surrounding forests, exploring them, enjoying them. Or they basked in the sun all day long, living for the green moment, while deer laid their heads in Sita's lap and peacocks ate out of her hands.

But one day, evil arrived in their lives, announcing itself comically. Surpanaka, the rakshasi, arrived in Panchavati. She was the spoiled sister of the Emperor of evil who lived on the distant island of Lanka, while his power spread from his throne like a great sickness through the world. Brought by fate, Surpanaka, on her hunt, came to the grove in Panchavati. She scented humans in the asrama. She saw Rama from behind a tree and she was smitten.

She looked at him; she turned and looked again. Her heart stood still at his unearthly beauty. She had never seen anyone like him. Surpanaka wanted him for herself. She longed to run her fingers through the tangled mass of his hair; she yearned to stroke his face and clasp him tightly in her arms. She wondered who this was: handsome as Kamadeva, and as dark and blue.

Surpanaka was as ugly a rakshasi as ever lived. She was old with sin and years of devouring human flesh. She was bloated and misshapen; her voice was a harsh croak; her hair was a dirty copper; her eyes were tiny, cunning, and cruel. She was fanged and altogether hideous, but she was a mistress of maya. She could change her form as she liked, though she could not change the evil in her soul.

With just a thought she turned herself into an apsaralike beauty. Ravishing now, she came up to the princes. She ignored Lakshmana and Sita but, fluttering her lashes at him, swaying her hips and bending low so he could see her cleavage, she said seductively to Rama, "Who are you, stranger? How have you come to this home of rakshasas, when obviously you are no rakshasa yourself?"

Rama looked into her eyes and knew what she was. He said, "I am Dasaratha's son Rama, and I have come to live in the jungle for fourteen years. These are my brother Lakshmana and my wife Sita. And who are you? You seem to belong here, for you are a rakshasi I think."

She blushed; she tittered. She said, "I am no ordinary rakshasi, Rama, but your equal in pedigree. I am Surpanaka. Ravana of Lanka, Emperor of the world, is my brother. I live in Janasthana with my cousins Khara and Dushana. I have two more brothers, who are in Lanka with Ravana: Kumbhakarna who sleeps all year, and Vibheeshana who is so full of dharma that he is hardly a rakshasa."

She smiled at him again. "But all that is beside the point, my delectable prince. Fate brought me here, and the moment I saw you, I knew I must have you for my husband. You are the most handsome man I ever set eyes on; I have maya and I can be as beautiful as you want. I am powerful, Rama, I will look after you. We are meant for each other. What can this pale Sita do for you? She, at best, is fit to be my morning meal!" And she laughed uproariously at her joke.

Rama said, "Exquisite Surpanaka, I am a married man and I love this pale Sita of mine. I don't think a great princess like you could bear to be my second wife. But my brother Lakshmana is alone. He is younger and fairer than I am. He will make the perfect husband for you. Marry him and you will have him all to yourself."

Surpanaka turned to Lakshmana. She saw he was handsome and strong, too; she saw the muscles rippling on his arms and his chest. She switched her attentions to him. Caressing the younger prince's face, the rakshasi said, "Lakshmana, we shall be happy together in the

Dandaka vana. Let us be married, charming Kshatriya. Ah, you are so sweet; let us be lovers!"

But Lakshmana protested, "I am only my brother's man. How will a princess like you be happy married to a mere servant? You should coax my brother a little more; persuade him with your maya sakti: better that you be his second wife than my only one. Woo him, lovely Surpanaka; he will leave his pale princess for you."

Surpanaka saw the wisdom of what Lakshmana said. She turned back to Rama. "You spurn me for this limp hag of yours. I will eat her and then we can be happy together."

With a roar, she rushed at Sita. Just in time, Rama sprang up and caught her. Quick as thinking, Lakshmana drew his sword and cut off her ears and her nose, so dark blood spouted from her. Screaming in shock, a demoness again, Surpanaka fled into the forest. The brothers dissolved in mirth. But Sita trembled. Though she said nothing of it, she had a powerful premonition of evil: as if, already, upon a distant throne she sensed a malevolent emperor, a terrible Being who turned his baleful gaze on them across vast spaces.

Howling like a storm, Surpanaka fled through the Dandaka vana. Birds and beasts scattered at her passage. Clutching her face she went, roaring and shrieking; while blood gushed through her claws and splashed onto her thick feet. Through the dim jungle she flew, all the way to Janasthana, the city of rakshasas. She fell in a heap before her cousin Khara, demon king of the forest.

When he saw what had happened to her, Khara roared louder than she did. Like some great serpent, he hissed, "Who has done this to you? Who courts his death so fondly? Who has tied a noose around his own neck? I will drink his blood today, and vultures and kites shall have his carcass to feed on. Tell me, Surpanaka, which Deva or Daitya has been such a fool?"

Surpanaka sobbed inconsolably for a while. Servants washed her wounds and stopped the flow of blood with poultices of herbs and leaves. Then, her green eyes flashing, she said, "Haven't you heard of the three strangers who live in Panchavati?" Her face grew dreamy. "Two are princes, handsome as if all the nobility of kshatriya kind has been gathered just in them. Their limbs are strong and graceful; their eyes are long as lotus petals. Their skins are bronzed, as if they have lived in the open for many years. They wear valkala and jata, like rishis, but say they are sons of Dasaratha of Ayodhya. Oh Khara, they are as enchanting as gandharvas. They have wonderful weapons with them and seem to be great archers. They are called Rama and Lakshmana."

Her face grew dark; a spasm of hatred twisted her coarse features. "Then, there is *she*. She wears no bark, but fine silks and ornaments not of the earth: diamonds and rubies the like of which I have never seen. Because of her, the friendly princes maimed me. Help me, Khara: I want to drink their blood!"

Khara sent for fourteen of his fiercest rakshasas. He said to them, "Go to Panchavati and kill the three humans you find there. Surpanaka wants to drink their blood."

With Surpanaka showing them the way, these rakshasas went to Rama's asrama. They came like rain clouds chased by the wind. When Rama saw them, he said softly to Lakshmana, "Watch Sita. It seems I have a battle to fight."

Fitting an arrow to his bow, he stood waiting. Rama hailed the rakshasas: "Why do you come armed with tridents and swords? We are kshatriyas living here in peace. We wish no one any harm."

The rakshasas leered, "We have come to drink your blood and have your woman."

Rama said, "I have heard the rishis of the jungle have no peace because of you. Look, here is the bow of Varuna raised against you. If you value your lives, fly!"

He stamped his foot as if he were chasing away some dogs. But those mountainous rakshasas roared like thunder. They rushed at the prince, casting their trisulas at him. He was so quick none of them saw Rama's hands move; but they saw his arrows smash their tridents in shards. Next moment, they themselves lay dead, their bodies turning to ashes with the heat of the serpentine narachas with which he had shot them. For a bowman like Rama, this was child's play.

Surpanaka stood open-mouthed at his archery. He smiled at her and playfully raised his bow again. With a shriek, she fled back to Khara. She said nothing to him at first, only sobbed incoherently.

Her abominable cousin growled, "Now what is it, Surpanaka? I sent my men to avenge you. What else do you want?"

Surpanaka managed, "There is a new pool in Panchavati: of your rakshasas' blood." She shivered. "I did not see Rama bend his bow or hear our men scream. One instant they rushed at him; the next, they lay dead with his arrows buried in them to their feathers."

Khara stared at her disbelievingly. Surpanaka hissed, "If Ravana or Kumbhakarna had been here, they would not let this pass. Are you afraid, you disgrace to our family? Khara, you are not fit to rule. Terrified of two humans: how Ravana would laugh if he heard this."

Khara's roar shook the jungle. "Don't taunt me, woman. Who says I am afraid? I only waited for my rage to break its shores like the sea in a storm. Come, show me these human worms, that I can send them to their ancestors in the sky."

Surpanaka fawned on him, taking back what she had said to provoke him, praising his valor now. Khara summoned his brother Dushana, who was also his general. "Let a thousand men march for each one this Rama killed. Fetch my chariot; we leave at once."

Ravana's cousin Khara was a splendid rakshasa. His golden chariot drew up, laden with an array of deadly weapons. His army of demons, short and tall, handsome and ugly, some straight and some twisted, flowed around their king like a weird sea. They cried out in fell voices, stamped their feet, and waved their swords and spears, bows and tridents in the air.

Khara of the rakshasas came forth from Janasthana with his formidable legion seething around him: a tide of darkness. But evil omens beset his going. A scarlet cloud appeared above them and a ghastly drizzle of blood fell on the demon force. The leading horse of the complement that drew Khara's chariot stumbled and broke its leg. When the anxious rakshasas looked into the sky, they saw the sun had a rim of darkness around it. A vulture flapped out of nowhere and perched on the flag above Khara's wooden castle.

His men began to whisper among themselves. But Khara stood up, tall and fierce in his chariot, and roared, "I am not moved by these vagaries of nature. Only the weak pay them any heed. I am Khara of the rakshasas, master race of the world. My men are the greatest warriors on earth and we will take death to the arrogant kshatriyas. Indra and his Devas dare not face us; what then of these human princes? Come, let me hear you roar when we march into battle!"

The emboldened rakshasas roared Khara's name. What indeed could two humans do against the fighting demons of Janasthana?

The celestial rishis, the Devas, gandharvas, siddhas, and charanas:

all the immortal ones gathered in the sky above Panchavati to watch the battle between Rama and the legion of night.

They said among themselves, "Narayana has incarnated himself to rid the earth of rakshasas. There will be great bloodshed today."

"It is his first battle against evil on such a scale."

"Lakshmana is with him."

"Rama is the sleeper on the waters. What can a band of jungle rakshasas do against him?"

"You forget Khara is Pulastya's grandson."

Pulastya was one of the original Saptarishi, the seven sages Brahma created in the beginning from his mind.

"Rama was not born to be killed by the likes of Khara. One day he will stand against Ravana of Lanka, and then dharma and adharma will be tested against each other on earth."

Khara drew near Panchavati. At the heart of his force, twelve ferocious demons ringed him round in their chariots. Enormous Mahakapala, Sthulaksha, Pramathi, and Trisiras rode behind the legion, and Dushana rode at its head. Like a horde of malefic planets came the rakshasa army, as if to harry the sun and the moon.

Rama saw the omens of the sky, the birds that flew in alarm before Khara. He saw the ring round the sun and the crimson cloud above; Varuna's bow hummed impatiently in his hands. Rama cried to Lakshmana, "My right hand throbs; my arrows are smoking in their quiver. I feel as I did when Parasurama stood before me. But we must be careful, Lakshmana, and today I must deprive you of the pleasure of battle. Take Sita up to the cave on the hillside; we must be on our guard against Surpanaka."

Rama watched them leave. He strapped on his armor, light as the breeze. As he strung his bow, the power of that weapon surged through him. His astras hot in their quiver, Rama stood like Siva before he razed Daksha's yagna.

Khara arrived in Panchavati. He halted his legion and, with a horrible roar, the rakshasas attacked. Like rays of the sun, the demons' arrows, tridents, and javelins covered the sky. They fell on Rama like lightning. The prince was struck but never wounded, because his thin kavacha was magical. Then he replied. His arms were a blur, so even the Devas and rishis above could not see them. Like mortal thoughts his arrows flared at the rakshasas and they fell in swarms, hardly knowing how they died.

Rama strung his bow with astras: nalika, naracha, and vikarni blazed starfire at the shocked demons. They could not bear the fear those missiles brought and fled back to Khara, some of them screaming, others whimpering like children.

Astounded by Rama's valor, Khara rallied his people and advanced himself. Collecting their scattered courage, teeming around their king, the rakshasas charged Rama again. But quick as wishes, he drew a gandharvastra from his quiver and, chanting its mantra, shot it at the demon army. The rakshasas saw a blinding fireball flare at them through the sky. The unearthly weapon broke, whistling, among them. The astra separated into a thousand arrows of fire and light; Rama's shafts filled the quarters. They turned into serpents with heads of flames and fell on the howling demons: one shaft for each rakshasa. And not an arrow but it took a life, consuming the fiend it struck, making ashes of him.

Sudden desolation overtook Khara's army. Then Dushana plunged out of the ranks like streak lightning in his black chariot. His fangs were bared; myriad sorceries flashed around him to show he was a rakshasa with great powers of maya. Dushana's demons, the occult phalanx of Khara's army, rushed at Rama. They cast their spells at him: flaming trees, rocks that exploded over his head, disgorging a thousand other sorceries, and fire-spitting serpents.

Dushana barely saw Rama raise his bow, or the four arrows that flew at him in the heart of an instant. They cut down his chariot horses. Another blinding shaft killed his charioteer; three more pierced his armor, hurling agony through his blood. Roaring in shock, Dushana raised his mace and rushed at Rama. But so calmly, that prince cut off the rakshasa's arms with two crescent-tipped arrows and slew him with another through his heart.

The rakshasas who remained alive stood frozen around Khara. How could one man fight like this? Like two armies. Rama shot two more astras at Khara's legions. The monster's soldiers all perished, like little mountains felled by Indra's vajra of a thousand joints. At last just Khara and his three-headed, loathsome, and completely fearless commander, Trisiras, were left alive amidst the smoking ruin of his army of fourteen thousand.

Speechless, Khara mourned his brother Dushana. Trisiras cried, "Leave the kshatriya to me. I will drink his blood today!"

Roaring from three mouths on three grotesque heads, Trisiras flew at Rama. He too was a mayavi, a sorcerer, and he struck the prince with three arrows, complex and quick as sunbeams. Rama could not cut them down; at the last moment, he made them harmless with a mantra. Yet they stung him, and he cried, "Rakshasa, you have struck me thrice. No ordinary archer could do this."

Fourteen arrows, deep as time, flew in formation from Rama's bow. They pierced the hearts of the rakshasa's horses and flew on up. They cut down the banner on his chariot, killed his charioteer, and finally they crashed into Trisiras's chest, so his six eyes bulged round. He rose screeching from the wreckage of his ratha and Rama cut his heads from his swollen body with three more lightlike shafts. The demon's blood flowed across Panchavati in three black rills while his heads rolled down the hillside.

Roaring louder than ever to keep his own courage up, Khara, king of the jungle, came to fight. He was even more of an archer than Trisiras and a fair battle broke out. The Devas above sighed, when from his whirlwind chariot Khara split Varuna's bow in Rama's hand. Rama seized up the Brahmadatta, and its jewels radiated shafts of fear into the rakshasa's heart. Now Rama's arrows sang as they flamed at the demon king. But Khara was a worthy adversary; it was true that Indra himself would have hesitated to fight him.

In the heat of battle, crimson-eyed Rama cried, "Serpent of the jungle, all your sins have borne fruit today. Prepare to die."

But Khara roared back, "You crow because you killed a handful of common soldiers. But I am Khara, your death, and this mace in my hand will send you to Yama. Bid farewell to your life, princeling; I mean to drink your blood before the sun sets. Only then will I sleep in peace tonight."

His dark mace raised aloft, he flew at Rama. But Rama shattered that dire weapon with a single shaft. He cried to the bewildered rakshasa, "Sleep you will, Khara: upon the earth as you would in the arms of a woman you have long desired. And the rishis of the Dandaka vana will roam the jungle in freedom again."

With maya, Khara grew tall as a hill. He pulled up a sala tree by its roots and flung it at Rama. But the prince dodged it nimbly and struck the rakshasa with twenty sizzling arrows, so he screamed and tore them out of his flesh like poison thorns. Rama stepped back, for the demon ran at him again with his bare hands. He strung the Brahmadatta with an aindrastra. Invoking the king of the Devas, he shot Khara through his chest with that final weapon.

One moment, the rakshasa rushed at Rama with his claws outstretched to seize his throat; the next, he screamed as the astra struck him and his flesh fell away from his skeleton in anxiety to escape the intolerable pain of that missile. His heart exploded, then his giant head, and nothing was left of Khara but patches of blood, skin, and a heap of bones on the ground.

This triumph of the Avatara was beyond the wildest hopes of the Devas, who rained down shimmering petals like fireflies on Rama. The sky was full of gandharvas' songs, and dancing apsaras cast their shadows on saffron clouds above the sunset. Rama looked around him and saw the ground strewn with the corpses of the rakshasas and their elephants and horses, as plentifully as a yagnashala is with darbha grass. He sighed and, suddenly exhausted, sat down among the dead.

Their faces shining, Lakshmana and Sita emerged from their cave. Sita ran to Rama and flung her arms around him. Lakshmana fetched water from the river and, with equal love, his brother and his wife bathed his wounds.

Again and again Sita would embrace her husband. Her eyes were full of tears: of sorrow to see his injuries and of excitement at his dazzling victory.

10. In Lanka

There was a rakshasa called Akampana who was part of Khara's army. He hid himself, out of sight, and escaped Rama's arrows. Akampana headed straight for Lanka in his chariot that flew through the air. He arrived at the massive palace gates of the Sovereign of evil.

Within the doors of that magnificent palace, in a splendid sabha at its heart, was a black crystal throne encrusted with priceless jewels that were tribute paid by royal vassals throughout the three worlds. Upon this throne sat the Master of darkness. In a weird cone upon his neck were ten heads of varying features and sizes, all of them savage. Ravana was a monster, the most sinister and powerful rakshasa. Nothing about him was ordinary; all his ten heads thought for him, and his intelligence and knowledge were unrivaled in heaven or earth. He was the grandson of Brahma's son, Pulastya Muni: thus the Creator's own great-grandson. And he had Siva's blessing.

Ravana was thousands of years old. But he was a tapasvin; so he did not look even a small part of his true age. He kept women of every race, the most beautiful and seductive women from all the realms. He was an expert of the arcane tantra vidya, and they helplessly gave him their youth in his bed. Often the virgin who spent just a week with him emerged from his harem looking ten years older than when she had been brought to the Rakshasa. He was insatiable, and his love-making was a diabolic ritual: he drained a woman of her precious years, of her very destiny.

Ravana was an awesome monarch. His instinct ranged over his domains as the sun does over the earth. Within his ten satanic heads, he sensed all that happened throughout his empire. What he did not sense, where goodness and dharma raised their hated visage, his servants, to whom he entrusted dominion in his dreaded name, reported to him. And at once Ravana dispatched some venal or murderous agent to subvert or suppress it without mercy. His was a complex kingdom and he ruled over it by his own lights, his own dark wisdom.

Today his side throbbed and three of his heads ached relentlessly since morning. The Demon knew bad news was on its way, even before Akampana burst into his presence and fell sobbing at his feet. Ravana sighed like a ravine full of the wind. He spoke from the mouth on his central face, the one with the coppery eyes. He said sonorously, "Tell me, Akampana, what news of my cousins and my sister?"

The rakshasa from Janasthana stood trembling that he, who brought news as bad as his, could meet a swift death. Ravana said again, "Have no fear, Akampana; you know you can tell me anything." Cajoling he sounded, almost gentle.

Akampana stared down at his feet. He drew a breath and said in a whisper, "My lord, all the rakshasas in Janasthana are dead. Khara is dead and Dushana; Trisiras is slain."

Deep in all Ravana's eyes, there was a flicker, as if some unimaginable serpent had stirred from its slumber in his heart. The smile did not leave his frontal face, though the others grew grim. In the same cajoling tone, still casually, he asked, "Akampana, who did this thing?"

Akampana thought Ravana had taken the news very well. He said, "I escaped in my chariot, Lord."

Ravana's eyes blazed briefly. "Who did it?"

"A man, Lord."

"But I heard of no army that came to Janasthana."

Akampana said nothing; he did not know where to look. Ravana said quietly, reasonably, "Whoever they are, don't they realize there is no escape for them? Not in Devaloka, because Indra fears me. Not with Kubera, Varuna, or Agni shall they find sanctuary; bold though they must surely be and gifted, to have razed Khara's army. I will find them, Akampana, and I will bring them here to Lanka."

Not even Akampana liked to think what his master did with those he brought to the dungeons of Lanka. Akampana said softly, "Not them, Lord. Him."

"What do you mean?" whispered Ravana, all his ten heads swiveling round to stare at his demon. Those heads were like an inverted bunch of macabre fruit. The one at the very top was the smallest and the most vicious; it was entirely puerile and malignant.

Akampana's voice rattled in his throat at the awful regard. Looking anywhere but at Ravana, he breathed, "One man killed them all."

A roar began on the littlest, purely demoniacal face. Then the ten heads roared together, last of all the central one around which the others budded. The palace shook; the king's guards came running to his door, though none dared enter. Akampana thought his end had come. The ten faces now spoke together, as they did when the Rakshasa was out of control.

In ten voices Ravana cried, "You say one human killed Khara, Dushana, Trisiras, and all the army at Janasthana? Are you sure you haven't been drinking cane liquor all morning, Akampana?"

Akampana swallowed; he shivered at the change in his Emperor. But he managed to say again, "One man, Lord of the worlds. Just one man with his bow and arrows."

Ravana stared from all his eyes, the heads cocked at many quizzical angles. He stared in disbelief at Akampana, who raised his hands to shield himself from that gaze.

He cried, "I beg you, listen to me, Lord." The devilish heads grew attentive. "There was once a king called Dasaratha. He belonged to the race of Surya, to the royal House of Ikshvaku. He has a son called Rama, who is as blue as a wild lotus. Rama came to the Dandaka vana. His shoulders are wide as a bison's and he is as strong as a lion. He is a master of astras, and he killed the rakshasas of Janasthana."

"Perhaps Indra sent a host to help him? Let us have the truth, rakshasa."

"I thought of Indra when I saw Rama's archery. But no, Indra did not come to help Rama. His astras were a thousand arrows each, and each shaft turned into a five-headed, fire-mouthed serpent. Janasthana is a desolation. Those of us who survived, the handful who fled, have no sleep any more, for Rama's face haunts our dreams. I believe he has a brother called Lakshmana, who is his equal. But he took no part in the battle."

Ravana sighed like the north wind on the mountaintop. His lips curled; fangs flashed at the corners of his mouths. He rose and crossed to his bay window, which looked out over the turquoise sea.

He said softly, "I will go to Janasthana myself to kill these brothers."

"Oh no! Before you do anything in haste, listen to what I have heard about this Rama. He can hold up a river with his arrows. They say that if he wants he can extinguish the sun and the stars with his astras. He can raise the earth out of the sea, if it is submerged, or plunge it into the deeps by breaking the bounds of the world. All the rishis say that he is Vishnu come as a man. He shone like a God when he stood facing our army. He was a blue sun, and he killed fourteen thousand rakshasas as if they were small children before him."

Akampana had been thinking feverishly on his way to Lanka, to save his skin as the bearer of the news he brought. Ravana was about to speak; but he saw the light of an idea in his rakshasa's eye.

"Finish what you were saying, Akampana."

"It would be foolish, my lord, to engage Rama in a duel, for you could not be certain of the outcome. But there is another way." He paused, and saw he had his master's interest. "Rama has a wife called Sita, who followed him into the forest. She is exquisite. He loves her more than his own life, and she, him; they are like prana to each other."

Ravana's topmost head hissed, "So what? What are you trying to say?"

Surer of himself now, Akampana continued at his ease. "She is the most beautiful woman in the world, Ravana. The apsaras of Devaloka cannot compare with her. Her face is perfect; her body is a vision."

"Say what you have to quickly, fool," said the Monster of Lanka.

Akampana blurted, "If you were to abduct Sita and bring her here secretly, Rama would die pining for her!"

The nine heads mulled over this, whispering sibilantly among themselves. Then in surreal chorus, they grinned, horribly and all together. They bobbed up and down, endorsing Akampana's idea, delighted with it. Ravana's main face smiled, showing four rows of fangs. "I like your plan. Tomorrow at sunrise, I will fly to the Dandaka vana myself to bring Sita back to Lanka."

Akampana bowed deeply and left the presence without turning his back on his Emperor. Ravana stood at his window for a long time, staring across sullen green waves. Then he turned back to his duties and pleasures of the day, and to his endless study. The Rakshasa was a profound scholar.

He retired early that night and he ordered no woman to come to him. He soon fell asleep, the eyes in all his heads shut fast.

The next morning, before the sun rose, Ravana sat in the strangest chariot. This ratha was made of gold, alloyed with a starry metal, and four horned mules were yoked to it. They were green creatures of sorcery and flew through the sky quick as thoughts, at their master's command.

When Ravana was ready, his chariot rose into the air. It hovered there, swathed in eerie luster, as the sun crept up behind the palace. The Demon raised a hand to wave to his rakshasas below. Next moment, the chariot vanished from sight.

Ravana flew across the sea of Bharatavarsha. He flashed across the plateau of the southern peninsula, over field and forest, mountain and river. He slowed his flying mules over a jungle below him that was his destination. He peered down to find the hermitage for which he was bound. Quite soon, he spotted Maricha's asrama: its wood fire's smoke curled into the sky. With a command that was just a potent thought, Ravana flew down smoothly as a bird and alighted in the glade where the rakshasa Maricha, now turned a rishi, sat in dhyana. It was the same Maricha whom Rama had once doused in the sea with the manavastra. Maricha was Ravana's uncle.

He gave a cry of welcome when he saw who had come to visit him. Quickly he laid out a darbhasana for the Emperor and set a bowl of fruit before him. Maricha was older than he, and Ravana paid proper, if somewhat hollow, obeisance to him before he settled into the grass throne.

Maricha blessed him and said, "What a pleasant surprise, nephew. Something important must bring you to my asrama. Tell me, what has happened?"

Ravana looked away from Maricha. He gazed at his humble hut; he gazed at the tree under which it was built, on which the wildflower garlands of worship hung. He took his time to begin, then said, "Uncle, did you know that all my rakshasas in Janasthana have been killed? Khara, Dushana, and all the rest. The entire army has been razed." He drew a talon eloquently across his throat. "In a day."

Maricha's eyes grew round. "How? When Khara led the army, how?"

Studying his dark, brutal hands, Ravana said quietly, "One man killed them all." He paused. Then, rolling the words on his tongue as if to see if they would conjure any magic, he said slowly, "A kshatriya. A Rama."

Maricha drew a sharp breath; his hair stood on end. He held up his hands and cried, "Don't say that name!"

Ignoring him, Ravana continued, "Obviously the human is powerful; such power is a threat to me." He took up a blade of darbha grass and began to pick his fangs. "This Rama must be killed. But we think he is too dangerous to face in battle."

Maricha, who had experience of Rama, nodded his head several times in assent.

Ravana continued, "We think his wife should be taken in secret to Lanka, without Rama knowing where she has gone. We know noble hearts like his; he will pine for her and die. Or he will think her dead and kill himself to join her in the next world. I need your help, Maricha."

But Maricha gave a moan. To his surprise, Ravana saw the old rakshasa's hands shook and his face was filmed in a sweat of fear. Struggling to compose himself, Maricha cried, "Whoever set you on this course is your enemy and wants to see you dead. Is one of your advisers trying to kill you? You would be mad even to think of it. This same Rama once shot me a thousand yojanas into the sea; and you find no one else to abduct but Rama's wife!"

Maricha breathed heavily; his eyes bulged in anxiety. "Ravana, you are the Lord of all the rakshasas and someone is envious of you. He is trying to have you killed. Rama will finish you if you go near him. He is like a sleeping lion. Only a fool will thrust his head into the lion's jaws and then awaken him.

"You are my nephew. I am your well-wisher and I want nothing from you. Return to Lanka, to your women. Forget you ever heard the name Sita. Go, Ravana; don't invite your death to you."

Ravana listened calmly. He was unmoved by the descriptions of Rama's prowess, unmoved even by Maricha's obvious fear. But he respected Maricha almost as a guru, and he had never heard him speak of anyone else as he did of Rama. Since there were such conflicting opinions about abducting Sita, he decided to let caution prevail.

Ravana said, "Very well, uncle; if you feel so strongly I will not take Sita. Though it rankles that a mere man treats us as this Rama has, and I have no fitting response for him. But no matter; there is no hurry. I am sure the chance will present itself one day, and I will crush this prince like an insect under my nail."

All his heads glowered at the thought. Ravana flew back to Lanka in his mule chariot.

11. Surpanaka again

A few days later, a more relaxed Ravana sat on his crystal throne, worked also with huge pearls and blood-red corals from the sea. He had another visitor, who changed that Emperor's mind again.

For days after the slaughter of the rakshasas of Janasthana, Surpanaka lived alone in the deserted city. The ghosts of the dead haunted her, wailing at her for revenge: after all, it was in trying to avenge the injury to her that they had died. She spent those days and their nights as inside a nightmare. Over and over again she saw Rama's face. She saw his smoking astras, and she heard the screams of the rakshasas she had led to their deaths. She dared not sleep any more except when she fell into an exhausted swoon.

If one of her brothers had been with her, he would have told her the fault was not hers. But here she was, alone in the midst of the Dandaka vana, and every leaf that stirred in the breeze reminded her of her guilt. At last she could not bear it any longer, the hallucinatory loneliness, and the wounds where Lakshmana had cut off her ears and nose still smarted fiercely. They were ill healed, with no one to minister to them, since all her rakshasis had fled.

In despair, she decided to go to her brother in Lanka. She arrived with witchcraft, having flown limply over the sea.

Let no one who speaks of Ravana forget his greatness. True, he was evil, none as evil as him, but he was magnificent as well. In fact, such was the greatness of Ravana that no other king on any world could hold a candle to him.

He sat upon his throne like fire in a crystal shrine. He was a master not only of darkness, but also of knowledge, classical and hermetic. Ravana sat bare-bodied in his splendid court, and his mighty chest bore the circular scar where, once, Indra's elephant Airavata had gored him. Another emblazoned wound showed where Indra's vajra had burned him. But Ravana was not killed by tusk or thunderbolt, which no other warrior had ever survived. Indra had fled when the adamantine vajra came back to him without claiming the Demon's life.

Despite the inverted cluster of heads, and of these just the topmost was purely evil, Ravana was handsome, as rakshasas are, and manly. Women felt faint when they saw him. Of course, he never hesitated to take any woman who caught his fancy, regardless of whose wife, sister, or daughter she was. What Ravana wanted, he invariably had.

He was a master of astras, and a favorite of Siva's. He had a boon of unequaled strength and a sword of power from Siva; with these he had established dominion over the three worlds.

On his way to the triune sovereignty, he had descended into the Patalas and vanquished Vasuki, Emperor of the nagas. He had then quelled his own half-brother, Kubera, Master of treasures upon the mountain, for lordship over the earth. The Rakshasa wreaked havoc in Kubera's pleasure garden, the Chaitra, molesting his yaksha women and plundering as much gold and as many jewels as he liked. From Kubera, Ravana also took the incomparable pushpaka vimana. This was not the mule chariot, but a wonderful ship of the firmament.

Finally, he attacked Indra in Devaloka and defeated the Ones of light. They also now paid him tribute: wealth and horses, elephants and women. The elemental Gods were his vassals. The sun shone softly for him, the moon never waned over his island. The wind blew gently on Lanka and the sea never dared rise there, for fear of Ravana.

But the Rakshasa had his greatest blessing from his grandsire Brahma: that he could not be killed by a Deva of the sky, a gandharva, a charana, Asura, Daitya, Danava, pisacha, rakshasa; or by any among the immortal races of darkness or light. But thinking them too puny, he had not asked for invincibility against mortal men. After all, he was Ravana, who had once lifted Kailasa in his hands to please Lord Siva. Holding the mountain aloft, accompanying himself on the vina, he sang the Sama Veda as no one had sung it before.

One should never discount the majesty of Ravana of Lanka. Evil he was, but he was also the greatest of all the created beings of his time. He had dominated the known universe for centuries, and even Deva women felt weak with desire just to see him. He was matchless at arms, in his generosity, in his intelligence and knowledge of the sacred lore, and in his indomitable courage. He was Ravana, the peerless, the invincible. There was no one like him, as complex, as powerful, or as wise, save the great Gods of the Trinity themselves. But let us not forget he was evil as well: a Beast of the night.

Ravana hardly recognized his sister when she stood fuming before him. She had no nose or ears, and her face was so much older. Her hair had turned gray in a week; her voice was different, sadder. If he knew her by anything, it was by the fire in her eyes. She stood with her hands on her hips, glowering at her brother.

She said shrilly, "You call yourself an emperor. You say Indra is your vassal. But you are only an emperor of your harem, since you don't seem to know anything that goes on beyond its doors. Ravana, you have grown arrogant and complacent. Janasthana is razed, everyone who lived there is a moldering corpse; and you sit here indulging yourself. Rakshasa, you are not fit to rule!"

Ravana said nothing. He let her vent her anger. She cried, "Do you know, O Emperor, what force razed the might of Janasthana as if it never existed? A man: one man, a Rama."

Ravana said quietly, "Tell me about him."

Surpanaka thought bitterly about the prince, his dark face and his mocking smile. Yet her expression grew wistful when she remembered him.

She sighed, "He is the son of King Dasaratha, who sent him to the Dandaka vana. His arms are long and so are his eyes. He is as handsome as Kama Deva. He wears valkala, and his hair piled above his beautiful face in jata. He wielded a bow that was not made in this world. He shot astras called narachas that burned our soldiers to ashes.

"I did not see him bend his bow or draw back its string. I only saw his arrows scorch the sky in a livid storm. And fourteen thousand rakshasas were cut down in a muhurta and a half. Khara was among those fourteen thousand, and Dushana and Trisiras. It was no army of weaklings that Rama wilted as if it were a field of green plants.

"He let me escape because I am a woman; but look what his brother did to me. Lakshmana is just a fair version of him; he is as powerful as Rama. I could tell by the weapons he carried and the speed with which he ruined my face. They are not just two men when they fight; they are two armies by themselves."

Another memory stirred in her. Her eyes glittered more than ever. "With them, also, is Rama's wife, Sita. She is Janaka of Videha's daughter and, oh, she is beautiful. Her hair hangs below her waist. Her nose is fine, and her body is lissom and perfect. Her skin is golden and I have never seen another woman like her. Hers is the beauty by which all other beauty may be measured.

"Ravana, you have had the apsaras of Devaloka in your bed, the slender gandharvis and yakshis of night who live in scented pala trees. But you have not seen Sita. She makes the charms of these others seem like stars twinkling vainly beside a full moon."

She knew her brother well, especially his weakness. Surpanaka leaned close to him and breathed, "She is the woman for you! She belongs in your bed. I tried to capture her for you; that was when Lakshmana cut my face. If you don't believe me, go and look at her just once. Then tell me if you don't lose your heart. She was born for you; your destiny is calling you, Ravana. Go and kill the arrogant kshatriyas, and bring Sita back to Lanka to adorn your harem and your life."

She saw the gleam in his eyes and knew she had aroused his desire. Surpanaka fell silent and, whimpering, gingerly felt her wounds. Ravana clapped his hands; he nodded to his court that it was dismissed.

12. Maricha persuaded

Ravana sat alone in his court. Light from the sea and the sky streamed in on him through the tall bay windows. Before his mind's eye there floated a face conjured by Surpanaka, which seemed to call out to him with unearthly perfection. Below the face he saw flawless limbs, like none he had ever caressed.

He sat thinking only of how he could possess the woman of his dreams: Sita, whom he had not even seen, but who already haunted him inexorably. Plan after plan rose in his ten heads, some absurd, some almost plausible. Plan after plan he rejected, in a spirit of complete solemnity. Ravana had decided he must have Sita: not only for revenge, but also for the pleasure of his bed.

After what he knew the kshatriya had done to Khara and the others, Ravana was not rash enough to confront Rama. Despite what Surpanaka said, the Rakshasa was neither complacent nor foolish. Rama was a dangerous enemy; he must be stalked cautiously. Ravana sat lost in thought for a while. Then he rose, strode out to his stables, and ordered his flying chariot to be yoked to the uncanny mules.

Over the smoky sea flew the Demon, bright as a jewel in the sky. His white silks flapped around him; his golden earrings shone in the sun. He was still deep in thought: he wanted to approach the one whose asrama he was headed for in just the right tone. The Lord of Lanka was bound, again, for his uncle Maricha's hermitage.

Ravana sat perfectly still in his chariot, unmoved by picturesque Bharatavarsha unfolding below him. Painted forests and flowing plains, rivers like silver threads laid across the earth and mountains thrusting up: all these he ignored. His thoughts were his masters, and they were far away. He wrapped himself against the wind and sat dreaming in the chariot, and scheming. At last he saw the Dandaka vana. As he flew low, shrouded in maya so he was invisible, he saw the giant nyagrodha tree on the branches of which Jatayu sat when Rama first saw him.

Maricha's asrama was not far. When that hermit rakshasa saw Ravana's chariot descending on him from the clear sky he trembled. Maricha guessed what must be on his nephew's mind that he had returned. But he was afraid of Ravana, and went to welcome him with a smile on his face.

With fruit, dark mushrooms, and soft venison, Maricha entertained his royal guest. When Ravana had settled himself comfortably and eaten two ripe red mangoes in silence, Maricha said, "I hope all is well in Lanka. The queens of my lord?"

Ravana gazed at him briefly. As was their way, nine of his faces were now hidden. But the inscrutable eyes of the main face were turned unwinkingly on poor Maricha. He blanched and offered his terrible guest more fruit. But Ravana declined, thrusting the bowl away with the back of his long hand.

At last, he said with a sigh, "Uncle, I have no peace of mind and I have come to you for comfort. A word from you is balm to my distress."

Maricha betrayed nothing of his thoughts. "Tell me, my king, what troubles you?"

"Oh, I am suffering, Maricha, and only you can console me. Surpanaka came to Lanka today. The prince who killed Khara had her nose and ears cut off. Not one or two of our people were slain by this Rama, but fourteen thousand. He is certainly a great archer. But just think, uncle: he must be a great sinner as well, that his father banished such a warrior from his kingdom.

"Now, in exile, he has crossed my path. He is a blot on the face of kshatriya kind and he must die. For no reason, he maimed my sister; then he murdered fourteen thousand of my best rakshasas and my cousin Khara. Maricha, I am a king. I cannot ignore such provocation or my people will lose respect for me."

Maricha thought, "Better that than lose your life." But he said nothing, only waited in silence to hear what his Emperor intended by way of revenge.

Ravana resumed softly, "He is evil, this Rama, and powerful. The only way to kill him is to take his wife away from him, so he does not know where she has gone."

Maricha's heart gave a lurch. Ravana saw fear leap into his demon's eye and ignored it. "Uncle, you must help me. With you at my side, I do not fear even the Devas. You are wise and gifted beyond anyone's common understanding. You are my hope in this enterprise; listen to my plan."

Maricha's hands shook; he had broken out in a sweat. It seemed to him his life was forfeit, any way he viewed his predicament. If he did not go along with Ravana, the Rakshasa would kill him; if he did, Rama would. Maricha shivered with strange cold this warm afternoon. He nodded numbly to Ravana, to indicate he would listen to his plan.

Ravana said, "Uncle, master of maya, turn yourself into a golden deer. If Sita sees you at Panchavati, she will ask Rama and Lakshmana to capture the creature for her. With all your guile, Maricha, lead the two princes far from the asrama and from Sita. And as Rahu does the light of the moon, I will seize her, and fly with her to Lanka.

"Rama's heart will break and he will become easy prey for me. I will avenge my cousins, my sister, and my dead fourteen thousand."

Not a word that, just hearing about her, he wanted Sita for his bed. But Maricha guessed as surely as if Ravana had confessed his lust. Maricha's mouth was dry. He licked his lips and stood goggling at Ravana as if his eyelids had lost their power to blink. At last he said slowly, "Ravana, nephew, you said you needed comfort because your heart was troubled. You have come to the right person. Now listen to me." He folded his hands to Ravana. "You are an emperor, and fawning courtiers surround you. They are not sincere. They will say anything to please you, even if their counsel leads you to your death. Of old it has been said that it is rare indeed to find an honest and blunt counselor, who truly cares for his sovereign. It is rarer still to find a king who listens to such an adviser.

"Ravana, your spies have been asleep, basking in your glory, believing you are invincible. Or surely you would have heard of Rama much earlier, and you might have prevented the slaughter of Khara and the fourteen thousand. Rama is more powerful than Indra or Varuna. He came to rid the jungle of our people. His work is done, and if you leave him alone, he will return peacefully to Ayodhya.

"This prince is no adharmi. No evil sits upon his heart; no sin stains his spirit that he will be easy to kill. He came to the jungle to keep his father's honor; he came forsaking a throne that was his for the taking. Rama is an embodiment of dharma. If you kidnap his wife, you might as well leap into a fire and save him the trouble of killing you: which, Ravana, he surely will.

"Go home to Lanka. Ask Vibheeshana's advice and you will find he says exactly as I do. I want to save you from death, Ravana. Listen to me. Don't be swayed by the moment's passion; take heed for your future."

Ravana said nothing, but stared calmly at Maricha, so that rakshasa said, "Once I lived in the northern forests at the feet of the Himalaya. What days those were. I was as strong as a thousand elephants, and we ate hermits' flesh, and ruined every sacrifice in the forest. For years, Viswamitra tried to perform a yagna in that vana. But each time it neared completion, Subahu and I would desecrate it.

"One day, we attacked the yagnashala where Viswamitra sat chanting the Vedas. With filth we went: blood, excrement, and rotten meat to cast at the holy fire. Suddenly I saw a young man, handsome as the moon, who stood guard over Viswamitra's yagna. He was no more than sixteen summers old, tender, and innocence was upon his face. For a moment I was arrested by his sheer beauty. Then, roaring, I hurled my filth at the agni.

"I scarcely saw that youth fit his arrow to his bow, and, Ravana, I was lifted from the ground and carried into the sky. My body and soul on fire, I was borne a thousand leagues by the astra with which he shot me, and flung into the sea. That was Rama. He was only a boy then, a stripling."

Maricha paused, his chest heaving. He prayed fervently that Ravana would be convinced. How could he explain Rama's prowess to his king? "You know your sister as well as I do," he continued. "I am sure she provoked the brothers, that they cut off her nose and ears. She must have taunted Khara into attacking Rama. Then what choice did the prince have, except to defend himself? I speak to you from my heart, as not merely my king but my nephew. Be guided by me, Ravana. You have vanquished many great enemies in battle, but this kshatriya is different. All the wise say he is Vishnu's Avatara."

Maricha fell silent, hoping good sense would dawn on his sovereign. But like one whose evil hour had come, Ravana was impervious to wise counsel. The older rakshasa's words fell by the way, like seeds in a desert.

After a moment's tense silence, Ravana said softly as ever, "I am not afraid, uncle. My mind is made up: Sita must be taken. I did not come to you for your advice but for your help."

His voice had an unpleasant edge to it now. He bared a fang briefly, and Maricha trembled.

Ravana said, "Don't let the freedom I give you as an elder go to your head. Don't forget who I am: obedience, unquestioning obedience to me, Maricha, is your dharma."

Those terrible eyes bored into Maricha's frightened ones. Some of the heads appeared briefly, in a haze, to glare at this insignificant demon that dared thwart Ravana.

Ravana said, "Uncle, be a golden deer with silver speckles for me. Enchant Sita's heart. When I have taken her, I want nothing more from you. Come, we will go in the chariot and arrive quickly."

Maricha still hesitated. Ravana studied his fingernails and said in deadly quiet, "If you value your life, Uncle Maricha, I think you should do as I say."

But in a final burst of courage and good sense, Maricha said, "Someone wants you dead. And it seems you yourself are keen to put an end to all your glory. Ravana, if you do this thing you will die, and doom will come to Lanka. As for me, it is foolish to speak of my freedom: the moment I see Rama again, I will die. He told me as much. But at least if I die at his hands I will find heaven for myself. Ah, Ravana, I see the stubbornness in your eyes and I know you will do as you have decided. This is the last chance you have to save yourself. You seek to embrace the lovely Sita, but you will clasp your death instead."

13. A golden deer

But Ravana was in no mood to pay any attention to Maricha's advice. He wanted to see Sita: to possess her as quickly as he could. Surpanaka had inflamed him well, and he had surrendered his reason to the seductive images that filled his mind. Ravana rose and fingered his sword meaningfully. He said, "Let us go."

He strode out of the asrama. Maricha cast a last sad look at the hermitage that had been his home for so long. He was sure he would never see it again.

Ravana called impatiently over his shoulder, "Hurry up, Maricha; my time is short."

Maricha mumbled to himself, "Ravana, you are the most arrogant and callous rakshasa, and you will lie dead upon the earth very soon, pierced by Rama's arrows."

With a sigh he went out to his determined king. Ravana embraced him. In febrile anticipation of seeing Sita, he cried, "Now you are my obliging uncle again. I will reward you when your task is finished, Maricha. I will reward you beyond your dreams."

They climbed into the chariot and flew like the wind toward Panchavati. The air in the higher reaches froze Maricha's blood, and much too soon for his liking they saw Panchavati from the sky. Ravana grasped his uncle's hand in excitement. He guided the chariot down into some woods near the princes' asrama.

The Emperor of the rakshasas helped Maricha out of the chariot. He whispered, "Now, uncle, change yourself!"

Maricha shut his eyes with a prayer. He focused his maya sakti upon his own body. In a moment he was transformed and a velvet stag stood there, its golden skin twitching. Even Ravana gasped: so graceful, so brilliant and beautiful was that creature. Silver markings shone like stars on its body; it was a treasure alive, with great, limpid eyes, curled antlers, and a delicate gait. Ravana stroked the golden stag's flanks and it quivered beneath his hand. After patting it a few times to quieten it, he slapped the deer sharply on its side and sent it dashing off toward Rama's asrama.

Maricha, the golden stag, came in enchantment to the asrama in Panchavati. Shy, playful, and tremulous, it approached the hermitage. Its skin was molten; its antlers seemed to be made from stalks of diamond and its silver markings glowed like bits of the moon. It pranced there, at times cropping lush grass and at others dancing on quicksilver hooves, as if for the rapture of being alive and being so lovely a creature.

There were other deer around Rama's asrama. The moment they saw this gilded beast they fled, barking in alarm at his smell. Maricha would have loved to sink his fangs into their throats and drink warm blood. But the pleasure was denied him today. Under the karnikara trees encircling the asrama, the golden stag strutted in disdain of those lesser creatures. Even the squirrels chattered down angrily at the predator they smelled clearly under his shimmering hide.

Sita came out of the asrama to gather flowers for her puja. She crossed to the karnikara and asoka trees, and the flowering bushes that grew in their shade. Suddenly the golden deer stepped out from behind a tree. Sita almost dropped her basket. Her eyes were riveted to the bewitching creature. She called to it, as she did to the other deer that frequented the asrama. But this beast appeared not to understand her.

Excitedly, Sita called Rama and Lakshmana. The deer stood quivering, quite near her, then ran a small way off when it saw the princes coming. When Lakshmana saw the golden stag he stopped in his stride, scowling. He said to his brother, "Be careful, Rama, this is no deer. I don't know why, but I feel strangely sure that this is our old friend Maricha."

But Sita cried, "Oh, Rama, just look at this creature. How beautiful he is. I have never wanted anything as I do this deer. He can be a companion for me here, and a wonder when we take him back to Ayodhya. I beg you, take him alive for me."

When Rama saw the deer, he too was bewitched. How could anything so indescribably beautiful be evil? He said to Lakshmana, "Not even Indra's Nandana or Kubera's Chaitra will have a deer like this one. Look at its tongue when it feeds: like a small streak of lightning. I must capture the creature for Sita. Even I am enchanted by it; how she must want it for herself.

"Besides, if it does turn out to be Maricha, I will kill him. But if it is not the rakshasa, then Sita shall have an exquisite pet. She never asks me for anything; I can't refuse her this."

Rama stopped speaking and stood staring at the golden stag. He gazed hard and shook his head as if to clear it.

His mouth was set tightly, and he said, "I think you may be right after all, Lakshmana. There is an evil feeling about this golden deer. The certainty grows on me also that he is Maricha. I will follow the beast, and I think kill it. All my instincts cry out warning: some great danger is very near. Keep your bow in your hand and fit it with an arrow. Watch over Sita as the mothers of the wild do their young. I will be back soon; Sita, be careful."

As if it had understood everything he said, the stag streaked away into the woods. Bow in hand, Rama ran after it. Sita stood waving to him. Rama waved back at her a last time and was lost to view, as he plunged after the golden deer into the thicker forest around Panchavati.

14. The dark mendicant

His sword strapped to his waist, his bow shining in his hand, Rama chased the golden deer through the Dandaka vana. It led him along so cunningly, he grew more and more convinced it was no stag, but an enemy disguised. The deer seemed to realize he would not kill it, until he was sure it was not a deer. It would stop in its tracks, gleaming under the trees of the dim forest. It would let him come quite close; then his heart would soften, seeing what a lovely creature it was, its eyes so soulful. But just as he drew near enough to make a spring and take it, the golden stag would prance away deeper into the forest, even as if it mocked him.

So the chase went on. The deer led Rama farther and farther from the asrama. It tantalized him by vanishing; he thought he had lost it and turned back. Then he glimpsed a flash of gold from behind a tree, like a crack of the moon through dark clouds, and he was off after it again.

An hour of this and Rama was convinced a rakshasa was leading him on this chase. He decided to kill it the next time it showed itself. If it was a creature of maya, as he suspected, an ordinary arrow would not kill the deer; and it would alert the golden thing that he had changed his mind about taking it alive. With a soft mantra, Rama drew an astra from his quiver. Now he waited; he knew it would return even if he stopped following it.

Rama stood very still beside a small clearing, and he did not have long to wait. The golden stag stepped into the glade, near enough to let him chase it again, too far to seize. Quick as a thought, Rama raised his bow and shot the astra through the creature's heart. With a horrible scream Maricha fell, his body a rakshasa's again, cut almost in two by the shaft of fire. He lay panting, dying. But before his life was gone, Maricha the sorcerer threw back his head and, in an uncanny likeness of Rama's voice, screamed piercingly, "Sita! Lakshmana! Help me!" Then he cried out again, and so convincingly because his agony was genuine.

The next moment he was dead. Hearing the rakshasa scream like that in his voice, dread gripped Rama. Some great mischief was afoot and he was so far from the asrama. Anxiety burning him, he turned and ran back at a lope.

In Panchavati, at the edge of the grove around the asrama, Sita heard Maricha scream and cried, "That was Rama. Fly to him, Lakshmana!"

But Lakshmana stood silent and would not answer her in the mood she was in. She trembled; her eyes filled with tears. Shaking him, she said angrily, "Why do you stand there as if you didn't hear Rama cry out?"

A shadow crossed her face; she backed away from Lakshmana. "O evil one!" she breathed. "So you don't love your brother, after all. You want him dead, don't you, so you can make me your wife?"

Hurt sprang into Lakshmana's eyes. He said patiently, "Sita, calm yourself. No rakshasa, Danava, gandharva, Deva, not an army of all these, can make Rama cry out like that. He will soon be back with the hide of the devil that turned himself into a golden deer."

But Sita's eyes blazed. "You are an anarya. You are a blot on the Ikshvaku name, that you can be so calm while your brother is being killed. You have waited patiently for this Godsend, either for yourself or for Bharata's sake, pretending to love Rama while you have always been his worst enemy.

"But if you think I will ever be yours, banish the thought, Lakshmana. I will kill myself rather than let you touch me."

Lakshmana cringed. He folded his hands to her and cried, "Sita, how can you even think this of me? The wounds of battle I can bear gladly, and arrows of fire; but not these savage words from you. I only waited here because he told me not to leave you for an instant, whatever happened. But I cannot bear to listen to you any more. I too am afraid; I feel grave danger very near. May the vana devatas preserve you from harm."

But she only glared at him and cried, "Fly! If you want me to believe you." Tears in his eyes, glancing back over his shoulder to see if she would relent, Lakshmana followed the awful cry into the jungle.

Ravana waited impatiently in a nearby thicket for Lakshmana to leave. He heard Maricha cry out in Rama's voice and a smile lit his dark lips. His uncle had served him well in his last moment. As soon as Lakshmana had gone, with just a thought Ravana transformed himself into a parivrajaka. He was a wandering mendicant, clad in ochre robes, a kamandalu and a battered umbrella in his hands, his hair matted in jata, wooden sandals on his feet, rudraksha round his neck and wrists. Only his eyes betrayed anything of what he truly was.

As night accosts evening, when the sun has set and the moon is yet to rise, Ravana came to Sita, alone in that asrama. He came softly, yet in a fever, to the door of the little hermitage and stood staring in at her. She had her back turned to him. Before he went, Lakshmana had drawn a magical line across this door, an occult rekha. It protected the doorway, so no one could enter the dwelling unless they were asked in. At this line of power, Ravana hesitated.

For the first time, the Demon saw Sita and he was inflamed. Jaded with the love of any woman he wanted casually, of the most beautiful women of all the races, it was an age since Ravana had been moved by a passion like the one that seized him now. In fact, he had never felt such desire: for never in all his years had the monster seen anyone like Sita. The very chasteness of her was fire to his blood. He was mad for her.

He knew his time was short; he coughed softly at her back. Sita whirled around with a cry, thinking Rama had returned. She had been on edge since she heard Maricha's inspired scream, and stood wringing her hands. The trees around Panchavati, and the spirits in their branches, all held their breath. The river stumbled over her bed at what Sita was about to do. She would invite the terrible mendicant inside and break the spell of Lakshmana's rekha.

Ravana stood utterly still when Sita turned and faced him. No fantasy he had of how lovely she must be had prepared him for her beauty. The moment the Rakshasa saw her face to face, whatever hope there might have been of his turning back was gone. His very soul was lost: an absolute love seized the Demon of Lanka.

He murmured some mantras from the Veda to calm himself; he had to restrain the blinding lust he felt. Sita folded her hands to the parivrajaka. If any instinct warned her that he was not what he seemed to be, it was blurred by her anxiety for Rama. Maricha's cry still echoed in her mind.

Barely keeping the hoarseness from his voice, Ravana said, "Who are you, young woman? Your skin is like burnished gold; you are as fragrant as a pool full of lotuses. Tell me, are you Parvati come unknown into this forest, or Indra's Sachi? Or Lakshmi, perhaps? Or are you Bhumi Devi, or Rati? Your teeth are pearls strung together; your body is so perfect I can hardly believe you are real. What can I say of your eyes, your face, your hair, your breasts, your waist I can hold in one hand? Save that I have never seen anyone whose beauty remotely approaches yours.

"Yet you are neither a Deva woman nor a gandharvi. Don't you know this forest is full of rakshasas? Go back to where you came from, lest any of them see you. For they are wild demons who must possess what they desire. Who are you? To whom do you belong? Tell me how you came to the vana."

Unusual talk indeed for a mendicant of a holy order. But Sita decided he spoke in good faith, for only in good faith had all the rishis she had ever met spoken to her, though none as this one did of her charms, and so warmly. On another day, Sita would have blushed to hear him; she may have resented what he said. But today, she merely fetched a darbhasana for him, as she would for any sannyasi, and said, "Come inside, Muni, and sit down."

At that moment, Lakshmana's rekha was broken and the forest heaved a sigh. Now fate would take its course. Ravana stepped, smiling, across the threshold. Sita had no eyes for her visitor. Time and again, her anxious gaze scanned the trees through her door to see if Rama and Lakshmana returned. Then, in her feverish state, she thought she must answer the parivrajaka's questions. She must please him, or suppose he cursed her?

Sita said, "I am Janaka's daughter Sita. I am Rama of Ayodhya's wife. Twelve years ago, Dasaratha was about to crown my husband yuvaraja. But his queen Kaikeyi held him to his word, given a long time ago for saving his life, that he would grant her two boons, whatever she wanted. She asked that Rama be banished to the Dandaka vana for fourteen years, and her own son Bharata be crowned yuvaraja.

"Have you heard of my husband Rama, my lord? He is famed for his dharma and his valor. Do be comfortable in our home. Rama and Lakshmana will return shortly and they will be happy to see you."

He saw her eyes darted repeatedly to the open door.

Now being so close to her, hearing her husky voice, Ravana said, "Sita, have you heard of a great Rakshasa called Ravana? All the beings of the three worlds live in terror of him; his very name strikes fear in their hearts."

He gazed at her with ineffable longing. He was wise enough to know he was a lost man. He put restraint behind him and said, "I, Sita, am Ravana of Lanka."

And when his eyes blazed darkness, she knew he spoke the truth. Abandoning pretense, desire naked in his voice, he cried, "Since the moment I saw you, my heart has burned with a love it has never known before. Come to Lanka with me; it is a jewel in the ocean. My city is built on a mountain, and if you look out of any window, you can see azure water stretching away to the horizon. Day and night you hear the wash of the waves, like ancient song. There are gardens in my palace such as you may dream of; they are lovelier than Indra's Nandana.

"This forest life is not for you. Come with me; become my queen. From now on, my heart is yours to command."

He spoke simply, without artifice, and Sita was angry when she saw he was completely serious. She said, "Listen to me, O king. Rama is everything to me: my life, my world, my sun, my stars. You know nothing about him; he is the greatest man alive. Your asking me to go with you is like the jackal importuning the lion's mate.

"You don't understand how dangerous your desire is. Rakshasa, go away from here. Save your life while you can, before my husband comes back and kills you."

Now the Demon's presence unnerved her. She sensed the enormous evil of him, and sensed his desire reaching for her across the room like a beast of prey. She saw how his eyes burned. Speech ebbed from her in fright, and her limbs shook as if she was in death's presence.

Ravana saw she finally realized who he was. With a smile on his assumed features, he said slowly, "You know nothing about me, Sita; let me tell you a little. I am Visravas's son. Kubera is my brother and I vanquished him in battle. Because of me, he abandoned his city and went to live on Kailasa. I keep his pushpaka vimana in my palace.

"I am Ravana, at whose name Indra trembles and sends me tribute. Vayu blows softly on Lanka for fear of me, and Surya shines gently on my island. Is that not enough for you, my perfect Sita? Forget Rama; he is just a man." Ravana laughed. "Just a boy, who hasn't the courage to defy his old father. What can he give a fascinating woman like you? You need a king to love you. You are born for greatness, Sita: to be my queen. Don't waste yourself; come away with me."

Sita shivered. But hearing abjectness also in his voice, she took courage, and cried, "You say Kubera is your brother. You say the great Visravas is your father. How can you, of all people, speak like this to another man's wife? Ravana, if he sees you here, Rama's arrows will cleave your heart. Begone, Rakshasa, fly!"

How she rued everything she had said to poor Lakshmana. But it was too late for remorse. Ravana rose in anger. He clapped his hands twice and stood before her as he was in nature: a Demon, his skin shiny and his fangs bared in a smile. Ten heads, all of them terrible, stared at her. Some licked their lips, some grinned, and all the eyes on ten heads shone with lust.

In his voice deep as the sea, harsh as the wind in a desert, and grave as death, the Rakshasa said to Sita, "Once again, I beg you, accept my love willingly. Now you see who I am. I swear to you, upon my honor which moved Mahadeva himself, that never once, tender one, will I displease you in the smallest thing. I will be your slave; I will love you forever. Rama has nothing to offer you. Turn away from him, Sita: be mine from today."

Sita darted for the door. With a growl, he caught her. Easily as if she were a child, he draped her across his shoulder and strode out to where his chariot waited.

Sita screamed, "Rama, save me!"

Ravana climbed into his chariot with her flailing in his arms.

"Lakshmana!" screamed Sita, but she had sent him from her.

Without a whisper, the mule chariot rose from the ground and Sita saw the earth fall steeply away. Panting like an animal caught in a hunter's snare, she cried to her karnikara trees, "O my friends, tell Rama that Ravana took me. Ravana of Lanka."

Then the chariot was high enough, and it flashed south through the sky toward distant, exotic Lanka.

15. The valor of Jatayu

Jatayu sat sleepy on the highest branch of a friendly tree, when he saw the chariot drawn by glowing mules fly above him, with a woman in it screaming for help. Languidly, the lord of birds flapped into the air and flew alongside the wizardly ratha.

Sita saw him and cried, "Jatayu, save me! Tell Rama that Ravana carried me away."

Wings tucked into the wind, gliding along easily beside the chariot, Jatayu warned the Evil One, "Rama is the Lord of the earth. You fly the way of death, Rakshasa."

But Ravana loosed an arrow at the great bird and singed his wing. With the ululating cry of a fighting eagle, Jatayu attacked the Demon. The bizarre mules brayed in terror and tossed the chariot about like a feather in a storm. Jatayu was old and nearly blind, but he was from an ancient and noble line. He was also willing to die to stop the Rakshasa from carrying Sita away.

Like light, the eagle raked the Rakshasa's hide with his talons. Ravana howled and his dark blood fell down to the earth below. Ravana shot ten searing arrows at Jatayu, who dodged them and rose high above the chariot. He swooped down like a fishing eagle for its silver prey beneath the waves. He snatched Ravana's jeweled bow out of his hands with his beak and snapped it.

Jatayu flew at the green mules. He fell on them with wings like swords. He raked their eyes with his talons, blinding them. He killed them in the air and the chariot hurtled down to the earth. Just before it shattered on the ground, Ravana snatched Sita up in his arms and leaped out.

He set her down. Baleful eyes on fire, roaring dreadfully, the Demon drew his great curved sword. Jatayu swooped on him again; but tiredly now, he was too old for this. With two strokes of his weapon Ravana hewed off Jatayu's wings. The eagle fell, blood spouting from his wounds, his life leaking out.

With a scream, Sita ran to the fallen Jatayu. She embraced him and his blood drenched her clothes. She kissed him again and again, crying, "Oh Jatayu, you have died for me."

Growling like a tiger, Ravana seized her again. Now with just his own power, he flew up into the air and home toward Lanka.

Holding her in his arms, he flashed through the cobalt sky. They say the sun lost his brilliance when he saw that crime, and the wind stood still. The Rakshasa carried Sita, wearing xanthic silk, as a thundercloud might the golden moon. The Devas wept at the sight; the rishis of Devaloka were terrified. Only Brahma was unperturbed. He sighed and said, "Fate takes her course now."

Sita was like a streak of lightning against the Rakshasa's dark chest. The lotuses she had worn in her hair fell away to the sad earth. She drooped like a plant pulled out from its soil. She still struggled, but barely now, against his mighty clasp. As she kicked her legs weakly, her anklet broke around her foot and fell shimmering like stardust.

"Rama!" cried Sita. "Lakshmana! Look what is happening to me."

She sobbed in Ravana's arms. She cajoled him; she threatened him. But he was just glad to hold her against him as they flitted across the sky. He was pleased his plan had worked so flawlessly. He did not consider Maricha's death a flaw, but a life well given in a good cause. Ravana shut his eyes in pleasure; he had what he wanted. Slowly, he would seduce her in Lanka, and she would see that he was right: that her destiny lay with him.

Sita begged him; she beat her fists against his chest. Then she fell silent and struggled no more, but watched the ground below her for some hope, any. When they flew over a mountain, she saw five monkeys on its summit. Quickly she undid her necklace and her earrings. Ripping some cloth from her sari, she tied the ornaments in the square of glowing silk and threw it down to the monkeys.

Ravana laughed. "In good time you will learn to forget about your Rama. Yes, you will learn."

Sita cried again, "Rama! Lakshmana!"

The monkeys heard her. Looking up, they saw a woman borne away by the Rakshasa; they saw the bright bundle she let fall from above. Ravana flew on. Across the sea he flew, holding her with just one arm now, and never suspecting it was his death he clasped to him. He held her firmly, though, knowing she might well kill herself by leaping out of his grasp.

16. Sita in Lanka

Over the darkening southern strait, Ravana came to Lanka with Sita in his arms. He alighted in his palace, big as a city itself, on the pinnacle of the hill upon which his capital was built. At once his guards surrounded him.

He called for the rakshasis of his harem. The Demon gave Sita into their care. "Look after her as if she is my life. Let no one approach her or speak to her without my consent. I will call for her shortly; take her away until then."

He clapped his hands and summoned eight trusted warriors. He commanded them, "Fly to Janasthana. Go armed to your teeth, for our enemy is deadly. Spy on Rama in the jungle and inform me of his every movement. Stalk him, and kill him if you can."

Ravana allowed himself a moment to gloat: he had some revenge now for the death of Khara and the others. Rama must already be heartbroken. Better still, the Master of evil had just abducted the most beautiful woman in the world. It was true she resisted him; but how long would her stubbornness last? In his considerable experience with women, the best of them, the most worthwhile of them, always resisted him at first. Perhaps they were afraid, or they did not wish to seem wanton. But not one had held out for long. Finally they all succumbed and were glad of it, once he took them to his bed.

The Rakshasa believed there was no exception to the rule, not even Sita, the most beautiful woman of them all. He would be gentle at first; that would win her over. But then, the Rakshasa was hardly himself today: there was already an important difference between Sita and all the others. The rest had been conquests, prey for the Beast. Today, he was the conquered one. The moment he laid eyes on her, Ravana had fallen hopelessly in love. He no longer knew what he did; only that his every moment was full of her: her eyes, her hands, her skin, her voice.

Like a skiff on a stormy sea was Sita surrounded by Ravana's rakshasis. Her face was streaked with tears and she still sobbed, her eyes cast down, long lashes covering them.

In a while, Ravana came haughtily to her and waved away the rakshasis. But Sita did not raise her face to him. He seized her arm and pulled her roughly through his palace. He dragged her up flights of silver stairs and stood her at gold-framed windows that gazed out at spectacular views of the ocean. He hauled her onto a lofty terrace, with carved pillars of solid gold, and flung out his arms to show how vast and how splendid were his island and his city. But she did not see the lakes or the sprawling gardens with their deer and peacock, exotic trees, and banks of rare flowers brought here from the world over. Her heart was frozen with fear.

Impatiently Ravana said, "I am the Emperor of ten million rakshasas across the earth. All of them shall be your subjects. You will have glory and power beyond your dreams: the thousand princesses in my harem shall be your handmaidens. Forget your Rama. He is too feeble for a woman of your beauty: a tapasvin at the whim of his father's queen! Compare us, and you will know the difference between a weakling boy and a great king.

"Forget him, Sita; you will never see him again. Accept that destiny contrived to place you in my hands: because you belong with me. Come, let me show you the pushpaka vimana; we will roam the sky in it. Accept my love, princess; no one has been offered it before. Let your eyes look at me and your heart be glad, knowing how much I love you."

The declaration of love came so naturally from the monster. Such tenderness was in his voice that he might have been amazed to hear himself. But Sita only sobbed more bitterly to listen to him; her hope grew dimmer with every word she heard. They went down the silver stairway again, and out into a walled pleasure garden.

He said softly, "You don't realize what it is I lay at your feet. But you will soon, when you see it is the earth I offer you. Look, I kneel before you, my precious one."

He did so, impulsively, and laid his head at her feet! But she leaped back from him, and set a long blade of grass she drew out of the ground like a green sword between them. Sita said coldly, "You know nothing of my Rama, that you compare yourself to him. He will come to Lanka and kill you as he did Khara. You have desecrated the sanctity of my body by touching me with your hands, Rakshasa. Rama's arrows will color the earth with your blood.

"You boast that you are more powerful than the Devas and the Danavas. But my prince will raze your city and feed you to the God of death. You say you are a great warrior; yet you have the character of a thief in the night, coward that you are who can kidnap a defenseless woman. Ravana, I have come to Lanka to become your death."

His face turned red at her taunts. He bared his fangs and snarled at her like an animal. Then, controlling himself, he said quietly, "I am not moved by the greatness of your little kshatriya. I have drunk the blood of a thousand princes like him. As for you, you have exactly one year to consider my love. Yes, I love you, or you would already be dead for what you have said to me. If you accept this love that consumes me, you shall be queen of the world at my side."

Now all ten of his heads appeared, and Sita gasped to see them again. The central one was silent, thoughtful. But the one right on top, the smallest, evilest one, sneered, "If you don't come to me in a year, you will be cut in small pieces and be my morning meal instead."

Nine heads laughed madly and fell to whispered discussion among themselves about which choice she would make. His main face dark, his lips still throbbing at what she had dared say to him, Ravana turned and stalked out of the asokavana where he had brought her again.

17. Rama's despair

As he ran back toward the asrama at Panchavati, Rama knew evil was about. Maricha must have known he would be killed; yet he had been willing to die. Either that or he dared not but give up his very life for the one for whose sake he had become the golden deer. Rama did not care to think what power could terrify a rakshasa like Maricha so much that he would rather die than cross its will.

He ran toward the asrama in panic. He was certain he had been lured away from Panchavati so that something unthinkably foul could enter it. But Lakshmana was there; what evil could pass his brother? Then Rama remembered Maricha's dying scream and he feared to think what it had been meant to achieve. He raced through the jungle and a jackal howled in his path, startling him.

"Grave danger waits for me!" he thought, and plunged along the twisting trail. Around the next corner he ran straight into Lakshmana running toward him: they both cried out and drew their swords. Rama saw his brother was sobbing and took him in his arms.

When the younger prince was a little calmer, Rama said gently, as he might to a child, "You were right; the golden deer was Maricha." But he was agitated himself. "You have left Sita alone; we must fly to her. Oh, I wonder if we will find her alive. I have seen such sinister omens on my way and I feel shrouded in darkness. Some implacable terror has come into our lives: evil one can only begin to imagine. You shouldn't have left her, my brother, not even when you heard Maricha scream."

They arrived at the asrama, and no Sita came out to greet them. A wounded silence lay over the hermitage. Rama ran in and saw the signs of a struggle inside. He saw the earthen vase of karnikara lying broken, its flowers crushed, its water spilled. He saw five lotuses from Sita's hair strewn on the ground, two of them trampled. A cry escaped poor Rama.

"She is gone, Lakshmana!" he wailed. "They must have been rakshasas come to avenge themselves on me. Why did you leave her when I told you not to? You should have known it was not I who screamed. I left you to watch over her, Lakshmana, and now she is gone."

He lost control of himself. He seized Lakshmana's shoulders and shook him. Lakshmana wept again. "I did not want to leave her. But she began to say terrible things to me when she heard the scream. She said, 'You won't go to save your brother, because you want me for yourself.' I could not bear it. She cried she would kill herself if I did not come to look for you. I had no choice, Rama: she was like one possessed; she would not listen to me."

But Rama was desperate. "Women are like that when they are frightened. You should have known better than to give in to her. And now she must be dead. Oh, Sita!"

Rama ran in and out of the kutila. He looked for her under her favorite trees. He called her name over and over again. He sobbed like any man who had lost his wife. Suddenly, he cried in hope, "She must have gone to fetch water."

They ran to the river, but she was nowhere on its banks. The trees seemed to droop around them; the deer were forlorn and the flowers all sorrowful. Rama, unhinged, went up to the trees.

"Have you seen her?" he cried to the kadamba and the tilaka, the asoka, the karnikara and the kritamala. But they stood mute, on the eloquent verge of speech.

He cried to the grieving deer, "She loved you so much. She must have bid farewell to you before she went." But the deer could not speak either. He looked at them, his tears welling over. "Her eyes are like yours," he said, and stroked their faces.

Grief making his movements stiff, he turned to Lakshmana. "I cannot live without her! But I can't die either: my father in heaven will not look at my face, because I did not protect Sita."

Lakshmana took him in his arms, and Rama sobbed against his brother's shoulder. Lakshmana stroked his head: "Don't give in to sorrow like this. I am sure she is not dead. This is such a vast forest; she may be hidden in any of a hundred caves. We must not despair, or all will surely be lost. Instead, let us search for her. Calm yourself; dry your eyes and be brave again."

Through his tears, Rama gave him a wan smile. He heaved a sigh and said, "You are right; we must not let despair conquer us."

"She could not have gone far, or been taken far," Lakshmana said. "It hasn't been long since I left her."

Again they searched the asrama for any sign of Sita. They sought her among the trees and on the riverbank. They looked for her in the cave where Lakshmana and she had sheltered when Rama razed Khara's army. They called her name, many times; but there was no response. Exhausted, they came back to the asrama and sat sunk in despair.

Rama's face twitched with anxiety. It was not radiant any more, but like the face of a corpse, ashen. His body was limp. At that moment he would have made easy prey, had anyone chosen to attack him. Sighs came from him like his very breath; his tears flowed.

Rama said, "Lakshmana, there is no greater sinner than me, that I am punished like this repeatedly. Who knows what I may have done in my previous lives to suffer such torment in this one? I have lost my kingdom, my father, and my family. My sorrow had just grown quiet in the peace of the forest, when now . . . Look, we used to sit on this slab of rock, she and I. We spoke of everything under the sky: about love and time, life and death, sorrow and dharma. No, she could not have gone to the river for water, or to the woods to gather flowers. She was too timid, my brother. We must face the truth: a rakshasa has taken her."

Panic took him again, and once more he ran to the edge of the woods. He cried out for her as a wild creature to its lost mate. But only the silence of the Dandaka vana answered him.

Lakshmana was terrified to see his serene Rama like that. It was so far from his nature, his brother feared he might lose his reason altogether. The younger prince put an arm around the older and led him back to the rock seat. He said, "Show me your fortitude now, Rama, or we are both lost. Let us seek her with patience and courage, and we will find her."

But Rama still had a faraway look in his eye. Jumping up, he cried, "There she is! I saw her behind that asoka tree. Quick, Lakshmana, before she gets away."

When they found no Sita there, he sent his brother to the river again. Twice Lakshmana went and returned, shaking his head. Then Rama went himself to the Godavari, and cried in anguish, "River, did you see where my Sita went? Tell me, who has taken my love from me?"

But the river only flowed, sorrowing. She could see into his destiny and she had no part to play in it. Rama cried to the deer and the trees around the asrama. But they only stood drooping with sadness and dared not say anything for fear of Ravana.

Rama howled, "When my father died, Sita was with me and I could bear the grief. For her smile made me forget everything else. But now what will I do? Who will keep my heart from breaking? Lakshmana, I can't live without her."

His brother winced to see Rama in such torment. But there was little he could do, save wait for him to recover some composure. Then some deer, which had been friendly with Sita, came and nuzzled their heads in Rama's hands. He caressed them blindly, crying, "Look at their eyes: they have something to tell us!"

In quaint chorus, the deer pointed their long faces to the southern sky, to show where Sita had gone. Quickly they lifted their heads, to show that she had been borne away like the wind. Numb with grief, Rama did not understand at first. But Lakshmana cried, "South! She was taken south and through the air. Rama, we must go that way."

They did not pause to think any more. Rama embraced the deer and the brothers set off toward the south.

18. Wrath

Scanning the trees and the undergrowth along the way, the princes came south in search of Sita. At the edge of the asrama, Rama pointed to some lotus petals that lay crushed on the earth. He whispered, "She was taken this way. I gathered these lotuses for her this morning, and she wore them in her hair."

Then his eyes rolled in his head and madness seized him again. Rama raged at the mountain, "Say where she went, silent witness, or I will crush you with an astra!" His eyes blazing, he turned to Lakshmana: "I will consume the river; I will smash the mountain into dust. Watch me, my brother: I will burn up the earth!"

He drew an awesome shaft from his quiver, an astra made of the fire that ends the stars, and began to fit it to his bowstring. Just then Lakshmana pointed to the ground with a cry. They saw splayed footprints in some soft earth where Ravana had trodden. Rama forgot his fury, and Lakshmana cried out again: ahead of them lay the Rakshasa's broken sky chariot and his dead mules, mutilated by Jatayu.

They saw blood everywhere, in great splashes. Rama breathed, "There was more than one rakshasa. They fought over her and devoured her."

Lakshmana said, "Look here."

On the ground, riven by Jatayu's beak, lay Ravana's gold-inlaid bow, the fire of its jewels put out. Rama picked it up and examined it. He said in amazement, "Only a great warrior could wield this bow."

They saw the white parasol that lay rent and broken. Rama breathed, "Sita was taken by a king."

Then they saw Ravana's sarathy, dead on the ground. "A rakshasa," whispered Rama, his courage ebbing from him. "We were right; it was a conspiracy of demons. But which king flew here in a mule chariot to abduct Sita?"

Lakshmana only stared mutely at his brother; the tragedy was plain to him. Rama said slowly, "If they meant to avenge the death of Khara and the slaughter of his army, they have succeeded beyond their greatest hopes." He laughed bitterly. "I cannot live without her, Lakshmana. I will kill myself." He grew silent and his face was dark. A rare glitter in his gentle eyes, Rama said, "Do you remember what you said to me that day in Ayodhya, after Kaikeyi had banished us?"

"How can I forget the day that changed our lives?"

"You said I was too soft, and I think you were right. That day I kept dharma in the face of all Ayodhya. From that day my family and, I think, even the Gods who rule our fates mistook my gentleness for cowardice: that now they allowed my Sita to be taken from me.

"But from today, I will be another man. Lakshmana, the softness of the moon will give way to the blazing heat of the sun. The rakshasas of the world will feel my wrath; the Devas, the gandharvas, and the yakshas will know who Rama is. I will burn up the earth; I will make ashes of heaven. I will dislodge the planets from their orbits, and consume fire and air. I will drain the sea with my astras. The darkness of eternal night will be complete, for I will put out all the stars in the sky!"

He was transformed before his brother. Rama became more awesome than he had been when he humbled stormy Parasurama; again he was more God than man. Lakshmana fell at his feet. "Rama, this rage does not suit you. Your emotions have always been your slaves. But now your anger rules you and I am afraid. I beg you, calm yourself; be gentle again. I dare not look at your face for what I see in it. The footprints on the earth are still fresh; I am sure Sita isn't dead. We will find her, if we only look for her."

But Rama stood above him, breathing hard. Lakshmana cried, "If we do not find her, you can burn up the earth. But at least let us look."

Rama seemed undecided what he wanted to do first: look for Sita or consume the world. His eyes were still full of pale light, and Lakshmana said, "You bore your sorrow like a kshatriya when our father banished you from Ayodhya. That fortitude was kingly. But if you succumb like this to grief, how will your subjects rely on you?

"Rama, who among the living has not had to bear suffering? Great Nahusha was made a python for a thousand years. Yayati was cast out of heaven. Even Viswamitra lost a hundred sons in just a day. The earth is convulsed by quakes and eruptions. The sun and the moon, the eyes of the universe, are eclipsed by Rahu. No one escapes fate's ordeals. But how often you have said to me that one should not let one's mind be broken by them.

"You, of all men, must never give in to sorrow. Be yourself again, Rama. How can you think of burning up the world for one man's sin? You should seek out the sinner, and consume him with your wrath."

Rama heaved a sigh, and the darkness left his face. Next moment, he hugged Lakshmana and there were tears in his eyes. "What would I do without you? You have shown me the way of dharma and I will do as you say. But anguish roils me and I cannot think clearly. Be the thinker for both of us: decide our next course, until I am calm again."

Lakshmana said, "Let us first comb Janasthana for some sign of Sita. If we don't find her, we will go south as the deer said to."

19. Jatayu dies

Rama struggled with a God's wrath, maddening him so he wanted to raise his bow and end everything. But when he looked at Lakshmana, leading the way resolutely, he swallowed his anger like bile.

Lakshmana walked ahead toward Janasthana. His eyes scoured the bushes, the ground, and the trees for any sign that might help them, any sign at all of Sita. Suddenly he gave a shout; they had come to a clearing where Jatayu lay dying. He was like a little hillock, drenched in crimson, unrecognizable. His blood was everywhere, seeping vividly into the earth. Quick as thinking, Rama drew an arrow and would have killed Jatayu had Lakshmana not caught his arm.

"It is the rakshasa who killed Sita!" cried Rama. "He is bathed in her blood."

But Lakshmana said, "It is Jatayu and he is dying."

Rama ran forward and took the eagle in his arms. Jatayu bent his head to ask the prince to listen to him. He could barely speak, and he had hung on by a last thread of his life, just so he could see Rama before he died. His eyes were bright with death, and blood flowed from his beak as he spoke in an agonized whisper. "Don't waste your time in this forest, Rama; the one who killed me has taken Sita far from here. It was Ravana who took her when you were away." His dying eyes grew wistful. "I fought him in the air. I broke his chariot so he plunged down to the earth. But he is fell and strong. He hewed off my wings with his sword and flew up into the sky with her."

Rama wept; tenderly he stroked the great bird's face. "Jatayu, noblest friend, you are dying for my misfortune. Why did Ravana take Sita? I have done him no wrong. Who is Ravana, Jatayu? What does he look like? Where does he live?"

Jatayu said, gasping, "He was like a black tempest and he carried her through the sky. He went south, child, south." The eagle's eyes closed in exhaustion. Opening them again, he said, "Hold me in your arms, Rama. My eyes have lost their vision and I am going now." He paused, breathless, then said, "It was the hour of vinda when Ravana carried Sita away. Anything lost at that time will always be found again. You will have Sita back from the Rakshasa. You will kill him and have her back. He is Visravas's son, Kubera's brother . . ."

Then life had gone from Jatayu; he was dead in Rama's arms. Rama whispered, "Jatayu gave his life to keep his word of protection. Only a father would die like this for his child. Collect some wood for me, Lakshmana, so I can cremate him with honor."

With the eagle's body in his arms, Rama walked slowly toward the Godavari. Lakshmana made a bed of darbha grass on the ground and Rama laid Jatayu upon it. Lakshmana fetched dry branches and twigs and covered the corpse.

Rama said solemnly, "Foster father, king of birds, may you fly straight into the heaven meant for the greatest tapasvins. Noble Jatayu, I, Rama, give you the freedom of that realm."

He kindled the pyre by rubbing two arani twigs together, and offered anjali to the departed soul. He offered pinda to pacify the spirits of the manes; he recited the slokas for srarddha. The brothers bathed in the Godavari and, standing in the river, offered tarpana for Jatayu. The great eagle rose into the Swarga of the most exalted rishis.

20. Kabandha

Jatayu's death, and cremating him, made Rama forget his anger. Even the grief of Sita's disappearance mellowed when he saw the golden eagle had died for her sake. Rama grew quieter and more determined. Lakshmana's terror subsided with his brother's brief madness. But he would never forget how fearsome his gentle Rama had been during the moments when he wanted to burn the earth. Lakshmana heaved a sigh of relief: he had no doubt his brother could consume the world.

They went south now, and a joyless journey they had without Sita. They missed her lively observations about this mighty tree and that tiny flower, and the little deer with eyes too big for his face. She was not with them to make the jungle come alive with the miracle of her endless fascination, and the Dandaka vana was a wan place, as forlorn as the princes themselves. Wrapped in gloom, they marched on. Though his tread was firmer now, not a word did Rama speak. Lakshmana walked in silence at his side, his eyes alert for any further sign of Sita.

They walked three krosas from Janasthana and came to the jungle called Krauncharanya. This was a black forest, with hardly a sunbeam breaking through the dense thatch of branches and leaves above. Often, they saw glowing eyes staring at them from behind a great tree trunk or a black thicket, as they went cautiously along. Their bows were fitted with arrows, ready in their hands. Their progress was slow because they stumbled along mainly through pitch darkness. Frequently, they sat on a convenient tree root or a smooth rock to rest. This was a dangerous jungle, and they needed all their wits about them to pass safely through it.

They went three krosas, laboriously, through that densest of vanas; while nameless creatures moved unseen through the thick undergrowth beside them, and above them through the matted branches. Then they saw sunlight ahead and came out into the open. They stood in a clearing, shading their eyes from the glare, until slowly their vision adjusted itself to the sun.

They saw a cave before them, and at its mouth stood a rakshasi gazing at them with interest. In fact, she stared just at Lakshmana. When she saw the princes noticed her, she detached herself from the cave mouth and came ambling toward them with long strides. She was all smiles and fluttering eyelashes.

Laying a hand on him enticingly, she said in her coarse, mannish voice to Lakshmana, "I am Ayomukhi. Come into my cave, fair stranger, I am a mistress of love. Let us range the green jungle and the hill slopes of Krauncharanya together, making love by daylight and darkness, moonlight and starlight."

She stroked his cheek; she let her hand rove over his chest. With a cry of rage, Lakshmana drew his sword and lopped off not just her nose and ears, but her heavy breasts as well, and she fled shrieking and gushing scarlet into her cave. They walked on into the jungle before them, forbidding as the one they had emerged from. They crept forward, with Ayomukhi's howls ringing in their ears.

Abruptly, Lakshmana stopped in the dark. He whispered to Rama, "My left side throbs and my mind is full of fear. Something evil lies in wait not far ahead."

A vanjulaka bird cried its thin, lilting cry. Rama touched his brother's arm: "By the omen of the vanjulaka's call, we will overcome whatever it is."

More carefully than ever, they crept along through the darkness. Ahead of them the forest thinned and again some light shone through. They went gingerly toward the light; the feeling of threat was now a palpable thing. Then two enormous hands flashed out from the trees like lightning and seized them. Dragged over leaves, scraping against tree trunks and branches, struggling but held firm, they were hauled a long way toward brightness and the strangest monster they had ever seen.

He was mountainous. But he had no head or legs, just a huge barrel of a trunk with these arms, nearly a yojana long, attached to it. A single gigantic eye was set in the middle of his hirsute body. Below it was a fanged maw. All around the rakshasa were splashes of blood, and bones picked clean, and the intestines and skins of creatures he had eaten, among them deer and boar, elephant and tiger. The giant eye regarded them hungrily and the slavering mouth grinned. The creature's breath was a fetid roar.

He said in a thick lisp, "Kabandha is lucky today. Long time since Kabandha has eaten human meat."

He licked his lips and, yawning his mouth wide, its stench unbearable, he brought his captives slowly toward it. He paused and manipulated his fingers, each one thick as a young tree, to loosen the deerskin and valkala they wore. These he did not want to eat. Momentarily, the princes' arms were free. Quick as light, they drew their swords and hacked off Kabandha's hands at their wrists.

His eye rolled in shock; his roars shook the jungle. Kabandha lived by hunting with his hands and his eye, for he had no legs. But life went out of him now, with the gushers of blood from his severed wrists. His eye streamed tears and, through the rest of his screaming, he cried shrilly at them, "Who are you, humans? Who are you?"

The younger prince said, "We are Rama and Lakshmana. And who are you, awful one?"

A bitter laugh came from Kabandha. He blinked his eye several times in some deep remembrance. At last, in a voice transformed, he said, "It is my good fortune that brought you to me today. I think my long suffering is finally over. I was not always as ugly as you see me now, O Lakshmana. Once my name was Dhanu, and I was as handsome as Soma. And I was arrogant. I would frighten the rishis of the forest with my maya. I would assume one monstrous form after another, and roar at them from behind the trees.

"But one day, I startled a hermit who had a quick temper, and he cursed me: 'Be this monster from now!' Since then, I have been like this. I begged him to take back his curse, and he said, 'When Dasaratha's son Rama cuts off your hands and you die, you shall have your splendor back.'

"I also offended Indra, and he struck off my legs with his vajra. Brahma said to me, 'Live hunting with your arms, Dhanu.'

"Cremate me, Rama; release me from my bondage."

Rama said, "My wife Sita has been abducted by a rakshasa called Ravana. We only know his name. Do you know any more about him? You have been here for so long; you must know many things."

Kabandha said, "Dig a deep pit and cremate me in it. Then I will have my old powers back and know all things. Don't hesitate, Kshatriyas: your apparent cruelty shall be kindness. For without my hands I will die anyway, and slowly. I beg you, hurry. Old memories already flood back into my mind, but I can't see them clearly."

The princes collected dry branches and twigs. They dug a pit deep enough to put Kabandha in and they burned him. The flames had scarcely begun to lick at the rakshasa when he was released from his curse. In a flash of light, a dazzling figure sprang up from that pit: Dhanu, the archer of the sky! Next moment a chariot, made of starlight and yoked to shining horses, flew down to bear him away to Devaloka.

Radiant Dhanu said, "Rama, I see all things again, in both place and time. I will show you the way that leads to Sita.

"There is a prince of vanaras called Sugriva. He lives on Rishyamooka, the mountain that casts its shadow over the Pampasaras. Your destiny and Sugriva's are bound together. You must find him. He is the son of Surya Deva, the Ancestor of the Ikshvakus; he will be like a brother to you. He will ask for your help, but in return he will do anything to help you find Sita. Like his father the Sun, he knows everything that happens on the face of the earth. Swear an oath of friendship with him by a sacred fire, and he will certainly help you."

Rama asked, "How will I find the Pampa?"

"This path we are standing on, which Kabandha once straddled, is lined with trees whose sires grow in heaven. At its end, you will come to a garden not less beautiful than the Nandana or Chaitra. Beyond that garden is as pristine a lake as you will find in this world.

"The lotuses that grow on it were once brought down to the earth by the Devas. The flowers of the Pampa never fade, nor do its fruit rot. Its water is as clear as the heart of a rishi, and you can see down to the white sand on its bed. Swans and cranes and birds from unknown lands come to drink from it. The Pampasaras is so sacred, Rama, that it will restore your faith.

"By that lake, once, the great Rishi Matanga lived, with his sishyas. In his asrama you will still find an old woman called Shabari." A smile lit Dhanu's face. "As I did when I was Kabandha, she also waits for Vishnu's Avatara." He laughed. "But only to worship you, not devour you! She is so pure that she has been called a hundred times to Swarga. But she waits to see the face and the human form of Rama of Ayodhya."

Impatient to be away among starry fields, Dhanu's horses tossed their shimmering manes. Dhanu patted their necks, and spoke to them in a resonant tongue.

He said to Rama and Lakshmana, "Farewell now, I have so much to do. West of Lake Pampa is the Rishyamooka. You will find Sugriva in one of the caves of that mountain. May your quest be fruitful, Rama. May you fulfill the destiny you were born for!"

The lustrous one bowed to the princes. Then his chariot rose into the air and flew straight toward the stars, leaving a silver trail across the sky.

21. Shabari

The path that Dhanu had showed them went meandering to the southwest. Rama was calmer now, and with every step they took he became more resolute. Scented flowering trees and trees laden with fruit flanked their way. They had left the dense and dark jungle behind them. They now walked through airy woods, their hearts lighter than they had ever been since Maricha died. Hope accompanied them again as they moved along as quickly as they could. When the sun had sunk low at the end of the harrowing day, the brothers settled at the foot of a hill for the night.

Rama had little peace even in sleep. Sita's face filled his dreams, and more than once he saw a leering, demonic visage beside hers, mocking him. He awoke bathed in a sweat of fear, and found Lakshmana vigilant at his side, stroking his brow in tender concern, his eyes full to see him suffering.

Morning came and they marched on. Thus they traveled for many days, until one midmorning they arrived at the banks of a great lake at the foot of a mountain. This had to be the Pampa that Dhanu described; surely there could not be two lakes as lovely as this one in the same part of the earth.

They knelt and bathed their hands and faces in the sweet, sparkling water. At once, their hearts were full of hope. For the first time in all the days since Sita had been taken, Rama put an arm around Lakshmana and favored him with a slow smile. Lakshmana hugged him, crying, "We will find her, Rama. We will certainly find her."

Rama nodded in belief. They walked around the lake and came to its western bank. There they saw what they had been looking for: a small asrama nestled in a cool grove of fruit trees. Shabari had sure intuition of their arrival and came out to welcome them, her wizened face wreathed in smiles.

She knelt at Rama's feet and then at Lakshmana's. Taking her hand, Rama said sweetly, "Shabari, has your service to the munis borne fruit? Has your karma been made ashes by your tapasya; have you found moksha?"

Her eyes alight to see him, Shabari said, "Today my tapasya is fruitful because I have seen your face. And because your eyes have looked at me today, I will find moksha as well. Rama, the rishis whom I served ascended into heaven in chariots of the sky. They said to me, 'Shabari, stay here until Rama and Lakshmana come to our asrama. Serve them, and only then come to Swarga.' Long have I waited for you, my prince; long have I plucked the fruits of our trees, to feed you when you came. They never become dry or rot, and I have kept them all for you."

Years and years ago, Shabari had been born a huntress, a vetali. Now Rama saw how clear and lambent her spirit was. He still held her hand in his, and said affectionately, "Shabari, you are the first of your kind to find the highest Brahmi. Dhanu told me about your tapasya and I would love to look around your asrama."

She laughed like a little girl. By his hand she led him around the hermitage, its meager dwellings and its rich garden. He was content to be shown around thus: the holding of hands was a sweet, sacred link between them.

Shabari said, "This place is called Matangavana, after the rishi Matanga, whose sishyas all the others were. Oh, they performed such penance and sacrifice here that their blessings will last a million years upon the earth. In the end, their hands so shook with age the flowers they offered on the vedi fell out. Come and see the vedi, Rama."

Moss covered the vedi where the rishis had made their offerings of old. Flowers lay upon it and grew wild around it. But when the princes looked, they saw that the stone altar blazed like a drop of the sun, and they had to shield their eyes.

Shabari said, "Finally, our rishis were so old they could not move, but they still made their offerings. They could not get up to fetch water for their worship; so the waters of the ocean fell out of the sky for them. That is how this lake was formed. They bathed in it, and look, here is the valkala they wore: the robes have still not dried. And look at the lotuses on the vedi. They were offered by those munis, and they have not faded. Nothing fades here. I, too, am much older than I even look!" She smiled again, toothlessly, and in ecstasy that they had come to see to her. "Come, Rama, Lakshmana; eat some of the fruit I have kept for you."

They sat with her and she brought an assortment of fruit: mango, purple grape, pomegranate, apple, pear, and some others that grew only in that place. They were as juicy as if they had just come off their trees.

Lakshmana said, "These are the sweetest fruit I have ever tasted."

"By far," agreed Rama.

Shabari glowed, and her gaze never left Rama's face. When they had eaten, her eyes still on him, Shabari said to Rama, "I am at peace now. I have fed you the fruit of Matangavana and I am ready to leave this world."

Taking her hand again, Rama said, "You are the purest of the pure. Being with you has renewed my heart and eating your fruit has made my faith strong in my time of fear. May you reach the heavens of the rishis whom you looked after while they lived in the world. Dear Shabari, you have my blessing."

She was a Brahmagyani, free of any attachment, and she worshipped Agni Deva now. She touched holy water with her fingers. Before Rama's eyes, she yoked the inner fire and, with agneyi, made herself a mass of flames. Soon she was white, murmuring ashes. From those ashes rose a youthful woman, of ethereal beauty, and prostrated herself before Rama. When he blessed her, Shabari rose immortal into Devaloka.

Rama and Lakshmana looked on, tears of exaltation in their eyes.

22. Rama's grief

As the brothers walked around the lake, with a fragrant breeze caressing their senses and their minds, Rama sighed, "Lakshmana, this place where the seven seas flowed has calmed me. I feel we are close to finding some news of Sita."

They walked briskly toward the Rishyamooka, which loomed ahead. Through charmed woods, through fragrant forests of asoka, punnaga, bakula, tilaka, and others nameless and resplendent with blooms, they came again to the banks of the Pampasaras, in another, wilder place. The lake was heavy with lotuses, some white as fresh snow and others dark as twilight skies. The water was transparent and they saw the spotless sand on the lake's bed.

Tiger and deer roamed the banks of the Pampasaras together, the predator calmed of his bloodlust in this zone of enchantment, where the ground was mantled with unfading flowers in every resonant hue. This place was nearer heaven than earth; touched by its deep rapture, Rama and Lakshmana bathed in the clear water while curious peacocks watched them, with royal plumage unfurled. Silvery fish nibbled delicately at their bodies, and little songbirds made a feast of music in the living trees.

When they came out of the lake, Lakshmana saw his brother's eyes were wet with tears. Rama said hoarsely, "Go alone to the

Rishyamooka. I will stay here; my heart is full of Sita. She smiles before my eyes, she whispers to me from the water. I feel her fingers on my skin!"

The tears spilled down his face. Spring was in the air. A malaya breeze blew down from Rishyamooka, velvet-fingered, and the lotuses, crimson, magenta, and dark cyan, swayed in it.

Rama cried, "Lakshmana, this mountain breeze unhinges me. My heart is weak, and my limbs. Go on by yourself, my brother, and seek out Sugriva. Spring is a cruel time for lovers parted by fate. The scent of the sandal tree makes my blood course. Kama seems to play with the flowers on the trees and vines, and the honeybees are in tune with him. The branches are entwined so they seem to make love. Looking at that karnikara in bloom, how can I not think of Sita?"

Lakshmana did not know what to say. But this grief of Rama's was gentler, and he saw no harm in it. His brother cried, "Listen to the waterfowl: how their awkward songs used to make her laugh. She once took me by the hand to show me these birds at their games. Ah, I can hear her laughter now and it burns me like fire."

There was a lively symphony by all the birds. Some honked in quaint voices; others warbled effortlessly, golden-throated and mellifluous. The peacocks were the most tuneless singers of all. Yet somehow, all together, the birds' music made strange and perfect sense: an atonal but sublime song.

Rama said, "The koyals are in pairs; the peacocks strut for their hens. This breeze of Vasantha is fire to my body. I ache for Sita, for her soft eyes, her voice and the touch of her hands. Oh, Lakshmana, she must also yearn for me. How will we stay alive without each other?"

Rama sat on the ground and sobbed. Lakshmana sat beside him and put an arm around his shoulders. So they remained, for a long time, and his brother let Rama cry out some of his sorrow.

After a while, Lakshmana said, "Your dharma is to tread the winding path that leads to Sita. Don't abandon your courage. Fate is leading you down a strange road. Rama, you are the kshatriya who gave up his kingdom for the sake of dharma; you don't need me to tell you that there is no resisting fate. Why you are led along this painful way is mysterious. But there it is, and you must negotiate all its twists and turns bravely. Don't give in to grief; remember this path leads all the way back to Ayodhya."

Lakshmana spoke softly, persuasively. "Let your sorrow flow out from you like a river to the sea. Believe me, you will find Ravana and kill him. And Sita will be with you again, forever.

"Shed your sorrow and arise. You are not an ordinary man, that you can let anguish overwhelm you. You are Rama, the king of this world. There is an enemy whom destiny has set before us, and our way winds on past his death. But we must find him first."

Rama heard him out in silence while he stared out across the waters of the breeze-stroked lake. Abruptly, he wiped his eyes and rose. He hugged Lakshmana and said, "Yet again you have restored my courage. It was surely written that you would come with me into exile. For without you I would have been lost long ago, and wandering the wastes of madness. Come, my wise, precious brother, let us find the monkey on Rishyamooka."

Arm in arm, they walked toward the mountain ahead.

BOOK FOUR

KISHKINDA KANDA

{In Kishkinda}

1. On Rishyamooka

Sugriva, the vanara, sat on one of the peaks of Rishyamooka. Beside him were four other vanaras who had once been his ministers. They had fled into exile with him when his brother Vali chased him from his kingdom. Sugriva was anxious and restless on the mountain. With keen jungle eyes, he had seen Rama and Lakshmana at the Pampa far below. When they began to climb toward him, he was afraid. Baring his fangs, Sugriva chattered his disquiet; his monkeys raised their faces and did the same.

Now these were not monkeys as langurs, baboons, or apes are, or any of the species of simians we find in our forests today. They belonged to an ancient race of jungle beings, rather human in their natures and very magical in their ways. Their blood was mixed of old with the blood of the Devas—for their women's charms were legendary—and they were an evolved and enlightened folk.

But just now, their king in exile, Sugriva, hopped about on his tree branch upon the mountain more like a common monkey than a great ruler of his people. He gibbered nervously, and stared down in terror at the two hermits who had begun to climb the slope. When the kshatriyas were halfway up the mountain, Sugriva lost his nerve completely. He tucked his tail between his legs and scampered into the cave where he and his friends had sheltered since Vali chased them out of their jungle city, Kishkinda.

Sugriva breathed in the darkness, "Tapasvins carrying bows and swords! I am sure Vali sent them to kill me. My brother won't rest until he has my head."

Sugriva whimpered pitiably. Of his companions, only Hanuman was unmoved. He was the son of Vayu, the Wind God. He said in his soft, calm way, "You know that Vali cannot set foot on this hill, nor anyone who serves him."

"You would also tremble, Hanuman, if you were hunted by your own brother!" Sugriva snapped. Then tears stood in his golden eyes, and he said, "And vanquished in battle, and your wife taken from you for your brother's bed."

"Vali cannot come to Rishyamooka," said Hanuman gently. "By Rishi Matanga's curse, this place is safe from him."

"But I am afraid, Hanuman! Can I help that? Did you see those strangers? They look more like Gods than men. Did you see their bows and the swords glinting at their sides? Kings have all sorts of people they employ to achieve their ends. I am sure Vali sent these two to kill me."

Hanuman said, "They may be harmless wanderers."

"How can we be sure? Go to them, Hanuman. Work your charm on them and find out who they are. If they are evil run back to me, and we must flee. But if they are good men, win their friendship and bring them here."

Hanuman already felt an inexplicably joyful instinct about the two splendid men who came slowly up the mountain. He went down gladly to discover more about them. Suddenly the princes of Ayodhya were accosted by a diminutive brahmana, clad all in white, with bhasma laid broadly across his brow and a beaming face from which two friendly, canny eyes shone out. Hanuman, son of the wind, could change his form as he chose.

"Good sirs, you seem to be rajarishis," he cried, before they recovered from their surprise. "No, you seem to be Devas! I have been watching you scour the mountain. At first I thought you were sannyasis, for you wear valkala and jata. But then I saw the noble weapons flashing in your hands."

Rama and Lakshmana stared at Hanuman. They felt strangely sure he was not what he appeared to be, but equally certain that he was harmless, at least to them. His shrewd eyes never leaving their faces, and sizing them up all the time, Hanuman went on chattily, "I see eagerness in your step, as if you were impatient to be somewhere else. But you are brave; I would venture that you are courage incarnate. Your radiance is like the sheen of gold. But every now and then a sigh escapes you as if some terrible sorrow sat on your hearts."

He was thoughtful for just a moment; then again the flow of exquisite language: "You are brothers, certainly. Though you are dark, good friend, and slightly the older, and you, friend, are fair. But otherwise you might be twins. Your arms are bare, but if my mind does not play tricks on me, golden ornaments belong there. But tell me, my princes, for that you surely are, why have you come to this desolate place? To guard Rishyamooka against some danger, perhaps?

"I can see your bows were not fashioned in this world. I am sure, when you loose them, your arrows are of light and flames; and your swords are like serpents slumbering at your sides. Hanuman sees a great deal, Kshatriyas, because his eyes are clever. But I must not be rude, asking all these questions and saying nothing about myself. I can see you are not merely good men, but uncommonly good men. I will tell you who I am, as my master instructed me to if I found you were good."

He went on, without drawing breath. "There is a just and valiant king of the vanaras called Sugriva. He was driven out of his kingdom by his brother, and Sugriva now lives upon this Rishyamooka in fear. I am his minister Hanuman, whom he sent to make friends with you. Yes, I am a monkey too. I became a brahmana to approach you, and to discover if you were good men or not. You see, I am Vayu's son and can assume any form I please."

And he stood smiling benignly at them. Rama gave a delighted cry when he heard who the little brahmana was. He took Lakshmana aside, and said, "How refined his voice is; how beautifully he speaks. Surely, he is a scholar of the Vedas. Nobody who does not have a sincere heart can speak so well. This Hanuman speaks from his heart, and he is intelligent and able. Sugriva is fortunate to have such a minister; success will attend all his endeavors."

Lakshmana came back to Hanuman and said, "We have already heard of your master Sugriva. Indeed, we climb this mountain to seek him out and have his friendship. We trust you, O Hanuman, and we will do as you tell us."

Hanuman clapped his hands happily, and the thought flashed through his mind that these princes had come seeking Sugriva with some woe of their own. Surely then, they could help his master against Vali.

Hanuman looked at Rama and said, "But how is it you wander these dangerous jungles that teem with wild beasts and rakshasas? Forgive me, Kshatriyas, for asking so many questions. But I am a monkey and my curiosity gets the better of me."

Lakshmana glanced at Rama, and his brother nodded that Hanuman might be told everything. Lakshmana said to the little brahmachari, "There was an emperor called Dasaratha who ruled the kingdom of the north called Kosala. He was a king of dharma and never strayed from the truth. This dark prince is his eldest son Rama. Rama's honesty and valor are a legend. But because of an old vow, Dasaratha sent his precious son into the jungle for fourteen years.

"For his father's sake, Rama went gladly to the vana. I am Lakshmana, his younger brother, as you rightly guessed. I came with him because he is my life and my God. But not just we two came to the forest: my brother's chaste wife, Sita, was with us. Ten days ago, a rakshasa abducted Sita from our asrama in Panchavati in the Dandaka vana.

"We came south in search of Sita, and in the Krauncharanya we came upon Dhanu, who told us to come to Rishyamooka and seek out Sugriva. Our destiny led this way, said Dhanu, and your king would help us. As you see, my brother is grief-stricken. If he can, let Sugriva help Rama who once needed nobody's help; but time has brought him to this sorry pass."

Hanuman saw that though Lakshmana spoke with restraint, and formally, his eyes filled with tears as he told their tale. Hanuman laid a hand on the prince's arm. He said, "Sugriva will be honored to help one so noble as I see your brother is. Come, let me take you to him, for you have much in common. He was driven from his kingdom by his brother Vali, and his wife was taken from him as well. Sugriva will help you. I, Hanuman, give you my word on it."

Lakshmana went back to Rama and said softly, "I trust this son of Vayu. Shall we go with him?"

Even as Rama nodded, Hanuman was a monkey again before their eyes: a towering vanara, tall as a tree! He scooped them up easily in his arms, set them on his wide back and set off up Rishyamooka for Sugriva's cave.

Sugriva stood at the cave mouth. His face was strained and his eyes were full of fear, so Rama immediately felt compassion for him. Hanuman set them down and said, "This is Rama, a noble kshatriya in exile."

Quickly, Hanuman drew the doubtful Sugriva into the cavern and told him the princes' story. As he spoke, the monkey king's face cleared of anxiety and his eyes shone in hope. Hanuman said, "And so, my lord, they have come to meet you."

Sugriva emerged from the cave and embraced Rama and Lakshmana.

2. A friendship sworn

Sugriva said warmly to Rama, "I have heard of your valor. It is my good fortune that brings you to Rishyamooka; you would honor me by being my friend."

He held out his hand. Rama took it, and they embraced again. At once Hanuman produced two arani twigs and lit a fire. He worshipped the flames with flowers and other jungle offerings. Hand in hand, Rama and Sugriva walked round the agni to solemnize their friendship. In the age-old way of the vanaras, they chanted together, "You are my friend. From now on we share everything, joy and sorrow."

They embraced again and there was a feeling of great auspiciousness upon them, of a friendship well struck up. Sugriva broke a branch from a sala tree. He laid it on the ground and made Rama sit on it. At once, Hanuman tore another branch from a sandalwood tree and set it down for Lakshmana, who smiled at his thoughtfulness.

But then Sugriva's eyes were full again, and he said to his new friend, "Rama, I am a miserable monkey. With fists like iron and fangs like daggers, my brother Vali drove me from my kingdom. And he has taken my wife, Ruma, for himself. Because of a rishi's curse, he may not set foot on this mountain, and I have sought shelter here. But my courage is broken and every breath I draw is in fear." He looked pleadingly at Rama. "Help me, my friend, I seek refuge in you."

With piteous little cries, he bent himself at the prince's feet. Rama was moved. By Sugriva's gentle appearance, he felt certain the monkey king's cause was just. He said, "Sugriva, I will kill your brother for you."

Sugriva danced for joy. "With your coming, Rama, I have hope again! I feel certain I will gain my kingdom back, and my wife. You shall be the end of my fear. After years, I will sleep in peace, without being tormented by dreams of death."

As Rama and Sugriva spoke, far away in Lanka, Sita's left eye, like a lotus petal, throbbed; and Vali's tawny eye in Kishkinda; and Ravana's coppery one as well.

Sugriva said, "Hanuman told me about you, Rama: how your Sita was kidnapped. My friend, whether she is hidden in Patala or in Swarga, I swear my people will find her for you." He smiled at the prince and stroked his cheek. Then he continued, "Have no doubt fate intended our paths to cross. Let me tell you what we saw a few days ago. We sat on the loftiest branches of that sala tree when, suddenly, the sky above was rent with the shrill cries of a woman. When we turned our eyes up, we saw a strange sight. A rakshasa, dark as a rain-cloud and as big, flew across the firmament. As the thundercloud does the streak of lightning, he held a beautiful woman in the crook of his arm. She wriggled like a queen of serpents to get free, but he held her fast. She cried, 'Rama! Lakshmana!' and we did not know who she was, or to whom she called. But all at once, a little bundle fell on us out of the sky. It was her ornaments, tied in yellow silk. We kept the bundle safely, in case anyone came for it."

Rama was on his feet. "Why didn't you tell me before? Show me the bundle, Sugriva!"

One of the monkeys loped into the cave and brought back a silken bundle. With trembling hands, Rama took it from the vanara. He saw at once that it was Sita's. He touched it to his eyes, and undid the knotted square of silk. When he saw the ornaments inside, poor Rama fainted.

The monkeys sprang away to fetch water to revive the stricken kshatriya. Slowly, at Sugriva's long-fingered ministrations, he regained consciousness. Rama held the jewels out to Lakshmana and said, "My eyes are blurred, child, but I think these are her ornaments. Do you recognize them?"

Lakshmana said quietly, "I don't know the bangles and the neck-lace, but the anklets are Sita's. All these years, I saw them every morn-ing when I knelt at her feet and she blessed me."

Rama sat up; his face was grim. He said to Sugriva, "Tell me more about the demon who took my Sita from me. Tell me where he lives and I will go and send him to Yama's city."

Sugriva, who was a loving and kindly monkey, wiped his own eyes. He touched Rama's arm and said gently, "I know nothing else, Rama, only that he was a rakshasa. But I swear to you, I will discover every-thing there is to know about him. Sooner than you think, Sita will be with you again and you will be rid of your grief. Calm yourself, my prince, sorrow does not suit you."

Rama was so touched at Sugriva's solicitude he fell quiet. He even managed a wan smile, and said, "I am sorry, my friend. Your concern warms my heart; and my heart tells me that, like seeds sown in fertile ground, your words will bear rich harvest. In adversity it is rare and fortunate to find a friend like you. From now, I depend on you to find Sita for me. And I swear to you on our friendship, I will do anything to make you happy, anything to remove your own sorrow."

Sugriva cried, "The Gods smile on me at last, that they brought you to me. Looking at you, I feel that with your love I can have heaven for the asking. What then is a mere monkey kingdom? I have your friendship sworn by a sacred fire; I could have no greater blessing. I will help you, Rama. I swear it in the name of our friendship."

3. The vanara brothers

For some time, Sugriva and Rama spoke together. Slowly Rama's composure returned, as if seeing someone else who suffered as much as he did restored his equanimity. Rama, Sugriva, Lakshmana, and Hanuman sat in a circle on branches laid on the ground. Now it was the vanara king's turn to recount his tale of woe.

"For years, since he chased me out of Kishkinda, I have lived in mortal fear of Vali. From forest to forest I fled, until I arrived here in Rishyamooka where he cannot come. But even here my mind is not at rest. Rama, I see my wife in my brother's arms and that vision torments me. I have nightmares in which Vali stalks me through evil forests. He ambushes me under eerie trees, cuts my throat, and drinks my blood. I cannot bear it any more. I must have peace of mind again, or I will go mad."

Rama said, "You are my friend and your grief is mine. Your brother is no brother any more, but an enemy." He laid his silver quiver before the vanara. "Look at my eagle-feathered arrows. Vali shall feel their points, Sugriva; he will lie dead at your feet."

Sugriva embraced the kshatriya and said, "He drove me from my throne and my kingdom. He imprisoned all my people who were loyal to me. He sent his own vanaras after me into the jungle; but we five killed them. When I first saw you climbing the mountain, I thought he had now found the help of men to hunt me. When I saw your weapons, I was sure you had come to kill me. How grief dements one: a man in dread is afraid of the breeze that blows by him. Rama, my days have been so dark that only the comfort of these four friends has kept me alive."

"Tell me more about Vali."

"He is my older brother. He was my father's favorite and I was devoted to him. When our father died Vali was crowned king, and no one was as pleased as I was. In those days we were united and happy." He sighed, remembering.

"In our forest, there was an Asura called Mayavi. For many years there was enmity between Mayavi and Vali, over a woman. One night Mayavi came to our city gates, roaring to my brother to come out and fight. When Vali heard the demon, he sprang from his bed.

"His wives and I begged him not to go out after the Asura at that hour; but he would not listen. I went with him. When Mayavi saw the two of us come out together, he ran. The night was lit by a full moon and we chased him easily through the pale forest.

"The Asura ran a long way, with Vali and me in pursuit, until suddenly he vanished before our eyes. He had run into a cave.

"Vali's blood was up. He cried, 'I am going in after him. Wait here until I return. Guard the cave mouth, Sugriva, let no one past you. I must kill him tonight!'

"He went in and then all was quiet. Rama, not for an hour or a day did I wait there for Vali, but a whole month. I ate whatever fruit I could pluck from the trees around me, and I waited in terror of what went on within the black cavern. But I did not leave my place.

"One day, I saw blood come seeping from the cave, and with it, I heard my brother's voice crying out in what I was sure were his death throes. I was terrified that the Asura would come and kill me also. I rolled a boulder across the cave mouth; with tears streaming down my face, I offered tarpana to Vali's spirit and came back to Kishkinda.

"At first I told no one anything; but slowly they prized the truth from me. Our ministers decided they would crown me king in my brother's place. For some weeks, I ruled Kishkinda peacefully; then Vali came back! You should have seen his face when he found me on the throne. I fell at his feet, and cried, 'How lucky I am that you have returned. Here, take the throne; it is yours.'

"I told him how I had waited outside the cave for a month; how blood flowed out one day and I heard what I thought were his dying cries. I told him of my fear of the Asura, who had slain as great a warrior as my brother, and how I rolled the boulder across the cave mouth and went home. Seeing his suspicious, angry face, I begged him not to doubt me.

"But Vali mocked me in court. 'This traitor told you only half the story. After a month's battle, I slew the Asura and it was his blood that flowed from the cave. But when I tried to come out, I found its mouth sealed with a boulder. I was too weak to move it and I called Sugriva's name; but there was no reply. I wandered through a maze of caves, seeking a way out; I could not find any. One day, when I had recovered my strength, I smashed the rock with my fist and here I am. And what do I find here, but this wretch upon my throne!'

"Vali threw the ministers who had crowned me into prison. He tried to have me killed, but I fled Kishkinda. He chased me through five forests, until I heard that by a rishi's curse he cannot set foot on Rishyamooka. My friends and I came here and took shelter. But I live in dread. I can still see my brother's blazing eyes, seeking me in the dark to have done with me."

Sugriva sobbed.

Rama said quietly, "It is plain that only Vali's death will bring you peace. And I swear to you, he will die."

4. *Dundubhi*

But Sugriva said, "Rama, my brother is no ordinary vanara. He can leap across the sea; he can break a peak from a mountain and cast it into the waves. When we roamed the jungle together, in our happier days, he would draw out great trees by their roots, in exuberance, as if they were blades of grass.

"Once, many years ago, there was another Asura called Dundubhi. He was as strong as a thousand elephants. He had sat long years in tapasya and had a boon of strength from Brahma. Dundubhi came to the ocean and cried to Varuna, 'Come out and fight. I can find no one else strong enough to do battle with!'

"But Varuna knew about Brahma's boon, and replied, 'You are too strong for me, Dundubhi. In the quarter of the Gods there is a mountain called Himavan. He is the lord of all mountains; he will fight you.'

"Like an arrow, Dundubhi flew to the Himalaya. He plucked off a few peaks from that icy range and hurled them down or smashed them to dust with terrific fists. Himavan appeared upon his loftiest massif, like a great white cloud. Like thunder, he said to the Asura, 'Why do you disturb my peace? I am a tapasvin and know nothing of war. I cannot fight you.'

"Dundubhi roared, 'Like it or not, you shall fight me! Or you must find someone else who will.'

"Himavan said, 'In the south, there is a beautiful city called Kishkinda. Vali the vanara rules it. He is Indra's son. You shall have little satisfaction from water, rocks, or trees. But Vali will give you the fight you crave.'

"Dundubhi assumed his favorite fighting form: a stupendous bull bison's. He flew through the air like a thundercloud in a storm and reached Kishkinda at twilight. At the gates of our city, he roared his challenge to Vali. He stood snorting and lowing horribly, and pawing the earth. When he bellowed, he sounded just like a grating dundubhi.

"Vali was in his harem when the Asura challenged him. He came storming out to the palace gates, bringing his women with him, his arms still around them. He cried, 'Stop your bellowing, Asura! Leave my gates if you love your life.'

"But Dundubhi had come for battle, and he replied, 'You can boast before your women if it makes you feel bold. You can even have a whole night with them; I can wait until morning. Just remember to indulge yourself to your heart's content, because this will be your last night on earth.'

"Vali bared his fangs and snarled at the Asura. To provoke him, Dundubhi cried, 'Himavan said you would give me a good fight. Looking at you, I doubt it. But we shall see as soon as you come out from behind your women's skirts.'

"Vali grew very still. He led his women back to the harem. Putting on the golden garland his father Indra once gave him, he came forth, chattering his rage as we vanaras do. Horns and long, mighty arms locked; they wrestled and gored and struck each other so savagely the earth shook around them. But slowly, that immense Asura, the bison, lost ground to my brother. With a ringing cry, Vali lifted the demon into the air and dashed him on the ground, and again, and again; until life fled his shattered body and Dundubhi lay dead at Vali's feet. The jungle rang with Vali's roars.

"But my brother was not satisfied, as if he wished he could have had a longer battle with Dundubhi. Still beating his chest, dancing, he lifted up the Asura's body once more. Whirling it round over his head, he flung it into the sky. It flew aloft for yojanas. But when it flew over Pampa and Rishyamooka, the black blood from the demon's corpse fell on Matanga's rishis. When the carcass struck the earth, the sage's precious trees and plants, which he thought of as his own children, were crushed.

"With mystic sight, Matanga saw who had done this. He cursed my brother: 'Let Vali and his vanaras die if they set foot in this forest or the mountain above my asrama.'

"All Vali's vanaras in the jungle around the asrama came scurrying back to Kishkinda. He was amazed to see them swarm to him in such panic. They cried out all together, so he could not make head or tail of what they said. He roared at them to be quiet.

"Then one old monkey said, 'You desecrated holy ground with the Asura's carcass. Rishi Matanga has cursed you that neither you nor any of yours may set foot in his forest, or you die.'

"Vali flew to the muni and lay at his feet. 'Forgive me, my lord, I did not realize what I did.'

"But Matanga only rose and walked away, and the curse remained. Vali fled back to Kishkinda: he felt his limbs grow weak as a woman's in the muni's asrama. Not since then has my brother come to Rishyamooka, or near the Pampasaras. Protected by that old curse, I live here today in safety. Come with me, Rama, I want to show you something."

He led the prince to a towering sala tree, its bole as thick as ten men. "Vali could shake all the leaves from this tree with his hands. He could pull it up by its roots. Rama, I feel anxious about your fighting him."

Lakshmana laughed, "You worry too much, Sugriva. But tell us, what can Rama do to convince you he is stronger than your brother Vali?"

5. Seven sala trees

Sugriva was briefly shamefaced; yet he knew he was right to doubt that any man could quell his awesome brother. He said, "Don't mistake me, Lakshmana. It isn't that I doubt Rama's prowess, just that I am so afraid of Vali."

He fell quiet for a moment, as if debating whether or not to speak his mind. He seemed to decide for it, and said slowly, "Once we came hunting together on this mountain, long before the curse was laid on him. You see these seven sala trees growing in a crescent? Vali shot them with seven arrows and the shafts went right through their trunks. Look, the scars are still on them."

His eyes darted from Lakshmana's face to Rama's. "Don't be angry, Kshatriyas. But I would hate to see my brother kill you: that would break my heart. Come with me."

Around the corner from the cave mouth lay the skeleton of a creature that had been as tall as five men. Its huge bones glinted dully in the sun. Lakshmana cried, "What is it?"

Sugriva said, "Dundubhi's skeleton. If Rama can lift this skeleton and throw it for a yojana, I will believe he is as strong as Vali."

Rama smiled kindly. "It is natural for you to be full of doubt after what you have suffered. I will do my best to convince you that I am stronger than Vali; though I fear it won't be easy."

He strode up to the skeleton and lifted it with one hand. Effortlessly he flung it high into the air. It vanished into the sky, and then they saw it as a dim speck, falling beyond the horizon ten yojanas away. Four of the vanaras gasped. Hanuman was the most round-eyed of them; he alone began to guess who this dark prince really was. But Sugriva hopped around the place where the rakshasa's skeleton had lain; he chattered to himself.

Finally he explained, "When Vali flung the rakshasa here from Kishkinda, Dundubhi was much more than a skeleton. He was immense with meat and gristle: at least five times greater than his bones and ten times as heavy. But if you can also shoot an arrow through one of the sala trees, I swear I will believe you are as strong as Vali. My brother shot seven arrows through the boles of all seven."

Rama put an arm around Sugriva. He said quietly, "I will try to convince you."

He drew an eagle-feathered arrow from his quiver. He strung his bow so quickly the vanaras stepped back a pace from him. Rama bent his bow in a circle and shot one arrow of uncanny trajectory through all seven trees. Sugriva gave a hoarse cry. His monkeys leaped into the air, gibbering in amazement. Rama's arrow, which had entered the earth beyond the seventh sala, flew up from the ground behind him and settled back into his quiver.

Sugriva whispered, "Vali is dead." Then he shouted so the mountain echoed with his cries: "Vali is dead! Rama has killed Vali!"

He turned to Rama and grasped his hands. He danced around

him, crying, "Forgive me that I doubted you. You are among archers what the sun is among planets, what Himavan is among mountains, what the lion is among beasts!

"But why waste time? Let the thorn in my heart, which has lodged there for so long, be removed today. Let me sleep this night in peace, knowing my enemy is dead. I can't wait a moment to be free of fear. Let us go and kill Vali!"

Rama smiled at his excitement. He embraced Sugriva fondly, and said, "Let us go then."

They set out for Kishkinda. At times the vanaras loped along beside the kshatriyas on the ground, and at others they swung through the branches of the trees, picking ripe fruit for Rama and Lakshmana on the way.

6. An arrow from the leaves

Sugriva stood at the gates of Kishkinda and roared a ringing challenge to Vali. Rama and Lakshmana hid themselves behind some trees and waited. Vali was amazed at what he heard: his cowardly brother, whose nerve he thought he had broken forever, had come to fight. He would show him; he would mangle him. He laughed aloud in his court. Great Vali cried, "Sugriva has come to challenge me. Has he gone mad? Or is he so sick of exile that he prefers to die?"

Vali came out of his city gates like the sun. He was Indra's son, a mighty vanara in his prime. He did not say a word to his brother. With a roar, Vali charged Sugriva as bull apes of the jungle still do, and knocked him to the ground. Emboldened by the thought of Rama hidden in the jungle, Sugriva jumped up and fought back.

As they fought, both vanaras grew tall as trees. They rained blows like thunder and lightning on each other. Like Budha and Angaraka, who fought across the sky in ancient times, the brothers battled in the jungle outside the secret city. Each blow was like Indra's vajra striking, and the forest shuddered.

Rama fitted an arrow to his bow. He drew the bowstring to his ear and waited his chance. But he could not tell Vali from Sugriva! They were like twins, as alike as the Aswins of heaven. Rama waited, trying to distinguish vanara from vanara in the hot fray of curses and blows; but he could not. When he saw that no golden arrow flashed out from the jungle to deliver him from his brother, cringed from the fight, and at once Vali unleas his head. Sugriva spat blood. He turned tail an the forest.

Vali chased him until he reached the boun He roared after his brother, "Don't come back

Not pausing even to look over his should ing back to Rishyamooka. He did not see Ran he had scampered up the loftiest peak did he betrayal on a wind-worn crag.

Shortly Rama, Lakshmana, and Hanuma tain. Sugriva was just a terrified monkey nov his fangs. He growled; he turned away from "You came here offering me friendship. You you were. But instead of killing Vali, you stood by while he almost killed me."

He was so angry he would have attacked the prince. He wiped the blood from his nose and mouth and studied it briefly, moaning. He shivered at how close he had come to dying.

Tears in his eyes, Rama cried, "I couldn't tell you and Vali apart! You look so alike; you walk and even fight exactly like each other. My bow was bent, my arrow was ready: but I could not tell if I aimed at Vali or at you. I did not want to kill you instead of your brother."

Sugriva stopped whining. He scratched his head and considered this. The vanara laughed nervously, as the truth of what had happened dawned on him.

Rama said, "You must not lose heart; we will kill Vali before to-morrow's sun sets. Lakshmana, make a garland for Sugriva with some gajapushpi vine. So I can tell him from his brother, and I will know which one to kill."

Drawing his sword, Lakshmana severed a length of the colorful elephant-flower creeper. Tying its ends together, he made a garland for Sugriva and draped it around the vanara's neck. They slept that night without much comfort. Often Sugriva groaned in his sleep, when his dreams showed him his brother, fangs bared, hands outstretched to throttle him.

The next day, the rising sun saw them at the gates of Kishkinda once more. Rama had to reassure Sugriva repeatedly, hugging the wounded vanara, comforting him. At last, Lakshmana said bluntly that the choice was either to trust Rama or to return to his life of terror on Rishyamooka. Again the kshatriyas hid themselves behind a tree entwined with a dense creeper. With them were Hanuman, Nala, Thara, and Neela, who was once Sugriva's Senapati. For a clearer view, Rama climbed onto one of the leafy branches.

Sugriva drew a deep breath. Taking the last shreds of courage in his hands, he rattled the wooden gates. He kicked those gates and roared his challenge to his brother within the city.

In his wife's bed, Vali awoke in surprise. The coward he had given such a thrashing had come back roaring for more fight. Vali leaped out of bed and clothed himself. He would not let Sugriva off alive today.

But his queen, the sage and comely Tara, said, "Only yesterday you gave Sugriva a beating, and he is back already. If I know him, he would sit licking his wounds for a year before he dared return. I am sure he has not come alone. Be careful, Vali, my every instinct warns me of danger."

Vali stared at her in surprise. Tara said, "Angada told me two kshatriyas have been in the jungle lately. Their names are Rama and Lakshmana. I am sure Sugriva has their help that he dares come so boldly to our gates. I have heard Rama has no equal as an archer, that he blazes like the fire at the end of the yugas. Listen to me today, Vali: befriend Sugriva and crown him yuvaraja; end this enmity, it will benefit us all. After all, he is your brother who once loved you. Perhaps he did not lie about the cave and the Asura. My heart quails for you, my love: don't make an enemy of Rama!"

But Vali was too angry at being woken from his morning dreams in her arms to pay Tara any heed. He cried, "How can I let him taunt me at my gates? What kind of king shall I be if I don't respond with a fight? As for Rama, I have heard he is an embodiment of dharma. Even if he could, how will such a prince kill me when he has no quarrel with me? But for your sake, I won't kill my foolish brother. I will only give him a sounder beating than he had yesterday, and he will never come back."

Tara came out into the passage with Vali. She had tears in her eyes as she clasped him tightly, her slim form quivering in his arms. He laughed, "You are frightened for nothing! Go back inside. I will come back to you as soon as I have chased that fool away with the thrashing he is howling for."

Helpless, Tara went back into her apartment.

Vali swaggered out of his gates, roaring for Sugriva. His brother sprang at him with fresh courage, now that the actual moment of battle was here. Raging like two storms they fought; their blows were like earthquakes.

Rama waited in his tree hoping that, by a miracle perhaps, Sugriva would kill his brother without his help. He knew if he shot Vali down with his arrow, that karma would cling to his name forever; and a stain on white cloth is always starker for being on otherwise taintless fabric. Tensely, Rama waited. Vali struck Sugriva with fists of thunder, and Sugriva uprooted a young sala and struck his brother back. They had grown tree-tall again, in titanic combat.

Rama waited for a miracle. But again, it was Sugriva who tired first: perhaps because he relied on the strength of another, while Vali counted just on himself. Suddenly courage failed Sugriva. Vali struck him three awful blows on his temples and his knees buckled. He swayed on his feet and began to fall. Then Rama shot Vali through the chest from his tree; the sound of his bowstring was like the end of the world.

The sky and the earth shook at Vali's scream when Rama's arrow pierced him like fire. He toppled like a great tree felled by an ax. With a crash, Vali fell to Rama's cunning shaft, and at once the sky was dark as dusk over Kishkinda. They say Vali the vanara fell as the Indra-dhanush falls onto the earth on the paurnima day of Asvayuja, when the rainbow is pulled down after the festival of the king of the Devas.

7. *Vali's anguish*

Vali looked like a fallen God with Rama's arrow in his chest. Kishkinda's heartbeat stopped around its stricken king; silence fell on the jungle kingdom. The trees strained down over the wild warrior. The birds in their branches were hushed; no vanara made a sound. Nothing stirred as Vali lay there like a sunset cloud edged with the gold of his father Indra's garland. His chest heaved; his breathing was agonized.

Magnificent Vali lay upon the earth like Yayati of old, who fell when his punya was exhausted; like the sun fallen into the world at the end of the yuga. He was a smokeless flame, incandescent and pure. A dancer in a dream, Rama emerged from hiding like a vision at the hour of dying. With Lakshmana at his side, he came softly toward Vali. The silence in that place was complete: an ocean of quiet, the heart of death. Rama stood over Indra's vanara son.

Vali had shut his eyes in anguish and disbelief. Now he let them flicker open and stared at Rama, who stood unstringing his bow. Vali waited for the prince to come near. Then the fallen vanara spoke, and his voice was clear though death was upon him.

"How did you shoot me down from hiding like a coward? I fought my brother, not you, and suddenly you struck me with your arrow. You have killed me, Rama. Why?" It was no empty question; life ebbed swiftly from Vali. "What do you gain by my death? You are a noble king's son, a prince from a renowned and flawless line. I have heard you are generous and brave, truthful and just. I have heard your compassion and your courage are hardly of this earth. Why, I have heard you are an incarnation of dharma.

"A kshatriya should be a master of his emotions. Patience should adorn his character, manliness, truth, and valor. Just before I came out to fight, my wife Tara warned me Sugriva must have made you his ally. But I scoffed at her fear; I thought you were a man of honor. What should I fear from you, with whom I had no enmity? But, oh, how wrong I was.

"You are the worst kind of sinner: the one who pretends to be dharma itself. You are a dark well covered with green grass; treacherous prince, no one knows what you really are until it is too late. I have done you no wrong. Did I come to your kingdom and insult you? Sugriva and I are not even of your human kind. We are vanaras, monkeys of the jungle, living here, fighting our own battle. Yet you have killed me today: you who are a kshatriya and know every nuance of dharma. You came here and took it upon yourself to string your bow with my death and strike me with it from hiding. *Why, Rama?*"

His eyes welled over. Vali shook his head slowly, from side to side. "We are monkeys of the forest. To us, fighting over a kingdom, a flashy bauble, or a woman is part of our nature. How does our quarrel concern you so much that you kill me for it? You have not even heard both sides of our story. And look at me: all my glory is as nothing now, that you have struck me down, Rama of Ayodhya. What will you say when the rishis of the earth ask you why you killed Vali? A king may hunt an animal of the jungle. But for what do you kill a monkey? Not his meat or his hide, not his bones or his hair. Brahmanas and kshatriyas may eat the flesh of animals with five nails. But look at my hand; it has just four. Why have you killed me, Rama?"

His chest heaved again and speech came tortured from him. "Dasaratha is cursed that he has a son who is addicted to killing; and killing by stealth and deceit. If you had challenged me openly, I would have crushed you. But you crept upon me like a serpent in the grass and you shot me down.

"I have heard something of your story from my vanaras. I know you want to please Sugriva, so he will help you find your wife. But if only you had come to me first, I would have brought her to you in a day, and Ravana with a rope round his neck. Instead, you have killed me. When I am gone Sugriva will have my throne; and that much, at least, is lawful. But not that you killed me. That torments my spirit as it leaves this broken body, because I don't know why I have been shot down like a beast on a hunt."

His eyes were blurred and his voice had grown weak. But Vali spoke quietly, with no rancor. He said, "Rama, tell me before I die why you have killed me. I want to know, I truly want to know."

Sugriva stood by, silent, his eyes not dry. Now that Vali lay helpless, all Sugriva's terror had vanished, and nostalgia and love surged in him again. Vali's breath rasped in his throat, and his natural splendor grew dim like a fire that had burned down.

8. The light beyond

For a long moment, Rama stood silent and grave over the dying Vali. Then he said quietly, "I fear you don't understand everything about dharma. Lakshmana and I belong to the House of the Sun. It is our dharma in the name of the king, my brother Bharata in Ayodhya, to punish those that sin. We are kshatriyas of the earth: the solemn power to judge is vested in us.

"You speak of dharma. But you don't seem to know that by dharma a man has three fathers in the world: his own father, his guru, and his older brother. In this world, an older brother should treat his younger brother like a son. Sugriva was a loving and obedient brother to you. But you drove him from your kingdom; worse still, you took his wife Ruma for yourself.

"That is why I shot you down today, Vanara: you broke dharma by taking your brother's wife. I could not but judge you, and kill you for what you made Sugriva suffer. He and I have sworn friendship by an oath of Agni. He is as dear to me as Lakshmana. If anyone treated my brother as you have done Sugriva, I would kill him. The oaths I swear are not empty; they bind me in honor.

"It is not appearances by which we judge, but by the soul. Sugriva is a pure and untainted soul; while you, who are so powerful, who are a great king of your people, are lost in darkness. You are beyond the pale of dharma: a king like you must not be left alive."

Vali's breath wheezed painfully, and his eyes shone with unworldly knowledge streaming into his heart at what the Avatara said. Now he heard transcendent echoes in the blue prince's words, and they enfolded him, consoled him on the threshold of death.

Rama was saying, "The princes of Ikshvaku rule the world. You say I shot you from hiding. But through time, the kings of the earth set traps for wild creatures of the jungle. We hunted them from trees or with nets. You are strong and valiant. But as you say yourself, you are a vanara, an animal. I did not break dharma when I hunted you."

Not by what Rama said was Vali assuaged, but by his unearthly voice, and the visions that unfurled in the vanara's head as he listened: like golden lotuses, thousand-petaled. Rama's love washed into him in a tide. The dying monkey saw hidden realms of life opening before him, and he knew Rama had killed him in compassion and in forgiveness of all his sins. He knew death was only the beginning of a deeper, more glorious existence. It was redemption. Rama's voice opened a path of light out of the bondage of the body; and when he had a glimpse of what lay beyond, Vali understood who this dark prince was, who stood before him. A smile touched his lips and his eyes softened. He knew Rama had not only killed him, but also delivered him to eternal life.

Then he thought of his son, and Vali was snatched back into anxiety. He took Rama's hand, held it tightly, and breathed, "Now I know who you are, my lord. Forgive me that I doubted you. But a great care holds my spirit back in this world. My son Angada is still tender. He is my only child; he has much to learn yet and he will pine for his father's love. I am not worried about anyone else, not even my queen.

"Who has you has everything, prince of light. What is a vanara kingdom, when he who has your love can be a king in heaven? Protect

247

my son, Rama; let him be as dear to you as Lakshmana or Bharata. And my Tara, don't let Sugriva harm her."

The light around Rama grew blinding, and the dying vanara saw it was the light of his own soul. His heart was awash on the sea of splendor, flowing in waves from the blue kshatriya; only Vali saw Rama as he truly was.

In ecstasy, Vali cried, "I answered Sugriva's challenge just to die at your hands! If I lived a thousand lives, each time I would not die any other way. Look after Angada, Lord; let your blessing be upon him."

Vali's breath came in ragged gasps as Rama knelt beside him and took his hand.

Rama said, "Only fate decides how a man shall die. When he is born, already deep in his body the secret of his death nestles; no man may live a moment longer than he was born to. I swear Angada shall have my protection, and he will be as dear to Sugriva as he was to you. I will see to that."

Suddenly, they heard heartbroken wailing from within the walls of Kishkinda. They heard the shrill yowls of the vanaras' panic when they learned their king was slain. The monkeys fled into the jungle in every direction, for fear that they too would be killed. Above the bedlam, Rama and Vali heard the ululating lament of a queen. Tara came out of the palace, bringing her son Angada with her.

9. Tara's grief

As Tara came wailing out of Kishkinda, someone cried to her, "Tara, save yourself and your son. Vali is killed, and our enemies are at our gates."

But she snarled at that vanara, "My husband lies dying outside the city and you speak to me of saving myself. My life has already gone from me."

Crying his name, she ran to where Vali lay with Rama's arrow in his chest. Never before had anyone vanquished Vali in battle. He had cast great rocks at his enemies as his father of light did his vajra of a thousand joints. He had killed countless Asuras. Vali's roar had been like thunder; his courage had been deeper than Indra's. Tara could hardly believe her eyes when she saw he lay on the ground, gasping his last, and his killer so terribly bright above him.

Tara fell on her knees beside Vali and clasped him to her. Angada wept as loudly as his mother. Tara gazed at the arrow plunged into her husband's chest. She felt it gingerly with her fingers, and sobbed. Vali's eyes were shut; he had drifted off on the sweet pain and the uncanny peace of his death.

Tara cried, "Why don't you open your eyes and look at me? It is I, Tara, your wife. Come, my lord, let us go back to the palace. I will wash your face with cool water and you can sleep for a while. Then you will be well again."

But Vali said nothing. Only his breath still rasped cruelly from him, rattling his torn chest. Tara stared at him for some moments, her tears flowing as if they had life and passage of their own. She sighed, "This bed you lie on is hard; you are not used to such a hard bed. But perhaps a more wonderful Kishkinda calls you from another world. Oh Vali, am I so unfeeling that I can see you like this and my heart doesn't break and my life fly out of my worthless body?

"Why didn't you listen to me when I warned you this morning? Vali, I am afraid: Angada will be at Sugriva's mercy now. Your brother cannot love you for what you have done to him. Angada, look at your father for the last time!"

She turned her face up to Sugriva, who stood hugging himself as if he was very cold. He crooned to himself, shifting from one foot to the other: a restless, anxious monkey.

Tara said to him, "How happy you must be, Sugriva. Your brother is dead and the kingdom is yours. With your human friend's help, your long ambition has been fulfilled.

"Vali, why don't you speak to me? It is I, Tara, who kneel beside you."

She sobbed; she cried she would fast to death from this moment. Hanuman came to her and said kindly, "All of us reap the fruit of our karma. Why should we mourn anyone else? When we are all pitiable, like bubbles riding briefly on a current until they burst. This whole world is a transient place, a dream. Tara, your dharma is not to die for Vali, but to live for Angada. Your husband was noble and gracious, save for one crime. He will find the heaven meant for the brave.

"Your people look to you for strength, and Angada must perform the last rites for his father. My queen, it is a time when your womanly strength must give solace to others. Let Angada fulfill his sacred dharma as a son, and then let him be crowned yuvaraja. Tara, compose yourself."

But Tara only sobbed louder. She called out to Vali again and again; she cried that she would die beside him. Suddenly, Vali's eyes flew open, blazing with death, and his gaze lighted on his brother who stood guilty as a murderer.

Vali called softly, "Sugriva, come near. I want to speak to you."

Sugriva padded warily up to him, on tiptoe. Vali whispered, "Now I feel sorry that I hurt you for so long. My arrogance and the fear in my heart made me mad. Fate was envious of our old love, my brother; she conspired to set us against each other. Take the kingdom from me, Sugriva. I give it to you gladly, because I know you will make a good king. But come nearer and hear my last wishes."

He reached out and grasped his brother's hand, and Sugriva's eyes brimmed over. Vali said, "Now Angada has only you to depend on; look after him like your own son. He is more precious to me than my life, and I leave him in your care. He is brave, if young, and a fine warrior; he will prove himself noble. And Tara. Sugriva, my Tara is wise and seasoned in statecraft. Consult her about everything you do: she has been most of my wisdom while I ruled."

He paused, in pain, before continuing, "Then there is this Rama who has come among us like providence. Be sure to help him with all your heart, for he is great and glorious beyond our understanding. He has come to the world to dispel its darkness. Help him with all your might: nothing is more important!

"Now take my garland and wear it round your neck. Take it quickly before life leaves me, or its power will fade."

Sugriva wept like an orphaned child. Gone was any joy he had felt that Vali was slain; gone any eager anticipation of kingdom. His hands shaking, he gently removed Indra's golden garland from Vali's neck and draped it around his own.

Vali called his son to him. He drew Angada close, and kissed him. "My child, your life has changed. Don't chase after pleasure any more. Accept whatever comes to you, joy or grief, calmly. From now you must please your uncle Sugriva. He may not cosset you as I did; but obey him in all things and treat his enemies as yours. Don't be too attached to anyone, nor coldly detached; adopt a middle course. Remember, listen to Sugriva and grow used to his guardianship."

Vali reached out to stroke his son's cheek a last time, and life went out of him. Tara screamed long and piercingly. The vanara chieftain

Neela went up to the dead king's body and drew the arrow from his chest. Tara made Angada prostrate himself at his father's feet.

Sugriva came to Rama with folded hands and tears flowing down his face. "You have kept your word and Vali is dead. But I feel no joy when I see Tara weep, Angada fatherless, and my brother lying on the earth as a corpse. I caused Vali's death from my greed, and I regret it bitterly. I want no kingdom any more; I must seek the peace of my soul. I will return to Rishyamooka and sit in penance for the crime of killing my brother.

"How many times we fought each other, Vali and I. How often he held my life in his hands, and always he cried, 'Leave my sight! I haven't the heart to kill you.' My brother loved me, but I did not understand him. I should never have wished him dead. I am a terrible sinner; I am not fit to rule."

Fingering the garland around his neck, he sobbed, "Look at my brother's generosity even after I had him killed: he made me wear this heavenly thing. Rama, I will tell my people to seek out your Sita for you. And they will find her. But I cannot bear to live any longer; not even on Rishyamooka will a sinner like me find peace. There is only one way for me: I will make a pyre for myself and die!"

Rama stood disconsolate to hear Sugriva raving like this. Tara rose from Vali's side and came to him.

"Rama of Ayodhya, I have heard you are merciful. Take pity on me and kill me with the same arrow that took my husband's life. We shall be united again, and he will be happy. You have been separated from your wife; you can understand my pain. Noble prince, you cannot want Vali to suffer as you do. Send me to him, Rama, he needs me. No sin will cling to you, I swear, not even the one of killing a woman."

Rama said to her, "You are a great king's wife: you should not give in so tamely to despair. Fate rules this world, and all that happens here is by Brahma's will. Once Angada is crowned yuvaraja you will be happy again. Fate is all there is in this world; all of us are her playthings. We begin and end by her dictates; then how can we resist her during our brief lives? Only fate knows what is best for us and what our ends are. Only she knows which fork on the long road we must take; only she knows why, and what lies around the next corner. All that is, is by fate. And at last, she takes us into heaven, as she has taken Vali today.

"Put away this despair. No woman whose husband was a warrior, and whose son is a warrior, should give in to grief. Be brave, O queen, and perform the last rites for Vali."

Lakshmana spoke to Sugriva, and they arranged for the royal palanquin to be fetched from the city. When they heard about the final reconciliation between Sugriva and Vali, and of Sugriva's remorse, the vanaras gathered around again. Near where Vali had fallen, they heaped a tall pyre with fragrant sandalwood. When they had bathed his body in the river, they laid their dead king upon it with honor. Holding back his tears, Angada touched his father's pyre alight with a flaming branch. They prayed for the peace of Vali's soul, as the flames licked him into ashes.

They went back to the river and bathed, and offered tarpana to the departed one. Then they returned to Kishkinda.

10. King of the vanaras

The vanaras gathered outside Kishkinda, outside the cave that led into the secret city. The monkey chieftains were all there; anxiety was writ large on their faces; it was plain in their uneasy movements and nervous chattering. At the cunningly concealed cave mouth Hanuman came to Rama, and said, "By your grace, Sugriva has the kingdom of his ancestors. Advise him what to do next. He feels guilty and talks of killing himself. Our people are alarmed; they want a strong king to rule them."

Rama said to Hanuman, "To keep my father's word, I may not enter any city, or village even, until the fourteen years of my exile are over. But let Sugriva be taken into Kishkinda and crowned."

Rama turned to Sugriva, and said aloud before all the vanaras, "Don't waste your grief. If you are truly sorry, go into Kishkinda and take up the reins of kingdom. Crown Angada yuvaraja. He is a noble prince and he will bring honor to Vali's name and yours."

Rama paused and looked around him at the trees of spring, festive with flowers, and the birds full of songs in their branches. He said slowly, "It is Shravana. The monsoon will soon be upon us. Lakshmana and I will find a cave on the mountain to live in until the rains have passed. For four months, it will rain without let. But when the month of Krittika arrives, you must keep your promise to me that you will find Sita. I will wait until then.

"But now, go into your city, O king of the jungle, and be crowned. It is a time of transition, when your people need you most of all. Be strong and sit upon your throne with dharma beside you. I know you will be a great king. Go my friend, go in peace."

Sugriva knelt at Rama's feet for his blessing. But Rama raised him up and embraced him. The princes of Ayodhya went back into the forest from where they had come. Sugriva entered the hidden city of Kishkinda and was crowned king of the vanaras. At the same ceremony, he made Angada the yuvaraja and embraced him as if he were his own son. Bitterness had melted from Sugriva's heart; only remorse for his brother's death remained.

Then, at last, his wife Ruma came to him. Crooning in joy, he clasped her to him and his life began anew. Sugriva began a long and happy rule as king of the olden and free race of the vanaras.

11. The rains and after

Rama and Lakshmana went to the mountain called Prasravana. They found a large, dry cave, its floor so smooth and clean that it may have been created just for the princes of Ayodhya to live in. They had barely laid out beds of grass for themselves when the heavens opened. For four months, with hardly a day when they saw the sun, it poured on the world. The wind howled in the valley below the cave and great trees bent their crowns to the power of Vayu and Indra.

The jungle grew visibly with the succor of the monsoon. When the sun did emerge from behind scudding cloud banks and shone down into the world for an hour or two, the brothers marveled at the lush creepers that wound themselves around giant trees, almost a fresh foot each day, and thrust gaudy flowers and sensuous pistils at the steaming forest. The trees were covered in soft new leaves, and the grass and the foliage all seethed with warm, wet life. The animals of the jungle mated in abandon during the rains, beside swollen rivers and on tangled hills. The birds in the trees were all lovers. Serpents entwined in damp nests, and insects mounted their mates under flowering bushes and slabs of rock, in fervent ritual.

Rama was lonely. His blood coursed madly for Sita during the nights of the waxing moon that flitted across the shrouded sky behind stormy rags of cloud. The prince lay sleepless at the cave mouth and every beam of renegade Soma was a shaft of longing in his heart, every streak of lightning a jagged impatience for the monsoon to end.

Once, past midnight, Lakshmana was roused from a deep slumber by the sound of his brother sobbing. He awoke to see Rama bereft at the silvery cave mouth: tears flowing down his dark face, grief having its way with him. In Rama's eyes was such torment it seemed he had taken the sins of all created beings upon himself, and suffered in their place. Lakshmana put his arms around his brother, as he would a child, and held him close.

Rama wept, "Our lives are ruined. Not without reason did Kaikeyi send us into exile. Sita, where are you, my love? With whom do you spend this night?"

Lakshmana stroked his head and said, "Rama, don't let your mind be swayed by wild suspicions, or your will broken by sorrow. The rains are almost over. In just a week, even sooner, Sugriva will begin his quest for Sita. Don't forget who you are in this dark jungle, O prince of all the world. You will kill the Rakshasa and have Sita back. Only be brave."

Rama grew quiet. He smiled at Lakshmana and took his hand. "It has passed now, child. Like a storm my sorrow has passed. Lakshmana, there is no one like you in all the world: no one else could have saved me as often as you have done. You are right. I will wait for autumn, and then Sugriva will keep his word to me." Rama sighed. "It is hard to wait, but wait I must."

Lakshmana said, "I am restless too. But it cannot be long now before these wretched rains pass and we can begin our search with the sun in our faces. How I long for the sun, Rama."

Rama cried, "My loving brother, best among men!" and he hugged Lakshmana.

The next day, the sun shone from a cerulean sky that had not a cloud in it. In Kishkinda, Hanuman looked up and knew it was time Sugriva kept his word to find Sita. But the first months of his kingship saw Sugriva mired in an orgy of indulgence. As if to make up for his stark years of exile, the vanara left the governance of his kingdom to his ministers, and steeped himself in wine and women, as if to live just by them, to heal the wounds of his years of terror by them, to forget Vali's death by them—even as if to find immortality through pleasure.

When the sky cleared, Sugriva had forgotten all about Rama and his promise to him. They had a month of clear weather, of days when the sun dried the sodden forest, of nights when a charmed moon hung low in a lucid sky. Still, Sugriva made no move to keep his word to Rama; indeed he seldom emerged from his harem.

One day, Hanuman went to see his king, who lay drunk among his women. The son of the wind said quietly, "My lord, you have a kingdom now and your wife back. All the pleasures of Kishkinda and the power of its throne are yours to enjoy. But have you forgotten the friend who gave you all these things? What about your pledge to Rama that you would find his Sita as soon as the monsoon passed?

"The sun has shone on us for a month. It is time you called your vanaras to you and combed the earth for the prince's wife. He waits patiently in his cave for your help. Don't delay any longer, Sugriva, lest Rama's love turn to anger."

Sugriva blinked his wine-red eyes. The merriment faded on his lips and he grew very still. For a moment, he seemed to struggle with some inner conflict; his eyes blazed briefly at being disturbed at his pleasure. Then his expression sobered, and he clapped his hands for a guard to fetch Neela, his Senapati.

When Neela came, Sugriva said to him, "Send our messengers abroad; summon my vanaras from every jungle in the world. In fifteen days, I want them all in Kishkinda. Those who do not come shall die. Let Angada collect our forces here in the city. Hurry, Neela!"

Sugriva turned to Hanuman with a smile, "Thank you, my friend, for reminding me. And now, if you allow me . . ."

Hanuman bowed and left the harem. Sugriva called for another flagon of wine as he turned back to the delectable Ruma and the others.

12. Grief and anger

More than a month had passed after the monsoon: a month of aching nights, when he lay awake, and Sita's face and her tender form drifted before his eyes like visions and stoked his despair. One day, Rama broke down.

Lakshmana returned from his foray into the jungle, where he had gone to hunt. He found Rama laid out at the cave mouth. His face was tear-stained and anguished; his mind had sought relief from its agony in unconsciousness. Lakshmana sprinkled sparkling stream water on his brother's face, and Rama revived. He sat up, shaking his head in misery, helpless pleading in his eyes.

Lakshmana cried, "I should never have left you alone. You must not torture yourself with memories; they only rob you of your courage. The rains are over. Sugriva must already have sent his people on the quest for Sita. Take heart, Rama, the way ahead is shorter than you think. You will be with her soon."

But Rama said, "The season and the mood of the forest inflame me with longing. There are times when I cannot help myself. Lakshmana, she is in the hands of a devil. My heart tells me he is no ordinary rakshasa, but a great creature of darkness. And I fear for her life.

"Sugriva swore he would begin his search for Sita as soon as the rains broke. Sharada has been with us for more than a month, and there is no news from the vanara. These four months have been like a hundred years for me; but it seems Sugriva has forgotten his promise. He is indifferent now that he has what he wanted. You say I must be calm. But I cannot help myself any more; my body is on fire.

"Go to Sugriva and tell him from me: 'The most contemptible man is he who forgets his friends after he has used them and has no further need for them.' Ask him if he wants to hear the sound of my bowstring again. Remind him how I killed Vali, and of the debt he owes me. Rouse him from his lust; wake him to my pain and my need.

"Tell Sugriva I said, 'The portal through which Vali left the world is still open. If you break your word to me, you will follow your brother out of this life. Hurry, Sugriva, before despair becomes my master and I come to kill you. You are still my friend; but don't mock my friendship any longer.' "

They had heard of Sugriva's long debauch from some wandering vanaras. Lakshmana said softly, "The monkey does not deserve his throne. I will go and kill him in his harem. Let Angada rule Kishkinda. Vali was right: he would have helped you sooner than his brother has cared to. Sugriva has forgotten he owes you everything he has today."

Lakshmana strapped on his quiver. At once, Rama said, "I wish I had not showed you my anger. You must not be hasty, Lakshmana. Give Sugriva every chance to justify himself, before you even think of killing him. Tell him gently that by the covenant we made with Agni as our witness, he and I are friends for life. He must have reason for his delay: be patient when you speak to him, speak kindly."

Lakshmana bowed to his brother, as formally as he might have in the sabha of Ayodhya, and strode away through the jungle toward the secret city of the vanaras. As he went, his mind swung between reason and anger. He must obey Rama and give Sugriva every chance to explain himself. But if the monkey king could not satisfy him, Lakshmana would not wait for Rama to come and kill Sugriva; he would do it himself. Didn't the knavish creature know Rama's plight? Had he place in his heart only for his own grief? Such a selfish heart should be cloven with an arrow.

Lakshmana could not bear to see Rama as he had been these past months. He couldn't bear the hunted look in his eyes, the lines of pain that had appeared on his face. As all men do who love another as intensely as Lakshmana did his brother, he felt Rama's anguish as if it were his own. At times he felt it even more than Rama did: during the long nights when he sat and watched his brother toss and turn in his sleep, and wept for him.

His bow clasped in his hand, gleaming like a sliver of a rainbow with its jeweled inlay, Lakshmana stalked grimly toward Kishkinda.

13. Lakshmana goes to Kishkinda

Kishkinda lay between two green peaks. It was cleverly concealed in a valley, into which the only way was through a long tunnel, high on one hillside. As Lakshmana climbed to the mouth of the tunnel, he saw the fierce vanara guard posted outside it. Those vanaras did not know him, and when they saw him coming, they began to jump up and down as monkeys do when they are alarmed. They bared their fangs and danced about, waving long arms, snarling—frightened themselves, trying to frighten him away.

When they saw he came on, they scrambled to pick up rocks and tear up young trees with which to attack him. But his face burning like the flames of yuganta, Lakshmana approached in quiet fury. In his hand, and sensitive to its archer's mood, his bow burned with its own fire. When he reached behind him to draw an arrow from his quiver, the vanaras lost their nerve. They dropped their rough weapons and fled.

These monkeys ran to their king's wooden palace. One cried, "A warrior with death on his brow marches on your city, Sugriva."

Another said, "His bow was not made in this world and his arrows shine like time."

Another whispered, "He is no ordinary man. He comes like Yama."

But Sugriva was drunk, and he was lost in the long embraces of Tara, his dead brother's wife, now his own favorite. Baring his fangs at them that they dared disturb him, he chattered angrily at the guards. He chased them out of his apartments, built quaintly half on the ground and half along the trunk and branches of an immense tree. But the king's ministers had gathered outside his palace. Terror-stricken, they called for Angada, and he quickly summoned his army to the several entrances to the city hidden in the mountain.

Lakshmana saw the vanara army marching out through the city gates. His eyes turned crimson and his hands shook on his bow. At the head of his legion, Angada came out to meet Lakshmana. The young vanara stood bravely before the kshatriya. But not a word came from him, because his tongue stuck to the roof of his mouth and his body trembled at the awesome power that Lakshmana exuded.

But the human prince said gently to Angada, "Go and tell your uncle that Lakshmana has come to his gates. Ask him why he has not kept his word to my brother. If he has a shred of dharma, he should not break his solemn pledge. Give him my message and tell me what he says."

Though the prince spoke gently, Angada sensed Lakshmana's mood and the menace of him. He turned and ran back to Sugriva, who was at his endless pleasure while death had come to his gates. Angada burst in on the king, his uncle, who was making love with the prince's mother Tara.

Angada turned his gaze away and cried, "Lakshmana is at our gates!"

But Sugriva was so drunk he could hardly open his eyes. By now, all the monkeys of Kishkinda were shouting outside the king's palace. Sugriva heard the noise through his stupor and it roused him.

Sugriva's ministers ran in to him in panic. Their king rose unsteadily. He asked for water, with which he splashed his arms and face. The water stung him; he squealed at its coldness and shook his fur. At last, the vanara king was more or less awake. He stood swaying slightly before his nephew and his ministers. But now his eyes were wide open, and he asked in a clear voice, "What is all the fuss about?"

Hanuman said, "Rama and Lakshmana are princes of dharma. You swore friendship with them and they helped you recover your kingdom. Lakshmana stands at your gates with his bow in his hand, and our army is terrified because the unearthly thing shines so brightly. The prince's eyes burn in wrath, Sugriva. Tell him you mean to keep your word to Rama, or we are all dead."

Suddenly Sugriva grasped the peril he was in. He gave a moan and cried, "I have done nothing to offend the princes of Ayodhya. Why does Lakshmana come here with anger in his eyes? Some enemy of mine has poisoned his mind against me. Not that I am afraid of him; I am not afraid of him or of Rama. But it pains me that our friendship is at risk. Oh, the mind is fickle, and the smallest slip is enough to kill sacred friendship. And you all know I owe Rama everything I have today."

Hanuman said, "You must reassure Lakshmana that you have not forgotten your debt of gratitude. Rama is not really angry, only anxious. But you have lost track of the seasons. The monsoon is over, when skies were dark and rivers turbid; it has been tranquil Sharada for more than a month. While you have been happy at love and wine, Rama has pined for his wife. He counts not the seasons and months, but each moment of his life that passes without Sita; and every one is like a wretched year to him.

"He has sent Lakshmana to you in anguish. Don't be offended if the messenger's words are harsh; he has cause to be aggrieved. You say you are not afraid of Rama. But if he strings his bow, the three worlds cringe, because he can extinguish them with his arrows. He loves you, Sugriva; keep that love. Rama is more than you or I can imagine.

"Forgive me if I speak too plainly, but it is my dharma to save you from folly."

Sugriva stood staring thoughtfully at his quiet minister. Slowly, the wine-sodden fog lifted from his mind. The vanara king bowed solemnly to Hanuman, to acknowledge his wisdom. Sugriva sent his doorkeepers to escort Lakshmana through the king's own underground passage.

Like the sun entering a rain cloud, Lakshmana came into Sugriva's palace. Along carved wooden terraces, curling corridors, and polished halls, he was led through the labyrinthine edifice. He paused at the threshold of the antapura. He heard exquisite music within, and saw the beautiful women of the vanara's harem. The tinkling of their silver anklets, the warm, breathy whispering of their voices, the fragrance of their delicate bodies invaded him like a seductive army.

Growing confused, he pulled violently on his bowstring and Kishkinda shook to its foundations.

14. *The diplomacy of Tara*

Sugriva turned pale when he heard the thunder of Lakshmana's bowstring. For all his boasting, he dared not face the angry prince. Terror gripped the vanara king and his fur stood on end. He turned to the lovely Tara and said, "My queen, this kshatriya's real nature is gentle, and he is as easily calmed as he is roused. Go to him, Tara; he will never show his anger to a woman. Pacify him, then bring him here and I will speak to him."

Lakshmana waited alone in a corner, away from the eyes of the women of the harem. When the lovely Tara came to him in the wooden hall where he stood, she sensed his tenseness and his fury. Hesitantly she came, her long eyes cast down and only half open from all the wine she had drunk with Sugriva. Her slender body quivered with fear, like a lotus in a breeze. Yet she came with great poise, and was entirely queenly. Lakshmana knew who she was, but not why she had come. Thinking, even, that she had been sent to seduce him, he turned his back on her and stood glaring out a window. But Tara came softly up to him.

She said, "Be welcome to Kishkinda, O Kshatriya. But, great Lakshmana, you come in anger. Tell me, what is the cause of your rage, at which our city trembles? Who has been foolish enough to light a fire in a forest of dry trees?"

She touched him swift and deep. What man could ignore Tara's beautiful voice or her utterly feminine presence? This was not the kind of battle Lakshmana relished. With an effort, he steadied himself and quietened the disconcerting tumult in his body.

He said to her, decorously, "My lady, your husband has sent you to placate me. But don't be blind to what he has done. Once he became king, he has forgotten my brother Rama, who restored his kingdom to him. Wine and women are all he remembers, and dharma is far from his mind. These months that Sugriva has spent indulging himself, Rama has languished in the forest, with grief driving him to the edge of madness. Is this the friendship that Sugriva swore, with Agni as his witness? He has betrayed us, and an ingrate comes to a bad end."

Lakshmana spoke quietly. But there was truth in his words and his eyes still smoldered dangerously. Tara did not reply at once; she considered what to say. Her task was a delicate and grave one, and she knew it.

At last she said, "Kshatriya, even great rishis fall prey to the temptations of Kama. What, then, of a fickle monkey whose nature you well know? After years of being denied in the wilderness, Sugriva could hardly help indulging himself. He fell so avidly to pleasure that he left even the governance of the kingdom to his ministers.

"But, noble Lakshmana, Sugriva had no desire to hurt Rama or you. It isn't that he does not value your friendship; he was merely lost in a sensuous dream. You have woken him from his stupor; now let Rama, who is tolerance embodied, forgive him."

Lakshmana looked at this bewitching queen, and thought, who could refuse her anything she wanted? But he also made no immediate reply, only gazed evenly at her.

Tara said, "I think you should also know, my lord, that Sugriva has already ordered his vanaras to come to Kishkinda. He means to send them forth in every direction on the quest for Sita. He did this even before you came here. Hundreds of thousands of monkeys from all over the world already fly to us at their king's command."

She saw Lakshmana give a start at this news she had subtly kept for the last. She saw his eyes soften and knew her little battle was won: she had saved Kishkinda and its king from immediate danger. Tara said, "Come with me to the antapura. I can see you are pure and strong, and will not be tainted by its sights. Sugriva is waiting for you."

She walked before him through winding, climbing, simian corridors, along knotted branches of the ancestral tree into which the complex palace was built; and they came to the antapura, Sugriva's harem. Inside, the vanara king sat upon a couch of gaudy brocade. He wore fine ornaments. He sat among his women, with his arms around the delectable Ruma. Lakshmana's fury sparked alive again, and Tara sighed to herself at how indiscreet her lord was.

Sugriva sprang up when he saw Lakshmana. The kshatriya's eyes sparked with anger. But the ways of monkeys and men are a world apart, and little could Sugriva understand that seeing him with Ruma could infuriate the human as it did. He came forward guilelessly to greet the fair prince, shambling up to him, his long arms trailing the floor. He folded his hands solemnly to Lakshmana, and stood silent, his moist brown eyes gazing at the warrior's face.

Between his teeth, Lakshmana said, "A compassionate king, who is concerned about the suffering of others, gains fame for himself in the world. A truthful king, who remembers favors he has received and is grateful for them, deserves his renown. But a king who strays from dharma, who forgets his solemn oath sworn to his friend: there is no one worse than him. There is redemption from every sin in this world, prayaschitta for even the murder of a brahmana. But where is the salvation for an ungrateful man?

"Sugriva, you lied to us when you swore you would help find Sita. Rama kept his word to you; for your sake, he took Vali's life. But when you had what you wanted, you ignored Rama's need. The gates through which Vali went are not shut. If you don't honor your oath sworn before Agni, Rama's arrows will send you after your brother. Rama bids me tell you there is still time for you to relent. But hurry, Sugriva; before both your time and his mercy run out."

Lakshmana spoke fiercely. It seemed the calmness that Tara had brought to his spirit was shaken at the sight of Sugriva at his dalliance, while Rama was waiting in anguish for the vanara to find Sita. Tara wanted Sugriva to be quiet, lest, in his inebriated anxiety, he say the wrong thing.

She said quickly, "You leap to the wrong conclusions, my prince. Sugriva is not a liar, nor has he forgotten his oath. Sugriva loves Rama. For Rama this vanara will sacrifice everything, even his kingdom. Why, he would gladly abandon Ruma and me, for Rama's sake. Even in my bed, my husband speaks of Rama. I have told you, mighty Lakshmana, Sugriva has already called his legion vanaras to him, to send them to the corners of the earth to seek Sita out. Shed your anger, good Kshatriya. The vanaras will discover Sita swiftly, wherever she may be hidden."

As Tara spoke of Sugriva's devotion to Rama, the transformation that came over Lakshmana was quite marvelous. His body grew calm and a smile lit his handsome face like the sun breaking through dark clouds. Sugriva breathed a sigh of relief; his drunkenness had left him.

He took Lakshmana gingerly by his hand and led him into his apartment.

He sat him down on a couch and, crooning in affection, said, "How can you ever think I would forget Rama, when I owe him everything I have today? Nothing can repay my debt to your brother. I may be just a vanara, but I am not such an ingrate. Not that a kshatriya who can shoot one arrow through seven sala trees needs my help. But for what it is worth, all my resources are Rama's to use. Why, my very life belongs to him.

"And when he sets out to kill the rakshasa who took Sita, I will follow him with my army. I will follow Rama anywhere: let him forgive me just this once." Wringing his hands, he stood before Lakshmana.

The vapors of anger had risen away from that prince's mind. He said slowly, "With you at his side, loving Sugriva, Rama will surely vanquish his enemy. But now come with me to Prasravana. Rama needs to see you to restore his faith. As for me, I spoke harshly only because I have watched my brother's anguish these five months and found it hard to bear. Sugriva, forgive me for what I said impetuously."

There was genuine sorrow in the vanara's eyes as he heard about Rama. He turned to Hanuman: "My monkeys from Vindhya and Himavan, Mahendra and Kailasa, march on Kishkinda even now. Send word to them to make haste. Fifteen days was the limit I set. Five have already passed. Rama is in pain; my people must be here in ten days."

Before he had finished speaking, they heard an alarm in the streets below them, and the noise came toward the palace. Through the window, Sugriva saw that his colorful people had begun to arrive from far-flung parts of the earth. They came to his door with gifts for their king, and he welcomed them graciously.

When he had seen to the comfort of those first troops, Sugriva called for his palanquin. He climbed into it with Lakshmana and they set out for Prasravana. The hefty, long-limbed vanara carriers loped through the forest, flying lightly through the lower branches of the trees when passage was difficult on the ground. They arrived at the cave to which Lakshmana guided them with jungle directions of tree, rock, and stream. By now he was no stranger to the vana, and he knew how those who lived here found their way.

Sugriva alighted from the wooden litter; he came nervously into Rama's presence. As soon as the vanara saw the prince, he gave a low cry and stretched himself on his face at Rama's feet, his tail coiled, his eyes lowered for shame. But Rama raised up the great monkey and embraced him. Only gently did he chide him, saying with a smile, "My friend, dharma, artha, and kama should be of equal importance in one's life. To be aware only of kama is as dangerous as falling asleep on the brittle branch of a tree. I hope you remember your promise to me, Sugriva, that you would find my Sita."

His eyes wandering everywhere except to Rama's face, Sugriva said, "You are like a God to me! Everything I have today is because of you. How can I forget what I promised you, Rama? Even as we speak, thousands of vanaras converge on Kishkinda. The first monkey tribes have already arrived. Soon the city and the hillside will swarm with my people.

"When they are all here, I will give the command and they will fly to comb the world. Wherever Ravana has hidden her, my vanaras will discover your Sita."

Sugriva took Rama's hand and stroked it. "You shall not have long to wait; bear with me just ten days more."

Rama saw he spoke the truth. He saw the monkey king's love in his eyes and, knowing his simple nature, he gladly forgave Sugriva. He put the delay down to his own karma, and hugged his friend. At least now he knew what arrangements Sugriva had made to find Sita. This was infinitely better than the hell he had been in, not knowing if the vanara meant to keep his word at all.

15. The quest for Sita

In swinging legions, the vanaras of the world poured into the cradle-land of their race. By the tenth day after Sugriva met Rama at Prasravana, the hillside reverberated with their exuberance at being all together in the forest of their ancestors, as they had not been for centuries. The trees flashed bright fur, shining eyes, glittering jewelry, vivid scarves, caps, and clothes. Indeed great, they said to each other, must be the cause that brings all the monkey people on earth together at their king's gates. They were not particular about shelter and every tree in the forest housed ten husky males.

Sugriva came again to Rama's cave that overlooked the sea of vanaras on the hill below. Bowing to him, the monkey king cried, "My people have answered my call. Think that I have a hundred thousand bodies myself; for it is my spirit that goes abroad as my people to seek out Sita. Rama, the vanaras of the earth and their king are yours to command!"

Rama said, "My loyal friend, let your people find where Ravana lives. Let them discover whether Sita is alive. But command your great army yourself, Sugriva: they are your people and you are their king."

Sugriva summoned a vanara chieftain called Vinata. He said to Vinata, "Take a fourth of our army and go west. On the mountains, and in their every cave, search for Sita. Seek her as you might seek your very life if it were lost. Seek her in jungles, across rivers, and upon hills. Cross the Ganga, the Yamuna, and the Saraswati on your quest; cross the Sindhu. If you still don't find her, cross into alien lands. Scour the frontier countries for her and fly back to me in a month. May success attend your search. For your life shall be forfeit, Vinata, if you do not find Sita."

Sugriva sent Hanuman to the south, with Angada to lead that expedition. He sent Tara's father, Sushena, to the east, with a teeming force, and Shatabali to the north. To each vanara chieftain, Sugriva described all the lands and nations he would search in astonishing detail. Rama wondered at how widely Sugriva had ranged over the earth, and how well he remembered everything he had seen on his journeys. This was not knowledge acquired from stories he had heard: it was the learning of sight and sound, touch, scent, and adventure.

Then Sugriva called Hanuman to him alone. "Wherever she may be, there is no one more likely to find Sita than you. Not the mottled face of the earth, not the sky with its realms of clouds, not the seven seas can contain you, Son of the wind. O ablest of all my people, not even the worlds of spirits are inaccessible to you, who can fly as swiftly as your father of light and air. Do you remember the day she dropped the bundle of her jewels down to us on Rishyamooka? The Rakshasa took her south that day. While all the others may fail, I know that you, Hanuman, will find Rama's Sita for him."

Rama went to Hanuman and put his hands on the loving monkey's shoulders. He smiled at Sugriva's wisest minister. "I believe that, of all the vanaras, you will find Sita."

Rama took a golden signet ring from his finger and pressed it into Hanuman's long hand. "Show this to her when you find Sita, and she will know you have come from me."

Deep peace came over the spirit of Rama when the vanara received that ring and prostrated himself before the prince. Rama was strangely certain that when Hanuman headed south to seek Sita, the quest for her would truly begin. Hanuman went down the hill and gathered his vanaras to him; and to Rama he seemed briefly like the moon with a thousand stars twinkling around him. Rama called out again to the vanara who had, from the first, impressed him as being the sagest of his kind.

"Hanuman," he cried, waving, "remember I count on you!"

Sugriva's army flashed away across the earth on its quest. The monkeys went through the world like fireflies through a jungle.

16. In the south

The vanara armies went in pageant from Prasravana, some under the trees, some over the leafy, nimble ways of their branches; and the hillside was emptied of a hundred thousand monkeys.

At the cave mouth, Rama turned to Sugriva and said with a smile, "When you described the far countries to your chieftains, I felt you had seen them all with your own eyes. How do you know so much about the earth, Sugriva?"

Sugriva said, "Rama, when my brother Vali pursued me in anger once, I fled through the world. Through forests and across rivers, over mountains and through mazes of caves I flew, with him after me. He chased me across the earth and I fled for my life with my four ministers. Finally, Hanuman reminded me of Matanga's curse, and we came out of the north to Rishyamooka. My eyes saw the world in terror. Fear held them wide open and every detail is engraved on my memory. For years Vali chased me, Rama, and for years I flew before him."

Teasingly, Rama asked, "Isn't it time you returned to your palace? Tara waits for you, Sugriva, and Ruma and many others. I will see you in a month, when the moon is full again."

In hope, Rama waited. When he grew dejected, Lakshmana was beside him to divert him from his grief. His brother took Rama on long walks through the jungle of endless fascination. Lakshmana would always say that sooner than Rama thought, Sita would be found.

Vinata in the west, Sushena in the east, and Shatabali in the north combed those quarters for Sita. Great vanara legions poured through forests and across rivers, over mountains and into deep caves, questioning the wild folk they met along the way, cajoling or threatening them as they saw fit. The monkeys scoured the corners of Bharatavarsha for Ravana's kingdom or lair. But they found no trace of him, or of her whom they sought. After the month given them was over, they came back, disappointed and apprehensive, to Kishkinda and Prasravana.

Sugriva stood on the hill's shoulder with Rama, overlooking his forces that had returned to him empty-handed. He said quietly, "These I never expected to find Sita. Didn't we see the Rakshasa bear her away to the south? Be of firm faith, Rama. Vayu's son Hanuman will return with news of your wife."

The force of vanaras that went south with Hanuman, Angada, and Thara at its head, traveled across all the lands that Sugriva had described to them. They were exactly as he said. The intricate caves of the Vindhya mountains, its thick jungles, the hidden fissures behind many falls that plunged down mountain slopes—they searched all these, but found no sign of Ravana or Sita, nor gleaned any news of them from the denizens of those parts. Forest after forest they combed, and with each one they passed without finding her their dejection grew.

Once they wandered into the strangest vana any of them had ever seen. The trees of that forest had neither leaves nor flowers. Riverbeds they saw here, but no drop of water between their banks. It was a dead forest, where no blade of grass grew, where no living creature drew breath. The silence of the lifeless realm was absolute and Angada's monkeys were unnerved. Huddling together, the vanara army crept breathlessly through that wasteland, and at its very heart they saw a rishi sitting in tapasya. His austere face shone, his jata was piled high, and near him was a charming pool on whose bank flowering trees grew, and trees laden with fruit.

They did not know it, neither did they dare disturb the solemn muni at his tapasya, but he was Kandu. Years ago, his son of sixteen summers had been lost in this same forest. When, after days of searching frenziedly for him, the rishi did not find the boy, he cursed the forest and everything in it to be desolate forever.

Silently, the vanaras passed through the eerie place. They went farther south. Quite suddenly, they saw trees ahead of them full of lush green leaves. They heard all the sounds of a living jungle: streams full of gushing water and branches full of birds that sang among brilliant flowers and their scents. Fierce tigers, elephant, and deer they saw, and the monkeys heaved a sigh of relief that the bizarre zone of death had ended.

But they had hardly entered the living jungle when a rakshasa, whose body faced one way and his head another, attacked them with a roar. Gibbering in fright, all the vanaras save Hanuman and Thara scampered into the nearest trees. Not that their perches were safe, because the rakshasa was as tall as any tree that grew there. Angada faced the strange monster alone.

In a wink, Vali's son grew as tall as the demon, and cried to Hanuman, "It is Ravana, uncle, and I will kill him!"

Before the rakshasa had recovered from his surprise, Angada smashed his head with a blow. The rakshasa fell, oozing blood and brains. As he died, he told them he was not Ravana, but the Rishi Marichi's son. Would they please release him from the bondage of his fiendish body by burning him? A thousand monkeys dug a pit for the rakshasa. In no time, they covered him with dry branches and set him alight. They saw a spirit form rise from the fire and, hands folded, ascend into the sky.

On they pressed. This was a jungle of endless hills, and each one had a honeycomb of caves scooped into its side. Patiently, the vanaras searched every hill and cave, flowing into those mazes in a tide of monkeys; and they came out again, shaking their heads, chattering in frustration. When they had combed that southernmost jungle without success, Angada's vanaras gathered around a great tree that grew in a clearing at the forest's limit. Restless and despondent, wave upon wave of the monkey folk stood around their prince.

Angada said to them, "The wise say that unwavering resolve in adversity leads to success. Don't be discouraged, we still have a week left. Let us forget our tiredness and begin again. We may have overlooked the one cave in which the Demon holds her."

The vanaras cheered him loudly. Like a golden river, they flowed away from the conclave around the solemn tree. Shouting encouragement to each other, they climbed the silver hill, Rajata, which was named for its pale color. Cautiously, they peered into every cave on that silvery hill. Each one they entered and searched, and they finally reached the summit. But they found no Sita, nor any clue of her.

They returned to Vindhya through the dead forest. Cave by cave, they searched that mountain, wood by wood; but not even here did they find the princess. The last week of the month Sugriva had given them elapsed. Hunger, thirst, and the weakness of the final week's frantic efforts had taken their toll on the monkeys. The army was exhausted. Great were the numbers and the appetite of that force, and they had denuded the jungles through which they passed of all their fruit.

Suddenly, a young vanara at the foot of the mountain they were combing cried to Angada and Hanuman, "My lords, come and look! A cave we haven't seen before."

They scrambled down the slope and saw that there was indeed a cave mouth, overgrown with foliage and flowering creepers, and veiled by a stand of trees, as well, as if nature had conspired to keep that cavern hidden from the eyes of strangers. As they stood gazing, they felt a gust of air blow at them. The bushes across the mysterious opening were agitated and the vanaras leaped back in alarm. But only a white stork and some painted teal winged their way out from the cave, squawking at the congregation of monkeys.

A delicious fragrance wafted around the vanaras invitingly. By now hunger churned their stomachs as much as failure did their spirits, and they were desperate to discover what lay within the cave mouth. They pulled away creepers, bent bushes and small trees, and in single file, slowly, and often painfully when some thorny plants scratched their hands and faces, managed to push their way in.

That cave was called Rikshabila; but Angada's monkeys did not know this. All was dark inside. When the creepers and bushes outside sprang back into place, no glimmer of light penetrated the blackness within. The monkeys held tightly on to one another's hands, forming a long chain of vanaras. Now they crept forward, so no one was afraid or lost in that perpetual night. Outside, hearing that an unexplored cave had been discovered, more and more vanaras arrived at the cave mouth. Bending back tree and bush, pulling aside creepers, they also crawled into Rikshabila.

For an hour and a yojana, the vanaras crept along the perfectly dark tunnel. Where the roof was low they were forced to crawl on all fours. As they went they were swathed in the ethereal scent, always wafted to them from ahead. Then Angada, who led the way, cried, "Light!"

The vanaras at the head of the chain emerged into another cavern with a high, sloping roof. They gasped when they shaded their eyes against the glare: before them they saw a garden bathed in mellow light. A profusion of trees grew here; but they were golden trees! Their blooms shone with colors that stirred the soul: calescent colors that were not any of the rainbow, nor of this world, but beyond both. From these flowers the quintessential fragrance that had swept over them seeped all the way to the cave mouth.

Clear pools dotted the garden, their water scintillating as if they were made of droplets of diamonds and pearls. An exuberance of water birds swam on these and warbled in joy. But there was more: imposing mansions of gleaming silver stood among the groves of golden trees. In awe, the vanaras stole forward. They saw the paths at their feet were of beaten gold and, like the mansions, encrusted with thousands of tiny precious stones. Apart from the bird's songs, a deep silence hung over the garden of enchantment, which was surely a relic from another age of the earth.

On soft feet, the wide-eyed monkey folk ventured cautiously into the first palatial edifice. They found it deserted. They came out and went into another; but that, too, had no living soul within its splendid walls. The vanaras roamed the wonderful streets for some time and they saw no one; until, all at once, Hanuman and Angada felt they were being watched.

Hanuman glanced at his prince. Angada's eyes roved up and down the airy street. He said, "Someone is here."

The next moment there was a quaint flash of light and a very tall woman stood before them: an ascetic wearing deerskin. She and they all stood still for a moment, staring at each other. Then she smiled at them and folded her palms. Hanuman answered her, folding his own hands and bowing deeply to her.

"Greetings, Swamini. We came through a dark tunnel and we do not know where we are. We were hungry and thirsty, and we saw water birds fly out of a cave mouth on the hillside. We followed their flight and arrived in this wonderful place. What is this garden, and who are you, holy one?"

She raised her fine hand in a blessing. "In olden days, great Mayaa, the architect of the Asuras, who built the fabled Tripura, created this garden. Mayaa worshipped Brahma with a long tapasya and the Pitama gave him the magical knowledge of architecture, which once only Usanas possessed.

"But Mayaa and Indra had battle between them over a woman, and Indra drove Mayaa from here with his vajra. Brahma gave that woman, Hema, these gardens and mansions. As for me, I am Svayamprabha, Merusavarni's daughter, Mena's friend, and the guardian of this Rikshabila.

"But we stand talking here and I make you weary travelers no proper welcome. You must eat some fruit from my trees and drink some wine to quench your thirst. Come, good vanaras."

They sat in a grove of trees that breathed quite plainly. Svayamprabha served them the gleaming fruit, which none of them had ever seen before—which, indeed, did not grow in the world outside. They were succulent and sweet. But famished though they were, no more than a single fruit each could the vanaras eat. The tasty flesh restored the monkeys' spirits and stilled their hunger completely. The wine Svayamprabha served them tasted unearthly too. It fetched the color back to their faces and made them light-headed.

Svayamprabha asked, "What brings you to the heart of our forest?"

Hanuman said, "We came in search of Sita."

He told her their story from the beginning, and of Rama's sorrow. When he had finished, he said, "You have been so kind, I am sure fate led us to you. If there is anything the vanaras can do to repay the debt, you only have to mention it, whatever it may be."

But she smiled, and shook her head. Hanuman said, "Much as we would love to, we cannot tarry, for our quest calls us urgently. We hoped we might find Sita in this hidden place; but it seems the tide of fortune still runs against us. Shall we return the way we came, or is there any other way back into the world?"

Svayamprabha looked troubled. "Usually, no one who enters here may ever leave. If you search for the tunnel through which you came, you will not find it. But I am moved by your mission and I will help you. You must all shut your eyes and not open them until I tell you to. Link your hands and sit perfectly still."

The vanaras obeyed her. Without feeling anything, never knowing how it happened, and so swiftly, they found themselves back in the outside world, though not in the jungle they had combed for Sita. Svayamprabha stood before them, tall and serene.

She pointed. "Beyond the shoulder of this hill lies the Mahodadi. Fare you well, and perhaps we shall meet again someday along the winding trails of time."

And she vanished before their eyes.

17. Despair

Angada and his people had not far to go before they found themselves on a beach. The sea, which many of them had never seen, stretched away to the horizon and roared in their ears. Unknown to them, and by an intuition of her lucid heart, Svayamprabha had brought them to the western shore of Bharatavarsha.

The yogini had called the sea before them Mahodadi, and so it was: vast, as they stood forlorn, staring across its interminable majesty. They stood a long time, feeling helpless. The month that Sugriva had given them to find Sita was over. Another week had passed in the world while they ate with Svayamprabha: time in her enchanted garden was also unearthly. Winter was almost over and spring would soon arrive in all his gaiety.

Angada's monkeys watched the rhythmical waves crash and ebb against pale sands, and they trembled to think of Sugriva's wrath when they returned to Kishkinda without news of Sita. Angada called a council of his chieftains.

He said to those leaders of his people, "Every one of you is a warrior and a hero. But who can stand against fate, when she is against us? We missed no cave on the hill slopes of the jungles; there is no grove or thicket we did not comb. But we have not found Sita and we have failed in our mission. Most of all, my friends, *I* have failed."

He drew a deep breath. "A sentence of death awaits us if we go back to Kishkinda. Sugriva will never forgive this failure. He is hard and cruel, our king. I know him; he has no love for me. It wasn't he who made me yuvaraja, but Rama who forced him to. At the first chance he gets, Sugriva will have me killed, as he did my father. I would rather stay here by this sea and fast to death than go back to Kishkinda and be murdered by my uncle."

The handsome Angada spoke softly, and not in anger but in sorrow and despair. His vanaras' hearts went out to their prince on the windy shore, where gulls wheeled whitely above and the waves washed frothing over their long feet. Some of the monkeys raised their voices to agree with what Angada had said.

"You speak wisely."

"Rama loves his wife so much that Sugriva will have our heads to please him."

"It would be foolish to return to Kishkinda."

"What prevents us from searching on for Sita?"

"If we fail, we can think hard of the world to come and starve to death."

The vanara chieftain Thara cried, "Why should we despair and kill ourselves for the sake of a man who means nothing to us? Besides, he killed our king Vali. Let us find our way back to enchanted Rikshabila, where our joy was so great that a week passed like an hour. We can live out our lifetimes easily on the fruit of Mayaa's trees. We need not fear Sugriva there. Why, we need not fear Rama, or even Indra, in Rikshabila."

There were murmurs of approval; then a silence fell. All the chieftains looked at Angada, asking silently for his opinion of Thara's plan. Hanuman did not like Thara's plan: it was the way of weakness.

He said to Angada, "My prince, you are as brave as your father. No, I think you are even braver than Vali was. You will be a great king of our people someday. Yet you have the youthful impetuosity of all the noble and the openhearted. Because they are afraid to face Sugriva, these vanaras agree with what Thara says. But we monkeys are renowned for our fickleness. What will happen when, tomorrow, these same vanaras begin to miss their wives and their children? And let me tell you, not all our common soldiers will like Thara's plan."

He paused and scratched his fur ruminatively with a fine finger. "Then some of us are such old servants and friends of Sugriva's that nothing could make us disloyal to him. Let me remind you, we should not make enemies of those who are measurelessly more powerful than we are. We should not act in bad faith toward Rama and Lakshmana. Thara may say what he likes, but I, Hanuman, tell you that no cave or garden in the three worlds shall be a sanctuary if we make enemies of Rama and his brother. Svayamprabha said that Indra's vajra drove Mayaa from his garden. Can you imagine, then, what one of Lakshmana's astras would do to us?

"When that time comes, Angada, all these monkeys will abandon you. And who could blame them? I say we should go back to Kishkinda like brave vanaras and tell Sugriva that, though we left no forest or cave unexplored, we could not find Sita. I know Sugriva better than anyone does. His manner is sometimes harsh, for what he has suffered. But having suffered as he has, his heart is kind. I don't agree that he made you yuvaraja only to please Rama. Didn't you see how he cried, when your father lay dying? He wanted to relinquish the kingdom.

"Also, think how much he loves your mother Tara; he will never harm you. Do not let fear cloud your judgment. Sugriva has no son and he loves you like his own child. We must take courage in both hands and go back to Kishkinda. All of us will go with you; we will beg Sugriva to spare your life."

But Hanuman had barely finished when Angada cried, "Your loyalty to my uncle blinds you, Hanuman! Sugriva is not nearly as noble as you make him out to be. He is neither pure nor kind; he is not straightforward or manly, but selfish. Just think how quickly he has taken his dead brother's widow for his wife—my mother. This is what he always wanted. Years ago, even, he sealed the cave where my father fought the Asura. He came home with the lie that Vali was dead. Is such a vanara trustworthy?

"What about this very quest? Rama secured a kingdom for Sugriva. But once he sat on Kishkinda's throne, did Sugriva remember Rama? You, Hanuman, reminded him of his dharma. And this after the fickle monkey had sworn friendship with Rama before a holy fire. Is such a vanara trustworthy? I tell you, but for the terror the sound of Lakshmana's bowstring struck in Sugriva's heart, we would not be here at all.

"Whatever you say, I will not trust a coward. Perhaps if we return, Sugriva will spare my life for my mother's sake, since she warms his bed. But he will imprison and torture me.

"I am not a fool that I will go back to Kishkinda. I will sit here and cast my life away before the sea. If any of you wants to return, he may. If you all want to go, do so with my blessing. Tell the princes of Kosala about me, then my uncle, and at last my mother. I hardly think she will survive this news."

As he spoke, tears filled Angada's eyes and trickled down his face. When he had finished, he began to pull up stalks of darbha grass that grew behind the sand line, to make a bed for himself to die on. Angada's impressionable monkeys were so moved that they, too, went and touched the sacred waters of the sea with their fingers. They sat around their prince, to die beside him themselves.

By the hypnotic wash of the waves the stricken vanaras sat, and they recalled the events that led to their being out here, in these dire straits. They spoke about Rama's childhood, of Kaikeyi's boons and of Dasaratha. These monkeys had roamed in distant lands, and they knew all about the blue prince of Ayodhya. About the exile of Rama, Lakshmana, and Sita in the Dandaka vana they spoke, about Panchavati and the massacre of the rakshasas of Janasthana. They reminded each other of the golden deer and the abduction of Sita. Then they spoke of Jatayu's death, as the scarlet sun sank into the sea, setting the waves alight. They remembered how Rama came to Rishyamooka, and the death of Vali. The wind carried their solemn narration, and twilight earth and livid sea heard the tale of Rama.

18. Sampati

On the mountain behind the vanaras, in a cave swept by ocean winds, lived Sampati the eagle. He was hungry, and when he saw the monkeys on the beach below his roost, he said to himself, "Fate is kind to me today. I don't have to go in search of my next meal: it has come to my cave mouth."

But Sampati was so old, and deaf as well, that he spoke aloud to himself. The wind, which blew at this hour from land to sea, carried what he said into Angada's sharp ears. The vanara prince jumped up with a shout. "Yama has come as an eagle to take us!"

Angada was so distraught he began to babble: "All the birds and beasts of the jungle loved Rama. Why, Jatayu gave his life for the prince of light. And for Rama's sake, we will also be devoured by death. But Jatayu was fortunate; the Rakshasa killed him and he didn't have to face Sugriva's wrath. But if you think of why we are about to die, Uncle Hanuman, it is because of Kaikeyi. She is the root of all this misfortune."

As he came nearer, for his dinner, Sampati heard everything Angada said. In his gravelly voice Sampati called, "Who speaks of Jatayu? Who says Jatayu is dead? It is a thousand years since I heard my brother's name. Who is the rakshasa that killed him? Who is Rama? I am old and weak, and I can hardly climb down this mountain. Help me, someone. Help me down to the ground and tell me about my brother."

At first the vanaras did not trust the eagle. But Angada went nearer and began the story of Rama again for Sampati's benefit. The ancient bird wept when he heard how Jatayu sacrificed his life for Sita. Angada told Sampati how Rama cremated Jatayu, and sent his soul to his ancestors. The monkey prince described how Rama came to Rishya-mooka, and their own fruitless quest for Sita.

At last, he sighed, "Searching for Sita is like seeking the sun at midnight. And we have come to this final shore to die."

The eagle, who had wanted to make his meal of them, now said gently, "Jatayu was my little brother. Once, I would already have flown to Ravana's city to have revenge. But, alas, I am too old and infirm now."

His feathers shook; he sobbed like a child, and all the vanaras gathered around the great bird. He saw their eager faces by the dying light; he saw their keen eyes. Sampati, who had lived alone for so long, was moved to tell the monkey folk the story of his own life, in his resonant, rambling way.

"I am old, ah, I am older than you can imagine, my vanaras. Would you believe me if I told you that with these eyes I have seen the Vamana Avatara of the Lord Vishnu, when he measured the worlds with three strides? Swarga, Bhumi, and Patala! And now there is Rama. I was there when the Devas and the Asuras churned the sea of milk to obtain the amrita from under the waves. I was there when the Hala-hala was churned up and began to consume the sky. I saw Siva quaff it, and it burned his throat blue; then they called him Nilakanta.

"I wish I could help Rama, who has come as a man now. But look, my wings are burned stumps and I cannot fly any more. It was at least a thousand years ago. Jatayu and I were much younger then; we were in our prime. We competed fiercely at everything. Once we challenged each other to prove who could fly higher, and nearest the sun. It was around the time when Indra slew Vritrasura. Angling our youthful wings, we flew into the sky like two arrows. Up and up we flew, for a night and a day, and the sun scorched us; still, we flew on. We were proud then, and each wanted to show he was the stronger one.

"As we matched each other, wing beat for wing beat, suddenly I saw Jatayu began to fall behind me. Dizziness overcame him, and I turned and clasped him in my wings. In our arrogance we had flown too near the sun: his body blazed with the wrath of the star. The moment I paused in my flight, the breeze no longer blew around me to cool my feathers. My wings took fire. Still holding the unconscious Jatayu in my arms, I plummeted down to the earth. A long, long time I fell, burning, and I also swooned. I awoke rudely when I crashed on this mountain. My wings were charred flightless, and there was no sign of Jatayu anywhere."

Again Sampati's eyes filled, as he remembered the vertiginous fall that had changed his life. He said, "Never since, have I seen or heard anything of my brother; until today, when you, my friends, bring these sad tidings." He wept with grave dignity, that aged bird.

Angada said, "You say that if you were younger and could fly, you would have attacked Ravana in his city. Do you know where the Rakshasa lives?"

The great eagle wiped his eyes with his ruined wing tips. He drew himself to his full height, and he was tall indeed; he towered over the vanaras. His eyes flashed a semblance of their piercing fire of old, and Sampati said, "I, too, saw the lovely Sita as Ravana carried her across the sky. She cried out and struggled, but the Rakshasa held her helpless. Her ornaments fell from her in a golden shower, and again and again she cried, 'Rama! Lakshmana! Save me!' Her garment was a streak of lightning against the ominous cloud that was the Demon. Now I remember; it must have been Sita: she cried out her husband's sacred name."

He paused; their eyes lighting up, the monkeys craned to him. Sampati said, "Indeed I know where Ravana lives; I know the place well."

Sampati looked around him again in the gathering twilight, and he saw hope flare on the monkeys' faces. The eagle continued, "Ravana is Visravas's son and Kubera's brother. He rules the island of Lanka, a hundred yojanas from this shore. Viswakarman created wonderful Lanka for the Rakshasa."

As he spoke, Sampati peered out across the sea and his eyes narrowed in concentration. With his burned wings, he waved the vanaras who blocked his view out of his way. The monkeys also peered where

Sampati did. They saw nothing except smoky waves stretching to the horizon. But Sampati stood very still, his eyes keened, his feathers quivering.

Suddenly he cried, "I see her! I see her in Ravana's garden, surrounded by rakshasis. I see her crying."

Then he grew slack again, and looked around at the disbelieving vanaras. His eyes shone. "I belong to the eldest race of eagles; Garuda is my kinsman. Our kind can see a mouse from the moon if we set our minds to it, for we hunt from the air. Though I am old and my vision is not what it used to be, at a hundred yojanas I can still see the lustful eyes on Ravana's ten heads, and the tears in Sita's, soft as lotuses."

Sampati's face grew dim again with his own grief, and he said, "Help me to the water's edge. I must offer tarpana to my brother."

When he had finished offering solemn tarpana, he came back to the shoreline of dry sand. He glowed with some ineffable joy. Angada, who saw this, cried, "O Sampati, a great light is upon your feathers! Can you tell us how we can reach Lanka in the sea?"

But the eagle shook his head. "My part in this adventure is over. This is the evening I have waited for, for more than a thousand years. My friends, in the old days a rishi lived on this mountain. Once, I despaired at my flightlessness and my dependence on my son Suparshva, who has looked after me as if he were the father and I the son. In that despair I thought, as you did just now, of taking my own life. But even as I stood in this very place and decided to walk into the waves to drown myself, that rishi came up behind me and took my wing.

"He said, 'You shall fly again one day, Sampati. Be patient, you have a great task ahead of you still: for one day, you will be the eyes that help Vishnu's own Avatara find his love. When that day comes and you have shown an extraordinary army the way to Lanka, your wings will sprout alive again. Sampati, be patient until then.'

"So here I am, my vanaras, and here you are; and I have shown you the way to Lanka. I feel a great burden lift from my spirit, I feel a light in my heart."

Even as he spoke, a golden lambency was upon the eagle's body and he shone like a piece of sun on that dusky shore. As the vanaras watched, Sampati's wings sprouted fresh young plumage before their eyes. His stooped back grew erect; his sunken eyes blazed again. He cried his shrill hunting cry in the ecstasy of his transformation, and the beach echoed with it. When the uncanny illumination left his body, it left Sampati young again and his wings whole once more.

"It is done!" he cried, dancing for joy. "Vanaras, look at me: nothing is impossible with faith. You will surely find Lanka, if only you believe you will."

Then, launching himself with a few running steps, he spread his splendid new wings and, crying out rapturously, flew up into the darkening sky and vanished.

19. Who will cross the sea?

The vanaras cheered Sampati on his way into the sky he had not flown in for a thousand years. They jumped up and down on that shore. Even when he had circled above them once and disappeared, flashing away like an astra, their joy did not wane. For they also celebrated the news Sampati had given them. At last they knew where Sita was; even if they did not yet know how to cross the dark sea that lay between themselves and her.

Shouting and dancing, as monkeys will, they leaped down from the embankment where Sampati had stood and went to the water's edge. They gazed out at the sullen, silver-crested expanse before them, and they fell somber and silent. The vista of waves was awesome and they did not have eagle's eyes that they could discern Lanka anywhere, let alone Sita in her garden of confinement.

Angada was quick to sense the despondency that gripped his people when they gazed out at the swollen waves. Turning away from that forbidding sight, he said to the vanaras, "Peering at the sea will serve no purpose. Our answer doesn't lie there, but within ourselves. We are tired. The day has been a long one and we have knocked at death's door. Night is upon us and this sand will serve as a soft bed tonight. When we wake up in the morning, we will think again of how to cross the ocean. Good night, my sweet vanaras. Sleep in peace tonight, because fortune finally smiles on our enterprise."

One by one, lulled by the drone of the waves, the vanaras fell asleep. The moon rose regally behind them, over the shoulder of the mountain. Long after the last vanara soldier was asleep, the leaders of that force sat huddled together around Angada, deliberating in quiet voices the impossible task before them: to cross a hundred yojanas of water. Past midnight, when the moon was at his zenith, Angada, Hanuman, and the other chieftains also fell asleep. The beach presented a strange spectacle as Soma Deva passed above: wrapped in his spectral light, a teeming army of monkeys covered the white sands.

The next morning, the vanaras rose with the sun's first rays slanting across their faces. They washed in the velvet sea, which lay like an interminable dream before them. There was no sign, even by daylight, of any southern shore to the ocean; no speck of island dotted the vacant horizon. Standing on the embankment, Angada raised his arms to call his people to him.

When they thronged around him, he said to them, "We are an ancient and magical race. Many of us have Devas for fathers and grandfathers. Some say the roots of the tree of the race of vanaras plunge deeper into time than those of the tree of men. I want to know who among you can leap across this yawning sea, find Sita, and leap back again? A hundred yojanas and death by drowning if you fail! Who can do it? Which of the vanaras will make the leap of faith?"

Only the dawn waves, washing ashore, answered him. Angada's call echoed there and the sea seemed to mock him.

He cried again, "I know there are great heroes among you; why have you all fallen silent? Let us hear of your prowess, vanaras. Let us hear how far each of you can leap."

Gaja of the monkey folk raised his voice above the ocean's ceaseless roar. "I can leap ten yojanas!"

Gavaksha shouted, "With my ancestors' blessing, I can leap twenty!"

Another vanara cried, "And I, thirty!"

Thus they shouted their abilities, one after another. Until one of the mightiest of them, Dwividha, cried, "I can jump seventy yojanas!"

Jambavan, the old king of the reekshas, the black bears, had journeyed from Kishkinda with the monkey force. Now he cried, "Once, I made a pradakshina around our Lord, the Dwarf Trivikrama of the three strides. And that was a great way indeed. Now the journey of my life draws near its end, and I stand on the brink of another ocean and another shore. Yet for Rama I will leap at least ninety yojanas, even at my age." He paused in doubt. "But a hundred, I wonder if I can leap a hundred. But if need be I can try!"

Then Angada himself cried, "I can cross the hundred yojanas easily!" His monkeys broke into loud cheers. He held up a hand for silence. "But I don't know if I can cross back again."

Jambavan said, "Angada, my child, I am certain you can cross to Lanka and back. Why, I am sure you could fly a thousand yojanas. For aren't you great Vali's son? But this task is not yours. It is not for a crown prince to risk his life, leaping into a strange land ruled by a rakshasa."

At once, Angada's eyes welled up. He said gently, "I thank you for your love, Jambavan. But who else will make this gravest leap? And you know it must be made. What is our solution, wise one? You think of a way."

Jambavan said quietly, "I shall, my prince."

He turned to where a solitary vanara sat upon a smooth rock, outside the throng of monkeys around their leaders. Hanuman sat all alone, gazing out over the implacable waves.

20. The son of the wind

Jambavan said to the moody Hanuman, "Why, O Son of the wind, do you doubt yourself so much? But it is the curse of all the greatest. Those who cannot do a tenth of what you can, those who haven't a shadow of your strength, stand up and boast about their prowess, while you sit here listening to them and say nothing. Hanuman, we need a hero to leap across the sea and bring glory to the vanaras."

But Hanuman was so unconfident, he said with a nervous laugh, "You have too much regard for me, good Jambavan."

"Do I indeed? Have you forgotten who you are, Vayuputra? Let me remind you of your ancestry, and let these monkeys hear who our modest Hanuman truly is. Once, Anjana, the apsara of heaven, was born as a vanari. She was so beautiful the wild wind was smitten by her. She could not resist him either, for their love was destined."

Jambavan grew thoughtful. "Yes, just as it was destined that one day you would sit here on this shore, doubting yourself with all your heart. Even as Anjana lay in Vayu Deva's coiling embrace, a voice spoke to her out of the sky: 'Anjana, a soul of matchless glory will be born as your son. He will have no equal in goodness or valor, wisdom or strength. Being his father's son, he will fly more swiftly than Garuda!'

"You have forgotten who you are, Hanuman. You have forgotten how, when you were just a child, you leaped into the sky because you thought the sun was a fruit you could eat. You flew three hundred yojanas into the air. Indra thought you were arrogant, and flung his thunderbolt of a thousand joints at you. But, Son of the wind, the awesome weapon merely grazed your cheek: for Brahma had blessed you to be immune to every ayudha. When the vajra fell away tamely, your people named you Hanuman: Invincible One.

"Vayu was incensed at Indra and he would not blow at all through the three worlds. At last, Indra realized it was only a child's fancy and not arrogance that had made you leap up like that. He was so charmed by your leaping for the sun that, laughing aloud at the thought, he also blessed you. He blessed you that you can summon your own death, like a servant, whenever you choose!"

Hanuman had risen beside Jambavan on that golden beach. Every word the king of bears said seemed to sever a link in the chain that bound his spirit. His eyes shone; his back was very erect. Hanuman smiled, and his doubts left him like mist before the sun.

Jambavan continued, "We stand not just on the shore of a sea, but at the brink of despair. You are Vayu's son, powerful as the wind himself. Don't hesitate, Hanuman: fate is calling you to make your name immortal. You are our hope; only you can save us all from death. Shed your unconfidence; your moment of glory has arrived."

There was a stirring of air above them. The vanaras sensed another implacable presence there. They huddled together and whimpered in fear. But caressed by his father's subtle fingers, Hanuman began to grow before the monkeys' eyes. His body shone with uncanny splendor and, moment by moment, as if Jambavan's words had unleashed the mahima siddhi, Hanuman grew bigger, and bigger still! As he grew, his expression also changed: from despondency to one of imperturbable joy. Now grown into a gigantic savior of his race, he smiled benignly down at the astounded vanaras.

He was tall as a hill; he was bright as the morning. He growled deep in his throat and shook his body like some unimaginable lion. The vanaras clutched at one another for comfort. They no longer saw Sugriva's wise and gentle, faithful and quiet minister Hanuman. This was another elemental being who towered over them, his great eyes glowing. This was Hanuman, the wind's magnificent son; and the challenge of the sea was no longer as daunting as it had seemed.

He was titanic already. Still he grew, until it seemed to the monkeys, dwarfed at his feet, that the sun would ignite his mane. He was like some great flame, and he bowed to the monkey elders and to his prince Angada. When he spoke to them, his voice was thunder.

"Agni's friend Vayu is powerful," boomed that immense vanara. "He is tameless, and he pervades the universe. I am that Vayu's son. No one can leap as far as I can. I can fly a thousand times around Mount Meru. I can fly around the world with the moon!"

It was as if a stranger spoke in their Hanuman's voice. The ocean trembled when he cried, "Do you know the strength of these arms with the sinews of the wind in them? I can thrust the mountains down into the earth and plunge the jungles into the sea. I can crush the greatest peaks into dust with my hands. And I, Hanuman, serve my Rama!"

The stupendous monkey smiled from ear to ear. "And now I will fly across this little sea to find Sita. I will cross the waves in a moment and carry her back to safety. If need be, I will draw Lanka up by its roots and bring it to Rama. I go now, I go!"

No monkey stood on that shore who was not slightly relieved that he went. Though he was always kindly, he was so awesome now they could not help being afraid of him. Yet they also rejoiced. Seeing him like that, they had no doubt that wherever she was, Hanuman would find Sita. It seemed that he was always intended to find her, none but he. Only he had to be pushed to the edge of despair before he summoned this other Hanuman from within himself: this pristine vanara who neither doubted nor knew the meaning of fear.

Jambavan, who alone was old enough not to be overwhelmed, cried, "We will wait upon this shore for you, Son of the wind. Remember our lives are in your hands."

Hanuman smiled. "Fear not, uncle, great Jambavan. My prince Angada, give me leave: I go now to find Sita in Lanka. But the soft ground will be riven if I leap from here. I must climb to the top of Mahendra where the rock is firm for a thousand hands. From there I will fly and cause the earth no injury."

With a few strides, climbing nimbly as monkeys do, he gained the summit he sought; his people stood on the beach below, watching him. He waved from his height, and it seemed to them he was bigger than the mountain. Far away were the eyes of the son of Anjana and the wind: in his mind, he had already reached Lanka and discovered Sita. With each foot on a different peak, he straddled Mahendra. Hanuman stood, swaying in his father's lofty gusts, whistling around him in exhilaration. Back and forth he swayed, readying himself for the leap of a hundred yojanas across the plumbless sea.

BOOK FIVE

SUNDARA KANDA

{Hanuman's adventure}

1. The leap of faith

Hanuman was a tremendous beast, straddling the Mahendra. As he craned toward the sky, the sinews on his neck and back stood out like cobras. Restlessly, the son of the wind paced the mountaintop. Tigers, bears, and leopards that lived near the summit scurried out from their caves and fled down the mountain: this was not a monkey they would care to contend with. Mahendra, which stood unmoved by tidal wave and typhoon, shuddered beneath Hanuman's footfalls. Elephants blundered down the slopes. Gandharvas and kinnaras who lived in some of the caves flew into the air in flashes, or fled with the animals.

The mountaintop swirled with gusts of wind, as Vayu enfolded his son in his airs. No one had made this leap before; only birds had ever gone this way to Lanka. Hanuman saluted the Lokapalas, the guardians of the four quarters: he worshipped Surya, Indra, Varuna, and Kubera with folded hands. Again he turned to the east and worshipped his father Vayu. He thought of Rama and Lakshmana; he prayed to them in his heart. He paid obeisance to the holy spirits of the rivers, and the mother of them all, the ocean. He worshipped Varuna Deva.

The trees on Mahendra shook at Hanuman's advent and the mountainside was covered with a colorful mantle of flowers that fell from their branches. Still, Hanuman grew. As he paced the mountain's summit, rocks cracked under his feet, while the peaks echoed with his quest for an unyielding place from which to launch himself. Smoke issued from those cracks.

Cowering in caves in the lower reaches for terror of the monkey a hundred hands tall, the animals of Mahendra gave throat to their fear. Some roared, some bayed, some howled; but they all huddled together: tiger and deer, elephant and panther, the great bears of those hills, Jambavan's cousins, and hissing, venom-spitting serpents. A thousand flights of birds flew screaming from their nests in caves and crannies, and the sky was full of their dark wheeling alarm. On the mountain's summit, Hanuman paced and paced, gathering himself.

It is said even the rishis of Mahendra scuttled off that massif, and secret vidyadharas flew into the sky and hovered there like strange birds to watch Hanuman's leap. Then the awesome vanara stood still on a spot that did not give below his feet, as if it had once been created just for him. He turned his face to the sky and roared like the wild creature he was, lord of them all, while above him the sky recoiled at the sound. Behind him, longer than the longest hamadryad pulled out of its hole by Garuda, his tail coiled and twitched with life of its own. Far below on the seashore, Angada's vanaras stopped their ears with their hands.

When the echoes of his roar had died away, suddenly Hanuman squatted down, his hands resting on two jagged peaks beside him. He thrust his neck out at the sky. He shook the final shred of doubt from his head and turned his eyes across the endless sea. He drew a deep, deep breath and crouched, quivering in readiness.

"God speed, Hanuman!" the vanara army cried from below.

He thundered at them, "Like an arrow from Rama's bow I fly to Lanka! If Sita is not there, I will fly to Devaloka to seek her."

A clap of thunder rent the air and the vanaras below saw the most amazing sight they ever had: swift and steep as a thought, gigantic Hanuman rose into the firmament. With him, pulled up by their roots by his velocity, rose a thousand flowering trees, as if to see him off on his auspicious journey and keep him company part of the way. Then their flowers fell out of the sky in a cascade, an enchanted shower onto the calm sea. The waves washed ashore in every color imaginable, and they carried their soft cargo to the sands at the feet of Angada and his army.

But above them, Hanuman did not fall back to the earth. Up he flew and away, carried by the power unleashed by his mighty legs and arms, borne on the swift currents of his father the wind: truly like the manavastra of Rama of Ayodhya. They heard the peals of his exhilarant laughter, floating down like more blooms from the sky.

Like a thundercloud sped along by a tempest, Hanuman flew through the air. His arms were stretched before him like two streaks of lightning. The Devas saw his flight and gathered on high to watch. On flashed the vanara, and they whispered among themselves in awe, the immortal ones. They said he might swallow the very sky with his cavernous mouth. Hanuman's shadow on the placid ocean was thirty yojanas long, as he flitted across the firmament like a mountain in the days before Indra sheared their wings.

Through fleecy clouds, like a plunging moon he flew; and eager for his success, the Devas showered unearthly petal rain over him. Not wanting him burned, the sun shone softly on his back as he arrowed along. And, of course, his father Vayu held him precious in his arms, heart to heart. Never before had he felt his son so near him, so much his own, and he sped him on with a timely gust.

Varuna, the ocean below, watched Hanuman's flight and thought, "I would not exist, but for the Ikshvaku kings; and this monkey flies on a mission for the finest prince of that line. I will give him a place to rest on, and then he can gain his destination with ease."

Varuna summoned Himalaya's son, Mainaka, who lay submerged deep below his waves. The Lord of waters cried to the mountain, "Rise up into the air; become a resting place for Hanuman."

That legendary mountain, with the peak of gold for which he was called Hiranyanabha, plowed up like another sun rising out of the sea, and stood gleaming in Hanuman's path. But the son of the wind thought Mainaka was a demoniacal obstacle and, with a nudge of his chest, thrust him aside. Suddenly, Mainaka's spirit appeared on his golden pinnacle, refulgent before the flying vanara.

Mainaka cried to the monkey, "Varuna bade me rise to be a resting place for you. The Lord of waves would like to be of use to you, Hanuman, and to the prince of the House of the Sun whom you serve. Your father Vayu saved me from Indra's vajra, when the Deva king severed the wings of all mountains. The wind hid me under the ocean when Indra hunted my kind. Look!" And silver wings shimmered behind that resplendent being. Mainaka said again, "Come, Hanuman, rest a while upon me. Then you can fly to Lanka from my summit."

Hanuman replied, "I am moved by your love and by the ocean's kindness. But my time is short and I have none to rest. Farewell, good mountain, we shall meet again someday."

Hanuman waved to the golden one. As Mainaka sank under swirling waves again, the vanara streaked on through the sky. But then the Devas of light are never content to leave any hero untested in his most difficult hour. They called Surasa, who is the mother of all serpents.

The Devas said, "We want to see how great this monkey really is. He is the wind's son; just this leap is too easy for him. But we can test his mettle if he finds someone dreadful in the sky barring his way. Become a rakshasi in the air, Surasa. Let us see how worthy Hanuman truly is."

Soon, spread across the sky like a thunderstorm, Hanuman saw a rakshasi who dimmed the brightness of the sun. She grinned, baring fangs big as hills. She licked her lips when she saw him, and bellowed, "How hungry I have been! But here comes a fair feast, flying into my mouth. Come to me, little ape, and be my lunch."

Hanuman folded his palms to the awful one. He said humbly, "Devi, I am on a sacred mission. On my way back I will fly into your mouth. You have my word."

But she cried, "By Brahma's boon no one can pass me without going through my mouth! Brahma's boon shall not prove false."

She yawned her mouth wide as the horizon. Exasperated, Hanuman cried, "Rakshasi, your mouth is too small to contain me. Open wider, so I can fit in it."

She yawned her firmament of a mouth still wider; she let it gape a hundred yojanas. In a flash, Hanuman was the size of a man's thumb and, before the demoness realized what was happening, he flashed in and out of her plumbless maw. Outside its darkness again, Hanuman grew vast once more.

He bowed to Surasa. "I flew into your mouth. Now let me pass."

Surasa laughed; she liked this clever monkey in the sky. She cried to him, "Pass in peace, Hanuman, it was only the Devas testing you. May your journey be fruitful; may all your missions succeed."

She vanished out of the sky and Hanuman flew on. His path was many thousands of feet high. It was the skyway of the birds he flew along, the subtle path of rishis and gandharvas. Vayu had wafted his son up to where he flew as swiftly as he wished. It was damp today, the celestial skyway, and raindrops fine as dew moistened his face pleasantly as Hanuman flashed along.

Farther ahead, there was a real rakshasi called Simhika who lived in the ocean. Suddenly Hanuman felt himself slowing and then coming to a standstill in the air. He felt himself being dragged down, and when he looked at the sea below he saw that a rakshasi's curved claw clutched his shadow on the water. Even as he watched, amazed, she parted the sea like another mountain and rose, lion-faced and terrible, out of the waves. Her mouth yawned from horizon to sky to swallow him.

Now Hanuman lost his patience. With a roar, he plummeted down into her jaws like a fishing hawk. Down her throat he plunged, becoming tiny again so she could not find him with her fangs. Down into her belly he flew. Beginning to grow again, he clutched two handfuls of her intestines and flashed back up again, dragging her stomach out through her mouth. Simhika died screaming, and her entrails floated like dark garlands on the waves.

Like Garuda himself, Hanuman flew on and the wind flew with him, making his passage effortless. He saw a dark speck appear on the horizon, and, at the speed at which he flew, it grew rapidly. Soon a lush island lay below him, a jewel in the sea. Within its undulating green confines, he saw a mountain that thrust its way up toward the clouds, and the sun-dappled gardens of that Mount Trikuta. Lower and lower he circled. He saw rivers, streams, and silvery waterfalls. He wondered at the richness of this Lanka he had reached after flying a hundred yojanas through the sky.

Quickly Hanuman thought, "I cannot land here like this. I am so big the rakshasas will never let me into their city without a fight. Then how will I find Sita?"

In the twinkling of an eye, he was a little monkey three feet high, and softly he set himself down on the peak of the Lamba hill. Round-eyed at the beauty of Ravana's island, Hanuman stood chattering approvingly at what he saw around him. He heaved a sigh of relief that his fantastic journey, his momentous crossing, was accomplished. To find Sita now should be no great matter.

2. Lankini

He had achieved the impossible; but the vanara was humble and he did not waste any time admiring what he had done. Indeed, apart from profound relief that he had not failed, Hanuman felt little else. That was his nature. In the distance, on the hill called Trikuta, he saw Ravana's city basking in the light of the afternoon sun and set out toward it. On his way, he marveled at the lushness of Lanka. He walked through thick grasslands, full of life, and swung his way through woods of flowering trees of fragrances he had never known before. To be safe, Hanuman had landed quite a way from the Rakshasa's city, and now he needed to cover a fair distance before he arrived at his destination. Gazing around with bright eyes, Hanuman loped along toward Ravana's city.

The sun was sinking on the horizon when, through the trees ahead of him, he saw its scarlet and golden shafts reflected from the crystal windows of the mansions of Lanka. He saw the deep moat that encircled the fortress city in protection, the vigilant patrols of rakshasas that guarded its entrances, the wide, clean roads that wound their way into the lofty gates; and he was all admiration for what he saw. Hanuman had the feeling that Lanka must be as beautiful as Indra's Amravati. And he was not far wrong; Viswakarman himself had built this city for Ravana.

At the foot of the Trikuta hill, Hanuman paused. Above him, in the evening mists that had gathered round it, the rakshasas' city seemed to float on air!

Lost in thought and in the grandeur of this Lanka before him, wondering what manner of demon its king was, who lived in such splendor yet could stoop to abduct Sita, Hanuman came to the city gates. The rakshasas who stood guard there were ten feet tall. They were fierce, and carried weapons of fire, nestling at their sides like organs of their bodies. There were so many of them outside the gates, hundreds, and Hanuman saw there were twice that number within. He thought that not even the vanara army, if it ever arrived here, could hope to fight their way past that guard; he saw every man of it was a veteran of many wars. All of them wore shining battle scars like ornaments on their arms, faces, and deep chests.

The vanara thought, "How ferocious they look; not even Indra's Devas could pass these rakshasas." Then, most awful thought of all, "Will even Rama be able to fight his way into Lanka? For sure, no more than four of our vanaras can make the leap across the sea: Angada, Neela, Hanuman, and Sugriva, our king."

He was perturbed. But he decided firmly that he would not be swayed by his branching anxieties. He would first tackle the immediate task at hand: to find Sita. Hanuman wasn't sure how to proceed, and he felt fear fluttering in his belly. If he was not absolutely careful, and very lucky as well, all would be lost; and his great leap would have been in vain.

Even if she was in the city, and still alive, how would he be able to meet her alone? The fear flared across his mind that after all Rama might have to return to Ayodhya without Sita; Hanuman shivered. He scolded himself and swore he would be calm. He decided he would enter Lanka after night fell, under cover of darkness. He climbed into the middle branches of a tree, sat hugging himself for the coldness in his heart, and watched the sun set in the ocean.

The last sliver of coruscant fireball sank below the horizon, and the sea was languid as a woman after love. Like a shroud pulled over her face before she slept, night stole over her and wrapped her in darkness. Hanuman roused himself and decided he was still too big to pass unnoticed into Lanka. He made himself smaller still; he shrank into a tiny marmoset-sized monkey, no bigger than a kitten.

Once more he crept to the gates of Lanka and, hidden in the shrubbery, peered into the wondrous city. It was like a city of the gandharvas. Lights were everywhere; glimmering jewels paved the road and encrusted the walls of the houses. Lanka lay before Hanuman like a piece of rich tapestry. As if to help him, the moon rose over the trees and ramparts into a sky full of stars. Like a king swan Soma Deva was, among lotuses on the dark lake above.

A high, gleaming wall ran all around Lanka, made of some unearthly metal so smooth it was impossible to scale. Hanuman stood gazing at it and it confirmed his fears that Lanka would be hard indeed to breach: protected by the sea, a moat, ferocious rakshasas, and this wall that a fly could not cling to.

Hanuman thought glumly, "I won't be able to deceive this eagle-eyed guard if I assume the form of a rakshasa. What a city this is; not even my father Vayu could enter it without Ravana's leave."

He counted on his fingers the vanara warriors who were strong enough to storm Lanka: Kumbada, Angada, Sushena, Mainda, Dwividha, Sugriva, Kusaparva, Ketumala, Hanuman, and Jambavan, lord of bears. Rama and Lakshmana would come, too; though he could not imagine how they would arrive here. But what could this mere handful do against the might of Lanka's rakshasa army? Hanuman shivered again with the chill in his heart.

He came to a drawbridge across the moat, guarded by another force of rakshasas. He crept stealthily along its underside and gained the far bank in the moonlight. He crept along another hundred feet, when suddenly he heard a hiss in the dark and a powerful hand snatched him up by the scruff of his neck. Two crimson cat's eyes glared at him from the shadow he was snatched into, and, dimly before him, he saw a luminous and dreadful female form.

It was a secret goddess who had caught him. Amused, but menacingly, she said, "What have we here? It seems to be no warrior, but only a little monkey. But not everything is what it seems to be, and you are very heavy for one so small. Who are you, and why are you trying to creep into Lanka? Don't lie to me; I saw you crawling under the bridge."

The necklace of rubies at her throat glowed like embers in the night. Hanuman pretended to be a terrified little monkey. He trembled in her grasp, and whimpered, "I will tell you, beautiful one, I will tell you. But who are you, Devi, and why do you terrify me with your fierce eyes and your deep voice? As you can see, I am only a little monkey. But who are you, and why do you stand here in the dark at Lanka's gate?"

She shook him. She bared pale fangs and said, "I am the spirit of Lanka. I am Lankini and no one may pass me, for I am the guardian of Ravana's city. Prepare to die, monkey. I will pluck your head from your neck with my nails."

Hanuman said, "I saw the beauty of Lanka from yonder peak, and I was so enchanted that I came to see it nearer."

But she was unmoved by his flattery. Her eyes glinting, she snarled, "Foolish monkey, you cannot pass into Lanka unless you vanquish me in battle."

Hanuman pleaded, "I will admire the sights of Lanka and go away as I came. I mean no harm to anyone."

With a soft howl, she struck him across his face. Then Hanuman lost his temper. Bunching his tiny paw into a fist, he struck her back, squarely on her mouth. Her eyes rolling up, she crumpled to the ground. Yet, since she was a woman, Hanuman had not hit her with all his strength. Soon she fluttered open her eyes and, shaking her head to clear it, sat up. But now she folded her hands to Hanuman and spoke to him in awe.

"So the prophecy has come true!" whispered dusky Lankini. "Brahma gave me a boon and said I would be invincible at these gates. But he also said that one day a little monkey would come along, and when he struck me down I would know the end of the rakshasas was at hand." Her voice fell lower. "And I know what brings you here. It is she, it is Sita who brings doom to Lanka."

Hanuman saw she was crying. With a sigh, Lankini gathered herself up and said, "It is no use my standing guard here any longer. Lankini does not bar your way any more; you are free to enter as you please."

Her red eyes streaming, the fierce guardian melted into the night. She left the gates of Lanka forever.

3. Lanka

Great Hanuman, the tiny monkey, leaped nimbly onto the glassy wall around Lanka. For a moment, he perched there, admiring the city that lay below him. Then, hardly able to find a firm foothold, he jumped down on the other side, into Ravana's capital. In quaint adherence to what the shastras said, he landed on his left foot, as it was written one should when entering an enemy's house or his country.

All around he heard music, of the night's carousers: string and wind instruments, and soft drums. From the windows of mansions so sublimely conceived they were magical, he heard a tinkling symphony of little bells of different pitches. They were hung out to sound in the wind, in their thousands, so all the city was alive with their charmed song. Hanuman fetched a sigh when he saw the wonder that was Lanka. Not for a moment was there any doubt that the city of lights had been created by a divine craftsman, its every mansion and street, all its grand and subtle design.

Hanuman leaped onto the roof of a dwelling so tasteful you could almost say nature herself had colluded in its construction: so serene, so effortless were its lines. He saw every home was different from the others, each as elegant as the next, every one a work of art. There was simplicity here in quiet abundance; but no wealth was lacking, either, from the houses and the streets of Lanka. Hanuman saw precious jewels that made his eyes grow round. He saw doors and, at times, whole walls of painted silver and burnished gold.

He jumped lightly from roof to roof. Everywhere, like an accompaniment to the little bells, he heard another ubiquitous tinkling: of the anklets the women of Lanka wore. He heard the rustling of their silken garments as they embraced their husbands or their lovers. He peered in through windows, the sea breeze blowing round his ears. By the butter lamps of the night, or by moonlight that streamed onto beds of entwined love, he saw that the rakshasas of Lanka were a noble and handsome people. Their tall women were tender as lily stalks; their men were virile warriors. Hanuman heard another immanent harmony of sighs and moans woven into the bells and the music. As the night advanced, this rhapsody swelled.

Another noise attracted him and he scrambled across the roofs. Round-eyed, he saw a quarter of worship where solemn brahmana priests, all rakshasas, ceaselessly chanted the Vedas. Hanuman sat listening to the chaste recitation and to the waves far below in the bay, washing upon Lanka's golden beaches.

Suddenly, he heard the tramp of military feet in the street below and drew back into the shadows. It was Ravana's vigilant night patrol. This was no merely formal force, but a powerful contingent of war. Hanuman saw the glinting weapons those rakshasas carried: macabre ayudhas in which dark fires slumbered. He did not like to think of what these demons would do to an intruder who fell into their hands. He shivered on his perch. When they chatted quietly or smiled, saber-like fangs gleamed on the rakshasas' bold, sensual faces, and wiry mustaches bristled.

From roof to roof sprang Hanuman, until, like a silvery hallucination before him, he saw Ravana's palace silhouetted against the sleeping ocean. It was as if a small slice of another, supernal world had fallen into this one. Shimmering towers and turrets reached for the stars on their way across the sky. That palace by itself was as large as a fourth of the rest of Lanka. Perched on a hill of its own, as if to complement the spirit of him who lived in it, all of Ravana's palace had just a single motif: it reached out to the constellations above, to whatever lay beyond its grasp, in constant yearning. It sought anything that was alien and majestic, just to touch perhaps, to enrich itself with a caress; but then, more likely, to conquer as well. Within that great palace, Hanuman sensed an implacable evil, a quenchless thirst to dominate.

Through a golden gate set with corals and pearls bigger than any he had ever seen, he stole on tiny feet into the antapura, Ravana's harem. The jewels reflected Soma Deva's light back to him in quiet iridescence. Incense hung in the cool air, laden with distant, breeze-blown dreams from the sea. In some rapture, Hanuman stood gazing at the crystal city below, where now the revelers and musicians fell quiet and began to seek sleep or love. As he watched from Ravana's roof, looming over the rest of Lanka, he saw the rakshasas turn their lamps out, one by one, and just the little bells still tinkled in the midnight breeze.

But it seemed the revelry in the king's palace had only begun. Ravana had more than a hundred guests tonight and their celebrations, in an enclosed garden and one of the glittering pavilions leading out into it, were far from over. Food, delicacies of all kinds, was kept warm with burners under silver dishes, so the guests could eat whenever they chose to. There was wild game and catch from the sea, and other meats the scents of which Hanuman had never smelled; he did not like to think what they were.

All the guests were obviously from the rakshasa nobility. They were taller than the others in the city outside, finer-featured, more richly attired; the ornaments these rakshasis wore would rouse the envy of the apsaras in Devaloka. Hanuman saw the women of Lanka were hardly less beautiful than he imagined the starry nymphs to be. Some were fine-boned and ethereal; others were more sensuous and earthy, but so seductive that even the little vanara in the terrace shadows sighed to look at them. The nobles of Lanka were both dark and fair, and some surely had very mixed blood: some of them had blue eyes and hair shot with auburn and gold.

The sprawling garden was dotted with clear pools, and Hanuman saw that already many of the revelers had peeled off their clothes and swam, naked, men and women together, laughing. Wine flowed there and no rakshasa was sober any more. In some amazement now, Hanuman of the jungle watched them as they paired off and wandered to quiet corners, where, with silver light streaming down on their beautiful, powerful bodies, they began to make love as unashamedly as animals of the jungle. Only, thought Hanuman, most wild beasts prefer privacy when they mate and enjoy it much more than these demons did their vacuous promiscuity.

Then his fur stood on end and his eyes stared in shock. He saw couples wander across to others and lie with them, four and six together. Like nests of serpents, thought Hanuman, shuddering. Soon, all Ravana's secluded garden writhed with naked rakshasas and rakshasis, at their soulless orgy under the trees and on the grass and even in the bathing pools of the perfumed garden.

From his windy height on the palace roof, Hanuman scrutinized every woman's face, and he heaved a sigh of relief. Though the rakshasis were beautiful, without exception, there was no doubt in the vanara's mind that none of these, whose bodies shone in the flowing moon, was Sita. No, her beauty would far surpass the superficial charms of these women; hers had to be an altogether more spiritual loveliness. Rama had described her to him and an image of her face was engraved on Hanuman's heart. He was certain he would know her as soon as his eyes saw her.

He turned away from the garden of lust and, through an open window, crept into Ravana's palace. Golden were its halls and its thrones. An opulence of jewels encrusted the ivory and sandalwood seats, beds, and couches with which the countless, lofty rooms were furnished. When he had roamed through the fine maze of corridors and apartments in one antapura, Hanuman emerged into the courtyard of another. He gasped. There, glinting gemstones of fascination that twinkled back at the stars in subtle converse, was a great ship of the sky: the pushpaka vimana!

It was a mysterious disk, wrought in Devaloka. Ten crack guards, more dangerous-looking than any he had yet seen, stood watch over the uncanny craft, which seemed so strangely alive. Hanuman scrambled quietly into the adjoining antapura, which he had yet to explore for Sita.

Again, rooms branched endlessly from the labyrinthine passages. Hanuman eased open numberless doors, one after another, and gazed at the sleeping women within; each was as beautiful as the others were, none was as beautiful as he knew Sita must be. Through Ravana's endless harem padded Hanuman, the little monkey, son of the wind, in quest of the peerless Sita. Now and again, the night's stillness was broken by the whinnying of a horse from the Demon's stables.

If there were a hundred women's apartments in each antapura, there seemed to be a hundred antapuras in Ravana's palace. Passing his hands in wonder over walls of smooth silver and doors of solid gold, Hanuman patiently searched them all. He found the Lord of Lanka was a collector not only of rakshasis. Some wings of the harem were full of sleeping gandharva women, lovely beyond belief; their hair glimmered with the natural starlight that is their elfin heritage, and their gossamer skins seemed to be woven from moonbeams.

In other antapuras slept strong-limbed kinnara women with high cheekbones, whose men are centaurs. In yet other apartments were chambers full of green and serpentine naga women, sinuously exquisite, with jewels embedded in their sleeping heads. It struck Hanuman that all these women were Ravana's lovers. It did not seem to the vanara they were restrained here as captives; they slept much too languorously. Hanuman thought, what a king this Rakshasa must be! However grudgingly, he felt a stab of admiration for Ravana.

The little monkey shook his head at the ways of fate. Here was a sovereign who had delectable mistresses from every race in the three worlds; yet he chose to court death at Rama's hands. And Hanuman believed that however impossible it might seem to him just now, death would come ineluctably for Ravana.

4. In Ravana's antapura

On and on, through the maze of corridors in Ravana's harem, tiny Hanuman wandered. Some had floors of marble, others of smooth glass, and yet others were tiled with tinted stone not quarried on earth. As he searched for Sita, wondering again what manner of rakshasa the Lord of Lanka must be for so many of the most beautiful women in the worlds to be in his antapura, Hanuman came to a taller door than all the others he had eased open tonight. Softly, he entered that apartment which was the only one in this wing of the seraglio.

The first chamber was a great living room, richly, tastefully furnished. No one was here. He tiptoed across its expanse and opened a door in the far corner. The vanara froze. Before him, in a bedroom as big as a court, upon a bed of crystal, ivory, and sandalwood, at the head of which he saw the white parasol of kingship, slept a rakshasa who could only be Ravana himself. He was darker than Hanuman had imagined; his sleeping presence was that of a thundercloud. Golden kundalas hung from his ears; his arms lay long at his sides, down to his knees. He was lean and powerful, with not an ounce of superfluous flesh on him. The clothes he slept in were of white silk, and the room was redolent with the sandalwood paste which had been massaged into his dark skin by women's fine hands.

Hanuman went closer. A potent emanation of evil from the sleeping Demon touched him fiercely, and like a frightened little monkey, he scampered back a few paces. The Rakshasa's arms lay like ebony pillars on the spotless sheets. That bed was made not just for one sleeper, but Ravana slept alone in it tonight. His breathing was slow and even; he slept deeply.

Hanuman raised his eyes past Ravana's sleeping form. He saw there was another bed in the room, as beautifully wrought as the king's was, but smaller. The chamber was dark and Hanuman could not see clearly. He crept around the first bed to the side of the second one. He sighed when he saw how beautiful the woman was who slept in it. Springing up onto the ivory headboard, he peered down at the sleeping queen, for so she must be.

She wore ornaments richer than any he had seen all this extraordinary night. The pearls she wore so carelessly around her neck were each a princess's dowry. When Hanuman saw her skin was softly golden, he felt a surge of excitement: thus Rama had described Sita's complexion to him. She was so beautiful that as he gazed at her, Hanuman grew convinced she was Rama's love. The vanara slapped his shoulders in delight; he scrambled up and down the pillars of that room. Then he went back to awaken her. Luckily for him, a warning instinct restrained him.

Hanuman thought, "By her beauty she must be Sita. But how does she sleep so contentedly in Ravana's bedchamber, with a smile curving her perfect lips?" He slapped himself again, across his cheek this time, as monkeys do. How, even for a moment, could he think that Sita would sleep in Ravana's bedchamber? She would rather die! He was right. The breathtaking woman, who slept alone in her regal bed, was Mayaa's daughter Mandodari. She was Ravana's queen, a rakshasi. Realizing his mistake, Hanuman crept out of that apartment.

Dejectedly the little monkey wandered again through the palace. Hundreds of sleeping women he saw, but none of them was Sita. He wandered into the kitchen, big as mansions, and the wine cellar, which stretched on interminably, with casks, vats, and sparkling bottles, in row upon row, shelf upon shelf. Hanuman was unhappy about having gazed at the lovely mistresses of Ravana of Lanka; not all of them were fully clothed, and some wore nothing at all.

The vanara said to himself, "But my mind is not moved by what I see, not by all the nakedness, not by what I saw in the garden. It is the mind that sins, not the senses. And I am unmoved, though I realize how easy it would be for anyone to yield to temptation."

Hanuman wandered out into the rambling gardens around the

palace. His eyes roved everywhere, in some despair now; he had come this far, and nowhere yet was there any sign of Sita. Through exotic, steamy greenhouses Hanuman ranged, whimpering to himself now and again, every bit the lost little monkey. The moon had sunk low over the satin ocean and would soon set into burning silver-gold waves. He realized he had wandered for hours in vain. Tears welled in his eyes; the vanara grew awfully certain that Sita was dead. Perhaps, when she refused to give in to him, Ravana had killed her.

Hanuman was tempted to make the crossing back to Bharatavarsha by darkness, before the sun rose. But then what would Angada and Jambavan say, who pinned their hopes on him? He thought of the shame of failure, and Hanuman persuaded himself to stay on and to search again, more thoroughly. Once more, the little monkey combed Ravana's palace. Scampering up and down the wide golden stairways, he searched all its floors of antapuras. He combed its gardens, its private arbors with their tonsured lawns, vibrant plants, and curling vines. He searched every inch of the palace; he even peered under the beds in each room to be quite sure he had not missed her. Yet no Sita did Hanuman find.

He thought, "Sampati the eagle said he saw her here from across the sea. Then where is she? Ravana must have killed her between then and now, and cremated her body. Or perhaps there are dungeons below the palace where he holds her. But I have looked everywhere, and I saw no sign of such a prison, or a stairway leading down to one."

Hanuman perched on top of a round pillar on a flight of stone steps outside the palace, and sat hugging himself. Then he thought of Rama. How would he tell the prince that Sita was nowhere to be found in Lanka, that she was probably dead? He shivered at the thought.

"Rama will certainly kill himself," moaned poor Hanuman. In misery, he wrapped his arms even more tightly around himself. He swayed from side to side, wondering what on earth he could do, short of putting an end to himself out here in Lanka. Wretched thoughts followed each other across his mind in a morbid procession.

"If Rama dies, Lakshmana won't stay alive; he will also take his life. Bharata and Shatrughna will follow them, and so will their mothers. The glory of Ikshvaku, House of the Sun, will be extinguished forever. And the purpose of that handsome Demon, who sleeps so soundly in his bed of crystal and ivory, will be well served."

He sighed, and again a serpentine evil seemed to reach out for him from the heart of the palace framed against the light of the setting moon. Hanuman's train of brooding continued, "If Rama dies, Sugriva will kill himself for not having kept his word that he would find Sita. Then, Ruma and Tara will also kill themselves. When Tara dies, Angada will hardly stay alive. And all this because I failed them!"

Hanuman wanted to cry. As the moon sank into the sea on silver fire, he began to mumble to himself in despair.

"Even if Sita is dead, it is better that I never go back to Kishkinda. If I don't return, they will at least live in hope; while if I do, their hearts will be broken. I will go into the jungle and take sannyasa. Or better still, I will take myself to an obscure corner of this island and set myself on fire. But they say it is a grievous sin to kill oneself, worse than murder.

"Whether I find Sita or no, Ravana I must kill for the grief he has caused. Or perhaps I should take him back to Kishkinda and let Rama deal with him."

Now and again he craned his neck to watch the luminescent spectacle of the setting moon. As the last sliver sank under foaming waves, suddenly a dying beam of moonlight lit a hidden copse at the very edge of his vision. Hanuman got up on to his toes and peered at the concealed wood. It was set cunningly in the shadow of the palace, so one could see it only as the moon set, by its last rays. At first, Hanuman did not peer with any great hope; by now, the night had taught him such despair he hardly dared let hope into his heart again.

But stretching on tiptoe, he saw there was certainly a grove of asoka trees below him. He decided he must investigate it, at least to satisfy his conscience. He slipped down from his pillar. As he scampered toward the hidden grove, the heaviness lifted away from his heart and a great, fresh hope surged through his body. Hanuman cocked his head from side to side, wondering. He silently invoked the eight Vasus, the eleven Rudras, the twelve Adityas, the seven Maruts; he solemnly saluted them all, begging their forgiveness if arrogance had entered his heart after his leap across the sea. With tears in his eyes, he begged them to lead him to Sita.

Hanuman prayed to Rama and Lakshmana; he prayed to Sita whom he had never seen. He bowed in the darkness to Indra, to his father Vayu, to Yama, Surya, and Soma. Then, cautiously, he began to seek a way into the asokavana. It took a while but he found one, craftily hidden between a flight of stone steps and a tall hedge. Hanuman crept along carefully. Though there were no rakshasa guards in Ravana's harem, out here in the open he might well encounter a night patrol. He knew this was his last chance; a stirring breeze blew around his face.

The asokavana lay beyond the high wall that encircled Ravana's palace. It stood between the palace and the sea. Thinking how beautiful Sita must be, Hanuman leaped up onto the wall. He saw the care with which that garden was maintained, its trees elegantly clipped and planted in the ground with knowing design. There were rare trees here, trees even he had never seen before. He saw those that were sons of ancient sires that grew in Indra's Amravati: great plants that stirred Hanuman's monkey's heart and spoke to him in silent and primeval tongues of living leaf, twig, and blossom.

He jumped lightly down into the asokavana. At once, the heady scents of a hundred different kinds of night-blooming flowers swept over him. He looked up and saw birds in dense flocks roosting in the branches, their heads tucked under their wings. He saw tame deer sleeping curled up under the bushes and on the lawns. Koyals and peacocks Hanuman saw, and they, who were sensitive to the smallest sound, raised their heads in annoyance that an intruder had found his way in here. Little Hanuman saw the eyes of chital and sambur glowing nervously at him from the pitched night.

When the birds in the trees grew disturbed and flapped their wings in half-sleep, flowers from the branches where they roosted streamed down to the ground in scented showers. Hanuman stood covered in petals, a bright little mound. Smiling, he shook the flowers from his fur and crept on through the darkness. It could not be long before the sun rose behind him, and then he must either hide or flee.

Shaking those trees with strength quite disproportionate to his size, parting creepers and peering into the dark crypts behind their lattices, Hanuman went along, a little storm of quest through the asokavana. Ahead, he heard the murmur of flowing water. Peering by just starlight into the gloom, he saw a small stream frothing down a hillock that loomed in the night. This rivulet fed a handful of lotus pools, which reflected the canopy of stars above upon surfaces still as mirrors.

Like jewels those pools lay, banked with white sea sand. There were stairways leading down to them, made of deep slabs of unworldly turquoise. Viswakarman of Devaloka had created them and conceived their sublime arrangement. By now, Hanuman was so tired he had to sit somewhere and rest. He saw a shimshupa tree before him. Its branches hung low; the creepers that clung to it cascaded from its highest twigs in a stream of dim color.

Hanuman sprang up into that tree and sat among its middle branches, hugging himself again in disappointment, thinking that the surge of hope in his blood as he entered the asokavana had deceived him. The little monkey whimpered; but he refused to abandon his quest, telling himself that when the sun rose he would see Sita under the bowers of this asokavana. Hanuman sat staring around him and often up at the stars strewn across the sky like silver lotuses on another lake. He prayed fervently that his mission might still not prove futile.

5. The little temple

Exhausted by now, Hanuman told himself, "Rama said that Sita loves flowers, trees, and all wild things, deer, squirrels, and birds. He said she spoke to them as if she knew each one's tongue. The stream is cool and pure. Perhaps she will come to touch its water and worship the sun at dawn."

He whispered on to himself like this. He dared not relinquish hope; his very life hung by just that thread. Like many creatures of the jungle, he could see almost as clearly by night as by day. As his eyes grew accustomed to the darkness, Hanuman marveled at the great garden he had come into. It was at least as lovely as Indra's Nandana or Kubera's Chaitra. The night flowers seemed to bloom back at the stars unfurled in the sky above.

The scents, which were wafted on the night, reminded him of Gandhamadana, the fragrant mountain to which Hanuman had once gone during Sugriva's long flight from Vali. Hanuman did not know this, but the scents of Ravana's asokavana were heavenly because the plants, shrubs, and trees that grew here had sprouted from seeds brought down from Nandana and Chaitra themselves.

As his eyes saw the night more clearly, Hanuman peered out sharply from his perch. Ahead of him, glowing through the darkness, was a little temple supported by white pillars all around, its arches overgrown with ivy.

Hanuman shinned down his tree and crept toward that temple. He stiffened in surprise when his feet encountered smooth coral, cool in the night. He saw that the pathway leading to the domed edifice was paved entirely with slabs of the red stone of the sea. He saw the steps that led up to it were also of dark coral. As he drew nearer, he saw that the little shrine glowed by starlight because its outer walls had been gilded with molten gold.

He heard heavy breathing within, and gingerly he glided through the shadows right up to its entrance. He saw the flickering light of the torches, which dimly lit the cloister. He heard the sound of snoring, and then someone sigh softly. In a flash, Hanuman darted his little head round the arched ingress. His eyes grew round and his heart gave a lurch. Her yellow silk was soiled, her face was stained with tears, and she sighed from time to time amidst the rakshasis who lay asleep around her. But she shone in that shrine like a wafer of the moon, and there was no doubt in the vanara's mind. This was Rama's love, this was Sita!

She had not eaten properly for days. But if anything, her beauty was heightened by her plight; it smoldered like fire hidden by ashes. Her face was tear-stained and unwashed. But not for a moment could any of Ravana's queens within their secure chambers, not even Mandodari by a long way, have held a candle to Sita. She had cast away all her ornaments and sat drooping like a wilted lotus. But she was the most beautiful woman Hanuman had seen, and would ever see.

Her great eyes were full of disbelief at what she now endured. Nothing in her sequestered past had prepared her for these brutal days and nights. Even as Hanuman watched, riveted, unable to tear his gaze from her, tears flowed down her face. Then, as if she sensed his presence in the shadows, she stiffened. She stared anxiously around her, and his heart nearly broke with the terror he saw in those gentle eyes.

Like a black snake, her hair trailed behind her, twisted into a single limp braid. Hanuman thought breathlessly, "Even like this she is more beautiful than I had imagined, more lovely than Rama described her as being. Though dirt and sorrow stain her face, the night shines with her beauty. Beloved of all the world is she who sits grieving on the bare ground because of the Rakshasa's cruelty. Ravana must pay with his life for what he has done."

His mind was a whirl. "Truly, she belongs with Rama; no other will do for her or for him. How do they live without each other? Their love is so strong it prevents them from dying of grief."

A breath of that sorrow touched Hanuman's imagination, and he shivered. "Only Rama could stay alive after being separated from this Goddess."

Hanuman thought worshipfully about Rama, as if only now, seeing Sita pining for him, did he begin to understand the prince of Ayodhya. He prostrated himself before Rama in his mind, and cried silently up at the stars, "Rama, Lord, I have found your Sita!"

Then he also fetched a deep, deep sigh, and said softly to himself, "Fate is powerful indeed. Look at Sita, so lovely, so chaste, and yet she suffers as the wicked never seem to. Ravana's haughty queen sleeps peacefully in her bed and so does the Rakshasa himself. Rama and the mighty Lakshmana were her guardians in the forest, and still she was taken. Such are the ways of fate, irresistible; or, perhaps, such is the beauty of Sita.

"Vali died of this fate, or for her beauty, and Kabandha. Rama killed fourteen thousand rakshasas, when Surpanaka turned on Sita. For Sita's sake I have leaped across an ocean, and I would not wonder if Rama stands the universe on its head for her; for she is the rarest jewel in all of it. Oh, nothing in the three worlds can compare with Sita's beauty."

Hanuman reflected on her character, more immaculate than her beauty. "She could have had any man or king, every luxury. She could have had the Devas at her disposal, had she been inclined to. But she followed Rama into the jungle, and she was happier there with him than she had ever been. Look at her now. What has she done to deserve the torment she suffers, the grief that savages her?

"She does not notice the charms of this asokavana. She is blind to everything save the vision in her heart, of Rama's face."

For a while he watched her weep silently. Then, fearful of the rakshasis who lay around her, and he saw two that were awake, he crept away into the night. Hanuman climbed back into his shimshupa tree. His heart overcome equally by pity and rage, and his body by great exhaustion, the little monkey fell asleep in a cleft branch of that tree.

6. In the asokavana

Dawn broke over the horizon, and the first shafts of pale light divided the sleeping ocean, full of dreams, from Ravana's island. Hanuman in his tree heard the Vedas being chanted loudly and was startled awake. Within his palace, Ravana had also awakened early. The image he woke with was of Sita's perfect face; he had dreamed of her all night.

The Lord of Lanka rose from his bed. He had no eyes for Mandodari, who, as she lay asleep with her lips a sigh apart, was a picture of sweet seduction. He pulled on the fresh robes of white silk laid out for him. Putting on a necklace and golden bracelets, so brilliant they dispelled the last straggles of night that lingered wistfully in the world, he left his apartment. He strode through interminable passages and arrived by his own private entrance in the asokavana where his heart lay captive.

But as he went like a storm through the antapura's passages, there were others already awake: lovely women, who had dreamed of his virile face and form. They wanted a few moments with him, if not in their beds, at least like this, out in the open. All along his way through the harem, they approached him with soft caresses; but he strode impatiently along. Those women followed him to the asokavana, in a small throng. Some brought chamaras to fan him with; others held lamps to light his way, since the corridors were still dark.

Like Indra surrounded by his apsaras, Ravana came out into the crisp dawn. Not looking left or right, without a glance at the silken sea that lay like a languorous woman herself below Lanka, the Rakshasa made straight for the little shrine of the white pillars, where Sita sat sleepless and distraught.

Hanuman hid himself behind a screen of leaves and peered down at Ravana. Now he saw even more plainly how magnificent the Rakshasa was: tall and dark, handsome as Kamadeva. His white robe was like froth at the crest of the turbid sea of presence and power that was Ravana. In his time, Hanuman had seen other kings of the world, but never one nearly as arresting, as awesome, as this emperor. Greatness sat lightly on those rippling shoulders; fame and measureless authority radiated from his central face. Ravana had the power to make his cluster of nine heads become invisible at will. At dawn today, he came out with just one face showing, because he did not want to risk repelling Sita.

For all the dark majesty it wore, Ravana's face was haggard and careworn. The single-mindedness with which he stalked to the little temple in the asokavana cried out that great Ravana was strangely vanquished: that his vast kingdom meant less to him than the woman who sat sorrowing within that retreat. She had become all the kingdom he wanted, all his heaven and earth. Ravana breathed the image of Sita; he slept and woke in her obsession.

From his perch, Hanuman could see into the little temple. He saw Sita grow pale, when she knew Ravana had arrived. Swiftly, in a reflex of fear and shame, she covered her body with her hands. Like frightened birds, her eyes flew this way and that, avoiding his smoldering stare as he came and stood tall and ominous before her.

He drank deeply of the sight of her with his red gaze. He did not appear to notice how disheveled she was, or the dirt that streaked her tear-stained face. Before him Ravana, master of the worlds, saw only his hopes, his life, his heaven and hell; and if he had known it, his death as well. She stared down at the bare earth she sat upon. She was like a branch, blossom-laden, but cut away from her mother tree, and sorrowing on the ground.

Ravana sighed. In his voice like somnolent thunder, he said, "Whenever I come here, you try to hide your beauty with your hands. But for me any part of you I see is absolutely beautiful. You are the perfect woman; beauty begins with you. Honor my love, Sita, and you will discover how deep it is. My life began when I first saw you, but you treat me so cruelly."

She said nothing, never raised her eyes up to him. Hanuman, little monkey in his tree, trembled with what he saw and heard.

"You say it was dishonorable for me to abduct you; but you forget I am a rakshasa. It is natural, and so entirely honorable, for me to take another man's wife if I want her. It is even honorable for me to force myself on her if I choose. That is a rakshasa's nature, and his dharma."

Sita gasped. At once Ravana regretted what he had said. He went on more gently, "I will never force myself on you, because I love you. I will wait for you to return my love, to give yourself to me willingly. You are my day and my night, and all my dreams. I feel I was never alive until I saw your face.

"Abandon this wretched grief; you were born to be a queen of queens. It does not suit you to sit on the bare floor like this, with your clothes soiled, your hair unwashed, your face covered by a screen of dirt, and starving yourself almost to death. When he made you, Brahma crowned his long quest of creation. You are the woman he labored through the ages to make. No man, no Deva or gandharva, why, not Brahma himself, can resist your beauty. No blame attaches to me for loving you as I do. The fault lies not in my love, but in your perfection."

Color, a flush of shame, touched her cheeks as if his words were fire in her ears. It was not her Rama who spoke them, but they came unhindered into her hearing.

"Wherever I look, asleep or awake, I see your face. Even when I am dead, I know my eyes will see nothing else. I do not ask you to return my love with the same passion I have for you. Not even a shadow of it. I only ask you to begin to think kindly of me, to care for me a little. I beg you, come and rule my palace as my only queen. All the others will serve you as sakhis, even Mandodari. I will be your servant.

"Everything that is mine shall be yours. Time and again, I have vanquished the Devas and gandharvas in battle. Apart from what they bring me as tribute, I have taken untold wealth from them. The rarest silks, and jewels you cannot dream of, will be yours, even as they should. They will adorn your perfect body as they were made to. All my endless kingdom will be yours; only, set aside this stubborn grief.

"Sita, fate is all-powerful. You and I were created for each other. Why else would you have come to me at all, by the long and winding way that you did? Brahma intends that we should be together. Don't resist the will of God. Shed your grief, my love. Bathe, and put on the finest silks on earth. Adorn yourself with the most precious ornaments in the three worlds. And let me look at you, ah, let me feast my eyes on you!"

He was helpless for this insane love. Already, whenever he was able to tear his thoughts away from Sita and consider what he had plunged into, Ravana realized it was no less than his death he courted so ardently. Six months of the year he had given her to yield to him had passed, and she was as obdurate as ever. Each time he came to her she gave him the same answer, and with each visit to the asokavana his obsession grew, and his despair.

Ravana had no joy or peace any more in the arms of his wives. Out of old habit, he had made love to them, desultorily, for the first month Sita was in Lanka. But he found such aridness in these couplings that he gave up seeking to quench his fatal desire elsewhere. He had not been in Mandodari's bed for five months, and the others could not hope to tempt him at all.

Initially, his frustration when he saw Sita so lovely before him, and so unattainable, would drive Ravana into a frenzy. He would growl and scream at her. But soon he grew calmer; for the first time in his life, he began to resign himself to his own helplessness. He realized the only way into her heart was if she decided to give herself to him.

He had exhausted all his arguments of power, wealth, and virility. He persisted in them only out of habit; there was no conviction in him any longer when he boasted to her. At last, he knew all he had to offer this most exceptional woman was his love. And while doing her best not to be cruel, because she saw that he loved her in his dreadful way, she spurned him over and over again.

Now, out of habit, Ravana said, "What can he give you that I cannot? You are denying your own nature, Sita. Other women have been brought here as spoils of war, as frightened as you were when you first came, more so. But when they knew me, none of them resisted me for more than a week. None, once they tasted my love, ever wanted to leave me. You are stubborn. It is only stubbornness and fear, not love, which bind you to your Rama.

"He is not my equal, in wealth or power, valor, or even tapasya. Forget your wandering hermit. By now he has lost his mind from sorrow. Be sensible, as your humankind always is. Just think there is no hope of Rama ever seeing you again, no hope that he can cross the ocean that separates Lanka from Bharatavarsha. Give up your stubbornness; it is all you have to lose."

His eyes roved over her slender form, and they blazed. He whispered, "Oh, Sita, give yourself to me! I will love you as women only dream of being loved. Rule my heart, and be queen of the worlds as you were born to be. We will walk hand in hand in this asokavana and you will discover the meaning of happiness."

But again she picked up the long blade of grass and set it between herself and him like a naked sword. She said, "I am the wife of another man, Rakshasa, and my husband is my life. How can you even think of me as becoming yours, when I am already given to Rama? Given not only for this life, but forever, for all the lives that have been, and all those to come. I have always belonged to Rama, and always will. You have many beautiful women in your harem; don't you keep them from the lustful gazes of other men? How is it, then, you cannot conceive that I would be true to my Rama? That it is natural for me, because I love him."

He looked away from her. Not that he saw anything except her face, even when he did. But he could not bear what she said. Never had he encountered such chastity, and to believe in it would mean denying everything he had lived for. A smile curving his dark lips, Ravana turned his gaze from her.

But Sita went on, undaunted. "You court death for yourself and your kingdom. Have you no wise men in your court, who advise you against your folly?"

Ravana laughed, "They all know I am a law unto myself. They know I am invincible."

She looked up briefly into his eyes and, her voice firmer, said, "You have violated dharma and punishment will come to you more quickly than you think. You don't know Rama; he is not what you imagine him to be. You speak of this sea being an obstacle between him and me. But I say to you, Ravana, even if the ocean of stars lay between us, my Rama would come to find me."

Something flickered deep in Ravana's plumbless heart, and she saw it in his eyes. But she did not know whether it was fear, or a sorrow too distant to fathom.

"But it is not too late for you, Rakshasa. Take me back to Rama and he will forgive you. I will tell him you did me no harm. I am part of Rama as the light of the sun is part of the star. Nothing in all the worlds, no cause in the yawning ages of time, will persuade me to give in to you. Take me back to Rama, before doom comes to Lanka."

Ravana stared at her in amazement. He looked at his women around him, and, throwing back his dark head, began to laugh. "Are you trying to frighten the Lord of the rakshasas, at whose name the universe trembles?"

"If Rama is angry, nothing in the universe can save you. You don't know who he is. Indra's vajra may fail to harm you, or even Yama's paasa. But when Rama strings his Kodanda and Lanka shudders, you will know the terror of your death has come for you. As the sun covers the earth with his rays, Rama will cover your city with his eagle-feathered astras; and each one shall be a flaming army among your people. And then it will truly be too late for you.

"Rakshasa, there is no escape for you anywhere. Take me back to Rama and ask his pardon. He is kind beyond your understanding; he will forgive you. Listen to me, Ravana, you do not know what you have done."

The smile vanished from his face. In a voice as menacing as a serpent's hiss, he said, "My love for you, which you scorn so arrogantly, preserves your life. No one else could speak one word of all that you dare to say to me and hope to live. I should have you tortured for speaking to me as if I were just anyone, but my love prevents me."

The veins stood out on his temples from the anguish she caused him. His skin turned a ghastly pallor, his lips twitched. Deep in his eyes, terrible wrath and untold tenderness hunted each other; shadows, dark and bright, flitted across his face. He clenched his fists and drew himself erect. He said to her in deadly quiet, "Two months more I will give you, out of my great love. Remember to be in my bed before those sixty days are past. If you are not, my cooks will serve you to me in pieces for my morning meal."

The women who had come with Ravana felt sorry for Sita, but none of them dared speak on her part. They tried to convey their sympathy to her with their eyes.

She flashed fearlessly at Ravana, "You have often called Rama a weakling hermit. When his arrow is buried to its feathers in your black heart, you will know who my Rama is. Very soon, Rakshasa, you will be just a few handfuls of ashes, and all your glory with you. Even as you dare look at me with lust in your eyes, you do not know that I could burn you up, and myself, with my paativratya. But I will leave you to Rama. Now that I have seen how evil you are, I think fate conspired to make you abduct me. So Rama would come to kill you."

His lips quivered. But having thrown herself at time's mercy, she mocked him, "You say you are the bravest man in all the world. You say you vanquished Indra and Kubera in battle. But you stole me from my asrama like a thief, when my husband was away. Rakshasa, you are more a coward than a hero."

Ravana's eyes were the color of the dawn that lay out on the sea. For a long moment, he said nothing, but grew very still. Then with a cry he drew his sword and stood over her, the weapon raised in both hands, glinting over her head. Hanuman almost fell out of his tree; he had no time to intervene. A smile tugging at her mouth, Sita raised her face and gazed calmly back at the Demon's terrible eyes. Thus they remained, locked in a silent struggle of wills, and the violence of it made the rakshasis around Sita scamper away, whimpering, and even Ravana's mistresses drew back in fear.

But at last, just as Hanuman was about to fly to Sita's rescue, Ravana threw back his face and howled abysmally, like a wild beast struck by an arrow. He thrust his sword back into its sheath, and screeched at her, "What do you want with that adharmi whom his father banished, that impoverished, half-naked tapasvin, when you can have my love?"

Turning on his rakshasis, he cried, "Coax her, threaten her; do anything you have to! Your task is to make her come to me. If you fail, I will have your lives as well."

Still, he stood staring at her as if his eyes would lose their vision if he turned them from her face. Then, one of his once-favorite women, Dhanyamalini, who grieved for both her lord and Sita, came to him in that little temple. As Hanuman watched in amazement, she wound her slender arms around his neck like green vines, and kissed him full on his lips, so even he turned to her in surprise. The fascination of Sita was briefly forgotten, and his rage. Dhanyamalini was terrified the duel of wills between Ravana and Sita would break out again. He was in the mood for it, and the next time he would kill her.

Dhanyamalini cried, "Why do you waste your time with her? It has been so many moons since you came to my bed. Every night, Ravana, I lie awake staring at the stars and wondering, will my king come to me tonight? Will he come to drink the fever that burns my body and turns my dreams away? But every night you lie alone, thinking just of Sita. She is not worthy of you, my lord. Come to my bed and let me take your anguish from you. Forget her for a while. Brahma has not willed that she be fortunate enough to lie in your arms."

Bemused, and realizing the peril of staying on there, Ravana allowed Dhanyamalini to lead him away. After he had left, Sita sat very quietly, drained. A rakshasi brought her some food and water. She ate a morsel and drank just enough to keep herself alive.

Later, inside the palace, Dhanyamalini turned crying softly from Ravana. Minister to him tenderly as she would, she could not arouse her king at all. Sita's face haunted him, and he lay quite impotent in that lovely rakshasi's bed.

7. *Trijata's dream*

When Ravana left, the rakshasis began to cajole Sita again. They knew their master would not think twice to kill them if Sita did not give in to him. These were not beautiful consorts, who ever warmed the Rakshasa's bed. They were coarse warrior women who guarded his female prisoners, his spoils of war. It fell to them to persuade the more desirable captives brought back to Lanka that the best course open to them was to go to Ravana's bed. No woman, ever before, not gandharvi or apsara, kinnari, siddhi, or Asuri, had held out against their persuasions for more than a few days. But this human princess was different. Six months had passed and there was no sign of her yielding.

After the morning's encounter between Sita and their master, the rakshasis of the asokavana were alarmed. They were determined to persuade her, by fair means or foul.

"The most beautiful women would give anything to spend a night in Ravana's bed; but you refuse him."

"She is vain."

"And foolish; she doesn't know what she is doing."

"Silly creature, your beauty blinds you to the truth of your plight. But beauty does not last long. Be Ravana's queen, arrogant one, and you will have wealth beyond your dreams."

"And power."

"Such pleasure in his bed that you could not dream of. Do you know how virile a rakshasa is? And this is not just any rakshasa, but Ravana himself."

They brought their fanged faces close, making her gag with their putrid breath. They smiled and snarled at her; they hissed in her ears like serpents. Sita wept. Little Hanuman sat in his tree, wisely restraining himself from committing any rashness; though his blood boiled and he longed to tear those rakshasis limb from limb.

Sita said, "I would rather die than be unfaithful to Rama."

They growled like a pack of wild dogs, snapping around her. Seeing that reason and argument had little effect on Sita, they began to threaten her.

"What a tasty meal she will make."

"She is too succulent to be left alive."

"She torments our king. He neither wakes nor sleeps in peace."

"Let us cut her up and divide her soft flesh."

Sita jumped up and, stopping her ears, ran out of the little temple. She stood panting under an asoka tree like a fawn at bay. The pack of rakshasis still growled and raged.

"Her flesh will be better for us to eat, than to warm Ravana's bed."

"She is so vain she will be cold in his arms anyway."

"When he knows she is dead, he will come to his senses again."

"We will be doing him a service."

"If we are to die anyway, let us kill her first."

"Let us do it now; this folly has gone on too long."

The rakshasis streamed out of the little shrine with murder on their minds.

"Rama!" Sita cried outside. "Lakshmana! O my mothers in Ayodhya! Why have you all forsaken me?"

She saw the rakshasis advance on her, their eyes full of death. She moaned. When they were just a few feet from Sita, an older rakshasi called Trijata awoke from a strange dream. She came flying out of the little temple. She slapped two of the younger ones resoundingly. "Have you gone mad? Do you want to die a slow death in the king's dungeons? Come away, you fools, and listen to what I have to tell you."

She was the strongest of them, their leader, and the ones she slapped whined. Trijata said, "Sita, come and hear what I dreamed."

Trijata had always been kind to Sita, since Ravana first brought her to the asokavana. As time wore on, and Sita resisted the Demon's every effort to seduce her, Trijata's kindness had grown into adoration. Now Sita was not averse to listening to the old rakshasi's dream, though she would not go any closer to hear it, but stood wiping her tears, still shaking from her near escape.

Her fierce eyes full of her dream, Trijata said, "I saw blue Rama clad in flowing white silk. He wore a garland of white lotuses, which were not of this world. Oh, he was handsome past imagining. He sat in a chariot of the firmament, an ivory vimana drawn by white swans. Our Sita wore royal white as well, and she sat beside him.

"Then I saw Rama riding a four-tusked elephant, a son of Airavata. As glorious as his brother, Lakshmana rode beside him through a deep forest. Someone waited for them in a glade hidden in the heart of that forest. I saw her face; it was our Sita, and Rama and Lakshmana came to her in joy. Rama set Sita on his elephant and they flew through the sky, for the children of Airavata go that way."

The other rakshasis, who were impressionable and superstitious for all their fierceness, listened raptly to Trijata, their thick mouths hanging open. Under her tree, Sita thought Trijata's dream had come like a Godsend to answer her prayer.

The rakshasi went on, "In my dream, they flew to the gates of Lanka. I saw Rama in a golden chariot drawn by eight mighty bulls. As I watched him, he opened his mouth and swallowed the earth. I was terrified. Then there was an ocean of milk everywhere, and a pale mountain rose out of it, majestically. Rama set his elephant upon that mountain, and Lakshmana and Sita rode with him.

"I saw Rama, resplendent, his body made of light, in a fabulous palace. He sat facing east on a golden throne. He was being crowned by an immortal rishi, and congregations of Devas and munis had gathered for his coronation. Sita sat beside Rama. It did not seem to me that throne was any of this earth, and I knew there was no throne in any of the three worlds loftier than the one on which dark Rama sat."

Lowering her voice to a whisper, Trijata said to her rakshasis, "Rama was Narayana himself, the Parabrahman, and this Sita was Lakshmi at his side. She is a Goddess, I tell you; don't even think of harming a hair of her. There was unearthly music everywhere, like nothing I had ever heard before, and the host of Devas surrounded Rama and Sita.

"I saw Rama, Sita, and Lakshmana again, in the pushpaka vimana, flying north through the sky."

Trijata paused. She glanced left and right to make sure no guard had entered the asokavana, no spy of Ravana's. Gathering her rakshasis closer, draping her long arms around their shoulders, she said in the softest whisper yet, "I saw Ravana clad in red, karavira flowers around his neck and his body glossy with oil. I saw him fall screaming out of the sky from his vimana. On the ground, he wore black garments and he was dragged along by a dark woman. I saw him sitting in a chariot drawn by donkeys, and it went south, ever south. He drank oil from a bottle in his hands and laughed insanely, as if he had lost his mind.

"I saw Ravana's brother Kumbhakarna sink beneath the waves. I saw our king's sons all slain."

Trijata was thoughtful for a moment. She resumed, "I saw Ravana's other brother, the gentle Vibheeshana, and he shone like the sun at noon. He sat with the royal parasol unfurled above him; he wore the white silks of kingship and a crown upon his head. Vibheeshana came with his head bowed to Rama on his elephant.

"By what I know of dreams, and they never lie, Rama will come to Lanka, kill Ravana, and take Sita back with him. Lanka's great army will be razed.

"Finally, just before I awoke, I saw a monkey, one of the vanara folk. He set fire to our Lanka and she burned down in ashes."

Open-mouthed still, the other rakshasis listened to her. Nearby, under her asoka tree, Sita sobbed quietly. Hearing Trijata's dream made her cry for joy. It was as if Rama reached a hand across the sea and stroked her face.

Sita's left eye throbbed, as did her left shoulder, piquantly, and a current of enchantment coursed through her body. It was a long time since she had felt any hope at all. But now, though there was no sign of it except the old rakshasi's dream, Sita thought rescue was nearer than she had imagined. She felt Rama had flown into the asokavana as a breeze and caressed her; she was certain it would not be long before he came for her.

In his tree, Hanuman still thought Sita was about to do something drastic to herself. He felt impelled to comfort her. But how could he approach her without being seen by the rakshasis? Yet if he went back across the sea without speaking to Sita, the prince would be sad. He might even be angry and burn Hanuman up with a look. Worse still, if he did not bring some hope to Sita quickly, she might take her own life before Rama even landed on the shores of Lanka.

"I am just a little monkey," said Hanuman to himself. "Even if the guards see me, they will think I am harmless. I only hope Sita does not think I am Ravana, who has become a monkey to trick her into his bed."

He grew pensive indeed, as his imagination raced ahead of him. "If she thinks I am Ravana or some other rakshasa, she might scream. Then, surely, the rakshasis will come to capture me. If I am killed, Rama and Sugriva will never land on Lanka, because no one else can leap across the sea. All will be lost. I must be very careful; careful indeed, Hanuman. You do not realize what is at stake here, what awesome affairs of the world depend on you. You must not startle her, little monkey; you must be subtle."

Then, as if someone unseen decided to help him, an ingenious idea struck the good vanara.

8. *The shimshupa tree*

The branches of the shimshupa tree, on which Hanuman was perched, grew out a good way from its trunk. Creeping surefootedly along those branches, the vanara went out as far as he could without showing himself. The rakshasis who had been ready to kill Sita were frightened by what Trijata said. Most of them wandered back to the little temple and had already fallen asleep under its round pillars. A few conferred together, and decided to meet Ravana to tell him that none of their persuasions had moved their ward.

Sita stood beneath the asoka tree, gazing out across the ocean with unseeing eyes. She stood fidgeting with her limp plait, torn between her instinct of hope and the terror of her predicament. Suddenly, out of the sky, a little voice spoke. Little but so solemn, it spoke half to her and half, musingly, to itself. Strange things this voice was saying or chanting.

"There once was a king called Dasaratha. He was a rajarishi; great was his power and radiant his truth. His wealth and valor were legend, famed in all three worlds. More renowned, yet, was the tapasya of Dasaratha of Ikshvaku, of the race of Surya Deva. He was as strong as Indra, kind as a father to his people, noble and generous. Not only among men, but among the Gods this king had renown and honor."

Sita looked around her in amazement and she saw no one. But the quaint chanting continued, like an intimate mantra.

"Four sons mighty Dasaratha had; the eldest was Rama and the king loved him more than his life. Rama is a kshatriya among kshatriyas. He is the greatest archer in the world, a terror to his enemies. A protector of his people, wise, compassionate, and immaculate in dharma is Rama of Ayodhya."

Sita quivered with joy waking in her; the tide of hope surged higher than ever. She stood rapt, listening to the charming voice rambling on: "To preserve Dasaratha's honor, Rama went to the jungle, renouncing kingdom and comfort, wealth and power. With Sita and Lakshmana, Rama went to the Dandaka vana. Clad in tree bark and deerskin, like any tapasvin, the prince of dharma went into the fearful vana.

"Fate brought Rama to the jungle where austere rishis, whose tapasya blesses the earth, were harassed by rakshasas. The demons desecrated the hermits' yagnas; they killed the munis and drank their blood. Rama slew the evil ones. The forest resounded with his bow-string and, far away, the Emperor of sin trembled on his crystal throne. Deep in his soul, he sensed a light come into the world, for its liberation from his reign of fear.

"From a dark stirring in the lord of savagery, his brothers attacked Rama at Panchavati. But Rama killed them all. Khara he dispatched, Trisiras, Dushana, and fourteen thousand others, with lucific arrows."

Sita stood motionless, the soft words binding her in a trance.

"When Ravana heard about the massacre of his people, he was furious. He decided Rama must die. But when the Evil One heard of Rama's prowess, he thought cunning and grief were better weapons than arrows to fight the prince of Ayodhya with. With the help of a golden stag, which was no deer at all, he kidnapped Sita from Panchavati."

Now she was agog to hear what followed. For, of course, she did not know what had happened to Rama after Ravana abducted her. Her face was alight with eagerness; her eyes darted all around her and up at the leafy branches. Still she saw no one.

The little voice went on serenely. "Grief-stricken, and consoled by his loyal brother, Rama wandered through the forest seeking his love. And on a mountain in the wilderness, he made friends with a monkey. The monkey was called Sugriva and he promised to help Rama find his Sita. In return, Rama killed Vali and set Sugriva on the throne of Kishkinda, from where he rules all the monkeys of the earth.

"At his command, Sugriva's monkeys combed the ends of Bharatavarsha for Sita. Nowhere did they find her. At last, on the southern shore of Bharatavarsha, an army of vanaras led by their prince Angada thought of killing themselves, because they had failed in their quest. But then an eagle called Sampati, who is Jatayu's brother, told them where she was. One of those monkeys leaped across the ocean to this Lanka, and he was the son of the wind. At long last, he found Sita in an asokavana. But he did not know how to approach her, lest he frighten her."

The voice paused, then said, "Devi, I am that vanara."

Sita quivered in amazement. Twisting her long plait in her fingers, her eyes full of wonder, full of fear, she peered up into the branches of the shimshupa tree. At first she saw nothing. Nervously, she looked around her: suppose the rakshasis had also heard the little voice? But they were all asleep inside the white temple. She peered more closely now; she scrutinized every branch of the spreading tree. Slowly, Hanuman climbed out on a leafless fork and smiled sweetly down at her.

Sita gasped when she saw a tiny monkey, clad in fine silk, his fur the color of the bricks that paved the paths in the asokavana. Fear had become so much part of her life, and the vanara saw it flash across her perfect features. For a long moment, she stared silently up at him. He was so small and affable, his eyes kindly and golden; there seemed to be no harm in him at all. But she looked up at him through her own suspicions and saw him as a sinister creature. Certain that he was evil, she turned away with a cry. She began to chant Rama and Lakshmana's names feverishly, under her breath.

"I must be dreaming," Sita told herself. "They say that to dream of a monkey is an evil omen. I pray no harm has befallen Rama and Lakshmana that this monkey speaks so knowingly of them. I hope my father Janaka is well."

Doubt had its way with her. She wrung her hands and said to herself, "But I am not asleep; it must be madness that grips me in my misery. I think of Rama so much that my imagination is playing tricks on me. I hear these words of hope in my desolation, though no one speaks them."

She paused, considering this for another moment. Then she whispered, "But what about the monkey? He is no figment of my fancy." She shut her eyes, and said in a quavering voice, "May the Gods help me; may Indra, Brihaspati, Brahma, and Agni have mercy on me. May what the monkey says be true!"

Hanuman slipped down the tree and prostrated himself, small and elegant, at her feet. When he rose, he held his hands folded together above his head, and said to her, "Devi, your soiled silk shimmers like sunlight; your eyes are like lotus petals. You seem to me to be quite perfect, yet you stand here so forlorn, clinging to a tree. As water drips from a lotus, tears spill from your eyes. Why do you weep, Devi? What ails you, what terrible sorrow? Who are you? Are you a gandharvi, or a naga kanya? Are you an Asuri, a yakshi, or a kinnari? Ethereal one, you are surely not of this world. Perhaps you are Rohini separated from the Moon, that you are stricken? Your eyes are so beautiful, they were not meant to shed tears.

"But I see that your feet rest on the ground; so you must be a human princess. The wife of a great prince perhaps? Even Rama's wife?

320

Yes, I do believe you are Sita. When I see your sorrow, I know that no other woman on earth grieves as you do."

Her hand still resting on the asoka's branch, she said, "I am Dasaratha of Ayodhya's daughter-in-law. I am Janaka of Videha's daughter. I am called Sita and I am Rama's wife. Once, Dasaratha wanted to crown Rama yuvaraja. But on the day of the coronation, fate took a cruel hand in our lives. When Rama was exiled by Kaikeyi, he told me to stay behind in Ayodhya. But I could not bear to be separated from him, and I went with him into the Dandaka vana. We were so happy together in the forest, until Ravana carried me away.

"For six months, I have lived in dread in Lanka. The Rakshasa gives me two more moons to submit to him. At the end of that time, when I do not yield, he will have my body served in pieces for his morning meal and my blood in a golden goblet to drink."

She stood distraught before Hanuman.

9. The way of dharma

Hanuman said, "Devi, Rama sent me here. I bring you news of him. He grieves every moment for you, and Lakshmana consoles him. Rama sends word to you, and inquires how you are."

A thrill of excitement swept through Sita. She cried, "I have heard that hope is always answered, and joy comes to the most miserable. Now it streams into my heart!"

They stood speaking softly about Rama for a while. When he thought Sita trusted him, Hanuman went nearer. With a cry, she released the branch she held and sat abruptly on the ground. She was certain Hanuman was Ravana in disguise, scheming to come near her, to touch her, perhaps force himself on her. She said defiantly, "If you are Ravana, trying to deceive me as you did at Panchavati, all I have to say to you is: stop tormenting me! Even you must think I have suffered enough." At once Hanuman lay on his face again at her feet. While her breath came in gasps, the little monkey lay motionless.

Slowly, she saw he meant her no harm, and understood her fear. She wept again. Then she grew quiet and said, "But perhaps you are just what you say you are, since you lie so humbly before me. Perhaps you are indeed a messenger from Rama. When I look at you my mind grows calm, and peace steals over my heart even in this terrible place.

If you are truly who you say you are, then arise, little monkey; you have my blessing. Arise and tell me about my Rama. Despite my worst fears my heart is drawn to you, for you appear to be a soul of great goodness. Tell me about my husband, vanara, tell me how he is."

Hanuman's eyes were full, but he said nothing. Suspicion flared up again in Sita's heart. Once more she was certain Ravana had become a little monkey to approach her. She withdrew again into silence.

Now Hanuman said so gently, "Trust me, Devi, I am not deceiving you. I have come from Rama. If you do not believe me, I will describe him for you. Rama is as brilliant as the sun and as tender as the moon. As Kubera is of the earth, he is Lord of all the worlds. His power is as profound as Narayana's, and his speech as wise and gentle as Brihaspati's. He is as handsome as Kamadeva would be, if the God of love took a human form.

"Though he is the noblest of men, and grows angry only when he is grievously wronged, he is a terror to his enemies and there is no archer like him anywhere. Soon, very soon, you will see Rama's arrows burn up the sky and bring death's justice to Ravana. Don't doubt me, Sita. Rama has sent me to find you; he grieves for you night and day.

"Lakshmana sends his greetings to you, and so does my master Sugriva. As soon as I take word back to them, Rama and Lakshmana will storm Lanka with a vanara army, and rescue you. I am Sugriva's minister, Devi, and my name is Hanuman. When Sampati told us you were held here, I leaped across the sea to find you. Don't doubt me; Rama sent me to you."

A smile dawned on Sita's face, and it was like the sun appearing from behind dark clouds. As if she had just woken from an evil trance, and saw Hanuman before her for the first time, she cried eagerly, "When did you meet Rama? Where did you meet my husband? Tell me, good monkey, how do you know Lakshmana?" Then, again, the shadow of doubt. "Describe them, describe them carefully. I must be sure that you really know them."

Hanuman launched into the story of how he first met Rama and Lakshmana on Rishyamooka; and how he took them to Sugriva, who hid in fear lest the kshatriyas were Vali's agents come to kill him. The monkey described the oath of friendship Rama and Sugriva swore, with Agni as their witness. He told of the slaying of Vali and the crowning of Sugriva. He spoke of how Rama and Lakshmana lived in the cave when the rains came; how Sugriva forgot himself in the pleasures of his harem, and the vanaras' quest for Sita was delayed.

He described Lakshmana's wrath and his arrival in Kishkinda. Sita sat enraptured before him, doubt gone from her for the time being. As Hanuman spoke about Rama, it was clear that the prince had come to mean everything to the vanara. Sita felt deep kinship with Hanuman. Adoringly the little one spoke of her kshatriya in his grave voice, and monkey and princess were bound in a trustful covenant of which Rama was the secret.

Hanuman said, "When the month Sugriva gave us to find you in the south had elapsed, we despaired and thought of ending our lives by the sea. But Sampati the eagle had seen Ravana bearing you through the sky to Lanka. With his hunting eyes, he peered across the ocean of a hundred yojanas and saw you in this asokavana. After that, it was just a matter of deciding which of the vanaras would make the leap across the waves. I was chosen, Devi, and I am so glad of it: that I can see your face and bring you some solace; that I can tell you Rama will be here swiftly to save you from terror."

As Hanuman spoke, Sita's face softened. Now he saw how beautiful she was; how kind her eyes were, and how serene, when he spoke about Rama. "I arrived here yesterday, and all night I spent searching for you in Ravana's antapura."

Sita shuddered to think of herself there.

Hanuman went on, "I saw many lovely women there, but none that was as sad as I knew you would be. I saw Ravana asleep on his crystal bed; I saw his queen nearby him. But I did not see you and I despaired. Then, as I sat on a pillar wondering how to end my life, a shaft of the setting moon pierced my eye and this garden at once. And suddenly, a great hope was upon me.

"I searched the asokavana for a long time but I did not find you, and my heart sank again—until I climbed this tree and saw the little temple. I crept up to the white pillars, then I saw you; and when I saw how you wept, I knew you were Rama's love. The rest of the night I spent in this shimshupa tree. By the light of dawn, I watched Ravana arrive and saw you keep him away. I grieved for you; but I dared not attack Ravana: if I was killed, who would take news of you back to Rama?"

Hanuman stood before Sita with his hands still folded, and he saw tears start in her eyes again. But these were tears of relief; he saw she did not doubt him any more. He said, "Rama sent this ring to you, so you could trust me."

He stepped forward and shyly pressed the signet ring into her hands. Tears streamed again from her eyes, dripping onto the golden thing that lay in her palm. She felt Rama so near her that she might touch him.

She cried to Hanuman, "Forgive me that I doubted you. I have been the Rakshasa's prisoner for so long that my faith has worn thin. Rama gave you this ring, or you would not have had it. I know he would never give it to just anyone, but only to one whom he trusted entirely. I see by your deeds that he was not mistaken; not the yawning sea, not Ravana and his rakshasas could keep you from finding me. Even when I received you with suspicion, you did not flinch from your mission. O Hanuman, I thank you."

Hanuman bowed solemnly to her, and a delighted smile lit his face. Sita continued, "Now I have no doubt that Rama will come for me, with Lakshmana beside him. And then not Ravana, not the host of the Devas could stand against them. I have wondered that I did not already see my husband's astras burning up Lanka's sky. But then I thought it was my fate to bear my suffering patiently, and the agony I have endured was written for me before I was born.

"Hanuman, since he did not come for me all this while, the evil thought crossed my mind that perhaps Rama had stopped loving me. You don't know how happy I am that you have plucked that fear from my heart. I have my faith back now, and the strength to bear Ravana's torments for as long as I must. For as I look into his fearsome face, I will know that sooner than he dreams, he will lie dead and his rakshasas' blood will stain the earth.

"Oh Hanuman, I hope my husband has not lost heart?"

Hanuman said, "He did not forget you or lose heart; he did not know where you were. Now, as soon as I return to Kishkinda, Rama will come to Lanka. Sita, he is grief-stricken without you; he cries incessantly. How can you ever think he has forgotten you? He lives with Lakshmana in a cave on the mountain called Prasravana. When he wakes, it is with your name on his lips. And Lakshmana said to me, when Rama falls asleep, exhausted, he still whispers your name, over and over. If he sees any sight in the forest that pleases him, he tells you about it, shares it with you. Not for a moment are you away from Rama's thoughts; just as I see that not for a moment is he out of yours."

Sita glowed. But she bit her lip, and her eyes filled again when she thought of Rama, that he was so far from her and heartbroken. She said, "Hanuman, when I hear he thinks of me, I am full of joy. But when I hear he grieves for me, I know the hell he must be in, and I am full of care for him. All this suffering is because of our karma of past births. The joy we have in this one, and the depths of grief, are wages for what we have done in lives gone by. No one, not Rama nor you nor I, escapes the fruit of karma, be they sweet or so bitter that they destroy us."

Hanuman marveled at her gentle wisdom, though her eyes flowed tears as if they were her life.

"Just think of Rama today, Hanuman. He has an ocean to cross and the rakshasa army to defeat before he can have me back. Like a boat lashed by a storm, my prince is tossed on fate's hostile tides. It is six months since Ravana brought me here."

She sighed. "Time is against us. Ravana has a wise brother called Vibheeshana, who tells him that he should take me back to Rama. But Ravana is blinded by fate, as if his death calls him urgently. Vibheeshana has a daughter called Anala and she told me this. When faith moves my heart, O vanara, I feel certain Rama will come to Lanka, kill the Rakshasa, and save me. But here in this city of darkness, faith is mostly far from me and my despair always near. And I fear my life is a ruined thing just for my having been here.

"Yet deep in my heart I always know my Rama's love is beyond being affected by time and its trials: that despite everything, the sorrow and the ocean, he will come and take me back."

Hanuman grieved for her. "Rama will be here sooner than you think. But if you like, I can take you out of here today upon my back. I could carry Lanka across the sea if I wanted."

Sita looked at the little monkey, and suddenly her laughter tinkled in that garden. "It is sweet of you to speak so bravely, Hanuman. But I think you are a little small to carry me out of here on your back."

Hanuman smiled serenely. "Devi, I am the son of the wind."

In a flash, he stood before her for just a moment in his other, awesome form, his golden hair brushing the sky.

Sita breathed, "O Vayuputra, you are greater than you say or I had dreamed. Small wonder Rama chose you to bear his ring to me. But I am afraid to go with you. Though Ravana brought me here through the sky, I am terrified by flight. Suppose I fell from your back? No, we must not risk such danger.

"More important, dear Hanuman, my heart insists that Rama must come to Lanka and slay its Rakshasa. There is no other reason that I am here, suffering like this. Ravana is part of our destiny and destiny must take its course. Rama must come to Lanka and kill Ravana, whose power stretches deeper and farther than we imagine. Then dharma will be established on earth, and Rama will be a king, as he was born to be.

"Besides, I would rather die at once than try to escape and be captured again." She looked down shyly and added, "Also, good Hanuman, you must forgive me, but I am Rama's wife and it isn't proper for me to cling to you while we cross the sea. It is true that Ravana held me as he flew through the sky; but that was by force and he will pay for it with his life."

She paused again, and great dreams lit her sad eyes. "Dharma is for Rama to rescue me himself. Cross the ocean alone, good Hanuman, and bring Rama back to Lanka. Let there be war, a dharma yuddha, as is honorable, and let my husband win me back. Fate has not brought me to this pass to escape like a coward. Rama must come and kill Ravana in battle. Then my sorrow will end."

She fell quiet and somber at these thoughts. Hanuman smiled to hear her speak so bravely. Knowing she was not alone had restored her courage beyond his expectation. He had a glimpse of the strength of her character, and he thought that here, indeed, was Rama's wife: she who suffered in the asokavana for the sins of the world, that it might be redeemed from the Rakshasa by her anguish. Why, Sita was like her mother, the Earth: she was Ravana's prisoner.

Hanuman said, "What you say is just; no one but Rama should touch you. I will fly back and tell him he has two months to rescue you. Have you a message for him, something by which he will believe that I have indeed seen you?"

10. The choodamani

Sita said, "Say to Rama, good Hanuman, that Sita reminds him of the day he lay asleep with his head in my lap, on Chitrakuta, on the banks of the Mandakini. A crow swooped down and pecked me. I threw a stone at the bird, but it came back again. It flew cawing above my head and repeatedly it plunged down to peck me.

"When he heard me cry out, Rama awoke. He saw my blouse had slipped from my shoulders and my face was flushed. He laughed, saying I had let a crow frighten me. The crow flapped away and perched in a tree some distance away. Rama went back to sleep, and the bird flew at me again. It swooped down thrice and raked my breast with its claws. Some drops of my blood fell on Rama's face, and he awoke.

"When he saw my blood, Rama pulled up a blade of darbha grass and invoked the brahmastra. That crow was Indra's son. Coming alive in a flash of fire, the brahmastra flew from Rama's hands and hunted the black bird through the sky. He flew quickly as a thought, but the astra stayed behind him, singeing his tail feathers; the moment he stopped, it could consume him. Through the three worlds that crow flew. At last, panting and terrified, Indra's son came and fell sobbing at Rama's feet.

"Rama said, 'I would forgive you, Deva, but what about the brahmastra? It must have its prey.'

"Growing into a figure of light, tall as the sky, that son of Indra said, 'Let it have my left eye!'

"So the brahmastra put out the dark bird's eye, big as a planet, and the ayudha was appeased. Indra's son fell at our feet again, saying he had been sent by his father to test the Avatara. He begged our forgiveness and returned where he had come from. Remind Rama of that incident, Hanuman. If he could send the brahmastra after a crow that pecked me, what will he do to Ravana who holds me his prisoner and torments me?"

Her eyes glinted. "Tell Rama that Sita asks why he has forgotten her. Why is Ravana still alive after what he has done? What does Lakshmana say to this, who is as much a warrior as his brother? For all their valor, and being matchless kshatriyas, they cannot comfort me in my misery. It must surely be the sins of my past lives that have come to roost in this one."

Her fine shoulders shook as she wept again.

Hanuman said, "Indifference does not keep the brothers from Lanka. If you saw how poor Rama suffers without you, all your doubts would vanish. Let me fly back to him now and he will be here swiftly. Ravana's corpse will adorn the earth and Lanka will be a heap of ashes, blowing in the sea wind."

Sita said, "Touch Rama's feet for me. Bless the noble Lakshmana, who is the rarest treasure on earth. Tell them I will survive in this place for another month, but not a day longer. After a month, Sita will be dead. Rama must come to Lanka before the moon returns to the nakshatra where he is tonight. Or he may never see me alive again."

Sita wiped her eyes. She untied a knot in one end of her yellow garment, and took out the choodamani she once wore in her hair. She gave it to Hanuman, who received it, bowing. His face lit up, and he circled round her in pradakshina.

Sita said to the vanara, "Give this to Rama. He knows it well. When he sees it, he will think of my mother, of his father Dasaratha, and of me: memories of us three are upon its jewel. Everything depends on you, Hanuman; my life is in your hands."

Hanuman bowed again to her. Again, Sita said to him, "Touch my Rama's feet for me. Tell him he has one month to come to my rescue."

Hanuman heard her out patiently while now she repeated herself, time and again, anxiously. At last he said, "Rama will be here sooner than you expect."

Then, thinking of the vanara gone, she cried, "Must you go today? Can't you stay another day and leave tomorrow?"

Hanuman looked uncomfortable. Sita sighed, "I will miss you when you have gone; you have lit my despair with a ray of hope. But I know that the sooner you leave the sooner Rama will come with the vanara army."

She bit her lip, as another unthinkable doubt rose in her mind. "Hanuman, how will an army of your people cross the yawning sea into Lanka? Vayu, Garuda, and Hanuman may cross the waves. But how will the others come? For that matter, how will Rama?"

Hanuman said quietly, "The vanaras who serve King Sugriva are a magical people. We have ranged the earth. Nothing can stop us; not rivers or mountains, jungles or oceans. There are many in Sugriva's army who are my equals, and many more who are greater than I. Between us, we will devise a way to cross the ocean. Devi, remember the march of dharma is always inexorable. As for Rama and Lakshmana, they will sit right here on my back, one on each shoulder, and fly over the waves to land in Lanka. Let your spirit be at peace; we will come for you."

"Like gentle rain on a field of green shoots has your coming been to me, kind Hanuman. Remind Rama of another time when we were alone and my tilaka was rubbed away. Remind him of how he took the dust of the manasila stone, and marked my brow with it. Oh, how does he live without me? Here, each moment my life is ready to seep out of me, since my eyes do not see his face. Only with a great effort do I hold it back."

11. The terrible vanara

Hanuman knew how short his time was. He prostrated himself, his little monkey's form at Sita's feet. When she had blessed him, he rose, and his eyes were full of promises and tears. He bowed again to her, deeply, and then he left her. When Hanuman had not gone far, a thought struck him with some force.

He said to himself, "I crossed the ocean to find Sita and I have found her, nobler than I had imagined, and sadder too. But I must not leave Lanka like a thief. I must make my presence felt. I must strike some fear into the hearts of these rakshasas. The best soldier is the one who achieves more than he was told to.

"I have already done what I was sent for. I have leaped the waves, found Sita, and given her the ring Rama sent. But how much more I will accomplish if I provoke the rakshasa army and discover how strong it is. How much cleverer I will be if I can meet Ravana face to face!"

He knew it was dangerous, but an inner voice urged him to be a little rash. Hanuman decided impulsively, "This asokavana must be Ravana's favorite garden. That is why he has kept Sita here. Let me ruin this pretty garden, with its clipped plants and trees. When Ravana hears of it, he will send his guard to attack me. When I crush that force, the Rakshasa will tremble on his throne. For if I can do this, who am only a messenger, what will happen to him when Rama arrives with Sugriva's army and Jambavan's?"

Growing vast in a moment, and roaring in the anger he felt at Sita's ordeal, Hanuman began to wreck the asokavana. He uprooted trees and snapped their trunks like twigs. He stirred whirlpools in the lily ponds, so they broke their banks and spilled over, muddying their crystal waters. He smashed down the carefully heaped rockeries. He trampled beds of exotic plants, brought here from distant corners of the earth.

In no time, he devastated the asokavana. Resuming his little monkey's form, he climbed onto the flat top of a stone pillar and sat waiting for word to reach Ravana. The rakshasis in the little temple had been startled awake by the commotion in the asokavana. They were terrified to see the great vanara, like a golden tempest, destroying the king's garden. The birds that roosted in the garden rose into the sky in screaming swarms, like clouds of doom. The deer, peacock, and other tame creatures dashed about in panic.

The rakshasis vaguely remembered having seen Sita talking to a little monkey, in what they thought was demented grief. Now they ran to her, crying, "Who is this creature?"

But Sita replied, "Ask one serpent about another. He must be a rakshasa, who can assume any form he likes. I know nothing of him and I fear him as much as you do."

The rakshasis fled to Ravana with their tale of the monkey who had wrecked the asokavana.

"We saw Sita with the creature," they said, "but now she denies knowing the monkey. He may be a servant of one of your enemies, Kubera or Indra, come to spy on your city. Or he may be Rama's messenger, for he sat talking to Sita. If you don't believe us, Lord, come and look at the asokavana. He has uprooted every tree in it, save one: the shimshupa under which Sita sat. He must die for this."

Tears of rage burned Ravana's crimson eyes. He clapped his hands and sent a company of his palace guard to deal with Hanuman. Ravana sent eight hundred rakshasas to the ruined garden. They surrounded the monkey who sat chattering and snarling at them on the round pillar outside the garden. At first, they laughed to see how small he was; they could not believe he had ravaged the asokavana by himself.

But the moment the rakshasas went to seize the little monkey, he stood up, stretched, and in a wink he was enormous. His head was in the sky and, his golden eyes blazing, he growled down at them dreadfully. The gigantic vanara beat his chest and that noise reverberated through Lanka, shaking Ravana's palace to its foundations.

Hanuman roared at the rakshasas, "Rama and Lakshmana are with King Sugriva of the vanaras; glory be to them! I am Hanuman, the wind's son, and I serve Rama. I flew across the sea to find Sita and I will make you sorry before I leave your infernal city."

Some of them growing huge themselves, the rakshasas rushed at him. Hanuman pulled up the pillar he sat on and smashed them with it, killing a wave of demons. Their screams rang through the sea air;

their blood and brains were spattered across the ruined garden; scarlet gore flowed in streams. In a trice, unbelievably, that entire contingent lay mangled and lifeless. Hanuman's roars of triumph rang through Lanka and the city quaked again.

Word reached Ravana, and he could hardly believe what he heard. He called his minister Prahastha's son, Jambumali, one of his ablest young commanders, and sent him forth with a bigger force. Crying again that he was Rama's servant, Hanuman wiped out this legion as well, beating it to bloody pulp with the pillar.

Jambumali himself was a great warrior, strong and arrogant, fierce and handsome. He came into battle roaring as only a noble-born rakshasa can. He shot a sizzling clutch of arrows at Hanuman.

His fur quivering, Hanuman stood very still at the first wounds he received. A slow smile spread on his face and, one by one, he plucked out young Jambumali's shafts from his flesh, like thorns. Then an earthshaking duel erupted between them. Seizing up boulders from the asokavana's despoiled rock gardens, Hanuman hurled them at the rakshasa. But Jambumali's arrows were wizardly, and they blew the stones into dust. Then Hanuman twirled his pillar above his head and flung it like a javelin at the young rakshasa, smashing him against a wall, crushing his chest; and he died with an incredulous look on his face.

From his window, Ravana watched in mounting fury. He roared to his ministers to send another legion against Hanuman, who stood towering and pleased as could be in the streaming sun. The remains of the first two forces lay around his feet, rakshasas' blood splashed everywhere as if in some horrible offering. Five ministers sent five warrior sons at the head of the biggest detachment yet. They marched up the cobbled streets of Lanka, like thunder rolling, to quell Hanuman. But the vanara was implacable; he was invincible. With the pillar he retrieved from Jambumali's chest, he razed that contingent as easily as the others.

Hanuman was enjoying himself. His fur was colored with rakshasas' blood and he danced among the dead, still crying out Rama's name and that Hanuman was his servant. He cried that he was just one among thousands of vanaras, most of them greater than he, who would soon descend on Lanka. Ravana was astonished; never had he encountered such prowess, save once, long ago.

The Rakshasa called for his own son now, the mighty Aksha. Wearing silver mail, his bow in his hand, Aksha was like the first flame that leaps up in the yagna pit when the brahmana pours libation onto the fire. Ravana blessed his valiant boy.

The splendid prince climbed into his chariot and rode at Hanuman. When he saw the vanara looming before him, he stood up in awe. With an echoing roar, Aksha attacked. Hanuman smiled. He thought how handsome and noble this boy was, and then, quickly, how marvelously he fought. Aksha's arrows fell out of the sky like deadly rain. In a wink, Hanuman was a tiny monkey, dodging those shafts. Then again he was enormous, and cast rocks and trees like lances at Aksha.

The ocean trembled to watch the battle between Ravana's son and Hanuman. On they fought, fiercely and cleverly, and Hanuman thought, "I like this dauntless boy so much I do not want to kill him. But what can I do? The fire that rages must be put out, or it consumes one."

With a sigh, Hanuman smashed down Aksha's horses with his stone pillar. Crying out weirdly, Aksha rose into the sky with maya. But as he drew back his bowstring, the vanara plucked him from the air as if he were an annoying fly. Blessing the young rakshasa in his heart, Hanuman dashed his head like lightning against a stone wall.

When their prince died, Aksha's legion panicked and fled back to their master of darkness in his sabha. Ravana sat, ten-headed and terrifying, before his ministers. He was aflame. A tremor ran through his lean body when he heard Aksha was slain. No muscle on his faces twitched, to show the grief that clutched him like a pang of death. But nine of ten heads shut their eyes in a prayer. The tenth, central one called for his eldest son: the awesome Indrajit, master of astras, said to be his father's equal in battle.

His lips pale at what the monkey in his garden had done—the streets of Lanka flowed rakshasa blood—Ravana said to his prince, "Your brother and your friends have died. It seems no legion can stand against this monkey, let alone take him. Go, my son, bring him to me." Softly, he added, "Bring him alive."

Indrajit walked around his father in pradakshina. Then that rakshasa prince went to tame the vanara in the asokavana.

12. The coils of an astra

Sweeping through Lanka in his chariot like a dark wind, Indrajit flew at Hanuman. When he neared the vanara, he pulled on his bowstring and Lanka echoed with the sound. Hanuman responded with a burst of wild laughter, that here at last was a worthy adversary. The exhilaration of battle was upon him and he longed for a keen fight.

They fought outside Ravana's palace, the rakshasa prince and the marauding monkey, tall as a tree. Like thunderstorms colliding, they fought, roaring exuberantly, the air between them thick with Indrajit's arrows and Hanuman's rocks and trees. Occasionally, both of them paused, panting, for neither gave any quarter or yielded an inch of ground. Indrajit was amazed at this monkey who shrugged off his most lethal missiles. And Hanuman wondered at the young Rakshasa, who was unharmed by his barrage of everything heavy he could lay his hands on. He tore up flagstones and steps of rock and flung them, spinning like chakras, at Ravana's son, only to see them shot into powder.

At last Indrajit drew an exceptional arrow from his quiver. He shut his eyes, invoking Brahma, the Creator, ancestor of the rakshasas. Once, out of affection for his great-great-grandson, Brahma had given Indrajit his own astra. Hanuman grew still at the Brahma mantra; he folded his hands. The astra flamed at him through the sky. Out of his bhakti, he would not escape it, but allowed it to bind him in hoops of light. He sprawled on the ground, apparently vanquished.

Hanuman said to himself softly, "The boy doesn't know that by Brahma's own boon to me, his astra can hold me only for a moment. But I want to see Ravana face to face before I fly out of Lanka, and this is my chance. I am not afraid. Vayu, my father, and his friend, Agni, protect me."

He lay unprotesting while they thought the astra's power had conquered him. The rakshasas crowded around, and bound him once more with the longest ropes and strips of bark they could find. As soon as the coils of rope touched Hanuman's body, the coils of the astra vanished. All the great astras are haughty; none will stand for other bonds beside its own. When he saw them running at the fallen monkey with their ropes, Indrajit cried out to his soldiers to stop. But they did not hear him in the commotion.

Ravana's son thought that now there would be no restraining

Hanuman. But to his surprise, the vanara lay where he had fallen, and allowed himself to be bound and dragged before the Lord of Lanka in his palace. Puzzled, Indrajit went with the monkey to his father's sabha.

13. In Ravana's sabha

When he was brought into Ravana's presence, Hanuman opened his eyes, which he had screwed shut as if in pain as he was hauled along the smooth floors of the palace. He saw Ravana smoldering above him: tall and darkly magnificent. A golden crown on his head reflected shafts of light from pearl, diamond, and ruby. The Rakshasa wore the same flowing white silk Hanuman had seen him in that morning. He sat very still on his throne above the vanara at his feet.

The scent of sandalwood paste, with which Ravana's body was anointed, filled his sabha. Noble, wise, and terrible, as well, were the Demon's eyes; they now searched Hanuman's face curiously, fiercely. Ravana wore a necklace of pearls around his neck, some big as a pigeon's eggs, and around his rippling arms he wore heavy bracelets of gold and coral. He sat on his throne of black crystal with his ministers around him, Prahastha, Nikumbha, and the others.

The rakshasas of Indrajit's guard had dragged Hanuman here roughly. But when he lay at Ravana's feet and looked up at the splendor that was this great Rakshasa, the vanara was dazzled. He stared at the Demon and, unable to tear his eyes from the king of Lanka, Hanuman stared on. He thought, "What strength, what majesty! Yet he is evil. If he had not taken the path of night, the left-hand way, this Rakshasa could have been king of the Devas if he wanted. I have never seen such presence, such power. But then, he is cruel and ruthless. He is a creature of darkness and his heart knows no mercy."

Ravana, who had his name because he made the worlds tremble, gazed down into Hanuman's tawny eyes, gauging him shrewdly and swiftly, so the monkey felt his very soul being scrutinized. The Rakshasa felt a stab of fear, and thought, "Is this Siva's Bull come to Lanka, as he swore he would when I hefted Mahadeva's mountain? Is this Nandi come as a monkey to announce my death? Or is it Banasura come to kill me?"

Slowly, the fire that slumbered in the depths of his eyes blazed up to their surface. In a fearful glower, Ravana turned ten heads at his minister Prahastha, who had also just lost a son to Hanuman. Sibilantly, the king said, "Who is he? Where has he come from? What does he want, that he destroyed my asokavana and killed so many of my warriors, that he killed my son? Ask him."

Prahastha turned to Hanuman, who lay trussed on the floor. "Answer without fear, monkey. You will not be harmed if you tell the truth. Did Indra send you here as his spy, or was it Vaisravana, Kubera, or Yama? Or perhaps Vishnu, the enemy of our people, sent you? You are not just a monkey. That much is obvious from your courage. Tell us who you are."

But Hanuman was not about to answer a mere minister. He indicated that he wished to stand. When he was helped to his feet, he turned and addressed Ravana. "Not Yama, Kubera, or Varuna sent me. Not at Vishnu's command did I come. This is no disguise but my true form, for I am a vanara. I wanted to meet you face to face, Lord of the rakshasas, and so I razed the asokavana. Your soldiers I slew only to defend myself, because they came to kill me.

"No astra may bind me, Ravana; for Brahma himself has given me that power. I allowed myself to be bound with these puny ropes, because I wanted to speak to you. Listen to what I have to say, and it may profit you, O Emperor."

Ravana said nothing. He only stared at the monkey, waiting for him to continue. Hanuman said, "Ravana of Lanka, I have come to your city at the command of my king Sugriva of the vanaras. He wishes you well and asks you to pay heed to the message he sends. This is Sugriva's message:

" 'There was a noble king in the House of Ikshvaku, whose valor and dharma were immaculate, and his name was Dasaratha. Rama is his eldest son. Rama is a kshatriya and a prince of truth. To keep his father's honor he went to the Dandaka vana for an exile of fourteen years. With Rama went his wife, Sita, and his brother Lakshmana. One day Janaka's daughter Sita was lost in the jungle. In anguish, Rama journeyed to Rishyamooka. There he met Sugriva, who had been driven from his kingdom by his brother Vali. Rama and Sugriva swore a covenant that Rama would restore his kingdom to Sugriva, and that in return, Sugriva would find Sita, wherever she was.' "

Ravana listened, twenty ferocious eyes turned unwinkingly on Hanuman. The monkey went on without pausing, "Ravana of Lanka has surely heard of the valor of Vali of the vanaras. Rama killed that same Vali with one arrow from his unearthly quiver, and set Sugriva on the ebony throne of Kishkinda. To honor their pact, Sugriva sent out an army of vanaras to find Sita; north and east, west and south he sent them. They are mighty monkeys of my ancient race. Some fly through the air like Garuda, and others as swiftly as Vayu. I am Hanuman, the wind's son by Anjana, and I leaped across the ocean in quest of Sita.

"Imagine my surprise, great king, knower of dharma, when I saw the lovely Sita grieving in your asokavana. I thought, how can one so noble and renowned as Ravana of the rakshasas, Ravana of matchless tapasya, hold another man's wife against her will? You are a person of superior intelligence; you should never have become entangled in such shame.

"Which Deva or Danava, Asura or rakshasa, Lord of Lanka, shall stand against the astras of Rama and Lakshmana?"

Ravana still said nothing. Hanuman stared straight into his eyes in cool defiance, as no one ever dared to. The vanara said, "I saw Sita. I am surprised that a king of your wisdom harbors a serpent in your palace with such tender affection. Like the choicest food mixed with poison, she will prove more than you can digest. Ravana, she will be your undoing. Heed what I say; return her to Rama who pines for her. Give her back today, she is dangerous.

"You are a tapasvin. For one who sat for as long as you did in penance, what is a woman, even the most beautiful one? I have been told it was incomparable dhyana that blessed you with invincibility against Deva and Asura; and you vanquished Indra and Kubera. But Ravana, you forget that Sugriva is neither a Deva of light nor an Asura of darkness. He is not a gandharva, a yaksha, or pannaga. Great Rakshasa, Sugriva is a monkey and Rama is a man. Are you invincible against these two?

"Think well, before it is too late and nemesis comes hunting you. Long have you enjoyed the fruit of your tapasya; but the time to pay for your sins is near. Will you be able to withstand the human princes and the vanaras, or will they bring you your death? I appeal to your wisdom, Ravana of Lanka. Remember how Vali died; think back on

Janasthana and the slaughter of Khara's army. Think of today, and what I have done to your garden and your army. I say to you, even I, who am just one small monkey, could raze your fabled Lanka. For I am on the side of dharma, while you are on the other."

Ravana's eyes were eloquent with fury; but he said nothing. Hanuman went on bravely, and calmly still, only quiet reason in his voice. "You think of Rama's wife as just another woman. But she is the deep and dark night that will eclipse the glory of Lanka; she will prove to be the end of all your majesty. She is the noose you have tied around your own neck, as if death were dearer to you than life. She is the fire of truth, which you kindle close to your deluded heart. Rakshasa, she will make ashes of you and your city.

"Rama is he who can incinerate the universe. He can put out the stars with his arrows and create them again. Save yourself from his wrath. Save your people, your women and children; save this beautiful Lanka. When Rama comes, what I did in your asokavana shall seem as a trifle compared to what he will do. Not Brahma, Indra, or three-eyed Rudra will save you then."

Ravana's eyes flashed. Like some unthinkable beast of prey, the Rakshasa growled low in his throat, "Kill him."

But his brother Vibheeshana cried, "My lord, to kill the monkey is against the dharma of kings. Don't let your anger get the better of you; you must not kill a messenger. Think of a less drastic punishment for him."

But Ravana snarled, ten heads at once, his eyes on fire. "There is no sin in killing a despoiler and a murderer. Hasn't he killed Jambumali, Aksha, and ten thousand others? Hasn't he desolated my asokavana? Haven't I sat here listening to his taunts and his abuse, which no king would tolerate?"

Vibheeshana said quietly, "On no account should a messenger be killed. He is our enemy and he must pay for what he has done. Whip him, maim him, even; shave his head and scar his body with your wrath. But do not have him killed; the law of kings does not permit it.

"Moreover, he is just a lowly messenger. If you have him put to death, all you gain will be an evil name for yourself. Send an army against the human princes whose emissary he is. That is just; and the wise will not censure you, but say that Ravana kept his temper even when he was gravely provoked."

The ten heads nodded slowly. But in his heart, Ravana wondered, "Is this Vishnu who has come as this monkey to kill me? Or is it Brahma, or the Parabrahman Itself, the Holy Spirit incarnate?"

With some effort, the Demon of Lanka curbed his anger.

14. The monkey's tail

Calming himself, Ravana said to his brother, "You are right, Vibheeshana; I will not have the monkey killed. But I must punish him for the havoc he has brought to our city."

The heads whispered evilly among themselves; then, a slow smile wreathed the central face. Ravana said, "Nothing is more precious to a monkey than his tail. Let this monkey's fine tail be set on fire. Let him be sent back with a burned stump behind him to show that he crossed my path. Yes, let the monkey's tail be lit and let him be marched through the streets of Lanka. Let my people mock him for what he did today."

He nodded to his guards, who ran out to fetch a length of cloth. They wound the fabric tightly round Hanuman's tail. At first, Hanuman glowered; he bared his fangs and snarled at his captors. But then he thought, "If I allow myself to be paraded through the streets of Lanka, I will be able to see the city by daylight. What I observe will be useful later, when we bring our army against Ravana."

He allowed his tail to be wrapped, dipped in oil, and set alight. He let Ravana's guards drag him out of the palace and into the dazzling sun. They hauled him through the city, while the rakshasas lined the streets, jeering and taunting him. Hanuman went quietly, as if no fight was left in him, while his tail blazed, though he felt no pain yet.

The rakshasis of the asokavana ran to Sita and cried triumphantly, "Your friend the red-faced monkey is being paraded through our streets, with his tail on fire!"

Tears springing in her eyes, Sita turned away from them. She began to pray fervently to Agni, God of fire. "If it is true that I have been faithful to Rama, true that I have kept my vows and that my mind has always been pure, then don't let Hanuman, who leaped across the sea to find me, who braved every danger to bring Rama's message to me, be burned by your flames. Let your touch upon his tail be as cool as the caress of his father Vayu."

338

At once, Agni was soft as sandalwood paste on Hanuman's tail, and Vayu blew gently around his heroic son. The vanara wondered that the flames that encircled his golden tail did not hurt him at all. He thought, "My tail burns fiercely, yet I feel only a wonderful coolness, as if someone anointed me with tender sandalwood paste. Oh, this is even more marvelous than the mountain that rose from the waves. But why should I marvel? Varuna of the ocean is so devoted to Rama that he bade Mainaka receive me. Why should I wonder that Agni has decided not to burn my tail, when he knows whom I serve?"

Then his wise heart informed him, "Sita prays for me! And, of course, Agni is my father's friend."

He felt he had seen all there was to see in Lanka. He gave a roof-rattling roar and, in a blink, Hanuman was as tall as the loftiest tower in that city. The next moment he was the little monkey of the asoka-vana again, small as a cat, and he leaped nimbly onto the nearest rooftop. The ropes that bound him fell away from his body in a use-less pile. He jumped down into the street again, growing as he fell un-til he was bigger than he had yet been in Lanka. Pulling up a pillar that stood at an intersection of streets, he struck out at the rakshasas who attacked him, felling a hundred; the rest fled. Great Hanuman stood roaring at the heart of wonderful Lanka and his tail blazed behind him like a quenchless torch.

Then, monkey that he was, he squatted on the ground, scratching his golden fur, wondering what to do next. What he had come for was accomplished. But another yearning tugged at his mind, the itch of the fire in his tail. Hanuman thought, "The asokavana is ruined. I have killed many of Ravana's best warriors today and their blood runs through this evil city. I have killed one of the Rakshasa's sons. Still my heart is not content. The fire in my tail has been kind to me, but it has been deprived of its fuel. Let me return the favor of my father's friend Agni. I will set alight these fine mansions of Lanka to feed his hunger."

Hanuman was a streak of lightning among the rooftops. He sprang from roof to roof, setting Lanka on fire with his burning tail, while the wind billowed around him fanning the flames. Houses caught and the palaces of the nobles blazed as the conflagration spread. Hanuman, roaring in delight, raced all over the city, touching it aflame with his tail as if he were lighting a thousand lamps for wor-ship at sandhya.

Rakshasa men, women, and children poured out of their homes.

All the city echoed with their cries as their fabulous dwellings, created by Viswakarman, crackled and burned. And everything within them, the spoils of a hundred wars, was consumed by Hanuman's inferno. Priceless silks, brocades, and tapestries were ashes. The gold of Lanka melted and flowed into the livid streets, and the hearts of precious jewels were snuffed out in the flames that enveloped Ravana's capital. Their pillars cracking in the incendiary heat, mansions came crashing down.

When he had put much of Lanka to the torch, Hanuman sprang high into the air and landed with a mighty tremor on the roof of Ravana's palace. The vanara ran across that roof, big itself as a city, touching every corner ablaze with his raging tail. Ravana's palace caught and burned like straw. The agni in the monkey's tail was fierce, and exhilarant the breath with which his father, the wind, fanned the flames. The harems disgorged their delectable women, screaming above the roar of the fire and the howl of the wind.

Hanuman was an apocalyptic beast, exulting as the city burned, roaring his joy to the sky, beating his chest like thunder, celebrating the triumph of the natural jungle over the city of artifice. From Ravana's palace roof, the vanara saw that most of Lanka burned; he saw more houses collapse in slides of rubble and sparks. Smiling to himself, still immense, he leaped straight from the king's palace to the nearby peak of the Trikuta. The wind wrapped himself lovingly around his son. Hanuman looked behind him and saw his tail still burned with the friendly Fire God's cool flames, his proud tail that had gutted magnificent Lanka!

He jumped down onto the white beach below, the cries of the stunned rakshasas still ringing in his ears. He dipped his tail hissing into the waves and put out the exceptional fire, which had not singed a hair of him. At the very moment when he thanked pristine Agni with all his heart, a terrible thought struck Hanuman like an arrow. He whimpered aloud at it.

"I have committed a sin of rage. The wise restrain themselves, but I gave in to anger. Sita must have burned with the rest of the city. Everything has been in vain; I have ruined Rama's life!"

Hanuman stood at the foot of the Trikuta and, turning his face to the blazing city, he howled long and mournfully, a grief-stricken animal of the jungle. But then a subtle light shone into his heart. He scratched his head; he cocked it to a side. He shook it, and he thought, "If the fire did not even singe my tail, it was because of Sita's prayer. Then how much more Agni would have cared for the princess herself. He couldn't have even warmed her, she is so chaste. She is divine; no flame could burn her."

Suddenly he heard voices above him and he saw three bright beings flying through the sky. Their bodies seemed made of shimmering crystal; their long hair blew, casting colorful waves of light behind them. He heard clearly what they said, as if fate had willed them to pass above him at that moment. One of the charanas of the air, for so they were, said to the others, "How amazing it was to see! Ravana's palace fell raging around her; all the asokavana was consumed. But Sita was calm at the heart of the fire. And the flames did not burn her at all, but washed over her like cool waves."

Hanuman jumped up and down. He danced; he shouted out Rama's name. He decided he would see Sita once more before he left Lanka. One great leap and he landed in her presence. Her face lit up, and she cried, "Oh, Hanuman! You alone are enough to wipe Lanka from the face of the earth. You are mightier than I imagined. But fly now, good vanara, fly to Rama with my message."

Hanuman said, "Don't be anxious, Devi. Rama will be here in a few days with the vanara army. Until then: may the panchabhuta, the very elements, protect you!"

Sita said, "Fly Hanuman, fly to my husband."

Hanuman leaped back onto the Trikuta's summit, and from there onto another mountain called Arishta. Now he grew as tall as he had been upon Mahendra across the sea; he towered into the sky like one mountain standing on another. As he paced the hilltop, seeking a hard place to launch himself from, Hanuman crushed the rocks under his feet to dust and Arishta shook just as Mahendra had. Facing north, the golden vanara stared for a moment at the foaming tide far below. He crouched down, every muscle taut for the leap. With a cry that made the ocean quail, Hanuman launched himself into the air, and Lanka shook as if with an earthquake. Like an arrow, the vanara flew north over the waves, flashing back toward Bharatavarsha.

Cobras and lions tore out of their holes and caves in terror when Hanuman leaped into the sky. Trees rose with him and fell back onto the earth and into the waves, their trunks floating like twigs on the surging foam. Before he arrowed into the outer blue, he seemed to hang in the air for a moment. His body lit by the last rays of the sinking sun, he filled half the firmament like a thundercloud streaked with lightning.

Then he flew effortlessly through the soft sky, along the way of the wind, joyful that he had accomplished what he had come for and, indeed, much more. Some clouds reflected the ocean below and such a sight it was: Hanuman flashing through them, his hair fluorescent with the sunset and flecked with sea green. At twice the speed at which he had flown to Lanka, the son of Vayu flew back to Rama with his news.

Once more, Mainaka rose before him, a golden pyramid, a vision out of the waves. Hanuman circled the mountain, crying out his success, blessing Mainaka, being blessed in return. He stroked the glassy sides of the mountain in affection, and, folding his hands to that ancient one, flashed on. Soon he saw Mahendra looming before him and the sacred coast of Bharatavarsha. Hanuman roared his exultation to the darkening sky and the clouds in it. The ocean shook, and the four quarters. The vanaras on the far shore, waiting so impatiently for him, pricked up their ears.

Their faces lighting up, Angada's monkeys scarcely had time to turn to each other when, with a whistling of the air and a quaking of the earth, Hanuman landed on the summit of Mahendra. He stood for a moment on that height. He beat his chest; he cried out a long and ringing triumph, and thanked his ubiquitous father for being with him on his journey. Then Hanuman shrank back to his ordinary vanara size and ran down the mountain, bursting with his news and the joy of it. He met Angada, Jambavan, and the others halfway, for they, too, were agog to greet him and came running up as eagerly as he ran down.

15. A hero returns

When they heard Hanuman roaring above them, Jambavan cried to Angada and his monkeys on the beach, "He has found her, or he wouldn't roar so loudly."

So the vanaras ran up Mahendra in a frenzy of hope. Pulling up plants and small trees around them, spraying the hillside with their joy, they scrambled shouting up the mountain. As they came they broke the most colorful branches from the trees and waved them aloft like a sea of flowery torches. And when they met the returning hero coming down the mountain, their excitement knew no bounds.

Angada embraced Hanuman again and again, and the others all bowed at his feet quaintly, with palms folded. Some of them had brought fruit and savory roots, which they had gathered on their way up. They offered these to Hanuman, guessing that perhaps he had not eaten since he left these shores. Hanuman bowed to Angada and Jambavan. As the sun sank below the waves, they fell silent and stood gravely around him, waiting for him to speak. Suddenly, a smile creased his kindly face, and Hanuman raised his voice and cried, so every vanara heard him and that place echoed with what he said: "In Ravana's asokavana, I saw Sita!"

The army of monkeys roared. They sprang high into the air. They turned cartwheels on the ground and the branches of the trees, and gibbered in delight.

Hanuman held up a solemn hand and said, "She sat surrounded by rakshasis, who guarded her night and day. Her face was covered with dirt, streaked with the tears that flowed ceaselessly from her lotus eyes. She was skin and bones from hardly eating; she took only enough food and water to keep her soul in her body. Her black hair was twisted into a braid like a serpent. It was grievous to see the noble Sita like that."

Angada cried, "There is no one like you in all the world. You have crossed the sea and come back with news of Rama's wife!"

Mahendra was splendid with the vanara warriors upon its slopes: a vivid army lit by the last rays of the sun. A pang of hunger seized Hanuman, who scarcely remembered he had not eaten at all since he crept into Ravana's city, a day and night ago. He took a fruit from one of the vanaras nearest him and began to chew on its flesh. Jambavan cried that Hanuman should be allowed to eat in peace; he must be hungry, indeed, after his adventure across the ocean. Once the first mouthful passed his lips, he knew how ravenous he was, and Hanuman ate quite a quantity of fruit and tender roots.

When he had filled his belly, he belched softly and smiled. Then Jambavan said, "Tell us everything now; just as you went hungry for food since you left, we have waited hungrily for your news. Tell us every detail of your adventure, so we may share in it completely. Tell us about Sita, and how Ravana treats her. Tell us all we should know, and decide in your wisdom whatever may not yet be told. But tell us, tell us; we are impatient to hear."

Hanuman rose. He paid solemn obeisance to the south where Sita was. Then he told them about his flight across the sea and all his adventures in Lanka. He ended by saying, "Then from the top of the mountain Arishta I leaped back to these shores, and once more Mainaka rose golden in my path to greet me. And I flew back swiftly and landed upon this Mahendra."

The vanaras shouted his name until the sky resounded with it. They kissed their tails and leaped into the air, turning somersaults forward, backward, and sideways.

Hanuman said gravely, "It is strange but true that the Rakshasa has not yet harmed Sita. When I think of how he has sinned by holding her his prisoner, I am astonished he has not been consumed by terror. But then, as I told you, he is no ordinary rakshasa. He is a tapasvin; otherwise, touching her would have devoured him quicker than fire."

His eyes brimmed with tears. Hanuman said, "Oh, when I think of how she laid a blade of grass between herself and him, like a sword, my heart bleeds that a woman as brave as she should suffer as she does. She could so easily make Ravana ashes with the fire of her chastity. But she wants Rama to rescue her; she believes that is the way of dharma. Why, when I offered to carry her out of Lanka, she refused, saying she could not willingly allow anyone but Rama to touch her. But how she suffers, every moment. We must hurry; we must not leave her there for long."

Angada cried, "Under Jambavan's command we can raze Lanka, or what you have left of it, Hanuman! I shall kill Ravana myself. I, too, am a master of the brahmastra, the aindra, and the vayavya; Indrajit I can kill easily, and Hanuman can finish the rest. Let us go with Dwividha, Panasa, Neela, and Mainda, who all have boons from the Devas. The handful of us will crush Ravana's legions and bring Sita back. If we return to Kishkinda and tell Sugriva that we found Sita but have not brought her back, he surely won't be pleased."

Jambavan smiled at the prince's eagerness. But he said quietly, "I have no doubt you will prevail against the rakshasas. But take thought that Sita herself wants Rama to come to Lanka to rescue her. She believes that is the way of dharma. I say we should go back to Rama and tell him everything. Let us leave the rest up to him."

Hanuman agreed with Jambavan, and Angada gave up his impetuous plan. Through the darkness of night, which had fallen around them, the monkeys set out at once, by starlight, on their journey home to Kishkinda.

16. The king's vineyard

Early the next morning, after traveling all night by jungle paths and treeways, Angada's vanara army arrived at the outskirts of Kishkinda. On the fringes of the hidden city, within the green valley in which it was built, lay Sugriva's jealously guarded madhuvana, his private vineyard. His uncle Dadhimukha tended to it, and here he made and stored the choicest wines for the king's cellar.

The monkeys who had come from the south were already in high spirits when they reached the madhuvana. Someone cried, "We bring joyful news for our king. He will not be angry if we taste his wine today."

"What about the guards of the madhuvana?" cried another vanara.

But Hanuman himself said, "Leave the guards to me. Today you shall drink to your hearts' content."

Angada's army stormed into the king's vineyard where his wines were stored in great vats. Like an invasion they came, and not in fine goblets, nor even from wooden bottles, did they drink. They tipped the vats over and swilled straight out of them. Dadhimukha's protests fell on deaf ears. When he tried to threaten them, they dragged him through the madhuvana, pulled his beard, and ripped his clothes.

The honeyed wine went potently to their heads, and in no time every vanara was drunk. Some sang, others laughed and wept; others jumped high into the air and turned somersaults and cartwheels. Most of them could not walk steadily any more, though they danced all right. They swarmed into the trees and played riotous games in the branches, swinging from tree to tree, leaping down and chasing each other, shouting at the tops of their voices.

Hanuman cried to that army, "Drink your fill; today is a day for celebrating."

The vanaras needed no encouragement; they drank Sugriva's finest wines in vatfulls. Dadhimukha tried again to stop them, because they were now doing fair damage among the delicate vines. They laughed and began to pick the sharp fruit, crying that the grape on the vine was headier than the wine in the vats.

Now Angada cried, "Let them drink. They come with joyful news for the king."

The desperate Dadhimukha ordered the guards of the madhuvana to stop the drunken monkeys. But they were no match for the fighting vanaras of the king's army. Roaring, Hanuman himself joined the fray and the guards beat a hasty retreat. The drinking and the revelry continued.

Dadhimukha withdrew, and said to his monkeys, "Let us go and tell the king. He is on Prasravana."

Through the nimble treeways, Dadhimukha and his monkeys flew to Sugriva. The vanara king sat with Rama, whom he now visited every day, to comfort him, and also because he himself found deep solace in the company of the blue prince: ineffable peace, which surpassed the pleasure he had in his queens' arms.

Dadhimukha prostrated himself at his nephew's feet and lay there, obviously distraught. Sugriva asked sharply, "What is the matter, Dadhimukha?"

Tears in his eyes, that solemn and elegant monkey told him how Angada's vanaras had stormed his madhuvana and were drunk in Sugriva's favorite sanctuary. He sobbed, "Hanuman and Angada attacked us when we tried to stop the others."

Lakshmana was standing nearby. He asked, "Why does Dadhimukha come here with tears in his eyes?"

Sugriva turned to Lakshmana, and a smile stirred on his lips. "He wants me to punish Angada's army for ruining my madhuvana and drinking all my best wine."

"And?"

Sugriva said, "I won't punish them: they wouldn't drink my wine unless they have come with good news."

Dadhimukha looked downcast. Sugriva went on blithely, "I am certain that Hanuman has found Sita." Sugriva turned to Dadhimukha: "Uncle, they must have found Sita, or they wouldn't dare drink my wine. Tell Angada, Jambavan, and Hanuman that I am impatient to hear their news."

A little dazed, poor Dadhimukha went back to the madhuvana. But Sugriva was elated he could keep his promise to Rama that, be she anywhere at all, his vanaras would find Sita. He was pleased that at least in some measure he could repay his debt to the prince. Most of all, he was happy that at last a ray of hope shone into his human friend's misery.

17. "Lord, I have seen Sita!"

When a chastened Dadhimukha came back to the madhuvana, he found most of the monkeys asleep, on the ground and in tree forks. He presented himself before Angada with folded hands and said, "Forgive me, my prince. Forgive my guards for trying to spoil your army's enjoyment. I have just been to the king to complain about you, but he said, 'Welcome them to my madhuvana, for I am sure they bring good news. Tell Angada, Hanuman, and Jambavan that Rama, Lakshmana, and I wait impatiently for them on Prasravana.' "

Angada blew a blast on his hunting horn and his army rose out of its stupor. Thousands of vanaras, scattered across those woods, shouted their prince's name and stood groggily before him. Some were unsteady on their feet, but every last one was ready to jump to his command. Angada called to his people, "Rama and Sugriva are waiting for our news. We must go to Prasravana."

Cheering Angada and Hanuman, Rama and Sugriva, that long-armed legion flew along to Prasravana. Through the treeways they swung, and where there were no trees to swing through, they loped along the trails the jungle folk had made on the ground.

Meanwhile, on Prasravana, Sugriva went to Rama and said, "They have found her. They must have found your Sita, or they would not enter my madhuvana. Besides, they have crossed the limit of time I set for them. They would not come home at all unless they had good news. Rama, I am sure our Hanuman has discovered Sita."

They heard the commotion of Angada's army, still far from sober, roaring its way up Prasravana. The excited monkeys chased each other as they came. With pride in his eyes, Sugriva watched his people swarm up the slope. Every vanara walked tall. They shouted their delight to the sun, the sky, and the wind, and whoever else cared to hear them. And if any doubt lingered in Sugriva's mind that they had found Sita, it vanished when he heard his monkeys climb the hill. At Sugriva's side, Rama sat hardly breathing.

With Angada, Jambavan, and Hanuman at its head, their faces shining, the army arrived at the cave mouth. The leaders prostrated themselves at the feet of Sugriva, Rama, and Lakshmana. Now Hanuman bowed again and again at Rama's feet, and he cried, "Lord, I have seen Sita!"

Like the sun at dawn after a long night of fear, a smile appeared on Rama's dark face. He touched Hanuman's head with his hand in a loving blessing. And a tumult broke out there, as every vanara ran forward to babble the tale of how Sita was found on Lanka, each one as if it was just his own story.

Some cried that she was unharmed; others how sad she was; others said she was like a doe surrounded by tigresses, among the rakshasis; others told of Trijata's dream; others how Hanuman savaged the asokavana; some described Hanuman's rout of Ravana's forces; then some spoke of Indrajit and the brahmastra; more, of Hanuman in Ravana's sabha; and others of the burning of Lanka. So it came out, abruptly and all together, the end, the middle, and the beginning, and no one could make head or tail of it.

His eyes moist with hope, Rama raised his hand. "I thank you! I thank you, my friends, for bringing me news that Sita is safe. Now tell me, what did she say to me?"

Hanuman had not told anyone about the message Sita sent. A little shamefaced, the monkeys made way for the son of the wind to stand before Rama once more, and relate his adventure himself. Embarrassed, they said, "You finish the story, Hanuman, you will tell it best."

Rama and Lakshmana stifled smiles, while joy tugged at their hearts. Hanuman came before Rama; he turned his face to the south, where Sita was Ravana's prisoner. He bowed in that direction with folded hands and said quietly, "Rama, I leaped across the southern sea to find Sita. With my father's power, I leaped a hundred yojanas. There, in the city of Lanka where Ravana rules, I saw Sita in an asokavana where he holds her prisoner. She hardly eats or drinks, but sustains herself by thinking of you. Some rakshasis guard her, and try to persuade her to yield to Ravana.

"She saw no way of escaping, nor any hope of you finding her. The morning I saw her, she had decided to take her life."

Smiling modestly, Hanuman told how he had sat on the shimshupa tree and chanted the history of the Ikshvakus; how, at first, she had been terrified that he was Ravana come disguised as a monkey; how, slowly, he won her trust.

Hanuman said, "Sita sent this message to you: 'Somehow, thinking of you, I will stay alive for a month more. But after that Ravana will kill me. Save me, Rama, before the month ends.'

"I gave her your ring, and she was as happy as if she had seen you standing before her."

He drew out the choodamani Sita had given him and handed it to Rama. Lowering his voice, Hanuman said, "She asked me to remind you of the day in Chitrakuta, when the crow attacked her. She asked me to remind you of the time when you marked her brow with the tilaka of dust from the manasila stone. She said she is waiting for you to save her, and that every moment apart from you is an abyss."

Rama held the jeweled choodamani and a sob wracked him. Choking, he said to Sugriva, "Her father gave her this when we were married, and she wore it at the wedding. How beautiful she was on that day. Indra himself once gave Janaka this heirloom. When I look at it, I see Dasaratha, Janaka, and my Sita before my eyes. I feel she is here beside me."

Rama shook as if with a fever, and cried to Lakshmana, "Lakshmana, I see her face when I hold this golden thing. She weeps for me, my brother."

He turned to Hanuman. "Tell me everything she said, noble Hanuman. What you say will be like water on the lips of a man dying of thirst. Oh, if she stays alive for a month, she will live longer than I will; for I will not last another moment without her. Oh, Hanuman, take me to my Sita now!" He calmed himself. "But first, tell me what she said; tell me everything."

Rama clasped Hanuman's hand, and Hanuman led him away into the cave. Alone, he told Rama everything he had seen and heard in Lanka; all that he had observed about Sita; all that she had said to him. He began with Sampati the eagle, who directed them to Lanka. Then he described how he crossed the sea, and how he found Sita. In painstaking detail, Hanuman dwelt on his meeting with her in the asokavana; every breath she drew, each word she uttered, he related carefully and vividly.

He said, "I have assured her that your love is constant, and that you will come swiftly to Lanka with an army of Sugriva's monkeys and Jambavan's bears, to rescue her from the Rakshasa. She waits anxiously for you, Rama, knowing you won't fail her, and that soon Ravana will be meat for the scavengers of the ocean isle."

Rama smiled bravely to hear what Hanuman said.

BOOK SIX

YUDDHA KANDA

{War}

1. On Prasravana

Rama's eyes shone when he heard Hanuman's adventure in Lanka. Hugging the vanara, the blue prince cried, "Before today, I had heard of Garuda and Vayu crossing the ocean. Now Hanuman the vanara has leaped across the waves out of his love. He has ravaged impregnable Lanka and returned alive to bring us his news. Matchless one, it saddens me that, poor as I am today, I can repay you only with an embrace."

Tears running down his face, he embraced Hanuman again. Rama controlled himself, and said quietly, "It is true we have found Sita. Yet, though Hanuman vaulted the ocean as if it were a puddle of rainwater, how will the rest of us cross the yawning sea?"

The vanaras all nodded their heads and murmured their agreement. Gloom settled on the company.

Then Sugriva cried, "Rama, it is not right that you fear these trifles as another man may. In dharma, this is nothing. Can just a sea stand between Rama and his love? Can Death, who is the widest of seas? I say no! We will cross the ocean, all of us. Look at the faces of my monkeys, Rama. Look carefully, and tell me if you see a single vanara who would not gladly leap into a fire for you. No, there is no one here who does not love you better than his life. Then how can you doubt the ocean shall be crossed?"

He paused, and saw Rama smile. The vanaras cheered their king deafeningly. Sugriva said, "To my mind, it seems a bridge must be built across Varuna's kingdom of waves before our army can cross into Lanka. I say to you, once the bridge is built you will see my vanaras' valor. You will see Ravana's corpse lie upon the earth. Only, do not succumb to doubt; don't let grief be your master. Rather, harness your rage fiercely in your heart and let it be your weapon. We will surely kill Ravana and rescue Sita. You must believe this, Rama."

The vanaras cheered again. But though what Sugriva said gave some heart to Rama, he was still somber. Then, shrugging off his despondency and drawing himself erect, he said, "You are right, my friend. We will find a way to cross the ocean, because we must. If we cannot build a bridge to take us over the waves, I will drain the sea with my astras and we will walk to Lanka on dry land to confront Ravana."

Rama turned to Hanuman. "Tell me all there is to know about Ravana's city. Tell me every detail you saw, when in your wisdom you decided to look it over. Omit nothing, my friend. Paint a picture for us so that Lanka rises before our very eyes and we see her turrets sparkling in the sun."

Hanuman described the Rakshasa's city, leaving out no sight he had seen, however trivial. He did not belittle Ravana's rakshasa guard; he praised them. But he said the vanaras, who could grow vast or tiny at will, and who were all fearless fighters, would be more than a match for that army of darkness: the vanaras, with dharma on their side and Rama of Ayodhya to lead them!

"Angada, Dwividha, Mainda, and the rest of us will not fail you, Rama. All you have to think of now is an auspicious time for us to set out."

Once more, the vanaras leaped into the air and cried out their king's name and Rama's, Hanuman's, and Angada's, and the names of all their chieftains, one after the other.

Rama and Lakshmana imprinted Hanuman's description of Lanka on their hearts, as if their lives depended on remembering each detail.

2. Below Mahendra

When Hanuman declared they must choose a proper muhurta to set out for Lanka, Rama shaded his eyes and stared briefly at the sky. He said, "The sun is at his zenith; this is the hour called Vijaya. If we set out at once for Lanka, our mission will not fail. Today the moon is in the Uttara nakshatra, but tomorrow he will be in Hasta. We must leave immediately if we are to take death to the Rakshasa across the sea. Let Neela go in advance through the jungle of fruit trees, with part of our army. But Neela, beware the rakshasas have not poisoned either the fruit or the pools in the vana you pass through. They may well do this, when they learn of our purpose.

"Let Gaja, Gavya, Gavaksha, and Rishabha lead armies from here, and let Hanuman carry me upon his shoulders, as Airavata does Indra. Let Angada carry Lakshmana, as Sarvabhauma does Kubera. Let us set out with courage and determination in our hearts."

Rama spoke bravely now. He was not dejected any more, but full of hope, like the noble kshatriya he was. A beaming Sugriva sounded a clarion blast on his jungle horn; he shouted orders to his people to set out. Like a wave across the hillside, a flash flood of monkeys, the vanaras swept down Prasravana and flew along the quick paths of the trees. Over mountain and through forest they swung with lithe, long arms, toward Mahendra and the sea beyond.

The sun began to sink even as they went, and from Angada's shoulders Lakshmana cried to Rama, "You will soon be back where you belong: upon the throne of Ayodhya with Sita at your side. Look, the omens of the sky, the beasts and the trees are auspicious all around us."

When Rama looked, he saw the sky was specklessly clear in every direction and the sun full of soft brilliance. Yet Sukra rose, glowing, behind them as they went. The seven rishis around the northern star Dhruva, and Dhruva also, were clear and shone down on them. In the south Viswamitra's galaxy, which he created for Trishanku, was plain. Visakha sparkled: the sacred asterism of the House of Ikshvaku.

Lakshmana smiled. "The breeze caresses us and the birds sing in joy."

Rama smiled back at his brother, and now a mood of elation took him also. He cried, "The forest streams run like crystal, and the scents of the flowers on the branches fill my heart with hope."

"The end of our misfortunes is near," said Lakshmana.

The vanaras pressed on south, cutting across the path of the sinking sun and bearing slightly to the east. Through the green awnings of many forests they flew easily through branches, over brown hill, and across frothing river. Finally, as the sun was poised above the southern sea, its rim touching the water, they stood breathless on Mount Mahendra.

From the summit of the mountain they stared across the smoky sea, which faced them again, roaring at their feet. Rama saw the stupendous obstacle in his path, and was reminded sharply how right he had been to have misgivings about the crossing to Lanka. On and on stretched the ocean, which thundered up at them in disdain. Waves crashed against the rocks piled round and smooth at the foot of Mahendra. Varuna seemed to mock them with his expanse, his depth, and his ancience.

Rama, Sugriva, and Lakshmana climbed down the hill to the small wood below it. Rama said somberly, "My hope wanes to see the ocean before us, with its island hidden by the horizon. Let us make camp and rest here. We must consider carefully how we will cross the formidable lord of rivers."

Like another sea themselves, the vanaras thronged the shore in tides that flowed down the hillside. They came to answer their king's call and gathered round him on golden sands lit by the last light of day. Briefly, Rama and Lakshmana were left alone together in the little wood.

Rama said quietly, "Nothing makes me as anxious now as the short time Ravana has left Sita before he kills her: only a fleeting month, of which three days are already gone. Lakshmana, my heart is weak with fear that we may not be in time to save her."

And Rama broke down and sobbed. "O Vayu!" he cried. "Blow from here to where my love sits, and stroke her with the very fingers of air with which you touch me. Then blow those same drafts back to me, so I see her clearly before my eyes and she knows I am coming. How piteously she must have cried '*Rama, save me!*' when the Rakshasa carried her away.

"My brother, they say time heals every wound. But this wound of being separated from Sita grows more painful with every moment that passes, as if flaming knives are being turned in it. It consumes me, Lakshmana; it robs me of my manliness. Can you begin to imagine how I long for her? Her touch, the look of her eyes, her tender caress, the sound of her sweet voice. Can you imagine how I yearn to be rid of this sorrow that feeds on my very life? To cast it from me like soiled clothes: to kill the Rakshasa and to have my Sita back. Lakshmana, hell and madness clutch at me, and I have to thrust them away with the knowledge that she lives—that, out there beyond this sea, my Sita is still alive."

Lakshmana took his brother gently by the hand; he led him out of those woods to the damp sand. A stirring wind blew around them. In the distance, the scarlet sun sank into the waves. Rama sank down on his knees in prayer. Quietening the anguish in his heart as best he could, he worshipped pristine Surya Deva.

3. The king's brother

Meanwhile, in Lanka, Ravana sat in council with his ministers. He was terrible to see in his fury: controlled and sinister. Ravana said softly, "A low creature of the jungle, a monkey, comes to Lanka and sets it ablaze. By himself, he wipes out a good part of my army and escapes with his life. The asokavana is burned down; our people's homes are razed. More than half my own palace is gutted and the temple of our Devi of Lanka is ashes."

All ten heads were clear in their malignant cluster around the central one, now as feral as the rest. Lips twitching, they glowered. He paused, drew a deep breath, and gazed around him, from face to blanched face in his sabha. Hanuman had shocked them all, as they never believed they could be within their smooth walls that no lizard could scale. In that court, which had escaped Hanuman's conflagration, silence reigned.

Restraining the rage that surged in him, Ravana continued in deadly calm, chilling his ministers' blood. "It is said a wise king is guided by his friends and counselors, who have his welfare at heart. A wise king knows the fruit of what he does depends on fate and the divine powers that rule men's lives.

"He who acts in dharma, but walks alone and pays no heed to his ministers' counsel, is less than the best of kings. But the king who pays no heed to the fruit of his deeds, who has no belief in providence, is a hasty one, foolish and doomed to failure."

Ravana's ministers sat tensely around their sovereign. Slowly, deliberately, he spoke to them; at times staring into this one's eyes or another's, then gazing out again at the blue-green sea below the wide windows.

Ravana said, "There are also three kinds of advisers: those who look clearly at every problem in the light of the wisdom of the Shastras; those who debate, argue, and disagree among themselves, yet arrive at the same conclusion as the first; and finally, those who obstinately follow their inclinations and prejudices, and will never agree with any opinion that differs from their own, however reasonably."

He scrutinized their faces. "My loyal friends, our spies tell me that Rama has gathered an army of vanaras and reekshas to attack our city. From what I hear of this man, he can drain the ocean with his astras and walk across its bed to our shores. Somehow, I have no doubt that he and his legion of apes will arrive in Lanka. We must defend ourselves, and I want to hear your counsel on how we can best do this. I want to hear how you think we should confront the danger that threatens us."

They glanced at one another. Then Ravana's chief minister, Prahastha, whose son Jambumali was killed by Hanuman, stood up and cried, "Only a foolish counselor will allow his king to be anxious when the greatest army in all the world is his to command. We were unprepared for yesterday's encounter with the monkey, and doubtless he was helped by some sorcery and an evil crossing of stars in the sky. But not every day is the same, and your army is the one you led into Varuna's city under the waves, Bhogavati, and we annihilated its great nagas.

"This is the army with which you vanquished Kubera on Kailasa and became Lord of the earth. My lord, you are Ravana who brought the Asura Madhu to Lanka in chains. Mayaa himself gave his daughter Mandodari to be your wife. The denizens of the Patalas tremble at the mention of your name. They know you are the greatest master of maya that ever lived.

"Why does such doubt beset you today, who slew Varuna's sons? Or do you really think this Rama, who is a mere human, is an equal of the enemies I have named?

"Remember how easily Indrajit captured the monkey Hanuman. Indrajit by himself can obliterate the race of vanaras. Or has my lord forgotten that your son is called Indrajit because he once brought the king of the Devas to your feet, bound in the crystal coils of his astra? And only when Brahma begged you, you sent Indra back to Amravati.

"Mighty Ravana, I don't know what darkens your mind with such anxiety today. Why do you even ask for our counsel, when it is not needed? It is obvious what the fate of this Rama and his monkeys will be when they land on Lanka's shores. I say send Indrajit to face them; then we will deal with what remains."

Another like-minded minister echoed what Prahastha said. "You conquered the Devas, the Asuras, the gandharvas, the pisachas. All the kings of Swarga, Bhumi, and Patala are your vassals. Why should Ravana pay any mind to a puny man who dares come to our shores with a ragtag army of monkeys?"

Prahastha, who was Ravana's favorite, cried again, "Send me into battle and see what I do to the upstart Rama. Send me before anyone else, and I will rid the earth forever of her burden of monkeys."

The grief of Jambumali's death weighed on Prahastha's heart. His eyes were full of fire when he spoke, and he meant each word he said. But then, the others were not to be left behind. Every minister there cried that he could single-handedly kill Rama and his vanaras. They cried how easy their victory would be. Had their king forgotten their courage? How they had fought at his side in a hundred battles and the heroes they had killed?

Ten smiles were beginning to brighten ten demonic heads of the Emperor of evil. But suddenly, Vibheeshana stood up and waited for the king to let him speak. Ravana raised an imperious hand to silence the excited sabha. He said to his brother, "Yes, Vibheeshana?"

"Ravana, three methods are advocated for success in any undertaking: sama, dana, and bheda: conciliation, gifts, and argument. Only when these gentler means fail should one use danda, force. I have heard so much about Rama that has touched my heart. He has conquered his passions, most of all, his anger. How can one oppose a man who is a master of himself? Not only that, but the Gods are on his side.

"If you truly want to understand what it is you face, think reasonably of what Hanuman achieved. He leaped across the ocean; was this an ordinary feat? Hanuman was only a messenger; surely, the one he serves is far greater than he. Think of what Hanuman did here, what he reduced Lanka to. Think calmly and without prejudice, however comforting it may be to deceive yourself.

"I beg you, do not underestimate this enemy; most of all, because he has done nothing to offend you. What he did to Khara and the rakshasas of Janasthana was not his fault. It was Khara who attacked Rama. And you know how cruel our cousin was. Someday, retribution had to come for his years of savagery to the rishis of the jungle.

"Dear lord, I know you will not like hearing what I have to say next. My words will not be music to your ears, as Prahastha's are. But you are my brother, and as I love you, I must speak the truth. Ravana, think of what you have done to Rama; for just a moment, reflect on the anguish you have caused him. You have taken his wife from him and brought her here as your prisoner. This is no ordinary sin, but the father of sins: the one that breeds all the others, which follow inexorably in its wake. Think, my brother, that if you had not committed this sin, no Hanuman would have crossed the sea to Lanka and gutted it.

"The Gods still love you for your tapasya, and they have warned you. It is not too late. Heed the omens; give Sita back to Rama and beg his pardon, before you and all our people are destroyed. Rama walks the path of dharma. He is that most dangerous of all enemies: the perfect man! The sin you have committed against him is like deadly poison to yourself. Not merely your life, your soul is in peril. Relent, Ravana. I speak as your brother and from my love for you. Listen to what I say, before it is too late.

"I speak for your people, who already murmur among themselves that their king should return to the ways of peace. They are afraid Rama's astras will end all this magnificence that is Lanka, and their lives with it. Give Sita back before Rama comes to take her. That is the way of dharma."

Twenty eyes on ten grim faces gazed unwinkingly at Vibheeshana. Not a muscle moved on any face to betray the feelings of the Evil One. Without a word, Ravana waved his hand to indicate that the council was dismissed. His ministers bowed low to their king and left the sabha without turning their backs on him. Ravana sat alone on his throne. He sat staring out at the sea from his windows, and tears like drops of fire rolled down his dark face.

The next day, Vibheeshana came early to Ravana's private chambers in another wing of the palace, which also had not been burned by Hanuman's fire. Outside, the first rays of the sun touched the sea awake to another morning. Vibheeshana prostrated himself at his brother's feet. Ravana spoke no word, only stared at him out of tired, sleepless eyes.

Vibheeshana summoned his courage and said, "Evil omens have gathered over Lanka. They were first seen, here and there, on the day Sita entered our city. But today they are everywhere, out in the open like some plague. In the quarter of worship, the fires of sacrifice billow with black smoke that reeks of excrement. The flames splutter with thousands of sparks and die out, repeatedly, so they have to be kindled every half-hour. The havis of offering crawls with ants and worms.

"Our animals are all listless and restive. The cows yield no milk and the elephants refuse to touch their feed. The horses cry in the royal stables and whinny in fear as if they saw specters of doom. You must have heard the crows keep up their raucous cawing through the night.

They roost on your squadron of vimanas. Our guards killed hundreds of the birds; but more flew down out of the darkness.

"If you look into the sky, you will see vultures and kites wheeling in it. They cry down shrilly, as if Lanka were already littered with corpses for them to feast on. Jackals and hyenas roam the city streets, by night and day, and never stop howling. The omens speak plainly, Ravana: that we will not be able to withstand Rama's wrath.

"Spare your city its life, O King, and your people their lives. Let us all live in peace. Relent, my lord, before the vanara army lands on Lanka's shores and the sky flames with Rama's astras."

He paused, his face flushed in his anxiety to convince his brother. Tears standing in his kind eyes, Vibheeshana took Ravana's hand imploringly.

But Ravana drew his hand away and said, "Listen to me, Vibheeshana, I will never let her go. She is more precious to me than all the world, and she was born to be my queen. Let Rama come not with an army of monkeys but with the host of heaven, and I will not give Sita up to him. Your counsel is the way of cowardice. How can a king like me heed such advice?"

Vibheeshana opened his mouth to speak again. But Ravana stood up tall over him and waved his brother away from his presence.

4. The rakshasas' council

Later that morning, under his royal white parasol, Ravana rode in his chariot to the sabha of the people. It was approaching noon, when the conches sounded to assemble the city's rakshasas. They gathered in the streets to watch their king pass. Ravana had always been a munificent sovereign to them, and they loved him fiercely. They shouted his name and "Jaya!" as he rode through their midst, with a small guard to precede him and an armed force behind to lend majesty to his progress. When he saw the havoc Hanuman had wreaked, Ravana's eyes smarted with tears. But the rakshasas of Lanka were dauntless; they had already begun rebuilding their city from its ashes.

The people's sabha stood under a dip in the hillside, and the vanara's inferno had not touched it; Hanuman had not noticed the edifice in its seclusion, around a bend in the king's highway that led into the city. The representatives of the rakshasas of Lanka had already gathered in the capacious sabha, which Viswakarman had also made for Ravana. Inside were a thousand of the wisest leaders of their people. Rarely indeed did their king call such a council; and after what the monkey had done to Lanka, every seat in the sabha was taken.

With long strides, Ravana walked through his people and ascended the jeweled throne set on a raised dais, amidst other ornate seats for his generals and ministers. Prahastha sat on Ravana's right, and Vibheeshana and the others around their king, each in his own lofty place. Ravana among his nobles was like Indra among his Vasus.

When the applause for him had died down, Ravana said quietly, "I have called you here because a crisis looms over Lanka."

Outside, the crowd surged around the sabha like another sea. They were not the only ones agog at the council Ravana had called; the Devas peered anxiously down at it.

Ravana went on, "Rakshasas, you have never failed me. I need your advice and I know you will lend me your wisdom. I did not call this sabha earlier because I wanted my brother Kumbhakarna to be with us. He is here today."

The immense Kumbhakarna half-rose in his throne beside Ravana's to acknowledge the lusty cheering for him. It was rare for him to be in their midst. The giant slept all year round and woke for but a day between two six-month slumbers.

Ravana continued, "I want to tell you about her whose name is on every tongue in Lanka. I want to speak about Sita."

Silence fell. Calmly he gazed around the people's sabha, daring them to challenge him. Then he began again, in his reverberant voice: "I brought her here from the Dandaka vana because I have never seen another woman like her. I need not tell you that the Dandaka vana is an ancient home of our people. I need not tell you what happened to Khara's army there. But let me say this: if, at first, I went to the jungle to gain revenge on her husband, the moment I saw Sita all that changed. I fell in love with her and wanted to make her my queen. For so she is fit to be."

He paused, trying to gauge the mood of his people. But they sat gravely below him, meaning to hear him out in silence. Only Kumbhakarna shifted in his throne.

Ravana said, "But she spurns me. Though I have become like her slave in love, Sita spurns me. She thinks only of her Rama, and will not even look into my face, let alone give herself to me. This has never happened to me before and I do not know what to make of it. But I confess, my friends, that I am helpless to stop loving her. I cannot live without her."

Still, there was silence, above which Kumbhakarna's sonorous breathing was clear.

Ravana said, "I gave Sita one year to accept my love, a year to come willingly to me. Just two months of that year now remain, and she is still obstinate. But I have not called you here to tell you about my misfortune in love. The fact is, even as I speak to you, Sita's prince has gathered an army of vanaras across the sea. He means to invade us.

"I do not know how Dasaratha's sons and their apes intend to cross the sea; but they do. As we all know, not five days ago a lone monkey somehow leaped the waves and came among us with havoc. It is true that then we were unprepared. But the fact remains that he did burn Lanka.

"I have called you here because together we are more likely to think of a solution to this crisis. Advise me, rakshasas; what shall I do? I want to kill the Kosala brothers and keep Sita for myself. I want to do this as quickly as I can, and I need your counsel to this end. I think we have known each other too long, and fought too often at each other's sides, for me to describe my valor to you. Equally, I need no one to tell me of your prowess. Consider carefully, all of you, ministers and warriors, and tell me what I should do."

Only a brief silence followed. Then the mountainous Kumbhakarna's rumbling voice filled the sabha testily. "You should have consulted us before you abducted Sita. No king who obeys the law of dharma will ever have cause to regret what he does. One who sets too much store by his own valor, and acts rashly, without thought for consequences, will rue what he does one day.

"As for me, I wonder that Rama has not killed you already. I wonder that you have not choked on the venom that is another man's wife. I marvel that you haven't yet tasted the suffering that is on its way to you."

Ravana's face grew dark. He opened his mouth to speak, but Kumbhakarna went on: "I am not saying I will abandon you. No. Whoever your enemy is, regardless of what is just and what is not, I will stand by you and fight. But only because you are my brother and

I love you; not because I agree with what you have done. The three worlds quake at the name of Kumbhakarna. The Devas of light shiver when I wake from my long dreams."

Now the giant laughed aloud and the hall of the people shook at that sound. He held up his prodigious hands and said, "You won't even have to come to battle, Ravana. I will crush your enemies for you. Have no fear; Kumbhakarna will save you from Rama and his monkeys."

Everyone was silent while the tremendous one spoke. His were no empty boasts, and not even Ravana dared to cross this brother of his lightly. At first, Ravana seethed at what the titan said. But soon he smiled to hear his protestation of loyalty. He knew what a boon it was to have Kumbhakarna fight for him: no army had ever stood before his untold strength, whenever he was awake and came to battle.

"When I have killed Rama," said the giant, "Sita will be yours."

There was a short silence. Then a minister called Mahaparshva said, "If Rama dares to come to Lanka, he will find a quick death here. But there is something I do not understand. Why do you beg Sita for her love? Why don't you just take her as you please?"

Ravana smiled. "I will tell you why. Once, some years ago, when I was flying in the pushpaka vimana, I saw an apsara who went toward Brahmaloka by a shining pathway of the sky. She was enchanting and I desired her. I accosted her, but she would not have me. I ravished her between heaven and earth, and her screams rang among the stars.

"I left her there in a swoon and came home. But she went to Brahmaloka with her tale, and the Pitamaha was livid. Brahma came to me in a dream and cried, 'If you ever force yourself on another woman, your head will burst in a thousand pieces and there will be an end to Ravana.'

"That is why, Mahaparshva my friend, Sita has not yet felt my flesh upon hers."

He paused again. Kumbhakarna's avowal of support had restored Ravana's spirits. He said to his people, "I am Ravana of Lanka. Rama does not know who I am, that he dares march against me. My valor is as deep as the ocean; I am as strong as Vayu. Rama knows nothing of the arrows of black agni that flare from my bow. We hear of this Rama's brilliance. But I will absorb his light as the sun does the stars at dawn."

Ravana, Emperor of darkness, threw back his head and laughed. His fangs flashed in the noon light that streamed, hushed and rich, through the windows of that sabha. He cried, "A mortal man, a mere human, dares to come to fight the rakshasas of Lanka. And with what? An army of monkeys!"

The mood infected his demons and their laughter rang out. When the crowd outside heard what the merriment was about, the laughter swelled into a roar. Women and children, old and young, all joined in the celebration of their king's and their own tameless might.

But in the hall of council, Vibheeshana rose to his feet. He shouted above the wave of laughter, *"Why don't you see that Sita is like a deadly serpent?"*

Silence fell. Ravana's eyes flashed dangerously, but he said nothing. It was the time-honored custom that any rakshasa of worth could have his say in the sabha of the people. Moreover, Vibheeshana was well loved; he was noble and wise, and everyone would want to hear him out. He spoke anxiously, like one who knew the truth, but also knew that he would not be heeded when calamity threatened: because the very stars were ranged against him.

Impassioned Vibheeshana cried, "The nape of her neck, which you adore, is the stem of the serpent's hood. Her sweet, wan smiles are the snake's fangs. And the deep sorrow in her heart is the venom that will be the death of us all. She is proud and she is terrible. Oh, my precious lord, send her back where she belongs, before doom finds us.

"Return Sita to her Rama before the vanaras come to Lanka. You saw what just one of them did. In Sugriva's army, there are many monkeys as strong as Hanuman and some even stronger. You speak of your arrows of fire, Ravana; but what do you know of Rama's astras? Every shaft of his is brighter than a sun flare, swifter than time or thought, and each one as potent as Indra's vajra. How will the rakshasas stand against Rama? Could Khara withstand him? My brother, as I love you, you must heed my lone voice of sanity in this sabha of self-deceivers. Send Sita back. Great Ravana, not even you can resist the tide of Rama's astras when they come blazing through the sky."

Vibheeshana turned on Prahastha: "Prahastha, you brag about your valor. Do you think Khara was killed with bragging, and his fourteen thousand at Janasthana?"

Vibheeshana was desperate to make his brother listen to him. "You are like blind men, and you are all wrong. Ravana, you are wrong. Kumbhakarna, you are wrong to support our brother in his folly, especially when you know this madness can be the death of him and of us all. Listen to me, my brothers, my people—none among the living can stand against Rama of Ayodhya. You do not realize who this prince really is. Not even the Devas of heaven can contain him.

"And you, the leaders of our people, where is your wisdom in this hour of crisis? How can you lead your king to his death with such foolish counsel? Are you tired of Ravana's rule, are you tired of your own lives? Are you his loyal subjects, his friends and well-wishers? Or are you his enemies, that you encourage him to tread the path to ruin? I swear to you, if Ravana persists in this folly, he will find death at Rama's hands.

"A serpent holds your king in its coils and throttles life from him. Instead of releasing him, you hasten him toward his end. Stop him, good rakshasas. Use force against your king if need be, for by his own admission he cannot help himself. Stop Ravana from drowning in the sea of fear called Rama. Tell him he is wrong; tell him to return Sita, and prevent him from bringing doom upon himself."

Indrajit had been fidgeting impatiently while his uncle spoke. Now he sprang to his feet and cried, "Father, these are a coward's words! Follow them, and find ignominy for yourself and all your clan. I pray that no one in this royal house will ever have to choose such a cringing course, as my uncle plots for us. Vibheeshana has always been different from the other men in our line. He is soft and weak; he lacks the natural manliness of our family."

Indrajit turned directly on Vibheeshana. "Why do you try and frighten us with tales of the valor of Rama and his brother? He is just a man. The weakest rakshasa, let alone Ravana or any of his blood, will easily kill the human prince. I brought the Lord of the Devas to Lanka, bound in coils of fire. Have you forgotten, uncle, how I seized Airavata's tusks and forced him to his knees? Shall I, then, be afraid of two human princes, and their band of monkeys that feed on berries and fruit? You insult me, Vibheeshana, and you insult my father. It is you who seem to have lost your reason, and tread a path of madness called Rama."

An indulgent smile on his face, Vibheeshana listened calmly to Indrajit. Then he said, "Child, Meghanada, you are young and your mind is not full-grown. I understand your enthusiasm and your courage; but strength and valor are not everything. You have not learned the lesson of discernment yet. You are so emotional that you don't see right from wrong, dharma from adharma. I know you think you are supporting your father with your foolhardy counsel. But in fact you are being his most dangerous enemy. When a man walks the way of sin, all his majesty falls away from him. As for you, young one, if you do not curb your rashness and your arrogance, your death will come to rid you of them.

"To my mind, Ravana has erred in allowing you into this council at all. Your place is not here, among the experienced and the wise. When you do not know how to speak to your elders respectfully, how can you presume to offer advice to this sabha? What do you know of Rama that you dare to belittle him? How do you think your uncle Khara was slain, as if he were a child?"

Indrajit's face was crimson at being put down. But Vibheeshana turned away from him and said to Ravana, "My brother, listen to me. Take a chest full of the rarest jewels you can find in your treasury. Take Sita with you in your vimana and fly across the sea to the shores of Bharatavarsha. Return Sita to her husband. Beg his forgiveness, which, knowing the prince, he will give you. Then come home in peace to Lanka and rule for many years more. Listen to me, Ravana, mine is the only reasonable voice in this sabha."

But Ravana turned, eyes blazing, on his gentle brother. "Today I realize the truth of the old saying that one may live in peace with an open enemy, but never a treacherous kinsman. You move with me as if you are my brother, as if you love me. But all the while envy consumes you and you bide your time waiting for the right moment to strike me down. Truly do they say that fortune is found in cows, continence in rishis, fickleness in women, and mortal peril in the hearts of one's own relatives.

"I have honor across the three worlds; I own their treasures and their fealty. I have trampled on the heads of my enemies. But I think you have hated my glory, though you never dared to show it before. Water drops rest on the lotus, but they do not belong to the lotus. The bee sucks its fill of nectar from the flower in bloom, but has no loyalty to the blossom. Your love is like spring thunder, full of noise but bringing not a drop of rain.

"Vibheeshana, if anyone else had dared speak to me as you have just done, he would have died before he finished. But you do not deserve even my anger; I would stain my hands by killing you. You are a disgrace to our family and a traitor to your king. Let me never see your face again."

It is said the grace of God was upon Vibheeshana and he was a saint. He looked stricken for a moment, but then a miracle came over him. His body grew lambent, and he rose into the air from where he sat and four of his faithful with him.

From his place at the height of a man's head, Vibheeshana said in a voice so full of goodness it was frightening for the others to hear, "You are my older brother, and you can say anything you like to me. The older brother is a father to his younger brothers. But you will not walk the way of dharma, even when it is pointed out to you. My only thought was to save you and my heart was clear when I spoke. But it seems that one who has embraced his own doom does not want to hear the truth, or to be saved.

"I did my dharma by you, Ravana, and I spoke plainly. But you would rather hear the sweet, false words of the rest of your sabha, which will tell you, 'Ravana is great, Ravana is invincible!' Even to the very moment when Rama's arrows break into your chest with death at their flaming points. I have prescient vision, and I have already seen many of these rakshasas, who beat their chests about how heroic they are, lying dead as carrion for scavengers."

Vibheeshana was radiant, and his voice echoed through the hushed sabha. Now tears glistened in his eyes. "I have tried to warn you, Ravana. I have tried to save your life. Forgive me if I spoke harshly, because I spoke in love. But you have turned on me in suspicion, and that is more than I can bear. Since you will not listen to what I say, since you doubt my love for you and think I am your enemy, I will leave Lanka and trouble you no more. But even as I go, my heart insists that I warn you one last time. Oh, my brother, I beg you, restore Sita to Rama! Make peace with the prince, and live long and happily after."

With that, Vibheeshana and his four followers blazed out through the windows like five comets. They rose high into the air and flew toward the shores of Bharatavarsha, trailing bright wakes behind them, which shone for a while, then faded like smoke in the sky.

5. *The good rakshasa*

Vibheeshana and his four rakshasas flew across the sea, and where land and sea met, Sugriva's vanaras saw the five demons in the sky above them. Vibheeshana's mace glittered in the sun, and the ornaments he wore, of the royal House of Lanka. Those vanaras cried to their king, "Sugriva, come and look!"

Shading his eyes, the monkey king gazed up at the shimmering five in the firmament, poised there as if they sat on the wind. He scrutinized them for a moment, and said, "They are well armed and seem powerful, especially the one with the mace."

Hanuman had come up beside his king, and he, too, shaded his eyes to peer heavenward. Sugriva said in a low voice, "The rakshasas have come to kill us."

Around him, excited vanaras began to pull up young trees to be armed. Suddenly Vibheeshana spoke to them from above, and his voice rang above the waves and echoed against the mountain behind. "A sinful rakshasa called Ravana rules Lanka, and I am his younger brother Vibheeshana. Ravana abducted Sita and holds her against her will. Time and again, I told him to return her to Rama; until my brother turned on me, saying I was a traitor. I have left my wives and my children to fly here; I have come to Rama for sanctuary. My friends, announce me to him. Let him who is the refuge of all the world be mine as well."

Sugriva came running to Rama and Lakshmana in the little wood. "There are five rakshasas in the sky. Their leader says he is Ravana's brother, Vibheeshana, and comes to you for refuge. He says he turned against Ravana because he abducted Sita. He says he told Ravana to return Sita to you.

"But these are demons who range the sky at will, at times plain to the eye, at others unseen. Be careful in your dealings with them. I am sure they are Ravana's spies, sent to assess our strength and discover our plans. This flying rakshasa Vibheeshana will inveigle himself into your trust. Later, when you are not on your guard, he will strike at you. I, a simple monkey, say this to you, Rama. But remember, the ways of war are the same among vanaras, rakshasas, and men. And of us all, the demons are the most treacherous. He is Ravana's brother, and says as much; lure him down and kill him."

Rama turned to the other vanaras who had come to him, Hanuman among them. "You have heard Sugriva. But in a situation like ours, there are often more opinions than one. I would like to hear them all before we decide what we should do about the rakshasas in the sky."

Angada raised his hand to speak. When Rama smiled and nodded at him, the prince said, "At first, the rakshasa must be treated with suspicion. If there is even the slightest doubt about his sincerity, let him be killed. But if after we examine his motives and watch him carefully, we are satisfied that he is true, let him be welcomed to our side."

Neela spoke and Dwividha, Sugriva again, and some others. Though each reached his conclusion by different arguments, they all agreed Vibheeshana was not to be trusted. Only Hanuman was silent. Rama turned to him and said, "How is it you voice no opinion, Hanuman? You have been in Lanka."

Hanuman said, "All of you are as wise as Brihaspati himself. But if you truly want to hear what I think, I will tell you: not to appear wiser than anyone, but because this is how I feel. Someone says a spy of our own should be sent to Vibheeshana. I don't agree. Someone else says that he has not observed the conventions of such a meeting. But I should think this goes in Vibheeshana's favor. His decision to come out here appears to have been a hard one; at first he tried to convince his brother of the error of his ways. Just think, would it not have been easier for him to agree with whatever Ravana did, since he is the king?"

A few vanaras began to interrupt. But Hanuman held up a hand, and continued, "Besides, I have seen Vibheeshana in Ravana's sabha. What I heard him say there inclines me to believe what he tells us. When Ravana wanted to have me killed, it was Vibheeshana who said a messenger should never be punished with death. Only then did Ravana decide to fire my tail and parade me through Lanka. I saw Vibheeshana close in Lanka, and I felt his face was honest and kindly.

"If you take my word for it, this rakshasa is neither deceitful nor cunning. He speaks his mind and deals in truth. We should take him for what he says he is. He is no spy, but has made a very hard choice: he chose the way of dharma over his own blood. Think of it another way. If he is honest, as I say he is, how difficult it must have been for him to come here, not knowing how we would receive him. Rama, he has risked everything to come to you in faith. This is the way I look at it."

Rama said quietly, "Vibheeshana comes to me with love and I must welcome him."

But Sugriva cried, "Rama, he is a rakshasa! He has abandoned his own brother."

A smile hovered on Rama's lips. He turned to Lakshmana and said, "Noble souls may be born among rakshasas as well. I think we must take Vibheeshana at his word. And then, not everyone is blessed with a Bharata or a Lakshmana for a brother."

Sugriva said, "You are too trusting. Vibheeshana is Ravana's spy, sent here cunningly. We must go into war with care; caution demands we kill the rakshasa."

But Rama smiled, "What does it matter if he is a spy? He can do me no harm even if he means to. Dear, loyal Sugriva, not all the rakshasas in the world can harm me, let alone one who comes to me for refuge. The way of dharma is clear on this: no one who comes for sanctuary should ever be turned away. If it were Ravana who came to me, I would give him a place in my heart. Go, my friend, and bring Vibheeshana to me."

Rama's tone was firm. Sugriva walked around in a circle. He pondered; he scratched himself and he frowned. He considered the matter at hand from every angle, talking to himself as he did. Then his frown cleared and, with a smile, the vanara king cried, "You may be right, after all. Perhaps he does come in good faith. Let us meet him. Let him be one of us, until he proves otherwise."

Sugriva strode out to where Vibheeshana and his four followers were still poised in the sky. He called up to the rakshasas, "Rama welcomes you; he grants you refuge."

Vibheeshana laughed in delight. In a flash, he and his friends had flown down to the wet sand beside the sea. Sugriva brought him before Rama. With no hesitation, not even bothering to look into the dark prince's face, Ravana's brother cried, "My Lord!" and prostrated himself at Rama's feet.

Standing up, and with eyes only for Rama, Vibheeshana said, "My Lord, I am your servant from now. I have left everything I have in Lanka and come to your feet. Ravana has strayed from dharma, and he does not want to return to it. Otherwise, he should have stood here before you himself and begged your forgiveness. I have left my friends and my family behind, Rama. From now on, you are everything to me. My life belongs to you, my fate is in your hands. My joys and sorrows are yours to bestow; my life is yours to take."

Rama stared at him for just a moment, then his face softened in a smile. He laid his hand gently, in acceptance, in blessing, on the good rakshasa's head.

6. *Suka*

Rama raised Vibheeshana up. The rakshasa was so moved that he wept through his smiles. Rama said, "First of all, tell me about your brother, whom I must face in battle. Who will know him better than you?"

Rama glanced quickly at Sugriva when he said this. The vanaras around them fell hushed. How much would the rakshasa tell? Would he hesitate? Understanding at once that this was a test of his sincerity, Vibheeshana began to relate everything he knew about Ravana. He described his prowess, his exploits, and his army.

As he spoke, a weight seemed to lift from the rakshasa's heart. It was as if magic was upon him, the grace of the blue one he spoke to. Also, Vibheeshana felt uncannily that there was nothing he said that the prince of light before him did not already know. He felt he could go on talking to this ineffably kind kshatriya forever. Indeed, he wanted to, not only about Ravana but about himself; he wanted to tell Rama all about his own life. And he felt certain that nothing he said would be new to the prince.

As it was, Vibheeshana spoke of Ravana's tapasya and Brahma's boon to him, by which he was invincible against Deva and gandharva, Asura and kinnara, naga and rakshasa. He spoke about Ravana's Senapati, Prahastha, and his formidable army of rakshasas; then of Indrajit, Ravana's son who had vanquished Indra himself. He told Rama how Indrajit could make himself invisible while he fought. He described the young Rakshasa's maya, saying it was a powerful gift from Agni, whom the demon prince worshipped.

Vibheeshana dwelt at length on the heroes in Ravana's army; his heart sank for Rama's sake, now that he had seen the force of monkeys that must confront Lanka's ominous legions. When he had told all he knew, Vibheeshana fell silent. No vanara there, not even Sugriva, could doubt any more that this rakshasa had come as a friend.

Rama was quiet. It seemed a battle raged within him when he heard what Vibheeshana said. But then his face cleared again and a new strength sat upon it. Rama said simply, "I will kill Ravana, Prahastha, and all the evil army of Lanka. It is for that I have come. Not in Rasatala, Patala, or Brahmaloka will Ravana escape me. I swear that unless the Rakshasa and his sons lie dead upon the earth, I will not return to Ayodhya. I swear this in the names of Bharata, Lakshmana, and Shatrughna."

Vibheeshana fell at Rama's feet again. "Accept me, Lord of light; I will fight for you. I will help you destroy Lanka. For sin rules from the throne of my ancestors and evil rules my brother Ravana's heart. I swear this by dharma and by my life."

Rama embraced Vibheeshana. He turned to Lakshmana. "Bring us water from the sea, my brother."

When the water came Rama said, "Lakshmana, sprinkle the holy water over Vibheeshana and crown him king of the rakshasas. For so he shall be."

Thus Vibheeshana was crowned on that windswept beach. Sea, sky, and land craned to the twilight coronation, because it was blessed by Rama. When they saw how pure Vibheeshana's faith in Rama was, and how transparent his sincerity, the vanaras felt a surge of affection for the rakshasa. They danced and sang, and shouted his name, Sugriva's, and Rama's together, as they celebrated the unusual crowning of a king. But the four demons who had journeyed here with Vibheeshana, leaving their own families behind in Lanka, were solemn, even as if they sat in Lanka's palace, in its royal sabha.

Sugriva said to Vibheeshana, "Noblest of rakshasas, tell us how we can cross this sea and reach Lanka."

His lofty brow furrowed, Vibheeshana thought for a moment. Then he said, "Rama should petition the ocean. Rama's ancestors, the Sagaras, gave the sea its very name. Bhagiratha's prayatna made Ganga's holy water flow into the ocean. Varuna will not refuse Rama what he asks."

Lakshmana said, "Not even the Devas or the gandharvas have gained the shores of Lanka; and neither shall we, unless a bridge spans the waves. But if Varuna wills it, we can surely pass over him."

Sugriva agreed, "Rama should worship the ocean."

Rama spread darbha grass on the sands, and he lay upon them to petition the Lord of the sea. He blazed on that beach like agni on the vedi of a yagna. Rama stilled his breath and his mind, and began to pray.

Just then, another rakshasa called Shardula was passing overhead, on his way to Lanka from Bharatavarsha. He saw the army of vanaras, and paused his flight to stare down at the force that lay spread over beach, foothill, and wood. He was Ravana's spy and hung invisibly in the sky. Keen eyes peeled, missing nothing, he assessed the vanara army. He noted its deployment, its commanders, and its size.

When he had seen what he wanted to, Shardula sped through the sky again and descended in Lanka. He came into Ravana's presence. He bowed to his sovereign and said, "I have seen an amazing sight, my lord. On the northern shores of the ocean, there is another sea of vanaras that swarms over the land in a tide. I saw the glorious Rama and Lakshmana, and a thousand chieftains of monkeys, all fierce and mighty. That other sea covers the pale beach, the hillside, and the woods below Mahendra, so it seems the very earth is made only of monkeys. The vanara army is ten yojanas square, my lord; you must act quickly."

Ravana clapped his hands, and ten guards came running to him.

"Fetch Suka to me," cried their king.

When Suka came, lean and wiry, his eyes like coals in his bearded face, his king said to him, "Fly to the northern shore of the ocean. You will find an army of vanaras there. Commend me to their king Sugriva. Tell him that Ravana of Lanka says:

" 'Vanara, you are the scion of an ancient and noble race. What have you in common with the sons of men and this prince of Ayodhya, that you bring your army to fight for him? What concern is it of yours that I have taken his woman? I have no quarrel with you; we are not enemies. Mighty son of Riksharajas, you are like a brother to me. Lanka is impregnable and I am invincible. Go back to Kishkinda and live in peace. It is not for the vanaras to take sides in this contention. Why should you risk the lives of your people for a human who treats you like a beast?'

"Make Sugriva understand he should not meddle in this war. If the vanaras leave, two men we can easily kill."

Across the ocean, with sorcery, dark Suka flew quick as thinking. He flew down into the heart of the vanara camp, where Sugriva sat among his monkeys around the campfires of night. The vanaras sat singing the timeless songs of their race: of tree and forest, of jungle river and mountain cave, of the green softness of branches and the terror of the night leopard. When Suka landed suddenly in their midst, they leaped up in alarm and surrounded the rakshasa. For so he plainly was, with his crinkled hair and burning eyes and the sharp fangs in his long face.

Sugriva motioned that they should not harm him; only restrain him, and allow him to speak. Suka did not bow to the vanara king, but delivered himself haughtily of Ravana's message. As he spoke, the vanaras' eyes glittered. They bared their teeth and snarled. And when they heard the cunning words about Rama treating them like beasts, the monkey folk growled in anger, for their hearts were true. They pounced on Suka, bound him, and beat him and kicked him while he lay screaming on the sand. Then Rama heard his screams and ran to the vanaras, shouting to them not to kill the rakshasa.

The monkeys tied up the lean demon and flung him at Rama's feet. His body covered in blood, his face bruised and swollen, Suka wailed, "I am only a messenger, Rama, don't let the monkeys kill me. It is not my own message that I brought, but my master's. Am I to be killed for that?"

Rama pulled the vanaras away from Suka. With a cry of relief, Suka rose into the air in a flash, out of the vanaras' reach. He hovered there, held fast by the long vine the monkeys had bound him with, helpless to release himself because his hands were tied as well. He cried down miserably, "Rama of Ayodhya, now I have seen you and you are noble indeed. Lord of monkeys, Sugriva, what message shall I take back to my king?"

Sugriva shouted up to the rakshasa, "Tell your master, Sugriva of the vanaras says to him: 'How can you be my friend? I don't know you, nor have you ever done anything for me. Rama is dearer to me than a brother; I owe him everything I have. You are his enemy, evil one, you are the enemy of all the world. Your rakshasas kill my people in the jungle, for meat and for sport; and you and yours will die for that. The vanara army will soon arrive in Lanka. We will burn your city and you shall be a corpse among its ashes, with all your rakshasas.

" 'You are a fool, Ravana. The Devas of light may protect you; you may hide in the sun; you may dive into Patala to seek shelter. But Rama will find you anywhere, and you will die as you deserve to. It is true you slew Jatayu; but he was old and feeble. Do not think the vanaras of Sugriva will be like him. Or have you forgotten so soon what our Hanuman did to your city?

" 'You are a coward as well as a fool. You dare not face Rama and Lakshmana, but cower on your island and send out your spies, as you did Maricha. You do not know Rama; who he is. The hour of reckoning is near, Rakshasa, and you must pay for all the sins of your long, evil life. Prepare to die!'

"Take my message back to your master, Suka."

But Angada cried, "This is no messenger, Rama; he is a spy. Let us torture him a little and see what he has to tell us. A spy should not be released. He will go back to his master and tell him all about our army."

He had hardly finished speaking when the vanaras lunged forward and hauled Suka down by the vine. The monkey folk would have beaten him again, but Rama stopped them, saying quietly, "Hold him if you must. But don't hurt him; let him be like a common prisoner."

Thus Suka was held.

7. Rama and the ocean

Rama lay on the bed of darbha grass. He laid his head in the crook of his arm and lost himself in dhyana. He decided he would either cross the sea or die where he lay. The moon rose and set, and the sun rose again, always westering. Then it was noon, and evening again; Rama had not stirred, slept, eaten a morsel, or drunk a sip of water. He lay unmoving on his bed of grass, and he prayed to the Lord of the sea.

His mind was like a lamp that did not flicker. Even the sky above seemed to strain down to the earth, when it sensed Rama's immaculate tapasya. He had the singleness of thought that rishis who sit with their every sense stilled for a hundred years seldom achieve. For three days and nights, Rama lay in prayopavesha, in perfect prayer. Around him, the vanaras fell silent, and then mournful, as time wore on. Yet the Lord of the sea did not appear before the prince.

The moon, which rose over the third night of Rama's tapasya, sank into the waves in the west. Dawn flushed on the horizon and the sun appeared behind Mahendra, the vanara army, and Rama, who lay in dhyana. But at dawn of that fourth day, with sunrise, Rama's eyes also blazed. He turned to his brother, who sat near him in padmasana, not eating or drinking himself.

Rama said slowly, "The ocean is arrogant, Lakshmana. It seems that in this age of the world, the pacific way of sama is ineffectual. Even the Lords of the elements have regard only for violence, and honor is to be had only from fear. Varuna does not understand my gentleness, or he should have stood before us by now. But since he seems to believe I am a weakling, whose prayers are not worth hearing, I will change my method.

"Bring me my bow, Lakshmana. Let us see what Varuna does when I make vapor of his waters with my astras, and all his fish lie heaving on an arid bed of sand. The vanaras will walk on dry land to Lanka, where my Sita waits in anguish for me."

Quietly, Lakshmana fetched the bow and quiver. Rama stood forth on that shore like the fire at the end of the yugas. He folded his hands briefly to the ocean. Assuming the archer's stance, alidha, he fitted arrow after arrow to his bow, and they flashed whistling at the waves.

The sky grew dark as twilight. Thunder echoed in the darkness, and supernaturally vivid lightning divided the sky in jagged gashes. Rama's shafts of light and flames flew hissing into waves risen like giant shields to meet them. His arrows pierced the waves as common barbs do flesh. In amazement, in fear, Lakshmana and the vanaras heard the ocean screaming above the roar of its tide, in a cavernous voice. They heard Rama roar like an angry God. They heard the report of his bowstring, again and again.

The earth shook. The sky was agitated and waves rose like mountains in the stricken sea, tall as Mandara or Kailasa. The monkeys lost their nerve at the awesome violence; most of them fled screaming up Mahendra. Rama stood like a flame himself on the shore. The ocean howled back at him in pain and fury. But the arrows raged from his hands, a river of fire in spate. Whales, sea serpents, and schools of brilliant fish leaped above the seething water in terror. But they could not escape; all the ocean burned. Hilly flames danced beneath its surface, in the belly of the Lord of waves.

A shocked Lakshmana fell at his brother's feet and clutched his hand. He cried, "Abandon this wrath, Rama! Return to the peaceful paths of our fathers. You can win this war without laying waste the sea."

From the dark sky there rose a great lament, and a hundred heavenly voices cried to the prince of light, "Rama, do not dry up the ancient sea."

But Rama heard neither his brother nor the supernal ones. He snatched his hand from Lakshmana, and the river of flames flowed again from his bow. In a terrible voice that was hardly his, gentle Rama roared, "Varuna! I will make a desert of you and the vanaras shall cross into Lanka over your dry corpse."

He paused his prodigious archery, then cried again, "I will consume you and the Patalas below you. All your denizens, fish and whale, shark and timmingala, will lie rotting under the sun."

Then, standing like a burning rock upon the tempestuous beach, Rama invoked the brahmastra. It seemed earth and sky would crack open when he chanted the mantra to summon that weapon into his hands. The twilight of the world turned to a night of dread. The sun and moon strayed dizzily from their orbits. At midmorning, stars twinkled down clearly on the earth. A thousand meteors scorched down into the hissing water. All the slow and stable elements seemed ready to come undone, at the very quick of themselves, where the grace of creation held them bound in time. Chaos verged on the world.

Gale winds from the sea uprooted knotted old trees and blew them about like wisps of straw. Streaks of lightning fell out of the heavens, their rutilant whiplashes seeming to begin in the stars. Woven into the roar of the storm rang the piteous cries of the beasts of the earth, among them Sugriva's vanaras. Lions and tigers whimpered like frightened cats, and great bears wept for fear in their caves. The weaker, gentler animals were in an absolute frenzy. They dashed about blindly, shrieking, but found no refuge from Rama's ubiquitous rage.

As Lakshmana watched in disbelief, the ocean receded from the shore; like a whipped cur the sea fled from Rama's fury. A yojana of dry seabed lay exposed, its pale expanse strewn with the piteous carcasses of its creatures. Dolphin and shark, great whale, whale-eating giant squid, and floundering fish of every hue and size all lay gasping their last on the desert of Rama's anger.

Then from the heart of the sea rose a wave loftier than all the rest, a mountain among mountains. It was cloven, and from it the Lord of oceans stood forth: Varuna Deva, tall as the sky. His body was made of water and light, his hair of shining foam. He was an uncanny sun risen in that twilight and he lit the darkened earth with his marine glory. He wore seaweed and gold on his body, pearls the size of islands and corals dark as night and bright as sunsets. The waves and the flowing locks of his hair were not separate from each other. The rivers, whose lord he was, rose around him: Ganga, Yamuna, and the others, luminous Goddesses. His people, sea serpents with flashing jewels in their heads, and his nereids and mermaid queens, all rose around that scintillant Deva. They stood treading the crests of waves.

Varuna walked slowly out of the water, his hands folded above his head. He dwindled as he came, and prostrated himself at Rama's feet. The God of waves cried to the Avatara, "You are the soul of peace and love; Lord, this wrath does not suit you. Whatever be your despair, it is not dharma that you should transgress the laws of the natural elements. It is the pristine and unbroken nature of the sun to shine, the wind to blow, the earth to turn around; and it is my nature that I am deep, vast, and uncrossable. Not even I can still the waves that flow from me. What could I do when you petitioned me? I cannot change my nature. I would have to destroy myself to please you, and the earth with me.

"This is why I was silent, and not from any arrogance. What I can swear to you is this much: when the vanaras cross over me, however they do, no shark or crocodile, no whale or any other creature of the deep will harm them. It is not in my power to grant you any more, Rama, or I surely would, O greatest of all kshatriyas."

The ocean stood humbly, hands still folded, before the simmering Rama. But Rama said, "You were so long rising from your deeps, my lord, that I have invoked the brahmastra. The weapon must have its prey."

Varuna said at once, "Drumakalya in the north is sacred in my name. The Abhiras are a tribe of mayavis who obey no law of God or man. The sins they please themselves with are too monstrous to tell. They quell these crimes in the holy waters of Drumakalya, and I bear the agony of retribution for them. For eons this has continued, since evil first came into the world. My torment is endless, like the crimes of the Abhiras.

"I beg you, prince of light, rid me of my ancient suffering with the brahmastra."

Rama turned his back on the waves. He drew his bowstring past his ear and the brahmastra flamed into the sky like another sun from his hands. Scorching the heavens, it flashed toward its mark.

The incendiary weapon parted cloud, sky, and time. The earth was riven deep where the astra flared down into it, and, out of chasmic fissures in the ground, the dark waters of Patala rose glimmering to the world's surface. The planet shuddered. The fissures cracked deeper and deeper, long after the arrow itself had bored through the earth and flew out from its other side, on an endless journey through the stars.

The water that gushed up to fill those plumbless fiords foamed and raged like the ocean himself. Gone were the demonic Abhiras, tracelessly, absorbed into the panchamahabhuta, the original elements of creation. Their sins were burned to nothing in the realm the brahmastra slew them into. The residual heat of the astra, which by now was a galaxy away, dried up those waters, and that place was called Marukantara from then.

From the shore of the southern sea, Rama blessed Marukantara. Sweet and sacral water, rare oshadhis, filled those clefts in the earth. Where they came from no one could tell, save that they did so by Rama's grace. But they healed anyone who bathed in them, of any ailment. Marukantara became a sacred tirtha on earth.

Rama's body still glowed with the power of the astra. Varuna said to him in awe, "I have a vision, Rama. Let me tell you how you can cross over my waves."

The Lord of the sea pointed a long, lucent finger at a monkey who stood behind Rama. He said, "That vanara is Nala. He is Viswakarman's son, and he carries his father's genius in his blood. Let Nala build a bridge across my waves. I swear it shall not sink and it will bear the weight of the army of vanaras when it marches over me. I bless you, Rama of Ayodhya. My torment of ages has ended. The sins of the Abhiras are not washed in my waters any more, but in the ocean of the stars. I am in your debt, O Kshatriya; you shall cross over me with your army."

The sky above that shore had cleared. The storm on the sea had subsided. Varuna bowed to Rama; his smile dazzled the quarters. He turned back into his waves and slowly sank beneath them again with his people, into his submarine domain. Soon the sea was as placid as a lake.

Rama heaved a sigh and turned back to the vanaras.

Nala stood shyly at his side, a slim, elegant monkey. He said, "What the ocean said is true. I have my father's gift. I will build the bridge for you, Rama, and it will sink only if Varuna wills it to. For my bridge shall be strong."

Not the sea, not the earth, not the wind or the sky ever forgot the wrath of gentle Rama on that wild shore.

8. *Nalasetu*

Nala stood beside Rama on the southern shore of Bharatavarsha. The young vanara had a smile on his face, and Rama asked him, "What makes you smile, Nala?"

Nala replied, "My lord, I was just thinking that danda, the way of force, is the best way to achieve what one wants. Whatever he might have said, it was your arrows that fetched Varuna out of his deeps. I did think, earlier, that I might build a bridge to make the crossing to Lanka. But then I wondered how we would keep it afloat. And it would take much longer than a month to build a bridge that rests on the bed of the ocean. But now Varuna has promised to keep our bridge above water. Shall we begin, Rama?"

Rama said, "Let us begin at once."

The vision of a natural bridge came to Nala in inspiration, and he began to issue instructions. It seemed as if the little wood at the foot of the mountain had grown there just to help build this bridge across the sea. The vanaras pulled up its trees, and then the trees that grew on Mahendra. They carried them to Nala, who was busy now, shouting where each trunk should be laid.

They must first make a pile of rocks on the shore, to be the bridge's support. Some of the vanaras grew on Mahendra's slopes: Hanuman and Dwividha, Neela, Angada, and Mainda. Effortlessly they hefted huge boulders and threw them down the mountain, where others caught them as if they were little stones. Nala was everywhere, at the head of the bridge, at its base, in between, telling the vanaras which tree trunk should be set where, and which rock.

Soon, the foundations of rock and stone had been laid and shored with timber. Then came the task of extending the bridge across the waves. And now, subtle magic was upon the sea where the vanaras worked. Varuna kept his word to Rama: a channel of perfectly still water stretched away to the horizon before the busy monkeys. No ripple stirred along that channel; it was like a mirror, though on both sides of it the waves swept on as always. In the tranquil groove across the water Sugriva's people labored, scurrying back and forth between the bridgehead and the land with trees and rocks. Quickly the bridge to Lanka took shape.

Not a twig of that bridge did the ocean disturb. Under the sun, and later the moon, the monkeys worked tirelessly. On the first day they built fourteen yojanas, and the far end of the bridge was barely visible from the shore any more. Nala neither slept nor rested, and Rama and Lakshmana stood beside him in turns, to encourage and advise him; though he seldom had any doubts about what he was doing. It was as if the undertaking was blessed, indeed: every rock, tree trunk, and branch seemed to have a preordained place, where each one fitted perfectly.

Those who saw Nala's bridge say that it spanned the ocean as the Milky Way does the sky. On both sides of it the waves roared; but no spray wet the still channel, and no branch was washed away, no stone sank. The zone in which the vanaras toiled was utterly calm; not even the wind blew there.

On the second day, growing more expert with every hour, they built twenty yojanas; though now the distance between the shore and the bridgehead was great, and the monkeys formed a long chain to carry their loads.

At noon of the third day, they saw Lanka's tallest mountain, Suvela, on the horizon and set up a cheer. But Rama said, "Let us rest now and work again after night falls. If we can see Lanka from here, the rakshasas can see us from Lanka."

The Devas of light and the rishis of Devaloka had gathered invisibly in the sky to watch Nala build his bridge. They smiled among themselves that it looked like a parting in a woman's hair, whose tresses were the endless waves. That night the bridge was completed, and the final rocks and trees were carried across to lie on the Lankan shore. The moon was high above, and the vanaras gathered on the beach at Bharatavarsha.

Sugriva said to Rama, "My lord, let Hanuman take you across the waves upon his shoulders. Let Angada carry Lakshmana. When they cannot walk, or if the ocean breaks his word, they can fly through the air with you."

They offered worship to the Gods on that shore. Rama prayed solemnly to Siva, his guru; he was full of anxiety as the hour of reckoning drew near. Rama was the first to set foot on Nala's bridge, the Nalasetu, then Lakshmana and Sugriva. Cheering loudly, singing, and dancing, the vanara army followed him: now to return to the sacred land only after the enemy was vanquished. Rama's heart was heavier than he cared to show.

The vanaras were exuberant. They shouted Rama's name, Lakshmana's, and Sugriva's as they went along, Angada's name and Hanuman's. Now another hero was added to their legends: Nala's name echoed beneath the moon, and was wafted by the night breeze among silver waves.

The monkeys did not just walk on the bridge of stone and trees. As the fancy took them, they dived into the calm sea beside the bridge and swam some way. Then they climbed back on, shivering with the crispness of the water and the breeze, and walked again along Nala's bridge through the tranquil band of the ocean. When a different mood took them under the bronze and timeless moon, the vanaras leaped up into the air, crying, "This is how Hanuman went!" and flew along, as most of them could because of the unearthly blood in their veins.

So great was the noise that army made, the moon above no longer heard the waves but only the tumult of the sea-crossing monkeys. High above that colorful, colossal force, the Devas and the celestial rishis, the gandharvas and apsaras showered blessings down on blue Rama: in the fervent hope that the Avatara's mission would succeed.

Their breath filled night sky and moonbeam, breeze and spray, as the heavenly ones whispered in starry tongues, "May you vanquish your enemy, Rama, and rule the world for ten thousand years."

Devaloka was more impatient than the earth even, that Ravana be slain.

Past midnight, when the moon sank low, the army of vanaras landed on the shores of Lanka, swift and quiet, wave after wave of monkeys. Rama hugged Lakshmana and cried, "Let us make camp here. The trees shine with fruit and the vanaras will be pleased."

The dark prince knew how to read omens; he had studied their lore with Vasishta. He said, "Did you notice the portents of land, air, and sea, Lakshmana? We shall win our war. Yet I see a calamity curled like a sinister fetus in the womb of time and growing rapidly toward its dreadful birth. Though I am certain we will prevail, I have a terrible premonition of tragedy. I see not only a million rakshasas being killed, and their blood staining this island; I see the death of so many of our merry vanaras and the solemn and mighty reekshas of Jambavan."

He grew silent. The last lines of monkeys gained the beaches of Lanka, and like shadows they hid in the dense groves of mango and banana trees.

Rama said again, "Listen to the earth; can you hear it prophesy the grim fate that stalks this island? I feel the sands of time on my cheek, blown in a warning breeze. I feel a hush upon the world and see blood drops in the clouds that gather across the face of the moon. Look up, Lakshmana. Who has seen so many crows and kites in the sky at midnight? And the stars are wrapped in ominous haloes.

"It is as if the end of the world is here. This will be more of a battle than we have dreamed, Lakshmana. I can feel it in my body: a million lives will be put out on these shores. Ah, not only to save Sita have we crossed the ocean, but to fight the greatest war of our times. We must not underestimate the enemy; we must be vigilant so he does not take us unawares.

"Uncanny visions rise in my mind: of timeless evil, and a battle older than the earth, which has been fought before on countless worlds, in forgotten ages. Even after this battle of Lanka, the war shall be fought again and again; until time ends, and dharma and adharma with it."

Rama grew somber and fell silent. After a while he said, "This Ravana is no ordinary rakshasa; he is more than we think he is. His soul is ancient and this is just one incarnation of his through eternity. But he must be killed. Much more than Sita's life is at stake here. The future of the world is in your hands and mine, and in the hands of these loyal, loving monkeys. *We must win this war.*"

The vanaras surrounded the princes again. Rama saw how excited they were, how devoted to him. Had they not crossed the sea for their Rama, and joyfully? They also knew, with unerring jungle instinct, that they had come to fight the eternal war between good and evil. But tomorrow, or the next day, the sky would be dark with the arrows and lances of the rakshasas, and the trees and rocks these monkeys would hurl back at the demons. Tomorrow countless brave vanaras and fell rakshasas would lie side by side, and their blood would stain the earth of this pristine island.

Rama wept for them all.

9. Spies

In another tide, the vanara army covered the southern shore of Lanka. Then, across the night's last yaama drifted the sounds of bugles and drums: Lanka was awakening to another day. As the sun rose, so did the vanaras, who saw the great city above them resting on its hills. They stood awed, gazing at its vivid flags fluttering in the dawn breezes, and its turrets of gold and silver.

In one immense voice, the monkeys roared their excitement at being here and the earth shook. The rakshasas in Lanka heard that noise, and were astonished.

Rama was pensive. He turned to Lakshmana. "Look at Lanka upon its hills. For almost a year now, Sita has been a prisoner there. Can you imagine the torment in her eyes? And the tears those eyes have spilled? Look at Lanka, Lakshmana: her turrets seem to stroke the sky. Viswakarman built his city for Ravana, in fear."

Morning mist drifted across the hills, and for a breathtaking moment it seemed Lanka floated on air like an island on another sea. The breeze wafted down the scents of its gardens, and Rama sighed, "Ah, this city we must attack is like Kubera's Alaka."

For a time, Rama stood rapt in the spectacle of Lanka poised above them. Then, quietly, he turned to the task at hand. He called the vanaras together around him. Rama said, "Let Angada and Neela be at the heart of our army. Let Rishabha be on the right flank and Gandhamadana at the left. Lakshmana and I will go at the head of our legions, and let Jambavan and Sushena bring up its rear."

When these instructions were being carried out, Rama came to Sugriva. "I think this deployment is the best we can hope for, my friend. Now it is time we set Suka free, to fly back to his master and tell him we are here."

Sugriva gave the command and the bonds at Suka's feet were cut. With a moan and not a glance behind him, the demon streaked away toward the imperial city above. Disheveled and shaken, Suka arrived in Ravana's presence. His king laughed to see him.

"Who bound your wings, my little rakshasa?" cried the Lord of evil. "Who marked your pretty face with bruises? Don't tell me you fell among Sugriva's vanaras?"

Ravana's guards cut away the vines around Suka's body. Suka stood before his master. Tearfully, the spy said, "I flew to the shores of Bharatavarsha as you commanded. But when I gave the vanaras your message, they tied me up and beat me without mercy. They would have killed me if Rama had not stopped them. They are ruthless creatures. They are quick to anger, and implacable when they are angry."

The spy trembled to think of the moment when he was sure his end had come: when he lay under a mountain of monkeys who beat him and kicked him, their fangs bared in his face.

Recovering himself under his king's ten-headed gaze, Suka said softly, "I saw him, my lord. I saw Rama, the scourge of Viradha, Kabandha, and Khara. I saw him amidst his teeming vanara army. Last night he landed that army on the southern shores of Lanka. The ocean posed him no obstacle, but came quailing before him when he burned the tide with his astras. Varuna told Rama how he could cross the waves with his legion of the jungle.

"Great Ravana, even now Rama's army marches on your city. Return Sita at once, or be prepared for war."

Ravana's roar echoed against the walls of his palace. The Demon thundered, "Let not only the jungle but all the earth and all the armies of Swarga and Patala come to fight me. I am Ravana, I am not afraid. Let the Devas and the Asuras arrive at my gates with their bright and dark hosts. I will face them. *But Sita stays here with me, she is mine!*

"As for this Rama, I will cover him with my arrows as bees do a flowering punnaga in spring. As the sun dims the stars and turns night to day, I will take Rama's glory from him. When he stands before me he will discover, and the world will discover, his worthlessness. My astras will consume him and he will be a heap of ashes before your eyes. I am Ravana. My valor is as deep as the sky; my speed is of thought and time. Rama does not know who I am, or he would not dare come to my island.

"No one has told him that not Indra or Varuna, not Yama who is death or Kubera who was Lord of the earth, could stand before me in battle. That is why Rama has come to Lanka like an ignorant boy, who has not bargained for the swift end he will find here."

His breath was harsh and heavy and his eyes burned crimson. The nine heads around the central face now appeared, now vanished, in their baleful cone. Suka stood shivering before his king. Ravana grew quiet again and his quietness was more menacing than his open fury.

Slowly, the Demon of Lanka said to Suka and another rakshasa who was there in his presence, "Suka and Sarana, my brave spies, the army of monkeys has done what I never dreamed they could. They have crossed the ocean. Now we must prepare in earnest for war. Go, both you clever ones; turn yourselves into monkeys and go among Sugriva's people. Bring back a detailed account of their numbers, their weapons, and how the army of apes is deployed; which vanara commands which part of it, and how powerful each one is. Go now, fly!"

They went before he had finished, for they read their king's mood clearly. Beneath all his bluster and roaring, they sensed the despair that consumed him. When Ravana was left alone, his nine demonic heads reappeared around the royal one, and all ten conferred sibilantly.

Turning themselves into monkeys, Suka and Sarana crept into the vanara army. They strolled along its length and width, chattering intently between themselves, so no other monkey spoke to them. They saw how the jungle force was arrayed: which vanaras commanded each flank, and which the center, the front lines, and the rear. But as they walked through that wild multitude, trying to count its numbers, Vibheeshana saw them. Knowing who they were at once, he pounced on them with a band of monkeys and dragged them before Rama. They cringed and cried that Ravana had forced them to come, that he would kill them if they did not obey him.

"Don't kill us, noble Rama," they wailed. "Your mercy is a legend in the world."

Rama smiled at them indulgently. "Have you finished with spying? Then go back to Ravana and tell him everything you saw. If there is anything else you want to know before you go, Vibheeshana will take you around and show you all our secrets. But return to your master, and tell him from me:

" 'You dared take my Sita from me. Now you will have to prove yourself in battle. Come out, Ravana; bring all your sons, your brothers, and your commanders; stand face to face with me. Tomorrow, Lanka shall be a ruin worse than Hanuman left it. Tomorrow you will find me at your gate and discover that Rama's arrows are more terrible than Indra's vajra. Tomorrow, Rakshasa, you will taste my anger.' "

Suka and Sarana fell a score of times at Rama's feet. They would rise and begin to go away; then, overwhelmed again that he had spared their lives, they would run back and prostrate themselves at his feet. At last the vanaras chased them away.

They fled straight into Ravana's presence and reported: "Vibheeshana saw through our disguise and the vanaras captured us. They dragged us before Rama, but the noble prince set us free. He said, 'Take all the secrets you have gathered, and if there is anything else you want to know, ask Vibheeshana or the monkeys and they will help you. But go back to your master and say I will be at his gates tomorrow. Tell him to meet me with his army, and all his brothers and sons. Let us see how they save him from me.'

"Ravana, we have never seen kshatriyas like Rama and Lakshmana. Greatness shines from their bodies like light from the sun. Lord, you have always taken our advice; listen to us now. We have never seen an enemy like this one. It is not wise to have war with him. We may not be great warriors like some others, but we have seen the world. We say return his Sita to this prince of Ayodhya. Make peace with him; he is terribly brilliant and dangerous."

Wordlessly, Ravana strode out through his windows onto the vast terrace outside. Sarana and Suka followed their master meekly. They saw how grim his face was. For a long moment, the wind blowing their hair, king and minions stood silently on the terrace, gazing out over Rama's army.

At last Ravana said, "Tell me which monkey chieftain is which; show me which one leads each legion of the jungle rabble."

Ravana's spies pointed out Nala and Neela to him, Angada, Hanuman, and many more vanaras. Then Ravana's red eyes rested on Vibheeshana. There was untold rage and pain in them, and Suka and Sarana trembled even more. The spies smoothly moved on to Lakshmana, who stood on the other side of Vibheeshana, and Sugriva, Sushena, and Jambavan, the lumbering king of bears. Gaja, Gavaksha, Gavaya, Mainda, and Dwividha they showed their sovereign. His eyes grew grave when he saw how radiant these monkeys were, how strong and agile.

Quite suddenly, at the heart of the knot of monkey chieftains, they saw Rama. Unearthly blue he was, and the bow at his back gleamed in the sun. Suka and Sarana saw their king's gaze riveted to the dark prince. Taking courage in both hands, they whispered together, "Lord, that is Rama."

For just a moment, when he saw Rama at the head of that merry force of the jungle, it seemed Ravana felt a pang of doubt. But then, quickly, his eyes were hard again. He turned snarling on Suka and Sarana, "You want to frighten me with this ragtag of foolish monkeys? Who but witless apes would follow a hermit into Lanka, to fight Ravana? As for you two, count yourselves lucky that I don't have your heads. Put it down to the services you have done me in the past. Now go, before I change my mind and reward you with the death you deserve for trying to sow fear in our hearts."

They bowed to him, crying, "Long live Ravana! May victory be yours," and fled from his presence, before he did indeed change his mind. They knew that, given the occasion, the lives of his servants meant little enough to the Rakshasa.

10. A mayic head

Ravana called a council in his sabha. He said to his ministers, "The enemy is at our gates; let our fighting rakshasas be armed."

His mood was strange: he was full of thought, which had never been his way just before a battle. The Rakshasa was somber, like a man who has incurred a heavier debt than he could ever discharge. The ministers hurried away to carry out his command. Ravana returned to his private chambers. He dismissed his servants and summoned Vidyudhjiva, his sorcerer.

Vidyudhjiva was a demon with occult powers, not least among them a gift for maya, the sorcery of creating illusions. Ravana said to him, "Make me a bloodied head, just like the prince of Ayodhya's. Make me a bow and a quiver that resemble his in every detail."

This was not hard for Vidyudhjiva, who had stared long and in some fear at the kshatriya below. Within the hour, the head and the weapons were ready for the king. Ravana went to the asokavana. That garden, which Hanuman had ravaged, had been cleaned up by a contingent of rakshasas. It had been planted again with saplings from other parts of the island.

Far away from her surroundings, borne on a daydream of her love,

Sita sat forlorn and bewitching under the lone shimshupa. Her head was bowed and her eyes were teary when Ravana stalked up to her. The moment he saw her his heart was on familiar fire. She was so quiet in her grief, so entirely regal and lovely. Hers was the beauty of one whose spirit had survived its severest trial; in her loneliness she was as deep as the Ganga. She was calm, as if the Rama in her dreaming mind was as real as the one who was missing from her life.

Standing above her, Ravana said tenderly, "Sita."

She was startled out of her reverie, like a sleeping doe awakened by a tiger. She blanched to see her captor, her breast heaved. Weak at the sight of her face, Ravana said, "Don't waste your dreams on your Rama any more. How often you extolled his valor and said he would easily kill me in battle. But you did not know Ravana when you spoke. You did not know who I am."

He paused to watch fear start in her eyes, but he saw nothing there. It was as if she had passed beyond the pale of fear by her long ordeal. Disappointed but undaunted, Ravana went on, "Your hermit prince, who killed my cousin Khara, is dead. Forget him now; he is gone forever. Turn your thoughts away from the past and to where it belongs, to where destiny has brought you. Turn your love to me, Sita. Look into my heart and see the flame that burns there for you. Touch me, and feel yourself loved as that boy could never have loved you.

"Arise, precious Sita, come to my antapura with me. I am your hope, your sanctuary. The prince of Ayodhya is dead. If you had not been so stubborn, and resisted me for so long, you might have saved his life. But that is over now. All your punya and your vratas could not protect your Rama. Now prepare yourself to be a queen, the greatest queen on earth: my queen, Ravana's queen in Lanka!"

She stared at him mutely. He went on, "Listen to me, foolish woman. Just as you prayed he would, Rama came to Lanka. He landed on the northern shore with an army of vanaras. But the monkeys were tired after their passage across the sea, and they fell asleep. When my spies reported this to me, I sent my rakshasas under Prahastha and he killed the apes while they slept.

"Your Rama was so tired after his journey, he slept on even when the monkeys died around him. Prahastha crept up to him. With a clean stroke of his sword, he cut off your husband's head and brought it to me. The traitor Vibheeshana has been captured. Lakshmana and the vanaras who escaped death have fled our shores. Sugriva's neck was broken, and Hanuman's jaw, before he was impaled on my warriors' lances. So much, Sita, for your last hope.

"The sands of our northern beaches are no longer pale, but dark with the blood of monkeys."

Ravana paused; he grinned fiendishly. The Evil One said, "I see from your smile that you do not believe me. I had thought as much, and I have brought something for you to see."

Ravana snapped his fingers at one of the attendant rakshasis. "Tell Vidyudhjiva to fetch the trophy from the battlefield."

Vidyudhjiva emerged from the shadows with a sack. Ravana nodded to him. "Show it to her."

The sorcerer opened the mouth of the sack and drew out the head he had created with his maya. Sita's eyes stared in shock. Vidyudhjiva set the bloody head down before her. Ravana drew a bow out of his sorcerer's bag, a replica of the radiant Kodanda, and said, "Even if you don't recognize your husband's head for what Prahastha's blade has done to it, you will know this bow of which so much was made. Until the bowman came to grief on Lanka."

Sita gazed at the bloody head, its eyes shut, its neck horribly severed, and she began to scream. "Are you satisfied now, Kaikeyi? The light of the House of Raghu is put out forever. What did my gentle Rama ever do that he came to such an end?"

She fainted and fell across the grisly head. For a long time, as Ravana watched her in satisfaction, she did not stir. Then she awoke and began to wail loudly, calling Rama's name over and over again. Brokenhearted, she stroked and kissed the mayic head.

Sita whispered, "They say that only the husband of a loose woman dies like this. But not for a day, not for a moment, have I sinned in deed or thought. Not once have I missed my vratas for Rama. Yet his head lies before me, hewn brutally from his precious body, and I have to see this sight with my eyes. I am cursed!

"Oh Rama, how will your mother Kausalya bear this? How did a common rakshasa do this to you, who were lord of all the earth? I should have allowed Hanuman to carry me out of this accursed place, and this would never have happened. I am the most unfortunate woman ever born. Just when I thought the end of our ordeal was in sight, a rakshasa has ended all my dreams.

"I will not live a day longer, Rama, and Lakshmana will be left alone in the world. His eyes streaming with a grief that will last the rest of his life, his heart full of guilt and dark confusion, he will go back alone to Ayodhya: to bring news of Rama's death to our mothers and our people."

Ravana stood watching her triumphantly, lust and hope stirring powerfully in his heart. Sita cradled the bloody head and sobbed. Then a messenger arrived in haste from Prahastha. He came running and breathless, and stood with palms folded before the king at his diabolical game.

Ravana glanced at him in annoyance. He was enjoying Sita's grief. He thought the moment had come when her spirit would break and she would turn to him for comfort; and his hardest battle would be won. But the messenger, who stood quaking before his master, obviously brought urgent news. Ravana snapped at him, "Speak!"

"Prahastha has arrived at the palace, my lord. He wishes to be announced immediately; his news is grave."

With a snarl, Ravana turned away from Sita, who had not once raised her eyes up to him as he so dearly hoped she would. Ravana strode out of the asokavana. At once, Rama's head made of Vidyudhjiva's illusion vanished out of Sita's hands, and the bow and quiver beside her. She gave a cry and fainted again.

A kindly young rakshasi among the others watched, day and night, over Sita. Her name was Sarama. She had heard how Vidyudhjiva had created Rama's head with sorcery. As soon as Ravana stormed away to the palace, Sarama ran to Sita, who lay motionless on the ground. Shaking her, the young rakshasi cried, "Didn't you see how the head and the weapons vanished? They were made of maya. Rama lives!"

At the magic words "Rama lives," Sita roused herself. They heard drummers and town criers out in the streets of Lanka, summoning the rakshasas to arms. The army of vanaras was at their gates. Sita looked at Sarama in desperate hope. The rakshasi stroked Sita's cheek and said, "Not a vanara is slain, let alone Rama. Your rescue is at hand, lovely one. Pray to Surya Deva that your Rama kills Ravana, and all the earth will rejoice with you."

Sarama went off again to the palace to glean the latest news from the servants there. She returned shortly, shaking her head. She said, "Yama comes for Ravana's life and the end of Lanka is near. His mother and his older ministers begged the king to give you back to Rama; but he would not listen to them. Like a man who has lost his reason, he cried that he would rather die than give you up: for you were dearer to him than life, many times over. Ah, Sita, you have come here to be the death of him."

Sita was consoled. She began to pray to all the Gods for Rama's victory.

11. *The enemy at the gate*

Nearer and nearer Lanka's walls came Rama's jungle army. Its trumpets and wild horns, its drums and conches, resounded through the sea air. Ravana sat in his sabha with his ministers and commanders. Repeatedly, he asked for their advice on how their campaign should be planned. But his rakshasas were anxious. They did not boast any more; they could hardly believe the vanaras had actually landed on Lanka.

But their king was still in high spirits. He mocked their silence; he laughed in their faces. He roared at them, "Cowards! Are the mighty rakshasas of Lanka terrified of a foolishness of monkeys? Are the conquerors of the Devas of Amravati and Kubera of the mountain panic-stricken that some long-tailed vanaras have gathered at our gates? Or is it the two human princes that make you so pale? Humans whom you would have as a snack in the morning.

"It is the rumors that terrify you. Just think: none of you has seen the prowess of this Rama and Lakshmana. None of you has measured their worth. But listening to some gossip, you sit here and tremble like women.

"I say to you, Rama is just another man. He may well be the strongest of his kind; but he cannot suddenly become a Deva, a gandharva, or an Asura. He is a puny human, and the strongest of his race is no match for even the least of our rakshasas. Your doubts have turned you against yourselves, and there is no fiercer enemy than one's own mind.

"If you calm your fears, victory will be ours, easily. And the jungles of Bharatavarsha will be rid of the menace of monkeys for good."

Malyavan was one of the oldest and wisest rakshasas in Ravana's sabha. He had fought countless campaigns at his king's side, and he had known Ravana since he was just a boy.

Now Malyavan said, "A just king rules his kingdom for many years.

But a king who turns away from dharma quickly loses his throne, and very likely his life as well. You have never needed me to tell you this before, Ravana, but it seems you do now: the most fatal mistake a warrior can make is to underestimate his enemy.

"Open your eyes and look at the sea of vanaras outside our city. There is a great chance that we will lose a war against them. If there are any more monkeys like Hanuman in their ranks, our defeat is a certainty. If you are sure that your enemy is weaker than you, fight him. But tell me, my son, are you certain you will defeat Rama and the vanara army? Somehow, I don't believe you are.

"Remember, though you are invincible against all the Devas, the Asuras, the gandharvas, the nagas, and the other immortals, you have no boon against men and monkeys. You spurned that blessing in contempt. It is a man, with an army of monkeys, who has come to your gates. No boon protects you against them. Wisdom demands that you give Sita back.

"I have heard that this Rama is Vishnu himself, who has been born as a human prince to kill you. Think with your intellect, Ravana, not your hopes. Could an ordinary man have done what Rama did at Janasthana? He killed fourteen thousand rakshasas, and Khara with them. Could an ordinary man have crossed the sea with an army of monkeys? Would Varuna not have drowned him? But Rama is no ordinary man. Give Sita back to him and, being who he is, he will forgive you. This is your chance to redeem yourself."

But Ravana turned on Malyavan, as he had never done before. "Old fool, you have joined the ranks of the doubters, who are so enamored of Rama! Why don't you and the rest like you go and join your human prince? Your fine kshatriya, whom his own father turned out of his kingdom, though he was the eldest son. Without wealth to gather a proper army, the upstart has brought a jungle of monkeys to my gates. And you think I should go in fear of him—this nobody, this mere man.

"Can't you see that Sita belongs at my side? She is like Lakshmi, come down into the world just for me. And you want me to give her back tamely to that mendicant? Because he brings a gaggle of monkeys to my island? Is this the rakshasa's way? Do you seriously advise Ravana, Lord of the earth, to go in fear of a human?"

He glowered at old Malyavan. "Hear me clearly—you, Malyavan, and all the others who are so afraid: it is not in my nature to submit, not to this Rama nor to anyone. One's nature can never change. I am Ravana, and Ravana I will remain, whether I live or die.

"You say the building of the bridge across the sea is a feat that shows Rama's prowess. I say to you, he will not return by that bridge. It shall prove the bridge to his death."

Ravana stood blazing before his hushed sabha. Malyavan saw it was no use trying to reason with him, and held his peace. He mumbled a customary blessing and left the court.

Ravana began to prepare in earnest to meet the vanara invasion. He issued orders to his commanders. "Prahastha, you guard the eastern gate; Mahaparshva and Mahodara go to the southern gate. Indrajit, noble son, you meet the monkeys in the west. I myself will see to the northern gate. Virupaksha, take your army to the heart of Lanka and kill any monkeys that scale our walls."

Those rakshasas went out to their places, with their monstrous legions.

12. Between two hills

Beyond Ravana's city gates, the vanara chieftains had gathered around Rama and Lakshmana. Sugriva said, "Rama, the walls of Lanka are lofty and smooth, and the rakshasas who guard her gates are fierce. Our war will not be an easy one."

Vibheeshana said, "Our spies have returned, the friendly birds with whom the monkeys palavered. They say Prahastha guards the east, Mahaparshva and Mahodara the south, Indrajit the west, and Ravana himself the northern gates of Lanka. Virupaksha and his rakshasas guard the fortress at the heart of the city."

Vibheeshana described the might of the rakshasa army in detail. There was little he did not know, whether of the characters of the demon generals themselves or the warriors each one commanded. He recounted the battle against Kubera: how each legion fought, which rakshasas were the bravest and most to be feared. He described again how Indrajit brought Indra to Lanka, bound in his livid astra.

Finally he said, "Don't underestimate my brother's army, or his courage and ability. But Rama, my heart knows you can win this war. It will be hard, but it is not beyond you. Ravana has never been tested by an enemy to whose arrows he is vulnerable. Brahma's boon does not protect him from you or your vanaras. Let us see how he fights a battle in which he knows he can be killed."

Silence fell on the chieftains of Rama's jungle army. The time for the assault on Lanka was not far. Unlike the Rakshasa within his walls, Rama instructed his soldiers calmly and gently. "Good Neela, you attack Prahastha at the eastern gate. Brave Angada, take your army south to confront not one but two great rakshasas. Let Hanuman go to the western gate against Indrajit. Lakshmana and I will assail the north; while Sugriva, Jambavan, and Vibheeshana remain at the heart of our army, guiding us with their experience and wisdom.

"No vanara should assume the guise of a man when we fight, or he may be mistaken for the enemy by our own soldiers."

He grew quiet, and Rama's was a resonant quietness. He said softly, "For too long this Evil One has been a curse upon the earth. Too long his rakshasas have drunk the blood of the rishis of peace, whose tapasya supports dharma in the world. His time has come: not for nothing was Sita abducted; not for nothing did Sugriva and I meet on Rishyamooka. The hand of fate is always upon us, and everything that happens in this world is by fate.

"My friends, Ravana's time to die is here, and the earth will be rid of a great burden when he dies."

The sun was sinking into the sea again, and evening settled around them. Rama said, "Let us climb Suvela and spend our last night before the war on it."

Rama, Lakshmana, Sugriva, and Vibheeshana climbed that hill. Below them Lanka lay like another galaxy, its lights twinkling like stars in its streets and homes as night fell.

Rama said, "It is so peaceful here, and how beautiful Lanka looks. But when I think Sita is a prisoner within those walls, I can hardly contain my anger. I wonder how a king who has as little dharma as Ravana has ruled for so long. He is a blot on the name of the noble family into which he was born. You, Vibheeshana, are his brother; you have left his side at this critical time, for what he has sunk to. I feel sad that all the rakshasas of Lanka must pay with their lives for their king's sin."

By the last light of day, Lanka seemed to float again in the air: a dream city. Then night was upon the island, and from the east, majestically, there rose a golden moon. A sea breeze, full of solemn news, plucked at the faces of those who had climbed the hill. Soft excitement gripped Rama as he sat silently on a rock. Lakshmana stood beside his brother, perfectly calm on the eve of battle.

Thus they sat, the human princes and the monkeys of the forest, staring out at Lanka and, beyond, to the silver and golden waves of the moon-drenched ocean. The rhythm and swell of the tide reached across the night and lulled them. They, and their army below them, slept deeply, and no dreams disturbed their rest.

The next morning they saw Lanka below them like a vision in vivid colors. The dawn breeze carried the scents of its gardens across to the vanara army. They saw, in wonder, that flowers that bloomed only in other seasons elsewhere in the world were all ablossom here: the dark roses of winter and the bright poppies of summer, at once. Wafted with the scents of flowers came the mellow songs of koyals in the branches of Lanka's trees and the lively noises of waterbirds that had flown here across continents to swim in Ravana's sparkling lakes.

Trikuta rose steeply from the rest of the island, and Lanka still seemed to be built into the wispy clouds of the early morning, a fantasy. Reverberant banks of many kinds of flowers decked the slopes of that hill. Rama and his vanaras stared out raptly at the spectacle shimmering before their eyes. Rama's gaze wandered over that city among cities, and rested on a palace that towered above every other edifice, as if it were a Kailasa among the Himalaya. Rama knew this was Ravana's palace.

A powerful intuition stirred in Rama when he saw that singular palace. He strained his eyes, and then on an open terrace he saw a white parasol unfurled. Suddenly a subliminal current, more potent than anything he had ever felt before, snaked out across the valley between the two hills. It gripped Rama's heart in a vise.

Rama felt a pang of panic. He saw Ravana across the vista that separated them. The Demon wore flowing white silk. He stood there, tall and sinister, staring out hypnotically, as if to destroy the human prince with his look. Rama felt the Rakshasa's hatred reach for him, to snuff life from him, and he shivered in that regard. But the prince of light did not turn away, as his flesh cried out to; he stood firm. The two of them, one of evil and the other of grace, locked stares like swords across the valley.

The tension between the two hills was a potent thing, and the vanara army fell hushed. Breathlessly, they watched the silent contest of wills between their Rama and the terrible one in Lanka. For a while, it seemed the very air might ignite; but at last, it was the Lord of Lanka who looked away first and abruptly turned his back. Rama stood as if he had been turned to stone by the contention. Then a cheer went up from the vanaras and a smile touched his face.

13. *Sugriva*

Rama turned to speak to Sugriva. To his astonishment, he found the vanara had risen bodily from the ground, and with a ringing cry flew at Ravana on his terrace. In a trice, Sugriva flashed across the valley that separated Trikuta and Suvela. Both armies watched, agape, as the monkey king hovered above Ravana and cried, "Rama is the Lord of the world, and I am his servant. Your end has come, Rakshasa, you won't escape."

The vanara swept down at the astonished Ravana, snatched the golden crown from his head, and flung it to the ground far below the terrace. But Ravana was perfectly composed. He said with a smile, "You must be Vali's foolish brother. Sugriva is the one with the beautiful throat; how unfortunate that throat will soon be slit."

With a cry, Sugriva fell on Ravana. Well prepared for it, the Rakshasa seized the vanara. But Sugriva was stronger than he had thought, much stronger; the blows he struck the Demon with were like thunderclaps. Panting and cursing, they fought. When Ravana saw the battle was a more equal one than he had bargained for, he began to use maya. He would vanish and reappear before the vanara's eyes. Sugriva grew confused and Ravana's eerie laughter mocked him.

But Sugriva had come only to taunt his enemy. As soon as the Rakshasa began to fight with sorcery, the vanara leaped into the air once more and, quick as a thought, flew back to Rama. The vanaras roared in delight.

Rama embraced Sugriva and cried, "How brave and foolhardy of you, my friend! If you had asked me first, I would never have let you go. Suppose you had been killed; what would I have done? Not Sita, not Lakshmana, not anyone could have made my life worth living again. While you fought, and my heart was in my mouth, I decided that if you died I would kill Ravana, crown Vibheeshana, and take my own life. Do you know that, Sugriva, dearer to me than my life?"

Sugriva blushed and mumbled shyly, "I saw Ravana standing there so haughtily, the devil who stole your Sita from you, and I couldn't help myself."

Rama smiled. "It is lucky you are as strong as Varuna himself." He turned to Lakshmana and said more quietly, "All the omens of the earth, the sky, and the sea cry out that we shall fight a great war. Let us not waste any more time."

Down the Suvela hill came Rama and his vanara chieftains. Rama sat in dhyana, praying and studying the position of the sun, as he had learned to, long ago in Ayodhya, from Vasishta. When the sun reached an auspicious place in the sky, he raised his bow above his head and gave the signal for the march to begin.

The vanaras had gathered rocks; they had pulled up young trees by their roots for the siege of Lanka. Excitement was upon them like a fever and their faces shone. Vibheeshana, Sugriva, Hanuman, Jambavan, Nala, Neela, and Lakshmana walked beside Rama. When they arrived at the gates of the city, they were arrayed again as Rama had ordered.

Rama himself went to the northern gate, where Ravana waited for him within his walls. No fine trees and gardens did the prince's eyes see in Lanka any more, but wave after wave of rakshasas, armed to their teeth, keen for battle. In turn the rakshasas looked out at the monkeys, and they were surprised that this was truly an ocean of vanaras. In contrast to the black-uniformed demon legions, the army of the forest was colorful with flowers in every hue, plucked from the trees and plants of Lanka, with which they had adorned their fur.

14. Angada's mission

The sea of vanaras strained at its shores to begin battle. The monkeys' roaring shook the ramparts of Lanka. They were eager for the dharma yuddha, the righteous war; but Rama restrained them. For, by the code of kings, and by dharma itself, a last effort should be made to strike peace: a messenger must be sent to Ravana, suing for it. After consulting Sugriva, Vibheeshana, Hanuman, and Lakshmana, Rama decided to send Angada.

Rama called Vali's son to him and said, "Angada, we must make a final attempt to find a peaceful solution. Take a message to the Rakshasa from me. Say to him:

" 'Your glory and your kingdom will soon be lost, and your life as well. You are the worst kind of thief there is, and you have abandoned the path of wisdom. For countless years, you have sinned against the rishis of the earth. You have tormented the Devas and darkened the elements of nature. But now the hour of retribution has come.

" 'Remember, Rakshasa, no boon of Brahma protects you against me. You were so brave when you abducted Sita because she was alone; let us see how brave you are when you face me in battle.

" 'I will give you a last chance to make peace. Return Sita to me, ask my pardon, and I will give it to you freely; and your life will be transformed. The Gods themselves send you this chance to mend yourself, and rule for another age. If you do not take it, Ravana, you will die. The choice is yours. There is the short, savage way of bloodshed and death, and the long, kinder way of repentance and dharma. Choose whether you want to remain a king, or if I must kill you and set Vibheeshana on your throne.

" 'If you choose the way of violence, Rakshasa, gaze deeply at your precious Lanka before you come out to fight. It will be the last you see of her before you die.'

"Take him my message, Angada, and tell me what he says."

With a cry, Angada rose into the air. He was clad in crimson and shone in the sky. The rakshasas gasped to see him as the vanara prince flashed over them and flew straight to Ravana's palace. Ravana stood in his sabha, putting on his armor and issuing final commands to his generals before battle was joined. Silence fell on that sabha when Angada blazed in through the window. He flew down into their midst, and the golden bracelet around his wrist was like a band of fire. Vali's son himself was a tongue of flame in Ravana's court.

Ravana had no time to speak before Angada declared himself: "I am Rama of Ayodhya's messenger."

Without pausing, he delivered Rama's message, exactly as Rama had given it to him. A growl grew in Ravana's throat as he listened. Time and again, his nine macabre heads appeared and vanished around his central face. They glowered at the vanara out of many malevolent eyes. When Angada had finished, Ravana roared so the walls shook around them and the floor under their feet.

"Seize him!" hissed the Lord of the rakshasas.

The demons nearest Angada sprang forward and grasped his ankles. Angada offered no struggle, but allowed himself to be held. Ravana screeched, "Torture him! that he dares come here with such a message."

The rakshasas fetched ropes and made to bind Angada, when he also gave a tremendous roar. He rose into the air with the four hefty warriors who had seized him and leaped out of the window through which he had come. Angada landed on a terrace and, still roaring, shrugged off the demons who clung to him for their lives. He cast them down to their deaths, onto the flagstones far below. Like a brittle twig from a dead tree, he broke a turret from Ravana's palace roof and smashed it to dust on the terrace. And roaring still, he flew back to Rama.

On both sides of Lanka's gates, the opposing armies stood, sizing each other up. At first the rakshasas were staggered by the sheer numbers of the monkeys. But then their commanders cried, "They are only monkeys armed with sticks and stones. Shall Ravana's army that conquered the Devas fear a nuisance of vanaras?"

Ravana strode out onto his terrace once more, to survey his own forces and the enemy's. He also cried to his troops below, asking how could the fighting rakshasas of Lanka fear a rabble of apes? He glowered out again at Rama and his wild legions.

Rama gazed into Lanka and the horde of demons within, who clashed their gleaming swords and shields together in the midday sun. He paused for only a moment after Angada returned to him with Ravana's answer to his offer of peace. Then, Sita's face, her eyes brimming tears, rose like a vision in his mind.

Rama raised the jeweled Kodanda above his head. Silence fell on both armies. Gracefully, the prince of Ayodhya brought his arm down. The roar of the vanaras was deafening as they surged forward, each monkey anxious to be the first one over the walls of Lanka.

15. A serpent bond

That first onrush of the vanaras was swift and decisive. In no time they demolished the eastern gate of Lanka. They perched in troops on the smooth outer walls of the city, which no other species could have scaled; for Sugriva's nimble monkeys, they hardly posed an obstacle. The vanaras attacked the western and southern gates, and the hills resounded with their battle cries. Then Ravana gave the signal to repulse the onslaught of the jungle.

The trumpets of Lanka blared; the drummers beat up a storm. Like another sea, the rakshasas surged forward to face the invading monkeys. The battle between those armies was like the primeval one the Devas fought against the Asuras on the shores of the Kshirasagara, when the amrita was churned up, and Mohini deceived the Asuras and gave all the nectar to the Devas.

Not for a moment did this battle pause; not when blood flowed in scarlet streams through the streets of Lanka; not when thousands lay dead, demons and monkeys, and the screams of the dismembered and the dying moved the blank sky and the voiceless rocks to pity.

Warrior locked with warrior in mortal combat. Strange and tortuous destiny had brought them face to face under the sun of just this day, for reasons as individual and inscrutable as time is old. Indrajit and Angada fought; their roars echoed through Lanka and bounced off the hillside. Hanuman and Jambumali fought, Neela and the ferocious Nikumbha. Lakshmana faced Virupaksha, and Rama, four rakshasas at once.

Indrajit struck Angada a glancing blow with his mace. Crying out in rage, the scion of Kishkinda smashed the demon prince's chariot down with a tree trunk and killed his horses. Indrajit fled. The battle between Lakshmana and Virupaksha was a brief one: Lakshmana slew the rakshasa with a humming shaft through his heart. It seemed that everywhere the vanaras had the day. Rakshasa chariots could hardly maneuver for the barrage of rocks the jungle soldiers rained on them. The demons used conventional techniques of war, which they had studied in their military schools and employed so successfully against enemies of the past. Now they found these quite useless; the vanaras respected no tradition of battle. They fought with uncanny strength, untamed instinct, and agility, to which the rakshasas had no answer.

The sun sank into the sea and the waves turned the color of the bloody streets of Lanka. Neither rakshasa nor vanara gave any thought to the night that fell. They fought on by darkness, and Varuna trembled in his shores. With the advent of night, the demons' strength and ferocity swelled. But the vanaras were dauntless. Their golden eyes gleaming by the risen moon, they fought on.

The tide from Rama's bow and Lakshmana's was lustrous in the moonlight; every shaft was a whisper of fate. The rakshasas shrank from the two kshatriyas: not an arrow of theirs failed to claim a life. It was as if Rama and Lakshmana were in contention to see which of them killed the most rakshasas. The demons fled from them; they would rather be anywhere than face the human princes. Rumor flew through the Lankan army about the brothers' unworldly archery.

Fighting with tree trunks and rocks, Angada not only wounded Indrajit's body but injured his arrogance, even as, once, his father Vali had Indrajit's father's pride; that day, long ago, Ravana had been humiliated. Unable to contain Angada face to face, Indrajit began using maya. He vanished before the vanara's eyes and fought invisibly.

Word reached Indrajit about Rama's and Lakshmana's valor, and how the rakshasa army was routed wherever the princes fought. Desperate to retrieve both honor and lost ground, he flew unseen into the sky. He loosed shafts of agni down on the brothers of Ayodhya, taking them unawares. Mantled in maya, Indrajit invoked a fell weapon: a nagapasa, a snake coil of darkness. He shot a clutch of arrows at Rama and Lakshmana, quick as light, and charged with the serpentine paasa.

Hissing through the night, the weapon bound the human princes in a flash. They fell like palasa trees flowered in crimson blooms. A cry of dismay went up from the vanaras; panic, like fire, swept through them. Their eyes shut, Rama and Lakshmana lay unmoving on the ground. In the sky, Indrajit roared his triumph.

"I am Indrajit, who conquered the king of the Devas! And two mere men thought they could fight me? Not all the rishis can wake them from the sleep I have sent Rama and Lakshmana into."

Tidelike and inexorable, his arrows pierced a thousand vanaras, wounding all their chieftains. No monkey could discern Ravana's son, or see from where his shafts blazed down. Only Vibheeshana saw his nephew veiled with maya in the sky. The uncanny serpents writhed, phosphorescent, around the felled kshatriyas. They lay motionless.

The vanaras had to force themselves to stand and fight, after Rama, who was the reason they were here, had fallen. Shock ripped through the monkey legions. Neither Sugriva nor Hanuman knew what to do; terror seized them also, and their jungle feet burned to run. They could hardly bear their own grief; how could they ask their vanaras to fight a battle that was already lost?

Indrajit was borne away to his father on a hundred rakshasas' shoulders. He was sure the war was won. With Rama and Lakshmana dead, what war was left to fight? But Vibheeshana knew more about the nagapasa than the others. He came running to Sugriva, who knelt sobbing beside the motionless Rama.

Vibheeshana said to the vanara king, "They are only unconscious. They will wake from this swoon, and evil shall not triumph so easily. Rally your soldiers, Sugriva. Rama lives!"

Vibheeshana called for water. When it came, he chanted some slokas over the monkey king and sprinkled the water on his eyes as if to wake him from a trance. When Sugriva rose slowly to his feet, Vibheeshana said to him, "This is no time for weakness; your army panics to see you crying. Rama and Lakshmana must be guarded carefully. When they awake from their sleep of sorcery, they will lead us to victory. Be brave, Sugriva. Give in to fear now and all will be lost."

Sugriva still stood numb and disbelieving. Vibheeshana took him firmly by the arm and said loudly, so all the vanaras heard him, "Look carefully at the princes' faces. They are not ashen with death, but still glow with life. No harm has come to Rama and Lakshmana; they will rise again to lead us to victory. Until then, Sugriva, take command."

Word flashed out that the brothers were not dead. Cheering loudly to reassure themselves, the monkeys were somewhat bold again. But would they really see their precious Rama leading them into battle again, with Lakshmana beside him? The vanaras carried the princes to a safer place, to protect them from further attack.

The fighting had stopped; the rakshasas thought victory was theirs. They ignored the stricken monkeys and followed Indrajit's triumphal march back to his father's palace. No demon heard the vanaras whispering among themselves, like fire in dry grass, that Rama and Lakshmana were not dead.

16. A ray of hope

Indrajit's march back to Ravana's palace was jubilant. Conches blasted his victory; singing and dancing broke out and Ravana waited keenly for his son's news. Indrajit jumped down from the shoulders of the ecstatic rakshasas who had carried him from battle. His severe, arrogant face wreathed in a smile, he bowed before his father.

Ravana asked his son, "Tell me, heroic child, what have you done that makes the rakshasas shout for joy, and even you smile?"

Indrajit replied, "Rama and Lakshmana are dead. I killed them from the sky with the nagapasa."

With a roar, Ravana jumped up from his throne. He ran to Indrajit and embraced him repeatedly. Even if he did not admit it, the Rakshasa had always been anxious about this first battle with an enemy against whom no boon protected him. Dark delight swept his heart at what his prince had done.

The vanaras stood around the fallen Rama and Lakshmana in an anxious crowd. Silence ruled them, and any leaf that stirred in the midnight breeze made them start for fear; so terrified were they of Indrajit. Hushed, the jungle army waited for Rama and Lakshmana to open their eyes.

Ravana sent word to the rakshasis of the asokavana. When they came to him, and Trijata was among them, he said, "Tell Sita that Indrajit has killed Rama and his brother. She will not believe you. So take her aloft in the pushpaka vimana and show her the bodies from the sky. Let her know it is time she forgot her prince, and came to my bed. Now she will come."

His eyes shone with absolute obsession. Trijata and her rakshasis forced a protesting Sita into the vimana and flew up with her. In the light of the moon and the torches of the two armies, Sita saw the havoc the marauding vanaras had wreaked, and she smiled. But when they flew nearer the earth, she saw how excited the rakshasas of Lanka were and how stricken the monkeys. She saw Sugriva and Hanuman below; she saw they mourned. Lower still flew the vimana, and in a clearing at the heart of the vanara army, Sita saw the sight that froze her blood. For the first time since Ravana had abducted her, she saw Rama and Lakshmana. They lay very still on the ground. Wherever Indrajit's arrows had pierced them, their bodies had blossomed in flowers of blood.

Heartbroken in a moment, Sita wailed, "The rishis who said that I would be a sumangali were wrong. Look where my husband lies, cut down by Indrajit's arrows. They said Rama would perform the aswamedha yagna and be king of all the world. But he has died without even being crowned in Ayodhya. The great Vasishta's prophecies were false; and my feet, marked with the auspicious padma rekha— they also lied. Fate is all-powerful; stronger than Yama even. Oh, Rama!"

She sobbed so piteously that the hardest rakshasi was moved. But Trijata stroked her face and said, "Hush, Sita, hush. It is the pushpaka vimana you are flying in. This chariot would never carry you into the sky unless you were still a sumangali.

"Indrajit's weapons are full of maya; they have plunged Rama and Lakshmana into a trance. Look how the vanaras strain to see when they will wake up. They are not dead, only asleep. Look at Rama's and Lakshmana's faces. Dead faces do not glow like theirs, and I have seen many. Trijata may be a rakshasi, Sita, but she has never told a lie in her life and she does not lie to you now. The princes are not dead, only asleep. They were not born to die at Indrajit's hands; great destiny has yet to be fulfilled through them."

Sita stared down more closely. She saw that indeed, there was still sacred life left in Rama and Lakshmana. Their chests rose and fell with prana and there was color on their cheeks. She wiped her tears. She folded her hands to the princes, and hugged Trijata. With its own will, the pushpaka vimana flew back to the palace of the Lord of evil.

17. The splendorous one

Gathered anxiously around Rama and Lakshmana, the vanara chieftains were terrified lest the princes pass on from swoon into death. Then Rama's lips twitched and he stirred. The monkeys held their breath. Rama moved his head, his eyes fluttered open. Turning on his side, he saw Lakshmana lying like a corpse, with blood flowers sprouted on his body.

Rama sat up and cried, "My brother is dead! Lakshmana, how will I live when you are gone? I may find another Sita if I comb the earth, but I will never find another Lakshmana. Not another brother like you, not another kshatriya like you. How will I face Kausalya and Sumitra? Oh, what will I tell them?"

He was still touched with the sorcery of Indrajit's paasa, efflorescent on his skin. His speech was thick, and he spoke like one who was asleep and having a nightmare. He stroked Lakshmana's face. "What will I tell Bharata, and Shatrughna, his twin? No, there is nothing left to live for. Rama will also end himself at Lakshmana's side. I should have cared for him like a father and I have led him to his death. When I left Ayodhya, my brother followed me without a thought for his comfort or safety. Now I must follow him to Yama's city."

Sobbing, still in a daze so he would not allow the others to speak, Rama grasped Sugriva's hand and cried, "Loyal friend, go back to Kishkinda with what is left of your army. When Rama and Lakshmana are both dead, you may find it hard to fight Ravana. Go in peace, dear Sugriva; we shall meet again upon some crossing of eternity. Fly, my sweet vanaras, fly back to the jungle across the sea. Farewell, I will never forget you."

Rama fainted again. The vanaras were frantic. When Vibheeshana ran out of the darkness with his mace in his hand, the monkeys thought he was a rakshasa come to kill them. In a wink, the ground was cleared of the jungle folk. Jambavan had to coax them out of the trees and shadows they had fled into, telling them it was only their friend Vibheeshana. Slowly they gathered around Rama again, while Vibheeshana sat beside him, holding his head, sobbing.

Sushena, the vanara physician, was summoned. He examined the princes. The night strained its ears to hear what Sushena would say; it seemed the very darkness mourned Rama.

After probing their wounds with long fingers and peering under their eyelids, Sushena said, "This is the same paasa that bound some of Indra's Devas, when they fought the Asuras beside the Kshirasagara. Brihaspati woke them from their trance with two herbs he raised from the sea of milk. It was the sanjivakarani and the vishalyakarani he used. Let our swiftest, most reliable vanara fly to the Kshirasagara, where the amrita was churned. He will find the hills Drona and Chandra there, rising steeply from white waves. On their slopes he will find the oshadhis we need; for the Devas left them planted there. Let him bring them back to me, and I will make Rama and Lakshmana well again.

"Let Hanuman go, so there is no mistake."

Now the writhing serpents that held Rama and Lakshmana in their coils were plainly visible. The vanaras stepped back in fear from those emerald thongs. Just before Hanuman could fly in search of the Kshirasagara, a great wind rose over the ocean. It howled across Lanka, pulling up small trees, blowing them across the island like blades of grass and out over the dark water. Huge waves smashed against the shores of Lanka.

Cowering in the storm, the monkeys heard the sound of unimaginable wings. Above the screaming wind, they heard the ululating cry of a golden eagle, greatest of all created birds. The vanaras around the fallen princes cried out: the glimmering serpents loosened their coils around the brothers. Turning into thin braids of lightning, they streaked away through the alarmed monkeys and flashed out across the sea.

Rama and Lakshmana sat up, rubbing their eyes. Still, the sky-churning wind swept closer. The monkeys scattered in fresh panic. The heavens themselves seemed to have opened, and from another mandala, awesome Garuda flew down to Lanka. His body seemed to be made of supernatural light, and his cry of love shook the island. Crystal wings tucked in, he glided down beside Rama. As the monkeys peered, wonderstruck, from tree and shadow, they saw Garuda assume a human form as soon as he landed upon the earth: a manly form, though his head remained an eagle's and his wings were folded behind him. He embraced Rama and Lakshmana. The brothers' bleeding wounds closed and vanished as soon as Garuda touched them.

The fabulous being stood before Rama, who said in wonder, "Who are you? I do not know you; but when you touched us our wounds healed, and I felt as if my father had caressed me. Who are you, mighty one? Your garlands and ornaments are not of this world."

Garuda said, "It is I, Garuda, your companion through the ages. Just once, during this incarnation of yours, I am meant to come to you. Not the Devas or gandharvas could have shorn the nagapasa with which Indrajit bound you. But all serpents fear me, even the subtle ones of agni. They fled when I came, or I would have made a meal of them, be they of flesh or fire.

"Your taintless dharma drew me down the mandalas. You will triumph now, Rama; no one will stop you. And when Ravana is dead, you will rule the earth as you were born to. But this world weakens me and I must return to where I came from: into timelessness from time. Don't perplex yourself too much with what I have said. One day, when your mission is accomplished, you will understand everything. Fear nothing, perfect Rama; Sita and you will soon be together again."

Then as the vanaras stood rooted, the miraculous one was a splendid eagle again. Unfurling shimmering wings he flew up and out of this world, still crying out in love. When Rama and Lakshmana stood up, once more, the monkeys' cries of *"Jaya Rama! Jaya Lakshmana!"* reverberated across Ravana's ramparts.

18. The jungle warriors

When Rama and Lakshmana were healed, earth, sea, and sky resounded with the vanaras' rapture. Lanka echoed with the monkeys' cheering, their wild horns, conches, and drums. Sugriva's people sprang high into the air; they turned somersaults and kissed their tails. Their hand clapping was like a tempest, and once more they rushed the gates of Lanka, eager for battle, confident of victory.

In his palace, Ravana heard the monkeys roaring. He raised his hands to stop the revelry around him. Then all the rakshasas heard it: the joy of the vanaras, a tide risen to drown the demons' celebrations. Ravana said, "Go and see what they are so pleased about."

The guards came back to their king and reported in low voices, "The human princes have been healed by a miracle: the nagapasa does not bind them any more. The hundred wounds Indrajit gave them have vanished from their bodies. No trace remains that they were injured."

As if to himself, Ravana said, "No one has ever escaped from the coils of the nagapasa before. Indra himself could not undo the bonds of darkness." He paused, seething, tormented. Then he cried, "Dhrumraksha, go forth with your army. Kill the Kosala brothers, brave rakshasa—you have never failed me before."

Roaring in great self-assurance, Dhrumraksha arrived on the battlefield beyond Lanka's gates with his fearsome legion behind him. But he saw evil omens in the sky, and Hanuman beyond, waiting with his indomitable monkeys around him. Dhrumraksha was one of Ravana's fiercest commanders and his rakshasas were some of the bravest in all Lanka. A pitched battle broke out between Hanuman and Dhrumraksha, the monkeys and the demons. And by night, the rakshasas were more powerful.

The vanaras fought with fang and nail; they fought with rocks and young trees they flung like lances at the enemy. At first, in the sheer joy of the resurrection of Rama and Lakshmana, Hanuman's monkeys killed thousands of demons. But the rakshasas came on and on at them, in wave after wave, fearless by night, ready to die. Sword, dagger, and arrow flashed under the moon, and hundreds of vanaras also fell. Slowly, they had to give way to the rakshasas; so many were they and so savage.

At the heart of the fighting, surrounded by a guard of his best men, was the seasoned Dhrumraksha himself. He fought from his chariot, flitting everywhere to strengthen the weaker lines where the monkeys threatened to break through. His arrows were like silver hail and his battle-ax was a thing of absolute fear, glinting crimson in the moonlight.

Hanuman saw that the demon at the heart of his men was the key to this encounter. He saw his monkeys forced back from the Lankan gate and he could not reach the rakshasa on the ground. He picked up a rock and flung it through the air at Dhrumraksha. The great stone flew down, whistling, from the bronze sky; just in time, Dhrumraksha leaped out of his chariot and saved his life. But the chariot was smashed and half the ring of fighting rakshasas around him was crushed. As he jumped away, Dhrumraksha himself tripped and fell. Before he could get on his feet again, Hanuman was upon him, snarling. With another rock, the son of the wind crushed the demon's head like an eggshell.

Ravana howled, long and loud, when he heard Dhrumraksha was dead. He called for another rakshasa, as ferocious.

"Vajradamshtra," cried Ravana to his lean, scarred demon. "Go to war; take maya with you."

Vajradamshtra took the field, with sorcery. He went everywhere unseen, and his sword and arrows spilled vanara blood copiously. He fought with cunning, but fate was ranged against him. Seeing the head of a monkey near him lopped off by an invisible enemy, Angada flailed out blindly with a blow like thunder. He knocked the invisible Vajradamshtra senseless. When the demon fell, his maya dissolved and the monkeys saw their tormentor clearly. They fell on him with cries of revenge, for he had killed many of them. Shortly, just a bloody mess of flesh and bone remained where that diamond-fanged rakshasa had lain moments ago.

Feeling his hand being forced more quickly than he liked, Ravana sent Akampana, maharathika, bane of Lanka's enemies and one of her boldest commanders. With his chariot guard, Akampana drove like a storm to the western gate, where Hanuman waited after killing Dhrumraksha. Now Hanuman knew exactly how to face the chariot-mounted enemy. Before Akampana could even begin to fight, he was crushed by a boulder that whistled down from the sky. Many of his rakshasas were crushed as well, under a barrage of rocks and tree trunks the monkeys hurled at them. The rest fled back to their king.

Ravana received the news grimly. He showed just his main face now; the rest were hidden. Forked serpent tongues darted in and out of their mouths, and not even his generals and ministers could bear that sight. Lifting his grave central face at last, Ravana said, "It is almost dawn. I will inspect the garrisons now."

He went around the city, speaking words of encouragement to his rakshasas, brave words he hardly felt himself. He saw his dead warriors lying in heaps; he saw that so far the battle belonged to Rama's vanaras. Stalking back into his palace, Ravana called Prahastha, his Senapati.

"Dhrumraksha, Vajradamshtra, and Akampana are slain, and our men are near panic. It is time one of our very finest went into battle. I would go myself, or send Kumbhakarna, Indrajit, or Nikumbha. But turning the tide of a war is your special talent. How will these chattering tree dwellers, who scratch themselves as they fight, contain Prahastha, the master?

"Perhaps the others could not see well enough in the dark. But now day dawns. Go, my friend; make a river, a sea of monkeys' blood for your king."

Ravana embraced his general. Prahastha said emotionally, "Ravana, I owe everything I am to you. My life is yours, my lord, and I will not fail you."

He bowed to his king. Ravana embraced him again, and Prahastha turned and walked out of the sabha. His commanders announced his coming to his army, waiting anxiously to sweep into battle. Prahastha went to the northern gate where Rama himself was. Seeing him come, at the head of his glittering legions, Rama turned to Vibheeshana. "Who is this rakshasa that takes the field against us? Surely he is a maharathika."

Vibheeshana said quietly, "I had not expected him so soon. It is

Ravana's Senapati Prahastha. He is a master of astras and he fought against the Devas at Ravana's side."

In a blaze of war that set the sky alight came Prahastha with his legions. He was an awesome rakshasa; his astras lit up the dawn. They fell flaming among the vanaras, and each one made ashes of a thousand monkeys. The vanara lines began to melt at his inexorable advance. Worry sat on Rama's face. Then he heard a roar from the trees above. Sugriva's Senapati, Neela, had silently watched Prahastha's advent. Now he jumped down to the ground to face the rakshasa general in his chariot of beaten gold.

Prahastha's horses reared in alarm at the stupendous vanara who loomed suddenly before them. With five lightning blows of the young tree in his hands, Neela felled those beasts. With another stroke he pulverized the chariot. Roaring as deafeningly as the vanara, Prahastha leaped down to the ground. They fought hand to hand, sword against tree trunk. That duel shook the earth: it seemed the vanara and the rakshasa fought with the elements as their weapons. Thunder, lightning, and tempest seemed to be in their palms; and they struck each other with these, roaring so loudly that the rest of the war was silenced. Monkeys and demons gathered round their Senapatis and watched them in awe.

Prahastha struck Neela down twice. The demons roared as loudly as their general. But Neela sprang up from the ground with a flat slab of rock in his hands. He leaped fifty hands into the air and, with all the force of his descent, smashed the rock down squarely on Prahastha's head. The rakshasa's skull was shattered and he lay twitching on the ground, his brains dribbling out.

The roar of victory of Neela, the son of Agni, echoed through Lanka. When they saw Prahastha felled, the rakshasas fled back to Ravana with fear pursuing them like a flash flood. The vanaras erupted in joy. They lifted Neela onto their shoulders and carried him back to Rama in a wave. Rama embraced the hero of the moment.

In his palace, Ravana heard Prahastha was killed. Tears scalded his eyes and he cried, "How can it be? Prahastha ravaged Indra's army when we fought in Devaloka. And now just a monkey has killed him? He was the most loyal friend I had; he was my finest warrior. I will come to battle myself. The vanaras will wish they had never followed their human prince to Lanka. They think they have victory in sight; when they feel my astras, they will know who Ravana is.

Prahastha is dead, but I swear the monkeys shall rue his death more than we."

19. Terrible mercy

Ravana ordered his chariot fetched. Surrounded by his warriors, the Lord of the rakshasas drove into battle in the golden ratha. Rama saw the demon army sweep toward him. He turned to Vibheeshana. "The rakshasas have recovered heart. Tell me, who are they that lead them onto the field?"

"On the elephant, white as Airavata, is Atikaya. The one mounted in the chariot with the lion banner is Indrajit. Mahodara rides beside Atikaya and Kumbha rides in the chariot with the serpent banner. Between them all, and the commander of this force, is Nikumbha. Narantaka is behind Nikumbha.

"But the lord of them all is the one beneath the white parasol: he who rides in the golden chariot; whom the rest surround; who looks like Siva himself coming to battle with his bhutaganas; whose kundalas send shafts through the day like the sun's; who wears the crown of Lanka on his head; who is built like Vindhya and Himavan; who is as bright as the noonday sun; who subdued Indra and Yama in Devaloka. Rama, that is my brother Ravana."

There was such feeling in that description, Rama turned to Vibheeshana with a smile. He saw the rakshasa was not past loving his terrible brother. Rama looked at the demon army that advanced on the vanaras. He had eyes only for the one who rode at the heart of that force. Long and admiringly the blue prince gazed at his mortal enemy riding toward him; long and hard Rama of Ayodhya stared at Ravana of Lanka.

In a low voice, he said to Vibheeshana, "He is like another sun risen over us. I have never seen anyone so splendid; it is hard to even look at him. See how his body ripples in power; look at the scars that adorn his dark skin. How handsome he is, how magnificent, Vibheeshana. Truly, if there was ever a king to fear on earth, it is your brother.

"I used to wonder how any warrior of this world could conquer the Devas and the Asuras. Now I do not wonder any more: no Deva or Asura could match Ravana."

Slowly, majestically, Ravana came toward them. As he gazed at the advancing rakshasa army and at its master, Rama's eyes turned red as blood. Between clenched teeth he said, "But he abducted my Sita and holds her his prisoner."

He quivered, and Vibheeshana was afraid when he sensed Rama's fury. Then Rama smiled again and said wryly, "But this anger is for Ravana. And I swear the Lord of Lanka will taste my wrath."

He drew an arrow from his quiver and fitted it to his bowstring. He stood waiting for Ravana to come within range. But at that moment, he saw the rakshasa army maneuver shrewdly, so its king was hidden from him. Like a shark hidden in a school of fish, Ravana fell on the vanaras. The Demon scythed through the monkeys, hewing off heads and arms and bisecting trunks with dreadful ease.

The first great vanara who confronted Ravana was Sugriva. Arrows from the golden bow of the Lord of evil sang around him in a storm. Sugriva hurled boulder after boulder at the Rakshasa; stone and shaft met in flight and shattered against each other. Ravana fixed an astra like a serpent to his bow and shot the monkey king with it. Sugriva cast a rock at the fiery serpent that flew hissing at him. But like a real serpent, the crooked shaft dodged around the stone and, straightening again, flashed into Sugriva's chest. He fell with a ringing cry and was rushed unconscious from the field.

Darkness took the vanara army. Ravana seemed to grow as tall as the sky; he loomed like a great cloud over the monkeys. Fifty vanaras charged the Demon. But they could not withstand him, and they either fled or were killed. Ravana's sinister laughter echoed through the battlefield, sending waves of panic through the monkeys. With no Sugriva to stand against him, the Rakshasa stormed, bloody, through the jungle army. Monkeys lay dead in his path like so many dolls, arms and legs hewn away, heads hacked from trunks; a river of blood flowed from his fearsome archery. Behind him, around him, swarmed the fighting rakshasas, their morale restored. They roared victory to their king and cut down the monkeys like stalks of tender cane in a field. The sky above the battle was dark; Ravana's volleys hid the face of the sun. His archery was not a thing of the times, but an arcane power, reminiscent of pristine ages when every warrior of the earth was like a God. The vanaras' screams rippled the river of blood that flowed through Lanka's streets and out her northern gate.

Rama picked up his bow, from where he had set it down when he saw Ravana was protected by the wheeling guards who never left his side. But a hand restrained him. Lakshmana said, "Don't go yet to fight the Rakshasa. Let me trim his arrogance first."

Rama smiled. "Go with my blessing."

Lakshmana bent at Rama's feet. He took the dust from them and marked his brow with it. Rama said, "Watch him carefully, Lakshmana. He is no ordinary warrior; no one in the three worlds has yet defeated him. When you fight him, remember your own weaknesses. Be careful, be vigilant; he is a great master."

Even as Rama spoke to Lakshmana, Hanuman charged Ravana, roaring. Dodging past the fire tide of arrows, the son of the wind came face to face, again, with the Lord of Lanka. No other vanara or rakshasa stood between them. Ravana's horses reared to see the towering monkey.

Hanuman said, "Rakshasa, you have Brahma's blessing that no Deva or yaksha, gandharva or Danava may kill you. But I am a vanara, Evil One, and you have no boon to protect you against this fist of mine. It shall be your death, Ravana."

But Ravana was calm. In his deep rasp of a voice he said, "Come, monkey, kill me with your blow if you can and you shall have everlasting fame. Come strike me, and let us see how strong you are. But remember, if you fail, I will strike you back and you will die."

Hanuman snarled, "Have you forgotten, taunter, how I killed your boy with a blow of this fist? Or perhaps he was not your own?"

Ravana's ten faces flashed into sight, snarling in memory of dead Aksha. Like dark lightning, he struck Hanuman on his chest and the vanara fell back, stunned. But shaking the fog of that blow from his head, Hanuman sprang up at once. Leaping into the air, he struck Ravana back like thunder exploding. Ravana roared; he collapsed against the side of his chariot.

In a moment the Rakshasa stood up again. He smiled at Hanuman. "Well done, monkey! You are stronger than I thought."

Hanuman cried, "Fie on me that you live after I struck you. But you shall not live after I do again!"

Once more, he leaped high to fetch Ravana another blow. But as he came down, swinging his arm, the golden chariot vanished with maya. Hanuman howled in frustration and looked around for the Rakshasa. He saw Ravana across the battlefield, engaging Neela.

But Ravana did not relish the fight against Neela, either: using the siddhis of mahima and anima, Neela made himself big and small, as he chose. At times he grew tall as a tree; but when Ravana attacked him, he shrank to the size of a little spider monkey, so the Rakshasa's arrows hummed harmlessly past him.

Tiny Neela jumped onto Ravana's banner and chattered down at him. Then he grew again and struck the Demon a bone-shaking blow. But when Ravana hewed at him with his sword, the vanara was a little monkey, gibbering at the king whose swinging blade came nowhere near him. The Master of Lanka was beside himself.

"Stand and fight, coward!" he raged.

But Neela grimaced at him and cried back, "Shame on you, Ravana, that you fight someone as small as me. No wonder you have taken to kidnapping women."

Ravana invoked the agneyastra and shot it at Neela, who was perched on the back of one of the Rakshasa's chariot horses, terrifying the animal. A flash of green fire flared out and engulfed little Neela. But instead of being consumed by the incendiary shaft, Neela only fainted briefly: Neela was Agni's son, and the father would not burn his own child.

Ravana thought the vanara was dead. Baying in triumph, he turned his chariot to where he saw his rakshasas fleeing the battle. They saw a warrior approaching that none of them dared face. Lakshmana had come to fight, and Lanka quaked at the sound of his bowstring. Lakshmana's challenge rang out across the field and Ravana advanced on him, smoldering.

For a long time they stood, demon king and human prince, staring at each other unwinkingly, locked in a duel of gazes before they fought with arrows. Neither looked away. Then Lakshmana cried, "Are you afraid to fight, Rakshasa, that you just stand staring?"

Ravana threw back his head and roared like ten lions. "Foolish human, dare you come to fight me alone? Prepare to pass through Yama's gates."

Lakshmana cried back, "I have heard enough about your valor and your prowess. Have you come to boast or to fight? Show me with arrows how great you really are."

Swift as light, Ravana's narachas flashed at Lakshmana. But quicker himself, the kshatriya cut away the burning heads of those shafts as they flew at him; they fell tamely around him, a rain of headless serpents. They writhed briefly on the ground and vanished. Already, Ravana loosed more smoking barbs at Lakshmana; quicker than the eye saw, the prince cut them down again.

So it went: a scintillating duel between two great archers, both masters. They admired each other's skill, and at times even shouted out their admiration across the long field where they fought. All around, rakshasa and vanara stood spellbound, watching.

Ravana tired of the battle of lesser weapons. He invoked an agneyastra and, with no warning that he had summoned a devastra, shot that deep shaft at Lakshmana. But from the first sound the astra made through the air, Lakshmana knew what it was. He cut life out of it with a clutch of fluid and feminine arrows. So that when the agneyastra grazed his brow, it merely dazed him slightly.

Roaring, Lakshmana loosed a coruscant volley that cleft the bow like an arc of night in Ravana's hand. Without his bow, Ravana was hurt often and sharply. Blood bloomed on his dark, smooth skin, where Lakshmana's barbs found their mark. Crying out in pain, Ravana invoked a more powerful weapon than any he had cause to use since his war against the Devas.

Ravana bent his head briefly in his chariot and invoked Brahma, grandsire of the worlds. He invoked a weapon of cosmic fire. Ravana invoked the brahmashakti and, in a wink, cast the howling thing at Lakshmana. Like a comet, the recondite missile flamed at the human prince. Quick as Lakshmana was, he did not have the speed or the power to cut the shakti down. A small sun, it took him squarely in the chest; with a cry, Lakshmana fell.

Swift as time, Ravana was at the fallen prince's side. He leaped down from his golden chariot and tried to lift Lakshmana into it. He wanted to parade his corpse through the streets of Lanka. But the Rakshasa could not budge the prince's body. Ravana, who had once drawn out Kailasa by its roots, could not move Lakshmana of Ayodhya. The Demon stood astounded. He saw that the fair kshatriya still breathed. The Rakshasa was thunderstruck. This human had been felled by Brahma's shakti; it still blazed in his breast, hissing and spitting fire. Yet Lakshmana lived.

With a yell, Hanuman flew out of the sky at the bewildered Ravana. He fetched him six blows like earthquakes across his chest and face. Blood welled in the Rakshasa's mouth; the ten heads roared and their owner reeled. Hanuman picked up Lakshmana easily, with love, and carried him through the air, back to Rama. Rama laid his blue hand on his brother's brow and he rose instantly as if from a slumber. Wailing in strange anxiety at Rama's touch, the shakti flew out of his brother's chest and back to Ravana. At once Lakshmana's wound closed, then vanished tracelessly.

Meanwhile, his pride stung by Hanuman, Ravana now went among the vanaras like Death himself. He fought with weapons and strength beyond their understanding, and thousands of monkeys were sacrificed to his fury. Wailing at the hell fire he attacked them with, they ran to Rama and cried, "We cannot stand against the Rakshasa. He is too terrible for us."

Rama picked up his bow and started toward Ravana. But Hanuman came running to him. "Ravana fights from a chariot; you should not face him from the ground. Allow me, Rama, to bear you into battle."

The son of the wind grew immense, and bent at Rama's feet. Rama climbed onto Hanuman's shoulders. And thus the prince of men first went to meet the king of the rakshasas in battle. The sound of Rama's bowstring silenced both armies. He cried across the field, "Ravana, prepare to die! Not Indra or Yama, not Agni, Surya, or Brahma will save you now, not Siva himself. You will not find sanctuary from me anywhere, Rakshasa. Did no one tell you what I did to your people at Janasthana, that you are fool enough to want battle with me?"

Glowering, red-eyed, ten-headed with a fiendish snarl on every face, now entirely a Demon from the pit, Ravana replied with a burn of arrows aimed not at Rama but at Hanuman who carried him. But Hanuman had Brahma's boon that no astra could harm him. Undimmed, he plucked those barbs calmly from his flesh and shook their embers from his fur. He loomed over the two armies, with Rama like a star on his shoulders.

Then, all at once, Rama was a blur, a dream of movement on Hanuman's back. No one could tell where he drew an arrow from his quiver or fitted it to his bowstring, or when he shot it at his enemy. But the report of his weapon was a crack of thunder. In a thunder-flash, Ravana's chariot was broken, his horses were killed, and his sarathy struck unconscious. Rama seemed to fight from another, un-worldly dimension of time. Ravana had no answer to the prince's tran-scendent archery, and a shaft as jagged as Indra's vajra plucked the Rakshasa's bow out of his hand.

Stunned silence fell on the armies of darkness and light. Serenely,

Rama fitted another shaft, with a glowing crescent head, to his bow-string. Languidly, he knocked Ravana's golden crown from his head. Gone was all the Rakshasa's glory, faded in a moment his majesty. He cringed beside his shattered chariot. On the beaming Hanuman's shoulders, Rama shone like a dark blue sun.

Then Rama lowered his bow! A smile touched his lips. Rama cried in awful gentleness to his enemy, so both armies heard him clearly, "I think you are tired after all the fighting you have done, all the vanaras you have slain. I could kill you now, but it would be too easy. Go home, Ravana. Be better prepared before you come to fight me again. Go now, Rakshasa."

Rama's mercy was more savage than any astra. His ten faces dark with shame, his spirit broken, like his chariot and his crown, Ravana crept back into Lanka with his worthless life, which he now owed his enemy.

The cheering of the vanaras woke the world from its swoon of disbelief. They yelled Rama's name, again and again, and yet again; oh, they believed in him completely now! Watching from above, the Devas wore smiles on their unearthly faces. For the first time, they actually saw that Rama was more than a match for the Demon of Lanka.

20. A monster is roused

Ravana sat trembling on his crystal throne. Again and again he saw Rama's arrows fly at him: shafts of time. He saw his chariot shattered, his horses cut down, and his crown broken. He saw Rama's dark, brilliant face above him and heard the beautiful voice that mocked him before both armies, "I could kill you now, but it would be too easy. You are tired. Go home, Ravana. Come back with a new chariot and another bow."

Ravana sat trembling with that humiliation. Grimly he spoke to his rakshasas. "You saw how a mere man shamed me on the field. It seems all my tapasya is worth nothing. When he gave me his boon against the Devas and Asuras Brahma said to me, 'Beware of man.' But I did not listen. I thought, which man would dare to stand against me in battle?"

He sighed, that matchless Rakshasa, humbled. Slowly he went on:

"Many are those who have cursed me. A yuga ago, I ravished a chaste woman called Vedavati, and she cursed me. Perhaps Sita is Vedavati, born again to be my death. When I look at her face, I feel I know her from another time. For long ages, I have ruled the world; once an Ikshvaku king called Anaranya foretold that a prince born in the House of the Sun would kill me. I paid him no mind then, but now I fear it is Dasaratha's son Rama he meant.

"Yes, many have cursed me, among them the mighty and the sublime. Parvati cursed me once, and Nandisvara. Varuna's daughter cursed me when I forced myself on her. My friends, today I have learned that the curses of the pure always come to pass."

The nine heads around his central face were not to be seen, as if they hid themselves for shame. Confessing his anxiety, sharing it, appeared to allay its intensity. Ravana said, "All this talk is of no use. Lanka is threatened as it has never been since I became king. I can think of only one solution: Kumbhakarna must be awoken; let us see how Rama faces my brother in battle."

Ravana ordered the guard at Lanka's gates to be doubled, and sent his messengers to Kumbhakarna's palace. Just nine days ago, his titanic brother had sat in the people's sabha and sworn to support his king in the event of a war. Eight days ago, the tremendous one had gone back to sleep.

Kumbhakarna slept deeply, but the messengers Ravana sent to awaken him were experts at their task. What they had to do was not easy; especially when it was just a week since he had fallen back into his slumber, which would last six months if he was not disturbed. Hillocks of food were heaped on great salvers carried by a small army of rakshasas. Among the dishes were young elephants, roasted whole. There was wine by the barrel and cartloads of garlands and incense. With these, and a train of nubile women, Ravana's servants came to rouse the king's brother. When Kumbhakarna awoke all his appetites must be satisfied at once, and all of them were enormous.

As they unlocked the door to his chamber with the golden key Ravana gave them, the gigantic rakshasa's snoring blasted in their ears. His breath billowed like a small typhoon around the cavernous room, whose ceiling was tall enough for the monster to stand under. Kumbhakarna lay naked, his chest heaving like an ocean, dreams flitting across his sensual face. Gently the women began to rub sandalwood paste into his smooth skin. His mountainous body was hairless.

The giant did not stir at the women's giggling ministrations, though there were ten of them, each one chosen just for him. They were tall, beautiful rakshasis, and rare: they alone in Lanka could bear his manhood. Quickly, they covered his massive body with the fragrant paste. They lifted his great head, four of them together, and the others draped the garlands around his neck. The food and the wine barrels had already been set down beside the bed, so there would be no delay when he awoke.

The servants brought conches, horns, and drums with them. They knew, from the experience of years, what an effort it was to rouse Kumbhakarna. When their loud talking had no effect, they began to shout in the hope that he might stir. But he slept on. When the anointing with sandalwood paste did not so much as break the rhythm of his snores, the servants began to blow on their conches, beat their drums, and blast on their horns. Kumbhakarna slept on.

Gingerly, they began to prod him and to shake his colossal form with their hands. He did not move. They tried to lift him from the bed, but could not. Then they began to slap his body in earnest. Not that they were pleased to do this; they feared that Ravana would have their heads if his brother did not wake up. They slapped him roughly and blew their conches into his juglike ears. They pulled the thick hairs in his nostrils. Suddenly, with a deep sigh, he rolled onto his side. Whatever dream he was smiling from left him, and his eyelids, long-lashed as a woman's, fluttered open.

With a roar that they had dared to interrupt his dreaming, Kumbhakarna sat bolt upright, red-eyed and growling horribly at them. Already, hunger raged in his hot body, and other lusts flamed through him as well. The servants jumped back some paces. They pointed to the heaped vessels of food and the barrels of wine. First his hungers must be fed; then they would tell him why they had come.

Tittering, the women came forward to feed Kumbhakarna. The menservants left them to their task. When half the food had been gorged, greedily, and three barrels of wine swilled down, Kumbhakarna began to fondle the women, who had disrobed for his pleasure. As always, the satisfaction of his desire did not take very long, though he took four of the ten women, one after the other, and their cries echoed down the long passages of the palace.

Kumbhakarna bathed, and the women dressed him and rubbed his body fragrant with the unguents and perfumes they had brought, to which he was so partial. Now the men were called back into the chamber. In his chasmal voice Kumbhakarna said, "You have woken me when I had barely fallen asleep. Tell me, who threatens Lanka? Is it Yama or Agni, Vayu or Indra?"

Just then a minister, Yupaksha, whom Ravana had sent after the others, came in. He said, "It is not Devaloka that threatens us. A human prince has laid siege to Lanka with an army of monkeys."

Kumbhakarna's expression was incredulous. "Ravana really needs me to fight a man and some monkeys?"

Yupaksha said, "Prahastha is slain, and this man Rama vanquished our king in battle."

Kumbhakarna growled in surprise. The women had almost finished dressing him. He brushed them aside and stood up, a mountain of a rakshasa, towering over the others.

Yupaksha said quietly, "Rama spared Ravana's life. He told him to come back to fight with a new chariot and another bow."

Kumbhakarna roared softly; then he laughed. "What! But this has never happened to my brother before. No Deva or Danava, yaksha or gandharva has ever humbled Ravana. Surely, no ordinary man has done this to him."

"Ravana dares not go out to face Rama again. He wants you to kill the Kosala princes."

Drawing himself erect, Kumbhakarna said, "I will. Tell Ravana that before the sun sets he will see the humans lying dead in the bloody sludge of the field. I will drag their bodies through the streets to his palace, that they dared to attack Lanka."

But Mahodara, who had come with Yupaksha, said, "Perhaps you should meet the king before you go out to fight. He is distraught; seeing you will restore his spirits."

Slowly, Kumbhakarna nodded. He loved his brother. He thought the world of him, and hated to hear that Ravana had been humiliated. Mahodara and Yupaksha hurried back to their master. Ravana sat alone and downcast in his sabha. They ran in to him, crying, "Kumbhakarna is awake, my lord. He wants to know when you will see him."

Ravana said dully, "I will see him at once, if he is ready to come to me."

The earth shuddered where Kumbhakarna set foot, on his way to meet his brother. Clad in white silks, his body embellished with glittering ornaments, heavy golden earrings in his ears, Kumbhakarna went to meet Ravana as Indra might go to Brahma. When he came out into the sun the vanaras perched on the smooth walls of Lanka, gazing in at what went on within the city, fled in fear. They had never seen anyone like him. He was full of raw splendor; his massive body blazed like a piece of the sun and it was hard to look directly at the leviathan.

When Kumbhakarna entered the sabha, he saw at a glance the damage Rama had done to Ravana's spirit. The haughty, regal bearing, which had set that king apart, had vanished. Instead, a forlorn Rakshasa sat on Lanka's throne, gaunt with defeat. When he saw Kumbhakarna, Ravana sprang up with a cry. He rushed to his brother and embraced him. He led him to the outsized throne beside his own, which was always kept there and was the giant's place.

Kumbhakarna said resonantly, "Who has tormented you, my brother? He will not live, be he not our Pitamaha Brahma himself. No one in the three worlds who has hurt you shall escape my wrath."

Ravana sighed; he was restive. He said, "So much has happened while you slept. These few days have been like years, ah, like centuries. As we feared, Rama came to Lanka with his army of monkeys. Vali's brother, Sugriva, is his ally. They crossed the sea and they have ravaged our island. Wherever the monkeys go they make a desolation of our orchards and gardens. No fruit remain on the trees, or flowers on their stems."

He sighed again, a deep fire flickering briefly in his troubled eyes. "They lay waste not only the plants and trees. The monkeys have killed many of our greatest warriors. Vajradamshtra, Akampana, and Dhrumraksha are dead." His voice fell lower still. "Prahastha is slain."

Kumbhakarna growled again in amazement. Ravana continued, "Thousands of our soldiers are dead. Indrajit bound Rama and his brother with the nagapasa; but the serpent noose did not kill them and their wounds healed miraculously. I struck Lakshmana down with the brahmashakti; it only stunned him. The moment Rama touched him with his hands, Lakshmana awoke from the sleep of the shakti, as no Deva could have."

His lips quivered, and the memory of his own humiliation filled his fierce eyes. In a whisper, Ravana said, "Then I fought Rama. His arrows were swifter than mine. He smashed my chariot; he killed my horses and my sarathy. He broke the bow in my hand and the crown on my head. He struck me down into the red mire of the field, and I was his to kill.

"But shining like my death above me, he said, 'Go back to your palace and rest. You are tired. Come again to fight me with a new chariot and another bow.'"

The Rakshasa choked, as if those words were flaming poison in his throat. A bitter laugh tore its way out of him. Desperate Ravana grasped his brother's hand and cried, "The hour of my direst need is here. I need your help today as I have never done before, or I would not have woken you. Go into battle for me, Kumbhakarna; go like Yama among Rama's army. You are my only hope now, only you can save me."

Unpredictable as ever, Kumbhakarna laughed. "We warned you in the people's sabha. Vibheeshana warned you, but his wisdom fell on deaf ears. There is no escape from the evil path you have chosen to tread. The hell you made for yourself has come seeking you.

"A wise king never disregards the Shastras. He does not ignore the truth for the sake of his lust. A wise king, Ravana, is never threatened by danger. But you, who have always been so cautious and so sage, chose to abandon dharma for the sake of this woman Sita. When you had lost your heart to her, you listened only to the flatterers in your court. But they, who turned wrong to right and sin to virtue, to say whatever you wanted to hear, they who ignored all the omens, were the worst traitors. And it was to them you chose to listen. You were deluded by the arrogance of your wealth and your power; my brother, you were deluded by your own vanity.

"Where is Prahastha now, who swore he would raze Rama's army by himself? Ravana, you ask me to fight against Rama. But it is my dharma as your brother, who loves you, to warn you. I will gladly go into battle for you, but I do not think this is a war you should pursue. Give her back, Ravana; my heart tells me we must return Sita at once."

Ten heads flashed into view. The lips on ten dark faces throbbed; twenty eyes glared at Kumbhakarna. Ravana howled in rage at what his brother said to him.

"How dare you! You are my younger brother; how dare you preach to me? You speak so glibly of the Shastras. But you seem to forget that an older brother is to be treated like a father, not scolded like a child."

Even the thought of giving Sita up was like dying to Ravana. But then he considered the truth of what Kumbhakarna had said; he knew his brother was right. Ravana softened, and nine heads withdrew out of sight.

He sighed again and said more quietly, "Perhaps you are right, and I have strayed from the path of kings. It may be true that I have been overwhelmed by love and deluded by power and wealth. But Kumbhakarna, the wise do not waste time mourning the past. Our lives are threatened; this is not the time to argue the rights and wrongs of our situation.

"I have sinned, I confess it today. I have sinned; otherwise, Rama's arrows would not have felled me as easily as they did. But he who helps a sinner out of love is noble indeed. Only you can save me now, only you can kill this kshatriya. Decide, my brother; will you fight my cause? I am sure that if you do, not the greatest vanaras, not Rama and Lakshmana, will stand before you. Help me, Kumbhakarna; it is the hour of my despair."

At once Kumbhakarna's whole manner changed. Gently now, he said, "I am not yet dead, am I, that you should tremble like this? No matter who is right or wrong, I will kill the kshatriya. He has come to our gates with war and I will kill him. I only said what I did out of love for you. Do not think I have forsaken you as Vibheeshana did. Fear nothing any more, Ravana. Kumbhakarna is awake now and he is ready for battle. Within the hour, I will bring you Rama's head and throw it at your feet."

A slow smile lit Ravana's face; hope stole back into his heart. Kumbhakarna went on, "You speak of danger, my brother. But I will rid you of this danger as the sun does the earth of night's darkness. Smooth the anxiety from your brow. Go to your harem, Ravana; order a flagon of your best wine and celebrate with your women. Victory shall be yours within the hour." Kumbhakarna smiled with surprising softness. "When Rama is dead, she will come to you, the one you are so hungry for. She will be yours forever."

Ravana cried, "When they see you with your trisula in your hand, they will think Yama himself has come to war. Go, my noble brother, bring me the heads of the princes of Ayodhya."

Kumbhakarna sent for his trident. It was carried by two rakshasas: a great and fell weapon, a thing alive. When Kumbhakarna took it from them, it glowed with uncanny light. Kumbhakarna smiled, "I need no army to go with me. I will go into battle alone."

But Ravana said, "The monkeys are ferocious. They hurl rocks at us, and trees that they pull out of the earth easily as blades of grass. If you let them near, they bite viciously and scratch with long nails. Take an army to guard your back and your flanks; the vanaras are savage and unafraid."

Ravana rose. He was certain the battle would turn his way once Kumbhakarna went to fight. The king took a golden chain from a table next to his throne. It shone with emeralds, rubies, and pearls, all huge and iridescent; all cut specially for Kumbhakarna. Ravana placed the shimmering necklace around his brother's neck and embraced him. An exquisite casket sat on the table. Ravana drew some bracelets from it, and a diamond ring set with a solitaire as big as a child's fist. He knew how much his brother loved jewelry—as a woman does. He adorned Kumbhakarna with these priceless ornaments. Kumbhakarna stood there, as resplendent as Himavan, Lord of mountains.

Finally, the king himself fastened his brother's impenetrable kavacha around his vast body. He hugged him as he might a child, with as much fondness, and kissed him on both cheeks. Again and again Ravana embraced him, and Kumbhakarna lay at his feet to receive his blessing. Ravana raised him up and clasped him once more.

It was time for Kumbhakarna to go into battle. Ravana went with him to the palace door to see him on his way.

21. The dreadful one

Surrounded by Lanka's most intrepid warriors, maharathika Kumbhakarna went forth to battle Rama and the vanaras. He rumbled at his rakshasas, "The human princes have made Ravana afraid. But I will kill Rama and Lakshmana, and the monkeys will flee Lanka, those we leave alive."

Their morale restored by the giant's presence, the rakshasas returned to fight. Evil omens gathered in the sky when Kumbhakarna appeared. But when they were pointed out to him, he laughed like thunder. "Who believes in these grandmother's tales? I am

Kumbhakarna. The natural laws that bind other men have no power over me."

Kumbhakarna came to the northern gate, and beyond it he saw the vanaras, countless, oceanic. But the sight did not dismay him. He had fought such armies before, and not of mere monkeys, but Devas and gandharvas armed with unearthly ayudhas. He had never lost a battle yet; he was elemental, no one could contain him.

When they saw him coming, the monkeys whimpered and those in front fled like clouds scattered by a gale. Like a night of terror, he advanced. His golden ornaments were streaks of lightning against his dark body; his pearls were moons. Some distance from the vanaras, the titan stopped. He was as big as ten men, and much bigger when he grew with mahima.

Kumbhakarna saw that the vanaras had recovered from the first shock of seeing him. Clutching onto one another for courage, somehow they stood their ground. The monumental rakshasa threw back his head and roared. Covering their ears, the monkeys scampered back to Rama. Growling, Kumbhakarna stood up in his chariot, his trisula burning in thick hands.

Over the heads of the fleeing vanaras, Rama saw the awesome giant who had come to battle. He asked Vibheeshana, "Who is this monster? He is as big as a hill and wears a crown on his head. His eyes blaze tawny fire, and I have never seen anyone like him before. What is he, a great Asura?"

Vibheeshana said, "He is Visravas's son and Ravana's brother; he is Kumbhakarna, my half-brother. Ravana has his strength by Siva's boon, but Kumbhakarna was born like this. They say he has no equal in battle; and though they love each other dearly, even Ravana is careful with him. Kumbhakarna is so strong that he has never known fear.

"In the war against the Devas, I saw him chase Indra and Yama from the field like children. The ones of light and the lords of the nine planets fled from him, thinking he was Rudra come to raze Devaloka. He is the biggest rakshasa ever created, and the strongest and bravest one.

"As soon as he was born, and he was full-grown in a day, Kumbhakarna felt such a hunger that it seemed only devouring all the world would satisfy him. Everything he saw, he ate. The people of the earth fled to Indra. Indra cast his thunderbolt at Kumbhakarna. But though the vajra struck him squarely, it did not harm him. Howling and laughing at once, the demon broke one of Airavata's tusks and chased the Lord of the Devas with it.

"Indra fled to Brahma. Brahma arrived on his swan and, seeing Kumbhakarna back at his endless gorging, the Pitamaha cried, 'Let sleep come over you and may you never awaken. For if you do, you will devour all my creation.'

"At once, Kumbhakarna fell into a deathlike slumber. But Ravana, who loved Kumbhakarna, worshipped Brahma. When the Creator appeared before him, Ravana said, 'Your curse is like letting a champaka tree grow to fullness, and cutting it down when it begins to flower. Mitigate your curse; let my brother not sleep forever.'

"Brahma said, 'Very well, let him awaken for a day after every six months. But only a day; otherwise, the world will hardly survive his hunger. He will wake for a day and sleep again for another half year.' "

Vibheeshana continued, "Rama, the day he wakes he eats like time itself, only more greedily. He devours whatever comes his way, beasts and men, elephants and tigers, anything at all."

Rama listened, astonished, to the tale of Kumbhakarna of the plumbless appetite. Vibheeshana said, "You have shaken Ravana, that he has roused Kumbhakarna and sent him into battle. But Rama, our army of monkeys flees just to see him. How will they stand and face him when he begins to fight?"

Rama called out to Neela, "Son of Agni, let the vanaras collect rocks and trees, and surround this enemy when he is near."

Hanuman, Gavaksha, Sharabha, and Angada climbed to the top of the mountain. Roaring their challenge, those mighty vanaras began the battle: they hurled huge rocks down at Kumbhakarna's army. Angada called to his soldiers, "Foolish monkeys, it is not a real rakshasa but a contrivance that roars to terrify you. Stand and fight, vanaras!"

They were not entirely convinced. But reluctant to let their prince down, the vanaras came back into battle. Hundreds of monkeys surged forward. With powerful sinews, they flung their wild missiles at Kumbhakarna. But tree and rock were blown to dust against his body. Kumbhakarna raised his head again, smiling. He roared once more and the advancing vanaras were rooted with fear.

Then he was among them like an evil storm; he was an army by himself; he was death. He burned the vanaras with his trisula, its flames leaping before him in a livid tide. That trident spewed three fires, emerald, scarlet, and blue. Each was a yojana long and half as wide, and the vanaras were ashed where they stood. Those whom he caught in his hands, Kumbhakarna ate, they screaming and he laughing uproariously at the feast of monkeys before him. He smacked his lips: he liked the taste of their flesh as well as any leopard of the jungle.

The vanaras ran screaming from Kumbhakarna. They flew back to the bridge across the moat outside the city. But Angada stood behind them and roared, "It is a shame on our race that you flee from battle! What are your lives worth once you run like this? Let us die with honor instead, and our fame will outlive us as a divine fragrance. Let us die and find a lofty place for ourselves in Brahmaloka. Stand and fight. Watch what happens to the monster when Rama comes to kill him."

But the immediate prospect of living was more attractive to the monkeys, and they pushed back in a wave to escape the demon giant. Angada stood between them and flight. He bared his fangs in such fury that suddenly they preferred to face Kumbhakarna, who was at least some distance away. Caught between terror and terror, the poor vanaras turned back to fight.

Dwividha came from behind the monkey lines with a piece of a mountain raised above him. Roaring to chill demons' blood, he cast the crag at Kumbhakarna. But it was heavier than he had thought, and his aim was false. A hundred rakshasas who surrounded Kumbhakarna were crushed with their horses and chariots under the peak. The monkeys were encouraged. Now Hanuman arrived at the front with a boulder in one hand and a tree trunk in the other.

But Kumbhakarna stood laughing at this paltry opposition. Hanuman's tree trunk, flung with force enough to mow down a legion, was burned to ashes by flames from the trisula. The vanara's rock was blasted into powder. Kumbhakarna came on in a wave of blood. He came feasting on vanara flesh, throwing the screaming monkeys into his jaws, two and three at once. His echoing laughter terrified the vanaras and again they turned tail. This was death, naked and inescapable, that swept them in its way. They were not foolish enough to stand and let it consume them.

Just then Hanuman maneuvered himself near Kumbhakarna and fetched him a stunning blow on his face with a tree trunk. Roaring in shock, blood breaking on his lips and through his nose, the rakshasa staggered where he stood. His laughter was stanched for a moment. But quick as light, Kumbhakarna thrust out his trisula like a striking serpent. The green flame from it took Hanuman in the chest, and he fell. In a wink Dwividha was at his side, staving off the giant with rock and tree. Hanuman rose groggily and fought on.

But the vanaras had seen the demon stagger when Hanuman struck him: they knew he was not invincible. The monkeys gained heart and came back to fight. But they could not stand against Ravana's gruesome brother. He slaughtered hundreds of them and his chariot waded through a lake of blood. Everywhere the vanaras lay dead and dying, the wounded screaming pitiably. The giant picked them up, thrust them into his maw, and chewed on them, rolling his eyes. The hunger of waking was still upon him powerfully, and he found he liked the new meat he had tasted today more and more.

The only vanara who could engage Kumbhakarna at all was Angada. He fought hand to hand with the titan whose body shone so eerily. Angada used speed and agility, rather than try to match the giant's strength. Quick as cunning, he dodged and weaved under the flames of the trisula. He found that even Kumbhakarna had to pause for breath, or, perhaps, to recharge his weapon. During those gaps in the fire the trident shot out, Angada would leap to the rakshasa's side and rock him with prodigious blows.

When the flaming trisula was lowered again, Angada was away, leaping out of range, ducking and weaving as Kumbhakarna roared in disgust. Losing patience, he flung the trisula at Angada. But the vanara prince had been goading the demon to just this indiscretion, and he dodged the trident nimbly. He leaped at the unarmed rakshasa and struck him a flurry of blows, each one enough to kill any other warrior. Kumbhakarna reeled; he even fell briefly. But then, growling, he struck Angada from where he sat on the floor of his chariot. Like a rag doll, the vanara flew back fifty paces and was carried unconscious from the field.

Seeing this, and Kumbhakarna without his fiery weapon, a hundred monkeys jumped on him. They clung to him, fastening long nails and fangs in his flesh. But this merely seemed to tickle him. He plucked them off, some with his own flesh clinging to their mouths, and ate them alive. When the lesser vanaras fled again, Kumbhakarna stormed after their king. He had seen Sugriva kill hundreds of rakshasas, away from where he himself fought.

When he saw the dreadful one looming at him, Sugriva seized a flat rock and leaped into the sky. Poised there, he called down to the blood-drenched monster, "You are a legend, Kumbhakarna. You devour my little monkeys and base your fame on your gluttony. But let us see how you wear this stone I crown you with."

Kumbhakarna smiled hideously, baring fangs longer than a tiger's. He growled, and that sound was like the roaring of an army. "Monkey, don't brag; I know who you are. You are Riksharajas's son and Brahma's grandson. But let us see your valor in battle, not just your boasts. Come, throw your little stone at me."

Sugriva cast the wind-polished rock down on Kumbhakarna's head like a thunderbolt. But it broke in a thousand fragments and fell harmlessly around the titan. Kumbhakarna threw back his head and laughed. Meanwhile, the trisula he had flung at Angada flew back to him. But Hanuman snatched it out of his hand and snapped the weapon of triune fires on his knee. Roaring to silence every other noise around him, and quicker than seeing, Kumbhakarna swept up a smooth stone from the ground and brought Sugriva down with it like a bird from the air.

With a triumphant yell, the demon bent down and picked up the unconscious vanara in his arms like a baby. He then started to lumber back into Lanka, having shrewdly decided to make the monkey king his hostage. He would bargain for his life with Rama and the vanaras: he would sell Sugriva back to them dearly. Hanuman saw him go. He wondered if he should fly to his king's help, but decided that Sugriva was canny enough, and strong enough, to escape by himself.

Kumbhakarna swaggered into Lanka with Sugriva in his arms. While the rakshasas lined the streets, shouting victory, the giant shambled toward Ravana's palace. Unknown to Kumbhakarna, Sugriva had woken from his faint. But he decided to lie still until he had full command of his faculties.

Suddenly the monkey king leaped up with a roar. He bit Kumbhakarna viciously in his nose and ear, drawing a font of blood. Screaming like a stricken elephant, Kumbhakarna dropped Sugriva. In a flash, the vanara flew up into the sky and back to Rama's side.

Stopping the flow of blood from his face with wet cloths that his rakshasas rushed out to him, Kumbhakarna turned back to the field. His body was streaked with monkeys' gore. Like a black cloud lit by red rays of a setting sun, he came back to battle. Now Lakshmana greeted him with a volley of arrows no army could have withstood. But Kumbhakarna stood unharmed. He blazed at the human prince with another trisula.

When Lakshmana stood unsinged by the weapon's three flames, the huge demon rumbled at him, "You are impressive, little mortal. Yama himself could not stand before me as steadfastly as you do. Indra fled sooner than you. But still, you are a child; your arrows do not harm me. Let me fight your brother; it is he I am after. Once I kill Rama, your army will be headless and our rakshasas can finish the rest of you. Then I can go back to sleep!"

Lakshmana said softly, "You want Rama, here he is."

He stepped aside. As soon as Kumbhakarna saw Rama, he roared like five thunderstorms and charged the kshatriya. Rama had been waiting impatiently. He met the giant with a brace of astras, weapons whose fires came from the Gods. Rama's shafts were feathered; but feathered as if in anticipation of a dim future, many thousands of years away. Then he would be born into the world again, as a very different blue savior of the times. The feathers on Rama's arrows were those of the peacock.

Rama shot silver arrows through Kumbhakarna's wrists and, screaming shrilly, he dropped his mace and his trident. The demon plunged forward, killing a hundred vanaras with every step he took, killing his own rakshasas if they came in his way. He hefted a rock in his hands and cast it whistling at Rama. But with a lucific shaft, Rama shot it to dust, or the very stuff of this world's illusion.

Five gold-tipped arrows flashed out from Rama's bow. Kumbhakarna's armor was disjointed at its seams, and fell away from him. Dazed by his enemy's supernatural archery, but still roaring, Kumbhakarna blundered on. The golden necklaces his brother had draped round him shone like heavenly treasure. His body bathed in scarlet with all the vanaras he had killed, Kumbhakarna came on.

Lakshmana cried, "He is blood-drunk, Rama, and not just on the gore of the vanaras but of his own rakshasas. Let the monkeys cover him; let them hold him down."

Rama nodded. The vanaras sprang at Kumbhakarna. In a trice, a hundred of them covered him. But the monster shrugged and they were thrown off with unbelievable power. Like Meru, the golden mountain at the earth's heart from where the continents unfurl,

Kumbhakarna rushed at Rama with his arms outspread: to seize him, to crush life out of him.

22. Weapons of light

Gorged on monkey flesh and the flesh of his own rakshasas, Kumbhakarna rushed at Rama. The prince stood as still as a mountain, as fierce as a flame that does not smoke. Rama strummed his bowstring, as if he caressed a vina.

He said to the demon, "Kumbhakarna, I am Rama. Are you ready to die?"

But the monster laughed like a volcano erupting. He roared back, "I am not Viradha or Kabandha. I am not Khara, Vali, or Maricha. I am Kumbhakarna; show me how sharp your arrows really are."

Quicker than thinking, Rama loosed a sizzle of shafts at him. But the demon stood smiling before him and most of the arrows fell tamely off his skin. The few that pierced him he pulled out like thorns. A hush had fallen on the field. Rama stared at his adversary in wonder: his arrows, which passed through the seven sala trees, which felled the invincible Vali, hardly punctured this rakshasa's skin. Both of them stood calm as hills on which it rains.

Kumbhakarna raised his own weapon, a mudgara of black fire. But the flames it spewed did not singe the prince of light. Rama intoned the mantra for Vayu's unearthly weapon; he had learned it a life ago from Viswamitra, on the bank of a river. In a rustling of breezes, an awakening of ancestral winds, the power of the astra filled the arrow in the prince's hand. It was a shining ayudha of time and air, charged with the power that denudes mountains.

The fires of the mudgara flamed around him. Rama drew his bowstring to his ear and Vayu Deva's astra, the vayavya, flashed from the Kodanda, howling like the simoom of the desert. With the force of a thousand years packed into a moment, that astra struck Kumbhakarna's right arm off at the shoulder in a crimson burst, and carried it up into the sky, still clutching the flaming mudgara in its hand. At first Kumbhakarna hardly noticed the pain: he had lost his arm so suddenly. Then he saw blood spurting in a geyser from his hollow shoulder, and he began to scream.

The rakshasa giant ran to a tree growing near him. He pulled it up with his left hand and raised it to hurl at Rama. But another shaft of the wind severed that arm as well, and the tree fell on the ground before it could be flung. Now Kumbhakarna's screams shook the sky and the dazed rakshasa army behind him.

Rama drew another arrow from his quiver. He said the mantra of the aindrastra over it. The shaft in his hand lit the world for a yojana around. It was Indra's weapon, subtler than time, also given him by Viswamitra. It hummed in Rama's hand, keen to fly from his bow and claim a worthy victim. No other kshatriya could have held that missile steady and drawn it back as effortlessly as Rama did; no one else could have shot it so truly. It blazed through the air like a burning sliver of a rainbow. It took Kumbhakarna's head from his body and carried it, still roaring, to the ocean below. Spuming blood at his severed neck like the spring of a red river, Kumbhakarna fell. The earth quaked.

In the sky, the Devas whom the dead monster had once humbled could not contain their joy. They showered unearthly blooms down on Rama, and the rakshasas fled the battlefield: they could not bear the fragrance of that soft rain. But released from terror, the vanaras danced on the petals that lay shining on the river of blood that Kumbhakarna had made outside Lanka. Rama stood among them, radiant, happy as Indra had been when he slew Vritrasura in time out of mind.

23. A king's despair

Messengers from the field of battle stood before Ravana in his sabha. He glared down at them from his throne. They stood trembling, speechless. He said impatiently, "Well? What news of my brother?"

The leader of the messengers said in a whisper, "My lord, Kumbhakarna assailed the monkeys like a storm at sea. He tossed them about, killed them, and ate them as if they were little dainties. He let flow a river of blood among the vanaras."

A smile dawned on Ravana's face. The first messenger fell silent. Not daring to look into his master's eyes, another one took up the tale. "Your brother was magnificent; he devoured a thousand vanaras."

"And I suppose a few rakshasas for variety?" said Ravana, still smiling. He knew how his brother fought.

The messenger bowed his head, then stood silent again. Ravana cried, "Well, go on! Has he faced Rama yet?"

"My Lord Kumbhakarna faced all the vanara chieftains on the field. He mastered every one, including Sugriva, their king. Then he came face to face with Lakshmana. Lakshmana's arrows fell away from him like wisps of straw."

Ravana rose from his throne and cried, "What did I tell you? They could not face Kumbhakarna! Has he killed the Kosala brothers? Tell me quickly, you take too long to deliver good news. Did he kill the humans with his hands, or burn them with his trisula? Has he impaled Rama's head? Is he carrying it through our streets to me in triumph?"

His voice quavering, the rakshasa said, "They fought a great duel, Rama and Kumbhakarna. But at last, Rama severed your brother's arms with two screaming shafts of the wind and his head with an astra of light. The Lord Kumbhakarna is dead."

Ravana fell where he stood. His sons Devantaka, Narantaka, Trisiras, and Atikaya had gone pale. Mahodara and Mahaparshva rushed to their fallen king; their faces were ashen.

When they sprinkled water on his eyes and held sharp salts under his nose, Ravana revived. He sat up unsteadily, and his ministers helped him to his throne.

Ravana whispered, "My precious brother, I sent you to your death. You have left me alone, Kumbhakarna. Did you forget you had a brother that you let yourself be killed? But Indra could not harm you with his vajra. How did a mere man's arrow cut your great head from your body?

"Ah, Kumbhakarna, I hear the Devas singing in the sky that you are dead. The vanaras are rapturous. They laugh at me, that my invincible brother is slain." He paused, then said more softly than ever, "This human prince who has come to our gates is truly terrible. He has filled our lives with such dread that I fear our end is at hand."

The Evil One shook his head sadly. "Vibheeshana told me Rama was powerful. I should have listened to him. But sweet Kumbhakarna, how did I know I would learn how powerful Rama is by your death? Vibheeshana was the only one who saw the truth clearly and I cursed him for warning me; I sent him away. And now it is the time for retribution."

He grew as still as the heart of night. He seemed to seek some deep strength within himself, to fight on. Again, ten heads were plain above his neck, whispering together in their cluster, in a devilish tongue no one else could understand. Ravana hushed them. They fell quiet and vanished out of sight. The Rakshasa sat in silence, trying to master the grief that wanted to break his spirit. He sat a long time, gathering his last resources, trying to find another frontier of hope within himself, beyond each defeat Rama inflicted on him.

At last, while his sabha waited, hardly breathing, the Demon sighed, "If something remains to live for, it is to avenge myself on my brother's killer. I swear Rama will die for this, and for Prahastha, and every rakshasa who has given his life for me."

Again, a pang of anxiety: Ravana shivered as if with a spasm of death. And indeed, he had already begun to die. Almost inaudibly, he breathed, "Sita, you are being avenged. My brother is dead because I love you. But you will not be satisfied with any death except my own. Oh, if you only knew how much I love you! I would still give up my life, before I gave you away. I cannot help myself: I would sacrifice a hundred Kumbhakarnas for you."

He fell quiet, and the sorrow of his brother's death was upon him once more. He murmured again, "Vibheeshana was right, and I would not listen to him. Kumbhakarna, what have I done to you?"

Now his son Trisiras, who could not bear to see his father in such despair, cried, "Our uncle lies dead on the battlefield. His arms are cut away, his head is gone. His body still glows with splendor, illumining the armies that stand gazing at him. The rakshasas of Lanka look to you for courage. How can you give in to grief now and leave your people helpless?

"Father, you still have your golden chariot, your great bow and Brahma's inexorable shakti. And I am proud to be Ravana's son! Send me into battle. I will go among the monkeys as Garuda went among the serpents, and bring you the humans' heads."

Ravana listened numbly to his son. He heard his other sons cry, "We will go with Trisiras. We will bring you Rama's head."

Devantaka, Narantaka, and Atikaya were eager to prove themselves worthy sons on the field. Their father clutched at this new hope like a straw in a gale. Perhaps his sons could achieve what Prahastha and Kumbhakarna could not? Was this the time of a new generation? Could it be that Lanka's stars of fortune now rose and set with the fortunes of these princes? Ravana did not think of how Hanuman killed Aksha. Neither did he consider returning Sita to Rama and begging his forgiveness. There was no turning back for the Rakshasa, though in his heart he knew his war was lost.

Absently, Ravana said to his sons, "You are all maharathikas, and masters of maya. All of you have Brahma's boons and command a hundred astras. Go, my sons, and bring glory to your father. This is your time."

They prostrated themselves at his feet. He blessed them, and sent them to war against Rama and the vanaras. But when they had gone, tears welled up in Ravana's eyes. He was certain he would not see his princes alive again. The Rakshasa cursed the insane love that held him in its clasp like death. Now he cursed that love for which he would sacrifice his own sons.

Ravana waved away his ministers. He sat alone on his throne, weeping, and the debt of karma he could never discharge choked his very life. Sita's face swam up before him, perfect as ever. Ravana looked into her eyes and, whimpering, cowered from her.

24. The sons of Ravana

Two more of their brothers, Yuddhomanta and Matha, went out to battle with Ravana's four sons. These fierce young rakshasas came mounted on elephants and in chariots, with a teeming army behind them.

Like a spirit of darkness Narantaka swept at the vanaras, who were in great heart after Kumbhakarna's death. The monkeys' faith in Rama, so crucial to winning this war, was stronger than ever. Now Narantaka arrived in a wave of fear. His arrows filled the sky like rays of a black sun, and a thousand vanaras fell before him.

Sugriva loped up to Angada and cried, "Kill this fell prince, Angada, before he kills us all."

Leaping into the sky, Angada flew down like a curse in front of Narantaka's chariot. The terrified horses reared and Angada snatched the bow out of Narantaka's hand. They fought with blows and by butting each other with their heads until Narantaka felled Angada with a stroke of his mace. But as the vanara sprawled on the ground, his hand fell on a rock. He saw the young demon draw a dagger from his belt. Angada sprang high into the air. Hurtling down, he crushed the rakshasa prince's skull with the stone.

Meanwhile, the battle of Lanka raged again at every city gate. Warriors' roars and the screams of the wounded and the dying rent the air. At first it seemed the rakshasas, renewed by Ravana's sons, would carry the day. They slaughtered the monkeys, who were a little complacent after the slaying of Kumbhakarna. Not only Ravana's sons but the legions they brought were magnificent. Also, by now the demons were more used to the vanaras' unconventional methods of fighting, and thousands of the jungle folk perished.

But shouting encouragement to his people, Sugriva sent some of his great warriors to fight Ravana's sons. Roaring through the air came Hanuman, son of Vayu, and Agni's son Neela, and with them Rishabha. They flew out of the sky like death. Like thunder and lightning, they fell on the princes of Lanka, who fought drenched in monkeys' blood. Hanuman killed Devantaka with six sickening blows to his temples. Neela strangled Yuddhomanta, and Rishabha fastened his teeth in Matha's neck. Roaring, screaming, but unable to shake the vanara off, the rakshasa died thrashing in agony.

Hanuman leaped on Trisiras, who was three-headed like his uncle after whom he was named, whom Rama killed at Panchavati. Two heads Hanuman smashed with a rock, and the third roaring one he silenced by beating it into a pulp with elemental fists. He bayed his triumph, long and loud, beating his chest in the ancient way of the jungle. The rakshasas fled from the fearsome vanara. With their princes slain, the demons panicked again. But from behind them, blowing an echoing blast on his war conch, loomed the last of Ravana's sons who had come to fight today. Mountainous Atikaya, built more like his uncle Kumbhakarna than his father, lumbered into battle on a caparisoned war elephant.

The vanaras fled back to Rama, crying that Kumbhakarna had risen from the dead. Rama turned to Vibheeshana with a question in his eyes. Vibheeshana said, "It is Ravana's son Atikaya. He is Dhanyamalini's son and a maharathika. He is a master of the brahmastra, and fought against the Devas and Asuras. He is incensed at his brothers' death; kill him quickly, or he will take many of our lives."

Even as he spoke a hundred vanaras died, in a moment, at Atikaya's hands. Neela and Angada charged him. But he brushed them aside with a fluent volley, so they were numbed. Then he roared, "I have not come to fight you monkeys. I can kill a thousand of you at any time. Send me a kshatriya who can match my skill. Send me someone whose death will change the course of my father's war. Or are the real leaders of this rabble too afraid to come to fight?"

Lakshmana turned to Rama, and his brother nodded to him. Pulling on his bowstring like spring thunder, Lakshmana came to face Ravana's gigantic son. But Atikaya drew a silver shaft from his quiver, and cried down from his elephant, "You are just a boy, Lakshmana. I am Atikaya of the rakshasas; not Indra or Varuna can stand before me. Not the earth, not Himavan, can bear my arrows. Go back and send me a grown man to fight."

Lakshmana answered him with arrows like light. For all his bulk and his bragging, Atikaya was a quicksilver archer. He shot down Lakshmana's shafts with his own. Lakshmana invoked an agneyastra and loosed it, flaming six fires, at the demon. But the rakshasa replied with a suryastra, and the fiery missiles locked above the armies. The dying day was lit by twin fires in the sky as if the sun had leaped back to midheaven.

Those shafts extinguished each other and fell hissing into the sea. Atikaya shot another astra, now of water, at Lakshmana, and the human prince replied with one of the wind. The missiles met in the air again, in night's gathering shadow; each charged with its archer's will, they struggled to prevail. But soon they were also spent and fell away harmlessly down the mountainside.

Lakshmana stood panting on the ground, Atikaya sat panting on his tusker: both drained by the duel of the weapons of will. A twilight breeze stirred among the forests of the hillside; it joined a quiet air from the sea and blew over the armies of light and dark. Vayu himself blew at the heart of that secret air, and he whispered in Lakshmana's ear, "Only with the brahmashakti can you kill this rakshasa."

Lakshmana drew a golden arrow from his quiver. He invoked the Pitamaha of the worlds and charged that shaft with his shakti. The elements fell hushed at Lakshmana's mantra, and when Brahma's feminine power suffused the arrow, the four quarters shook. The sun, the moon, and the planets wobbled on high.

The arrow Lakshmana aimed at Atikaya was like a flame of the fire that incinerates the universe when time ends. The rakshasa tried to stop it with ten shafts of his own. But licking the enemy's arrows from the sky, the brahmashakti came on inexorably. It flashed into Atikaya's chest, consumed him, and nothing remained of Ravana's son but white ashes. His jeweled crown rolled down from his elephant's back, and in a celebrant gust Vayu scattered his remains over land and sea.

Once more the vanaras turned cartwheels on thin air. They kissed their long tails and leaped up at the moon rising in the east. The rakshasas fled back to Ravana.

25. Brahmastra

Ravana was numb when he heard that Trisiras, Atikaya, and all his other sons who had gone to battle against the vanaras were dead. He had no tears left to shed. All night, he sat alone in his court, plunged in dark grief, near madness. Again and again, one thought plagued him, phantasmagorically: "What if this Rama is really Vishnu, come as a man? Who can face him and his monkey army?"

At dawn, as if in answer to his despair, he heard urgent footfalls in the passage outside. Ravana's son by Mandodari, the peerless Indrajit, stalked sleek and feline into his father's presence. Indrajit was shocked to see the change in the king who sat so defeated on his throne. This was not even a shadow of that Rakshasa of immeasurable power, his father Ravana. The Demon before him was a broken old man; he had aged ten lives in a night.

Standing haughty and assured before his sire, Indrajit said, "There is no cause for you to despair as long as I still live. I bound the humans with the nagapasa and I cannot think how they escaped. But this time they will die. Let heaven and hell be my witnesses, father, I will bring you the heads of Rama and Lakshmana."

Ravana sat bemused, lost in a fearful reverie. At last he blessed his great son woodenly, not saying a word, not even rising from his throne. Knowing the only specific for the king's malady was Rama's death, Indrajit strode out of the palace. His chariot waited for him outside, silvery as the moon and fleet as wishes.

The rakshasas knew Indrajit had bound the Kosala princes with his coils of serpent fire. They knew he was the one to reverse the disastrous course this war had taken. They cheered him lustily when he came out. Prahastha and Kumbhakarna were forgotten for the moment, and all the others who had died. This was Indrajit who had come to lead them into battle: invincible Indrajit, said by many to be a greater warrior than even his father. This was Indrajit, their next king. The rakshasas roared, *"Jaya Indrajit! Jaya! Jaya!"*

Emboldened again by their crown prince's presence, blasting on conches, clashing swords and spears against shields and armor, the rakshasas came back into battle. Like a soft storm Indrajit's army swept toward the field. As it swayed in the morning breeze, the prince's royal parasol was white as wave froth or the inside of a seashell. At the edge of the city of Lanka, Indrajit raised his arms to stop his army's march.

He jumped down from his chariot and summoned the brahmana priest he had brought with him. That old rakshasa kindled a fire on the threshold of the field. Indrajit worshipped his God, Agni, with oblations and offerings. This was usually done before any battle; but before this one began, Ravana had been so confident he had not bothered to perform the ritual. With rice grains, with flowers and incense and resonant mantras, Ravana's eldest son now worshipped the sacred fire and the Navagraha, the nine planets.

The fire burned high. When the rakshasas saw no smoke came from it, they set up another loud cheer: it was an omen that Indrajit would be like smokeless fire, implacable! As the priest chanted his mantras and Indrajit stood very still beside him, Agni himself stepped out from that fire. Flames were his tawny body; flames were his face and his hair, and he stood iridescent before his bhakta. With his own hands, like lotuses ablaze, the Fire God received the havis from Indrajit. What more auspicious omen could the rakshasas have hoped for?

"Victory!" they thundered. *"Jaya Indrajit! Jaya!"*

Indrajit invoked the brahmastra. He worshipped it, and his bow, his arrows, and his silver chariot. The sky blanched when he performed these rituals; the earth shook and the sea rose in hilly waves to dash against the shores of Lanka. When his worship was complete, Indrajit climbed into his chariot, flashed up into the air, and vanished. Roaring, for this was their signal, the rakshasas flew at the marauding monkeys.

As the sun was climbing toward his zenith, the rakshasas fought fiercely for their yuvaraja. And from on high, where his chariot flitted at his will, fell a hot deluge of arrows. As banks of sunrays do the night at dawn, Indrajit's shafts pierced the vanara army.

The monkeys did not die in hundreds now, but in thousands, each moment. The field at Lanka's gates was strewn with corpses of the jungle folk, their long-limbed bodies askew, piquant in death. Indrajit's arrows were made of pure and smokeless fire. Each one scorched the earth and ashed a thousand vanaras. Their screams echoed in Ravana's ears as he sat so dismally in his palace. He knew they were monkeys dying. He rose painfully, and came out onto his terrace to watch his son do battle.

Ravana saw Indrajit fly down to the ground and fight where his aim was truer and his arrows still more terrible. The father saw the devastation his prince brought to the enemy. Hope sparked alive again in his heart: perhaps not all was lost. From his terrace, Ravana shouted his son's name.

The vanaras attacked Indrajit with trees and rocks, but in vain. He was such an archer they hardly saw his hands move; yet arrows flowed from his bow like light from the sun. Rock and tree trunk were smashed in flight, and the incendiary shafts flew on and stuck in the monkeys' chests, immolating them. Gandhamadana, Nala, Neela, Mainda and Gaja, Jambavan, Rishabha, Angada, and Dwividha had come to face Indrajit. But they were all helpless against his wizardly archery. They could not come near him; his chariot was always protected by an uncanny ring of fire arrows.

He struck them all, at times with fire and again with plain sharp points. Then he vanished, and just his arrows of green, blue, and scarlet flames still streamed at the vanaras. One moment they rose from the earth, then they fell from the sky; now from afar, now from near. The spectacle was so brilliant and beautiful that at times the monkeys stood gazing at it, while death came humming down at them.

It was all the sorcery of the brahmastra that Indrajit had invoked before the sacred agni. The young rakshasa flew down toward where Rama and Lakshmana stood. He shot a hundred arrows at them; but those shafts turned weak and fell tamely around the brothers. Cursing, he flew back on high and killed five thousand monkeys. The demon prince's hubris was boundless. He hated to think anyone could withstand his arrows as Rama and Lakshmana did.

Rama said to his brother, "It is his ancestor Brahma's power he fights with. All this is the maya of the brahmastra. He wants to break our spirit by fighting invisibly. He wants us to panic, and that we must never do."

Now a cloud of sorcery appeared in the sky, crackling with thunder and lightning. From it issued a million shafts, formed into great flowers, deadly rainbow flowers, all of sleep. Whispering susurrantly, they floated down on the vanara army and, one by one, every monkey fell into a trance. They would have all been killed, except that at the last moment before the petal fire fell on them, Rama cried out to Lakshmana and the princes drew the brahmastra's deepest power away from the forest folk and upon themselves, and they also fell in a swoon.

Thus the vanaras' lives were saved. They only slept, and dreams of Brahmaloka swept them far from that battlefield into incredible mandalas they would remember nothing of when they awoke: if ever they did awake, for the slumber of the brahmastra could last until the universe dissolved in the pralaya.

Darkness fell on that field, a moonless night when there are no stars in the sky. Indrajit's triumphant roars echoed through Lanka, and he was borne away once more on the shoulders of his ecstatic rakshasas. They had all seen how the vanaras had fallen, every last one, and how Rama and Lakshmana had fallen with them.

Vibheeshana, who was a tapasvin and possessed considerable spiritual powers, was unaffected by the astra. He stood alone, surrounded by abysmal silence and darkness. He looked around him, and as far as his eyes could see, monkeys lay unbreathing on the ground, trapped in the limbo of the astra. He saw a lone torch weaving its way toward him. Vibheeshana drew his sword. The bearer of the torch came nearer, and he saw it was Hanuman, glowing in the unnatural night.

They embraced fervently, and Vibheeshana said, "Truly, Brahma has blessed you that his own astra has no power over you."

Hanuman said, "I worshipped the Pitamaha and his weapon, and I am safe. But what about the others?" He gasped, "Rama and Lakshmana!"

Vibheeshana said, "They have absorbed most of the brahmastra's power, but they are not dead. Let us see who else is awake."

Vibheeshana also lit a rushlight of dry grass from the one Hanuman carried, and they set off through the unmoving vanaras and their rocks and trees fallen beside them. When they had stumbled along some way, a voice hailed them weakly, "Vibheeshana, is Hanuman alive?"

Hanuman and Vibheeshana ran to the voice. It was Jambavan, writhing on the ground with the agony of the astra; but he was conscious and recovering his strength rapidly. They helped him up and gave him water to drink. He revived at their ministrations, and the stupor seemed to ebb out of him.

When Jambavan had his breath back, Vibheeshana said to him, "How is it, great reeksha, that you ask after Hanuman, and not Sugriva or Rama, both of whom have fallen?"

26. Oshadhiparvata

Jambavan said simply, "If Hanuman lives, there is hope for all the rest."

Vibheeshana and Hanuman stood, curious, beside the grizzly jungle warrior. Suddenly overcome, Hanuman knelt beside Jambavan and set his head at the reeksha's feet. Since infancy, Hanuman had known and loved the old one like his own father. Shaking the miasma of the brahmastra from his head, Jambavan rose.

He said, "You must cross the ocean for us again, Son of the wind. Only you can save Rama, Lakshmana, and our fallen army. Hanuman, fly to the Himalaya. In the very north of that range, beside white Kailasa, you will see another mountain as splendid as sunrise.

"Neither sacred Kailasa nor golden Rishabha is your quarry, but a third peak that nestles between these two: Oshadhiparvata. Miraculous plants of healing grow on that mountain, and if you reach there after dark, you will see them light up the night with soft luminescence.

"We need four herbs to revive our army: the mritasanjivini that Sukracharya always uses to call back his dead; the vishalyakarani, the savarnyakarani, and the santanakarani, which heal all wounds, however grievous, with their very fragrance. These are the eldest herbs of healing that grow upon the earth, and their secrets are known only to the few who have studied their lore.

"Fly to the Oshadhiparvata, Hanuman, and bring back the four oshadhis."

Even before Jambavan had finished speaking, Hanuman began to grow, as he once did on the shores of Bharatavarsha. The spirit of his father, tameless Vayu, was upon him again, and his love for Rama, who lay as if dead on the darkling field. Hanuman grew tall as a tree and, with a few strides, gained the pinnacle of Mount Suvela. Not once did he turn back, but leaped off that peak straightaway. The son of the wind soared above the resinous darkness of the brahmastra and into sunlight again. With Vayu's blessing coursing in his every fiber, he flew north in the direction of the Devas.

Swiftly as his father flew Hanuman, who is called Maruti for his speed—quick as the Maruts. Like a thought, he sped through the blue vaults of the sky. It was a fine day everywhere, save in Lanka, and as he flew higher the air around him was cold. Below him the blue-green ocean lay like a woman languid, dreaming. He thought how innocent the elements seemed of the tragedy from which he came: that the Lord of the earth lay unbreathing on a fateful field from Indrajit's brahmastra.

Soon the sacred peninsula of Bharatavarsha, which had once been a vast island in the sea and had drifted north manvantaras ago, appeared under him. Sprawling jungles, rivers, plateaus, hills, and gleaming plains appeared below Hanuman as he flashed on and on, ever north. But he had no eyes for any of those excellent sights. Absorbed in his mission, he flew on, pushing himself until he flew quicker than the wind.

As evening fell, Hanuman saw the Himalaya ahead of him, stretching from horizon to horizon, like a necklace of crimson and gold across Bhumi Devi's throat. As he flew on, the great range grew taller with every moment, its majesty lit by the last shafts of the setting sun. Over the first peaks flitted Hanuman, over sheer white gorge and glacier, pale river and silvery waterfall. Night fell quickly around him.

The cold clutched at him, but he hardly noticed it. All he saw in his mind was Rama's face, its eyes shut and plunged in darkness. On flew Hanuman and crossed the jutting massifs of Himavan. He came beyond them to a tableland where a hundred lakes sparkled with reflected starlight. One of them was so magical he could feel its wonder reach up to caress him with mystic fingers. That lake perched between heaven and earth; Hanuman guessed it was the fabled Manasa sarovara, which Brahma created long ago, with a thought.

Now myriad flames dotted the hills under him, where fires burned in a hundred asramas to keep the biting cold at bay. This was holy country, where the greatest rishis of Aryavarta lived in tapasya. Ahead loomed two mighty peaks that stood apart from the rest of the Himalaya. In the starlight he navigated by, to Hanuman they seemed the most sacred and mysterious of all. One was tall and white as goose feathers, and Hanuman knew this was Kailasa, where Siva lived.

Thrice he circled that holiest mountain, and it seemed to him that a blessing greater than earth and sky reached out to touch his heart from the white eminence.

Beyond Kailasa, he saw another taller mountain of burnished gold. Its sides were smooth, and it glowed like an occult and unknowable yantra: the heart of the earth! Yet it was not towering Meru that attracted Hanuman, but a third mountain that lay between pale Kailasa and the golden one. It was much smaller than the other two, and dark by comparison. But it shone with a million twinkling phosphorescences. When Hanuman looked closer, he saw these were not the night fires of rishis, but the leaves of the plants that grew here, leaves like silver tongues of flame.

Hanuman flew down toward the glowing leaves. But as he drew near, they vanished from below him and the little mountain lay in darkness. Hanuman sprang up again and flew back into the sky; once more the plants of healing glimmered below him. Again the son of the wind flew down. But even as his feet sought solid ground to land on, the light of the plants disappeared.

Hanuman knew that the plants and the mountain colluded to conceal the oshadhis from him. Thinking of Rama, who lay unmoving on distant Lanka, the vanara gave a roar that the planets above heard. He struck the mountain with his fist in rage. Growling, great Hanuman grew greater still. In hands grown vast beyond imagining, he grasped Oshadhiparvata by its sides. Hanuman shut his eyes; he gritted his teeth and pulled that mountain out of the earth by its roots.

The vanara's body blazed. He flashed through the sky, bearing Oshadhiparvata above him in immense palms. Like light, Hanuman flew with the mountain. He flew so fast he vanished from the starlit sky and arrived almost at once in Lanka. Like a falling meteor, the son of the wind descended to the earth. Gently he set the mountain of herbs down beside Sugriva's unconscious army in the zone of the brahmastra, where it was neither day nor night, but bizarre twilight.

A kindly breeze blew into the limbo and filled it with the scents of the oshadhis. At once Rama stirred, and then Lakshmana. They shook their heads and sat up. The darkness of the astra dissipated. One by one, rubbing their eyes, all the vanaras awoke. Sugriva awoke, Angada, Neela and Nala, Rishabha and Mainda, and the others. Every vanara the brahmastra had felled revived. The stars shone down again, and the rising moon, like balm. As the rich fragrances of the oshadhis caressed them, even the monkeys who had been killed in battle rose from the dead, to fight again for Rama against the legions of evil.

But no rakshasa rose from the dead, because none lay lifeless on the field. It was Ravana's command that the body of any demon who died was to be cast into the sea. Rama blessed Hanuman who stood before him with tears of joy in his eyes.

Rama said, "Mighty one, return the mountain to its roots. Let Oshadhiparvata stand where it has always stood, between Meru and Kailasa. Lest another hero like you fly there someday in quest of the healing herbs."

Hanuman grew vast again; he lifted the mountain. While the vanaras cheered him wildly, he rose into the sky and raced away across the face of the moon, along the paths of the Devas and the wind, toward the Himalaya. Hanuman flew quickly as a wish once more, and returned in time too brief to tell, after planting Oshadhiparvata back in its place in the north.

Sugriva called Hanuman. He said, "The night is ripe for deeds. We must strike back while the rakshasas celebrate our death. Let some of our bravest monkeys enter Lanka with torches in their hands."

An army of flames, the vanaras approached the drunken, triumphant rakshasas. Some demon guards saw the torches the monkeys carried appear on top of Lanka's smooth walls. They thought it was all the wine they had drunk that made them see things that were not there. Then they thought perhaps it was some of their own people waving lamps in celebration. For they had seen the vanara army laid low by Indrajit's astra. The monkeys scampered along the rooftops, so recently restored after Hanuman's inferno. Before the rakshasas had time to gather themselves or repulse the shadowy intruders, Lanka was on fire again.

Like a nest of sin being exorcised, Ravana's city blazed with monkey fire. Before they knew what flames consumed them, mansions and palaces caught and burned down, and thousands of rakshasas died in their sleep. Women perished, and children; this was war. When the vanaras had set the city of night alight, they came flying back to Rama. The screams of the burned and the burning swelled above the crash of waves against the shores of Lanka. Snatched back from the dimension of sleep, into which the brahmastra had plunged them, Rama and Lakshmana raised their bows and pulled on their bowstrings like echoes of the apocalypse.

Finally, the rakshasas realized the monkeys had risen from the dead. They poured out of their homes and swarmed, shouting, into the streets. All around them flames licked at the sky and the moon, like some macabre festival of lamps.

Outside the gates of Lanka, Rama stood with his bow in his hand, even like Siva with his Pinaka.

27. The sons of Kumbhakarna

It was an infernal midnight when Ravana was roused from sleep. Earlier, from his terrace he had seen the vanara army lying still on the field. He went to the gates with Indrajit and saw that no life stirred under the brahmastra's canopy of darkness. Heady celebrations swept Lanka. Now at midnight, suddenly the city was ablaze. Messengers rushed to Ravana's apartment with the incredible news: the monkeys had risen from the dead, and they had set Lanka on fire.

Ravana sent another army against Rama. He sent dead Kumbhakarna's sons, Kumbha and Nikumbha, to war. Under moon and stars, in the hour of the rakshasas' greatest strength, the two princes attacked, with a swarming legion around them. The demons' weapons and the jewels at their throats, chests, and arms shone like a river of stars fallen to the earth; through Lanka on fire, the river of rakshasas flowed. Their savage faces lit by the moon and the flames, they came to fight for their city and their lives. Their women and children had died tonight, and they came grimly, for revenge.

But the vanaras were exuberant. Hadn't they just risen from the dead to fight again for Rama and the army of dharma? They felt invincible, that not even death could stand between them and victory. Roaring, Angada leaped at three rakshasas who marched at the head of the demon legions. In a wink, he smashed their heads with a rock. The rakshasa army parted like a river with an island in its stream, and Kumbha of the rakshasas stood forth to confront Angada of the monkeys.

Kumbha was tall and lean, like his uncle, the king, and his valor was lustrous. His arrows were gashes of lightning in the sky, and even Angada could not stand against him alone. Mainda and Dwividha rushed to his side. Still, Kumbha's blinding archery beat back the vanaras. Dwividha was pierced with arrows of dim green light, and Mainda as well; both fainted. Angada sprang to them; but he, too, was shot swiftly with shafts of sleep.

From behind the vanara lines loomed Jambavan, fangs and claws flashing in the moonlight, and beside him stood Sushena; but they could not even reach Kumbha. Then the vanara army parted again and another warrior, greater than Angada or Mainda, Jambavan or Sushena, came through it. Sugriva, king of the vanaras, son of Surya, arrived to battle in the night.

He stood before the demon prince and cried, "Kumbha, you are the pride of the rakshasas. You are as mighty as your father and your uncle; why, you are like Bali and Prahlada, Indra, Kubera, and Varuna. Your archery is like Indrajit's and your strength like your father's. You are a jewel of your line. Yet, my brave prince, now you will die; for even against my will, I must kill you. Come, fight me hand to hand, unless you are afraid without your bow."

At that taunt, following the cunning praise, Kumbha flung down his bow and sprang from his chariot to fight Sugriva with bare hands; which was just as the canny vanara intended. The two armies fell hushed around them, as vanara king and rakshasa prince locked with each other, and the muscles stood out on their bodies like tree roots.

Kumbha and Sugriva fought long and wildly, and Lanka shuddered with their roars and blows. But suddenly, Sugriva jumped back a nimble pace, clenched his fist, and struck Kumbha on his temple. One blow and the rakshasa sank to the ground, his skull crushed, blood and brains oozing from the wound. Crying out in terror, that yet another of their princes was slain, the rakshasas fled from Sugriva. The vanara king beat his chest; he gave the victory call of the deep jungle.

"*Aaoongh! Aaoongh! Aaoongh!*" roared Sugriva, echoingly.

His army responded echoingly with "*Jaya, Sugriva! Jaya! Jaya!*"

Nikumbha, ferocious as the dead Kumbha, rushed into battle, roaring to drown Sugriva's cries. Nikumbha was built more like his father than his uncle; he was another giant. Armed with an unlikely weapon came that prince of darkness: he came with a great pestle in his hands. The ayudha glowed in the night, now deep green, now dull red.

Nikumbha raised the weird thing above his head and began to spin it round; until it seemed to catch the movement and whirled, humming, with a will of its own. Nikumbha loosed the wheel of fire at the monkeys, a chakra of a thousand burning blades, a whirlwind of death. The vanaras fled shrieking from it, but it pursued them, quick as thinking. Thousands of jungle folk fell, headless, sliced in two or made ashes by that weapon of both blades and fire. Blood flowed in a gleaming rivulet under the moon.

Against the fleeing tide of monkeys came another vanara hero to confront Nikumbha dominating the field of death. The son of the wind came and stood before the prince: Hanuman, grown taller than the rakshasa. The wheel of death in Nikumbha's hands shone with new light. It shone like a red and green sun. Round and round, chanting an evil mantra, Nikumbha whirled the pestle weapon above his head. It seemed to grow in his hands. It flashed another hundred glinting blades; its flames were twice as livid as they had been before. Now the pestle howled in Nikumbha's sorcerer's hands like a spirit in torment.

He whirled it round so rapidly that it was an unbroken orb of light, a dark moon risen on the earth. With a cry that froze the blood, Nikumbha cast his weapon at Hanuman. It floated wailing through the moonlight and the vanaras fell on their faces. Like a comet, it blazed straight into Hanuman's chest. There was a white explosion, followed by stillness and silence.

Slowly the monkeys lifted their heads, expecting to see Hanuman blown to shreds. But he still towered above them, as he had been when he flew across the ocean. Of the pestle of fire, only some embers floated down from his chest, where that weapon had blown apart. Like a mountain trembling at an earthquake, Hanuman shook the embers from his fur.

Growling in his throat, an unimaginable beast of prey again, Hanuman sprang at the stunned Nikumbha. The son of Vayu bunched a fist and struck the rakshasa a staggering blow on his chest. Nikumbha's armor was riven; it pierced his flesh and blood flowed down his body. In a wink, Hanuman wrestled him to the ground, sat on his chest and strangled him with inexorable hands. Then he wrenched the prince's head off his neck, and anointed himself with the spouting gore.

28. Indrajit

When Hanuman killed Nikumbha, Lanka resounded with the vanaras' jubilation. The rakshasas shrank back in occult fear; they said that surely this battle could never be won. This was the ancient war between dharma and adharma, and they were fighting on the wrong side, the one that always lost in the final reckoning. Not all their dark weapons, not even their trained maneuvering or their greatest warriors were potent against the crude army of the jungle, armed with not just rocks and trees, but with dharma as well. Not a vanara knew how to hold a sword, a bow or arrow; yet victory so far was certainly theirs. It was as if the monkeys were protected by a power greater than the demons could fathom.

After Nikumbha was killed, another rakshasa, and a master of astras, Maharaksha, came forth. He invoked the agneyastra and shot it at the vanara army. It lit up earth and sky, and flew to consume the army of the jungle in primeval flames. But Rama came forth from the vanaras' side. Swifter than the agneyastra was his shaft in reply: a suryastra from the heart of the sun. The two weapons locked in the night sky, bright as midday with their garish splendor. But the will of Maharaksha was small match for the will of Rama, and the demon's astra fell away into the sea. Rama's arrow spumed on into Maharaksha's chest and consumed that rakshasa in an instant. The demon army fled again.

Ravana sat in his sabha, and strange strength was upon him. All his sons and nephews, save Indrajit alone, had been killed; the enemy turned every defeat into a reverberant victory. It was perhaps the last strength of despair; but Ravana no longer sat like a broken man on his throne. He had little left to lose now save his own life, and new courage surged in him.

He called Indrajit. Ravana said to his son, "It seems you are the only answer to the monkeys. Whenever anyone else has gone out to face them, they have been killed. But both times you went to fight, you came back with victory. Each time, Rama and Lakshmana escaped by a miracle. Go forth again, my son; take death with you this time.

Fight with any weapon you must, fight subtly with maya. Bring me Rama's head."

Again Indrajit rode out with his army. He lit a fire of yagna, and worshipped it with oblations and mantras. Once more, Agni came out of the flames and received the havis in burning palms. Indrajit chanted slokas to pacify the Devas, the Danavas, and the Asuras, and his demons brought him his silver chariot, yoked to steeds of unearthly pedigree. It was no common ratha, but the chariot of Maharathika Indrajit, bearer of the brahmastra, and it was proof even against Rama's and Lakshmana's astras.

When he had worshipped the fire, Indrajit cried, "Today I will kill the false hermits who roamed the Dandaka vana. Today the world shall be rid of the race of vanaras."

Bristling with weapons, Indrajit came to fight; hidden with maya, he flew into the sky. On the ground, battle had been joined again. As a cloud does the earth with rain, Rama and Lakshmana covered the attacking rakshasas with arrows. But then, from on high, Indrajit loosed his own storm of fire. His missiles fell on the vanaras like meteor showers. They flamed down from every side as if there were a hundred invisible archers in the air. The rakshasa's chariot was as quick as time and he hid himself behind some clouds.

Stealth and terror rode with the demon prince. He shot screeching narachas down on Rama and Lakshmana. They began to return his fire; they now tracked him with the quickness of instinct and by the trails his astras left. Ravana's son filled the sky with smoke and fog from his bow, so his arrows left no trails any more. Yet with intuition shrewder than sight, the kshatriyas shot their shafts at him, blindly, and drew blood. Now Rama did not shoot at the prince in his evanescent chariot; he only cut down Indrajit's astras, as soon as he saw them. But Lakshmana aimed at him and the rakshasa was hard-pressed to evade his arrows, though he rode through the sky like a gale.

Many of Indrajit's shafts found their mark, and Rama and Lakshmana soon looked like palasa trees in bloom. But not for a moment did they catch a glimpse of Ravana's son. He kept himself hidden behind his veil of maya. Indrajit assailed not only the princes; around them, thousands of monkeys fell.

Dismayed by the numbers of jungle folk who were dying, Lakshmana cried, "It is adharma, Rama, that a warrior like Indrajit burns the helpless vanaras with astras. They have come to Lanka to fight for us, and thousands of them perish each moment. I will bring this unnatural bird out of the sky with the brahmastra."

Though his bow flared arrows, Rama said gently, "It is not dharma for us, either, to kill a million rakshasas with the brahmastra. This is an ancient war. It has been fought by vanara and rakshasa on many worlds, in ages gone by and deep among the stars. And it shall be fought again. It is not only for us that the monkeys fight or die; it is for themselves, for their deathless souls. Lakshmana, you cut down his arrows now. Let me test Indrajit with astras that are less terrible than Brahma's, but still fierce."

But this was total war: of mind, will, and instinct. No sooner did Rama say this, than Indrajit sensed his intention and vanished from over the field. He flew back to Lanka, with a cowardly plan forming in his violent heart.

29. Vile deception

Indrajit did not leave the battlefield for long. Briefly, he stood on the ramparts of his father's palace, glowering out at the fighting beyond the walls of Lanka. He wept for his rakshasas whom Rama and Lakshmana had killed. If he had cut down ten thousand vanaras, the kshatriyas had killed twice as many demons. Indrajit was furious that this puny enemy had proved so indomitable. He fumed at their resilience. The rakshasa prince knew that all wars are won or lost in the minds of the generals; and the spirit of Rama of Ayodhya was immaculate.

Rama seemed invulnerable to weapons of fire and serpentine evil. But Indrajit had a plan by which he would carve the kshatriya's heart without breaking his skin. A master mayavi, Indrajit conjured up a lifelike, breathing Sita of maya beside him; with her in his chariot, he went to battle once more. Hanuman now led the storming vanaras. When they saw Indrajit ride out again, the soldiers of the jungle seized up rocks and trees to use against him.

But before they could begin their attack, Hanuman cried that they should not cast a stone or a twig at the young rakshasa. Hanuman saw that Indrajit had brought Sita out onto the field; the vanara stood very still, his hackles raised, growling. A hush fell on the war. Hanuman saw Sita wore a soiled yellow garment, just as she had in the asoka-vana. Her ruined plait hung limp behind her, and her face was streaked with dirt and tears. The vanaras froze when Indrajit brought the maya Sita onto the field. She was entirely lifelike, and she sobbed as if her heart was broken.

His fangs bared in a grin, Indrajit held Sita by her hair. Between the two armies, he began to fondle her. She struggled, she screamed, but Indrajit slapped her face. Hanuman sprang forward with a roar. In a flash, Indrajit drew his sword. The demon saw the hot tears in the vanara's eyes.

Hanuman cried, "Dare you touch the Devi? Vile rakshasa, you will die!"

But Indrajit cried back, "She is the cause of all this misery. She came as death to Lanka. When I kill her, my revenge will begin for every rakshasa who has lost his life here. After she is dead I will kill the rest of you, and somehow I think it will be easy. Don't preach dharma to me, vanara. Thousands of our women and children died when your monkeys set fire to our city as we slept."

Hanuman started forward again, but Indrajit was quicker than he was. With a blinding thrust, he buried his sword in Sita's breast; gasping, she sank down in the chariot. There was a moment of perfect shock, when Indrajit killed his maya Sita between the two armies. Hanuman and the vanaras stood turned to stone.

Gleefully, Indrajit called, "Come and see what I have done to your master's wife! Monkey, you crossed the ocean for nothing; all your trials have been in vain."

Panic, like a wave of death, flared through the vanaras. Their cause betrayed, all their valor so pointless now, the unnerved monkeys fled shrieking in every direction. The rakshasas chased them and cut them down easily. Hanuman grew gigantic again. Roaring dreadfully, he slaughtered the advancing demons. He trampled on them like insects. Bending down, he swept away whole phalanxes with a blow. Berserk with grief, the son of the wind ran amok among Indrajit's army. He was at them like Yama and the rakshasas fled.

But as soon as they ran, Hanuman grew dispirited. He turned to his jungle warriors. He sighed deeply; tears stood in his eyes. He said, "Sita is dead and I do not know if we should fight on. Come, vanaras, come away to Rama and Sugriva. Let us take them the news, and let them tell us what to do next."

Heads bent, the vanaras went back to Rama. Seeing them go, with a triumphant smile Indrajit turned his chariot back to his father's palace. At his feet, the body of the phantom Sita had dissolved into the stuff of dreams of which it had been made.

30. The yagna at Nikumbhila

Indrajit believed in the power of yagnas as much as he did in his own valor. He went directly to a tapovana called Nikumbhila. In that sacred grove he kindled another fire. He sat before it, his body bare and his demons around him. He fed the fire with ghee that had been purified with mantras. Like a fierce priest he was, absorbed in his sacrifice: a flame himself, and his ritual precise and flawless. He offered havis, and the agni blazed like a fragment of the sun.

Meanwhile, back on the battlefield, Rama heard the outcry from Hanuman's warriors. He sent Jambavan and another force of monkeys to the son of the wind. The battle around the western gate had been abandoned and Hanuman had just turned back when Jambavan came lumbering up to him. Jambavan saw tears streaming down the vanara's face. Barely pausing to greet the reeksha, Hanuman said, "I must see Rama."

The last rakshasa had fled into the city, and the massive gates clanged shut behind them. Hanuman came with Jambavan to where Rama and Sugriva sat. Bracing himself, the vanara wiped his eyes, and said as bravely as he could, "There is terrible news, my lords."

Then he looked into Rama's face and could not go on. Sugriva cried, "What is it? What is your news, Hanuman?"

Choking, Hanuman said, "Indrajit brought Sita to the field in his chariot. Before my eyes, he killed her with his sword."

Rama collapsed as if he had been cut down with an ax. The vanaras rushed to him. They sprinkled water on his face while Lakshmana held his brother's head in his lap. The dazed Lakshmana whispered, "Dharma is of no use in this world. My brother has been a savior to the munis of the forests. He killed thousands of rakshasas, so the holy ones could live in peace. But his dharma has not saved him from evil.

"And that monster Ravana still lives in his palace."

Lakshmana's handsome features twitched in a dark rictus. He

cried, "Gentleness and dharma are of no use in this world. But I swear Ravana will not live another day, and his city will be ashes when I have finished with it. Rama, rouse yourself; the hour of revenge is upon us. Sita may be dead, but Ravana will not escape with his life."

Rama lay unmoving. Then Vibheeshana came up to them; when he saw Rama unconscious, he wanted to know what had happened. Lakshmana sobbed, "Indrajit murdered Sita on the battlefield."

Looking doubtful, Vibheeshana asked, "Who brought this news?"

"Hanuman."

Still, the good rakshasa was unperturbed. "I know how much Ravana loves Sita. He would never let her be killed. But then . . ." He grew thoughtful. The vanaras and Lakshmana hung on his every word, and now on his silence. Suddenly Vibheeshana gave a cry. "Rouse yourselves, monkeys, hurry! We must fly to Nikumbhila. Indrajit created a maya Sita and killed her on the field to shock you. As you grieve over a death that has never been, my spies have brought word that Indrajit has lit a fire at Nikumbhila. At this moment he sits at a yagna that will make him invincible. We must stop him, or the war is lost!"

Rama's eyes fluttered open; he asked for water. He sat up and sobbed when he remembered Hanuman's news. But Vibheeshana said, "Sita is not dead. Indrajit made a maya Sita and killed her, so he could gain time for his yagna. Ravana loves Sita too much to let a hair of her head be harmed. Indrajit would die if he dared touch her."

Rama smiled wanly. Vibheeshana hurried on, "There is not a moment to lose. Indrajit already has Brahma's astra and the horses the Pitamaha gave him. If he completes the yagna at Nikumbhila, he will have invincibility as well. Then not you, Rama, or Lakshmana will be able to kill him, and everything will be lost. Give me an army of vanaras. Lakshmana, come with me. Indrajit is the key to this war; only he stands between us and victory. He must die, and my heart insists that Lakshmana will be the one to kill him."

Rama said quietly, "Lakshmana, go with Vibheeshana. Kill Indrajit and bring us victory. My brother, this is the battle you have prepared for all your life. But be careful; remember your enemy is a master of maya. Go with my blessing, sweet prince, your triumph at Nikumbhila will win this war for us."

31. Ambush

Lakshmana picked up his bow. He put on his armor and took the padadhuli from Rama's feet. His moment of destiny had arrived. He said, "Bless me, Rama, who are my brother and my God. Let my arrows drink Indrajit's blood."

Rama laid his palm on his brother's head. Lakshmana embraced him tenderly; then he followed Vibheeshana and the vanaras toward Nikumbhila. Jambavan went with them, with a hundred great bears who had crossed the ocean into Lanka.

Swiftly, stealthily, they arrived in Nikumbhila. They heard the yagna fire crackling; they heard Indrajit chanting mantras of power. All else was silence. Vibheeshana said, "We must attack them before it is too late. The vanaras must take the rakshasas unawares. When Indrajit comes out in anger, let him find Lakshmana waiting for him."

Rising out of the jungle around the yagna, armed with rocks and trees, the monkeys attacked Indrajit's demons. Savagely came the vanaras, and in a moment a hundred rakshasas lay dead, their heads crushed with wild weapons. The demons seized up their swords and fought back, and the yagnashala turned into a battlefield. Blood splashed everywhere; hewn-off limbs flew at bizarre trajectories, and Indrajit's solemn chanting was drowned by the roars of monkey and demon. More deafening than these were the roars of Jambavan's bears, who flew at the rakshasas in a black storm; their fangs and claws were death's lightning.

His sacrifice ruined, Indrajit jumped up with a cry. Red-eyed, he stalked out from the yagnashala, and that prince was terrible, even to look at.

Vibheeshana said to Lakshmana, "He is beside himself with anger; you have the advantage."

Hanuman, who had come along for the battle, had grown huge again. He pulled up a knotted tree for his weapon and battered the rakshasas to a pulp before they could run from him. Growling to see the son of the wind, Indrajit sprang at him. But then Lakshmana pulled on his bowstring. He stood behind the great old nyagrodha tree under which the yagna fire still burned, neglected. The forest echoed with that sound. Turning away from Hanuman with a snarl, Indrajit faced Lakshmana.

Vibheeshana stood beside the kshatriya. Indrajit realized at once who had brought the vanaras to this secret place. Choking with rage, he hissed, "Traitor! You have eaten the salt of Lanka all your life and you shall be damned forever. No rakshasa child will ever say your name except as a curse. You have betrayed your brother and your nephew. How could you, coward?

"You are Rama's slave; but remember, Vibheeshana, you are dealing with the enemy. Once his use for you is over, he will not spare your life. He will kill you like the cur you are."

Vibheeshana cried, "You are the evil spawn of an evil father. Ravana had every chance to save himself and his people. But he would not walk the way of dharma. You may be a great warrior, but you have no wisdom, only arrogance. It is true I was born a rakshasa, but I never loved violence as the rest of you do. And though he is a greater warrior than you or your father, Rama shuns violence whenever he can. He knows the way of violence is not the way of dharma.

"The wise have always said that to lust after another man's wife is madness; it is the sin that ruins a man. But Ravana has always reveled in sin, making a life of it: whether murdering rishis for his sport or reviling the Devas who are the guardians of the earth. But now the time has come to pay; neither your father nor you will escape.

"Look, Indrajit. Lakshmana guards the nyagrodha tree where your agni burns. Not you, but he. Dare you approach it, dare you tempt your death?"

For the first time in his wild and heroic life, Indrajit felt a cold pang of fear.

32. *Indrajit and Lakshmana*

Hissing like an angry cobra, Indrajit mounted his chariot.

Hanuman appeared at Lakshmana's side and lightly lifted the kshatriya onto his shoulders. The horses Brahma had given Indrajit shone like silver in the midmorning sun. The rakshasa cried, "Foolish mortal, have you forgotten how you and your brother twice lay in a swoon of death? No one can save you from me three times."

But Lakshmana was calm, now this moment of fate was upon him. He said quietly, "Brave words and brave deeds are not the same thing. Besides, each time you came to battle, you came invisibly. Only cowards fight like that, because they are afraid of their enemy and afraid to die. Let me see your valor now that we are face to face."

Before he had finished speaking, Indrajit shot a clutch of searing arrows at him. They covered his fair body in a blossoming of blood. With a cry, Lakshmana loosed five narachas at the rakshasa. They stung Indrajit and he roared; but they did not wound him gravely.

On they fought, the prince of Lanka and the prince of Ayodhya. Both were quick as light, both were masters of archery. Like two lions for the lordship of a jungle, they battled. Soon astras flared from their bows and lit up the hillside as if other suns had risen into the day.

Arrows stuck in each one's body and blood flowed richly from their wounds. They fought on, unmindful, upon the edge of death. The forest was hushed at the sound of their bowstrings, and all the rakshasas, vanaras, and reekshas around them grew still, as if they realized how pointless their lesser contentions were. They stood gazing at the mythic duel. And it seemed primeval phalanxes fought from the two princes' bodies: timeless legions of darkness and light.

A hum of subtle shafts from Lakshmana's magic quiver clipped the joints of Indrajit's armor. Like a snake's skin, the light silver mail fell away from the demon prince's body. Crouching bared, Indrajit shot twenty arrows in a blur, not only at Lakshmana but now at Vibheeshana as well. Taken unawares, Vibheeshana was struck down; he bore no arms against his nephew. But he recovered quickly and plucked the barbs from him. Yet his cry of pain distracted Lakshmana for a moment. In a flash, Indrajit shot his armor away also, and he was as unprotected as his adversary.

By now Vibheeshana had joined the fray. He killed a hundred rakshasas, but not an arrow did he shoot at his brother's son. Blind and deaf to everything around them save each other and their missiles, Lakshmana and Indrajit fought on. War was their art; they were masters, absorbed in their arcane craft. Both were so far above any other warrior there that only the princes themselves, one of grace and the other of evil, fathomed the dimensions of their duel. This was a trial of superior wills: a contention of two great spirits, to the death of one.

The wind did not stir when Indrajit and Lakshmana dueled at Nikumbhila; the birds and beasts of the forest were hushed. Slowly an unnatural twilight fell on that place, because the very sky was veiled with arrows. They loosed their shafts with the swiftness of inspiration, and both warriors were hardly visible for this speed. Indrajit fought from the air and the ground; and when he flew up, Hanuman rose with him. Finally the demon saw that fighting from the sky was no advantage to him: the son of the wind was quicker through the air than his magic horses.

Not merely that forest or island, but all the earth held its breath when these princes fought. In the deepest jungles and on the most exalted, faraway mountains, fires of sacrifice flickered and died down, when Indrajit and Lakshmana dueled on Lanka.

Then, as if with strength and will he had saved for this moment, Lakshmana struck Indrajit's horses with eight scorching arrows; so they whinnied in agony and blood spurted from their flanks. As those fine steeds faltered for a moment, Lakshmana killed Indrajit's charioteer with another shaft through his heart. With a curse, Indrajit leaped onto the chariot head. Thrusting his dead sarathy out of the way, he seized the fallen reins and drove the silver horses himself, while in the same hand that gripped the reins he held his bow and covered Lakshmana with fire.

But now Ravana's son's prowess was constrained, and the vanaras jumped onto his horses' backs. Indrajit could not hold them off while he fought Lakshmana and drove the chariot at once. With fangs, nails, mighty sinews, and rocks, the monkeys killed Indrajit's horses.

Night fell on the jungle. No one saw where Indrajit melted into it and vanished back to the city of Lanka. Lakshmana killed a thousand rakshasas, while his eyes always sought their prince. His ire was risen now; Indrajit and he had battled at the ends of their genius. It was a tide in him, the spirit of that elegant and mortal duel, and Lakshmana could hardly contain it.

Fortunately for his rakshasas, Indrajit traveled on a wizard's feet to Lanka. He did not tarry there for even a moment; no one saw him come or go. He mounted another chariot, fleet as the one the monkeys had destroyed. It was yoked to horses as marvelous as those that had died: Brahma had given him a whole stable of them.

Like Yama's wrath, the rakshasa flew back into battle. In fury at what they had done to his horses, he fell wildly on the monkeys. He killed countless vanaras before Lakshmana stood before him again and drew his fire. Fortune smiled on Lakshmana for an instant, and he broke Indrajit's bow in his hands.

But quick as fear, Indrajit picked up another bow and loosed a sizzle of arrows at Vibheeshana and Hanuman. Having exhausted the lesser astras, having gauged each other, the two archers now summoned more powerful weapons. Indrajit invoked a pale shaft of death, a yamastra, and shot it at Lakshmana. But Lakshmana cut it down with an artful weapon of the mountain yakshas: great Kubera's astra. Joined in momentous flames, the two ayudhas plunged into the sea, to be extinguished in the deep, after hours.

Lakshmana invoked the varunastra, of cold and watery death. But Indrajit met it with a fiery raudra; screaming in the sky, the two put each other out and fell in gray ashes to the earth. Lakshmana loosed the agneyastra of a thousand flames, but his enemy's calid suryastra erupted against it. Fire consumed fire on high, and both subsided.

Indrajit fitted an asurastra to his bowstring, a demoniacal weapon and close to his heart; it was the astra of his race. But Lakshmana met it with a mahesvarastra, as it came keening at him, and smashed it into shards of darkness. It was each other's knowledge, as much as each other's strength and quickness, that the two warriors plumbed: their gyana of the devastras. For every suryastra would not put out every agneyastra; nor would all mahesvarastras cut down any asurastra. Myriad were the astras and infinite their variety. Only the greatest archers, who had been instructed in their lore by the most knowing gurus, could match one another missile for missile as Lakshmana and Indrajit did. Only those blessed by the guardians of the occult weapons could survive a duel like this one for as long as these princes did.

Unseen, in the ethereal akasa, the fifth element, the rishis and the pitrs gathered in the sky and poured down their blessings in subtle waves over Lakshmana, who fought like a lion below them. He heard a voice in his heart, whispering urgently to him, "The moment of his death has come. Summon the astra of the king of the Devas; kill him with Indra's weapon."

Lakshmana invoked the aindrastra, relucent ayudha. He whispered a fierce prayer: "If it is true Rama has never strayed from dharma, let this arrow have Indrajit's life in my brother's name."

Clearing the darkness, lighting the faces of the ancestors and the sages with unearthly luster, the astra flared from Lakshmana's bow. And Indrajit had no answer to it. It took his lean head from his neck in a scarlet flash and his scream echoed through the shocked forest. When the light of the astra faded, the severed head lay on the red earth of Lanka like a golden lotus sprouted from the soil.

The vanaras' triumphant roaring shook Ravana's palace and fell on Rama's ears across the mountain. Like the sun fallen to the earth, Indrajit's head lay glowing in death: a star burned down. His pale body lay apart, like the moon cursed by Daksha to wane forever. Wailing, the rakshasas fled back to Ravana on his lonely throne, to tell him his last hope had been dashed.

Once Mandodari's brilliant son had brought Indra himself, bound in hoops of fire, to Lanka. He had paraded the Lord of the Devas through the streets of his father's city. Today Indrajit lay dead, his head plucked from his body by Indra's astra.

33. *The hero*

Lakshmana stood drenched in blood; his bowstring still quivered from discharging the aindrastra that killed Indrajit. Petal rain fell out of the sky, as if the Devas had crushed a rainbow and showered the pieces down on the kshatriya. This was the most critical victory yet. Indrajit had been the key to this war, the only rakshasa who had seemed invincible.

Joy coursed through heaven and earth. But Ravana was not yet dead. Glowing with his achievement, Lakshmana came before Rama. When Vibheeshana told him Indrajit was dead, Rama jumped up and cried to his brother, "Now are you a man!"

Rama clasped Lakshmana to him and kissed him repeatedly. He said, "This is the greatest triumph of our war. As long as Indrajit lived, victory was just a dream. Now it is within reach."

Then, his eyes filling to see Lakshmana's wounds, Rama began to clean them himself, like a mother. Though Lakshmana blushed brightly, Rama would not let him move. "What you have done will break Ravana's heart. Indrajit was his last hope; now Ravana is as good as dead."

When Lakshmana told him what Hanuman and Vibheeshana had done, Rama hugged them also. He said, "It won't be long now. Ravana will come to fight me."

Sushena arrived there. Rama handed Lakshmana over to his care, for the younger prince was in pain. Hanuman and Vibheeshana were wounded as well, and some vanaras and reekshas. Patiently and gently,

Sushena went to work on them all. Soon their pain was eased and their wound mouths were closed by his attentions. In those days, the healing herbs of the earth were truly effective; it is only in the kali yuga they have lost so much of their potency.

Shaft by shaft, the duel between Lakshmana and Indrajit was described to an avid Rama. Indrajit's courage and skill were praised, and the fact that he never used maya while he fought. Man to man they had battled; the better warrior prevailed and the one whose death was written was vanquished. Vibheeshana, who knew Rama worried about Lakshmana's quick temper, said how calm Lakshmana had been on this, the great occasion. And that was what had given him victory; because Indrajit had fought with anger.

Not once or twice but ten times Rama made them repeat each detail of the battle, as this was indeed music to his ears. A hundred times he hugged Lakshmana, making him blush, in embarrassment and joy.

34. Wrath

Ravana's ministers did not know how to break the news to their king. When they stood wordlessly before him, he fixed them in a glare and said, "Speak! What have you come to say?"

"Lord, Indrajit fought Rama's brother at Nikumbhila. He made the human's body a home for his arrows. Lakshmana was covered in his own blood."

"Your son fought Hanuman and Vibheeshana."

A slow smile appeared on Ravana's face. "How did Lakshmana die?"

But the ministers made no reply. Ravana cried, "Did Rama's brother escape with his life, that you stand so silent? Tell me!"

They said in a whisper, "The duel was fierce and even, Lord. But at last, Lakshmana killed your son. Indrajit has been gathered to his fathers."

For a moment was there such silence in that court you could hear the heartbeats of those who stood in it. Then a long wail burst from Ravana. Again and again he howled his son's name, as if to call him back from the dead; until compassionate nature intervened and Ravana slumped from his throne in a faint. They let him lie for a while before they dared to fetch water and sprinkle his face with it. Crying his son's name, the Rakshasa awoke from oblivion into a nightmare, the ruin that was his life.

"Indrajit, my little child! You have died before me. I thought you were invincible, or I would never have sent you into battle. You brought Indra bound with your serpent fire and marched him through our streets. And now a mere man has killed you? How could I have foreseen this, even in my dreams?"

Ravana groaned; his glorious life had become a living hell. Just one sin had brought him to this pass, one terrible error of judgment. Or perhaps it was the weight of all his other sins, his dark and arrogant past, that had finally pulled him down. In his time he had truly borrowed more from life than he could afford to pay back.

The last few days had turned Ravana's hair pure white. Softly he said, "My son, to die in battle is the best kind of death. It is better than dying of old age in your bed, helpless and dependent on someone for every breath you draw. Those who die as heroic a death as you did find heaven for themselves. You died fighting for your father, and you will have an exalted place in Swarga."

Ravana smiled bitterly. "Today all the Devas, the Danavas and Daityas, the gandharvas, charanas, kinnaras, and kimpurushas rejoice: because Indrajit, whom none of them could face in battle, is dead. Devaloka celebrates this day; Indra's cup of joy brims over. Ah, Meghanada, my cloud child, it seems just yesterday that you were a baby and I cradled you in my arms. I feel this earth is an empty dream now that you are dead, and the only truth is the anguish in my heart. My son, my sweet son, how will I live without you?"

He wept like a child himself. "How will I tell your mother you are dead? Will you be loved better in any heaven, that you have chosen to leave us and Lanka, whose very life you were? Weren't you meant to offer tarpana for me, when I died? To set the first flame to my pyre? But you have changed all that. You have made me the son by dying before me. Oh my precious child, forgive me. I never thought my sin was so heinous that I would have to face this grief."

Ravana wept as if it were as natural as breathing to him now. He spoke in a low voice, to himself, though he did not care any more who heard him. "No, not even she is worth this. But I could not help myself, once I had seen her face. No, Indrajit, it is not a warrior's arrows, but a woman's beauty that killed you. As she is the most beautiful woman on earth, she is also the most dangerous. She is Lanka's nemesis."

He sat sunk in his throne, hovering between grief and madness. But then his innate courage returned to him, and anger. The eyes flashed. Nine sinister heads glowered in their cluster around his central face. There was wrath in those eyes that death itself would not put out. His ministers shrank from their king; his breath blazed even like Vritrasura's of old.

Ravana whispered, "She has brought me nothing but pain and misfortune. And for what? She did not return my love. She came into Lanka like a curse. For her sake, I have lost my brothers and my sons, my nephews, Prahastha, and a million devoted rakshasas. They have all died for her, and she does not care even to look into my face."

His chest heaved with feelings too powerful to think about or even contain. Ravana said, "She must die." He shouted it aloud, until the palace rang with his roaring. "She must die! She must die! Sita must die!"

The nine fiendish heads bobbed up and down, chanting, "She must die! We told you she must die!"

His ministers had never heard those heads speak before. They shivered to listen to their loathsome chatter. Molten tears ran down all Ravana's faces. He drew his sword, blue and glinting. Without another word, his main face set in a mask, he strode out from his sabha. Down the lofty corridors of his palace went Ravana, heading for the asokavana. His steps rang along those passages, and his women and ministers followed him fearfully. Though they had seen his rage through the years, on and off the field of battle, never before had they seen their king like this. He was entirely demonic, a Spirit of darkness. No one dared try to stop him.

His sword a streak of lightning in his hand, Ravana stalked toward Sita to kill her. It was as if his great love had turned into the darkest hatred. His ministers and some of his wives began to speak to the Rakshasa, to beg him, all together, not to commit the crime he seemed bent upon. Sita saw Ravana striding toward her; she sensed his wrath across the asokavana. She saw the naked blade in his hand and knew her death was coming.

Her life lurched in her, a thing of perfect fear. She thought, desperately, that he came to kill her because she spurned him. She thought Rama was dead. She wished she had allowed Hanuman to carry her out of Lanka. All this in the space of a moment.

Ravana was deaf to the pleas of his women and his ministers. Grimly, he strode toward Sita. When he was halfway across the asokavana, she saw another figure dart out from a side door of the palace and run toward the Demon. She did not know him, but this was Suparshva, one of the last of Ravana's trusted ministers left alive.

Suparshva clutched his king's arm and cried with no thought for his own life, "My lord, what are you doing? Have you lost your mind, that you even think of killing a woman?"

Ravana stopped, and for a moment it seemed Suparshva's death had come. His king turned on him, snarling, and raised his sword. But as if he was compelled by fate herself, that rakshasa cried, "What use is it turning your wrath on a helpless woman, and one you love besides? The war is not lost and the greatest warrior is on our side: you, my lord. Don't give in to despair. When have you ever lost a battle? Turn this rage on Rama and victory shall still be yours."

Suparshva saw he had his king's attention. Ravana growled horribly, but he lowered his sword. He blinked his eyes and the cluster of nine heads vanished from sight, as if he had mastered them once more, and himself. Waking from madness, the Rakshasa shook his head to clear it and grew attentive. He seemed to see the world around him again; he seemed to hear what Suparshva said. More, he seemed to doubt his own anger and to realize the sense of what his minister was saying.

Frantic to convince his king, that rakshasa went on, "My lord, today is the fourteenth day after the full moon. Tomorrow is amavasya, the night of the new moon. Fight Rama tomorrow, and you will surely kill him."

Hope sparked alive again in Ravana's eyes and clutched at his wretched heart. From across the asokavana he saw Sita's face, and it shone like a bit of a higher world fallen into this one. Seeing that face, Ravana knew he would not have been able to kill her, anyway, when he was actually faced with the moment. He still loved her more than anything else: his son's lives, his brother's, his people's, his own.

Suparshva saw the yearning in his king's face and said gently, "My lord, when Rama is dead she will be yours."

35. *Moolabala*

With a last, lingering look at the woman who had ruined him, Ravana thrust his sword back into its sheath and stalked back into his palace. In the little temple, Sita sobbed in relief. She had a clear sense of being saved, yet again, by forces beyond the ken of reason. Without knowing who he was, Sita blessed Suparshva with all her heart.

In his sabha, Ravana paced the white marble floor, from bay window to bay window, from the tall doors to his throne, feverishly. Often he had to wipe his eyes: the tears for Indrajit had not stopped flowing. Yet the enemy was at his gate, and he must face him. At last he stopped his pacing. He went to his throne and sat in it, and a great decisiveness came over the Rakshasa. After he turned back from the asokavana, he had not spoken a word to anyone. His ministers and commanders stood by, waiting for his command.

Ravana rose again. He went to the rakshasas who were the leaders of his moolabala. This elite guard was the root of his power; these were his best warriors. He said, "Take horses, chariots, elephants, and foot soldiers. The human has killed my son; I want his life."

Every rakshasa in Ravana's moolabala was a great warrior, and there were a hundred thousand of them. This was the force Ravana had saved until the end of the war; none of these demons had yet gone to fight. They were all masters of astras, and had been taught by Ravana himself. The moolabala was the scourge of the worlds, the bane of the Devas. Now the Rakshasa unleashed it on Rama and the vanaras.

Bristling with occult weapons, Ravana's crack legion went to war. The rocks and trees the vanaras hurled made no impression on that force. They smashed those weapons of earth and jungle with riptides of astras. These rakshasas were unlike any others the vanaras had faced before: they fought like one man. As the monkeys perished, in hundreds every moment, it seemed an army of Indrajits had come to slaughter them.

The vanaras fled to Rama, crying they could not face the moolabala. Already, twenty thousand monkeys' corpses lay strewn across the field and not a single rakshasa had fallen. Without a word, Rama stood up, dark and tremendous. He raised his bow, and next moment the prince of Ayodhya was a blur before his vanaras' eyes.

Rama's archery against Ravana's moolabala was like Siva's tandava. He was a cloud, and his arrows were the livid rain that lashed the rakshasa legion. He was a sun and his shafts were beams that lit the darkness of the moolabala with iridescent death. In no time, twenty thousand rakshasas lay beside the vanaras they had slain. Rama's archery was unfathomable; it was transcendent, not of time but of infinity. And of Rama himself, while he waged immaculate war, there was no physical sign save his bow. Bent in a circle of flames, the Kodanda seemed to hang on air. No visible hand wielded it, but it consumed the moolabala in its firestorm.

Even as we, the deluded in this world of samsara, do not see the living Jivatma in ourselves, so too vanara and rakshasa no longer saw Rama. But the death he brought was everywhere. Elephants fell, horses and chariots were shattered, and, most of all, rakshasas fell, thousands of Ravana's best warriors, to astras that hung fire in the sky, and fell on them with erupting hearts of flame, each one made of a thousand deadly shafts. Not an arrow fell tamely; every one claimed a demon's life.

Time seemed to stand still, awestruck. The blue prince raised the battle into another, supernal dimension. The rakshasas cried that he was invisible, so they could not shoot back at him. Rama loosed a subtle gandharvastra at the moolabala and it came upon them like a fragrant breath of spring. But it was full of hallucinations and it mastered their minds. Suddenly those rakshasas saw a thousand Ramas. They saw him everywhere, smiling, his radiant bow calling them to death, which they knew was such a tender ceremony at his hands. Then again, they did not see him, but only the luster of his arrows: a single, ubiquitous light, engulfing them. They no longer knew or cared when they died; the rakshasas sighed, and were all at strange peace. Many even died with Rama's sweet name on their lips.

In just a muhurta, all that legion was razed. Just a handful, at the very rear of the moolabala, fled back to their master in his palace. It was a repetition of Panchavati. But the force of rakshasas this time was much greater, and they were not merely forest demons who tormented rishis of the vana; these were Ravana's finest troops, handpicked and trained by the king.

In a short hour, the invincible moolabala was annihilated. The widows of the dead streamed into the streets of Lanka, and their lament filled the city.

Some cried, "All this is Surpanaka's fault; she began this war."

And others, "Ravana should have been warned when Khara was killed, and the fourteen thousand at Janasthana."

"But he was smitten blind with the human woman."

"He does not care who is sacrificed. Ravana doesn't love his people any more, only Sita."

"Kumbhakarna, Atikaya, and Indrajit died. Still he sent our men to their deaths."

Once the streets of Lanka were full of vina nadam, soft flute notes, women's voices singing, the tinkling little bells and anklets, and the moans and sighs of rakshasis at love: all of which Hanuman heard when he first came. Now the same streets were riven with screaming and wailing, the gnashing of teeth and bitter accusations. There was not a house in that city which had not lost a son, a father, a brother, or a husband, slain for the sake of what the women saw as their king's madness.

The handful of his moolabala that escaped Rama came, shocked and bloody, before their sovereign. Ravana sat coiled, hissing like a king cobra on his throne. He bit his lip and trembled; deep lines of anguish were etched on his ashen face. He had not dreamed his finest legion could vanish as it had, like snow in a desert. Now his body glowed with the fury in him, like the pralaya.

He had already learned of the rout when the remnant of the hundred thousand returned to him. He did not look at them, but whispered, "Let Mahaparshava, Virupaksha, and Mahodara come to me."

When these rakshasas came, Ravana had controlled himself. He said to them softly, but with intense purpose, "I am going to war. I will cover the sun and the moon, the sky and the earth with arrows. Let those who will, that remain alive, come with me. I do not command it; I, Ravana, ask it. I am going to avenge Kumbhakarna and Prahastha, Atikaya and Indrajit. With my own hands, I will wipe the tears of every woman in Lanka who weeps. I will avenge every rakshasa who has died for me. Tell them. Not a vanara shall live, not Rama or his brother, not Vibheeshana, Hanuman, or Sugriva, or any of the others. Those of you who will march gladly with me, come!"

He strapped on his armor, light as mist. He strode out from his sabha and into the sun, where his chariot waited for him, with piles of bows and arrows laid in it. Not a living rakshasa stayed behind in Lanka when Ravana went to battle. Every demon accompanied his king; even the wounded went back to fight. For long ages he had brought them glory, and they would share death with him before they betrayed his trust.

As soon as he came out into the sun, his anxiety and sorrow fell away like shreds of night. This was the hour of reckoning, and the Rakshasa was a great warrior. He did not fear battle; he loved it. Only the waiting had been unendurable.

Awesome Ravana stood up tall in his ratha, to wave to his last army. In one voice his rakshasas roared his name.

"*Jaya!*" they thundered. "*Jaya, Ravana!*"

36. An infernal shakti

Ravana went to war like a fire sweeping the earth. Around him were Mahodara, Mahaparshva, and Virupaksha. In waves around their chariots swelled the rakshasa army, a million demons. Like the God of Death came Ravana. But as soon as he emerged from his palace, darkness filled the sky; it seemed the sun had been plucked out of the day.

The earth shuddered as if with a tremor of fear and ill omen. Strange birds had gathered in the trees, birds of night at midday. They gave rasping throat to some great evil, an imminent calamity they saw plainly with vision that pierced the veil of time. Eerie clouds scudded across the face of the sun and rained down glutinous drops on the Lord of Lanka and his army, a drizzle of blood. An eagle, of a species never seen on the island, flashed down like an astra and perched on Ravana's black banner, obscuring the golden vina he flew there.

Jackals howled in dismal chorus as if this were not day but the deepest night. Ravana's left eye and that arm throbbed; they twitched in febrile spasms. But if Ravana read these omens, and he was a knowing master of their lore, he did not acknowledge them. Or he was past caring. He rode on, roaring revenge in the names of all his slain.

Truly as death incarnate came Ravana among the vanaras, and none of their paltry rocks and trees was of any avail against his fury. The Demon's astras were twice as fierce as anything they had yet seen. They blazed from his bow; they blinded the monkeys and consumed them so not even ashes were left of the dead. Like an evil star loosed upon the earth, Ravana came hunting the vanaras and they could not stand before him. They fled as beasts of a jungle do, when the jungle burns.

But flying high into the air, Sugriva leaped cunningly into battle behind Ravana. He flew out of the sky at Virupaksha and that rakshasa was taken unawares. With one blow of his open palm, a blow like fate, Sugriva broke Virupaksha's neck, so his head lolled loose and he fell out of his chariot. Ravana shouted to Mahodara to take Virupaksha's place near him; his back was unprotected.

Though at first the monkeys fled from the Rakshasa, they soon collected themselves. Nimbly skirting his chariot, they went behind Ravana's back to fight the army of Lanka. But Mahodara, who was also a master of astras, attacked the monkeys who dodged his king. He attacked them with eerie fireballs that flew out of his hands, and with jagged streaks of lightning. He burned a thousand vanaras in moments. But then Sugriva, king of the jungle, saw him. He leaped at Mahodara, snatched the sword from his hand, and, using a blade for the first time in his life, struck off the rakshasa's head with his own weapon. Its scream cut off, Mahodara's head flew from its trunk and fell among his terrified horses. They bolted from the field, bearing their master's body away in his crimson chariot.

Sugriva's jungle roar echoed above all the other roars and screams of battle, and brought a smile to Rama's lips. Then Mahaparshva was at the vanaras, his chariot everywhere, dealing death as if the monkeys' lives counted for less than nothing. Angada came through his legions, parting them like a sea, to face the rakshasa. Long the two fought, with arrows against rocks and trees, and both of them streamed blood from all their limbs. Finally, with an impatient cry, Angada grew tall as a tree himself and struck Mahaparshva a blow on his chest that broke his ribs. One rib pierced his heart and he died, his eyes rolling up white on his bloody face.

The vanaras cheered deafeningly. They yelled their king's name and their prince's, and the battleground echoed with their cries of joy. Ravana screeched at his sarathy, "Fly at Rama! He must die today, even if the war is lost."

Like a nightmare that haunts waking, realer than daylight, the memory of how Rama humiliated him rose in Ravana's fragmenting mind. He screamed at the memory, as if to erase it from time. To rid himself of its burning shame, he invoked an astra called tamasa. It had been given him by Brahma, and he loosed it at the vanaras: a shaft of black flames. It came among them like a forest fire among the dry trees of summer, and their piteous screams rang across the field. The smell of charred monkey flesh filled the air.

At last, Rama stood forth against Ravana. Blue and serene, the prince of light faced the king of darkness. Rama of Ayodhya stood forth, bright and fearsome on that fateful day. The Kodanda was in his hand, a faint smile was on his lips. Lakshmana was at his side, and they were like Mahavishnu with his brother Indra beside him.

For a moment their gazes locked, Rama's fine, clear eyes and the Rakshasa's sallow ones. A chasmal hush fell on Lanka. Like twin moments of time being born from Brahma, the human and the Demon raised their bows at once and the duel began.

When Rama and Ravana fought, even Lakshmana became just an onlooker. The bowstrings resounded across the field like cracks of doom. The sky was lit up by a hundred comets, which met in pairs, unerringly, and exploded. Those shafts that were not intercepted flashed down, blazing, at the enemy.

But both warriors were great tapasvins: not even the devastras could burn them, with light or fire, darkness or sorcery. Rama shot a raudrastra at Ravana; but the flaming thing was extinguished against the Rakshasa's kavacha, his silver mail. Ravana had a macabre asurastra for Rama, one the prince had never seen before. It flared at him, then turned into savage prides of lions and tigers; they came bounding at him out of the sky in a bloodthirsty hunt. Rama remembered how frightened the beasts of the jungle are of fire. He loosed an agneyastra at them, and those creatures of maya were consumed.

On they fought, untiringly, on the threshold of death where this world and the next seem like one realm; where darkness and light, time and timelessness are the same. They fought with orbs of flames and night, each a little sun, each a void. Some were calorific, some freezing; some were arrows straight as time; some were little globes, worlds in miniature, enchanted and uncanny. Both their armies stood awestruck when Ravana and Rama dueled. Some missiles brought dreams, or visions in the sky, meant to lull the enemy. Others brought soft songs, but quietly maddening, so one could lose one's mind hearing them.

But for every astra there was another that made it harmless, no more than a spectacle in the sky. They fought on as if they made unknown music together, those mortal enemies. They fought as if they were both made of the same cosmic breath, two halves of a single genius. But suddenly, another archer, impatient to be part of that battle, stormed into the fray. Lakshmana was not willing to be left out. He must join in what seemed almost like a celebration, a festival of arms; though, of course, it was a duel to the death. Lakshmana cut down the banner on Ravana's chariot with two lightlike arrows.

Spitting flames, the Demon turned on Rama's brother. But Lakshmana split the Rakshasa's bow in his hands and shot his sarathy dead with an arrow through his temple. Now Vibheeshana was among them, roaring. He sprang at his brother's unworldly steeds, and killed them. When he saw Vibheeshana, Ravana's rage blazed up.

The Lord of Lanka leaped lithely down from his shattered chariot. In his arms there shone a bizarre shakti. Ravana spread his arms wide, wide, and the shakti yawned in the space between his hands, an emerald darkness. It spun humming there: a thing of perfect evil. Crying a ringing devil's cry, in an old and harsh tongue that only Vibheeshana knew, Ravana cast that weapon at his brother. But in a wink, two arrows of light flashed from Lakshmana's bow and the shakti was blasted into dust.

Ravana roared more horribly, a Beast cornered. Another shakti blazed in his arms, and it was brighter than the other. Abruptly, it vanished and his hands seemed empty. Yet Ravana whirled them round and round, for the weapon was still there. It was a shakti of maya that Ravana now spun, a feminine ayudha of untold power. He glowered at Vibheeshana again with fulminant hatred. But the moment Ravana cast the shakti at his brother, Lakshmana leaped between Vibheeshana and the invisible weapon. Rama cried out a warning; but the infernal thing flashed into Lakshmana's chest and he fell as if he had been struck by a thunderbolt, blood spouting from him.

Roaring exultantly, Ravana seized another bow from the remains of his chariot and strung it to finish Lakshmana. Rama gave a strangled cry, as if he had been felled, not his brother. He sprang between the Rakshasa and Lakshmana, who lay pinned to the earth by the shakti. Rama's eyes glittered, so even the vanaras slunk away from him. His body was livid and his arrows were molten.

In a voice the monkeys had never heard before, the plumbless voice of an angry God, Rama said, "Not both of us shall remain alive, Evil One. It was to kill you that I was banished when I was still a boy; to kill you I wandered the jungle for thirteen years. It was for your death that you took my Sita from me. All my life has been a preparation to rid the earth of you. Die now, Rakshasa, there is not room enough in the world for us both."

Rama's golden arrows were made from flames of the apocalypse. They flared in tide at the Demon of Lanka. Ravana was tired. He had no answer to Rama's archery; it was a profound thing of the prince's sacred heart. The Rakshasa climbed into one of his warriors' chariots and rode back into his city. The lofty gates rang shut behind him. The triumphant shouts of the vanaras echoed through the battlefield, and the rest of the rakshasas fled.

With a sob, Rama sank to his knees beside the fallen Lakshmana. The color had ebbed out of the younger prince's face. The shakti still writhed in his chest, a fire serpent swallowing its tail, and his blood gushed thickly from the wound. Carefully, because it was a thing of dire evil, Rama reached for the shakti. The moment he touched it, it burst apart in his hands and vanished. Lakshmana groaned. But he did not open his eyes and the blood still poured from the wound that yawned right through his body. Rama took his brother onto his lap. A score of Ravana's arrows stuck in Rama's own arms and chest, but he seemed unaware of them or their pain.

In a moment, Sushena, the vanara physician, was at Rama's side. Frowning, Sushena explored Lakshmana's wound with knowing fingers. Rama whispered to him, "Sushena, I have no will left to fight. If Ravana had not fled just now, he would have found me easy prey. My heart is weak; my body seems not to belong to me any more. The bow is heavy in my hands and I can hardly lift it to fight on. Noble vanara, Lakshmana is dead and I mean to take my own life."

Sushena signaled to some monkeys. They ran forward to help carry Lakshmana to a safer place, farther from the field where a hundred thousand lay dead, their blood congealing upon the earth.

37. Sanjivini

Rama sat sighing helplessly beside his unconscious brother. He sobbed Lakshmana's name, crying where would he find another brother like him. It seemed Ravana had won his war when his shakti struck Lakshmana down.

But Sushena said, "Lakshmana is not dead. Here, feel his hands,

Rama; there is life in them, buried in a deep slumber. Besides, his is not the face of one who has a short life on earth. Lakshmana has the face of a long-lived man. He is still alive, as surely as you and I are."

Sushena looked up. Among the vanara chieftains thronging around them stood Hanuman. He was calm, ready to be of service. Sushena said to him, "Only the vishalyakarani can heal this wound and bring Lakshmana back to us. Hurry, Hanuman, bring the oshadhi, or bring the mountain again."

The son of the wind grew vast once more. He flew up into the sky. Across holy ocean and sacred continent, the vanara flew like Rama's arrow. Like a vimana he sailed, and landed for the second time upon the little mountain, also called Sanjivini. It was daylight now and he could see the plants of healing, some shaped like tiny men, others like little stars. He breathed their scents and felt his own body begin to glow with new strength and hope like magic in his blood. But by daylight Hanuman could not be sure which of the glowing plants was the vishalyakarani.

Once more, bracing himself and growing big as half the sky, Hanuman plucked up the mountain by its roots and flew through the air with it. Some say the Sanjivini mountain allowed him to pick it up so easily because in its primeval heart it remembered the younger days of the earth, when all mountains had wings and flew through the air, the days before Indra severed their wings with his vajra of a thousand joints.

Hanuman flew back to Lanka with the mountain in his hands. Lanka rocked when he set the Sanjivini down on her shores. Sushena ran up those cold slopes with Hanuman, and his knowing eye soon picked out the vishalyakarani. Sushena crushed the man-shaped herbs between his fingers and held them under Lakshmana's nose, where breath still came and went faintly. The monkeys saw the yawning wound in Lakshmana's chest close like a flower at dusk. They saw its every trace vanish from his skin.

Lakshmana stirred; his eyes flew open. He jumped to his feet and reached for his bow as if he were still in the thick of battle.

With a cry, Rama hugged his brother. "I thought you were gone! What would I have done? Not kingdom or victory, not even having Sita back, would have meant anything to me. I would have killed myself if you had died."

Lakshmana frowned to hear him. He said, "You should not yield to grief like an ordinary man. Your mission in this world is not an ordinary man's."

As long as his brother lived, Rama was prepared to listen to anything from him. He hugged Lakshmana again, laughing in great joy, humoring him as one does a sweet and solemn child. But Lakshmana said gravely, "Listen, Rama. In my swoon, I saw many wonderful dreams and omens. Challenge Ravana today; you must kill him before the day is over. Tomorrow is amavasya, when the moon's face is hidden by the shadow of the earth. Tomorrow is the day of the Rakshasa's greatest strength."

Meanwhile, Hanuman lifted the mountain out of the sea again and flew with it to the Himalaya. But before he went, ten thousand monkeys, killed in battle today, rose from the dead and were ready again for the dharma yuddha, the war of truth. Their shouts of *"Rama! Sugriva! Jaya! Jaya!"* filled the air.

A great ocean conch booming drowned the monkeys' shouting. The gates of Lanka flew open. Clad in dark blue silk, with a new sarathy holding his horses' reins, Ravana rode into battle again, as if in response to Lakshmana's wish.

38. *The two great enemies*

Ravana shot ten smoking arrows at Rama. They flew at him, burning up the sky. But Rama plucked them from the air with one shaft of his own and smashed them into dust. In a wink, Ravana was on the other side of Rama and more arrows flamed at the prince, now from behind him. Whirling round, Rama shot them down. But again Ravana was already somewhere else.

The Demon rode in Brahma's flashing chariot, yoked to unearthly steeds; though Rama's bow streamed fire, Ravana was never in one place so they could find their mark. Quick as wishes, his chariot bore the Lord of evil over land and through the air. Now he was above, then upon the earth, but across the field; while Rama fought from the ground, where he made an unmoving target.

The Devas, the immortal rishis, the gandharvas and apsaras, all the celestial ones had gathered in the akasa to watch the fateful battle. Indra cried, "They are almost equal as archers. But the Rakshasa has his chariot, while Rama fights on foot."

He called Matali, his own sarathy, and sent him down to the blue prince. In the midst of the stunning duel, a chariot from another world appeared, shimmering, before Rama. Jewels shone at its pillars, its green horses glowed, and their manes seemed to be made of moonlight. The golden thing did not rest on the earth, but hovered two hands above the ground, pulsing. Silver moon bells tinkled on its roof, the garlands around the emerald horses' throats were lambent. Matali stepped down from that ratha and folded his hands to Rama.

The starry sarathy said, "My Lord Indra has sent you his own chariot, his golden bow, and his arrows that are lightning. He sends you his shakti. Rama, my horses will obey your thoughts."

Rama smiled at Lakshmana; this was the same chariot they had watched secretly outside Sharabhanga's asrama in the Dandaka vana. Rama remembered what Agastya had said, that when the time came Indra would send his own chariot to him. While Lakshmana held the storming Rakshasa at bay, Rama worshipped the ratha. After folding his hands to it, he climbed in. Like light Matali flashed away into the sky, with Rama behind him, splendid as Mahavishnu.

Ravana greeted Rama with a cool and deadly gandharvastra. Rama loosed a gandharvastra of his own. Full of hidden flames, the weapons fused in the sky. But neither could quell the other, and they fell away into the sea far below, where they burned blood red beneath the waves until they were extinguished in the deep.

Rama shot a devastra at the Rakshasa; but he had one of his own. These, too, locked together in a fervid duel of their archers' wills. But the astras' fires were exhausted before either warrior would submit. Ravana summoned a rakshasastra of a thousand shafts. It spumed into the sky and fell on Rama's chariot, its every barb a serpent; their hoods were flames and they spat smoking venom. The sky was full of shining hamadryads, flying at blue Rama.

But Rama was enthralled with the duel in the air. He admired his enemy's prowess, which for once matched his own. He relished being finally tested to the limits. The kshatriya strung his bow with a garudastra. Suddenly a thousand birds of prey were in the firmament. The monkeys and demons on the ground below cried out in wonder, and the golden eagles hunted the green serpents with crystal claw and beak.

Ravana turned back to common arrows. Whistling and sharp, they flew at Rama and Matali; and not even with the unearthly horses' fleetness, nor Indra's sarathy's dazzling skill, could all the shafts be dodged. Many found their mark, painfully, and one cut the banner from the Deva's chariot. When Ravana's arrows pierced Rama, it is told the sea swelled in tidal waves, as if to reach up into the sky to tend his wounds. They say the sun grew dim, as if he had a fever. Mangala reached out to stroke Visakha, the star of the Ikshvakus, over which Indra and Agni rule.

Ravana was as magnificent as Himavan's son Mainaka. The Rakshasa pressed Rama hard, and for a moment it seemed the prince could find no answer to him. Gentle Rama had not imagined Ravana would be quite such an adversary. He glared at the Rakshasa across the sky, as if to burn him up with his gaze. The earth quailed at Rama's anger. Tigers and leopards scuttled into their caves. The birds of the air wheeled in frenzy, screaming, because the very sky shrank from the rage in Rama's eyes. For a moment even Ravana shivered.

Roaring to drown his doubts, nine heads seething around the central one, the Demon seized up a pale trisula. Triune fires glowed at its points when the Rakshasa's hand touched it. The quarters echoed with Ravana's roar, at the bolt of power that surged through his body. The trisula was a great and olden ayudha; no one had ever withstood it.

Whirling the thing of white flames in his hands, Ravana cried, "Here comes your death, human. All the rakshasas you killed are waiting for you in the next world!"

With a howl, he cast his trident at Rama. Like the agni from Siva's eye it flew, a gash of fire through the sky. The report of its flight was of a hundred thunderclaps. It seemed the stuff of time would be torn asunder by that weapon. How could even the Avatara withstand its awesome power? Spewing invisible flames, the trisula came for Rama's life.

The Devas and rishis shut their eyes. They could not believe any man of flesh and blood could stand before that weapon, which not only burned the body but consumed the soul. Time stood still in the sky between the two chariots, and the fate of the worlds hung in the balance. Slowly, taking a lifetime, Ravana's trisula flew at Rama. In that frozen moment, Rama strung his bow and shot a hundred arrows at the macabre thing. But they were burned to ashes and fell away. The missile came on, inexorably.

Rama's face twitched in despair. Hardly knowing what he did any more, reaching blindly into the depths of his will, he found Indra's shakti in the chariot. Just in time, the last shred of an instant he had left, he cast it at Ravana's trident. The explosion in the air was as if the sun had blown apart. On the ground, the rakshasas and the vanaras covered their eyes with their hands; or they would have been blinded. Rama and Ravana shut their eyes. But the shakti of light put out the trisula of darkness, and both fell away to the earth. The unbearable splendor died out of the sky; demon and prince fought once more.

Ravana was shaken. He lurched briefly in his chariot, and at once Rama found him with three golden barbs. The Rakshasa screamed in rage. He stood like an asoka tree in bloom, crimson flowers unfurled on him. But no vital organ was struck, and his wounds were not deep or inflicted with any astra. Ravana plucked out the shafts and fought on. But the duel drained him. Now his face and his hands were those of an ancient beast's, thousands of years old; his skin was like dry parchment.

The chariots dazzled with their speed; they were like the magic wind. They flew on earth and through the air, their unearthly horses in blinding contention, spurred by just their charioteers' thoughts. Often, both stopped at once, as if by tacit agreement that their warriors needed to rest. After a panting pause, one archer would loose his stream of arrows again, and the other would reply.

Into one of those intervals Rama cried, "I have heard you were a great tapasvin once. Today you are just a thief, and like a thief you will die."

Rama's aim was as true as when the battle began; but Ravana fumbled at his bow. His arms were sluggish and his aim was wayward. He dared not acknowledge it, but he was tired. Each moment, Rama covered the Rakshasa with a hundred arrows from his superb bow. Then Ravana fainted. Instantly, his sarathy vanished out of the sky with his king. He landed in a quiet grove, on another hillside across the island.

When the Demon revived, he sat up in the chariot and looked around him. He gave a hiss of anger when he saw they had flown the battle. He screamed at his sarathy, "What have you done? Does a warrior ever run from war? Because you were terrified by Rama's arrows, the world will say I am a coward. Fool, fly back to the fight!"

But his head still spun with weakness. Gently his sarathy said, "I am no fool, my lord; nor am I afraid. For centuries I have served you faithfully. Today, for the first time, I saw you were tired and in mortal danger. It is a sarathy's sacred dharma to protect his warrior's life.

Omens of death were all around us, and Rama's arrows flew at us like time. You were hardly yourself after he cut down your trisula. You were full of age and then you swooned. I had to fly you out of danger; what else could I do?"

That loyal rakshasa spoke calmly, and at once Ravana softened. He said, "You move me with your love. But I have recovered now. Brave friend, fly back into battle. I must drink Rama's blood today."

The rakshasa turned to lash his horses again; Ravana stopped him, laying a hand on his shoulder. When the sarathy turned around, he saw his king had taken a bracelet studded with diamonds and pearls from his wrist and was offering it to him in gratitude. Bowing to his great master, tears in his eyes, the charioteer accepted the gift and turned his chariot back to the battle.

Agastya watched the relucent duel from the akasa between heaven and earth. He saw Ravana faint and his sarathy make the ratha invisible and leave the field. It was then that rishi came to Rama in Indra's chariot. He came in a sukshma rupa, a spirit form like bright vapor.

Agastya said, "Rama, worship your ancestor the Sun. The Adityahridaya is one of the oldest of all mantras. Worship Surya Deva with it, whom the Devas and the Asuras both revere, and you will kill Ravana today."

Agastya taught Rama the pristine mantra, and then vanished. Rama flew down to the earth. He asked for holy water; thrice he dipped his fingers in that water, and thrice, as Agastya taught him, he chanted the Adityahridaya, the heart of the Sun. It seemed the star blazed more brilliantly in the sky. Deep peace came over Rama, a living tide enfolding him. He felt his lucific ancestor had heard him, and touched him with a powerful blessing.

Then Ravana came flying back into battle. For a moment, Rama thought he saw Surya Deva appear before him and whisper, "Hurry!"

Rama flew up in Indra's chariot to face the Emperor of evil.

39. At the twilight hour

Ravana's black horses frothed as he stormed back into battle. Rama said to Matali, "Look, he comes the inauspicious way of apradakshina. He ignores all the omens and gives in to his deepest desire: to die."

Matali urged his horses forward; he came from the right, the way of pradakshina. The dust from Rama's wheels covered Ravana's chariot. Flying up, the Rakshasa shot a cloud of arrows at Rama. Now Rama put down his own weapon and picked up Indra's golden bow.

The sky was full of Devas and gandharvas, kinnaras and maharishis, gathered in the ethereal zone, breathlessly, to watch Ravana die. More omens appeared in the sky; they all favored Rama. The way the wind blew was for him. Ravana's chariot was covered in a red sheen, as if it was painted in blood. Kites and vultures wheeled around it, as though it already flew with the dead. The rakshasas of Lanka saw these omens and were terrified. Rama sensed victory.

Spellbound, the rakshasas and vanaras stood motionless, like figures in a mural of frozen time. None of them fought any more; their battle would be decided by the duel that raged between the two flitting chariots. But as if fate had petrified his gifts, Ravana's prowess had deserted him. Cursing the unaccountable stupor, he aimed repeatedly at Rama's horses and his sarathy. But his shafts were wayward and great weakness was upon him. It seemed that at last all the debts of karma he owed had overtaken Ravana, at once.

His hands trembled, and his body; Rama had drained his will. Even the effort of drawing back his bowstring was almost more than the Rakshasa could manage. He felt his vast age intensely; the deaths of all his brothers and sons had breached his soul. He gritted his teeth and roared to embolden himself. Though he knew his time had come, he was determined to die a heroic death. All his ten heads plain, chattering and screeching around the central one, Ravana fought on.

They battled in the sky and on the ground, and at times the chariots flew out some leagues over the sea. Air, earth, water, fire, and ether were hushed when Rama and Ravana dueled. Primordial forces of light and darkness, dharma and adharma, battled through the two warriors: yet again, in endless time. The wind did not blow any more. The sun was dim as if he, too, held his fiery breath.

The Devas grew anxious that despite all the portents, the duel was lasting so long. They began to wonder if Rama could kill Ravana, actually finish him. For hadn't all of them tasted defeat from the Demon? Always serene, and aware of the deeper purposes of fate, the rishis of Devaloka began to chant timeless mantras to bless creation.

"May darkness and evil be overcome, and men live without fear in the world. May danger leave the earth today; may Rama kill Ravana."

A gandharva whispered to the enchanting apsara beside him, "The sea is just its own metaphor, and the sky, also. And this duel between a man and a monster can only be compared to itself."

One of Rama's arrows whistled perilously near Ravana's heads; in a flash the cluster of nine faces vanished. Just then, another golden shaft from the Avatara's bow struck Ravana's central head from its neck. The Demon's scream rang through the sky. But he did not fall. As Rama watched, in shock, another devilish head sprouted from the Rakshasa's gaping throat, like a hideous flower from its stem.

This grotesque green face grimaced, three-eyed, at Rama. A forked serpent's tongue flickered across its lips. Its eyes were lidless, yellow, and utterly malignant. Ravana raised his bow again. Now he fought with fresh vigor, as if the beheading had renewed him!

Rama loosed another silver shaft at his enemy and took the second head off in a scarlet burst. Ravana's roar echoed down among the monkeys and demons; the sea rose in crested waves. The Rakshasa staggered in his chariot, almost falling. But then, once more, like a weird plant thrusting forth its horrible fruit, another grisly head pushed its way out of Ravana's neck. Now it was a less demonic visage that roared at Rama in the sky; it was a head more like the first one.

So these were not the heads of the sinister cone. It was not to be that Rama would sever ten heads and victory would be his. For the first time doubt gripped the prince. With each fresh head that sprouted on the Rakshasa's neck, he seemed rejuvenated; after the second head was struck off, he fought as if he had just come into battle. The shafts from his bow were a virile stream between the chariots. Ravana's face, his hands, and his skin were unwrinkled and young again.

Still wrapped in a pall of dread, the sun began to sink into the western sea. Twilight fell. Now the chariots were luminous, their horses glowed, and the warriors were illumined by the light of their arrows. Once more, Rama struck off Ravana's head. Again, the Rakshasa sprouted a fiendish one in its place and fought on, chortling in mirth.

Matali turned to Rama and cried, "This is Ravana you are fighting, and it is the new moon tonight. As night grows, his strength will be ten times what it is now. If you do not kill him quickly, Rama, you yourself will die."

Rama looked at Matali with a silent question in his eyes. The sarathy said, "Only the brahmastra."

Rama saw Agastya's austere face before his eyes again, and the rishi seemed to smile, endorsing what Matali said. Rama invoked the astra that Brahma had once created for the king of the Devas.

He murmured its hermetic mantra, and that ultimate weapon, which could extinguish a world, appeared before him brilliant as an aurora in the twilight. Vayu was its wings, Agni its head; Akasa was its shaft and it was as heavy as golden Meru.

With a prayer, Rama stretched out his hands to receive the astra. At once it lay as a golden arrow in his palms. He set it to his bowstring, and the sky shook as if its end had come: all the elements feared that astra. But Rama did not pause now; the shaft was as heavy as time in his hands. He clenched his teeth and, though his heart pounded out of control, he drew his bowstring to his ear in a fluid blur. With Sita's face before his eyes, Rama shot the brahmastra at Ravana.

A crack of thunder rent the air, and for a moment wrenched the earth out of her orbit. Briefly it was day again, as if the sun had leaped back into the sky after setting in the sea. But the other sun, the legendary ayudha, blazed into Ravana's chest. With the Demon's terrible scream, as it struck him, night fell on the world.

The brahmastra tore open Ravana's armor with fire. It ripped through his chest in an eruption of blood. Then it blew his heart to shreds. It bored on, through him, flashed down into the earth and pierced deep into her. It flamed on down, through rock and lava, to the core of the world, and the earth's molten heart could not contain that weapon. It rose again, through all the layers of the earth, and flew back into the sky and Rama's quiver. There it grew still.

The two charioteers brought their chariots down to the ground. In one Rama stood triumphant, and in the other Ravana lay dying. Blood gushed from the wound in his chest, but his body still shone like a piece of star. Not once did Ravana cry out as life ebbed from him through the gaping wound. But as he died, his eyes gazed with strange longing at the Blue One, standing so calm in Indra's chariot: Rama, so merciful in victory.

Visravas's son, Pulastya's grandson, the great-grandson of Brahma himself, he who had been sovereign of the three worlds for longer than the Devas cared to remember, great, great Ravana lay dying from Rama's arrow and from fate. As his burning eyes misted over, the rakshasas and vanaras, who had gathered around him in a hush, saw his lips move. Repeatedly they tried to form a single word, a name: the name of her who had become his death. Her perfect face filled the Rakshasa's last moment. Then his lips did not move any more; his torn chest did not heave. Life had left Ravana.

Even in death, his body glowed for hours, like a dark flame on Lanka.

40. The fallen king

Like the sun that falls on the earth at the end of the ages, Ravana lay on the field of battle. For a moment the rakshasas stood petrified to see him. Then, roaring in terror, they fled back into Lanka. The vanaras' jubilation echoed across the hillside. Unearthly music broke out in the sky, as Deva and gandharva, kinnara and apsara, exulted. A rain of heaven's flowers fell on Rama and his army of the jungle, and its fragrance was borne on the wind across island and sea. Quickly, that fragrance spread through the world, like joyful news. Mountain and river, forest and bird, plant, animal and knowing sage rejoiced.

The moon rose over the earth and bathed the momentous battlefield in silver. Rama stood radiant among his vanaras: he had fulfilled the mission of his life, the reason he was born. He had done the impossible. Sugriva, Vibheeshana, and Lakshmana gathered around him. Slowly they walked to where Ravana lay, his chest bloody where the brahmastra had torn him open, but his dark face finally at peace. Even in death, the Rakshasa was absolutely majestic. When Vibheeshana saw his brother lying there, as if asleep in the moonlight, he began to cry.

Rama laid a hand on Vibheeshana's arm. He said compassionately, "He was fearless to the last. Not even at the very end, when all his sons, brothers, and commanders were dead, did he try to bargain for his life. Kings like him are never mourned, not since the beginning."

Vibheeshana said wistfully, "No one could face Ravana; Indra and his host could not stand his valor. But against you he was broken like a wave against a shore. Yes, his life was a full one; he tasted all the pleasures of the earth, to surfeit. He was generous to a fault. Such gifts he gave away when he was pleased: jewels the size of a man's fist, gold in caskets.

"And he was more than merely a great king. He was a master of the Vedas, more learned than most brahmanas. But at last, fate wanted to bring him down, because he was unfeeling and cruel as well. He became selfish and arrogant, and time hunted him.

"With your leave, Rama, I will offer my brother's spirit tarpana."

Rama said, "With death enmity ends; now Ravana is as much my kinsman as yours. By all means, offer him tarpana."

Then, the news having reached them, the women of Ravana's harem streamed onto the field. They came wailing, their hair loose. Crying his name in a piteous lament, they came for a last look at their lord. These were women whom not even the sun had seen; now they poured out from the palace and the city, demented with grief.

Like a great tree uprooted, Ravana lay under the moon. Like creepers that cling to such a tree even when it has fallen, his women clung to him. Their cries echoed through the grim field. Some fell at his feet and kissed them; some stroked his riven chest with shaking fingers. Others fell in a swoon when they saw him like that, his blood spreading in a stain under him. One fair rakshasi took his head onto her lap.

As if to herself she whispered, "This was Ravana whom Indra could not face. This was our king from whom Yama fled."

Another took up her litany, but louder now: "This was Ravana who vanquished the king of yakshas in battle, and took Kubera's vimana and his nine treasures for himself."

Another said, for the dead must be extolled, "Not the rishis of Devaloka, not the gandharvas dared face him."

Another beautiful one: "The Devas couldn't face him. But look where he lies, killed by a mortal man."

"If only he had listened to those who wished him well."

"Sita was the death of him."

"And of all the rakshasas. But Ravana would not listen to anyone."

"It was fate. His time had come."

"It was decided long ago that he would die at the hands of a man. Fate deluded him even then, or he would have asked for Brahma's boon against men as well."

"It was fate that the greatest king of all, the bravest, the most tender and generous one, should lie dead today, his breast torn open by a fearful weapon."

And they sobbed inconsolably.

41. *Mandodari*

Suddenly, a hush fell on those women. They arose from the king's body and stood aside. Last of all, Ravana's queen, Mandodari, came to mourn her husband. She had not yet shed any tears. She came only now because the messenger who had gone to her had found her at prayer. When he gave her the news, she received it calmly, as if she already knew Ravana was dead.

Now for a long moment she stood staring at her husband. Slowly, she sank down to the ground beside him. Her body shook with grief like an ocean storm. She began to speak to Ravana as if he were alive and lying on his bed in the harem. She spoke quietly, not as if death separated them with its abyss.

Mandodari said, "How did this happen, my lord? That a mere man has killed you, Ravana, whom Indra could not contain. As I prayed for you today, I saw you in my mind as I have always imagined you at war: your eyes full of fire, your roars shaking the sky, your hands reaching for arrow after arrow to bury in your enemies' hearts. Instead, here you are, lying in this sleep you will never wake from."

She stroked his lofty brow, his face touched with a peaceful smile, now that all his conflict was over. She said, "Ravana, this silence does not suit you. I see you with your chest torn open and the great heart in it stilled. I see you before my eyes, but I cannot believe what I see. It will take me a long time; perhaps I shall never believe it; possibly I am dreaming.

"Ah, my lord, I warned you when I heard how Khara had died. I told you this Rama is not just a man. But you scoffed at my fear; you thought I was jealous and said I had lost my reason. I was jealous of her, yes, but it was not I who had lost my reason. Precious Ravana, it was you: that you could deceive yourself that a kshatriya who could kill fourteen thousand rakshasas by himself was just another man. Look at the price you have paid. Oh, look at the wound in your chest. Who will heal this wound?

"No, Rama is not just a man. He is someone else come as a man to kill you. But we were warned. When Khara, Dushana, and Trisiras were killed, we were warned. When Hanuman flew into Lanka, where the wind hardly comes, we were warned. When the monkey set our city on fire, we were warned. Would a hero like Hanuman serve anyone who was not immeasurably greater than himself? Ravana, there were those in your own sabha who told you that Rama is Vishnu born as a man, just to kill you.

"But you would not listen. He is the Paramatman, the Ancient and Eternal One, who has no beginning or end. His army of the jungle are all spawn of the Devas. They are the Devas themselves come down as monkeys to finish you. But if I told you this while you lived, you would have said I was fanciful and envious.

"Ravana, it is not a man who has killed you. How could a man ever kill you? Narayana has taken your life back to himself. Once you were a master of yourself. You sat in a tapasya such as the world had never seen, and Siva and Brahma blessed you with great boons. But when your evil time came, and all of ours, your own mind turned against you. When a king isn't a master of himself any more, how will he rule his kingdom?"

Her voice was a whisper. "You should have worshipped Sita. She is as pure as life itself, as sacred. Instead, you lusted after her. You should have sought her blessing, but you wanted her for your bed."

Deeply, deeply, the lovely Mandodari sighed. "Your antapura was always full of the most beautiful women of all the noble races. Look at me, my husband; in what way am I less beautiful than Sita? In what way am I less well born? But fate deluded you, and Sita came into your life as your death. No man can turn his death away, and you could not resist her.

"But now Sita will go back to Rama and they will be united again. While I . . . Oh, Ravana, how will I live in this cruel world without you? How will I bear the sorrow that tears my heart just as Rama's astra tore yours? Answer me, my lord, answer me!"

She sighed again, "No, you will not. You lie here, with all the glory drained from your fierce face. Your eyes, which blazed like suns, are shut forever; never again will I have the look of love from them you once used to turn on me. Or your smile of so much humor and majesty. Ah, look at the dust that already covers your face in its heartless film."

Mandodari trembled under the moon, as if a great cold was in her bones. Softly, she went on, her eyes never leaving Ravana's face. "How arrogant I was; I thought no one could ever kill you. My father is Mayaa, Lord of the Danavas, my husband was Ravana of the rakshasas, and my son was Indrajit, who hauled the king of the Devas through the streets of Lanka. Great was my pride, great my security.

Now, in a few savage days, I have lost both my husband and my son. Look at you; I cannot even hold you in my arms for the arrows that pierce your body. Ravana, is this really happening, or is it a dream from which we will both awaken?

"When Indrajit died, death called me in my heart. But how could I kill myself when you were still alive? But you did not feel the same love for me. Or you would not lie here like this, not speaking or stirring. Did I offend you that you have chosen to punish me so bitterly? Oh, this is the curse of the thousands of women whose husbands you killed.

"When I think of how you abducted Sita, that was not like you at all. You behaved like a coward and a thief, luring Rama away and then stealing her from him: you, who have never been afraid of anyone. It was your death come for you and we did not see it. Look at you, husband, lying there as if it is the earth you love and her arms you would rather sleep in than mine."

Only now tears welled in her eyes and rolled down her face. Grief overwhelmed her; without another word, Mandodari fell unconscious across Ravana's corpse. The other women came forward to revive her.

Then Rama came there, and said to Vibheeshana, "Before his body begins to decay, let him be carried into the city and prepared for the last rites. Let the women be persuaded to return to their antapura."

Vibheeshana coaxed Mandodari and the others back into Lanka. They went, crying aloud, with a hundred last glances at their fallen king, heartbroken because they knew they would never see his face again.

42. A new king in Lanka

Ravana's dark body was washed and prepared for the final tarpana. But suddenly Vibheeshana cried, "I will not perform the last rites. He was not a man of dharma, but a liar and a killer. He was not my brother, but my enemy. He was conceited and lustful. He was a monster: his eyes always strayed to other men's wives. An older brother should be worshipped like a father, but I did not respect Ravana. I will not offer tarpana for him; he does not deserve it."

Laying a hand on the noble rakshasa's arm, Rama said gently, "It is your dharma, and you must do it, my friend. True, your brother was a sinner, but he was also a great king. Now he is dead, and you must offer him tarpana, so his spirit is gathered safely to his fathers.

"Look at him now: the past is finished; death has released Ravana from himself. See how peaceful his face is."

Vibheeshana found solace in Rama's voice. He spoke so mercifully and so truly, there was no resisting him. Vibheeshana ordered his rakshasas to lift his brother's body onto the pyre that had been piled at the edge of the city. A fire was lit with mantras, and Vibheeshana touched Ravana's body alight with the flames. With sesamum and holy water, Vibheeshana offered solemn tarpana to his brother, to slake his thirst on the journey he had embarked upon.

Vibheeshana bathed in cold water to purify his body. Wearing a wet cloth round his waist, he mixed sesame seeds and blades of green grass with holy water. He offered these for anjali to Ravana's soul. Facing south, he prostrated himself on the ground. Ravana's women still came crowding near the crackling pyre. Vibheeshana asked them to return to the antapura, saying, "It is not proper for you to be here."

Rama stood with Hanuman, Lakshmana, Sugriva, Angada, and the other vanara chieftains around him. With folded hands, Vibheeshana came to Rama. Above them, the subtle akasa was empty again. The Devas and the other celestials had gone back to their glorious cities and timeless gardens, to celebrate Ravana's death. Rama was being hymned in all the tongues of grace, which have been spoken since before the world was made and are the ancestors of our earthly languages. The wisdom of Sugriva was being praised, the loyalty of Lakshmana and Hanuman. In their airy halls, gandharvas sang and apsaras danced; for at last it was true that Ravana was indeed dead. The darkness they had been plunged in for eons had been broken, and their spirits soared in freedom.

On earth, Rama went to Matali and embraced him. At the critical moment, it had been Indra's inspired sarathy who told him to invoke the brahmastra. He walked around the unearthly chariot in pradakshina, and stroked the wonderful horses' heads. "Swift as light you were," Rama said to them. "My victory is at least half yours."

They nuzzled their faces against him. Then Matali folded his hands to Rama, flew up into the sky in a blaze of splendor, and flashed across the threshold that divides the earth from the realm of the Gods.

Rama came to Sugriva and hugged him, again and again. He cried, "We have won, my friend. My loyal friend, we have won."

With Sugriva beside him, Rama stood at the heart of the vanara army. He said aloud to Lakshmana, "Child, Vibheeshana is a true friend. Without him, and his timely advice on so many occasions, we could never have won this war. Take him into the city, and crown him king of Lanka."

Lakshmana asked for a golden urn to be filled with water from the sea. Surrounded by the triumphant vanaras, Lakshmana entered Lanka. He set Vibheeshana on the crystal throne, on which Ravana had sat, and drenched the new king with the water in abhisheka. The priests of the island kingdom intoned sacred mantras. As the ceremony progressed, the rakshasas who had survived the war came out of their homes, where they had hidden in fear. They streamed through the streets to the palace to witness the crowning.

Around Vibheeshana, and now as his ministers, sat the four loyal rakshasas who had flown out of Lanka with him. When the coronation was over, the people showered fried rice grains on their new king and the brightest, most fragrant flowers from the forests and gardens of the island. Vibheeshana came out of the city with these and offered them to Rama. Smiling, Rama received the auspicious gifts from the king of the rakshasas.

43. Hanuman and Sita

Rama turned to Hanuman. He said, "Wise one, ask Vibheeshana's leave to enter his city. Go to the asokavana and tell Sita that Ravana is dead. Tell her I am alive and well, and Lakshmana and Sugriva also. Tell her Vibheeshana is king in Lanka, and bring back her message to me."

Hanuman rose and flew to the asokavana. Sita sat there under the same shimshupa tree where he had first approached her. Surrounded by rakshasis, she sat sorrowing still. Unhappy as Rohini separated from the Moon sat lovely Sita. Hanuman came and stood before her with folded hands. The rakshasis sprang up in fear and backed away from the son of the wind. They had seen what he did when he last came here.

For just a moment, she stared blankly, not knowing him for her grief. Then she recognized him and a small tumult of hope broke out on her face. Hanuman said softly, "Devi, Rama is alive and well. Lakshmana and Sugriva are with him. The war has been won. Your prince has killed Ravana, as you asked him to, and he has crowned Vibheeshana king of Lanka. Rama says to you:

" 'It is my good fortune you are alive to share in my victory. Let peace be upon you, Sita, your enemy is dead. Vibheeshana is king in Lanka now and you are in your own brother's house. He will come to you shortly, to bring you to me.' "

Sita was speechless. Hanuman stood before her, waiting, but she only shook her head from side to side and spoke no word. Anxiously, he asked, "What is it, Devi? Is my news not good, that you give me no message for Rama?"

Then she cried, "It is my joy, my boundless joy, Hanuman, which ties my tongue! How shall I reward you for bringing such news to me? No gift, no words can express what I feel. Nothing is good enough for you, nothing can repay my debt to you, for everything you have done."

Blushing, Hanuman said, "Devi, your affection shines like heaven's light. For me all the treasures of the earth cannot equal your affection. I see the smile on your face; I see Rama happy and my heart is full. I feel I have conquered the three worlds."

Sita smiled, bewitchingly, and said, "Hanuman, there is no one in all those worlds who can speak to me as sweetly as you do! Oh, you are the noblest, bravest, and kindest friend anyone could have."

Now Hanuman looked around him with a glitter in his eyes. "I have one favor to ask you. These rakshasis have tormented you for so long; let me have the pleasure of tearing them limb from limb."

He growled and the rakshasis shrank whimpering from him. But Sita laughed and said, "They were only servants of their master, and obedient to his will. They themselves are blameless. They will not ill-treat me any more, now that he is dead. Let us not judge them; I must have sinned in my last life, that I was condemned to suffer for a year in this one, to suffer captivity and terror and, worst of all, being separated from my Rama. I must have sinned heinously, that I made him suffer so much.

"But all that is over now. Rama always says that mercy and goodness are the only ornaments worth wearing. No one is sinless, Hanuman; let us be forgiving."

Hanuman struggled with himself for a moment. Finally he said, "You are truly the wife of the greatest man who ever lived. Let me go back to Rama and tell him how pleased you are. He waits impatiently for me."

Sita rose. Sensing she had something more to say, Hanuman paused. Her eyes turned down, she said shyly, "Tell Rama I am eager to see him."

Hanuman said, "Devi, in no time you and he will be together again, even like Indra and his Sachi!"

She whispered, "Fly, sweet Hanuman."

Hanuman rose into the sky and flew back to Rama.

44. Another Rama

Hanuman brought Sita's message to Rama. When the prince heard she was waiting to see him, his eyes brimmed over. Then he fell silent and was plunged in thought.

At last he turned to Vibheeshana and said, "My friend, I have no wish to see how she suffered. I could not bear it. Let her bathe, put on silks and ornaments, and come to me as she used to be."

With his women, Vibheeshana went to Sita in the asokavana. They brought silks and jewelry for her. But with grave dignity she said, "I will go to Rama as I am. He must see me like this."

Vibheeshana said, "Rama asked me to bring you holy water to bathe in, and silks and gold. How can I disobey him?"

Sita did not protest further, but went with the women. She allowed them to wash her filthy, tangled hair, and comb it out as gently as they could; for it was matted like jata. She allowed them to wash a year's dirt from her thin body. They draped her in fine silks and adorned her with ornaments fit for Rama's queen. They dabbed subtle perfumes over her, and made up her eyes and lips. When she looked at herself in the mirror they held up, Sita smiled: she was beautiful again for her husband.

Vibheeshana ordered a royal palanquin fetched, to carry Sita to Rama. He went before her, back to the prince. Smiling, he said, "She has come, Rama."

A wave of excitement rippled through the vanara army. The monkeys were agog to see her for whose sake they had come to Lanka. But Rama was distraught; there was dark conflict on his face. One moment, he felt ecstatic at the thought of seeing Sita again, and the next, a nameless rage gripped his heart.

Finally he said, "Let her come to me."

The vanaras and rakshasas gathered there surged toward the golden palanquin. Vibheeshana signaled his guards and they began to beat back the crowd with the staffs of fire they carried. They overdid this, hardly being well disposed toward the monkeys. The crowd roared its anger at them like a sea.

Rama jumped up and cried to Vibheeshana, "What is this? These are my own people, my kinsmen. They cannot be treated like this.

"A woman's chastity is her protection, not walls and weapons. Let them look at her, even as they look at me. And let her see me surrounded by those who helped me rescue her. In exceptional circumstances, the people may look upon a woman: in war, or when she is in trouble; during her wedding, or at a yagna." He bit his lip. "There has been a war for Sita's sake, and she is in trouble."

Lakshmana, Sugriva, and Hanuman stared at him in amazement. Vibheeshana went quietly to the palanquin to fetch Sita. With each moment that passed, Rama's disturbance grew. He frowned; he clenched his hands and stood taut as a streak of lightning. Vibheeshana helped Sita down from the litter and led her slowly to Rama.

She shrank from the thousands of eyes that stared at her. She blushed at the gasp from the crowd, when the monkeys saw she was more beautiful than they had dreamed. She covered her face. At long last, she stood before Rama. She saw his dark face, and stood gazing at what she saw as if it was her very life, which she had lost and regained. She whispered, "My lord!"

Her eyes swam with tears and her heart beat as if it would burst for joy. But Rama avoided her gaze. There was no smile of love or welcome on his lips. Looking away, and in a voice he did not use even with his enemies, he said to her, "Devi, I have vindicated my honor. Ravana wronged me and I killed him."

His tone was cold and his words were like needles in her bewildered mind for their haughty aloofness. Sita still trembled, but not with joy any more. In the same icy voice she could hardly believe was his, he went on, "Great was Hanuman's valor when he leaped across the ocean, and Sugriva's and Lakshmana's in war. Vibheeshana came to me, abandoning his own brother; without him, victory could never have been ours."

She shivered like a deer before a tiger, and her eyes were full of very different tears now: hot tears of anguish sprang in them. He looked at her briefly, and the sight of her face only fed his strange fury, as butter does a fire. He seemed to summon courage for what he had to say to her next.

He drew a deep breath. "I came to avenge Ravana's affront to me, and that I have done. For my honor and the honor of the House of Ikshvaku, I came to kill him. I came because of dharma."

He paused. Then, as if plunging a spike of ice into her, he said, "Do not think for a moment, Sita, that I came for your sake. Your name is a stain on our family. It pains me to even look at you. You can go wherever you like. I have rescued you, as I swore I would; I owe you nothing more. No man of honor can take home a woman who has lived in his enemy's house for as many moons as you have.

"I feel nothing for you. You can go with whomever you choose: Lakshmana or Bharata, Sugriva or Vibheeshana. It will not matter to me. Seek your fortune, since you have already been with Ravana for so long."

A hush had fallen; the stunned crowd hardly breathed. Just once more, helplessly, Rama looked into Sita's face, as if to seek something there that he could not bear to find. Then he turned away, red-eyed. Sita stood before him, as stricken as Ravana had been by the brahmastra, her heart breaking with each searing word he said, before all those vanaras and rakshasas. Tears flowed down her face and fell to the ground. She bowed her head down, right down, as if to bury it.

45. Agni pariksha

The vanaras could not believe this was the gentle prince they knew speaking. At last, Sita herself cried in a ragged voice, "You are full of wretched suspicion, Rama, and speak like any ordinary man. Don't you believe that I was faithful to you? Ravana touched me only once, when he dragged me from our asrama and flew with me to Lanka. And then, surely, the fault was fate's, that I was not strong enough to

494

resist him. How can you suspect me like this? I have been in torment being apart from you.

"I swear to you, I was entirely chaste; every moment I thought only of you. If you were so full of doubt, why didn't you tell Hanuman to bring your true feelings to me? I would have killed myself at once, and you would not have had to fight this war. Instead, you sent him with lies. Not for a moment did I know this is how you felt, this despicable jealousy. You have ruined me with your suspicion, Rama; how could you think this of me?

"Everything is futile: your victory, Ravana's death. At least he was not a hypocrite with me. I followed you to the forest when you were banished. I lived there with you for thirteen years, and still you doubt me. Or is it yourself that you do not trust, Rama?"

Her breath came in gasps; tears streamed down her face. And now, anger was in her voice. Her eyes flashing, she said, "You are meant to be a man of perfect dharma. Some say you are Vishnu's own Avatara. But you are just common, Rama, as base as any other man. You say again and again that you are born into a noble house; you boast of your great honor. But what about my honor, that you have humiliated me like this, after everything I have endured?

"I am Janaka's daughter, don't forget, and the Earth is my mother. Once, you took my hand and called me your wife. Have you forgotten that now? Or have I been a bad wife to you?"

Rama did not so much as look at her and his face remained a mask. With a wail, Sita turned to Lakshmana.

"Lakshmana, you have always done whatever I asked. I cannot bear the accusation that I am tainted. Your brother has abandoned me in the midst of this crowd. I have nothing to live for any more, when Rama tells me to go where I please, with whomever I choose. I choose to go to my death. Make a fire for me, Lakshmana; my place will be at its heart."

For the first time in his life, Lakshmana turned darkly to his brother. But Rama was made of stone; no flicker of feeling showed on his face. He stood staring at the ground. Lakshmana looked at him with the mute question: should he obey Sita? With awful silence, Rama said he should. Helpless, his eyes also streaming, Lakshmana began to build a pyre.

The vanaras stood mute, staggered by this Rama they now saw.

The fire caught and blazed. Sita made a pradakshina around her cold husband. She folded her hands to him and approached the flames.

She folded her hands to the agni, and said in a ringing voice, "If it is true that I have never for a moment been untrue to Rama in thought or deed, protect me, ancient Agni, witness of the world. Rama says I am tainted. If the sun, the moon, the wind, and my mother, the Earth, know I am pure, let these flames not burn me. Let the world know Sita is sinless."

Completely beautiful, she walked grimly around the fire, another flame herself. Then without a trace of fear or a backward glance, she walked into it. A gasp rose from the vanaras, and Lakshmana cried out. The flames were twice as tall as the slight, exquisite Sita; in the shocked silence, she stood at their white heart. She was the color of her golden ornaments, and the screams of the rakshasi women of Lanka filled the air.

In the sky, the Devas and gandharvas saw her, molten, in Agni's burning clasp. She was like a Goddess cast into hell by a curse. The ones of light, the witnesses of the ages, had never seen anything like this before. Though his eyes were now full of tears and his mind full of anguish, Rama did not stir. He stood staring at the ground.

46. The miraculous sky

Out of the sky Brahma's sons, the Saptarishi, cried to Rama, "How can you stand there and watch Sita burn? You are the Avatara. You are the Ancient One, the embodiment of all the virtues, the Compassionate One."

There was a flash of light from heaven, then another and another. A miracle unfolded above: golden vimanas appeared, a flotilla of gleaming ships of the firmament. In them rode Kubera, Yama, Indra, Varuna, and Siva. Brahma was there, mounted on his white swan. Ineffable splendor filled the sky.

But Rama said humbly, "As far as I know, I am just Dasaratha's son. I have heard about the prophecies, and it is true Ravana is dead. But I have never thought of myself as being anyone more than Rama, or of my life as being exceptional. If there are any deep and fateful reasons for my birth, let the Lord Brahma enlighten me about them."

The four-faced Creator, iridescent in the sky, said in his voice of ages, "Rama, you are Narayana. You are the Parabrahman, without beginning or end, who came as Matsya and Kurma, Varaha and Vamana, Narasimha and Parasurama.

"Rama, you create, nurture, and consume the universe. You are the sanctuary of the Devas; you are He who pervades the galaxies.

"You are oblation and fire, sacrifice and sacrificer. You are the blessed AUM, the inscrutable, fathomless one. I, Brahma, am your heart, and Saraswati is your tongue. When you blink, the stars are put out and lit again. The Vedas are your sacred breath; the mandalas are you body.

"The sun is your anger and the moon your tenderness; you were Vamana who asked Bali for three paces of land.

"Your Sita is Lakshmi. You were born as a kshatriya to kill Ravana. You have delivered the earth from evil; your mission is accomplished."

But Rama stared astonished at the refulgent Creator in the sky, ringed by the Devas in their marvelous disks. When Brahma had spoken, there was a great rustling from the fire in which lovely Sita stood. His body blue-green flames, his hair crimson tongues of flame, Agni himself stepped out from it. He was great and bore Sita, unsinged, like a child in his hands, and came before Rama.

"Here is Sita, blemishless as she was born. Like a serpent Ravana tempted her; but the thought of you was always in her heart. Not for a moment, not with a fleeting thought, has she sinned. Rama, she is purer than I am."

Now tears flowed down Rama's dark face, and, crying out in joy, he clasped Sita in his arms! Vanara and rakshasa watched this, more astonished than ever. Fire and moon cast their light over the auspicious field, and the vimanas were scintillant in the sky.

Rama said, "Forgive me, my love, that I was so cruel to you. Not for a moment did I doubt your chastity. I know what you are. I know you are pure enough to wash the three worlds of all their sins. No one else could have resisted Ravana as you did. He was evil incarnate, subtle, and the great tempter. And that is why you were chosen to be his captive. Oh, Sita, more than my arrows it was your chastity that was Ravana's undoing. You were invincible to his every blandishment and threat; and that broke his spirit."

Her eyes wide, she cried, "Then why . . ."

Rama was her familiar, gentle prince again. The rage he had assumed was gone from his face. With untold tenderness, he said, "My love, if you had not passed through the agni pariksha, the world would never have believed you were chaste. For the world always judges by its own norms and the world is far from perfect. The people would have said, and so would posterity, that Sita lived in Ravana's antapura and, surely, the Rakshasa enjoyed her. They would have said Dasaratha's son was blinded by love, and he took back a sullied woman. But now, my Lords of the air, the world knows my Sita is purer than the fire. That she is purity incarnate. And she is just Rama's, and will always be."

Siva appeared in the sky like a midnight sun. "As long as Ravana ruled from Lanka, the world was plunged in darkness, a night of the spirit. Dread was in every heart and even the guardians of the earth were helpless against Visravas's son. The long night has ended. Rama, you are the light of the world, its rising sun.

"The time has come when Ayodhya will rule the earth, with you as king. Bharata waits for you at home. He pines for you, Rama; it is time you went back.

"But first, look, here is someone who has come to bless you."

Beside Siva's immense vimana was another sky chariot, a crystal disk that had been dark until now. At Siva's sign, it grew brilliant and flew down to the ground among the wonderstruck vanaras. Rama and Sita now stood hand in hand. Like a dream, a panel on that craft slid open and out stepped a familiar figure. Rama gave a cry; Sita and he prostrated themselves at the feet of that great kshatriya, Dasaratha, come from beyond death to bless his son.

Lakshmana appeared at his brother's side and also fell at his father's feet. With hands of light, Dasaratha lifted Rama up, and the tears that welled in his eyes were drops of light, too.

Again and again he embraced his son, and Dasaratha cried, "Rama, Devaloka is glorious all right; but I am not content even in heaven because I am apart from you. I have never been able to forget what Kaikeyi said to me: 'Banish Rama for fourteen years.' But now, because of what you have done, I am free of my sorrow and the echoes of pain have left my mind. Now I see the greater purpose of your birth and your exile. My guilt has left me, because I know it was all fate's ploy: so Ravana could be killed. Ah, my son, your destiny was greater than I ever dreamed."

Tears still ran down his face, which was made of the light of the sun and the moon. Dasaratha went on, "How happy Kausalya will be when she sees you back in Ayodhya. How fortunate the people of our city are that you return to them as king. Today the fourteen years of your exile have ended. Go back home, my son. Rule long and joyfully; be the greatest king the world has ever known."

Rama was thoughtful for a moment. He said softly to his father, "I have something I want from you. Our greater purpose has been achieved, and Ravana is dead. You must forgive mother Kaikeyi and the innocent Bharata. Father, your own spirit will find peace if you do."

A shadow flitted across Dasaratha's face. Then with a smile, he nodded. "So be it."

Dasaratha embraced Lakshmana. He stroked the fair prince's face. "As long as Rama's name is remembered on earth, so shall yours be. Never has this world seen devotion like yours. Let heaven's choicest blessings be upon you, loyal child."

He embraced Sita and blessed her. "Your heart will forget the harsh words Rama said to you. He never meant them, but only wanted your name to be as taintless as you are, forever. Precious child, I have watched you: Rama could not have found another wife like you."

They knelt again at their father's feet. After laying his hand on their heads, he climbed back into the vimana and Dasaratha left the world, never to return. Siva and Brahma also melted out of the sky. Now Indra, king of Devaloka, flew down to Rama.

Indra said, "I remember how curious you were when you saw my chariot outside Sharabhagna's asrama. But it would have been wrong for us to meet then. Now what you came for has been accomplished, and here I am before you. Ask me for any boon, Rama. And it shall be yours, if it is in my power to give it."

Rama stood with folded hands before the Deva king. Not for a moment did he hesitate before he said, "My lord, a hundred thousand vanaras have died for me during this war. Their women wait for them in Kishkinda and in far corners of the earth. Give the people of the jungle back their lives. And wherever the race of monkeys lives, let there always be plenty of sweet water and an abundance of fruit."

Indra made a sign of life-giving across that battlefield, and by the streaming moon every slain vanara rose again to life. The dismembered were whole and no trace of the wounds that had killed them remained on their bodies. Seeming to wake out of a deep slumber, they came to Rama and stood around him in adoration.

Indra climbed back into his chariot. He said, "It is time you went back to Ayodhya and ruled the world. Bharata and Shatrughna are waiting impatiently for you, and so are your people. Rama, go home now."

Indra gained the silver sky, and for a moment the monkeys and the demons witnessed an awesome spectacle: all the Devas together in their chariots of the mandalas. Then, in a whisper, they vanished. For a long time, vanara and rakshasa stood staring at the heavens. But the Gods had gone.

47. The pushpaka vimana

They spent what remained of the night under the stars, gazing out over the solemn sea, hearing the wash of the waves for the first time since they had landed on Lanka's shores.

At dawn, Vibheeshana came to Rama. He brought silks, sandalwood paste, and scented water. "Rama, these are for your coronation. Take them from me and make all of Lanka happy, especially her king."

But Rama said, "Give them to Sugriva for my sake, he deserves them richly. As for me, my heart is full of Bharata's face. I have no place in it for coronations; not until I see my brother. I must leave at once, Vibheeshana: the road home is long and hard."

Vibheeshana said, "Let me shorten your journey for you, Rama, so you can be back in Ayodhya in a day."

Rama smiled, "How is that?"

Vibheeshana said, "Ravana once vanquished Kubera in battle and took the pushpaka vimana from him. It is still here in Lanka. You can return to Ayodhya in the crystal ship. But Rama, stay here with me for some days."

Rama took Vibheeshana's hand. "My friend, without you I would never have won the war. But my heart is with Bharata, whom I have not seen for fourteen years. I can still see him in Chitrakuta. He stood before me, wearing valkala, his eyes full of tears, and begged me to take the kingdom while he took my place in the wilderness. That memory haunts me. I see my mothers, my guru Vasishta, and my people, who think of me as their own. They are all waiting for me. Besides, Vibheeshana, when you have taken me to your heart, I will

500

always be with you. But for now, forgive me if I do not stay on in Lanka."

Vibheeshana gave orders for the pushpaka vimana to be fetched. It came gleaming and silent through the crisp morning air, its smooth sides mirroring the green and the blue of sea and sky. When the wondrous craft had landed, softly as falling petals, Vibheeshana asked, "Rama, what shall I do now?"

Rama was thoughtful for a moment. Then he said, "I owe Sugriva and his people a deep debt of gratitude. For my sake, give them fine silks, jewels, and colorful chariots they will love. Let your generosity be a legend among the jungle folk, and let the brief enmity between your peoples end forever."

Vibheeshana gave lavish gifts to Sugriva, his chieftains, and his people. Every monkey of that army was rewarded for his valor. Chattering happily at the treasures they received, the jungle folk cried out Rama's name, Sugriva's, and Vibheeshana's, all together. The sun was high now, directly above the vimana.

Rama came to Sugriva. He put his hands on the vanara king's shoulders. "What shall I say to you, my friend? How can I thank you, or ever repay my debt to you?"

Angada had come up beside his uncle. Rama put his arm around the prince. "What can be said of your valor, Angada? You were magnificent. And you, Vibheeshana, how will I ever repay you for everything you have done for me? My thoughts will always be with you, my dearest friends."

They stood before him, their hands folded. Choking, Rama said, "Go back to Kishkinda now, Sugriva. Your women and children are waiting for you. Farewell, my friends, I will never forget you!"

He began to climb into the vimana, but Sugriva called, "Wait, Rama!"

Rama turned back; he saw the vanara crying. Sugriva blurted, "We want to be in Ayodhya with you for your coronation! We swear we will behave ourselves, and be careful in your streets and your forests. We will not harm a tree, nor pluck a single flower. Please, Rama, let us meet your mothers, see you being crowned, and then return to Kishkinda."

Vibheeshana said, "I and my four friends who came out to you, we would also see you being crowned."

Such a smile broke out on Rama's face. He gave a delighted laugh at Sugriva's quaint promise that the vanaras would behave. He clasped the monkey king and cried, "How I wished you would say this! And you, noble Vibheeshana. Of course you must come to Ayodhya with me; but for you I would not be going back myself."

Glowing, Vibheeshana said, "Rama, the pushpaka vimana can carry all the vanaras, and me and my friends, too. Shall we leave?"

Rama said, "Shouldn't you arrange for Lanka to be ruled while you are away?"

Vibheeshana replied, "I have already entrusted the task to Suparshva and some other ministers. You see, Rama, Sugriva and I decided some time ago that we would go with you."

The vimana was a miraculous ship, and soon it was full of vanaras, who streamed into it. Amazingly, every monkey had a place inside, though it would not have seemed possible to look at the gleaming thing from the outside. Those who know the pushpaka vimana say that seen from without it was a great flying disk, but from within it was a dazzling city. Sugriva and his people, Vibheeshana and his four ministers, and finally, Rama, Lakshmana, and Sita climbed into the vimana. When they were all seated, the door slid shut by itself, soundlessly.

The ship flew at Rama's thought. When he willed it to, it rose into the sky. Though you could not look into it, the vimana was perfectly transparent from the inside. The vanaras laughed like children as they flashed up toward the clouds.

Rama turned to Sita. "There lies Lanka: the city Viswakarman built, the city of our destiny. Look at the battlefield outside its gates."

Dead rakshasas still lay heaped on that field, their blood drying around them in dark stains upon the earth. Rama took Sita's hand and whispered, "For you I killed Ravana, and fate willed it so."

They hovered above the momentous field. Rama pointed. "That is where Kumbhakarna fell. And there Hanuman killed Dhrumraksha."

As they rose higher, someone else cried, "Look at that nyagrodha tree. That is Nikumbhila, where Lakshmana killed Indrajit."

Rama said quietly, "That was the turning point."

As if they were sailing on the wind, they flew over the sea, gathering speed. Rama pointed down at a faint line upon the waves, stretching away to the horizon. "Nalasetu: the bridge Nala built for us. The bridge across which we came by moonlight to rescue you."

Now he smiled to think of the anxiety of those days. Sita said in a low voice, "This is the sea that Hanuman leaped across to bring me your message."

Golden Mainaka rose from the ocean to watch them pass. Waving to him, they arrived swiftly at the other shore, of sacred Bharatavarsha. The vanaras set up a cheer.

Rama said, "Sita, that beach is where Vibheeshana first flew out to me."

They flashed along now. Their speed was incalculable; the earth below was a blur of brown and green. Not long after, they were flying over a deep jungle. As they slowed, at Rama's will, they saw a familiar ring of hills and the secret entrance that led into Kishkinda. The monkeys roared in joy to see their home.

Rama pointed again. "That is where Vali died. And there is Kishkinda, where Sugriva rules."

Sita said, "Rama, let us take Tara and all the vanara wives with us to Ayodhya. They have given us so much; it is the least we can do in return."

Quiet as light, the vimana landed outside Kishkinda. The reunion of the vanaras with their families was rapturous. With his arms around Ruma and Tara, Sugriva ordered his people to hurry into the ship with their women. Soon they set off again, north to Ayodhya.

As they were still climbing, and before they went too quickly, Rama pointed out a mountain below, which shone as if a rainbow had broken on its slopes. He said to Sita, "Rishyamooka is iridescent for its colored rocks. That is where Hanuman first met us, when he came disguised as an artful brahmana, smooth of tongue and sharp of wit. On Rishyamooka's summit, Sugriva and I first swore friendship before a fire we lit."

Later, as they flitted along, Sita cried, "Look, Rama, Panchavati, where you killed Khara and his rakshasas."

Her voice caught in her throat; she saw a familiar glade in the jungle. Her eyes filling quickly, she whispered, "That is where Jatayu gave his life for me."

A shadow crossed Rama's face when he saw the asrama from where Ravana had taken Sita: a terrible memory of how life had been without her; how despair had coiled itself around his heart like a serpent. He remembered what a strength Lakshmana had been during those days. Rama said softly, "When we saw you were gone, my love, Lakshmana and I went south from Panchavati."

She saw how much he must have suffered. Tenderly, she took his hand. On they flew, over dense jungle, and Sita murmured, "From up here one would scarcely guess at all the wonders that lie hidden below: streams and flowers, ancient trees and charmed pools, and birds and beasts out of dreams."

Rama squeezed her hand, and such joy flowed between them at being together again. In a wide clearing they saw Agastya's asrama, and then Sutheekshna's. They saw where Viradha had died, at the very edge of the Dandaka vana. Their minds were full of memories of the forest, all their adventures. From the uncanny vimana, which flew this route after Rama's own heart, they saw Atri's asrama. They folded their hands in obeisance to the rishi and his gracious Anasuya.

Like a comet, the pushpaka vimana plunged across the sky with its tail of light. Now they flew low above Chitrakuta of the sparkling waterfalls. Rama said, "Do you remember how Bharata came to see me here, with his hair tangled in jata?"

On they flew and the Yamuna appeared below them, a silver thread laid across the earth. They went lower still, and Lakshmana said, "Look, Bharadvaja's asrama."

Sita cried, "The Ganga!"

Rama said, "Shringiberapura, where my friend Guha rules."

And then the three of them cried excitedly and at once, "The Sarayu!"

Lakshmana said dreamily, "The Sarayu, which cradles Kosala in her arms."

Now they saw the golden turrets of a city that lay like a vision below them. Rama heaved a sigh and whispered, "Ayodhya, city of my fathers."

Rama, Lakshmana, and Sita folded their hands and bowed to the royal city of the Sun.

Rama flew them back to Bharadvaja's asrama. It was quite incredible: they had come all the way here in a few hours. The vimana landed outside the rishi's asrama. Without a whisper, the crystal panels slid open, and Rama and the others climbed down into the sunlight.

Rama went before the muni and lay at his feet. Today was the first day after his exile ended. Bharadvaja blessed him and raised him up. He had already seen Rama's triumph on Lanka, clairvoyantly.

Rama asked, "My lord, how is my brother Bharata? And my mothers? And not least, O Muni, how are my people?"

Overjoyed, Bharadvaja put his arm around Rama. He said, "Ayodhya waits for you. Bharata is well; he wears jata and the same valkala you last saw him in. He sleeps on the ground, and all day long speaks to the padukas you gave him, just as if you sat before him. He counts not only the days, but the very moments before he sees you again.

"And your mothers are well, Rama. They also wait impatiently for you."

Suddenly, the sage's voice was tremulous, "These have been such a long fourteen years for us all. I can still see you standing before me, wearing deerskin, your hair freshly matted, and so solemn. Do you remember, you had just lost your kingdom? Yet dharma was all you thought of. Ah, you were like a God cast down into the world for some slight fault. I see it all so clearly; you had given away everything you owned as alms.

"I strive to be detached. But that day, when I was alone, I wept. Least among all the created did you deserve what had happened to you. But there was a great purpose behind it all. And even then Ravana's name came to my mind. But I could say nothing, for your encounter with him was still fourteen years away.

"From witnesses who are not of this world, I have already heard your story. Word of everything that happened to you in Chitrakuta, in Panchavati, on Rishyamooka and Lanka, came back to me. Your destiny in exile is fulfilled, Rama. Now it is time you claimed the throne of the world.

"But I will not let you go today. Tonight you must spend here with me, all of you, as my guests."

Rama bowed. He took Hanuman aside and said to the vanara, "I cannot refuse Bharadvaja; and perhaps this is a heaven-sent opportunity. Dear Hanuman, fly to Ayodhya for my sake. Go first to Shringiberapura, which we saw; from there, Guha will show you the way."

All attention, Hanuman stood gravely before Rama.

Rama went on, "Go to Bharata in Ayodhya; tell him about my life during these past fourteen years. Tell him everything you know, and tell him I have returned. As you speak, watch him carefully, Hanuman. Most of all, watch for the slightest flicker of disappointment on his face.

"Power and kingdom are mighty things, and the best of men are tempted by them. If you see the faintest sign of regret in Bharata's eyes that I have returned, fly back and tell me. I will return quietly to the jungle, while my brother rules Ayodhya in peace."

48. *The wonderful news*

Hanuman's was a delicate mission. He decided to go to Bharata disguised as a human being, just as he had first accosted Rama. Outside Bharadvaja's asrama, it took him no more than a moment, and a thought of his father Vayu, to effect the transformation. Then he flew up into the sky as a diminutive brahmana with a shining face. He flew across the holy Ganga, across the Sangama, where her golden waters flow into the midnight-blue Yamuna. He saw Shringiberapura beyond the rivers.

Hanuman flew down from the sky into Guha's court, astonishing that king of hunters. He cried to Guha, "Rama of Ayodhya has served his exile and returns home in triumph!"

Guha sprang up and embraced the quaint messenger. Hanuman told him about Sita's abduction and Ravana's death. Guha wanted him to stay on in his city, so he could hear all about the war of Lanka. But Hanuman said he must meet Bharata urgently, and asked the way to Ayodhya.

With directions from Guha, the little brahmana flew up again, while Guha's people stared after him. Ayodhya was near enough for one who had carried the Sanjivini mountain from the Himalaya to Lanka. Guha had described Nandigrama, the village a krosa from Ayodhya, where Bharata still lived like a hermit, though fourteen years had passed.

Hanuman flew down a short distance from Nandigrama and walked the rest of the way to Bharata. The canny vanara hid behind some bushes and stood watching the prince for a while. Bharata was quite alone, like a solitary rishi.

Hanuman saw he was as handsome as his brothers. But he hardly looked like someone who ruled a great kingdom. He wore a ragged deerskin, his face and his body were caked in dirt; only his dark, piercing eyes shone through that mask. But even these were half-closed, as if Bharata was absorbed in some fervor that kept all his thought turned within himself. Above his face, his hair was piled in thick jata, as wandering rishis wear who are unconcerned about their bodies. He was lean, as if he hardly ate.

Bharata sat at the foot of a splendid throne set in a roofed, but otherwise open, pavilion, and spoke incessantly to that throne. When Hanuman crept closer, he saw that a pair of padukas lay on the seat of the golden throne. It was to these that the emaciated prince spoke. When he had watched Bharata carefully for a time, Hanuman came out from hiding and approached him. Bharata stood up, a little startled to see the wiry, cheerful mendicant. The kshatriya sensed at once that the little brahmana before him was not quite what he seemed.

Hanuman smiled at Bharata. He said solemnly, "Your brother Rama, for whose sake you live like a muni, has sent me. He is well and his exile is over. Rama killed the great Rakshasa, Ravana, and he is on his way home to Ayodhya to quench the yearning in your soul."

The little brahmana spoke in the finest, formal language. At his first words, a great smile lit Bharata's face. By the time he finished, the prince gave a shout and actually fainted. In a moment Bharata revived. He clasped the little mendicant to him, crying, "Brahmana, for this news I will give you wealth you have not dreamed of!"

Bharata hugged Hanuman and planted kiss after kiss on his cheeks, and he wept and laughed at once for stark, unblemished joy. "This is not just good news you have brought me, my friend. This is my life you have brought me, who have been dead for fourteen years. Tell me what you want, anything at all, and it shall be yours."

Bharata saw the little brahmana before him also wept. Bharata hugged him again. He spread a seat of darbha grass for Hanuman and, taking his hand, made him sit close beside him. "My friend, we have had no word of my brother since I left him at Chitrakuta. Now you say he is coming back. And, oh, this is such wonderful news, I can hardly believe it is true!

"You know what they say, good messenger: 'Stay alive for a hundred years and happiness will come at the end. Even if it is late!'

"That is my story. I have grown so used to sorrow and only just keeping my spirit in my body, I cannot believe my fortunes have changed. You have made me so happy I feel I am dreaming and this cannot be true. Forgive me, kind friend, your news is too good to absorb at once."

Bharata still held Hanuman's hand, as if it were a living link with his Rama, more precious than life to him. "Be kind to me again, friend brahmana. Tell me all about Rama's life since I last saw him. Leave nothing out; tell me everything you know."

Sighing wistfully, as if Rama's story was part of his own life, Hanuman told that strange tale to the avid prince. Bharata sat rapt, and shut his eyes to listen to the little brahmana. For two hours the story lasted. Finally, after Ravana was dead and Sita tested by fire, Hanuman ended, "And Rama has reached the banks of the Ganga. He is spending the night with Bharadvaja in his asrama. Tomorrow is an auspicious day. It is panchami, the fifth day after amavasya, and the moon will be in Pushyami. Tomorrow, Bharata, you will see your brother."

Shouting the news aloud, Bharata ran into Ayodhya. He called Shatrughna and together they began to prepare for Rama's return. Ayodhya was decked out in flowers and banners. The roads were sprinkled with elephants' ichor and fragrant water, and strewn with festive petals and garlands. The news spread like light, and the people poured into the streets.

All the forlorn mantapas were cleaned out, for the first time in fourteen years, and festooned. Ayodhya was as colorful as a rainbow over Amravati. Songs were in the air and laughter, as if a curse had been lifted from the city that had been as somber as a burning ghat.

The army must receive Rama: the road between Ayodhya and Nandigrama had to be leveled in a hurry. The women of Ayodhya drew auspicious and exotic yantras with colorful powders, all along that royal highway. Urns with holy water, incense, and masses of vivid flowers were set out under the sky.

The next morning, after a day and night of frenzied preparations, the people gathered in Nandigrama to welcome Rama home. No one stayed back. They came laughing, singing, and dancing in the streets, as if all their destinies had turned around in a night. None of them had slept a wink and each one came to see just his or her Rama, the soul of Kosala.

They were curious: Had he grown older? Was his long hair streaked with gray now? Was he as handsome as before; was Sita's beauty deeper with the years? How did Lakshmana look? Would he still be the reluctant darling of all the young women? And the older ones too! After fourteen dead years, Ayodhya throbbed with life again. The faces that had been grim for so long were all wreathed in smiles.

At dawn the queen mothers arrived in Nandigrama in their silver and golden palanquins. Everyone waited, on edge, and Bharata stood before them all, with his brother's padukas in his hands. The white parasol had been unfurled for Rama and the royal chamaras had been fetched out. The crisp morning air was fragrant with incense and flowers; later, as the sun rose, it boomed with deep conches.

Bharata stood breathless with anticipation, like all the others: the loving people of Ayodhya come to welcome home their prince of grace.

49. Rama returns

Bharata stood impatiently in Nandigrama, with all Ayodhya behind him. Hanuman had flown back to Rama and back again, bringing word of the hour of his arrival. He stood beside Bharata now. That prince was anxious and restless, as if he still could not believe Rama was indeed coming home today. Slowly the sun crept over the horizon. Bharata fidgeted where he stood.

He turned to Hanuman. "There is no sign of my brother, or the army of vanaras."

Hanuman was back in his own splendid vanara form. He craned his neck, smiled, and said, "Indra granted the vanaras a boon: that wherever they went the forests would bloom and the trees hang heavy with fruit. My ears are keen, Bharata. I can hear the monkeys feasting around Bharadvaja's asrama. But now Sugriva gathers them into the vimana, and they will be here as quickly as you wish."

They stood together, scanning the horizon. Hanuman pointed a long finger and said, "That cloud of dust is where my people are with Rama."

Then, it seemed a full moon had risen above that distant cloud: a golden moon that flitted across the sky toward Nandigrama. A sigh went up from the people.

Hanuman said, "The pushpaka vimana was once Kubera's, but Ravana took it from him."

But the people of Ayodhya hardly cared. Their ecstatic shouts of "Rama! Rama!" rose into the sky and reached the dark prince inside the vimana. He squeezed Sita's hand. Silent as time, quick as thought, the magic craft flew to Nandigrama. Rama saw Bharata standing below, his face radiant and tears flowing down his cheeks. The next moment the ship landed. Its opalescent door slid open and Rama stepped out first of all.

With a sobbing cry of "Rama!" Bharata ran to his brother and fell at his feet. Repeatedly, he lifted his head and set it down in the dust. He sobbed and he laughed, and he would have danced for joy if it had been proper to his station. But with as fond a cry, Rama lifted Bharata up, hugged him, and covered his face with kisses, as a father would his son.

Bharata prostrated himself before Lakshmana and Sita, crying, "*Abhivadye!*"

Formally, Bharata went around to all the vanara chieftains, introducing himself, embracing them one by one. To Sugriva he said, "King of the jungle, you are our dearest friend. For friendship is reckoned by what a friend does in a time of need."

Bharata embraced Vibheeshana. He cried, "Lord of Lanka, without you, I have heard, our cause would have been lost. We owe you a debt of gratitude we can never repay."

Then Shatrughna was with Rama, crying for joy, prostrating himself before his brother. Rama raised him up lovingly. When Shatrughna had greeted Sita and Lakshmana and the vanaras and rakshasas, at last Rama came to his mother Kausalya. His tears flowing, his smile so tender, he knelt before her and clasped her feet. She was older and frailer; but now that she saw him before her, it was as if her spirit found another youth. Over and over again she embraced him and covered his face with kisses.

Rama prostrated himself at Sumitra's feet, and she embraced him and blessed him. At last, he came diffidently before the third palanquin that had brought dead Dasaratha's queens to Nandigrama. Before it, her head bent and her face covered, stood Kaikeyi.

Rama said gently, "Mother, it is I, Rama."

She gave a cry as if her life had come back to her. She flung her arms around him and cried, "How can you ever forgive me, my child? I was mad, Rama, and I have paid for it these fourteen years. I beg you, my son, try to forgive me."

But Rama had already fallen at her feet. When she raised him up, he saw her eyes were clear; no trace remained of the hatred and greed he had last seen in them. Her face was marked with deep lines and she looked older than either Kausalya or Sumitra. Kaikeyi's face had softened now, and Rama thought, "My father has forgiven her."

He embraced her and said, "We are all fate's puppets. Only the strongest of us are chosen to play the hardest roles upon this stage of life. If you had not done what you did, Ravana would be alive and the world still full of danger. It was not you who sent me away from Ayodhya, but my destiny that took me. As for forgiveness, it is not for me to forgive you, but for you to understand you had no choice in what you did. You must forgive yourself, little mother."

Rama made Sita and Lakshmana prostrate themselves before Kaikeyi. Now he saw Vasishta, and the kulaguru of the Ikshvakus also wept for joy. Vasishta embraced Rama, Lakshmana, and Sita, while the people of Ayodhya stood watching all this in a happy daze.

Bharata came to Rama again, and he held Rama's padukas in his hands. He knelt and placed his brother's feet in those sandals. Bharata said, "Rama, your padukas watched over me while you were away. With their inspiration, I ruled the kingdom in your name. And Ayodhya has not fallen into anarchy. Though grief was always near us, we looked at your padukas and dreamed of the day you would return. Rama, look into the granary and the treasury; their stores have increased tenfold. The army of Ayodhya is the greatest fighting force in all Bharatavarsha."

Rama said quietly, "Not once during my years of exile did I worry about Ayodhya. I knew that Bharata's rule would be a golden one."

Rama turned back to the mystic vimana, which loomed beyond him. He said to it, just as if he spoke to a friend, "Return to Kubera now. I set you free from Ravana's yoke."

The wonderful craft quivered as if it understood him perfectly. It rose silently into the air. It hovered there for a moment, and spun thrice on its axis, like a planet. Then, without a sound, the vimana flashed out of the sky and toward Kubera's kingdom in the mountains of the north.

Rama stood near his guru Vasishta, like Indra next to Brihaspati.

Bharata said, "My mother's sin has been forgiven, Rama, that you have come home. Her suffering and ours are over. My brother, I now return what you left in my care: I give back the kingdom of Kosala to you. My burden is removed and I feel light again. I have discharged my task to the best of my ability. But I do realize that my ruling for you was like a crow swimming for a swan.

"Now, Rama, be crowned, and let the world see the glory of Ayodhya again. As long as there are men on earth, as long as the sun and moon circle in the sky, precious Rama, rule!"

Rama greeted his people, moving through the delirious crowd, which reached out hands of love and blessed him, Sita, and Lakshmana. Then the brothers went off to the river, just they four. They cut away their jata on the banks of the Sarayu and bathed in the cool water, laughing and splashing one another, euphoric to be together again.

Their long arms smeared with sandalwood paste, wearing resplendent silks and priceless ornaments, the princes returned to Bharata's asrama like four Devas. Meanwhile, the three queen mothers had taken Sita in for her bath, and they clothed her in the finery they had brought out of Ayodhya. Their long ordeal had wrought a miracle among Dasaratha's wives: they were as fond as sisters now that fate's purpose had been fulfilled. The past seemed like a bad dream, from which all of them had woken.

Kausalya called the vanara wives, Tara and the others, and embellished their long hair, combing it out and twisting it into elegant coiffure.

When they were all together, princes and queens, an old man drove up before Rama in a fine chariot. When Rama saw him, he gave a cry and ran to embrace Sumantra. Rama and his brothers climbed into the royal chariot. With the vanara army, led by Sugriva, Hanuman, Vibheeshana, and all the people of the city, the festive procession set out from Nandigrama for Ayodhya.

50. Pattabhisheka: Rama's coronation

Asoka and Vijaya, ministers of Ayodhya, went formally to Brahma's son Vasishta, kulaguru of the House of Ikshvaku. Solemnly they asked him to crown Rama king of Kosala.

Bharata drove the chariot in which Rama came from Nandigrama to be crowned. Vibheeshana and Lakshmana sat on either side of him, with the chamaras, the whisks of pale silk thread. Shatrughna held the sovereign white parasol. The people were a colorful sea around the chariot, and the vanaras mingled with them joyfully.

Shatrunjaya, the white tusker, had come with tears in his old eyes to receive his prince. Rama made Sugriva ride on his back. Like the moon surrounded by the stars, Rama came to the city of his fathers to be crowned. The royal road was a long carpet of flowers; incense and perfume hung in the air, and hymns from the Vedas. Led by caparisoned cows, the procession made its way through the streets. Rama rode at its heart in the great royal ratha, with the rishis of the sabha and the older ministers accompanying him. As they went, he described his adventures in exile to them in his soft voice.

Speaking of how he met Sugriva and of Hanuman's valor and devotion, Rama came within sight of Ayodhya. He climbed down from the chariot and folded his hands to her golden turrets. At the gates he prostrated himself and touched the earth with his brow; his eyes were full, and so was his heart.

After fourteen years, which were another life, another dream, Rama came to his father's palace. Slowly he climbed the polished marble steps, where he had last seen Dasaratha in the flesh, heartbroken. Sorrow perched on Rama's heart for a moment, that his father could not be here for his coronation. But then he saw the lucent face and form he had seen in Lanka; he felt Dasaratha's presence near him, and Rama smiled again.

When he had been blessed by all the elders of the palace, some of whom were too infirm to come to Nandigrama, Rama turned to Bharata. "My brother, take Sugriva to my palace with his people and see that he wants for nothing."

When he was comfortably ensconced, Sugriva sent some of his vanaras to the ocean to bring back its holy water in golden vessels. Led by Hanuman, they went and returned quickly as the wind.

Finally, the auspicious hour had arrived and everyone gathered in and around the palace. Vasishta made Rama, who wore the purest white silk, sit on the ancient throne of the Sun, with Sita at his side. Vamadeva, Jabali, Kashyapa, Kartyayana, Gautama, and Vijaya were beside that great guru, who, it was rumored, was as old as the earth. Vasishta poured the water from the ocean and from the sacred rivers of Bharatavarsha over Rama in abhisheka.

The ritviks of the court gave the prince his ceremonial bath. Shatrughna held the white parasol over Rama's head, and now Sugriva and Vibheeshana held the silken whisks.

Suddenly there was a swirling of wind and a blinding luminescence at the door. A shining pathway materialized, flashing down from the sky. Along it came a Deva whose elemental airs whirled murmuringly around him; his brilliance swathed the sabha of the coronation in supernatural glory. He came softly; his footfalls made no sound. His body was lucid, so you could see the tempest of light whirling around his heart. It was Vayu, who had come bearing gifts from Indra in Devaloka.

The Wind God brought a garland of unfading lotuses from the scented pools in Indra's Nandana, and a necklace of pearls that were like drops of the moon. Then down the celestial path came more irradiant Devas to bless Rama. They all brought unearthly gifts, and Ayodhya shone for leagues around.

The Earth glowed when Rama was crowned king in Ayodhya. Nature was a riot of color; the forests burst into unseasonable flower, the rivers seemed to sing. The sky was clear as the hearts of rishis, and the sea blessed Rama's coronation with hymnal waves.

When the Devas returned to their mandalas by the sky paths of light, Rama gave away lavish gifts to the brahmanas of his sabha. Cows and horses he gave, gold and priceless ornaments. He gave Sugriva an invaluable necklace of gemstones, which he had inherited from his Ikshvaku sires. With his own hands Rama tied golden bracelets around Angada's arms, and another shimmering necklace around Vibheeshana. The four ministers of Lanka, and Neela, Nala, Dwividha, and the other vanara heroes, all had fabulous gifts from him.

Seated on her throne beside Rama, Sita undid a string of pearls from around her own throat. A hush fell on the sabha. Rama glanced at her, and he knew what was in her heart.

He said aloud, "Give your necklace to the one in this sabha who you think is all that an immaculate warrior should be. Let him be endowed with the rarest gifts of character the Gods bestow. Let him be calm and famous, valiant and skillful, truthful and persevering, intelligent and wise. Place your necklace around him whose vision is prophetic and whose insight is deep as the ocean. Think carefully before you give away the ornament you hold; for it has come to you from your mothers."

Sita rose and with no hesitation tied the priceless heirloom around Hanuman's neck. The sabha burst into applause. Hanuman stood blushing brightly, his heart alight.

All the vanaras who had fought on Lanka were given precious gifts by Rama and Sita and by their mothers and brothers as well. Now the feasting and the other celebrations began, and they lasted a month. Rama's people took their new friends from the jungle into their homes and their hearts.

At the end of the month, Sugriva and Vibheeshana came to Rama in his palace. Embracing him, they took tearful leave, promising to visit him again soon and eliciting his solemn word that he would also visit them in Kishkinda and Lanka.

Most poignant was the leave-taking between Rama and Hanuman. In a rare show of emotion, the son of the wind fell sobbing at Rama's feet. Then he prostrated himself before Sita. Only when they had both blessed him did he rise, wiping his eyes.

Like a great river, the vanaras flowed away to their jungle in the south. By now they were eager to be home. They were wild folk, and longed to be in the bosom of the earth again, among living plant and tree, beside charmed pools, along flowing streams, and under sage mountains, where their natural, primitive lives waited for them.

Rama saw Vibheeshana off in his own chariot, with Sumantra as his sarathy and a small army to see him safely to the shores of Lanka. Rama and his brothers stood for a long time at the gates of Ayodhya, waving to the friends who had become so intimately involved in their lives and their destiny. Rama had tears in his eyes, remembering that but for Sugriva's vanaras and the timely wisdom of Vibheeshana, victory would have eluded him. And Ravana would still be ruling the earth.

When the last wave of monkeys and their women had passed out of sight, Rama turned back to his palace. He called Lakshmana. The king took his brother's hand and said, "Rule this ancient land with me. Let me crown you yuvaraja."

But Lakshmana smiled and gently withdrew his hand. "Kingdom is not for me. When you sit upon the throne of Ayodhya, it is as if I sit there myself. Bharata has experience of ruling; he deserves the crown of the yuvaraja more than I do."

Rama pressed him again and again. Bharata came and begged him;

but Lakshmana would not hear of it. Quietly he insisted that Kaikeyi's son be crowned yuvaraja.

Thus began Rama's reign, Ramarajya, when Vishnu's Avatara ruled the world for ten thousand perfect years. And Swarga above and Bhumi below, heaven and earth, were truly as one.

AUM SHANTI SHANTI SHANTI.

BOOK SEVEN

UTTARA KANDA

{The book of the north}

1. In Rama's sabha

When Rama was crowned king in Ayodhya, the rishis of the four quarters came to bless him. Kaushika, Yavakrita, Gargya, Gadava, Kanva, and Muni Medhatithi's son: all these holy ones who dwelt in the east came to the sabha of the House of the Sun. From the west came Nrisangu, Kavasa, Dhaumya, and Kauseya. From the south came Swastayatreya, Namuchi, Pramuchi, Agastya, Sumukha, and Vimukha. From the north, and with their disciples, came Vasishta, Kashyapa, Viswamitra, Atri, Gautama, Jamadagni, and Bharadvaja: seven sages.

Led by Agastya, the rishis were announced and led into Rama's sabha. They were radiant as the rising sun, and Rama offered them padya and arghya. Soon they were seated in his ancient court on darbhasanas covered in deerskin.

One of the wise said, "We have heard about your great exploit in Lanka, Rama; we are amazed that Lakshmana and you could kill Ravana's son Indrajit."

In mild surprise, Rama asked, "Munis, does it surprise you more that we killed Indrajit than that we killed his father Ravana and his uncle Kumbhakarna? Why, my lords?"

With a smile, Agastya said, "Indrajit was invincible. But Rama, perhaps you do not know very much about that rakshasa prince, or even his father. Let me tell you about their clan.

"It was in the krita yuga, an age ago, that the Muni Pulastya lived in the world. He was Brahma's son, and resembled the Pitamaha in every quality. All the Gods blessed Pulastya and he came to Mount Meru, to an asrama that belonged to King Trinabindu upon the slopes of the golden mountain, and dwelt there in tapasya for an age.

"But the Rajarishi Trinabindu's asrama was like a bit of heaven fallen into the world. Unearthly trees grew here, and there were lakes and pools whose water was like amrita. So it was that the daughters of rishis, and naginas, gandharvis, kinnaris, and apsaras came to bathe, sing, and frolic in the enchanted hermitage. The young women disturbed Pulastya's dhyana, and he said in anger, 'Let any woman whom my eyes see here become pregnant.'

"And in fear the apsaras, kinnaris, gandharvis, rishis' daughters, and the other young women no longer visited that asrama. But King Trinabindu's daughter did not hear about Pulastya's curse. She arrived in her father's sanctuary on a clear morning in spring, and she heard the Vedas being chanted sonorously in a voice more fine and reverberant than any she had ever heard. Innocently, the princess came and stood before the godlike rishi she saw sitting under an unworldly nyagrodha tree.

"Pulastya's angry gaze fell upon Trinabindu's exquisite daughter, and at once she felt the strangest sensation in her loins and her belly. She turned as pale as a lodhra flower and ran in fear from the sage under his tree. The princess came trembling before her father, and he asked her, 'What happened to you, my child?'

"Tears in her eyes, she said, 'I do not know what happened to me, father. But I wandered into Pulastya Muni's asrama, and when he looked at me I felt my body change, even as if it was not my own any more.'

"Trinabindu lapsed into dhyana, and in his meditation he saw what had happened. He learned of Pulastya's curse. Taking his daughter with him, he went to the rishi's asrama. He said to Brahma's son, 'Lord, I have brought my daughter to you. She will serve you faithfully and look after your every need.'

"Pulastya, who saw clearly through time, knew it was destined that the princess should remain with him. He looked at her for just a moment before he said to Trinabindu, 'Leave her with me.'

"Thus King Trinabindu's daughter became the Muni Pulastya's wife. She looked after him so lovingly that one day soon the rishi said to her, 'You are a good wife and I am pleased with you. You shall be the mother of my son.'

"And in time she gave birth to a truly brilliant child. Since she had listened every day to her husband chanting the Veda when she was pregnant, their boy was named Visravas. He was a remarkable boy, knowing and gentle even when he was young, and compassionate to every living creature.

"Visravas learned the Veda from his father, and quickly he also became a master of tapasya. He was pure and restrained, above every temptation of the flesh, and the great Bharadvaja gave his daughter, Devavarnini, who was as lovely as any apsara, to be Visravas's wife. Visravas fathered a splendid son on Devavarnini, and that boy resembled his father so much the rishis of Devaloka named him Vaisravana.

"Vaisravana went into a tapovana and sat in dhyana in that forest's heart like a flame upon the earth. He grew like a sacred fire fed with ghee. For a thousand years he sat in unflinching penance. He began by living on just water, then on only the air he breathed; and finally he did not respire any more, but was perfectly quiescent. The thousand years passed like a single one.

"At the end of a thousand years, Brahma himself, and Indra and his Devas, appeared before Vaisravana. The Pitamaha asked his great-grandson, 'My child, tell me what boon you want from me. You can have anything.'

"Vaisravana said, 'Lord, make me a guardian of the world, a Loka-pala. And let me be a protector of the earth, a Lokarakshaka.'

"Brahma said, 'I was about to create the fourth Lokapala. So now, you be that guardian. Be the Lord of wealth; be an equal to Indra, Varuna, and Yama.'

"The Creator raised his hands in a mystic mudra, and suddenly the most wonderful ship of the sky appeared above him, quiet as flowers, bright as a sun, quick as light. Brahma said to Vaisravana, 'This is the pushpaka vimana. From now on, you shall travel in it, wherever you wish to go.'

"Raising their hands over the kneeling Vaisravana, Brahma and the Devas vanished from the forest of his tapasya. Just then, Visravas arrived there to bless his son.

"Vaisravana said to his father, 'Brahma has made me a Lokapala. He has given me this marvelous vimana. But he has not told me where I will live. You tell me where I can dwell without harming any living creature.'

"Visravas said, 'A hundred yojanas out on the southern ocean, and to the east of Bharatavarsha, there is a mountain called Trikuta. Upon its summit is a splendid city called Lanka. Viswakarman created Lanka for the race of rakshasas to live in, just as he made Amravati for the Devas. Lanka has battlements of gold and silver moats surround it. Its portals are encrusted with precious cat's-eyes. Long ago, the rakshasas fled Lanka for fear of Vishnu, and the city lies empty. You can live in Lanka, my son, without harming any of the living.'

"And so, Vaisravana, the pious Lord of treasures, began living in the deserted city of Lanka, upon the jade island of that name. Such was his dharma that he shone like another sun on the earth. Soon, drawn by his grace, a race of unearthly beings, the nairritas, came to Lanka, and they became Vaisravana's people. His fame, and his city's, spread through the world like the scent of flowers upon the wind. Lanka was a focus of fortune on earth. Its master journeyed wherever he pleased, through the three realms, in his pushpaka vimana. Most of all, he went frequently to visit his mother and his father in their asrama in Bharatavarsha," said Agastya Muni in Rama's court.

2. The race of rakshasas

Rama seemed surprised by what Agastya said. He asked, "My lord, I had heard the race of rakshasas was descended from Pulastya. But now, you say the rakshasas lived in Lanka before Vaisravana went there. Were those rakshasas as powerful as Ravana and his clan? Who was their ancestor, Muni? Why did Vishnu drive them out from Lanka?"

Agastya replied, "In the beginning, Prajapati was born of the first waters of the origin, in the lotus sprung from Vishnu's navel. He entered the sacred waters and created the first creatures in them. Those great creatures were savaged by hunger and thirst, and they came howling to their Creator. They cried, 'We are in pain; what shall we do?'

"Laughing, Prajapati said to them, 'You must protect the waters with your very lives.'

"Some of his creatures said, 'We shall.' Others cried, 'We must eat!'

"Prajapati said to those who would be protectors, 'You shall be called rakshasas.' To those who would eat, he said, 'You shall be called yakshas.'

"Among the leaders of the rakshasas were two mighty brothers, Heti and Paheti, who lived at the same time as the dreadful Madhu and Kaitabha. Paheti was a pious rakshasa, and he went into a tapovana and sat in tapasya. Heti wanted a wife. He was married to Yama's sister, Bhaya, whose very name meant fear. Heti fathered a son called Vidyutkesa.

"Vidyutkesa grew like a lotus in the holy and original waters. When he was full-grown, Heti had him married to Sandhya Devi's daughter, Salakatankata, and Vidyutkesa enjoyed his bride as Indra does Paulomi. She conceived, and climbed Mount Mandara to give birth. Just as Ganga brought forth the Lord Karttikeya when Agni left Siva's seed in her water, Salakatankata delivered a powerful child on the mountain. But she was so eager to make love again with her husband, after her long pregnancy, that she abandoned the child and returned to Vidyutkesa.

"The child, bright as the autumn sun, put his hand into his mouth and cried softly. That sound was like the rumbling of the thunderheads of the dissolution. It happened that Siva and Parvati were passing in the sky at that moment, riding on Nandisvara. Parvati heard the abandoned rakshasa child, Sukesa, crying; she was so moved she made him full-grown in a moment and immortal as well. Uma also blessed all rakshasa women with a boon: that their children shall be born as soon as they are conceived, so they would not be deprived of even a day's lovemaking, which they are so addicted to. Also, Parvati blessed the race of rakshasas, that all their children shall be full-grown as soon as they are born.

"Then Siva also blessed that demon Sukesa with untold wealth. And he gave him a luminous city to live in, a city that flew through the air and went anywhere at the rakshasa's wish. Sukesa flew through all the worlds in his city, and he became arrogant because of the boons he had. Yet he was not without the dharma that flowed in his very blood from his pious sires.

"When Gramani, the gandharva, saw Sukesa with his wealth and his city of the air, he gave his daughter Devavati to that rakshasa to be his wife. The lovely gandharvi was as pleased as a pauper who finds a treasure and the rakshasa was as delighted as an elephant in musth that finds a mate.

"Sukesa sired three sons on Devavati: Malyavan, Sumali, and Mali. They were as brilliant as the three fires of sacrifice, as steadfast as the three worlds, as powerful as the three Vedas, and as dreadful as the three diseases that afflict the body. Those boys knew their father had his boons from the Lord Siva by his dhyana. Those three young rakshasas climbed Mount Meru and began a tapasya that terrified all the created.

"When their penance threatened to ignite the very earth, the Lord Brahma appeared before the rakshasas in a vimana and said, 'I have come to bless you with the boons you want.'

"The rakshasas, whose bodies shook from their long privations, answered him, 'Lord, let us be long-lived, invincible, and may we all love one another.'

"Brahma granted them those boons and vanished from the sky like wealth won in a dream. Delivered from fear now, the demon brothers went where they liked and did as they pleased. An immense army of rakshasas followed them through the three realms. They had their way with every kingdom they came upon; none could resist them, and all creation went in fear of them. Finally, when they grew tired of their conquests, they came to Viswakarman, the divine builder, and said, 'Master of edifices, build us a home as magnificent as Indra's or Siva's.'

"Viswakarman said to them, 'In the southern sea, upon the island of Lanka, there is a mountain called Trikuta. Beside Trikuta is another mountain, Suvela. On Trikuta's central peak is a fortress city that seems to float on air. Once I built that city at Indra's behest. Its walls are so smooth only the birds of the air can come into Lanka. Rakshasas, you are the masters of your race, even as Indra is the lord of the Devas. As Indra lives in Amravati with his people, you may dwell in Lanka from now. And no enemy will reach you in that impregnable city, for its deep moats and its walls like glass.'

"Thus, Malyavan, Sumali, and Mali went to Lanka with their people, and when they saw the unearthly city, its streets paved with precious vaidurya, its mansions built of solid gold, they did not hesitate to make it their home.

"In that same time there lived a gandharvi called Narmada, and she had three daughters. Narmada knew Malyavan, Sumali, and Mali had gandharva blood in them, through their own mother. She knew they were masters of the earth by the boons Brahma had granted them. On a day when the Uttara Phalguni nakshatra was plain in the sky, she gave her three daughters to the rakshasas to be their wives.

"As the gandharvas of the air do with the apsaras of Devaloka, the young demons made love with their enchanting brides. Malyavan's wife was called Sundari, and she was as beautiful as her name proclaimed. He gave her a brood of fierce and handsome sons: Vajramushti, Virupaksha, Yajnakopa, Durmukha, Suptaghna, Matta, and Unmatta. He also gave her a beautiful daughter, Anala.

"Sumali's wife, Ketumati, was lovely as a full moon and dearer to her husband than his life. Their sons were called Prahastha, Akampana, Vikata, Kalikamukha, Dhrumraksha, Danda, Suparshva, Praghasa, and Bhasakarna. Their daughters were Raka, Pushpokata, Kaikasi, and Kumbheenasi.

"Mali's lotus-eyed wife, Vasudha, the gandharvi, bore him two daughters, Anala and Anila, and two sons, Hara and Sampati. The boys became Vibheeshana's ministers.

"With Brahma's boon, and sons as mighty as they had, Malyavan, Sumali, and Mali soon conquered the Devas, the rishis, the nagas, and the yakshas. They ranged the worlds like the wind, and they ruined every yagna they found and killed the rishis who performed them. Their hubris and savagery grew with their power, and the terrified Devas came to Siva, the Un-born, the God of Gods, and cried, 'Mahadeva, Sukesa's sons are the bane of the worlds. We have no sanctuary anywhere in creation. They come to Amravati when they please, drive us from our homes, and cry that they are Brahma, Vishnu, and Siva; that they are Indra, Soma, Surya, Vayu, Yama, Agni, and Varuna! We beg you, Lord, kill the rakshasas for our sake: there is no peace left in creation.'

"But Sukesa was Siva's bhakta. Sankara said to the Devas, 'The rakshasas' death is not written at my hands. Go to Narayana; he will find a way to rid you of them.'

"The Devas flew to Vaikunta, to the home of the Blue God who lies upon the sea of eternity. Piteously, they said to him, 'Vishnu, save us. Sukesa's sons have Brahma's boon and they torment us as they like. We beg you, cut open the rakshasas' faces with your chakra; give them as a gift to Yama. Melt the fear from our hearts, Lord, even as the sun does the frost upon the mountain.'

"Slowly, Vishnu said, 'Yes, I know Sukesa has Siva's boons and I know his sons have Brahma's blessing. I will kill them all for you, Devas. Be at peace.'

"When Malyavan heard what Vishnu had promised the Devas, he called his brothers and said, 'The slayer of Hiranyaksha and Hiranyakashyapu, of Namuchi, Kalanemi, Samhrada, Radheya the mayyavi, the just Yamala, Arjuna, Hardikya, Sumbha, and Nisumbha, and a thousand other great Asuras and rakshasas, has said he will kill us, as well. How will we resist the terrible Vishnu?'

"Sumali and Mali said to their brother, their king, 'We have imbibed the Vedas, we have been just rulers to our people. We have observed our rakshasa dharma and we have no enmity with Vishnu. It is the craven Devas who have poisoned Narayana's mind against us. It is for their sake he has sworn to kill us. Let us kill the Devas and remove the very cause of Vishnu's anger toward us.'

"A vast rakshasa army was mustered, with awesome commanders like Jambha and Vritra, and the demons prepared for war. Riding in vimanas and chariots, on elephants, horses big as elephants that trod air, sorcerous mules, bulls, camels, dolphins, serpents, crocodiles, tortoises, fish, swarms of great birds, vultures, eagles, and ravens big as Garuda, lions, tigers, panthers, boars, bears, and deer called srimara and chamara, the teeming demon army gathered in Lanka. Then, with legions of millions, the rakshasas set out to kill Indra's Devas, by earth, sea, and air.

"Dreadful omens appeared everywhere. Clouds, formed suddenly in a clear sky, rained down pale bones and steaming blood. Jackal packs swarmed around the rakshasa legions and howled dismally. An uncanny ring of vultures wheeled above and breathed fire through their hooked beaks. All the creatures of the earth seemed disturbed, and the shrieks of a thousand races of birds rent the air, as did elephant herds' terrified trumpeting; and jungles of great cats roared their anxiety above the sounds that every other living beast made. It seemed the very elements, the panchabhuta, would dissolve and the worlds would be undone. Scarlet-footed pigeons and vivid mynahs darted above the rakshasas in frenzy.

"But the rakshasas were the sovereigns of the three worlds. They were swollen with the pride of their conquests, their wealth, and their power. They paid no mind to the omens that would have moved a blind and deaf man to fear for his life. The demon army rode on, and Malyavan, Sumali, and Mali at its head were like the three flames of the apocalypse. And the rest relied on these three as the Devas do upon the Trimurti.

"The rakshasas streamed on toward the Devas' city. Vishnu saw them and he filled his twin quivers with arrows, mounted Garuda, and flew down to fight. He was as bright as a hundred suns, his armor gleaming, the Panchajanya and the Sudarshana, the Saringa and the Kaumodaki glittering in his four dark hands. He wore a shining garment, like a wrap of lightning across his body blue as a thunderhead.

"Some legions of the rakshasa army were blown away by the wind stirred by Garuda's wings. The golden eagle was like a flying mountain. Then, roaring, the rakshasas rallied. They surrounded Vishnu and assailed him with every manner of ayudha and astra. As locusts fly into a paddy field, bees into a jar of honey, moths into a great flame, crocodiles into the sea, and the worlds themselves into Mahavishnu at the dissolution, the demons' arrow swarms flew into blue Narayana.

"They struck him, they even drew blood; but they did not harm the Blue One. Then he drew back his own bowstring and loosed a tide of arrows at the rakshasas. Narayana's cloudbanks of arrows, his streams, his rillets, his rivers of arrows, cut down the demons in thousands, in hundreds of thousands, in an eyeflash, in a wink. Blood, too, flowed in waves, in frothing brooks, in rivulets, in a sea, at Purushottama's cosmic archery.

"Vishnu raised his sea conch and blew a blast on it deep as the sky. The rakshasas' mounts turned tail in absolute terror. The greatest demons were struck by his impossible volleys and fell like mountains riven by thunderbolts. Blood flowed from their wounds like the red cataracts of the monsoon flashing down the Himalaya. But the God did not tire; he reveled in his yagna of death: he severed their necks, smashed their banners, their chariot wheels, their bows, their limbs, stopped their screams. Like rays from the sun, waves from the sea, serpents from a mountain, rain from a cloud, his arrows flowed in torrents from his miraculous Saringa.

"The rakshasas fled from the dreadful Hari, like lions from the Sarabha, like elephants from a hunting lion, like leopards from a tiger, like dogs from a leopard, like cats from a dog, like rats from a snake. They fled down to earth, back to Lanka.

"Vishnu flew after them. Then Sumali covered Vishnu in a drifting mist of arrows. He rode up to the Blue God and roared at him, waving his arm above his head even as an elephant waves his trunk. With a smile, Janardhana severed the head of Sumali's sarathy. The rakshasa's horses bolted. Now Mali charged Vishnu. As the birds of dusk streaked with the last rays of the day fly into the caves of the krauncha hill, Mali's gold-tipped arrows flew into the Blue One's darkling body, thousands of shafts.

"Vishnu aimed his own volleys at Mali, and they drank the demon's blood thirstily, as serpents drink nectar. Vishnu cut down Mali's banner, smashed his bow in his hand, shattered his chariot, and killed his horses. Leaping down with a fulminant roar, the rakshasa struck

Garuda on his golden head with his mace, even as Yama once struck Siva. The eagle quivered; he spun round in pain and turned his back on the battle. Thinking for a moment that Vishnu had turned to flee, the rakshasa army roared its delight, like a sea at night when the moon is full.

"Even with his back turned, Vishnu cast the Sudarshana chakra at Mali. Time's wheel, blinding as the sun, the disk cut Mali's head from his throat and it fell on the ground, spouting blood even as Rahu's head did, when Mohini gave the Devas all the amrita to drink. Above, the sky erupted in peals of thunder, and petal rain fell down from Devaloka as Indra and his people were swept by joy.

"Roaring like ten prides of lions to see their brother killed, Malyavan and Sumali fled. They fled back into their city with what remained of their legions. Even as they went, Garuda recovered and began to flap his wings again, so thousands of rakshasas were blown into the sea. Some had their soft, handsome faces cut in two by the wheeling, ubiquitous chakra. Some had their chests crushed by a blow from the Kaumodaki. Some were dissected by arrows like bolts of lightning from the Saringa.

"Demon entrails floated like garlands upon the crimsoned waves. Like clouds driven by Vayu, the rakshasas fled before the terrible Vishnu. And he slaughtered them all around him and they lay in death's final postures like blue mountains.

"Seeing the massacre of his people, Malyavan came back to fight, as waves do to the sea after briefly touching the shore. His eyes bloodshot, his great body shaking, the king of the rakshasas cried to Vishnu, 'Padmanabha, is this dharma? That you continue to kill my people, when they have abandoned all thought of war? They flee before you and yet you hunt them like animals. You will not find heaven for yourself with this murdering. If you must fight, Narayana, here I am before you. Fight me, if you dare!'

"Vishnu said softly, and his voice drowned every other noise of land, sea, and air, 'I must keep the word I have given the Devas that I will exterminate your race. I will sacrifice Swarga to keep my word.'

"With a growl, Malyavan cast a shakti at the Lord, striking him squarely in his deep blue chest. It glittered there like a streak of lightning across a cloud. Smiling, Vishnu drew out that shakti and flung it back at the rakshasa. It struck his jeweled chest as a thunderbolt might a mountain. Malyavan fell in a swoon; but he rose at once, and rushed at Vishnu and struck both him and Garuda blows like thunderclaps with a fist clenched around an iron band studded with long, sharp spikes.

"Garuda flapped his wings and blew the demon back into the city of Lanka, and his brother Sumali and his legions with him. With that, somehow, the rakshasas' spirit was broken. They knew they could not stand before blue Narayana. The demons fled with all their people down below the earth, into deep, glimmering Patala, where their kind belong," Agastya said in Rama's sabha.

3. The birth of Ravana

Rama said to Agastya, "Muni, tell us how Ravana was born."

The maharishi resumed: "Sumali wandered the Patalas for an age. When his terror of Vishnu receded, he rose to the surface of the earth again and ranged the sea-girt world of humans for another age.

"One day, he saw the splendid Vaisravana flying above him in the pushpaka vimana, on his way to see his father Visravas. Vaisravana had come to Lanka and lived there with his nairritas. Sumali said to his daughter Kaikasi, 'My child, you are a young woman now and it is time you were given in marriage. Remember, the honor of three families rests in the hands of a daughter: that of her father's clan, her mother's, and her husband's, as well. See that you preserve all three, my Kaikasi.'

"She asked, 'Father, to whom do you mean to give me?'

" 'To the Muni Visravas, so you will have sons as splendid as Surya Deva.'

"Kaikasi bowed to her father, and she took herself to the tapovana where Visravas was performing agnihotra. The young rakshasi did not know that it was an inauspicious time to approach the rishi. She came and stood near him with folded hands while he was absorbed in the ritual. She stood staring down at her feet, bashfully, and scratched the ground with her toe to attract his attention.

"Visravas looked up from his puja and saw a young girl standing near him, her face like the full moon. He said slowly, 'Who are you? Whose daughter? And why have you come to my asrama?'

" 'Brahmarishi, I am Kaikasi. I have come because my father Sumali told me to. I beg you, divine the rest for yourself.'

"Visravas sank into dhyana. Then, emerging from his trance, he said, 'I see why you have come to me. You have come to have sons by me. But you have come at the wrong muhurta. So, O woman with the gait of a she-elephant in rut, you will have savage rakshasas for sons.'

" 'Brahmavadi, I beg you, let not all my sons be like that.'

"The rishi paused a moment; his face softened, and he said, 'Young woman, your last son shall be a man of dharma, like all the rakshasas of our clan.'

"Then the muni took Kaikasi unto himself and gave her children. Kaikasi was first delivered of a dreadful infant, with ten heads in a cone, with great fangs in them. His hair was like strands of fire; his lips were coppery like his eyes. When he was born, all the fell creatures of night gathered round that asrama and they circled his mother from left to right, in a bizarre and ominous ritual.

"Eerie clouds scudded into the sky and rained down showers of blood. Flaming meteors, thousands of them, fell onto the earth, making great craters and hissing into the sea, so the waves stood up like mountains and smashed against the shore. The very earth was agitated, as if with some terrible fear, and strayed from her true orbit.

"Kaikasi's first child was born roaring fiercely from all his ten heads and his father named him Dasagriva. Soon after, Sumali's daughter had another son, and he was the biggest baby ever born. His ears were like great jars, so he was called Kumbhakarna. Next, Kaikasi gave birth to a perfectly hideous daughter, and she was Surpanaka. Last of all, a serene and handsome infant was born to the rakshasi and he was called Vibheeshana. He was hardly like a rakshasa, by his appearance or his nature, and soft flowers fell out of Devaloka to bless his birth.

"Those children grew up in the forest where Visravas lived in dhyana. From the first, Dasagriva and Kumbhakarna had restless, lustful natures, and they spent their days in satisfying their every appetite. They hunted for sport and for food, and when they were a little older, they did not hesitate to slake themselves on any woman, of any race, whose path crossed theirs in the forest. Vibheeshana was a restrained, wise youth from the first; he spent his time at study and serving his father.

"Dasagriva, also, gave some of his time to studying the Vedas and other ancient revelations. And to his own father's surprise, that wild and ferocious Rakshasa outstripped his brother Vibheeshana, easily, at learning. But while Vibheeshana lived by what he learned from the Shastras, Dasagriva did not.

"One day, Vaisravana, who is also called Kubera, the Lord of the nine treasures, arrived in his vimana to visit his father. Kaikasi called her eldest son and showed him how lustrous and fortunate his half-brother was. She said, 'Look at his vimana, how it shines. He flies anywhere he likes in it. And he is a Lokapala: the master of all the wealth in the world. My son, I want you to be Vaisravana's equal. That is what your mother wants for you.'

"Dasagriva was thoughtful for a moment. He stared long and hard at Kubera's pushpaka vimana. He pursed his lips and said quietly, 'I will be more powerful than Kubera. He is the Lord of but one-quarter of the earth. I will rule the three worlds.'

"His mother embraced him fervidly. She kissed all his ten heads, which appeared and vanished, uncannily, around his central face. So it was that Dasagriva first decided to sit in tapasya. He went with his brothers to an asrama at sacred Gokarna and began his intense penance. And once he set his heart to it, that rakshasa's tapasya was past compare. It was his ancestor Brahma whom Dasagriva worshipped."

4. Dasagriva's tapasya

Rama asked Agastya, "Tell me about Dasagriva's tapasya, Muni, and his brothers'. "

The rishi said, "Their penance lasted an age and each of the brothers had his own method.

"Kumbhakarna stood amidst four fires in searing summer, and the fifth was the blazing sun above, until the skin peeled from his body. He never flinched. During the monsoon, he knelt on the ground, often in the middle of a river, while the rain and the floods swept over him ceaselessly, and he was truly wet to his bones. In winter, too, he stood on, never stirring, in icy water. For ten thousand years, Kumbhakarna performed tapasya.

"The gentle Vibheeshana stood on one leg for five thousand years, even like dharma in the kali yuga. At the end of his penance, apsaras danced on clouds and fine showers of unearthly petals fell on the good rakshasa. Vibheeshana spent another five thousand years imbibing the Vedas, until he knew them backward. He recited them while he stood with his face and his arms raised heavenward and stared at the sun, the stars, and the moon, never blinking, never looking down. And this rakshasa experienced only delight during all his ten thousand years of tapasya, as if he were in the Lord Indra's Nandana.

"Dasagriva, the eldest, went without food for ten thousand years. And at the end of every thousand years, he offered one of his heads into one of the four fires he had lit around himself. Thus nine thousand years passed and finally the Rakshasa was about to offer his tenth head, and his life, to the flames, when Brahma appeared before him like a sea of grace, with all the Devas around him.

" 'Dasagriva,' said the Pitamaha, 'a tapasya like yours must be fruitful. Never has this earth seen such a penance. Ask me for any boon, Rakshasa, and it shall be yours.'

"Dasagriva bowed solemnly before the four-faced Creator of the universe. He said, 'Pitamaha, the root of all life's fear is death. Make me immortal, so I shall never be afraid.'

"Brahma said, smiling, 'Immortality is not mine to give. I am not immortal myself. Ask me for anything else, something I can give you.' Dasagriva thought for no more than a moment, then said, 'Let me not die at the hands of any of the greater races of heaven or earth. Let no suparna, naga, yaksha, Daitya, Danava, rakshasa, Deva, gandharva, kinnara, charana, siddha, rishi, muni, or predator of the wild kill me. As for mortal men, puny humans, I have no fear of them, they are like straw.'

"Brahma said thoughtfully, knowing where this boon would take the Rakshasa, 'So be it, then. And I grant you another boon: that your nine heads, which you offered me in the fire, shall be restored to you. And Rakshasa, you will have the power to assume any form you choose.'

"There are some who say that the Rakshasa offered his heads not to Brahma, but to Siva. Both versions are true: for different kalpas.

"Brahma now turned to the good Vibheeshana. 'I am pleased with your tapasya, as well, Vibheeshana. What boon would you have from me?'

"Vibheeshana said, 'Lord, my life's purpose is already fulfilled and I am a kritakritya, that I see you before me. But if you are pleased with me, grant me that my mind remains steadfast and virtuous in the midst of life's greatest trials. Grant me that the knowledge of the brahmastra dawns on me of itself. May every thought that enters my mind, during every stage of my life, be of dharma. Let me fulfill my dharma, however hard it is. For if a man has dharma, he has everything.'

"And Brahma said to him, 'Though you are born a rakshasa, your nature is like a maharishi's. Noble Vibheeshana, I bless you that you will be a Chiranjivi. You will live as long as the earth.'

"Brahma turned to Kumbhakarna. But the Devas cried, 'Lord, you must not grant him any boon. All the worlds already live in terror of him. You know he came to the Nandana, and devoured seven apsaras and three of Indra's servitors. There is no count of the rishis and men he has eaten, Pitamaha. Instead of a boon, cast a spell over him, that the worlds may be safe.'

"But Kumbhakarna's tapasya had been as compelling as his brothers' and Brahma had to grant him a boon. With a thought, the Creator summoned the Devi Saraswati. When she stood, shimmering, before him, he said softly to her, 'Goddess of the word, be the speech on Kumbhakarna's tongue.'

"When she had subtly entered the giant rakshasa's mouth, Brahma turned to him and said, 'Kumbhakarna, I am pleased with your tapasya. Ask me for any boon you want.'

"Saraswati spoke from the demon's mouth: 'Lord, let me sleep for years and years.'

"Smiling to see the startled look on the giant's face, Brahma said, 'So be it,' and vanished from there with the Devas.

"When Sumali heard of the boons that Dasagriva had from Brahma, he rose from the Patalas, with Maricha and Prahastha, Virupaksha and Mahodara, and a host of other rakshasas. Sumali embraced his grandson and cried, 'Not even Vishnu can harm us any more! Vaisravana lives in Lanka, but Lanka rightfully belongs to you. Dasagriva, you shall be the Lord of all the rakshasas, and our race will be restored to glory under you.'

"Dasagriva said, 'Kubera is my older brother. We should not speak of him like this.'

"But his dreadful eyes shone with very different thoughts. Reading his heart clearly, Prahastha said, 'Among kings, there is no brotherly love. Listen to what I have to tell you, Dasagriva.

" 'The Devis Diti and Aditi are sisters, and they are both Kashyapa

Prajapati's wives. Aditi bore the great muni the Devas of day and light, the Lords of the worlds, and Diti bore him the Daityas of night and darkness. Indeed, the Daityas were Kashyapa's first-born sons, and once all this earth, full of mountains, seas, rivers, and forests, belonged to the sons of Diti. They were the masters of the world.

" 'It was Vishnu who helped the Devas usurp the power of the Asuras and rakshasas. That was long ago, in another yuga. But now you are the first of our kind who has a boon like the one Brahma has given you: that you shall be invincible to all the immortal races of heaven and earth. Yours, Dasagriva, must be an unrivaled destiny in the history of our people. You must not forsake that destiny, but seize it with both hands.'

"Dasagriva did not think long before he said simply, 'I shall.'

"The same day, with a legion of rakshasas who had pledged allegiance to him, Dasagriva arrived on Lanka, and Mount Trikuta. From there he sent Prahastha as his messenger to Kubera, Lokapala, master of wealth. Prahastha brought a courteous message to Vaisravana from Dasagriva:

" 'Lord of treasures, O my half-brother, this city of Lanka belongs of old to the rakshasas of my clan. Malyavan, Mali, and Sumali ruled Lanka. I am Sumali's grandson. I beg you, leave our city now, for I, Dasagriva, mean to be a king of our people here.'

"Prahastha brought his new sovereign's message to Kubera's court. Kubera welcomed the messenger with every courtesy, and when he had listened to the rakshasa's message he sent a reply through him:

" 'Dasagriva, this Lanka was given to me by my father, and I have peopled her with my nairritas, whom I brought here with generous gifts of gold and homes. You are my brother, and you are welcome to come to live in Lanka and to share its bounty with me.'

"While Prahastha took this message back to Dasagriva, Vaisravana flew to his father Visravas in his pushpaka vimana. He said, 'Father, Dasagriva sent me a message through Prahastha, asking me to leave Lanka, because he means to be a king in our city and a king of the rakshasas of the world. I replied asking him to live with me in Lanka, to share the wealth of Lanka with me. But I am not sure how he will receive my offer.'

"Visravas's heart misgave him. He said, frowning, 'Ah, he is an evil child, your half-brother, both by his birth and now by the boons he has from Brahma. He will never agree to share Lanka with you. My advice to you is, leave Lanka and go to Kailasa with your people. The Mandakini flows beside Kailasa. Golden lotuses that shine like the sun float upon her waters: lotuses as blue as Vishnu's eyelids and those as white as moonbeams. Devas, apsaras, gandharvas, nagas, and kinnaras come to sing and dance and make love beside the Mandakini. I fear that with his boon, Dasagriva is so powerful that you must not make an enemy of him. Yes, my son, I am certain the best course is for you to leave Lanka with your nairritas and make yourself a home near Kailasa.'

"And so Kubera did. He founded the secret city of Alaka to the north of the Himalaya, and its marvelous pleasure garden, the Chaitra, which rivaled Indra's Nandana in Amravati. And with the Lord Siva's blessing, he was happy there.

"Meanwhile, Prahastha heard that Vaisravana had abandoned Lanka, and he came excitedly to Dasagriva, shouting, 'He has left Lanka! Vaisravana has left Lanka for you to rule!'

"Dasagriva embraced him and roared, 'You, my friend, shall be my chief minister in our city!' And indeed, Dasagriva and Prahastha have been as close as brothers ever since.

"So the enemy of the Devas, Dasagriva, entered the magnificent city of his mother's people. He was crowned king of Lanka, king of all the rakshasas, and his people flocked to him from across the earth and swarmed up to him from the deepest Patalas to the city of their fortune, to their invincible sovereign of night," said Agastya Muni.

5. *Dasagriva marries*

Agastya continued: "When Dasagriva had been crowned king of the rakshasas, he decided it was now time to give his sister Surpanaka away in marriage. He gave her to a Danava chieftain, a great mayavi: Kalaka's son Vidhujjiva.

"Shortly after this wedding was celebrated in Lanka, with pomp and ceremony, Dasagriva went off to hunt in a forest of Bharatavarsha. He had grown up in a jungle and was always drawn to the wilderness. Now, fatefully, in the darkling vana, he came across the Asura Mayaa, Diti's son. Mayaa was passing through that forest with his daughter.

"Dasagriva saw the young Asuri, who was the most beautiful woman in creation in those days, and he was smitten. He asked

Mayaa, 'Who are you? Who is the young woman you lead through this dangerous forest?'

"Mayaa looked at the Rakshasa before him and felt a current of fate stir in his heart. He said, 'Have you patience to listen to my story?'

"Dasagriva replied, 'I have.'

"Mayaa launched into his tale. 'There was an apsara called Hema, perhaps you have heard her name. Even as Puloma's daughter, Paulomi, was given to Indra by the Devas to be his wife, so, too, Hema was given to me. I lived with her for a thousand years and she was like my very breath to me. I am Mayaa, good Rakshasa, and I am the builder of the Asuras, even as Viswakarman is of the Devas. With my siddhis, I built for Hema a secret city in a jungle's heart. I made it with gold and paved its streets with cat's-eyes, topaz, diamonds, sapphires, rubies, and emeralds. I lined them with trees with silver leaves and built many mansions in which just we two lived.

" 'She bore me two sons, Mayavi and Dundubhi, and one daughter: this child you see. But fourteen years ago, my Hema left me because the Devas wanted her back in Amravati with them. My daughter was just a child then. I lived in my hidden city, until she grew into a young woman; and now I am abroad with her, for I must find her a husband. As you can see, Rakshasa, she is uncommonly beautiful, like her mother, and it will be hard to find the man who can contain her. I fear for my honor, with my child being so beautiful.

" 'But, stranger, you seem to be an exceptionally noble and strong rakshasa. Tell me who you are. Whose son are you?'

"All the while he spoke, the Asura Mayaa's dark and glowing eyes scrutinized Dasagriva with deep interest. When he finished speaking, he had no doubt the Rakshasa before him was an extraordinary young man: even a king, perhaps a king of destiny. Mayaa, also, had been a great king of his people once, in time out of mind. That was when three miraculous cities he built had circled the earth, and he and his two brothers had ruled from those fabled cities, the Tripura, which finally the Lord Siva torched from the sky. But that is another story.

"Dasagriva said humbly, 'I am Pulastya's grandson, Visravas's son. My name is Dasagriva.'

"When Mayaa heard who the Rakshasa was and when he saw how this Demon gazed at his daughter, the Asura said to Dasagriva, 'This is my daughter Mandodari. Will you have my child to be your wife, Dasagriva?'

"With no hesitation, Dasagriva said, 'I will marry her now,' and his eyes blazed with love.

"There in that vana, Dasagriva kindled a sacred fire and he married the Asuri Mandodari by the wild rite of gandharva vivaha. Mayaa had heard of Dasagriva before; he even knew how Visravas had cursed his mother Kaikasi. He also knew Dasagriva was Brahma's great-grandson, and he knew about the boons he had from the Pitamaha. Mayaa gave his son-in-law an occult shakti, which he himself had received from a God after a long tapasya. It was with Mayaa's shakti that Dasagriva struck your brother Lakshmana down, Rama," said Agastya.

Rama shivered to recall that moment. He asked the muni, "And what of Kumbhakarna and Vibheeshana? Did they not marry?"

"Indeed they did. Dasagriva had Kumbhakarna married to Vajra-jwala, who was the granddaughter of great Bali, the son of Virochana. Vibheeshana was married to a gandharva king's daughter. He married Sailusa's pious child Sarama, a child of dharma, who had been born near the Manasa sarovara. It was when the lake was about to break her banks during the monsoon that the pregnant gandharvi cried, 'Saro ma vardhayata!' [Lake, don't flood!] affectionately. And her child was named Sarama.

"Once they were married, the three rakshasa brothers came home to Lanka and were absorbed entirely for a time in their young, nubile wives. Then Mandodari, who was the most beautiful woman on earth by a long way, gave birth to a magnificent son, who would be Dasagriva's heir. When he was born, this child made a noise like spring clouds rumbling in the sky, and they called him Meghanada. This is the rakshasa Lakshmana killed: this was Indrajit.

"Cosseted by a hundred women in his father's harem, Indrajit grew in the palace of Lanka like fire hidden under a stack of wood."

6. The crimes of Dasagriva

Agastya continued, and no one in his audience stirred. "One day soon, Brahma's curse began to take effect on Kumbhakarna. He yawned for an hour and felt a fathomless slumber coming over him. He said to Dasagriva, 'My brother, I feel a great sleep come over me. Have a palace built, in which I can lie undisturbed.'

"At once Dasagriva commissioned the finest builders in Lanka to

537

raise a matchless edifice for Kumbhakarna. It was a yojana wide and two yojanas long. It was supported by columns of crystal on every side and pillars of gold and silver. Its stairways were encrusted lavishly with padmaraga. Its terraces were of ivory and its latticed windows were hung with little bells that sounded together in the breeze.

"Gently Dasagriva led his brother, whom he loved no less than his life, into the extraordinary palace and laid him down in its central chamber. There Kumbhakarna fell asleep on a bed of fragrant sandalwood, and he did not awaken for a thousand years.

"In rage, and missing his brother terribly, Dasagriva set about distracting himself from his sorrow by conquering the three worlds. He smashed Indra's legions; he slaughtered rishis, gandharvas, and yakshas without favor. He anointed himself with their blood, because he blamed them for the endless slumber Kumbhakarna lay in.

"Dasagriva arrived with his demonic army in the Nandana, outside Amravati. He devastated the enchanted garden like a rogue elephant on the rampage. He sullied its clear pools and rivers; he cut down its trees and savaged its flower banks. Then he and his rakshasas stormed Indra's city and pillaged it as they pleased. With wild yells they forced themselves upon the apsaras of heaven, in their homes, in the streets, as the nymphs of Devaloka tried to flee from the horrible invaders. Indra fled before the Rakshasa. He gave him an immense treasure as tribute, and Dasagriva returned to Lanka.

"Vaisravana sent a messenger from the Himalaya to his half-brother in Lanka. This yaksha first arrived in Vibheeshana's presence and was welcomed by the good rakshasa. Vibheeshana brought that strange being into Dasagriva's court. The messenger bowed and said to the Lord of Lanka, *'Jaya vijayi bhava!'* Be ever victorious.

"Dasagriva received this with a resounding silence. In a moment, the yaksha continued, 'My Lord Vaisravana, Kubera of the mountain, sends you a message, mighty Dasagriva. Your brother says to you, "Dasagriva, rule the worlds not with fear, but with dharma. Only the rule of dharma will bring you lasting fortune; only dharma will save you. I have seen what you did to the Nandana. It is a disgrace to our noble family. I have heard that you kill the rishis of the vana as if they were beasts made for hunting. I have heard your rakshasas drink their blood and eat their flesh.

" ' "Beware, my brother, their curses will fall on you. I warn you again, as an older brother must when he sees his younger brother fall into danger: turn back from this folly! Or terrible punishment will come to you.

" ' "Dasagriva, you have also killed my nairritas and yakshas upon the mountain. Listen to what I have to say to you. When I sat recently in a tapasya to the Lord Sankara, on a tableland near Kailasa, I saw a Devi, who was the very embodiment of beauty, walking past the place where I sat. She lit up the mountain with her lambency and I gazed helplessly at her. Indeed, I could not turn my eyes away from her, though I saw she resented my regard. In a mere moment, my left eye burst in my face, and my right eye was turned the color of ashes.

" ' "As I jumped up with a cry, I saw the Lord Siva appear before me, at that perfect woman's side. They seemed to be a single light, blinding, and they filled me with such peace that I hardly remembered my eye had burst.

" ' "Siva said kindly to me, 'Suvrata, Dharmajna, I am pleased with your tapasya. Why, yours is the finest penance performed upon this mountain since my own, when I won Uma for myself. Be my friend, Kubera, you have conquered me with your worship. This is Parvati; she is like your mother from now. We bless you, Vaisravana, you shall live next to us forever.'

" ' "The Devi Uma also raised her hand over me in a blessing, and they vanished before me.

" ' "Siva himself swore friendship with me. I warn you, leave the earth in peace, or you will pay for your crimes." So said my lord Kubera to you, O Dasagriva.'

"And the messenger fell silent. Dasagriva sat as if graven of stone. Not a muscle moved anywhere upon his person; only his eyes turned the color of ripe plums; that, and all his nine heads appeared and vanished, again and again, in their malignant cone around his central face.

"He scratched his cheek with a long talon, then said very softly, 'I do not like the message you dare to bring to my sabha, yaksha. Your master sends word through you of his friendship with Mahadeva. Does he mean to threaten me? I have held Vaisravana in honor because I have thought of him as my older brother. But time and again he taunts me, he insists on provoking me. And now he dares to send you to my sabha with this haughty message. He is arrogant that he is a Dikpala, and that Siva once gave him some gold and a ship of the air. But I am Dasagriva, and I am invincible. And after hearing your master's message, I have decided that I will conquer the three worlds.'

"Now he rose, tall and ominous, his eyes like flames, and his ten heads were plain in their evil cluster. Only now did the yaksha realize how angry the Rakshasa was. Only now did he realize that he might be in danger. But too late. His breath aflame, Dasagriva drew his curved sword and cut his half-brother's messenger down before his throne. He had the yaksha's body dragged out into the street, and gave it to his scavenger rakshasas to devour.

"Dasagriva summoned the brahmanas of Lanka and had them perform an elaborate ritual for his well-being and the success of his next enterprise. Without further ado, he took a fierce legion of demons with him, mounted his chariot, and rode out of Lanka like a black wind, to attack Vaisravana, Lord of treasures, in his city in the north."

7. In Kubera's city

Agastya continued: "With six ferocious rakshasa commanders, Mahodara, Prahastha, Maricha, Suka, Sarana, and Dhrumraksha, in a ring around him, Dasagriva flew north through the air toward Mount Kailasa. He flitted over rivers laid like blue threads across the earth and plains like jade with brown hills jutting from them, flashed over unexplored jungles, and crossed the formidable Himalaya. In just a few hours that army arrived at Vaisravana's gates and made camp.

"The yakshas of the mountain heard of Dasagriva's advent and fled to their master's city, Alaka. Meanwhile, news of what Dasagriva had done to his messenger also reached Kubera. The Lokapala stood before his teeming legions, raised his hands high above his head, and roared, 'Kill the Rakshasa! Kill all the rakshasas, that they dare to murder our messenger and come to attack us here. No matter that Dasagriva is my brother; he must die.'

"Crying their strange cries, like a sea roused to break its shores, the army of nairritas streamed out from their white city fortress and charged the rakshasa legion camped below them. They outnumbered Dasagriva's demons by a hundred to one, but the force from Lanka, especially its commanders, fought a spectacular battle. Each of the six who surrounded their ten-headed king killed a thousand yakshas, and Dasagriva killed ten times as many.

"Wave after wave of brave yakshas swept at the Rakshasa. He stopped them as a great cliff does the tide. He let flow a river of yakshas' blood, staining the white mountain scarlet. They beset him with a veritable night of maces, clubs, javelins, arrows, and other, more mysterious missiles Kubera's people are masters of. They cast sorceries at the Lord of Lanka, and drew blood on him like the wild roses of spring. For a time they arrested Dasagriva's frenzy of slaughter. They managed to check the bloody career of his chariot.

"With a roar that stopped the wind on the mountain, Dasagriva seized up a huge mace, like Yama's danda, and leaped out of his chariot straight into the midst of the thronging yakshas. Like a volcano he erupted on them. His arms were a blur, the mountain air was a denseness of piteous shrieks: the yakshas fell all around him and their blood lapped around his feet.

"Mahodara, Prahastha, and the other rakshasa chieftains were hardly less dreadful than their ten-faced master was. Like snow on the Himalaya at the arrival of summer, Vaisravana's army melted at their onslaught. Limbs hewn from their trunks flew through the sunlit air, borne by invisible hands, and fell far away from those to whom they belonged. Severed heads rolled giddily down the mountain slope.

"Some of the rakshasas struck off their enemies' heads and then seized the headless trunks and swilled greedily from the open necks, their eyes as red as the blood that gushed into their wild mouths and flowed down their chests. Other rakshasas tore out the entrails of slain yakshas and wore them as macabre garlands. Soon the delicate nairritas could not bear the invaders' brutality, and fled back to their master in his city of gold and ice.

"A magnificent yaksha chieftain, Samyodhakantaka, killed a thousand rakshasas. He felled Maricha with a keening chakra, and knocked him down a sheer gorge, where the demon lay senseless for an hour; and Samyodhakantaka thought he had killed that rakshasa. Then, even as the yaksha cut down a thousand common rakshasas with some breathtaking archery and their gore flowed, mingling with yakshas' blood, Maricha flew up from the gorge he had fallen into. Roaring to shake the snow from the loftiest peaks, he hacked thrice at Samyodhakantaka with his curved scimitar, drawing three crescented fonts of blood from the yaksha. Howling, Kubera's commander fled.

"Now no yaksha or nairrita barred Dasagriva's way into his half-brother's city. The Rakshasa entered the golden portals of Alaka, contemptuously cutting down the last line of resistance: a meager, frightened company of dwarapalakas. At the next, inner door, Vaisravana's main dwarapalaka, the powerful Suryabhanu, stood in Dasagriva's way. With a growl from ten faces, the Rakshasa hewed at him with his sword. But the yaksha pulled up a stone pillar next to the door and struck Dasagriva across all his faces, drawing ten geysers of blood.

"Now Dasagriva's roar shook the white city down to its foundations of rock and up to its turrets of ice. He leaped at Suryabhanu like a tiger, snatched the pillar out of his hands, crushed his head with it like a mushroom, flattening the skull, and was sprayed with the yaksha's brains. All the other yakshas who crouched within the doorway melted away into the inner labyrinth of caves and streams within Kubera's secret city.

"Seated in his sabha, Vaisravana watched the rout of his army. He saw them run like children before the Rakshasa, who had breached his city like some plague. Beside him stood Manibhadra, his yaksha Senapati, his general of generals. Manibhadra stood quivering with rage, and Kubera, his master of the gray eye, said to him, 'Go, my friend, kill this Rakshasa and become the sanctuary of your people.'

"Taking his palace guard, four thousand of them, Manibhadra went to battle. These yakshas were the finest of Kubera's fighting men. They were all masters of maya, and fought with mysterious ayudhas, spewing banks of spectral flames. They killed a thousand rakshasas. But infused by their master's power, the rakshasa maharathikas seemed invincible. Prahastha killed a thousand yakshas by himself, and Mahodara, another thousand. And Maricha was implacable: he killed two thousand nairritas.

"Manibhadra himself faced Dhrumraksha on the pale and crimson field. Dhrumraksha struck the yaksha squarely in his chest with a great pestle weapon. But like a mountain struck by lightning, the yaksha did not flinch. He swung his own mace at Dhrumraksha's head, and the rakshasa fell spouting blood from a deep wound. Dasagriva rushed toward him. Manibhadra aimed three lightlike shaktis at the rakshasa king, but they fell off the Demon like the stems of flowers.

"Dasagriva knocked Manibhadra's gleaming crown askew with a

thought-swift arrow, and the stupendous yaksha was called Parswa-mauli since. Unable to withstand the ferocity of the fight Dasagriva offered, Manibhadra turned away from his adversary. Then a gasp went up from the advancing rakshasa legions. They stopped in their tracks, rooted, trembling. Dasagriva turned his head to where his sol-diers gazed, where a dazzling light shone now, as if a bit of the sun had fallen to the earth.

"There, his mace in his hands, swathed in the refulgence of a Loka-pala, stood Vaisravana himself, with two of his ministers, Sukra and Prausthapada, and two of the demigods who ruled two of Kubera's nine treasures: Padma and Sankha. In a voice that shook the palace, Vaisravana said, 'Dasagriva, you fool, what have you done? Don't you know these crimes will lead you straight to hell? How often I have warned you, but you are blind with arrogance and you will not listen to me. I will say no more; come let us fight.'

"And the Lord of the yakshas, the Dikpala of the north, was at the rakshasas like a force of nature. Dasagriva's warriors wilted before that assault of light. Maricha, Prahastha, Mahodara, and the others fled be-fore Vaisravana; only Dasagriva stood his ground. Kubera fetched him a blow like the end of time on his central head, but his half-brother re-ceived it as a God might an offering. His ten heads now flashed into view and ten horrible laughs filled the courtyard where they fought.

"For a while they fought with maces and blows like earthquakes. Kubera loosed an agneyastra at Dasagriva. But the Rakshasa doused its fires with a varunastra; and now the Rakshasa began to fight with maya. He assumed a thousand different forms: some terrifying, others deceptively gentle; some human, some almost divine, and some bes-tial. Dasagriva hunted among the yakshas like a tiger, a boar, a cloud, a hill, a sea, a tree, a yaksha himself, a Daitya.

"Then suddenly he vanished altogether, all his thousand forms. But Vaisravana's soldiers still died in waves around him. Dasagriva had made himself invisible; he still stalked the enemy, unseen, cut their heads from their necks, and drank their blood with all his ten mouths. Often you could see a headless corpse suspended in midair, and the blood gushing from its naked throat would vanish eerily.

"Finally, Dasagriva appeared again, in sinister splendor. He held a sleek iron club in his hand and, quick as light, he struck Kubera on his head with it. Flowing blood, the Lord of treasures, the Lokapala,

Siva's friend, the rishi who was equal to a Deva, fell unconscious. He fell like an asoka tree in scarlet bloom, which had been cut down at its roots.

"The Devas who were present, Padma, Sankha, and the others, spirited Vaisravana away to the Nandana in Amravati, where he was restored with magical herbs and poultices. But that was the end of the battle, and Dasagriva had vanquished his half-brother. Roaring his triumph, the Rakshasa entered Kubera's palace and plundered whatever took his fancy. But the prize he cherished most was the pushpaka vimana.

"The fabled vimana had pillars of gold; its arched doorway was made of vaidurya and padmaraga. Nests of pearls covered its dome, and inside were trees of the most pristine strains, which bore ambrosial fruit in every season. The ship of the sky assumed any form its master chose, and it flew anywhere in the three worlds at his very wish. Viswakarman had created that vimana, and now Kubera's conqueror, his brother Dasagriva, night-stalker, Lord of the night, flew down from Kailasa in the peerless pushpaka. And Dasagriva did not doubt any more that he would soon be master of the three worlds."

8. Dasagriva gets a new name

Rama asked keenly, "And what did Dasagriva do next, Muni? We knew so little about the Rakshasa, and yet it was our destiny to face him in battle."

Agastya resumed. "When he had vanquished Kubera, Dasagriva wanted to see the legendary thicket of sara reeds in which Siva's son, the Lord Karttikeya, had been born. He flew to the banks of the Ganga in his newly taken treasure, the pushpaka vimana, and he saw the bed of reeds that shone as if pollen from the sun had been scattered over it. The vimana flew up to a hill above the sacred thicket and would not move even when the Rakshasa willed it to.

"Dasagriva cried, 'What has happened? Someone on this hill has arrested our flight.'

"Maricha ventured to suggest, 'Perhaps, my lord, the pushpaka vimana will not bear anyone save Vaisravana?'

"Just then they saw a hideous being approaching them. He was a Siva gana, sallow-complexioned, dwarfish, thickset, misshapen, his head shaven, his arms short and massive, and obviously strong. And from his face, it was plain that he was full of unearthly joy, always. It was Nandiswara, Siva's mount, in his human form.

"Nandin said in a ringing voice, 'Turn back, Dasagriva. My Lord Sankara is with Uma on this hill, and none of the created may come here, not the gandharvas, nagas, yakshas, Devas, suparnas, Asuras, or rakshasas.'

"Dasagriva climbed down from his vimana; his kundalas quivered for the wrath he felt, and his eyes were the color of dusk. His voice quivering, he breathed, 'Who is this Sankara of yours?' At that moment he saw Nandin grow as refulgent as Siva himself, and he saw the gana had a monkey's face and held a flaming pike in his hands. Dasagriva threw back his head and roared with laughter that was like lightning exploding in the sky.

"Nandin grew very still, then said, 'Dasanana, ten-headed Demon, you dare laugh at my vanara form today. I could kill you even now, little Rakshasa, for you have no boon to save you from me. But I curse you instead. I curse you that you and your arrogant rakshasas shall be razed by the wild race of monkeys. They shall have my strength; they shall be as radiant and full of faith as I am. Claws and fangs shall be their weapons. They will have the mind's swiftness, and they will be like a legion of mountains come to your gates to crush your rakshasas. As for you, Dasagriva, your sins shall come hunting you as your death.'

"When Nandiswara pronounced his curse, a battery of drums sounded in Devaloka, as Indra's people rejoiced. But Dasagriva was not moved. He said evenly, 'Bull-like, what power does your master Siva wield that he sports like a king all the time? How does this hill arrest my vimana's flight? Does Siva not know that I, Dasagriva, have come here? Doesn't he know danger is near him?'

"With that, Dasagriva bent, thrust his hands under the hill, and drew it out of the ground by its roots. The hill shook violently. Siva's ganas on its summit trembled; Parvati slipped, and clung to her lord. Siva laughed; playfully he pressed down on the hill with his toe. Dasagriva's arms like columns were broken and thrust into their sockets. His roar of pain reverberated through creation, like the thunder of the pralaya. In Devaloka, Indra and his lambent people quaked to hear that sound. Oceans rose in mountainous waves and crashed against their shores. The earth wobbled in her orbit.

"Yakshas, gandharvas, and vidyadharas cried in alarm, 'Hah! What sound is that? Is the world ending?'

"Dasagriva wailed on. Birds wheeled in panic and animals dashed through their jungles in a frenzy of fear. Dasagriva still did not stop his dreadful howling, and an asariri said to him, 'Worship Siva, Rakshasa. He is kind, and he will bless you if you worship him.'

"It is told that, standing on one foot, Dasagriva then played on the vina, while he held that hill aloft with his broken arms and, for a thousand years, sang hymns from the Samaveda, which praise the blue-throated Nilakanta, Uma's Lord. And all the while, he wept.

"Siva sat with Parvati on the crest of the hill and enjoyed the Rakshasa's singing. When a thousand years had passed, the Lord said kindly to Dasagriva, 'Rakshasa, I am pleased with your worship and your valor. I will grant you a boon. But first, I will give you a name. Since you terrified the creatures of all the worlds with your wailing, I name you Ravana. From now, let the beings of the three worlds know you by that name. Go where you will, Ravana, go without fear.'

"Ravana's arms were healed. He set down the hill, gently, and prostrated himself before the God of Gods. He said, 'Lord, if you are truly pleased, grant me a boon. O Siva, I already have a boon from Brahma. You grant me a long life, Lord, and give me a great weapon.'

"Siva granted Ravana the boon he wanted, and gave the Rakshasa a glittering sword called the Chandrahasa. Then Siva and his ganas vanished from before the Rakshasa's eyes. Named anew by Siva himself, and with the Lord's inexorable blade in his hands, Ravana climbed back into the pushpaka vimana and now it flew wherever he wanted it to.

"No one could resist the Rakshasa any more and he soon conquered most of creation. Those that dared oppose him, he dealt with mercilessly, and the others yielded, saying, 'We are vanquished,' and he lost further interest in them.

"The Devas and all the races of heaven and earth sent Ravana tribute, and he was, indeed, the undisputed sovereign of all he surveyed. A tide of evil, whose font was Ravana of Lanka, swept the earth."

9. Vedavati's curse

"Ravana was a restless spirit. He never tired of ranging through the world, his domain. Once he went into the heart of a deep jungle and saw a sight that riveted him. Under a nyagrodha tree sat a young woman at dhyana. She wore the hide of a black antelope; her hair was matted in jata, like any rishi's, and she shone like a goddess in the dimness. She was in the sensuous bloom of her youth, and beautiful past describing.

"The Rakshasa stood staring helplessly at her for a while. Then he approached her and said softly, with a laugh, 'What are you doing here, young woman? Your youth and beauty do not belong in this forest of hermits. Why, a rishi could go mad just to look at you. Who are you, my beauty? Who is your husband? Ah, he is a lucky man that lies with you. And, tell me, why do you sit here in dhyana? Tapasya is not for the likes of you, auspicious one?'

"As any sannyasi should, she welcomed Ravana and made him comfortable. When he sat at his ease, she said, 'I am Kusadhvaja's daughter, and my father was Brihaspati's son and a brahmarishi himself. My father spent his life chanting the Vedas, and I, O Lord of the rakshasas, am called Vedavati. For I am the Vedas embodied in a woman's form, and I was born out of my father's bhakti.

" 'Many gandharvas, yakshas, pannagas, and rakshasas have begged my father for my hand. But he will never give me to any of them. Would you hear why, O Ravana?'

"And he was so enchanted with her that of course he would. Vedavati said, 'My father said he would only give me to the Lord Vishnu. When the Daitya king Sambhu heard this, he was furious. He arrived in our asrama one moonless night, killed my father in his sleep, and melted back into the darkness of which he was born. When my mother saw my father dead, she made a pyre and burned herself on it with my father's body.

" 'I have lived here in their asrama ever since, and I have kept the image of Narayana, the sleeper on the waters, in my heart. For my father's sake, I am determined I will marry Vishnu and no one else. It is to bring him to me that I sit here in tapasya. So now you know about me; I beg you, leave me to my dhyana.'

"But Ravana already quivered from wanting her. He said, 'You waste your youth for this foolishness! There is no woman in the three worlds as beautiful as you are. How can you do this to yourself? Anuttamaa, peerless one, only an old woman will sit like this in dhyana; not someone like you, blessed already with every gift a woman could want. Look, I am Ravana and I am the Emperor of the rakshasas. Why, I am Emperor of the three worlds because there is no one in any of them who can match my valor or my strength. Come, Vedavati, be my queen and enjoy every pleasure, as you were born to.

" 'And, tell me, who is this Vishnu for whose sake you desolate your youth?'

"Mortified, she said, 'Vishnu is the Lord of the three worlds. Only you would ask who he is so contemptuously.'

"With a terrible growl, Ravana sprang toward her. He seized her by her hair, to slake himself at once on her sinuous body. But she cried out in grief and rage, and her very hand turned into a blade. She sheared her hair off with it, leaving him holding her tresses. Still, he came after her. He laid his coarse hands on her. He forced himself upon her virgin, exquisite body. When he had spent himself in a paroxysm of violence, she rose and stood over him like a fire.

" 'Rakshasa, you have violated me and my life is a ruined thing. I will not live another day. But I swear I will be born again, and I will be your death, Ravana of Lanka. Alas, that I may not curse you, even now. You have sinned on my body, and if I curse you I will lose my own tapasya shakti.'

"With the power of her yoga, she kindled a fire and walked into it. As the Rakshasa watched in mild curiosity, Vedavati became ashes before his eyes."

Rama asked, "And was she born again?"

Agastya Muni said, with a smile, "Indeed she was, Rama. She was born in the next yuga, from a furrow in the earth, and her father who found her in a field named her Sita. And she did truly come as Ravana's death, and she also had Vishnu for her husband even as her father Kusadhvaja had wanted."

"What did Ravana do after Vedavati killed herself?"

"Ravana slept for a while, after he had enjoyed Vedavati, and also enjoyed watching her die. Then he climbed back into his pushpaka vimana and ranged the sky again, as he pleased, going wherever he chose to, as slowly or as quickly as he liked.

"One day, he came to Usirabija and the Rakshasa saw a great sacrifice under way below him. King Marutta of Ikshvaku was the sacrificer, and his ritvik was Brihaspati's brother Samvarta. All the Devas attended the yagna upon the mountain. When Indra and his illustrious people saw Ravana in their midst, they were terrified. In a wink they transformed themselves into beasts and birds and tried to hide from him.

"Indra became a peacock, Yama was a crow, Kubera a chameleon, and Varuna a swan. So, too, all the others; Vayu, Agni, Surya, Soma, the Aswins, and the rest were all wild, and some exotic, creatures. Ravana walked into the yagnashala like an unclean dog.

"The Rakshasa stalked up to King Marutta and said with untold menace, 'Either fight me or admit I am your master.'

"Marutta asked, 'Who are you?'

"Ravana laughed. 'So you don't know me, even when the Devas slink away as beasts when I arrive? You don't know the pushpaka vimana, which I took from my brother Kubera? I am Ravana of Lanka. I am the Lord of the three worlds.'

"Marutta said calmly, 'He who vanquishes his older brother in battle deserves to be praised, indeed. Why, he who rides in the pushpaka vimana is a matchless one. Tell me, Ravana of Lanka, what tapasya did you do that you are so powerful? Come, sit here beside me for a while and tell me everything about yourself. We have time, Rakshasa, for you will not leave here alive.'

"And Marutta picked up his bow and quiver and made ready to attack Ravana, but his priest Samvarta restrained him. 'If you leave your yagna unfinished, Siva's curse will consume your very race. He who has been consecrated for a sacrifice shall not let anger approach him.' The knowing Samvarta lowered his voice: 'Moreover, the Rakshasa before you is invincible, Marutta. It is far from certain that you will win a battle against him.'

"Marutta bowed to his guru and laid down his weapons. He turned back to his yagna, at which Suka gave a shrill shout, 'Victory to Ravana!'

"Ravana, meanwhile, had devoured many of the august rishis and munis that had gathered at Marutta's yagna. With all his ten faces leaking sages' blood, he left the yagnashala and climbed into the pushpaka vimana once more.

"As soon as the Rakshasa left, the Devas, the gandharvas, and the other celestial folk resumed their true and brilliant forms. Indra, who had been a peacock, said to that bird, 'You shall never have to fear serpents again, for a thousand eyes like mine will adorn your tail. And whenever you want to dance, just think of me and I will send you down a shower of fragrant rain.'

"The Lord Yama, who is death and justice, said to the crow that was perched on the pragvamsa of the house in which Marutta and his queen dwelt during the yagna, 'I am pleased with you, dark bird. The diseases of the earth, which torment every other living creature, will have no sway over you. Besides, you will know no fear. Death is your friend from now, and the fear of death is the cause of every other fear. You will never die of old age or sickness, but only when you are killed. And, O crow, whenever you eat in this world, all the spirits in my realm who are hungry shall feel sated, they and their families.'

"Varuna said to the swan that glided upon the pool of the Ganga, 'King of birds, your feathers will glow like the full moon. And no other creature shall be as beautiful as you. Whenever you are in water, you will feel unequaled bliss.'

"Rama, did you know that once swans were not purely white, but had brown wing tips and breasts? And the peacock was just blue and had no eyelets on his feathers."

Rama smiled and shook his head, that he had not known this. Agastya went on, enjoying his tale, "Then Visravas's son Kubera said to the chameleon sunning himself on a rock, 'I am pleased with you, my friend. Let your dark head have a golden hue from now.'

"Marutta duly completed his yagna, and the Devas returned to their Swarga on high, with their king Indra," Agastya concluded the tale of Ravana and the Devas at the ancient king Marutta's famous sacrifice. And Marutta was, of course, an ancestor of Rama, born in the House of Ikshvaku, the royal House of the Sun, and he also cursed Ravana, when his yagna was complete.

10. The curse of Anaranya

"Ravana ranged the earth and went to the cities of all its kings. He would say to each one, 'Give me battle, or say I am your master.'

"The kshatriyas who had heard of the boons the Rakshasa had from the Gods were wise enough not to fight him. Through the ages, awesome monarchs like Dushyanta, Suratha, Gadhi, Gaya, and Pururavas admitted: 'You are my master.'

"Then, Ravana came to Ayodhya, where Anaranya now ruled, and demanded, 'Give me battle, or say I am your master.'

"Anaranya replied, 'I will fight you, night ranger.'

"Anaranya had gathered an immense army, with ten thousand elephant, a hundred thousand horse, many thousands of chariots, and countless foot soldiers. A pitched battle began between the forces of darkness and light. But with Ravana leading them, and Siva's sword flashing like an arc of the sun in his hands, the rakshasa legions consumed the legions of Hastinapura, even as the fathomless sea does every stream and river that flows into him. Anaranya's forces perished like a swarm of moths flying into a forest fire.

"Anaranya himself plunged at Ravana. On his way he put Maricha, Suka, and Sarana to flight, as a lion might some jackals. Anaranya shot eight hundred scorching arrows at Ravana. But they harmed the Rakshasa as much as raindrops do the crown of a mountain. Ravana rode at the king of men, and, with a growl, struck him with his hand across his face, and the kshatriya fell out of his chariot like a sala tree struck by lightning. He lay dying on the ground.

"Mocking him, Ravana said, 'So, Kshatriya, what have you gained by fighting Ravana? Perhaps you were so steeped in the pleasures of your harem you never heard who I am? There is no one in the three worlds, puny human, who can vanquish Ravana of Lanka.'

"Anaranya breathed, 'My life leaves me as a summer breeze does a forest at twilight. But you have not conquered my spirit, Rakshasa, as you did the other kings'. And I say to you, at this moment of my death, that even as I have been generous to anyone who came seeking my help, as I have poured oblations onto a sacred fire, as I have ruled my people justly, and as I have sat in dhyana every sandhya of each day of my life: Demon, a prince born into this same House of Ikshvaku shall kill you.'

"As he pronounced his curse, a drumroll of the Devas sounded in the sky and petal rain fell out of Swarga. Anaranya's soul left his broken body and rose into Devaloka in a blaze of light. Ravana stood grimacing over the king's corpse for a moment; what the dying man had said disturbed his savage heart. He planted his foot briefly on the dead king's face and turned away from yet another conquest, bloodthirsty still," said Agastya Muni in Ayodhya's sabha.

The rishi paused briefly, then, because no one stirred in the court but waited raptly for him to continue, he resumed.

"Once, even as he terrorized the denizens of the earth, the Rakshasa met Narada Muni. He was crossing the sky in his vimana when he saw Narada sailing blithely along on a cloud.

"Ravana hailed the wanderer, 'Narada! How have you come down to the earth today?'

"The brahmarishi said to the Demon, 'O Son of Visravas, tarry a while with me; I would speak to you. I have followed your exploits and I am pleased with you. Why, I compare your conquests of the gandharvas and the nagas with Vishnu's victories over the Daityas. But my son, I have some advice for you. The mortal beings of the earth hardly deserve your attentions, O Ravana whom even Indra and the Devas, the Danavas, and the yakshas cannot subdue! They are too puny. Why waste your time with these insignificant, weak, and transient creatures, who fly into death's clasp anyway?

" 'I beg you, greatest of night stalkers, don't prey on these petty, unfortunate beings, who are already victims of hunger, thirst, old age, fate, disease, and every kind of anxiety and grief. Look at this unjust, absurd world of men, Rakshasa. Here you find some men steeped in wine, song, and women, and hardly a stone's throw away, others of the same race shed bitter tears of hunger, deprivation, and torment, unheeded by their brothers.

" 'These humans are slaves to every kind of delusion. And they are your subjects, Ravana, who can doubt it? Deceiving themselves that they are immortal, they plunge headlong toward Yama's gates. They are blind creatures, of no wisdom and full of folly. I tell you, the only real Lord of all mortal men is Yama, the Lord of death. Ravana, subdue Yama and you will be master of all this dying world.'

"Dreadful smiles dawned on the Rakshasa's ten faces. He did not pause to reflect for a moment before saying, 'Narada, I will fly down into Rasatala and conquer the worlds of nether. I will quell the nagas, the Devas, and the other immortals, and rule the three realms. After which, Muni, I shall churn the ocean for the amrita which will make me immortal: Lord of all creation, forever!'

"Narada murmured, 'Then why do you fly on another path through the sky? Set yourself on the path that leads to the city of the Lord of death. Your fame shall truly begin when you have vanquished Yama.'

"The ten-headed one laughed like the rumbling of an autumn cloud. He said, 'Yama is as good as vanquished, Muni. I have already sworn I will crush not only Surya's son, but also the Lords of the four quarters, the Lokapalas. But first let me fly south to Yama's kingdom, and when I have conquered him, the living beings of the earth shall be free of their torment of the fear of death.'

"With a deep bow and a wave, the Rakshasa flitted away south, leaving Narada pensive on his cloud that shone like a full moon with the radiance of his body. Narada wondered, 'How will the Rakshasa defeat Yama, who knows every creature, his gifts and deeds; who metes out justice to each one; who is the terror of the worlds? And if, indeed, he does conquer the son of Surya, what new order will the Rakshasa create for the earth?'

"Narada shook his head in some wonder at the thought. Then, he said to himself, 'I must not miss the encounter between the Demon and the Lord Death.'

"He, too, flew quick as a ray of light toward Yama's city."

11. Ravana and Yama

"Narada arrived like an effulgent thought in Yama's sabha, and saw Death on his throne. Yama welcomed the muni with every courtesy, and when Narada was comfortably ensconced in his court, he asked him, 'Brahmarishi, to what do I owe this honor today?'

" 'Pitriraja, King of the manes, the Rakshasa Ravana is on his way here and he means to challenge you. If you are vanquished, O Yama, who will wield the dharma danda?'

"Even as he spoke, they saw the pushpaka vimana fill the sky like a sun. It scattered the natural darkness of the kingdom of death.

"Ravana saw the dead in Yama's kingdom; he saw them reap the fruit of their karma, intricately, variously, good and bad. He saw Yama's servitors torment the sinners who had come to him; he heard their cries. He saw thousands of evil men being devoured by worms and packs of slavering dogs; and of course they did not die because they were already dead, but only suffered endless agony.

"He saw other souls ceaselessly crossing the Vaitarani, the river of blood: back and forth, again and again. Others walked through interminable deserts whose sands were like burning dust. Yet others were being cleaved with gleaming swords from the crowns of their heads to the forks of their legs, and their screams filled the air. Others wept for quenchless thirst, and others for ravening hunger that fed on the starving souls.

"Elsewhere, the Rakshasa saw those that had done good enjoying the fruit of their punya. They lived in lavish houses, from whose windows delectable strains of music floated. They were attended by the most charming women and ate the finest food. They wore gold and jewels on their bodies, and were illumined by the light of their own purity.

"With a roar from ten heads, Ravana flew at the dead who suffered dreadful torture. He fell on Yama's soldiers who tormented them, and let flow a river of their blood. Yama's servants fled and Ravana liberated the sinners from their suffering. These shouted his name so the sky of that naked realm echoed with its three syllables. They rejoiced at the undreamed-of release the Rakshasa brought.

"Again, Yama's dark legions swarmed at the invading Demon, now from every corner of the kingdom of death. In their millions, like hives of angry bees, they attacked the pushpaka vimana with all sorts of weapons. It would have fallen out of the sky; but Brahma's power and the power of the Devas, who were embodied in amsa in the mystic craft, kept it aloft. The wounds it received from naracha and astra, shakti and every missile cast at it, cleared miraculously, as if great healing hands were laid on it, constantly.

"Ravana and his demons flowed blood from all their limbs. Yet they fought on as if they were unhurt, their roars fiercer than ever, the stream of arrows from their bows thicker and more livid with each moment. For their part, Yama's soldiers fought as fiercely as the enemy. As storm clouds will a mountain, they encircled him. They cut Ravana's armor from his dark, lean body and his blood sprayed out of it in geysers. For a moment he fell unconscious on the floor of his vimana.

"But Ravana's boon protected him and he was soon on his feet again, truly roused now, and fighting more powerfully than ever. He leaped out of his flying ship and shot an infernal mahesvarastra at Yama's legions. It swept at them like a flash fire in a dry forest in summer. Strange beasts of the astra came bounding after the flames at Yama's soldiers. The legions of the Lord Death were consumed like a field of straw. Ravana threw back his ten heads and emitted a roar that convulsed the three worlds.

"Yama heard that roar, and his eyes turned the color of a setting sun. He knew his legions had been razed, and, in a low and terrible voice, he said, 'Fetch my chariot.'

"His sarathy brought his golden ratha to his palace steps. With a lance that was alive with a hundred secret fires and a hammer of flames in his hands, the Master of death, into whom all the worlds and their

554

creatures are absorbed when their time comes, climbed into his myste-rious chariot. Beside him the staff of time, the kaaladanda, stood em-bodied: a great and terrible spirit, bright as sun flares. On his other side was a burning noose, a flawless and primeval paasa. When the three worlds saw him like that, silent and furious, he who is Time per-sonified, they trembled.

"Blazing horses took to the sky, swift and smooth as wishes, and Yama flew at Ravana. When Ravana's ministers saw Death flying at them, quicker than time, when they saw how entirely dreadful he was, they either fainted or fled. But Ravana himself was imperturbable. He did not flinch at the sight of Yama; indeed, ten savage smiles lit his dark faces.

"Yama loosed a burning fusillade of every sort of weapon at the Demon. Ravana replied with a storm of arrows that covered the son of Surya's chariot in light and fire. A mythic battle ensued, a tumultu-ary battle, and it seemed the end of creation had come betimes. Brahma arrived there with the Devas and gandharvas to watch that battle of battles.

"Ravana's bow gleamed in his hands like Indra's vajra. He shot Yama with four smoking shafts through his vital organs, and his sarathy with seven. There issued from Yama's chasmic mouth a roar as of the ages ending; from his jaws gaping as wide as the firmament there erupted a roar more reverberant than any of Ravana's. From the jaws of Death sprang fires of wrath, with white flames for their peaks. They spumed out as if to consume the universe, and dark smoke with them.

"Those flames licked themselves into a sky-straddling black form, an embodiment of terror. In a voice of the storm clouds of the pralaya, that form, the Kaalatman, spoke to the refulgent Yama: 'No creature that I mark shall live. Why, Hiranyakashyapu, Namuchi, Sambara, Nishandi, Dhumaketu, Virochana's son Bali, Sambhu the titan, Vritra-sura, Vaana, all the rishis, gandharvas, and great nagas, yakshas, all the hosts of Devaloka, this Bhumi with all its oceans, mountains, rivers, trees, and creatures: all these I devour, when their time comes. Yama, now leave me alone with this Rakshasa. He shall not live another hour; that is nature's law.'

"Yama, who is the Lord of dharma, said, 'Stand apart, Great Spirit, for I will kill the Rakshasa today.'

"And Yama Deva stood forth with the kaaladanda, with its circle of flames like a crown, and with the embodied hammer and a thunderbolt quivering with cosmic ire. When Yama took the staff of death in his hands and raised it to strike Ravana of Lanka down, it glowed with a horrible sheen and all the rakshasas fled that battlefield in panic. Even the Devas, watching unseen, felt a tremor of fear.

"Suddenly, Brahma materialized before the Lord Death and said to him, 'Yama, you must not kill the Rakshasa with the kaaladanda. If you do, I will become a liar, because I have given him a boon that no immortal, no Deva, gandharva, rakshasa, Asura, or Daitya shall cause his death. If I am proved a liar, O Yama, the three worlds shall perish.

" 'I fashioned the danda you hold in your hand, O Lord of dharma. If you strike Ravana with it and he does not die, the three worlds shall fry to a crisp in the flames of your staff. I beg you, though your cause is just: desist. If you use the kaaladanda against the Rakshasa, my creation will be destroyed, regardless of whether Ravana dies or not.'

"And the pious Yama set aside his weapon. He said, 'If I cannot kill this Rakshasa because of your boon to him, why should I fight him any more?'

"And Yama Deva vanished like a great cloud from the field of battle, with his chariot, his horses, and his legions. Ravana's roar of triumph, that he had quelled Death, rocked the world. Like a sun from a tower of thunderheads, Ravana flew up from Yamaloka in his gleaming vimana. Yama, meanwhile, rose into Swarga with Brahma, Narada, who had watched all this avidly, and the other Devas."

12. The Nivatakavachas and others

"When Yama left the field, Ravana's ministers and commanders, who had fled in fear of the Lord Death, flocked back to their ten-headed king. They saw their master covered in his own blood. They saw the great gashes with which Yama had marked his body. They saw some broken bones protruding, ghastly, on his arms. Yet Ravana smiled at them, and they roared his name to the sky: that he was invincible and that he had conquered Death himself.

"Maricha, Prahastha, and the others fetched their king back into the pushpaka vimana and tended his wounds with rare and potent specifics. They sang his praises, and that was sweet music to his ears.

Now Ravana said they would enter Rasatala, the deepest of the Patalas, and subdue the netherworlds, as well: so he would truly be sovereign of the three realms.

"The only way down into Rasatala was through the ocean's bed, and Ravana set the pushpaka vimana on a course to plunge down into the blue waves, which are the domain of the marine titans and the nagas, who have both human and serpentine forms. Varuna is their Lord, and he protects them.

"Ravana erupted on Bhogavati, Vasuki's city. Battle-hardened by now, it did not take the Rakshasa long to subdue the city of serpents. He plowed on through the deepest ocean and arrived in Manimayi, city of jewels and of giants. The mysterious changeling titans, the Nivatakavachas, lived in Manimayi. These strange and powerful sons of Diti had impenetrable armor for skins and Brahma's boon that protected them.

"Undaunted, Ravana stormed their marvelous city. The Daityas were overjoyed: they are always ready for a battle. They fought back with every kind of weapon and with indomitable courage. The battle between the rakshasas and the Danavas churned the belly of the ocean. They fought for a year and neither prevailed, and the water around the jewel city was scarlet with blood.

"Finally, Brahma, who had blessed both Ravana and the Nivatakavachas, appeared in their midst, lighting up the ocean waves like a sun risen in the womb of the deeps. In an echoing voice he said, 'Not if you fight until time finds its end will either of you conquer the other. Let there be friendship between you, instead.'

"And so Ravana and the Nivatakavachas made peace with each other. They swore friendship by a sacred fire, and the marine demons welcomed the ten-headed Rakshasa into their city like a brother. He remained with them for a year, enjoying pleasures that were hardly to be tasted upon the surface of the earth. And from his new friends he learned a hundred mayic sorceries each day.

"Finally, almost reluctantly, Ravana left the city of the gigantic ocean Danavas. He ranged Rasatala, the deepest Patala, hidden away in the navel of the earth. Now he sought the secret city of Varuna, Lord of the sea.

"On his quest he saw the glimmering city of Asmanagara, where the Kaalakeyas, sons of the golden witch Puloma, dwelt. He invaded them like a curse. The Kaalakeyas were arrogant of their strength and streamed out of their fastness to give the Rakshasa battle. He killed more than four hundred of the quicksilver demons in an hour, his sword that Siva gave him flashing like some sleek and silvery predator from another time.

"He smashed his way through the Kaalakeyas' city, leaving a trail of blood that rose slowly to the surface of the smoky sea. Fourteen thousand Kaalakeyas perished; among them was the husband of Ravana's sister Surpanaka. Past the city of the Kaalakeyas, Ravana saw another city that looked like a white cloud under the waves. It shone like an immense pearl, like another Kailasa. He saw Surabhi there, the mother of Siva's bull Nandisvara, and milk flowed from her teats into the mystic white sea that is called Kshiroda, the ocean of milk. The moon rises from that sea, and the greatest munis of the universe live on the froth of the milk of Surabhi, the cow of wishes. The amrita, which is the food of the Devas, arises in that sea, as does the swadha, the food of the pitrs, the manes.

"Slowly, dazzled by her dappled beauty, Ravana alighted from his vimana and walked slowly round Surabhi, in pradakshina. Then he entered Varuna's ineffable city. Varuna's guardsmen challenged him. He struck many of them down, and roared at the others, 'Go and tell your master that Ravana has arrived in his city. Tell him he must either kneel before me with folded hands and acknowledge my sovereignty, or come and fight me.'

"The guards flew to their king, the Deva. Some of Varuna's sons and grandsons, powerful princes of the deep, issued from their gates and attacked Ravana. An intense battle broke out, but it hardly lasted some moments before Ravana and his rakshasas had razed the submarine legion, and the water turned softly crimson. Only Varuna's sons escaped the demons' virile onslaught.

"Those sons of the sea gathered themselves and fought back with stunning speed, strength, and occult siddhis. They rose above the pushpaka vimana and attacked Ravana all together, so fiercely that even he was forced to turn away from the encounter. The ocean princes' roars of triumph rocked Rasatala to its depths.

"In fury, Mahodara flew at the celebrant young immortals. He took them by surprise and briefly beat them back, smashing the chariots they had come to fight in. Still, they trod water and air; they swam like great fish; and now they turned on Mahodara with such cohesion and force that he fell in a swoon, blood pouring down all his limbs. With a roar that raised tidal waves around him, Ravana covered Varuna's sons with a tempest of astras. They could not stand the invincible Demon. They fell to his storm, and their merman warriors rushed to the watery field of battle and carried their unconscious princes back into their father's city.

"Ravana cried again, 'Announce me to Varuna, Lord of the ocean.'

"One of Varuna's ministers, Prahasa, came to the gates of the wondrous marine city and said, 'You have defeated Varuna's sons. Our Lord himself is away in Brahmaloka. It is in vain that you call for him here.'

"Ravana shouted in ten voices, 'The coward Varuna has fled before me! I am master of the Patalas, too.'

"And he rose again through six netherworlds and flew back to his Lanka. Now he had no doubt that he had subdued the three realms: Swarga, Bhumi, and Patala. He was master of all creation, or so he believed."

13. Women

Agastya Muni said in the sabha of Rama of Ayodhya, "The pushpaka vimana was full of the spoils of war the Rakshasa took from those he conquered in battle and those who yielded to him in fear. He took gold and jewels past compare, the rarest treasures wrought in the three worlds. And then there was another kind of spoil of war that he filled his ship of the sky with, generously: women. The most beautiful women of every race he subdued, any woman who caught his eye—he tore them away from their people and their families, their fathers and mothers, their husbands and children.

"Serpentine, seductive naga wives he took; young virgins and mothers, too. He filled his ship with exquisite gandharvis and Deva women, with dark and incomparable Asuris and rakshasis. The daughters and wives of human kings and the holiest rishis he wrenched, screaming, from their natural lives. And they crouched in the capacious vimana, which the Rakshasa turned into an aerial antapura, his harem in the sky.

"Their faces shone like the moon, their bodies were voluptuous and fragrant, and their tears fell onto the jewels that studded the floor of the magic craft, which Siva once gave Vaisravana, the Lord of treasures.

"One slender gandharvi shook like a leaf, wondering, 'Will the Rakshasa devour me?'

"Some sobbed more desperately than others did; they were mothers who had been torn from their small children, for the Demon's pleasure. But already there were some women who cursed their husbands for being conquered so easily, and who, despite their shock, let themselves admire Ravana: his lean, battle-hardened face and body, his dark and reverberant presence. Despite themselves, despite their predicament, they thought, 'Ah, he eclipsed a million great warriors, as the sun does the little stars at dawn.'

"And these would be the first to submit to the Demon, and they would taste a truly overwhelming and terrible love. But there were virtuous women among the thousands the Rakshasa abducted from across the three worlds, and these cursed him in their hearts, from the depths of fear and sorrow. They said, 'Evil One, this is the sin that breeds every other; this is the mother of sins. And as a thousand women shed tears of despair at what you have done to them, a woman shall bring your death to you, Ravana, in your very Lanka.'

"Briefly Ravana felt an unaccustomed coldness clutch his heart at these women's silent, potent curse. Briefly his face lost its radiance, and a shadow flitted across it. The pushpaka vimana landed in Lanka. Word of their king's sweeping conquests filled the streets, and the rakshasas came out in singing and dancing crowds to celebrate his victories and their own new power as the master race of the worlds. Suddenly, forgotten, mysterious Lanka was the focus of creation.

"Ravana was being borne to his palace on a thousand rakshasas' shoulders when he heard a keening sound, which echoed over every other in his noisy streets. It was the shrill ululation of a woman deranged with grief. Ravana saw his sister Surpanaka, her hair in disarray, her clothes torn, her face streaked with tears and dirt where she had rolled on the ground, unhinged that her brother Ravana had killed her husband Vidhujjiva, the Kaalakeya.

"When Ravana took her in his arms, he saw her eyes were the color of cherries, and he asked her, 'What has happened, little one? Who has brought these tears to your eyes? Just tell me his name and he shall not live another hour.'

"When she could speak, Surpanaka said, 'You killed my husband, O Rakshasa who call yourself my older brother. I loved him more than my life and you cut him down like any other enemy. What use is it my living any more, wretched Ravana, when you have made me a widow in my youth? Monster, I heard you killed him with your own hands. I am your younger sister and my husband is not just your brother-in-law, but meant to be like your own son. And you killed him.'

"He wiped her tears with his long fingers. He smoothed her hair and said gently, 'My child, my child, in the heat of war every enemy seems alike and just a target for arrows. Every enemy is one who would kill me, if I did not kill him first. I shot my arrows without looking whom I aimed at, for the Kaalakeyas rushed at me in a wave and every Asura was an indomitable warrior. I did not know whom I killed when I fought, Surpanaka; believe me I would never have killed him if I had known. You know how much I love you: why, I gave you away to Vidhujjiva with my own hands. How could I have killed him, when I knew it would break your heart? I never knew he had returned to his city. I thought he was here in Lanka with you.'

"Gradually, her sobs subsided. When she had calmed down a little, she said, 'I cannot live in Lanka any more. Everywhere I look, I see his face. I cannot bear it; what shall I do?'

"Ravana thought for just a moment, then said, 'I have decided to send our cousin Khara to the Dandaka vana, to rule the wilderness in my name. I will send fourteen thousand of my best rakshasas with him, so he can establish a city in the jungle's heart and spread my power through the land of Bharata. Khara's rakshasas will all be mayavis and you shall be safe with them.

" 'Dushana will go with him, as his Senapati, and our cousin Trisiras as well. Khara is our mother's sister's son, and he has grown with us. Why don't you go with him to the Dandaka vana? You will be distracted from your sorrow by the beauty of the jungle and all the wild marvels you will see there.'

"And so it was that Ravana himself set a distant chain of fate in motion. Khara went to the Dandaka vana with a legion of some of the fiercest rakshasas in Lanka. And there, in the depths of that impenetrable forest, he built a wooden city called Janasthana, from which he spread a reign of terror through that jungle where countless rishis lived, whose prayers were the very support of the world. The bloodthirsty Khara and the sinister Trisiras and Dushana, and, indeed, all their demons began to prey on the rishis, at first desecrating their yagnas, which brought grace down upon the earth, then killing and devouring the munis.

"Thus they sought to choke and in time to destroy the very roots of dharma in the world, and to establish the rule of hell in monstrous Ravana's name. And surely, at first, they succeeded in good measure. The Dandaka vana became a home of evil upon the earth, and the evil spread subtly from the jungle, borne on the wind, into the hearts of men. And it seeped into the earth as the sacred blood of rishis which the rakshasas spilled and drank."

14. The abduction of Kumbheenasi

"Hidden deep in a forest on Lanka there was a most auspicious tapovana called Nikumbhila. When Khara and his fourteen thousand had left for the Dandaka vana, taking Surpanaka with them, Ravana went to Nikumbhila. There he saw an altar of sacrifice, and standing before it he saw his son Meghanada, wearing the hide of a black deer, a tuft on his shaven head, and holding a kamandalu and a staff. A yagna fire blazed in its pit at Meghanada's feet, and Usanas, the guru of the rakshasas, the Asuras, and all beings of darkness, sat beside it, feeding the fire with oblations, chanting arcane mantras, himself a flame.

"Ravana approached his prince, clasped him fervently in his arms, and asked, 'Child, what are you doing?'

"But Meghanada had taken a vow of silence, mowna, and to break it would spoil his sacrifice. So it was Usanas who replied, 'Your son has performed six great yagnas, Ravana. He has already performed the agnistoma, the aswamedha, the bahusuvarnaka, the rajasuya, and the vishnu yagna. He has just completed the maheswara yagna, and already Siva Pasupati, the Lord of embodied souls in bondage, who are like beasts, has blessed your son with a vimana and the tamasi maya, which makes the one who knows it invisible in battle. Not even the Danavas or Devas can see the warrior who is mantled in the tamasi maya.

" 'Sankara has also given Meghanada a bow, a pair of inexhaustible quivers, and a mighty astra. Your prince was waiting for you, Lord of the rakshasas, for a father's blessing.'

"But Ravana was not entirely happy. He murmured, 'Indra and the

Devas are my enemies. They have been worshipped, and that hardly pleases me. But what is done cannot be undone; let us think of it as having been well done. Come, my child, let us return to our city.'

"Ravana blessed his son. He took the blessing of Usanas, who then vanished before their eyes. Arm in arm, father and son returned to Lanka and to their palace, where now the pushpaka vimana disgorged its cargo of the most beautiful women of all the races of the worlds, whom Ravana had brought here to grace his harem and warm his bed.

"But now, his pious brother Vibheeshana greeted Ravana, with shock and anger in his eyes. 'What have you done, my lord? Already, your sin has brought nemesis to our clan.'

" 'What do you mean, Vibheeshana?' Ravana was annoyed that his triumphal return was tainted by any imperfection.

" 'You have sealed all our fates by bringing these women here. Don't you see them cry? Don't you hear them curse you, my brother? How will their curses fail to bring punishment down on you?'

"Ravana growled, 'It is the way of war; it is the way of the rakshasas. You are born a rakshasa, but you have never been like one of us, Vibheeshana.' He smiled. 'And the women shall be well cared for and they shall be well satisfied with their lives here.'

"But Vibheeshana said, 'Then perhaps you will be content to hear that our cousin Kumbheenasi has been abducted by Madhu, just as you have abducted these women?'

"Ravana seemed surprised. He asked mildly, 'Who is Madhu?'

"Kumbheenasi, of course, was the daughter of Malyavan, who was the eldest brother of Sumali, their mother's father. Also, Kumbheenasi's mother, Anala, was their own mother's younger sister. Kumbheenasi was hardly less than a sister to those royal rakshasas.

"Vibheeshana said, 'While Meghanada was away performing his yagna, while I lay submerged in water, at tapasya, and Kumbhakarna slept, the rakshasa Madhu came to Lanka one moonless night. He killed many of our guards, entered the harem, and carried our cousin away. Even when we heard what had happened, we did not pursue Madhu or kill him. For once he has enjoyed her, Kumbheenasi will be his wife by rakshasa vivaha; and it would break her heart if we killed him.

" 'So, my brother, even as you took a thousand women from their homes and their men and children, we, also, have been punished here in Lanka.'

"Ravana's ten heads flashed into view, snarling. His breath was hot; his eyes were the hue of kimsuka flowers. Through clenched fangs he said, 'Let my chariot be fetched and my weapons be laid in it. Let my brother Kumbhakarna be roused. Let any others who would ride with me fetch their chariots and bows. I will go at once to kill Madhu, and then to crush Indra in Devaloka!'

"Four thousand aksauhinis rode with Ravana, every rakshasa of them hungry for battle. Meghanada rode at the head of that horrible force, Ravana at its heart, and Kumbhakarna at its rear. Vibheeshana, who had little taste for battle, though he was a great warrior and un-afraid, remained in Lanka.

"Across land and through the air they went, on fair mounts and strange; and it is told that when the Daityas of the air saw Ravana fly-ing to Madhu's city, the Asuras, who are the enemies of the Devas, joined his host.

"Ravana arrived at Madhu's city, entered violently, and found Kumbheenasi in the palace. She saw her cousin and began to cry. He took her in his arms with great gentleness and said, 'Don't be afraid. I am here now. Tell me where Madhu is; he shall not live another day.'

"At which she only sobbed more piteously and cried, 'If you bear me any love, don't kill my husband. The unhappiest woman on earth is a widow. I beg you, my brother, swear you will not hurt him.'

"Ravana paused in his anger. He wiped her tears. 'I have told you not to be afraid. Take me to your husband. I will not kill him, but take him with me to Devaloka to fight beside me against Indra. Madhu will be like my own brother from now.'

"She led him deep into the palace, where her husband waited in some fear. Madhu sprang up when he saw Ravana, whose presence was like death's. Kumbheenasi said, 'This is my brother Ravana. He accepts you are my husband. He loves you like a son, my lord. He wants you to fly with him to Devaloka, with your legions, to take bat-tle to Indra.'

"Madhu smiled in relief. He bowed to the Master of all rakshasas. He knelt before Ravana, kissed his hand, and said, 'I will go with you, my lord.'

"Ravana embraced him and he stayed in Madhu's splendid city that night, to celebrate his cousin's marriage. The next morning, Ravana flew north again, with an even greater army now than the one with which he left Lanka. He arrived at the foot of Mount Kailasa and made camp there. Kailasa, as you know, verges on Indra's realm."

15. *The violation of Rambha*

Agastya continued, "The moon rose over Kailasa. Ravana's army lay asleep, swathed in its light. But Ravana did not sleep. He climbed to the top of Kailasa, alone. As he went, he saw karnikara, kadamba, and bakula groves that seemed lit not just by the full moon but with luster of their own. Their flowers shone in the silver light like the phosphorescent blooms of Devaloka.

"The Rakshasa saw lotus pools that shimmered with the waters of the Mandakini, and were mantled with the flowers of the champaka, asoka, punnaga, patala, and lodhra trees that grew beside them. Here and there the brighter blossoms of priyangu, arjuna, and ketaka floated beside the others.

"Ravana heard the soft, breathtaking songs of kinnaras. He saw these wondrous folk in dreamlike snatches, appearing and disappearing not just in and out of his sight, but the dimension of this world. He saw knots of delicate vidyadharas, their eyes dyed with wine. He saw them at love, their naked limbs shining, their subliminal cries like music.

"From across the white tableland that lay around him, the Lord of night heard apsaras who sang across the valley in the city of Alaka, in his brother Kubera's enchanted halls. As he climbed on, often a caressing wind shook free tender showers of petals that fell over him, and their fragrances clung briefly to the Demon, as if in strange yearning, then fell away onto the pale ground. Ravana felt a soft and mighty sweetness steal over him.

"He walked on, an evil presence through such loveliness and purity. Then, inexplicably, he felt his blood quicken. He smelled a new fragrance on the breeze, unlike every other he had known tonight. It eddied around him, wrapped in the scents of a hundred wildflowers and in the aroma of the sandalwood paste ground from the chandana trees of Devaloka. But this was no exotic flower's perfume that made his heart go so fast. It was the scent of a woman's body.

"Ravana advanced carefully. He did not want to alarm whoever it was who inflamed him by just the scent of her skin. At least not until he was near enough so she would not escape him. He crept forward toward a circular glade of kadamba trees from where the fragrance issued. He could see another pool of mirror water through the trees, laden with a soft frenzy of lotuses in echoing colors.

"Ravana arrived at the circle of trees. Peering around the bole of the one he was behind, he thought he might swoon from the sight that met his burning eyes. She was not of the earth; no, she was certainly no human woman. She was too tall, too slender, and far too beautiful. And the brightness that swathed her long, perfect limbs was not of the moon or the stars, but of heaven. She was so lovely, she was barely corporeal. Yet her breasts were full and high, her waist slender as a lotus stalk, and her hips flared away from it as he had never seen on any other woman, of any race. For all her obviously unworldly charms, she was unbearably seductive; why, she was seduction embodied and displayed before him upon Kailasa.

"Her skin was anointed with golden sandalwood paste; her hair was adorned with mandara flowers from Devaloka. Her face was as the full moon above. She wore supernal ornaments and garlands woven with blooms of the six seasons. Her eyebrows were like Kama's sugarcane bow. The girdle around her flaring waist scintillated with gemstones cut in Indra's realm. Her hands were as tender as fresh leaves on the trees of spring.

"Ravana could not resist that apsara, for so she was; how could he, a rakshasa, when the Devas themselves and the holiest rishis had yielded to the charms of Rambha, the most beautiful of all the nymphs of heaven, their queen?

"He watched her for a while as she sang softly and danced in that grove. Then he could not contain himself; he darted forward and took her hand. She quivered, she blushed, and he said to her, 'Where are you going? What tryst are you going to keep tonight? Whose fortune smiles on him so brightly, that he will sip the amrita of your mouth? Who is he who will feel your breasts against his body tonight? Who will ride your hips, like a disk of gold that is heaven to enter?

" 'Tell me, who is more fortunate than I am tonight, that I have seen you here? No, not Indra, Vishnu, or the Aswins are. Ah, you draw your hand away; but stay, lovely one! Don't you know who I am, that I am the master of the three worlds? Look, I fold my hands before you and beg you: stay!'

"But Rambha shuddered, and said to him, 'How can you speak to me like this? You are like a father to me. You must protect me like your child, not say such things.'

"Ravana gazed at her and he, also, trembled with a shock of desire. Smiling and keeping her hand in his, he murmured, 'How am I like your father, perfectly beautiful one?'

" 'Why, you are Ravana, and I am Nalakubara's wife. He is your brother Kubera's son, and so I am like a daughter to you. It is he I have come to meet here, on this mountain, and I love him like my very life. Let me go to my husband, O greatest of rakshasas.'

"But he replied, 'Truly, you would be like my daughter, if you had only Nalakubara for your husband. But you are Rambha, an apsara, and none of your kind in Indra's realm is bound to just one man.'

"He said no more, but pushed her down on the velvet grasses that grew around the lotus pool, and Ravana ravished Rambha. Her garlands and ornaments lay broken around her; her lips were swollen with his savage kisses. Her breasts were covered with the marks of his fangs and her womanhood was a raw wound. Heedless of her cries of anguish, he had thrust himself brutally into her, again and again, as if he wielded a blade of war.

"When he had slaked himself, he rose and walked away into the night. She lay in a swoon for a while, her jewels scattered around her like the blooms of a delicate creeper that had been shaken by a storm. Then slowly, moaning, she rose and made her way through the trees to where Nalakubara waited for her. She came sobbing before him. He took her in his arms and asked, 'Why are you crying, my love?'

"She said, 'I was on my way to meet you when ten-headed Ravana accosted me. He asked, "To whom do you belong?"

" 'I told him, and I said you were his brother Kubera's son, so he was like my father. But he stared at me with eyes like fire. He took me by force beside the lotus pool. He was so strong I could neither stop him nor escape. I beg you, forgive me, for my mind is pure.'

"Nalakubara shivered. He shut his eyes and sank into dhyana to discover if what she said was true. When he saw with inner vision what had happened to her, he opened his eyes again and they blazed in anger. He poured some holy water into his left palm and sprinkled it over himself, all his limbs. Then he cursed his uncle Ravana: 'If you ever violate another woman against her will, all your heads will burst like ripe fruit.'

"When he had uttered his curse like a searing flame, a shower of petals of light fell out of the sky and the dumarus of the immortals sounded on high. Brahma and the Devas celebrated the curse, the rishis of the earth were full of joy: at least now the women of creation would have some protection from Ravana. As for the Rakshasa himself, when he heard of Nalakubara's curse, he shook in every limb, and never again did he force himself on any woman who did not want him herself. And these were more than enough for him to enjoy a new woman every night of his life. He was Sovereign of the three worlds, his wealth and power were measureless, and few indeed were the women who could resist him.

"Why, not one of the thousand women he took as the spoils of war failed to come to his bedchamber, in time.

"Of course, the tale of Rambha is told differently by some, who say it was Brahma Pitamaha himself who cursed Ravana, when he ravished Rambha," Agastya Muni said.

16. The invasion of Devaloka

"Flying up from Kailasa, the frontier of the earth, Ravana arrived with his seething host in Devaloka. The noise his legions made as they surrounded Indra's city from every side was like the sound the Kshirasagara made when it was churned for the amrita.

"Indra heard that sound in his sabha, the Sudharma, and he rose from his ruby throne, which the worlds worshipped. All the Devas were gathered in the splendid court. The twelve sons of Aditi were there, the eleven Vasus, the Rudras and Sadhyas, the Lokapalas and the forty-nine Maruts. The gandharvas, kimpurushas, and kinnaras were there, the celestial nagas and countless other refulgent beings, all fabled Lords of the earth and the sky.

" 'Let us prepare for war,' said their king Indra, as bravely as he could. But his voice quavered with fear, because he knew about the boons Ravana had.

"Indra flew quickly as a thought, as all immortals do whose bodies are made of light, to Vaikunta. He came before blue Vishnu, and said abjectly, 'Lord, it was with your blessing I killed the Asuras Namuchi, Vritra, Bali, Naraka, and Sambara. Bless me again, Narayana, because the Rakshasa with ten heads is at my very gates; and you know

Brahma's boon protects Ravana from me and my Devas. Tell me how this Demon can be slain.'

"Mahavishnu said slowly, 'No Deva or Asura can kill Ravana, because of Brahma's boon. I see the Rakshasa will subdue the worlds, for he is truly an awesome spirit. I myself will not face him in battle, when I know I cannot vanquish him. Yet I will kill him when the time comes, because his death is written at my hands.

" 'As for you, Indra, the Demon is at your gates and you must fight him. Fight him and do not be afraid; I will protect you. But do not hope to quell Ravana in battle: that you cannot do.'

"Indra went back to his city, and soon the Deva host issued from the gates of Amravati like a glittering cloud and faced the legion of the night outside. At the head of the sinister force of demons were Prahastha and Maricha, Mahaparshva, Mahodara, Akampana, Nikumbha, Suka, Sarana, Samhrada, Dhumaketu, Mahadamshtra, Ghatodara, Jambumali, Mahahrada, Virupaksha, Suptaghna, Yagnakopa, Durmukha, Dusana, Khara, Trisiras, Karavirajsha, Suryasatru, Mahakaya, Atikaya, Devantaka, Narantaka, and a thousand others as ferocious. Their eyes glowed like torches in the twilight.

"Surrounded by these rakshasas, Ravana's grandfather Sumali took the field and scattered Agni, Vayu, Surya, Soma, Varuna, the Rudras and Vasus, the Aswins, Dharma, and Indra himself and their blithe legions of gandharvas, kinnaras, and the other warriors of Devaloka. The Deva forces fled in every direction.

"Then the eighth Vasu, Savitra, the mightiest of them, took the field. He arrived like a legion of light himself to dispel the macabre darkness that had fallen over Amravati. At his side came two magnificent sons of Aditi called Tvashtar and Pusa. The air was a denseness of weapons, of wild yells and roars, and screams when some missile or other found its mark. Blood flowed in rivulets and lapped at the dark and bright warriors' feet.

"For a while it seemed Tvashtar and Pusa were containing the rakshasas, and they killed thousands. Then Sumali returned to the field, mounted in his chariot drawn by winged serpents. He came armed with every astra and with maya. Like a black tempest he blew at the Deva host and routed them. Gandharva's blood and kimpurusha's precious blood flowed with rakshasa's gore. Sweet, musical screams mingled with coarse yells and curses.

"Only Savitra stood unflinching before the terrible Sumali, and matched him shaft for shaft, spell for spell. The Vasu shone like a rising sun upon the dark field. He shattered Sumali's eerie chariot with a volley of astras like a bank of lightning bolts. Before the chariot was consumed, and its serpents reduced to charred ropes, Sumali leaped down to the ground. As he stood panting, with no escape, Savitra advanced on him.

"Sumali had no weapon left, and raised his sorcerer's hands to defend himself. Savitra seized up a great mace, whose flaming head made it seem like Yama's danda. The gada blazed like a meteor as the vasu raised it high, then brought it down in a crackling arc squarely on Sumali's head. It was like Indra's adamantine vajra falling on a pale mountain. There was a blinding flash of light; then an echoing silence fell on the battle. Nothing remained of Sumali save a soft heap of gray ashes that the wind already bore away.

"The rakshasa army howled like some vast horde of wolves, in one dreadful voice, and they ran headlong from battle."

17. The battle in Devaloka

"Roaring when he saw his great-grandfather Sumali die, Ravana's son Meghanada took the field. Mounted in his gleaming chariot that rode as easily through the air as it did on the ground, he swept at Indra's army like a summer fire in a dry forest. None of the Devas, gandharvas, or Vasus could stand against the invincible Indrajit. They soon ran from him any way they could.

"Indra cried after them, 'Cowards! Come back and fight. Look, I am sending my own son to tame the Rakshasa's boy. Come back, Devas, come back!'

"Indra's son Jayanta flew at Meghanada like a sleek comet. Heartened, the other Devas rallied round him and came back to fight. They surrounded Ravana's prince, whose bow streamed arrows as a star does light, and felled a thousand soldiers of the host of heaven, every moment.

"Jayanta's sarathy was Matali's son Gomukha. Meghanada struck him with a storm of a hundred gold-tipped arrows. Jayanta drew blooms of blood on the rakshasa prince's charioteer. Roaring like thunderheads, the two princes attacked each other with every kind of astra and shakti. Devaloka was lit by their battle, as if by a score of new suns. But these weapons also brought an unnatural night in the wake of their incendiary paths.

"Darkness fell over the battle in Swarga: an utter darkness. Now shrill cries echoed on every side, for in that blind night Deva fell unwittingly on Deva, and rakshasa on rakshasa. Suddenly, an awesome and incandescent demon materialized on the panic-stricken field. He was a great Asura who lived below the sea: Sachi's father Puloma. Quick as a thought, Puloma seized his grandson Jayanta in his arms and spirited him away from the battle. He plunged into the turquoise waves, below which he lived in a fabulous city.

"Some light broke again on the battle. And now, with the heroic Jayanta gone, Meghanada broke on the hapless army of Devaloka again, like a terrible calamity. He let flow streams of blood on every side and the Deva host soon fled again before Ravana's indomitable prince.

"The next morning at dawn, within his palace, Indra, Lord of the clouds, rose from his throne that was carved from a single ruby. He said, 'Let my chariot be fetched. I will go to war myself.'

"Matali brought the fabled ratha to the palace steps. As Indra prepared to ride, formidable thunderclouds scudded into the sky above him and were gashed with jagged streaks of lightning and deafening peals of thunder. Gandharvas sang and played on marvelous instruments and apsaras danced in his court when the king of Devaloka went to war.

"Indra came majestically to battle, and around him were the eleven Rudras, the eight Vasus, the twelve Adityas, the forty-nine Maruts, the Aswins, and the Lokapalas, who are the guardians of creation. A shrill wind began to moan across Devaloka, cold and fierce. The sun was shorn of his splendor and hundreds of meteors fell out of the sky in evil omen.

"Ravana also climbed into his vimana, fashioned by Viswakarman. Now immense serpents were coiled around that disk of the sky, to strike fear in the enemy's heart. The vimana itself appeared to be in flames, for the fiery breath of those nagas. Ravana came to battle surrounded by dense swarms of winged rakshasas and some Asuras, too.

"Ravana advanced to the head of his army and faced Indra of the Devas. Meghanada gave way to his father, and fought behind him now. Battle was joined and Kumbhakarna, the leviathan, erupted on the legions of Devaloka. He hardly cared whom he fought, but slaughtered anyone who came in his way, drank their blood, and wore their entrails round his neck like horrible garlands; and his heaven-shaking roars silenced every other sound on the field.

"But with Indra leading them, the Devas were infused with new resolve. Despite Kumbhakarna's dreadful advent, the first hour of the encounter swung surely the Devas' way. The Gods cut down the demons' front lines with fusillades of astras. Still clutching their common and strange mounts, rakshasa and Asura lay limb-severed and twitching their last on the ground. A river of gore swelled between the two armies, and vultures and crows drank from its scarlet flow.

"In a brief hour, a hundred thousand rakshasas perished. Then Ravana, with his ten heads in plain sight, all of them breathing fire, leaped down from his chariot and plunged at the Deva host. Hewing his way through those lines of shining warriors, the Demon rushed at Indra in a blast of crimson. Indra raised his bow and, shaking the ten directions with its potent twanging, shot a clutch of arrows with the power of Agni and Surya at Ravana's roaring cone of heads.

"Ravana raised his own bow and replied with shafts of darkness and fear that were no less potent than the Lord of Devaloka's were. Another unnatural night fell over the battle. Still, rakshasa and Deva fought on, as if they could not stop themselves; they fought blindly, scarcely knowing if they slew friend or foe. It was a sorcerous night that had fallen, and just three of the warriors who fought at its heart saw through its darkness.

"Indra, who consumed the legions of evil as he pleased with his astras, saw. Ravana was not blinded by the mayic dark, and neither was his son Meghanada. Ravana saw millions of his rakshasas burned alive by Indra's prodigious missiles; he saw his army dwindle before his eyes. He screeched at his sarathy, 'Ride at the Lokapalas! I will cut Indra's head from his neck today, and Varuna's, Yama's, and Kubera's. And I will rule from Amravati.'

"The host of heaven, it is told, Rama, stretched from the Nandana, which is just below Amravati, to the eastern mountain Udaya. The Lokapalas fought upon that mountain. Ravana's sarathy flitted like a fiendish thought through the legions of rakshasas, gandharvas, charanas, and the rest. Indra saw the Rakshasa coming, and cried to his Devas, 'Ravana cannot be killed. Let us take him captive and hold him instead!'

"From the north, the Demon plowed his way deep into the Deva army, as he would violate a woman. From the south, Indra thrust his way into the rakshasa army. After a hundred bloody yojanas, the two came face to face. Seeing his forces decimated by the Rakshasa, Indra attacked him with such ferocity Ravana was forced to retreat.

"A great cry went up from the other rakshasas and the Asuras: 'We are undone!'

"Meghanada watched all this, quivering with ire. He jumped into his chariot and, using his tamasi maya, flew into the fray invisibly, sowing death all around him. The Deva army scattered like straws in a gale. Meghanada flew at Indra himself, and the Lord of the Devas could not see his adversary for the maya he was cloaked in, which was Siva's boon to the rakshasa prince.

"Indra saw just the storm of arrows Meghanada loosed at him, the storm that smashed his chariot in shards and wounded Matali. Indra fled the field. He returned to battle, now mounted on his white elephant Airavata, who trod air.

"Still, Meghanada's maya was beyond him. He could neither penetrate its opacity nor catch a glimpse of his assailant. Indra felt dizzy from the deluge of arrows that fell on him from the sky; the torrent of arrows that besieged him from every side; the geysers of arrows that rose from below him when he took to the air.

"Indra felt himself being bound by inexorable hoops of power. He felt himself being made fast by Meghanada, master of maya; and the king of the Devas, the Lord of the immortals of Devaloka, Master of the elements, was helpless to resist the rakshasa prince's sorcery. In a daze, in disbelief, Indra allowed himself to be snatched from his elephant's back by immaterial fingers, to a remote corner of the war.

"Meanwhile, Ravana fought like an aksauhini of demons, by himself, and faced the Adityas and the Vasus. But those Devas contained the Rakshasa effortlessly: they drove him back with shining valor. For the first time ever, Meghanada saw his proud father shamed on the field. He saw him uncertain and fumbling at his bow. That prince called across the field to Ravana, 'Father, come away: the war is won! Indra is my captive. Rule the three worlds as you please, my lord. You are their only sovereign now.'

"When the Adityas and the Vasus heard Meghanada, they laid

down their weapons and fought no more. Ravana rode up to his magnificent son and clasped him in his arms. He cried, 'You are the savior of our race!'

"He cast a triumphant glance at Indra, held fast in the shimmering coils of Meghanada's astra. Ravana said, 'Meghanada, my heroic child, take your captive home to Lanka. I will follow you with Prahastha, Maricha, and the others.'

"The victorious Meghanada came home to a delirious reception from his people. Women and children lined the streets, when they heard who it was that their prince had brought as his prisoner. Not a rakshasa or rakshasi stayed home. The old and infirm had themselves carried out to celebrate this impossible victory of their king and his son, their own incredible victory: the triumph of the race of the rakshasas, the firstborn race of creation."

18. *Brahma intervenes*

"The Devas came in disarray to Brahma and told him how Meghanada had taken Indra captive. Brahma went with the Devas to Lanka. Like a four-faced sun he appeared in the sky over the city of the rakshasas, and, in a voice of ages, said to Ravana, 'Your son has truly made you Lord of the three worlds. He is your equal, Rakshasa; perhaps he is even greater than you are. For what he has done today, I name him Indrajit and the worlds shall know him by that name from now.

" 'But Indrajit, you must not incur the sin of holding the king of Devaloka a prisoner. Look, the Devas have come here with me; they are willing to pay you whatever price you ask to release Indra.'

"Without a moment's hesitation, Indrajit replied, 'Give me immortality and I will release the Deva!'

"Brahma said, 'There is no immortality for any of the living. Why, when my time comes, I myself will die.'

"Indrajit grew thoughtful. Slowly, he said, 'I will accept another boon from you, Pitamaha. Whenever I go out to battle, I worship Agni. Let a chariot of power emerge from the flames, and as long as I sit in that chariot, let me not die. If, however, I fail to worship Agni before I go out to fight, then I may be killed, if there is a warrior who can kill me.'

"Brahma said, 'So be it.'

"Indrajit spoke an ancient and secret mantra. The coils of the astra that held Indra vanished, and the king of the Devas was free. How miserable that splendid God was, how utterly vanquished in spirit: that a rakshasa stripling had conquered him, shamed him, marched him, the Lord of the Devas, through the streets of Lanka. Even death could hardly be worse than this. And now, their mission fulfilled, the other Devas flew up into heaven. But Indra could not ascend. He was leaden; his body had turned gross.

"He stood mute, with his head hung before his Father, Brahma the Creator, in a jungle in the world. Finally, the Deva said in a whisper, 'Pitamaha, what happened today? How was I, Indra, king of the Devas, defeated in battle?'

"Brahma's eyes were full of deep memories. He said gently, 'My son, you have forgotten an old sin you once committed. You have forgotten Ahalya and the Rishi Gautama's curse.'

"Indra shuddered to remember. He had lain with the rishi's perfect wife, who was like a tongue of fire, and the sage had cursed him. Gautama had cursed Indra to show a thousand organs of lust upon his body, because this was the first time in creation that sin had been committed and Indra was its perpetrator. Thereafter men, too, would commit this mother of every other sin, and the worlds would decay in time, through the four yugas.

"After Indra had performed a searing penance, Brahma had mitigated the curse, so Indra had a thousand eyes upon his body instead of a thousand phalluses. But Gautama had also cursed Indra that half the sin of every adultery committed in the world would accrue to him, for being the first adulterer; the other half would be borne by those that committed the sin. And this would weaken his power, until, one day, he would fall into an enemy's hands in battle. Gautama had also said the throne of Devaloka would never be secure from then: Indra would often be driven from heaven, and some Asura or other would rule in his place.

"Ahalya had been the first perfect, and perfectly beautiful, woman. But when she sinned, all the world shared her beauty and there were other women as lovely as she. And of course, you know, Rama, that Gautama cursed her to be a heap of dust in their asrama, until your blue feet touched her, and she was forgiven her sin and reunited with her husband.

"Brahma said again, 'Indra, do you remember the sin you committed that turned all the ages dark? This is your punishment.'

"Indra whispered, 'Pitamaha, how can I be rid of the curse? How can I rise into Devaloka again?'

" 'Perform a yagna in the name of Vishnu and you shall ascend from the very yagnashala.'

"Tears filled the Deva's eyes. He said, 'Pitamaha, my son Jayanta is dead.'

"Brahma said, 'No, Puloma has hidden him under the sea. Jayanta will return to you when you have performed the yagna.'

"With that, Brahma vanished. Indra performed the Vishnu yagna, and as soon as the last mantra was chanted and the last oblation offered into the sacred fire, he felt a pulsing and ecstatic radiance enfold him. He felt the grossness he had acquired in defeat melt into that blue and loving illumination. His body purified into a form of light, once more Indra flew up into Devaloka. He ruled from the throne in Amravati again.

"And so it is, Rama, the wise say that Indrajit was greater than Ravana. For in battle it was not the father but the son who conquered the Deva king. But however that may be, after Indra himself was vanquished, who else in creation would dare stand against the might of Ravana of Lanka?

"And so, ever since, Ravana was Master of the three worlds: of Swarga, Bhumi, and Patala. All their denizens, all their greatest monarchs, paid the Evil One homage. They sent him tribute, lest he come again to their kingdoms with his dreadful legions."

19. Ravana worships Siva

But now Rama asked the Muni Agastya in mild surprise, "O jewel among all the twice-born, were the kshatriyas of the earth all cowards, then, that they allowed Ravana to tame them and rule them so easily?"

Agastya smiled. "Once, during his endless campaigns, Ravana arrived at the gates of a splendid city of men called Mahishmati. Mahishmati in the world was said to be no less magnificent than Amravati in heaven. The king of Mahishmati was called Arjuna, and his clan was the Haihaya. Arjuna was a bhakta of Agni Deva, and with the Fire God's blessing Mahishmati became a wonder upon the earth. In return, Arjuna always kept the sacred agni burning in a great pit and the agnikunda filled with kusa grass.

"The day Ravana came to Mahishmati, Arjuna of the Haihayas had gone with his women to the Narmada, to bathe and to sport.

"Ravana said to Arjuna's ministers, 'I have heard your king is the mightiest kshatriya in the world. I have come seeking battle with him. Where is he?'

"But the ministers, who were wise men, replied that they did not know where Arjuna was, nor when he would return. Ravana took himself to the Vindhya mountains of a thousand peaks, mantled with emerald forests and infested with lions and other beasts, of whom the tawny ones are the lords. When rivers fell here in cascades, from sheer summits, they seemed to utter a horse laugh!

"Devas, gandharvas, apsaras, and kinnaras came to the Vindhya to sport and to make love, and the mountain that stood rooted like Anantashesa with his thousand hoods—the peaks, and the mountain streams were his forked tongues—seemed truly like a piece of Swarga fallen into Bhumi below.

"Ravana sought the greatest river that flowed down the Vindhya-chala, the blessed Narmada, which made its shimmering way into the western sea. It was a warm day, and he saw bison, elephants, herds of deer, bears, and lions quenching their thirst at different pools along the Narmada's course. He saw the rippling currents laden with goose, duck, ibis, teal, and every sort of water bird, some that had flown across the earth to arrive here.

"The river was crowned with a crest of trees in full bloom. Her breasts were two flocks of chakravakas; sandbanks were her hips, floating swans her girdle; her limbs were anointed with brilliant pollens, as if with the paste of the sandalwood tree. Full-blown lotuses were the eyes of the Narmada.

"Ravana saw her from above and was seized by a compulsion to bathe in her; he felt it would be like being embraced by a Goddess. He flew down in his petal-quiet vimana, with his ministers, and sat on the banks of the holy and beautiful river. Sitting there on velvet moss, enchanted, he murmured in adoration, 'Ah, she is the Ganga!' Then he turned to Suka and Sarana, who sat closest to their king. 'Look, the sun has dimmed himself in reverence to see me. He who sears the earth has turned mild as the moon to see Ravana.'

"He seemed to be carried away in this vein. 'Can you feel how Vayu the wind blows gently around us, for fear of me? And, despite the birds, fish, and crocodiles she bears on her currents, even the river seems like a timid young girl before me. My friends, you bear upon your bodies the blood of a hundred kings of the earth, each of whom would vie with Indra in might. Even as the Diggajas do in the Akasaganga, bathe now in this lovely Narmada. She will take your sins from you, my rakshasas. I, too, shall offer worship to my Lord Siva in her waters.'

"Prahastha, Mahodara, Suka, Sarana, Dhrumraksha, and all his other ministers entered the clear river, and she quivered with their virile presences even as the Ganga does when the elephants that bear creation upon their backs bathe in the golden river of the north. When they had finished their ablutions, the rakshasas fetched flowers for their king, for his worship. Soon there was another small mountain of resonant blossoms piled high on the sandbank, which shone like a white cloud lit by the noon sun.

"Then, Ravana himself waded into the lucid flow, just as the lord of the elephants enters the Ganga: majestically and last of all. He offered flowers on the water; he chanted the Gayatri mantra a thousand times; he dipped his head under the cool, clear flow. When he had finished this purifying ritual, he stepped out, set aside his wet clothes, and put on a white silk robe.

"Ravana offered more flowers to a golden Sivalinga he had brought with him and now installed in an altar of sand. He anointed it with the finest sandalwood paste. Then he raised his hands to heaven and sang and danced with abandon to Siva, who removes the suffering of the virtuous and bestows the greatest boons.

"As Ravana danced, so did his rakshasas, like swaying mountains. For all their girth and bulk, they were surprisingly graceful, and their worship was soulful and queerly elegant.

"Now it happened that quite near, and downstream from where the invincible Rakshasa offered his flowers on the water, great Arjuna of Mahishmati, the son of Kritavirya, sported in the Narmada with his women. He stood in the swirling current like a bull elephant among his cows.

"Arjuna was a thousand-armed kshatriya, and to show off his awesome strength to his women, he stretched all thousand arms out across the gushing river, bank to bank. Soon the water no longer flowed: Kartaviryarjuna's arms arrested its tide like a dam. The river rose in one place and then flowed back upstream, laden with fish, tortoises, and crocodiles, and with copious armfuls of kusa grass and the flowers of Ravana's worship.

"In that unnatural flood, the water swept back toward where Ravana was at his worship. Ravana's eyes turned red as poppies. He glared at the river as if he were gazing at one of his wives being enjoyed by another man. The birds were calm enough in their trees; the elements seemed at peace. He could find no reason why the water flooded back to him.

"Ravana was forced to abandon his incomplete worship. He spoke no word, only pointed a long and imperious finger downstream; he looked at Suka and Sarana, that they should investigate what or who had dared interrupt him. The river flowed west, and Suka and Sarana set their faces in that direction and rose into the air.

"When they had flown just a few moments, and half a yojana, they saw a thousand-armed kshatriya playing in the water with his women. He was as great as a sala tree. The river swelled round him, tossed his hair on its transparent currents like moss, then flowed back from him, as if in fear of that warrior. Suka and Sarana hung invisibly in the air. They saw that the kshatriya in the river was formidable, his eyes red-rimmed, his body hard as rock, his every movement proclaiming that he was a great king, never to be trifled with.

"Suka and Sarana flashed away, still unseen, back to their master. They flew down before Ravana and said breathlessly, 'Lord, there is a man we do not know in the river, half a yojana downstream. He is as tall as a sala tree and his arms are countless, even like the branches of a tree. He has a thousand women around him, and to amuse them he has spread his arms like a dam across the Narmada. And she cannot flow past him, but breaks her banks as if in terror and flows back toward us.'

"Ravana growled, 'It is Kartaviryarjuna.'

"At once he set off down the flooding river, hungry for a fight. The wind rose and howled around the Lord of the rakshasas, blowing up a pall of dust. In moments, dark clouds filled the sky, shook with thunder and lightning, and poured down a drizzle of blood. Bright as antimony in the fallen gloom, Ravana arrived at the recalcitrant pool on the river, which Arjuna had created with his thousand arms.

"In a voice like ten peals of thunder, Ravana said to the kshatriya's ministers, 'Tell your king, Haihayas, that Ravana of Lanka has come to seek battle with him.'

"The ministers replied, 'You are a shrewd judge of the time to fight, O Ravana, that you have come when our king is drunk and sporting with his women. You come like a cunning tiger, which chooses to attack a bull elephant when he is in rut, among his cows. We say to you, Rakshasa, if you are a man of honor remain here with us tonight, and tomorrow our king will fight you. But if you are impatient and must fight at once, you must face us first, because we will not let you pass to our king.'

"And they drew their swords and stood defiantly before Ravana and his rakshasas. That battle did not last more than a few moments before the Haihayas were all slain and most of them eaten by the demons from Lanka, who by now were hungry. More ministers and soldiers from Kartaviryarjuna's camp came rushing to face Ravana. They poured in like an angry sea, from every side, loosing tides of fierce missiles at the marauders.

"The Haihayas drew first blood; but then, roaring to shake the mountain, Prahastha, Maricha, Suka, Sarana, and the other great rakshasas began to cut them down, so the flooding Narmada was tinted with their dark gore. The rakshasas still ate their adversaries, as they fought on.

"Some of Arjuna's soldiers fled the battle in the forest and went flying to their king, at languorous love in the river. They babbled out their story and he came out slowly from the water. He said to his women, in perfect calm, 'Do not be afraid.'

"Kartaviryarjuna's eyes were slits of copper. His anger flared up like the fire at the end of the yugas, which consumes the world. He picked up a mace and set out to hunt the rakshasas. Arjuna of the Haihayas scattered the rakshasa front lines as the sun does the night's darkness at dawn. He came among them like a twisting tempest, the mace in his hands striking out in every direction, felling a thousand demons each moment.

"Then Prahastha loomed in his path like another Vindhya, with what seemed to be a great pestle in his hand. Roaring like death, Prahastha cast the occult weapon at Arjuna; as it flew at him its tip burned with a mysterious red fire, formed like an asoka flower. But Arjuna flung his own mace at that weapon: he flung it with five hundred arms! The two ayudhas exploded against each other. Kartaviryarjuna still held a mace in his hands, and he rushed at the astonished

Prahastha and struck him a blow like doom on his head. Like a bull struck by Indra's vajra, Ravana's Senapati crumpled.

"Seeing Prahastha overcome so quickly, so easily, Maricha, Suka, Sarana, Mahodara, and the rest slunk away from the field like dogs. Only Ravana remained to confront Arjuna. Like two stormy seas, two agitated mountains, two suns, two apocalyptic fires, two bulls fighting for a cow in heat, two thunderclouds, two lions, like Rudra and Kaala, Kartaviryarjuna and Ravana rushed at each other, maces in hand.

"Their blows were like erupting volcanoes, like earthquakes, like the world being cloven. When Arjuna swung his gada at his enemy's chest, it was a gash of lightning that briefly turns a dark, ominous sky golden. And when Ravana swung his mace at the stupendous kshatriya, it resembled a meteor falling through the sky onto a mountain.

"Neither combatant seemed to tire, though they fought like two rivers in spate trying to drown each other. Why, they fought even as Indra and the Asura Bali did, of old. Suddenly, the Haihaya cast his mace at his opponent like a bolt of fate. That blow would have killed any other warrior in the three worlds; but the mace smashed to dust against Ravana's chest, protected by Brahma's boon. But Ravana staggered back a bow's length and sank to the ground, crying out in pain.

"Seeing his chance, Arjuna darted forward and seized the Rakshasa in his thousand arms, as Garuda would a serpent. Kartaviryarjuna bound Ravana, even as Vishnu once did Bali. From above, there fell a delicate shower of fine petals from Indra's garden, from the immaterial hands of the siddhas, charanas, and Devas.

"When he had Ravana firmly, as a tiger a deer or a lion an elephant, mighty Kartaviryarjuna flung back his head and roared again and again: echoing thunder! Meanwhile, Prahastha, whom Arjuna had felled earlier, had come to his senses. Seeing his precious lord held fast in a thousand arms, he sprang up and charged Arjuna. Following their Senapati, celebrating his recovery, Maricha, Suka, Mahodara, Sarana, and all the other rakshasas rushed at Arjuna from many sides.

"Prahastha, the main assailant, loosed every sort of weapon at the kshatriya who held his master helpless. But with his thousand hands Arjuna plucked them from the air as they flew at him. Then he, also, held countless bows in numberless hands and shot such an extravagance of missiles at the rakshasas that he scattered them as the wind does the fleecy clouds of summer.

"Victorious, the great Haihaya brought Ravana, immobile in the thongs of a thousand arms, back to his city: Mahishmati like a jewel upon the earth. Along his triumphal march through his streets, women and brahmanas showered seasons of flowers over their conquering king and harvests of rice-grains," said the matchless Muni Agastya in the court of Ayodhya, in the perfect Rama's sabha.

20. Ravana and Vali

"In lofty Brahmaloka, Pulastya Muni, Ravana's grandfather, heard the Devas tell with relish how Kartaviryarjuna had taken Ravana prisoner, which they said was hardly easier than capturing the wind.

"Pulastya arrived in Mahishmati by rishi patha, the ethereal skyway of the sages of heaven. When Arjuna's ministers saw the muni, who was as splendid as a sun and hard even to look at, they ran in to their king to tell him that Pulastya himself had come to their city. Kartaviryarjuna folded his palms above his head and came out to receive the holy one.

"The Haihaya king came with arghya, with his own brahmanas going ahead of him, as Brihaspati does when Indra comes to the gates of Amravati to greet Brahma. Arjuna offered Pulastya Muni madhurparka, a cow, and water to wash his feet with, then said to him in some rapture, 'O Prince among rishis, today my Mahishmati is as blessed as Amravati. My life is fruitful today that Pulastya Muni has come to grace my city. My kingdom and my people are yours to command; all that I own is yours.'

"And he prostrated himself before the rishi. Pulastya laid a hand on the king's head and raised him up. He asked after the welfare of his kingdom, his family, his children, and his people. Then Pulastya said, 'You have no equal in strength and valor anywhere, O Kartaviryarjuna, that Ravana himself is your prisoner. Only you have ever vanquished my grandson, in awe of whom the sea and the wind stand still. You have consumed his glory, and I, Pulastya, have come to beg you to set my child free.'

"Arjuna did not say a word. He clapped his hands to have Ravana fetched from the dungeon where he held him, and set him free without condition. Why, that kshatriya gave Ravana lavish gifts of unearthly ornaments and clothes, and swore a covenant with him, before a sacred fire, that neither of them would attack the other.

"With this, Arjuna bowed low to Pulastya, took the padadhuli from his feet, and went back into his palace. The rishi, too, blessed his chastened grandson and vanished in a flare of light, back to Brahmaloka. Ravana returned to Lanka. Now that he had sworn friendship with Kartaviryarjuna, there was truly no king left in the three worlds who could pose a threat to the Rakshasa. He ruled as he pleased and extended his sinister sway as far as he ranged. He never hesitated to drink the blood of anyone who dared oppose him; and if he ever heard that any king or warrior, anywhere, of any race, was powerful, he made it a point to visit him and either kill him or have his abject surrender.

"Once, Ravana heard that there was a peerless hero in a jungle of Bharatavarsha. He was a vanara of untold valor and strength, a king of his people, and his name was Vali. Vali ruled the secret city of Kishkinda, and when Ravana heard about his prowess and his exploits, he went to Kishkinda and roared out a challenge to Vali.

"At this, Vali's wife and chief minister, Tara, her father Sushena, who was Vali's physician, and his brother Sugriva came and said, variously, to Ravana, 'Lord of Lanka, Vali is not in Kishkinda and no one else in this city is even remotely a match for you. Our king has gone to the shores of the four seas to say his sandhya vandana. We beg you, wait, and he will return shortly.'

"Ravana gazed in some curiosity at a great pile of glistening bones heaped outside the hidden gates of Kishkinda. He saw some bones were intact, but others had been crushed almost to powder.

"Tara said to him, 'These are the bones of those who sought to test their strength against Vali. Not even if you have drunk amrita, Rakshasa, will you escape death if you fight him. Ravana, if you are in a hurry to die, go to the shore of the southern ocean and you will find my husband there at his sandhya vandana, glowing like Agni Deva come down to the earth.'

"He growled at her, 'We shall see how a monkey fights Ravana of Lanka.'

"Climbing back into the pushpaka vimana, he flew quickly as a thought to the southern shore. There he saw an immense figure seated on the sands, like a small golden mountain, entirely absorbed in his twilight worship. His face, which shone like a rising sun, was turned toward the scarlet sea into which the sun sank like treasure. Ravana, black as night, crept up behind the vanara to seize him. But Vali sensed him coming; he saw him out of the corner of his eye.

"Vali showed no anger; rather he smiled serenely when he glimpsed the ten-headed Demon creeping up on him like a thief. He was like a lion that spied a rabbit, or Garuda sensing a snake. He did not pause his chanting of the Vedic mantras, but he prepared himself for Ravana. He was also determined that he would complete his worship, at all the four seas, this very evening.

"Unaware that he was discovered, Ravana crept up close behind the vanara. But when he raised his arms to seize Vali, quicker than light the great monkey spun around and gripped Ravana's neck in his armpit. The Rakshasa roared, he struggled; he flailed out at Vali, but he could not get free. The vanara held him fast; he held him as easily as he would a child.

"The other rakshasas now leaped out of the vimana and rushed at the vanara to rescue their king. But holding Ravana dangling from his armpit, Vali rose steeply into the sky, lit by the last shafts of the setting sun. The pursuing rakshasas flew up after him, but they could not match Vali's thought-like speed.

"The mountains of the earth swayed out of Vali the vanara's way as he sped toward the three remaining oceans, worshipping the Goddesses of dawn and dusk, being honored by the birds of the air. He alighted on the shore of the western sea, with Ravana dangling helplessly from his armpit like a rag doll.

"Vali immersed himself in the western ocean and chanted the sandhya mantra, standing waist-deep in the water. He flew up again, flitted away to the northern sea, and worshipped there, as well, immersing Ravana as if the Rakshasa were a strange limb of himself. He worshipped at the eastern sea, also, then flew home to Kishkinda and down into a sylvan garden just outside his city. Now Vali felt a trifle tired, having carried Ravana across the length and breadth of Bharatavarsha.

"He lifted his arm, scratched himself as monkeys do, and let the Rakshasa fall from his armpit; and, pretending to notice him only now, began laughing uproariously. 'From where did you spring?' he asked.

"Ravana said, humbly by now, 'Vanarendra, I am Ravana, and I came seeking a duel with you, for I heard of your prowess. But I never dreamed there existed in this world anyone who could do to me what you have done today. And, ah, how swiftly you flew! I thought only the mind, Vayu Deva, and Garuda flew so fast.

"'O jewel among monkeys, having seen you and felt your strength, I would not have you as my enemy. I beg you, let us be friends forever; let us swear friendship before a sacred agni. Let all our lands, our women, our soldiers, our food, all we own, belong to the both of us, jointly. Let us be allies, like brothers!'

"And, laughing, Vali agreed. They lit a fire, embraced, and the Lord of the monkey folk of the earth and the Emperor of the rakshasas swore to be friends unto death. Then Vali led Ravana into Kishkinda, like one lion leading another into his cave. For a month Ravana lived in Kishkinda and was treated even as Sugriva was in that wonderful, hidden city."

Agastya glanced at Rama in some wonder, and said, "It was that invincible Vali whom you killed with just one arrow, Rama."

Rama sighed, and Sugriva had tears in his golden eyes.

21. Speaking of Hanuman

Rama said brightly, "Truly, Muni, Vali and Ravana were powerful beyond all measure. But neither was as strong as our Hanuman! Neither of them could have accomplished what he did, in the most difficult circumstances: when Angada and the vanaras despaired on the shore of the southern sea; when, later, Hanuman leaped into Lanka and could not find Sita; and, of course, when he killed some of Ravana's best warriors and his son Aksha, and set Lanka on fire, all by himself.

"And in the war, too, he was invincible. Why, not even Kaala, Indra, or Kubera have done what Hanuman did, and I am sure that but for him we could never have triumphed. But I realize, O Agastya, that I know precious little about this dearest friend of mine. He is so humble that he never speaks of himself, almost as if he is not even aware of how great he is. Not only I, but also many others here would like to hear about his valor. My lord, though Hanuman himself perhaps would not have it, I beg you: tell us all there is to know about him."

Hanuman already squirmed shyly where he sat. Agastya smiled to see him, and said, "Rama, truly, there is no one on earth to match our good Hanuman in speed, intelligence, or even strength. But as you have observed, he himself is hardly aware of his greatness; which is why he did not consume Vali as a fire does a dry tree of summer, but instead watched Sugriva suffer in the wilderness. And there is a reason for this, besides his natural humility. You see, once the rishis of the forest cursed Hanuman that he would never be fully aware of his own powers. For even as a small child, he performed such feats that they were afraid of him, and what he might do when he grew up.

"You know, Rama, the mountain Sumeru has a golden hue because of Surya Deva's blessing. Hanuman's father, Kesari, ruled on Sumeru. His wife was the lovely Anjana, and upon her Vayu sired Hanuman, who was born with the color of the bristly heads of paddy sheaths. When he was just a mite, his mother left him sleeping and went into the forest to find some soft fruit for her child to eat. Hanuman woke up when she was away, and began to cry from finding her gone and from hunger, even as Karttikeya did in the thicket of sara grasses.

"Just then, he saw the sun rising on the rim of the world, like a mass of japaa flowers. He thought it was a great fruit and sprang up into the air to pluck it! Hanuman flew up like an arrow. The Devas, yakshas, and Danavas saw him flaring up like an effulgent thought, and were amazed.

"They said to one another, 'If he flies like this when he is just a baby, what will he be like when he is a youth?'

"Vayu flew with his son, enfolding him in a cool wrap of air, so the sun would not burn him. With his father's power, Hanuman shot up through the sky for a million yojanas and he drew near the blazing sun. Surya Deva knew this was a child of great destiny, who would one day be the messenger of Vishnu's Avatara: he did not consume the young monkey.

"At that very time, Rahu tried to seize the sun and devour him. Little Hanuman saw the Asura and attacked the demon who was trying to steal his fruit. Rahu was terrified by the awesome child and fled to Indra. Simhika's son, the Asura, complained to the king of the Devas, 'O Indra, you have said that I can feed on the sun and the moon, to still my perpetual hunger. Today is the day after the new moon, but when I was about to seize Surya, another Asura attacked me suddenly and laid hold of the star.'

"Indra, tall as a peak of Kailasa, his golden necklace blinding, mounted the four-tusked Airavata, set the aggrieved Rahu before him, and flew to where Surya Deva was with Hanuman. When Rahu saw the sun, he leaped off Airavata's back and flew at the blazing star. When Hanuman saw Rahu flying toward him like a great black cloud, he thought this was another velvet fruit, worthy of his attention. He sprang at Rahu to eat him.

"Rahu screamed, 'Indra! Help me!' and fled from the splendid monkey child.

"Indra cried, 'Never fear, Rahu, I will kill him!'

"Hanuman heard Indra's roar, and, turning his head, saw the Lord of the Devas. He saw white Airavata and thought that here, indeed, was the finest-looking fruit of all. He now flew at the Deva king and his mount. Roaring louder than ever, Indra cast his vajra at the infant vanara.

"The thunderbolt struck Hanuman squarely, and he fell unconscious through the chasms of the sky, down, down to the earth below. He fell onto a great mountain and broke his jaw. When Vayu saw what Indra had done to his son, he withdrew the precious prana that sustains every living creature; so they all choked and gasped for breath. Snatching up his wounded baby, the Wind God flew into a deep and secret cave.

"With every creature breathless and turning blue, it seemed creation would end. The worlds were plunged into panic, into hell. The Devas, gandharvas, and Asuras, those that could still move, came panting to Brahma. They cried, 'What sin have we committed? Why does Vayu choke us today? Ah, Pitamaha, we will all perish if you don't save us!'

"Brahma said to them, 'It was Vayu's son that Indra struck with the vajra.'

" 'What shall we do, Pitamaha?' wailed the Devas.

"Brahma said, 'We must seek Vayu out.'

"So, with all the created, the Devas, gandharvas, yakshas, nagas, siddhas, rishis, men, and all the rest, Brahma went to the cave where Vayu had hidden himself. They found him there with the infant Hanuman in his lap, radiant as the sun, but lifeless. And the Deva wept.

"Vayu saw Brahma, and he rose mutely, his eyes streaming, and stood before the Creator with his dead child in his arms. Vayu's golden kundalas and his unearthly crown were dim with his grief. Still without a word, he prostrated himself at Brahma's feet. Brahma reached out and stroked little Hanuman with his palm. At once, the vanara child awoke like a wilted plant that had been watered.

"When Vayu saw his son alive, he gave a mighty sigh of joy, and all the created breathed again: they gained back their life breath, their prana. Why, they were like lakes that were laden with lotuses, when the icy wind stops blowing across their waters. Brahma possesses three pairs of divine qualities: strength and glory, power and wealth, wisdom and dispassion. He appears in three forms: as Brahma, Vishnu, and Siva. He dwells in the three worlds: Swarga, Bhumi, and Patala. He is worshipped mainly by those who know but three stages in life: infancy, boyhood, and youth: the immortals. Now Brahma spoke to the Devas.

"He said, 'O Indra, Agni, Varuna, Rudra, and Kubera, grant this child great boons; for one day your own purpose shall be served by him. Grant him boons, also, so his father will forgive you for what you did to his son.'

"Indra removed the garland of lotuses he wore and set it around Hanuman's neck. He said, 'Since my vajra broke your chin, O tiger among monkeys, you shall be called Hanuman from now. And from now you shall be invulnerable to every weapon lesser than my thunderbolt, and to my vajra as well.'

"Surya, the Sun, said, 'You shall have a hundredth part of my radiance. And when you are old enough, little one, I myself will teach you the Shastras and no one in the world will know the scriptures, or live them, as perfectly as you will.'

"Varuna blessed him that he would never die in water, in a million years. Yama said Hanuman would not die from his danda, and no illness would ever touch him.

"Then Kubera, of the one tawny eye, said, 'Not my mace, nor any weapon less than it, shall cause your death. I bless you that you will never know tiredness in battle.'

"Rudra, the greatest, laid his palm on Hanuman's head and blessed him. 'No weapon of mine, or any I have power over, will harm you.'

"Viswakarman, who creates every astra, said, 'No weapon of heaven or earth shall kill you and you will be a Chiranjivi.'

"Brahma said, 'You shall not be killed by the weapons of Brahma or the curses of any brahmana.' He turned to Vayu, who by now was beaming. 'Your son shall be a terror to his enemies. He shall be invincible, and anyone that remembers his name, through all the ages, will be free from fear. I bless your son that he will be able to change his form at will, to assume any guise he wants. He will be able to fly to any part of the worlds at his wish, and he shall be a thorn in the side of Ravana of Lanka.'

"And having variously blessed Hanuman Vayuputra, Brahma, Rudra, and the Devas returned to their supernal realms. Vayu, wafter of fragrances, brought Hanuman home to his anxious mother on Sumeru. He told her about all that had chanced with her marvelous child, when she went to pluck fruits in the forest. And Vayu left Hanuman with Anjana, dissolved into a breathy wind, and vanished into his ubiquitous airs.

"Replete with great boons from the Gods, Hanuman grew into a young vanara, bursting with vigor, strength, and often mischief. He was not always as humble and self-effacing as when you met him, Rama. He was even in the habit, as a youth, of disturbing the munis of the forest at their solemn yagnas. At first he would rip to shreds any valkala he found hung out to dry. Then, as he grew bolder, he would leap down out of a tree and snatch a ladle from a rishi about to pour oblation into a sacred fire, or break the sacrificial vessels, full of holy water or other offerings.

"The rishis knew the young vanara was proof against their direst curses because of Brahma's boon to him. They came and complained to Anjana's husband Kesari, Hanuman's foster father, and to Anjana herself. But despite their admonishing Hanuman, he continued with his profligate ways. The rishis took their complaint to Vayu himself, invoking the Wind God with worship. But Hanuman was arrogant and tameless.

"The greatest rishis, born in the line of Bhrigu and Angiras, decided to curse Hanuman. They did not, however, curse him with death, but only to a long forgetfulness: of his own strength, of who his father was, and of the boons he had from the Gods.

"They said, 'When you remember these things again, Hanuman, at a great juncture of destiny, when you are on a mission for Vishnu's own Avatara, then your glory will return to you. But by then you will be a mature vanara, and your wisdom will have grown so you will never again abuse your powers as you have done in your youth.'

"From that day, a sea change came over the young monkey's nature. He grew mild and placid, because he did not remember any more who he was or how strong he was. He would go to the very asramas he had ravaged in his wild days, sit at the rishis' feet, and learn from them. He now became the embodiment of patience and gentleness. The sages who had known him in the past, as an irreverent whirlwind of a monkey, were astonished at the transformation, until they learned what had happened.

"Those were the days when Vali and Sugriva's father, the magnificent Riksharajas, was the Lord of all the monkey people of the earth. He was as splendid as Surya Deva was; but then, inevitably, time conquered him and he passed on. Vali became king, and Sugriva the yuvaraja. You know of the enmity that developed between the brothers, and how Vali chased Sugriva from his kingdom and took his wife Ruma for himself.

"It was the rishis' curse that kept Hanuman from avenging the wrong done to Sugriva, whom he loved as dearly as the wind does the fire. For in truth not even great Vali was Hanuman's equal. Ah, who is there on earth who is Hanuman's equal in strength, in vitality, in amiability, in wisdom, cleverness, virility, and discernment?

"Did you know that once he turned his face to the sun, when he wanted to learn the ancient wisdoms; and gazing thus at his blinding preceptor, he walked from the eastern mountain to the western one, where the sun sets? It is said that Hanuman knows as much as Brihaspati does, of both gyana and dhyana.

"And, Rama, what is perhaps not commonly known is that like Hanuman, the other great vanara chieftains, Sugriva, Mainda, Dwividha, Neela, Angada, Nala, Gaja, Gavaksha, Gavaya, Sudamshtra, Prabha, and Jyotimukha, were also Devas' sons and born to help you achieve your purpose in the world. Without them, very likely, Ravana would still be alive, and his shadow would cover the earth in fear."

Thus, in Rama's sabha, Agastya revealed many things that had been kept hidden so far. At last the muni smiled and said, "Now, Rama, you must give us rishis leave: our tapasya is never complete and the earth is always in need of our prayers."

Rama rose with tears in his eyes. He said, "My lords, your blessings must always be upon my kingdom and on me. I have another favor to ask you, holy ones. I mean to perform many yagnas, in time, to thank the Gods for my good fortune, and to have their grace upon my land and my people. I beg you all to come to my sacrifices and sit over them."

One by one, the rishis blessed Rama and left Ayodhya, some walking away from the city of destiny, where Vishnu's Avatara ruled, others flying into the air and vanishing by glimmering sky paths. Night had fallen, and Rama went in to Sita, waiting in his antapura.

22. In Rama's sabha

The next morning, his second day as king, Rama was roused by the vabdhis and magadhis, with songs as sweet as the kinnaras sing. They woke him with fulsome praise.

"Awake, O King, who are the joy of your mother Kausalya; for, Lord, all the world remains in a stupor while you sleep. O you are as powerful as Narayana, handsome as the Aswins, wise as Brihaspati, and regal as Brahma. Your patience is like the earth's, your glory is like the sun's, your swiftness like the wind's, and your heart is as deep as the ocean. In war you are as invincible as Siva, and yet your nature is as gentle as the moon's.

"Arise, O Rama, and shine upon your kingdom and your people!"

And Rama awoke and rose from his bed, even like Vishnu from Ananta. As the three Vedas wait on a great yagna, Rama found Lakshmana, Bharata, and Shatrughna waiting for him in his chamber. A hundred muditas, servants, waited on his pleasure as well. The twenty vanara chieftains, and Sugriva their king, waited for him, too, as did Jambavan and his wild and noble reekshas. Like yakshas attending on Kubera, Vibheeshana and his four loyal rakshasas waited for Rama.

And many others, besides, were there, among them important ministers of his court. All these sat in his royal apartment, waiting for him to awaken. Some illustrious rishis also waited for Rama, and he rose and came to them even as Indra does to his Devas in Amravati.

And so it was every day; and Rama would go with these loving friends and counselors to his sabha, to minister to his people; and his grace spread through all the kingdom.

Then, one day, he folded his hands to King Janaka, the rajarishi, and said, "My lord, you are our greatest, immutable support. It was by the power of your tapasya that I was able to kill Ravana. I beg you, father, accept these humble tokens of my love. I know you want to return to Mithila; let Bharata and Shatrughna ride with you as your escort."

A treasure of gifts was presented to the king of Mithila. A beaming

Janaka blessed Rama and said, "I am too old to enjoy these precious things. If you allow me, I will leave them for Sita."

Rama bowed to Janaka, and that august king embraced his daughter and then left for his own kingdom in great contentment. Having seen Janaka off at the palace gates, Rama now turned to Kaikeyi's brother, the noble Yudhajit, who had come from the kingdom of Kekaya to represent his father, Asvapati, at Rama's coronation.

Rama said gently to that kshatriya, "Uncle, you, too, must leave today. I am certain that at his age, your father misses you sorely. I will send Lakshmana with you and he will bring some gifts from us to your father."

When Yudhajit saw the priceless gifts Rama meant to send to his father, he remembered how Rama had been banished to the forest. He said, "Rama, let these gifts remain here in Ayodhya with you. It is only just."

Rama embraced him, and Yudhajit walked in a pradakshina around Rama and then set out with Lakshmana.

Now Rama went up to his friend Pratardana, the king of Kasi. He said, "My lord, I know you tried, with Bharata, to send me a legion of soldiers to Lanka. Alas, they did not arrive in time for the war, but I can never forget your intention. I must not keep you any more, my friend, from your wonderful city. I thank you with all my heart for having come for my abhisheka."

They also embraced, and then Pratardana set out for home with the guard he had brought with him. Rama turned to the three hundred other kshatriyas who had come for his coronation and to declare their loyalty. To them he said, "My brothers, it is your prayers and your unflinching dharma that helped me prevail against the enemy. While I was away, you have all been of such support to Bharata that I can never forget your love and your generosity."

They replied, "It is our greatest fortune that you killed the Rakshasa. It was not only for Sita that you fought, you and your jungle army; but for us all, for all our kingdoms: why, for the very earth herself, to set her free from Ravana's dark bondage.

"From now on, our kingdoms are yours to rule. You are enshrined in our hearts, noble Rama, and all we ask from you is your love; because we know how incomparable a possession that is."

And they, also, those noble three hundred, who had always resisted the yoke of Lanka, left for their kingdoms spread across Bharatavarsha. But before they went, they had the invaluable gifts they had brought for Rama's coronation fetched into the sabha of Ayodhya.

When those kshatriyas left, the earth shook at their going, so immense were their legions, flowing like rivers across the earth. When they had seen Janaka and Yudhajit back to their kingdoms, Bharata, Shatrughna, and Lakshmana returned to Ayodhya laden with horses, chariots, precious stones, elephants, intricately carved sandalwood chests, servants, gold by the cartload, and other treasures those kings had given them. They brought these home to Rama.

Rama gave most of them away to the vanaras, who wore the jewels and ornaments with such delight, and to Vibheeshana's rakshasas. Rama called Hanuman and Angada to sit beside him in his sabha. He unfastened his own ornaments from his person and tied them on the two vanaras, saying to Sugriva, "But for them I would never have won the war, my friend."

He called Neela, Nala, Kesari, Kumuda, Gandhamadana, Sushena, Panasa, the great Mainda, Dwividha, Jambavan, Gavaksha, Vinata, Dhumra, Balimukha, Prajangha, Sannada, Darimukha, Dadhimukha, Indrajanu, and many others, and, his eyes moist, gave them more gifts such as they loved. Rama said, "You are all like my brothers, why, like parts of myself. Jungle dwellers, you are the greatest friends a man can have!"

And the monkey folk stayed on in Ayodhya for a month, drinking sweet honey and being fed royal delicacies. And Rama and his brothers spent many happy hours with the vanaras, who could, many of them, change their forms at will; and with the rakshasas, who were a truly magical people, blessed with all sorts of occult siddhis; and with Jambavan's great bears, who were as loving and patient as they were strong.

But soon it was obvious that the vanaras and the rakshasas had begun to long for their own homes. The monkeys yearned for the forest and the primitive spaces of the wilds: for charmed pools and lakes, for sparkling rivers, for mystic mountains and star-crowded skies, under which their true and free lives lay in wait for them. The rakshasas also longed for the din of waves that was like the very rhythm of their days and nights, in the jewel that was Lanka.

So one day, when a month had passed, Rama said to Sugriva, "My friend, I see your people are growing restless in our city. I know you are loath to tell me you want to return to your forests, lest you hurt me. It is true I would love to keep you here with me forever, but I know you would soon be unhappy away from your home in the wild. So reluctantly, my brother, I give you leave to go. Take your noble, noble vanaras with you, Sugriva, and my undying love and gratitude. How can I thank you all, who risked your lives for me with no hesitation? No, I cannot, not in a hundred lifetimes."

With tears in his gentle eyes again, Rama turned to Vibheeshana. "And you, my dearest Vibheeshana, who to me are one of the wisest of the earth: you must also leave for home, for I see in your face that you long for Lanka and your wives and your people. And they have need of you. Ah, my friends, I would keep you all here with me and never send you away, but I know you will hardly be happy away from your homes. So I will let you leave now, all of you. But you must promise me you will return soon to Ayodhya, for I will miss you all more than I can say.

"It is only perhaps once in a lifetime that fate forges such friendship as we have. We have walked together through death's valley."

And every vanara and rakshasa had tears in his eyes. Hanuman came and knelt before Rama. He said, "Rama, may my love for you last forever. May my bhakti for you never turn to anyone else. And may this body of mine continue to live as long as your story is told upon the earth. Let me hear your life again and again, from the lips of apsaras, so that I feel your presence near me and see you before my eyes whenever I long for you."

Rama embraced Hanuman fervently and said, "So be it, O best among vanaras. Let your fame live in this world for as long as my story is told in it, and let there be life in your body for as long. And, Hanuman, this tale shall be told in this world for as long as the world lives. And so shall you live, as long as the earth turns round, O Chiranjivi.

"As for me, I would gladly give up my life for every favor you have done for me; and they are so many! Vanara, I am forever in your debt. But let me never have to repay any service you have rendered me, because it is only when one is in trouble that one needs to recall the debts one is owed."

Rama untied a string of pearls that shone like small moons from his neck, with a mystic cat's-eye in their midst, and fastened it around

Hanuman's throat. And the vanara was as splendid as golden Meru with the full moon risen over him.

The vanaras rose, one by one, and knelt before Rama, touching their heads to his holy feet. So, too, did the rakshasas and Jambavan's reekshas quaintly kneel. Rama blessed them all and he clasped Sugriva and Vibheeshana to him. As they, his friends dear to him as his life, bid farewell to Rama, they seemed stupefied with grief. It is told that the vanaras, the four rakshasas, and the mighty black bears left Ayodhya and its king as reluctantly as a soul leaves a body that it has lived in for a lifetime.

23. The pushpaka vimana

By noon, the vanaras, reekshas, and rakshasas had all departed. Rama and his brothers sat out on an open terrace to take the soft afternoon sun, when suddenly an indescribably sweet voice spoke out of the sky.

"Rama," it said, "look on me with love in your eyes of light. It is I, the pushpaka, returned from Kubera's city where you sent me."

They looked up in surprise and saw the disk hung in the clear azure above them. Rama asked, "What happened, O vimana?"

"I returned to my Lord Kubera, but he said to me, 'Rama of Ayodhya killed Ravana in battle. You rightly belong to him from now. Go back to Rama, gentle friend; bear him wherever he wants to go. There is nothing that would please me more, because Rama is the protector of the worlds.' So I flew to you from Alaka. I beg you, Rama, let me bear you through all the realms for as long as you remain in this world."

Rama said, "I thank you, sublime spirit, O best of all vimanas."

He worshipped the crystal ship with fried rice grains, flowers, sandalwood paste, and incense. Rama said, "Go now to your subtle realms, and come to me whenever I call you."

The vimana circled Rama thrice, in the sky, and vanished into the dimension of the siddhas. Now Bharata folded his palms to Rama and said in wonder, "Beings that are not born of Manu speak like men to you! It is just a month since you sat upon Ayodhya's throne, and already disease and death have vanished from the kingdom. Even the eldest of men are full of health and vigor. Women feel no pain when they deliver children. The rains that fall are sweet as amrita. And I am told this uncanny grace exists not only in Kosala, but in every kingdom of Bharatavarsha. The people all say, 'May Rama rule us forever!' "

And Rama stroked his brother's head and smiled.

24. The terrible decision

When the pushpaka vimana had gone, Rama went to a private garden in Ayodhya, where a profusion of chandana, aguru, deodar, champaka, punnaga, madhuka, asana, and other trees grew: the finest of their kinds. Unearthly parijatas here were like a mass of smokeless flames, with the sap of their sires that grow in Devaloka.

Lodhra, nipa, arjuna, naga, saptaparna, atimuktaka, mandara bakula, kadamba, jambu, and kovidara grew here as well, covered with feasts of fruit and flowers and slender creepers clinging to their mighty trunks. Bees and sunbirds, shining miracles hanging in the air, sipped their honey. Other birds, kokilas and bhringarajas, were like flashing, many-colored jewels in the branches, some golden-leaved, others like scarlet fires, and still others like kohl, darkling.

The great garden was dotted with scented pools, which had flights of steps leading down to transparent water, stairs paved with rubies that ended in crystal platforms beneath their surface. Carnivals of lilies bloomed on these pools, and chakravakas swam among them, as did teal and ibis, moonwhite goose, duck, and royal swan. Cranes stooped over the pellucid water.

All that secluded garden seemed like an immense, indescribable jewel. Stone benches were laid under the spreading, interwoven trees, and these bore thick flower cushions in every color of the season. Why, this vanika was as lovely as Indra's Nandana in Devaloka and the Chaitra that Brahma created for Kubera on the Alaka mountain.

Rama came into this garden and found Sita at its heart, waiting for him on a stone seat. Rama wrung some sweet nectar from a few flowers, a drink as heady as maireyaka wine, and gave this to Sita to drink: even as Indra makes Sachi drink.

Food and fruit were laid out for the king and his queen, and when they were alone, a troop of apsaras materialized before them and sinuous naga women, with gandharvas and kinnaras. They drank with Rama and Sita; they sang and danced for them. When the mood was set and the drink high in the royal couple's veins, the unearthly minstrels and dancers vanished as they had come. Rama turned to his love and drew her tenderly to him.

Thus their time passed. Rama would spend half his day attending to the affairs of the kingdom; then he would come to Sita in their garden. She, for her part, would spend her mornings seeing to her domestic chores, and especially looking after the needs of her three mothers-in-law, without favor or distinction. Then she would keep her daily assignation with Rama in the charmed grove.

One day he said to her, "It is time you bore me a child, my love."

And she turned her face shyly from him and whispered, "I want to go and spend a night in the forest in an asrama. I want to have the rishis' blessings."

He cried in joy, "You will go tomorrow!"

In Rama's sabha, there were some of the most brilliant men in all Bharatavarsha: not merely wise munis, but scintillating raconteurs with a fund of profound and amusing tales for their king. Vijaya, Madhumatta, Kashyapa, Mangala, Kula, Suraji, Kaliya, Bhadra, Dantavakra, and Sumagadha were some of the finest among these.

Later the same evening of the day Sita said she wanted to spend a night in a muni's asrama, Rama sat in his sabha with these bards. Today the sparkling Bhadra had everyone in splits of laughter.

Suddenly, unaccustomedly, Rama interrupted him, "Bhadra, tell me what our people say about me these days. Do they love me as they used to before I became king? And what about Sita, Lakshmana, Bharata, and Shatrughna? What do our subjects say about them? What do they say about mother Kaikeyi now? Tell me truthfully, Bhadra. A king must know what his people think of him. Don't spare me anything they say, good or bad."

Bhadra's eyes flickered briefly, then he folded his hands and said, "My lord, it is mainly about the killing of Ravana that the people speak. They say what a mighty deed it was."

But Rama said again, "Tell me everything they say, Bhadra. Don't spare me anything unpleasant you have heard. How will I become a better king if I do not know what shortcomings I must overcome in myself?"

Bhadra's seemed to collect himself for a moment. He drew a breath and said, "Then listen, Rama, to everything the people say, both good and bad. At the crossroads, in the markets, on the streets, and in the forests, they say, 'Rama built a bridge across the southern sea to Lanka. Which other king, indeed, which Deva or Asura, has done such a thing?'

" 'That was nothing, when you compare it with the killing of Ravana and all his fiercest rakshasas.'

" 'Yes, and he brought Sita back with him and he loves her just as he always did.'

" 'But isn't the pleasure he feels being with her a depraved joy? When he knows the Rakshasa carried her away and kept her with him for many months, and surely . . ?' "

Bhadra glanced anxiously at Rama, but there was no hint of any surprise or grief on that noble face. Rama merely nodded, impassively, that he should continue.

Bhadra continued, "My lord, they say, 'Why does Rama keep such a woman beside him? Doesn't he realize that we, too, will have to endure our wives straying, because the people always follow what their king and queen do?' Rama, this is what your subjects are saying, in the streets of Ayodhya and in every town and village in your kingdom."

Now Rama's lips quivered in anguish, and he looked around his sabha at his counselors, from one face to the next. They all turned their gazes from him. At last he asked them, "Is what Bhadra says true?"

As a man, all of them whispered, "It is, my lord."

For a moment he seemed to have turned to stone. Then he said to them, "Leave me for a while, my friends."

When they had gone, he said to his dwarapalaka, "Bring Lakshmana, Bharata, and Shatrughna to me."

They came at once, and saw their brother's face was like an eclipsed moon, a withered lotus; they saw his eyes were tear-laden. They bowed deeply to him, and he embraced them and made them sit in their thrones set close to his own.

He said to them, "You know how Sita entered the fire on Lanka, and Agni himself returned her to me; all the Gods appeared to attest to her purity. And I brought her home to Ayodhya, knowing she was perfectly untainted, in body and mind. But the people are not convinced. They judge her by their own lives, their own beliefs."

He broke down now, and sobbed, "The people say how will their wives be faithful to them when the king has brought home a woman who was abducted by the Rakshasa and kept in his asokavana for so many months? They say surely Ravana enjoyed Sita. They are saying she has sinned, that she is not fit to be their queen or my wife."

Lakshmana cried in anger, "You don't mean to take what they say to heart? The people will talk, Rama; they are common. They cannot understand chastity like Sita's."

But his brother raised a hand that he should stop. Rama said, "I am the king. I cannot disregard what the people say. My first dharma is toward them, Lakshmana."

Lakshmana and Shatrughna looked incredulously at Rama. Bharata was very quiet. He had ruled the kingdom for fourteen years; he alone seemed to understand the dilemma Rama faced. But it seemed Rama had already made up his mind about what should be done.

Very softly he said, "It is easy to slander anyone, and infamy is what casts one into hell. Dishonor in a king or a queen is intolerable. Why, I would sacrifice my life and even yours, my brothers who are like my very breath to me, for my reputation. If a king does not have honor, if he cannot hold his head high before his people, he cannot be a king."

He fell quiet and his tears flowed. His brothers waited to hear what he would say next, for they saw that he had not called them to ask their advice. Finally, he wiped his eyes and said evenly, "Lakshmana, Sita said to me she wants to visit a great rishi's asrama and to spend a night there to have his blessing." His voice sank to a whisper. "She is with child."

His brothers gasped. Rama went on, "Lakshmana, you must take Sita out in Sumantra's chariot tomorrow. Cross the Ganga and ride beyond the frontiers of Kosala to the Rishi Valmiki's asrama on the banks of the Tamasa." He paused as if to say the next words would cost him his life. "And, Saumitra, leave her there and return to me."

He looked at his brothers' faces, which were aghast, and continued more softly than ever. "Do not say a word to me about what I have decided. He who speaks against what I have said shall be like one who betrays me to my death. I am your king, Lakshmana; if you do not obey me, you shall be guilty of treason. She said to me, 'I want to visit an asrama on the banks of the Ganga.' Her wish must be fulfilled. Yes, it must. As for me, I cannot bear to see her before she goes. Tell her I was called away urgently from the city."

With that, Rama walked out of the sabha.

25. Lakshmana's anguish

Late that night, Lakshmana called for Sumantra and said to the king's sarathy, "Prepare the royal chariot, Sumantra. I must take Sita to visit Valmiki's asrama tomorrow."

When, at dawn, the chariot was fetched, Lakshmana went to Sita and said, "Rama has asked me to take you to the rishis' asramas."

She was as happy as a girl. She said, "Let me take some ornaments and silks for the rishis' wives, Saumitra."

And when she had everything she wanted, they worshipped at the temple in Rama's palace and set out. They rode for two days and arrived on the banks of the golden Ganga. Sumantra unyoked the horses and led them to drink. Lakshmana had hardly spoken all through their journey, and Sita was so excited she barely noticed his unusual silence.

Now they sat together, sharing the meal she had brought for them; suddenly, she saw his eyes fill and he gave a sob, as if his heart was broken.

She looked at him reproachfully. "Why are you crying in this blessed place, Lakshmana? Just because you haven't seen Rama for two nights! I have also not seen him for as long, but my heart feels no pang here, beside the Ganga."

Then she felt sorry for him, and said kindly, "Come, let us cross the river. I will give away the gifts I have brought for the yoginis and we will go back to Ayodhya. Oh please, Lakshmana, don't cry now. This is a joyful journey we have come on; for me, perhaps the happiest of my life. But then you don't know why I have come here today."

Lakshmana controlled himself with a great effort and called the nishada boatmen who waited to take them across the sacred river, she that once fell from the sky. Lakshmana helped Sita into the painted boat, climbed in himself, and they cast off. Sumantra would wait on this bank with the chariot and horses.

When they were in midstream, Sita folded her hands and prayed to Ganga, the Devi. However, when they reached the other bank and stepped ashore, Lakshmana broke down again and began to sob. Sita cried, "Again, Lakshmana! Whatever is the matter with you?"

He could not hold back any more. He cried, "Ah, that I were dead, rather than have to do this dreadful thing! Why me? O dear God, why me? I have done nothing so terrible that I deserve to have this vile task entrusted to me. O perfect Sita, I beg you, do not for a moment think that this is what I want, or that I am responsible for this monstrous crime. Oh, Yama, why don't you come for me and save me from the sin I am being forced to commit?"

Sita frowned and said, "What are you saying, Lakshmana? Why don't you speak plainly? Ah, you seem to be in agony. Has Rama been angry with you for something? Tell me what it is; I command you!"

He kept his face turned from her and his eyes streamed tears. Choking, he said, "Janaki, the people say that you are tainted and not fit to be Rama's queen. When Rama heard, he said to me, 'Lakshmana, a king's first dharma is to his subjects. Take Sita to the Rishi Valmiki's asrama and leave her there. She cannot be queen in Ayodhya any more."

Sita fell, as if he had cut her down with a sword. He sprinkled river water on her face and her eyes fluttered open. Weakly, she sat up with his help. She said, "Ah, Lakshmana, God has created this body of mine only for it to suffer. Today I feel as if sorrow has incarnated himself in me. What have I done, Saumitra, that my husband has abandoned me? What sin have I committed? I followed Rama into exile in the forest, and I was happy there that he was with me.

"Lakshmana, tell me, when the rishis ask me for what sin Rama has banished me, what shall I tell them? Oh, except that I am pregnant, I would drown myself in this Ganga."

Lakshmana stood before her, utterly miserable. He did not say a word, only wept.

Sita said, "I know you must leave me here, as your brother has commanded. But tell him from me that I will pray for him every day, as I have always done. For who else can save him from the curse that must fall on him, for what he has done to me today? Go, Lakshmana, go and tell Rama that even as his Sita is pure, she still loves him. Tell him to rule wisely, to love his subjects just as he does his brothers. Tell him not to grieve for me. Say that my spirit is always with him, and that his seed grows in me. Go, dear Lakshmana, go now before your heart also breaks."

Lakshmana walked round her in pradakshina, sobbing helplessly. He lay at her feet for her blessing and whispered, "I cannot see you like this, Sita. Ah, let me go now, I cannot bear this."

When she had blessed him, he rose quickly, and without looking at her climbed back into the boat and told the nishadas to row back to where Sumantra waited on the northern bank of the river. When he gained that shore of solid sorrow, he got into the chariot and said to the bewildered Sumantra, "Ride, Sumantra. This is Rama's command, that we leave her here. Never look back at her, ride for Ayodhya as if death rides after us!"

Across the sad and knowing river, Sita strained for a glimpse of the royal chariot that flitted away from her like the last thread of her life. When the chariot vanished, all too quickly, she stood crying dementedly on the banks of the eternal river and her sobs mingled with the puzzled cries of peacocks in the woods around her. And it seemed the sky would shatter and time would end, for what had been done to that sinless woman.

26. Valmiki's asrama

As some young disciples of Valmiki were going to the river to fetch water for the asrama, they heard heartbroken sobbing. Cautiously, they drew nearer and saw a woman as perfect as Lakshmi, who stood on the bank of the river, wringing her hands in some final despair.

They were not sure their guru would like them to talk to a young woman alone; so they ran back to the asrama and came breathlessly before their master.

"She is like a Goddess come down to the earth and she stands sobbing as if the world has ended!"

"It is not safe for her to be out alone."

"You must give her sanctuary until we learn more about her."

Valmiki gazed into his mystic heart, and he saw who it was that stood beside the Ganga and wept. He rose and, as his sishyas had never seen him do before, ran through the woods toward the river, as if his own life was at risk. Arriving, he saw Sita had collapsed on the ground and still heaved with sobs, as if she would die.

Gently Valmiki said to her, "I know who you are. In my dhyana I have seen why you are here. I know you are pure, and have been left here for no sin of yours. Janaki, from now you are in my care. Near my asrama is the asrama of the yoginis of this forest, the rishis' wives. I will take you to them. They will look after you like their daughter. Their home will be like your own."

Slowly, Sita's crying abated. She raised her teary face up to the kind and powerful muni that stood before her. She folded her hands to him, then touched his feet, as she had always done whenever she met a rishi. Sita whispered, "So be it, my lord."

She followed him to the asrama of the rishis' wives. They crowded round that great sage in joy. "We are blessed that you have come to our asrama today! What can we do for you, Valmiki?"

Sita stepped out of the trees and the rishis' wives gasped to see her, so luminous, so stricken. Valmiki said, "This is Rama's wife. Sita is sinless, but her husband has abandoned her in the forest for what his people say about her. Look after her; she is more than what any of us realize. Care for her better than you do yourselves, and you shall have my blessing and a great reward of punya."

The women said, "She is so exquisite, it will not be hard to do as you ask."

They put their arms lovingly around Sita and led her into their hermitage. Valmiki stood for a moment, staring after them. Then he turned and walked back to his own asrama with his disciples.

27. Sumantra's tale

As they drove back to Ayodhya in the chariot that seemed made of ashes, Lakshmana said to Sumantra, "No one suffers more than Rama does. He whose wrath could consume the Devas and gandharvas, the Asuras and rakshasas, is plunged in grief without a cure. Sumantra, how will my brother endure being apart from Sita? Tell me, which king has ever sacrificed so much for his people?"

Sumantra did not reply at once. Then, slowly, he murmured, "What Durvasa foretold long ago has come to pass, and what the astrologers in your father's sabha read in Rama's horoscope. I was there, and so was Vasishta; and Dasaratha made us swear we would not tell any of his sons about the prophecy.

"But today, fate has overtaken us all, and what the rishi saw in the stars has come to pass. If you want to hear what Durvasa said that day, I will tell you. But you must swear you will not breathe a word of it to Bharata or Shatrughna."

Lakshmana whispered, "Tell me, Sumantra. Tell me the whole truth and I swear not a word of it shall pass my lips."

Sumantra began, "When your father was king and you were small children, Atri's son, Durvasa, who many say is an amsa of the Lord

Siva himself, would spend the four months of the monsoon in Vasishta's asrama. Once, your father came to visit Vasishta and saw Durvasa seated at his left, like a star. Dasaratha prostrated himself before the two great munis, and they offered him madhurparka and fruit and roots from the forest.

"There was a satsangha of holy men there, and the rishis and the king spent their time listening to some ancient lore. And Dasaratha folded his hands and asked Durvasa a question that was burning his heart.

" 'Muni, for how long will my sons rule Ayodhya? How many years will my Rama live, and his brothers? How long will Rama's sons live and rule?'

"Durvasa gazed at Dasaratha for a long moment, as if considering whether he should tell the king a matter of some importance. Then, deciding, he said, 'If you truly want to know, listen, O Dasaratha. Once, in time out of mind, the Devas vanquished the Daityas in a great war and scattered them everywhere like chaff in a storm. The Daityas' women fled to the Maharishi Bhrigu's wife for refuge. She gave them sanctuary; she protected them from the Devas. But when Vishnu, who is the enemy of the Asuras, saw this, he severed Bhrigu's wife's head with the Sudarshana chakra.

" 'Bhrigu cursed Narayana, "You, Vishnu, have fallen prey to anger, which is a mortal passion. And you have killed my wife. So be born as a mortal man, and you will also be separated from your wife and feel the same anguish that I do today."

" 'And when the rishi had cursed the Blue God, he felt a searing agony in his soul, an indescribable torment. Then, through his pain, he heard a soft inner voice impelling him to worship Vishnu, whom he had cursed. When Bhrigu worshipped Narayana with a fervent tapasya, the Lord appeared before him and said, "I accept your curse, Mahamuni, it is just. I will be born into the world as a mortal man."

" 'So it will happen, Dasaratha. Your eldest son Rama is Narayana himself, born to fulfill Bhrigu Muni's curse. He will overcome evil on earth and rule for eleven thousand mortal years. But one day, he will be separated from his wife and suffer the anguish Bhrigu did.'

"Your father asked anxiously, 'Will my son have sons of his own before he loses his queen? Will they rule after him?'

"Durvasa said, 'Your son's wife will bear him two sons and they will rule after him.'

" 'And their sons?' asked Dasaratha.

"But the rishi would say no more."

Lakshmana clasped Sumantra's hand. He did not speak, but it seemed he found deep solace in the sarathy's tale. The darkness had left his face; he did not cry any more. The sun sank below the shoulder of the western mountain, and they arrived on the banks of the river Kesini. They stopped for the night beside her velvet flow and slept under sad stars, locked into the night's vast silence.

28. Lakshmana and Rama

It was noon of the next day when Sumantra's chariot returned to Ayodhya, with a somber Lakshmana. They rode up to Rama's palace and Lakshmana alighted at the steps. Wishing time would stop, he made his slow way into his brother's presence. He entered Rama's court, and tears sprang again in his eyes when he saw the king, who sat on his throne as if he were dead.

Lakshmana knelt at Rama's feet. He said in a barely audible voice, "I left her on the banks of the Ganga, near Valmiki's asrama."

He looked up into Rama's face, and his brother neither spoke nor stirred. He sat entirely absorbed by his grief. Lakshmana mumbled, "All this is fate, Rama. And you are no ordinary man, that sorrow should shake you. How often you have told me all things in this world are fleeting, and joy inevitably brings grief in its wake. No relationship in this world is permanent; not that of father and son, husband and wife, lover and beloved. But you are a great king. You are Rama; not even this final sorrow must leave its mark on you."

Rama saw how distraught, how terribly sad his brother was. He remembered all the times in the forest when he had lost his own composure and Lakshmana had consoled him, snatched him back from the lip of the abyss. Now Rama saw how much Lakshmana needed to be consoled himself. He stirred. He smiled wanly, and ran his hand through his trembling brother's hair.

Rama clasped Lakshmana to him and said, "Of course you are right. I am a king now; I must not let anything shake me. No, not even being parted from Sita. A king's only dharma is the welfare of his people. They must rule whatever I do; my life belongs to them."

Hearing his brother speak, Lakshmana gradually stopped trembling. Rama held him, for a long time.*

29. Stories in the night

The two brothers spent the night together in the empty sabha. Grief held them close, like the night's darkness. When they were boys, and later during Rama's exile, Lakshmana always loved to listen to ancient tales from his brother. And this night, seeing how distraught Lakshmana was, Rama said to him, "Child, it is four days since I performed my dharma as a king. Do you know how King Nriga was cursed, because he paid no heed to two brahmanas who came to his gates?"

Immediately, Lakshmana's face brightened. Like a boy he said, "No, Rama. Tell me."

"Once, an age ago, there was a king called Nriga, a God among men. He was pure, and always spoke the truth. His fame spread from the mountains to the sea, and he was a protector of the world and of his people. His generosity was a legend not only on earth, but also in heaven. Why, he once gave away a million caparisoned cows, draped in precious jewels, as charity at a yagna he performed at Pushkara.

"Among these cows was one he gave to the poor brahmana who lit the yagna fire. But as soon as the yagna was complete, the brahmana found his cow was missing. He set out in search of it, and roamed the length and breadth of Nriga's kingdom, often ravaged by hunger and thirst; but he did not find any trace of the white cow the king had given him.

"Finally, he arrived in Haridwara and walked on wearily to Kanakahala. There, he saw his cow in the yard of another brahmana, and now she had a lean, ill-fed calf beside her. Tears springing in his eyes, the brahmana called out to the cow, 'Shabale! My daughter, I have found you.'

---

*Another version of this story, in folklore, has it that Rama orders Lakshmana not merely to abandon Sita in the wilderness, but to kill her and bring back proof that he has. Lakshmana cannot bear to do this and leaves her in the forest instead. He brings back the blood-soaked ear of a deer, folded in a leaf, to a heartbroken Rama, and says it was Sita's. Rama does not look inside the leaf and never knows until his final meeting with Sita that she is alive and has borne him twin sons.

"And she tossed her head in joy and ran out to him, with her calf at her heels. The brahmana stroked her face, her flanks, in absolute rapture. He set off for home, with his white cow and her calf. He was like a sacred flame, as he went, that brahmana. But then the other brahmana, in whose yard he had found his cow, came shouting after him, 'Where are you taking my cow, you thief?'

"The first brahmana replied hotly, 'She is mine! The king himself gave her to me.'

"But the second brahmana cried, 'You are a liar! I found this cow abandoned on a roadside. I brought her home with me, and I have fed her and looked after her and her calf.'

"They almost came to blows. Then the first brahmana said, 'There is only one person who can settle this dispute: the king himself. Let us take our quarrel to him and do as he tells us to.'

"The second brahmana agreed, 'Let Nriga decide whose cow she is.'

"So the two brahmanas set out for the king's capital and his palace. They came to his gates, but found them barred. The guards said to them, 'You cannot see the king now. He is busy.'

"The brahmanas said, 'We must see Nriga; we will wait for him. Please take word to him that we are here to see him on an urgent matter.'

"Though they waited some days and nights outside Nriga's palace, the king did not see them. Finally, in anger the brahmanas cursed Nriga: 'You have forsaken your dharma as a king, that you do not care to see your subjects who come to petition you. Be a lizard, cowering in a hole. Be a lizard for a hundred thousand years. And one day, at the end of the dwapara yuga, when Vishnu is born into the world in the House of Yadu, he will free you from our curse. But only when Nara and Narayana are both born into the world to deliver it from the bondage of sin.'

"With that, the two brahmanas presented their old and weak cow to a third brahmana, and walked away from that city, and, indeed, this world."

Rama said in the living night, "So, Lakshmana, no king should neglect his dharma, for his people are his first and only dharma."

Lakshmana said, "That was a harsh curse for so small a crime, Rama. What did Nriga do?"

"Nriga was aghast when he heard of the brahmanas' curse. But he was a rajarishi, and controlled his grief. Calmly, he had his young son, Vasu, crowned king. Then he ordered his artisans to build him a marvelous pit below the earth, protected from the cold and the rain, and pave it with the brightest jewels. He had a secret garden fashioned above the ground, and the finest fruit and flowering trees planted in it, among which he could bask in summer.

"He blessed his son, and told him to be always attentive to the needs of his subjects. Then Nriga entered his secret hideaway, and at once he felt himself being transformed by the brahmanas' curse. He felt himself becoming a great monitor lizard. And, my brother, Nriga of old still dwells in his secret hideaway, that no man knows, and he waits for a dark savior to be born into the world. But, Lakshmana, that time is still very far."

Lakshmana laid his head in his brother's lap and sighed. When Rama had finished his strange tale and fell silent, it seemed the night's immense grief closed around them again, reaching for them with cold fingers. The breeze that stole in through an open window sobbed in the dark.

Lakshmana shivered. He rose and shut the window. He came back to his brother, and sat at his feet again. Rama was truly like a God now, so serene was he. Still, his sorrow filled the night like a sea. The brothers sat thus, in silence, for a long time. Then, Lakshmana whispered, "Rama, tell me another story."

Rama smiled. "Have I told you about King Nimi of our line and how he cursed our kulaguru, Rishi Vasishta, and how Vasishta cursed him?"

"Perhaps you have. But tell me again, Rama."

"Nimi was the twelfth son of Ikshvaku. He, too, was a rajarishi. He founded a city as splendid as Amravati, near Rishi Gautama's asrama, and he called it Vaijayanta, city of victory. When he had finished building, Nimi thought he must perform a yagna to please his father. He went to Manu's son, Ikshvaku, and asked if he could undertake the sacrifice. With his father's consent, Nimi began to prepare for the yagna.

"First, he chose Brahma's son Vasishta to be his chief priest. Then he asked Atri, Angiras, and Bhrigu, also, to sit over his yagna. But Vasishta said to Nimi, 'Indra has already asked me to be his ritvik. I beg you, wait until I finish Indra's yagna before you begin your sacrifice.'

"Nimi agreed. But when Vasishta went to Amravati, the impatient king asked Gautama to be his main ritvik, until Vasishta returned. King Nimi's yagna was soon begun, outside Vaijayanta, in the lap of the Himalaya. Nimi was consecrated as the sacrificer and his yagna would last five thousand years.

"Meanwhile, as soon as Indra's yagna was completed in Devaloka, Vasishta returned to the earth and to Vaijayanta. He found that Nimi's yagna was already under way, with Gautama as the ritvik. Vasishta trembled with anger. He asked to meet the king, and sat for a muhurta before the yagnashala. But Nimi was exhausted that day and he had gone to sleep.

"Vasishta's rage grew, and he cursed Nimi: 'May you lose your body, vain and treacherous kshatriya!'

"When Nimi heard of Vasishta's curse, he also cursed the brahmarishi, crying, 'You defile yourself with anger, Vasishta. I curse you, that you will also lose your splendid body!'

"And so, Lakshmana, both the king and the rishi lost their bodies. They became forms of air. Vasishta flew up to his father, Brahma, and said, 'Pitamaha, how can I fulfill my destiny in the world when I have lost my body, which was created from your immaculate thought? I beg you, O Hiranyagarbha, let me have a body again.'

"Brahma said, 'There will soon be occasion for Mitra and Varuna to spill their seed. Enter that seed, my son, and you will have a body again. You shall not be born of a woman's womb, so your life will still be mine to influence.'

"Vasishta bowed to the Creator, and he flew away in his spirit body to the Kshirasagara, where Varuna, Lord of all oceans, dwells, and is worshipped by the four Lokapalas. It happened that the Deva Mitra was there as well, sharing in his friend Varuna's sovereignty. Vasishta arrived in Varuna's submarine kingdom, and awaited his chance.

"Not a day had passed when the apsara Urvashi came to Varuna's realm with her sakhis. She was seductive past reason, she was beautiful past imagining, and the good Lord Varuna was smitten! Varuna found her alone in a secluded grotto, where she had been bathing, naked, and he said hoarsely to her, 'There is no one as lovely as you are in the three worlds, Urvashi. Ah, I must hold you in my arms, apsara, I must feel your body under mine.'

"She flushed, and said to the aroused Deva, 'My lord, I have come here to meet your friend Mitra, for I have already promised myself to him. He is my lover now; I cannot betray him.'

"But Varuna was beside himself. The white sea swelled around them in mountainous tides at the desire he felt for her. He was past helping himself; he shook with lust. He must have some release, or he would drown the world in his despair.

"He said, 'You see how I am, apsara. I beg you, if you cannot make love at least help me to some release. At least touch me, Urvashi, and I will spill my seed into this urn.'

"She was not so cruel that she would refuse him this. She laid her exquisite hands on him, and he ejaculated like a tide of flames into the golden urn. She vanished from there, a fragrant mist, to where Mitra, her lover, waited for her. But even as they made love, Mitra felt that the touch of another Deva had been upon her. Pulling away, the Deva Mitra, also, ejaculated outside Urvashi's enchanting body, into the golden urn that appeared, fatefully, to receive his seed."

By now the story absorbed them, and for the moment, grief seemed distanced. Rama said, "It was the same golden urn into which both Varuna and Mitra spilled their seed. There was a blaze of light from the urn, when Mitra's seed fell onto Varuna's, and a rishi of blinding splendor rose from that urn. He was Agastya; bowing to both Urvashi and the God Mitra, that already realized sage sought the Himalaya to sit in tapasya.

"No sooner had the peerless Agastya vanished than Vasishta, who had subtly entered the golden urn in his spirit body, rose, embodied and resplendent from the mingled seed of Mitra and Varuna. He stood with folded hands before Urvashi and her lover and said, 'Mitra Deva, I am not only your son!'

"And he vanished from there. Mitra now saw clearly in his mind's eye what had transpired between Urvashi and Varuna. He cried in despair, 'Unfaithful woman, I curse you to live half a mortal life in the world of men! Go down to the earth and be the wife of Pururavas of Kasi.'

"Pururavas was Budha's son, and by Mitra's curse Urvashi became his queen for a time. In his city, Pratishtana, she bore him a son of great prowess, called Ayu. Ayu's son was Nahusha, who was hardly less glorious than Indra; and, indeed, Nahusha ruled Devaloka for a hundred thousand years, when Indra was cursed after he killed Vritra-sura treacherously.

"When she had lived with Pururavas for some years on earth, Mitra's curse ended and Urvashi returned to Devaloka, to Indra's realm, where she is a dancer in his court."

Lakshmana wanted to know, "What happened to Nimi, Rama?"

"When Vasishta had his new body, Ikshvaku asked him to be the kulaguru of the royal House of the Sun, this ancient house of ours.

"As for Nimi, the rishis at his yagna saw the king had died. They embalmed his body in oils to preserve it. They clothed him in white silks and draped garlands made from unfading flowers over him. Then they completed the yagna he had begun, and Bhrigu spoke to the king's spirit that hovered over the yagnashala as a shimmering vapor.

" 'The Devas are pleased with you, Kshatriya. If you like, I can fetch your soul back into your body. Otherwise, I can bless you so you will dwell anywhere you choose. Ask for any boon you want.'

"But having tasted the freedom of death, Nimi did not want to be imprisoned in a single body any more. He said from the air, 'Holy ones, let me dwell in the eyelids of every living being. Let me see all the earth at once. But first, let me have a son to rule my kingdom.'

"The rishis and Devas blessed King Nimi of old that he would live as subtle air in the eyelids of all the living, and when he stirred in their eyes, they would blink. Lakshmana, before King Nimi of old lost his body, no living creature blinked.

"When the Devas had blessed Nimi, they vanished. And now, the holy rishis began to rub the king's lifeless body with their hands, as if they were rubbing arani sticks to make fire. They chanted secret mantras as they did this. Soon, Nimi's corpse was as hot as fire and suddenly a child sprang from it.

"The munis called that child Videha, since he had been born from a dead body. They also named him Mithi, since he had been born at their rubbing Nimi's corpse. Since he had no mother, he was called Janaka, and his city was named Mithila, where Mithi ruled."

Now Rama's eyes filled; for, of course, he spoke of Sita's father.

30. Sukra curses Yayati

Lakshmana said, "Why did Nimi and Vasishta curse each other, Rama? How is it such great men were not more forgiving?"

Rama said, "Forgiveness often deserts the greatest men, when they are tested with anger. Would you hear the story of Yayati?"

Lakshmana nodded eagerly.

Rama began yet another tale of ancient times. "Yayati was a king in the royal House of Soma. He was Nahusha's son, and he was a sovereign without equal in his time. He had two wives, each one as beautiful, accomplished, and virtuous as the other. The first was Sarmishta and she was Diti's own granddaughter, Vrishaparva's child. Yayati loved Sarmishta dearly, like his very life.

"His second wife was Devayani, to whom the king was indifferent, though she was in no way inferior to Sarmishta. In time, two sons were born to Yayati, one to each of his wives. Sarmishta bore Puru, and Devayani, Yadu. Yayati, of course, openly preferred Puru, since he was Sarmishta's son, and neglected Yadu.

"As Yadu grew up, he saw how unhappy his mother was. One day, he said to Devayani, 'You are the great Sukra's daughter. How do you tolerate being treated so wretchedly in your own husband's house? The king does not care if you live or die, mother. He is my father, as much as he is Puru's; but he has time only for my brother. I am treated like an unwelcome guest in this house, often like a servant. You may be able to bear this, but not I. I mean to put an end to myself.'

"In anguish, Devayani invoked her father, the awesome Sukracharya, the guru of the Asuras, who, being Bhrigu's son, is also called Bhargava. Sukra appeared before his distraught daughter and asked the cause of her misery. However, she would only shake her lovely head, as tears flowed down her face, and say, 'I mean to drink poison, or drown myself.'

"Repeatedly, Bhargava asked her, 'But tell me what the matter is, my child. You have never complained before.'

"Finally, she broke down and cried, 'You do not know how I am treated in this house. My husband humiliates my son and me. He always prefers Sarmishta and her Puru, and ignores Yadu and me.'

"Sukra Bhargava's eyes turned red as blood. He went to Yayati and cursed him: 'You have tormented my daughter. Be an old man from this moment. May your body lose its strength and may you be impotent!'

"And Sukracharya stormed out of Yayati's city. The moment Usana pronounced his curse, the mighty Yayati felt his limbs grow weak. He felt vast age upon him. His hair turned white, his skin became wrinkled, and he felt many thousands of years old.

"Yayati called for his son Yadu and said, 'I have become an old man by your grandfather's curse. But I have not satisfied my desires; they burn like fire within me. My righteous son, lend me your youth so I can enjoy my life and grow old naturally.'

"But Yadu said to him, 'How is it, father, that you have remembered me today? Puru is your son whom you love. Ask him to give you his youth.'

"Yayati called for Puru and asked him for his youth. Without a moment's hesitation, Puru said, 'I am honored that I can serve you. Take my youth and let me be old in your place.'

"So it was. Yayati shed his unnatural age, and Puru received it like a blessing, while he gave his virile youth to his father. Now the son was an old man and the father a young one. Yayati ruled the earth and lived a full life for many thousands of years. He performed a hundred aswamedhas and rajasuyas.

"One day, he called Puru and said, 'My son, give me back the age I burdened you with so long ago. And receive your youth back from me. You, my faithful child, shall be king.'

"He turned to Yadu and cursed him: 'You could have been king, if you had obeyed me. But you refused what I asked. You are a rakshasa born from my loins, and you shall father only rakshasas and yatudanas. Your sons shall not belong to the House of the Moon and they will be as evil as you are. I banish you from our city and our kingdom.'

"Yayati himself left Pratishtana and went away to the forest. He took vanaprastha. Puru ruled over the kingdom of Kasi from his throne. In time, after many years of tapasya, Yayati left this world and found heaven for himself.

"Yadu roamed the Krauncharanya: a wild and powerful beggar, a great kshatriya without a kingdom, wealth, or a family. He sired a thousand yatudanas on the demonesses of the accursed jungle. It was rage, my brother, which was the root of the tragedy of Yadu. He pitied himself too much and abandoned his noble nature from anger."

Lakshmana smiled wanly, "So we must be brave, Rama?"

"We must not commit Nriga's crime. A king's first dharma is toward his people, and I have not behaved like a king for four days now.

I have plunged myself in my own grief; I have forgotten that I am a king."

The night was in its last yaama, the quietest hour. The brothers sat wrapped in a deep, living silence, which bore the grace of ages at this magical hour. It seemed to Rama that his loss had brought him closer to his own soul, and even that his love for Sita had been a subtle and powerful obstacle that stood between himself and his destiny. Now, at the heart of the night, he saw this clearly, and his way ahead as well.

But he also knew that in another sense, his own life had ended. What he had done was irretrievable: from now, Rama the man would hardly exist, only Rama the king.

31. The Asura Lavana

The next morning, with the sun, the princes opened the lofty doors of the sabha and came out onto the white marble terrace outside to give audience to the people.

Just then, Sumantra hurried in to them and said, "Rama, some munis have been waiting to see you. They have come from their asramas on the banks of the Yamuna. Bhrigu's son Chyvana is with them and they want to meet you as early as they can."

Rama said, "Bring them in at once, Sumantra."

Soon, more than a hundred rishis, their bodies alight with tapasya, filed into Rama's sabha. They brought sacred water in earthen vessels, which they had drawn from all the most blessed tirthas in Bharatavarsha. They brought fruit and rare roots from the forest for Rama of Ayodhya.

Rama received these gifts humbly and in joy. He offered them silken seats in his court, and then asked, "Holy ones, tell me what I can do for you, that you have blessed my city with your auspicious presence. My kingdom and my life are yours to command, O Munis who are the support of the world."

Chyvana said, "Best among men, greatest of all kshatriyas, we know you will do as you say, unlike some other kings of the earth. Noble Rama, we live in terror and we have come to ask you to deliver us from the fear that stalks our lives."

Rama said in concern, "What fear stalks your lives, Brahmanas? Surely, we must all fear whatever threatens you."

Chyvana replied, "It is an Asura. Once, in the krita yuga, Diti, the mother of the Daityas, bore her first son, the awesome Madhu. Madhu was an Asura of flawless dharma, and a Sivabhakta. Rudra appeared before Madhu, who sat in tapasya, and from his own trident the Lord extracted another trisula that shone as if the fire of the sun were held captive within it.

"Siva gave this weapon to Madhu, saying, 'This ayudha is yours, for your perfect dhyana, Asura. As long as you do not turn against dharma and the Devas who are the guardians of the world, this trisula will make you invincible. For the weapon will turn your enemies into ashes.'

"Madhu prostrated himself before the God of Gods. He said humbly, 'Lord, may this ayudha be with my race forever.'

"But Siva answered him, saying, 'That cannot be, because the ayudha is too powerful. However, it shall belong to one of your sons and he shall also be invincible.'

"And the Lord vanished before his devotee's eyes. In joy, Madhu returned to the world, and he built a splendid city and a shining palace at its heart. In time, Madhu married the legendary beauty Kumbheenasi, who was the daughter of Ravana's sister Anala and the wise Malyavan.

"Madhu sired a mighty son on Kumbheenasi. He was called Lavana. As the child grew, his father saw he was entirely violent and evil. Heartbroken that his only son was a creature of darkness, Madhu left his city and his kingdom and sought refuge in death by walking into the ocean. Siva's marvelous trisula he left, reluctantly, to his monstrous child.

"Ever since, Lavana has been a terror in the world, most of all to the rishis who live in prayer and are the holders of the earth. Rama, no other kshatriya can rid us of Lavana. He desecrates our yagnas; he kills our brother rishis and feasts on their flesh. He is like death himself, with jaws agape. We have no peace; you must save us from the Asura."

Rama turned to his brothers and asked, "Which of you will kill Lavana?"

Bharata said eagerly, "I will, my lord."

Then Shatrughna rose from his golden throne and knelt before Rama. He said, "Bharata has already fulfilled his life's dharma. He ruled Ayodhya when you were away. With a broken heart, he ruled like a lion from Nandigrama. He slept on a bed of grass, ate only fruit and roots, wore his hair in jata, and ruled even as you would have.

"No, Bharata has endured enough for a lifetime. And as for Lakshmana, he went with you into exile. He fought the great war at your side. But I have done nothing yet of any note for you, my brother. I beg you, let me be sent to kill the Asura."

And his brothers smiled when they saw how he had tears in his eyes. Rama glanced at Bharata, who nodded to say that Shatrughna might be sent to kill Lavana.

Rama said, "Shatrughna, I will make you king of Madhu's sacred kingdom. Take an army with you, go to the banks of the Yamuna, kill Lavana, and establish a city there. And rule from that city, Shatrughna. Yes, you must also be a king."

He saw Shatrughna hesitate momentarily, and said, "It is my command. I am your older brother and you must do as I say."

Shatrughna flushed. He protested softly, "But it is not dharma that a younger brother be made a king while his older brothers live. Yet you say I must not disobey you. I should never have spoken when my brother Bharata had already said he would go to kill Lavana. Let this be my punishment: to be sent away from Ayodhya, away from all of you."

Rama said to Bharata and Lakshmana, "Let everything we need to crown Shatrughna a king be fetched. Call Vasishta and the other brahmanas; they must perform the rituals."

And so Shatrughna, the scourge of his enemies, was made a king in Rama's sabha, in Rama's name. And he shone even as Karttikeya had, in time out of mind, when he was made Senapati of the army of the Devas. Chyvana and the other rishis felt certain that Lavana was as good as slain.

Rama called Shatrughna to sit beside him, on his throne. Embracing his brother, kissing him as he used to when they were children, Rama gave him a glittering astra, like a band of sun. The sabha gasped when Rama materialized the blinding arrow in his hands out of thin air. Shatrughna shivered as he received the golden thing, and the moment it lay in his palms, it vanished from sight.

Shatrughna breathed, "What is it, Rama?"

Rama said, "You will kill Lavana with this astra. This is the astra with which Vishnu killed Madhu and Kaitabha of old, upon the primordial sea. It was after Vishnu killed those Asuras that he created the worlds and the creatures in them.

"But Lavana has Siva's boon and his trisula. The demon keeps the trisula in his palace. Shatrughna, as long as Lavana wields Siva's trident, he is invincible. So be sure you challenge him outside his city and kill him with this astra. Take an army with you; take our singers and dancers to entertain you. Take gold to pay all those who go with you, so they are never discontented; they must leave their families and homes to go with you to war. But when you go to kill Lavana, be sure you go alone. Go in stealth, Shatrughna, and ambush the Asura, because there is no other way in which he can be killed."

Rama grew thoughtful, as if he looked deep into his spirit to see the future. He said, "Wait until summer passes before you attack Lavana; his time to die is during the rains. Take your army now to the banks of the Jahnavi. Cross the Ganga and wait in the good munis' asramas for the rains to come. Only then, go alone to kill Lavana."

Shatrughna gathered an army of four thousand horses, two thousand chariots, a hundred of the greatest elephants in Ayodhya, and countless foot soldiers. He collected the bravest kshatriya chieftains to lead his army, and sent them ahead with the rishis to the Ganga.

This done, he went to Kausalya, Sumitra, and Kaikeyi, and took their blessings. Tearfully, he prostrated himself before Rama, Lakshmana, Bharata, and Vasishta, also. Once more he fell at Rama's feet, and Rama raised him up and embraced him. A month after his army had gone to make camp in the wilds, Shatrughna set out from Ayodhya to kill the Asura Lavana and to establish a kingdom for himself, so he could protect the holy country of the Ganga and the Yamuna, and the sages who lived in tapasya in those lands and were the support of all the world.

32. In Valmiki's asrama

When he had ridden for two days, Shatrughna arrived at Valmiki's asrama on the banks of the Tamasa. He prostrated himself before the muni and said, "I am Rama's brother Shatrughna, my lord, and I would spend the night here with you, if you let me. Tomorrow I will ride west again. I have come on a dire mission."

Valmiki said, smiling, "Welcome. This asrama is your own, O prince of Raghu."

And the rishi's disciples brought padya and arghya for Shatrughna. When his feet were washed and he had tasted the madhurparka they offered him, and eaten some of the fruit and roots, he sat on a darbhasana beside Valmiki.

Shatrughna asked the muni, "As I approached your asrama from the east, my lord, I saw a yagnashala for a great sacrifice. Whose is it, Swami?"

Valmiki did not reply for a moment, and his eyes were bright with the memory Shatrughna's question had evoked. Then, slowly, the muni said, "Once, in the House of Ikshvaku there was an ancestor of yours called Sudasa. He had a son called Virasaha, a pious and bold kshatriya. One day, when he was hardly more than a boy, Virasaha went hunting in the forest and saw the strangest thing.

"Two rakshasas had assumed the forms of two lions, and they were devouring every living creature in the vana. Bones and half-eaten remains were strewn everywhere under the sorrowing trees, amidst splashes of blood. But the rakshasas were not satisfied; their carnage continued unabated.

"In rage, Virasaha stalked the demons and killed one of them with an astra of fire, so he became a pile of ashes. The young prince ran feverishly at the mound and scattered the ashes with his foot. Just then, he heard a dreadful, heartbroken howl behind him. Turning, he saw the second rakshasa: a lion no longer, but reverted to his own evil form.

"The creature's jowls still dripped the blood of a hundred beasts he had killed; but also, his fierce eyes streamed tears for his dead companion. In agony the rakshasa screamed at the shocked Virasaha, 'You have killed my brother, who never harmed you. I will have revenge on you one day, Kshatriya!'

"And before Virasaha could raise his bow, the demon vanished. Virasaha never forgot the absolute grief he heard in that rakshasa's voice and saw in his terrible eyes.

"Virasaha went back to Ayodhya. The years passed and the prince's father Sudasa died. Virasaha became king of the Ikshvakus. Like all the kshatriyas of your august line, Shatrughna, Virasaha, too, was a king of dharma. Like all his mighty sires before him, he also performed an aswamedha yagna, which lasted years and was as majestic as a yagna of the Devas.

"Vasishta was the ritvik at King Virasaha's yagna, and it was as the sacrifice drew near its end that the rakshasa, whose brother a young prince had once killed in the forest, took his revenge. The rakshasa possessed Vasishta himself, and spoke in that muni's voice to Virasaha.

" 'When the yagna is over, offer me some fine flesh to eat. Don't hesitate, do as I tell you.'

"Virasaha said to his best cooks, 'Prepare the best dishes you know, with freshly slaughtered, succulent meat. Offer them to Guru Vasishta.'

"But his chief cook hesitated. The rakshasa entered that cook's spirit, and he prepared an aromatic dish of human flesh and brought it to the king. Virasaha and his queen, Madayanti, themselves brought that dish to Vasishta, who sat with his eyes shut, in dhyana, waiting for the ritual offering of food that would formally bring the yagna to its conclusion.

"Vasishta sniffed the air. He opened his eyes and saw the king and queen proffering the golden salver on which steaming human flesh was piled. The muni's eyes turned red, and he said in deadly quiet, 'Since this is the offering of food you have brought to me, O Virasaha, be sure you eat it yourselves, you and your queen. Let this be your daily meat from now.'

"He took the dish from the king's hands and flung it on the ground. At which, Virasaha flew into a rage and was about to curse his kulaguru in return, when Queen Madayanti clutched at his hand in which he had scooped up some holy water to throw into Vasishta's face. The king had chanted a potent mantra over the water.

" 'He is our guru!' cried the queen. 'He is like God to us; you cannot curse him.'

"With a moan, Virasaha sprinkled that cursed water over his own feet, and in a flash his feet turned every color under the sun! From then, he was called Kalmasapada: he whose feet were of many hues. Virasaha and Madayanti fell at Vasishta's feet and told the rishi how he himself had asked to be served with flesh.

"Vasishta pondered this for a moment, and he saw a rakshasa had caused the mischief. The mahamuni said, 'I cannot withdraw my curse. But it will last for just twelve years, and when the twelve years are over, you will remember nothing of them.'

"He laid his palm on the king's head and his queen's. And so it happened, Shatrughna. The yagnashala you see was Virasaha's."

Shatrughna spent the night in Valmiki's asrama. It was on the same night that, in a nearby hermitage, Sita gave birth to brilliant twin sons: Rama's sons. At midnight, some of Valmiki's sishyas woke their master with the news.

With a rushlight, the muni hurried through the darkness to the yoginis' asrama where Sita lived. The message the munis' wives had sent to Valmiki was to come at once and chant mantras over the precious children, to keep them safe from bhutas and rakshasas, and every evil spirit that might be lurking in the forest. And to make the sign of the sacred yantras over them, so they would always be protected.

Valmiki arrived breathless at Sita's hut of labor, and how his face lit up when he saw the two perfectly formed infants who lay beside her. He sensed unseen and ominous presences crowding that spare dwelling. Valmiki took up a handful of kusa grass and passed it over the children—the upper half of the blades, called Lava, over the child who had been born a few moments before his twin, and the lower, called Kusa, over the second child.

Chanting ancient and powerful mantras of protection, Valmiki said, "I name these princes, Rama's sons, Lava and Kusa."

The older yoginis of the asrama received the sacred grass from the rishi, and they too stroked the infants with them in blessing. Meanwhile, Shatrughna heard the news in Valmiki's asrama and he arrived at the sannyasinis' hermitage. He took the splendid children, his nephews, the heirs to the throne of Ayodhya, in his arms, and wept for joy and deep sorrow. He only gazed mutely at the tired, radiant Sita, and could not say a word to her.

Thus Rama's sons were born in the wilderness, in an asrama of yoginis, and they would grow up in the care of the Rishi Valmiki. Shatrughna remained in Valmiki's hermitage until the full moon of the month of Sravana, when the monsoon ended. The next day, at crack of dawn, he bathed in the Tamasa, still as a lake, took the dust from the rishi's feet, and set out west for the banks of the Yamuna and the asramas of the munis who had come to Ayodhya to ask Rama to kill the Asura Lavana.

Seven days and nights Shatrughna journeyed, until he saw the Yamuna before him, wide as a small sea. Chyvana and the incomparable Bhargava welcomed him, they and their rishis of the sublime gifts of the spirit.

33. *The killing of Mandhata*

When Shatrughna had rested and eaten, after his long journey, he sat talking with Chyvana Muni, pure as agni. Shatrughna asked, "Brahmana, can you tell me about Lavana, his trisula and his strength? I must know as much as I can about him, before I go to kill him for you."

Chyvana said, "Let me tell you a small story about an ancestor of yours. Mandhata was, like you, a scion of the House of Ikshvaku. He was Yuvanasva's son, and there was no king on earth as mighty as Mandhata of old.

"He ruled all this world, and one day he decided he would like to conquer Devaloka and rule Indra's kingdom as well. He gathered his army of kshatriyas, each of whom was hardly less than a Deva, and set out for Amravati. Such was Mandhata's renown that Indra quailed to hear he was coming. Indra appeared before the awesome king and said, 'Mandhata, your lordship of the earth is hardly secure, that you have come to take my kingdom from me.'

"The noble Mandhata was puzzled. 'I am king of all the earth. Who disputes my sovereignty over the world of men?'

"The thousand-eyed Lord of the Devas replied, 'Madhu's son Lavana is not your subject, Mandhata. He does not obey you.'

"Mandhata's face burned with shame. He hung his head and, without a word, turned back to the earth with his legions, now to conquer Lavana. Mandhata sent a messenger to the Asura. He sent a haughty kshatriya, with instructions to speak roughly to Madhu's son, to frighten him.

"Lavana listened for a while to what the king's messenger had to say, then calmly seized the warrior and ate him. Mandhata surrounded the Asura with his legions and attacked him from every side, covering him in a night of arrows. But the Asura raised the trisula, which Siva had given his father, and it shone like a sun in the darkness.

"The solid banks of arrows from Mandhata's bowmen were made ashes by flames from the burning trident. Lavana cast his trisula at the encircling army, and it went among them like the fire in which the worlds are consumed, when time ends. In moments, just whispering mounds of ashes remained where the Ikshvaku king, Mandhata, lord of the earth, and his vast, invincible forces had stood.

"The trident flew back into Lavana's hand, and his laughter filled the spaces of the earth and the sky."

Shatrughna looked stricken. Chyvana smiled, and gently took the prince's hand. "Shatrughna, Mandhata sought to kill Lavana for his own glory, for undisputed kingdom. You have come at our bidding, and not out of any ambition. Rama has blessed you; you will not fail. Only remember you must not fight him when he wields his trident, and tomorrow Lavana will die."

That rishi spoke with such quiet conviction that Shatrughna smiled.

The night passed quickly, and Shatrughna rose with the sun. He bathed in the deep-flowing river, took the rishis' blessings, and, with his bow in his hand and his quiver strapped firmly to his back, Rama's brother crossed the Yamuna.

Meanwhile, in the marvelous city that the Asura Madhu had once built, his son Lavana rose with an unaccustomed hunger roiling him. The Asura wondered at this, for he had eaten well the previous night. He did not, of course, dream that this was the final pang of hunger of his very life, death's greed.

His belly on fire, Lavana rose, took up a great cudgel, and strode out of his palace. He made for the forest in the heart of which his dark city was built. Every living creature in that jungle heard Lavana's footfalls and fled from his approach. But not all of them escaped him. Soon, a small glade in the forest began to fill with corpses. Lavana hunted without favor for species; and a mound of leopard and tiger, peafowl, deer, rabbit, boar, bison, and even elephant, grew in that glade, and its grass was stained crimson.

As he hunted Lavana ate, and blood leaked down his huge body from the beasts he devoured, often hardly chewing on their varied flesh, but only swallowing them with a perfunctory bite or two. However, today's raging hunger would not leave him; it burned his insides with irresistible compulsion.

Lavana slaughtered a thousand animals and birds. He stuffed their carcasses into a large net he had brought with him, and, by noon, dragged them along jungle trails toward his city. As he approached the gates he saw a lean, powerful kshatriya waiting for him. Lavana blinked; it seemed to him the young warrior was swathed in a pulsing light and the bow in his hand was like an arc of the sun.

Lavana felt a stab of fear when he saw Shatrughna; but he thought it was the strange hunger that possessed him today. He said in his rumbling voice, "Young fool, why have you come to my gates seeking death? Don't you know I have killed a thousand young kshatriyas like you?" He laughed, pointing at the bow in Shatrughna's hand, "And is it that puny thing you mean to fight me with? Ah, I am so hungry today, and it is some time since I ate sweet human flesh. But before I eat you, tell me who you are."

Shatrughna quivered with anger, and light like flames spewed through the links of his armor, like rays from a red sun. He said evenly, "I am Shatrughna of the House of Ikshvaku. I am Dasaratha's son and Rama's brother, and I have come to kill you. Your vile life has lasted long enough. You are the bane of every living creature in the world, and you shall not escape me today."

Lavana grew thoughtful. Then wild laughter erupted from him again, triumphant laughter. The Asura said, "Ravana of Lanka was my uncle and your brother Rama killed him for a woman's sake. Rama killed so many of Ravana's people, my kinsmen. And today you have made my revenge easy, Shatrughna. You have come to me yourself so I can drink your blood. I have sworn to kill Rama and all his clan; let my revenge begin today. Wait here for me while I fetch my trisula from my palace. Then we will fight, Kshatriya."

But Shatrughna raised his bow, and replied, "You will not pass me. Look upon this mortal world a last time, Lavana. Fill your eyes with these green sights, before I shut them forever. And when you are as dead as your uncle Ravana, there shall indeed be peace on earth."

Lavana clapped his hands together like thunder. He pulled up a tree from the ground and flung it like a bolt of lightning at Shatrughna. The prince cut it in a thousand slivers with godlike archery. But quicker than thinking, Lavana drew out another tree and, rushing at Shatrughna, struck him over the head with it.

Some rishis had gathered in the surrounding forest to watch the battle between the prince and the demon. They cried out in alarm when Shatrughna fell so quickly, and the Devas, gandharvas, and apsaras, who had gathered invisibly in the sky, shivered.

Lavana thought he had killed the human and turned back to his net of the carcasses of the beasts he had hunted. The terrible hunger ravaged him again, and he began to drag the dead creatures into his city to begin his noon meal. He gave a howl when he saw Shatrughna stir and then jump up, his bow still grasped in his hand. The long hairs on the Asura's bloated body stood on end when the prince drew a glittering shaft from his quiver and fitted it to his bowstring in a blur.

That was the arrow Rama had given Shatrughna, and it shone as if the fires of the apocalypse were contained in it. Time seemed to give a lurch and stand still when Shatrughna fixed that astra to his bowstring. The kshatriya's body was blinding now, and Lavana covered his baleful eyes.

The Devas in the sky cried to Brahma their father, "Hah! What is this, Pitamaha? Are the worlds coming to an end?"

Brahma said, "Shatrughna's astra is the very form of Narayana. Vishnu killed Madhu and Kaitabha with it before the worlds began. Rama gave the ayudha to his brother, and Lavana shall die with it today."

The Devas crowded the sky below which the prince and the monster faced each other. Shatrughna saw their shadows and glanced heavenward. He saw the Gods above and, turning back to Lavana, gave a roar like a pride of lions. Lavana roared back, so the earth shook and the sky. With claws outstretched, his red maw yawning wide, the Asura rushed at Shatrughna to devour him.

In a flash, Shatrughna drew his bowstring to his ear and shot Rama's astra at the demon. With a report as if the sky had cracked open and the world had ended, the flaming missile flew into Lavana's chest wide as a hill. It cut through gristle and bone like a dagger slicing through butter, and, leaving that mighty chest in scarlet shreds, bored down through the earth and into darkling Patala. Lavana swayed briefly on his feet like some thousand-year-old tree that had been cut down. Without a sound, but his ochre eyes full of surprise, the Asura fell onto the earth with a crash and was still.

Shatrughna stood shaking from awe of the astra that he had loosed. The sky filled with uncanny, blissful light; the world seemed swathed in it. Blooms of light fell from above on the victorious kshatriya. The Deva host appeared plainly on high, with refulgent Indra and Agni at their head.

The Gods said to Shatrughna, "O Lion among men! Ask for any boon you want and it will be yours."

Shatrughna said, "Let these lands be called the kingdom of Surasena and let this city of Madhu's, Madhura, be its capital. Bless my kingdom and my city, O Devas!"

And the Gods blessed Shatrughna. Soon he had a great army of men living with him in his city shaped like a crescent moon. No sickness entered Shatrughna's city, and Indra sent the rains on time, so the harvest in that kingdom was always bountiful. Quickly, the fame of his city spread through the lands of Bharata, and men of all the four varnas arrived to live in Madhura and flourished under King Shatrughna of Surasena.

Twelve years passed thus, and truly, Madhura and the kingdom around it were like a bit of Devaloka fallen into the world of men. The dharma of Shatrughna of Madhura was immaculate, and his people were prosperous past imagining. Then, one day, as he sat in his sabha, where incense always burned for the Gods, an inexorable yearning came over Shatrughna. He longed to see his brother Rama and take the padadhuli from his feet.

The same day, the master of the city that the Asura Madhu once founded gave orders for a small force to gather at his gates, to accompany him to Ayodhya. He would ride at once; it seemed to him he heard Rama's voice calling him clearly in his heart.

Shatrughna set out, and, after he had ridden seven days and nights, he arrived in Valmiki's asrama. The muni received Rama's brother with arghya and madhurparka; when Shatrughna sat comfortably with him, Valmiki took his hand and said feelingly, "The earth is free of darkness, that both Ravana and Lavana are dead."

The sage embraced Shatrughna and kissed the top of his head affectionately, blessing him. Later, as dusk gathered, some young rishis, Valmiki's sishyas who were musicians, came and sat around the muni and his guest. They brought their vinas and mridangas with them, and began to play. The singers among them began singing the Ramayana, while Shatrughna sat astonished and enchanted. It seemed to the prince that his brother's young life was being played out before his eyes again, in all its glory.

It was past midnight when the singers brought their audience to Lanka, where Rama killed Ravana with the brahmastra. Shatrughna sat as if turned to stone by the magic of the Adi Kavya. All his soldiers who had come with him felt as if they were in the midst of a wonderful living dream and the rest of the world had ceased to exist around them. It truly seemed that Valmiki's mystic song was, uncannily, realer than the world around them.

When the singers arrived at Rama's pattabhisheka in Ayodhya, Shatrughna fainted away, so powerfully did the past return to him. After the Ramayana had been sung, Shatrughna's soldiers begged their king to ask the Rishi Valmiki what the strange and powerful song was and who had composed it. But Shatrughna said it would not be proper to ask their host that question, unless he told them himself.

The king of Madhura said, "This asrama is full of all sorts of great secrets. It is beyond the likes of us to unravel any of them. Let us sleep now, for I long to see my brother and we must leave with first light."

But he could hardly sleep at all, for the visions of Rama and the Ramayana that filled the night. With dawn, he came to Valmiki, and, with folded hands, said, "My lord, my heart is full of my brother. Give me leave, Muni, that I may go at once to see Rama."

Valmiki blessed Shatrughna, and the kshatriya rode out again. He reached Ayodhya, his father's city, built into a coil of the Sarayu, its golden towers reaching for the stars: Ayodhya of dharma, where perfect Rama ruled. After so many years, Shatrughna came into his brother's presence and saw Rama again, who sat like Indra among his Devas, resplendent as a God.

With a cry, Shatrughna rushed to prostrate himself before his brother. As always, Rama raised him up tenderly, kissed him, and made him sit beside him on his throne.

Shatrughna said hoarsely, "Lavana is dead, my lord, and Madhura is renewed in dharma, just as you wanted. I rule that city in your name, Rama, and no evil passes its gates or comes anywhere into the kingdom around Madhu's ancient city."

Suddenly his eyes were full of tears, and Shatrughna said, "I have been away from you for twelve endless years and no punishment could be more cruel. I cannot stay away from you any more. I beg you, Rama, don't send me back."

Rama stroked his hair and said with a smile, "You are a king now, my little brother, a great kshatriya sovereign upon the earth. I have heard yours is one of the noblest cities in all Bharatavarsha. What will your people do if you desert them? A king's first dharma is toward his subjects, Shatrughna: they are like his own children. Everything else is secondary, insignificant. A king has no life of his own. So, O King, I will keep you here with me for seven days; but after that you must return to your kingdom, to Madhura where your dharma and your destiny lie."

Sadly, Shatrughna said, "So be it."

And after seven days and nights with his brothers, Shatrughna set out once more for Madhura. Bharata and Lakshmana rode a long way out of Ayodhya with him, and then stood watching until their brother's chariot disappeared in the distance.

34. *A brahmana and his son*

A few days after Shatrughna left Ayodhya, an extraordinary thing happened in the city of grace. It was known through all Bharatavarsha that since Rama sat on the Ikshvaku throne, no evil dared approach his people: no sorrow, no sickness, no misfortune of any kind. The kingdom was, truly, heaven on earth, that Vishnu's Avatara ruled it.

But then, as if to remind the people, and the king himself, that this was not Swarga but Bhumi, one day soon after Shatrughna came and went, a terribly distraught brahmana arrived at Rama's gates. He was sobbing, heartbroken, and in his arms he carried the dead body of his son, a child of fifteen summers. During Ramarajya, Rama's rule, the death of a child of just five thousand days was unheard of.

Loudly the brahmana cried, "What dreadful sin did I commit in my past lives that my child is snatched from me like this? Surely, I have not sinned in this life to deserve such savage punishment. He was my only son, and look at him now. He was meant to light my funeral pyre when I died; instead, he has made me the son and died before me. Oh, I cannot bear this grief! I will die of it myself, in a day or two, and my wife as well.

"Rama, they say you are a perfect king and sinless; and so there is no sickness or untimely death in your kingdom. But I say Rama must have sinned, or why has my child been snatched from me like this? My wife and I will die at your very gates, O King, unless you bring my child back to life! And you will be guilty of brahmahatya."

The brahmana was beside himself. "Damned is the House of Ikshvaku that a king like Rama rules it! Your subjects live in death's shadow, sinner. Who can be happy in a kingdom of such darkness? The sins of the king kill the children of a kingdom. You have sinned, you have sinned terribly, Rama of Ayodhya. I demand redress from you for the death of my child."

And the brahmana held his son's lifeless body to him, and sobbed and sobbed. Rama heard the man weeping, and came out of his palace and saw the pitiful spectacle at his gate. Tears flowed down his noble face and a cold pang clutched his heart. Rama staggered back into the palace, shaking.

He called for a guardsman and said to him, "Bring Vasishta and Vamadeva to me at once, and the other munis. Send for Bharata and Lakshmana too. Hurry."

Rama sat waiting, ashen-faced. He could still hear the brahmana's thin wailing outside and his wife's stifled sobs. The brahmana sat down in the middle of the path that led into Rama's palace, blocking it squarely. He held his dead child in his lap and railed against the king.

Soon, Vasishta, Vamadeva, Bharata, Lakshmana, and some prominent citizens came hurrying into Rama's sabha. Following them came Markandeya, Maudgalya, Kashyapa, Katyayana, Jabali, Gautama, and Narada, the greatest rishis in the world.

When they were seated, Rama said to them, "The brahmana's son has died, holy ones, and he says I am to blame. He means to kill himself at my door, because he says it is my sin that has killed his child."

The rishis saw the tears in his eyes and that his hands shook. Rama said, "Surely, some unspeakable sin has caused the child's death. But am I to blame, Munis? Ah, if I am, it is I who must kill myself. Tell me, have I sinned? What is my crime?"

It was Narada, the wanderer, who answered Rama. In his blithe and deep way, he began, "Listen to why this child has died. In the krita yuga, only the brahmanas of earth performed tapasya, only they ever sat in dhyana. It was a blemishless age, and the brahmanas of the earth were the support of the world; they were like Gods. All of them were born from the bloodlines of Brahma himself, and so they were called brahmanas. They were men of vision who saw through time as clearly as the men of the later ages see the world around them.

"Rama, the krita yuga was ruled by the brahmanas, with the ways of peace, and it was a taintless time. There was no sin in the world. Then came the treta yuga, and adharma was born. The first sin was committed from pride; and violence, greed, and deceit entered the lives of men. The Gods created the kshatriyas, to rule other men and to establish dharma again in an earth that sought to turn its blessed face from the ways of truth and vision. Manu divided humankind into the four varnas.

"Annrita, agriculture, came into men's lives, and this was the first step the rajoguna set upon the earth. Then came the dwapara yuga, and adharma, the beast Sin, now set his second foot upon the world, emerging further. In the krita, tapasya had belonged only to the brahmana. In the treta, both the brahmanas and kshatriyas were allowed dhyana. In the dwapara yuga, the traders, the vaisyas, also could sit in meditation and prayer, which was forbidden in the first three yugas.

"It is only in the kali yuga, when dharma survives only on one foot, and evil has sway over the earth, having set three monstrous feet upon it, shall the sudra perform tapasya. For there is no sin, say the wise, as heinous as for the sudra to sit in dhyana in our yuga."

Narada paused, then said very quietly into the fallen silence, "Yet, Rama, a sudra sits in long and fervent tapasya on the very hem of your kingdom. And by his dhyana, the shadow of sin has fallen over us all, even you. His forbidden tapasya has killed the brahmana's child. For you, O King, partake in a sixth portion of every pious deed and every crime committed in your kingdom. And because of this sudra's dhyana, you have incurred sin.

"You must go to him and right this wrong."

For a long moment, Rama gazed at the muni, Brahma's son, born when the earth was made; and he knew exactly what Narada meant that he should do. A chill gripped his heart as he said, "I will right the wrong, my lord."

Narada smiled grimly, "And the brahmana's son shall live again."

35. The death of a sudra

Rama said to Lakshmana, "My brother, go and comfort the brahmana. Have a tub of oil drawn and let his child's body be preserved in it."

Rama came out into the sun and stood briefly in prayer in his palace yard. With a silent mantra, he summoned the pushpaka vimana. At once the crystal ship appeared in the sky and alighted near the king.

The shining stairway was unfurled at Rama's feet, and he climbed aboard. Rama carried his bow and quiver, and a sword. At his very thought, the vimana rose steeply away from the ground and flitted westward, above heavy emerald forests, and then turned north subtly, to fly toward the Himalaya laid like a pale necklace across Bhumi Devi's throat.

It is told that, all the way he flew, Rama did not see a single sin being committed in his lands. West, north, and east he flew, and nowhere did he see any taint of adharma below him, but a pure world, with his grace permeating the sacred earth and the hearts of men.

At last he turned the pushpaka vimana to the south. Drawn surely by instinct, the enchanted ship came to the Saivala mountain, upon whose northern shoulder a great lake sparkled as if its waters were strewn with a million gemstones. Peering down, Rama saw a nya-grodha tree, a sire of its race that grew beside the water. And standing upon his head in sirasasana below that tree, in intense tapasya, he saw an emaciated ascetic, with jata and a long beard and his eyes shut fast.

Rama set the vimana down on the ground. He alighted from it and approached the strange hermit. Folding his hands to the yogin, Rama said, "I am Rama of Ayodhya. Tell me, Sannyasi, why do you perform such a trying tapasya? Is it for some boon? Or to attain Devaloka? You stand on your head, O Yogin; your tapasya is rare and stern. Tell me, are you a brahmana or a kshatriya? Or are you, perhaps, a vaisya? You could not be a sudra, Muni; for a sudra never sits in dhyana."

The ascetic did not move from his asana. But he opened his deep black eyes briefly, and answered Rama in a level voice, "I am a sudra, Rama; my name is Sambuka. And I stand upon my head in dhyana because I want to conquer Devaloka and be Lord of the four quarters."

Sambuka shut his eyes again and was lost in meditation. Rama stood numb before the hermit. Then he folded his hands once more to the absorbed Sambuka, drew his sword, and cleanly severed the su-dra's head from his body.

Suddenly the sky was full of lustrous presences. Indra, Agni, and the entire host of Devaloka appeared as bright shadows on high. Fra-grant petal rain fell on the avenging Avatara. The Devas cried that he had done well to end Sambuka's dreadful sin. But as he wiped his blade clean on some long grass, Rama had tears in his eyes.

Bowing to destiny, he said aloud, "If I have indeed done well, let the brahmana's son have life again."

Agni Deva said to Rama, "The moment the sudra was killed the brahmana's son breathed again. But now, Rama, we want to visit

Agastya Muni in his asrama. He has slept on water for twelve years, and today his tapasya is complete."

Rama and the Devas arrived at Agastya's asrama in their vimanas and he worshipped them all. The Devas blessed him, and then vanished from the sky. Agastya said to Rama, "Stay this night with me, Rama."

The rishi went into his hut and came out with a small bundle of dark silk. When Rama unwrapped the silk, he saw a jewel that shone as if the light of a crimson star had been captured within it. Agastya said, "This was fashioned by Viswakarman, Rama. In all this world, only you are fit to wear it. It will bring great fortune to you and to all your kingdom."

Rama bent his head and Agastya fastened the red gemstone around his neck by its golden chain. Rama asked, "What is this stone, Mahamuni? It fills me with such peace, such power!"

Agastya said, "Once, in the krita yuga, the men of the earth had no king. They went to Brahma and said, 'Pitamaha, Indra rules Devaloka, but we have no sovereign to guide our destinies. Give us also a king, Brahma. We have decided we must have someone to rule over us, someone as great as Indra.'

"Brahma summoned the Lokapalas, the masters of the four quarters, Indra, Varuna, Kubera, and Yama, and said to those Devas, 'Each of you give me a portion of your authority.'

"The guardians gave him a part of their power. As he received the majesty of the four Gods, Brahma sneezed. A splendid king appeared from his sneeze and he was called Kshupa. Brahma invested him with the power of the four Devas, and made him lord of the earth.

"Kshupa ruled with the power given him by Indra. He nurtured his people by the grace given him by Varuna. He shared with them the wealth and glory which he had from Kubera, and he punished them when they sinned, using the power of Yama."

Agastya Muni said, "Rama, now you are king of this earth. All the power of Kshupa is vested in you. The power of Indra, Yama, Kubera, and Varuna is vested in you. This jewel is the power of Indra. Keep it from now, Kshatriya, and let my spirit find its final peace."

The gem shone on Rama's chest as the sun does in the sky. Rama asked, "Where did you get this stone from, Muni?"

Agastya's eyes were full of light, the light of another age. He said,

"It was in the treta yuga that I got this jewel, Rama. Then, there was a jungle here in Bharatavarsha, a hundred yojanas long and wide, and no living creature dwelt in it, no beasts and no birds. No men lived there either, only the trees. I sat in tapasya in that vana.

"How shall I describe to you how wonderful the trees of those times were, how brilliant their leaves were, or how ambrosial their fruit? They were the sires of the trees that live in the world today, and they were closer to heaven. In the very heart of that forest, there was a lake, one yojana wide on every side. Only on its waters would you find duck, teal, swan, ibis, and chakravakas.

"A feast of lotuses and water lilies mantled its surface, blooms in colors you no longer see in this darkening world, Rama. Beside this lake, there was an ancient asrama. No one knew when it had been wrought, for it had not been built by any human being and no one lived in that hermitage.

"One summer's night, I found myself beside the lake and spent the night in that asrama. The next morning, I rose with the sun and went to the lake for my morning ablutions. I saw a corpse floating on the water, a plump, white, naked corpse. I stood rooted, staring at the body, when, all at once, the sky seemed to be lit by another sun, and a vimana flew down, yoked to the most incredible swans.

"In that open vimana, I saw an immortal, and with him were a hundred gandharvas and apsaras. They sang in unearthly voices; some danced by the first light of the sun, even as if this were the first day of creation. Perfect mridangas and vinas I heard, and from them unearthly music flowed.

"Rama, as I stood watching, unable to move, the lord of the vimana rose from his golden seat, even like the sun on the crest of the eastern mountain. He alighted from his ship of the sky and drew the corpse in the lake toward him with occult power. And then, I could not believe my eyes: he devoured that corpse, licking up its blood that leaked down his fine chin, crunching its bones, sucking out their marrow, chewing raptly on the flesh and plentiful white fat that decked them.

"When he had finished, and he discarded only a few shreds of skin, hair, and bone, he went down to the water and bathed, long and thoroughly, and all the while I saw that he wept. As he returned to his vimana, I emerged from where I had hidden myself to watch him, and said, 'Who are you, O Godlike? How is it that someone as noble as yourself feeds on dead human flesh?'

"I spoke in great wonder, my heart churning within me, for never had I seen such a strange thing. He folded his hands respectfully to me, and said in chaste, high language, 'Brahmana, I am the son of King Vaidarbha, whose name was known throughout the three worlds as Sudeva. He had two wives, and a son by each. I am Sweta, his eldest, and my younger brother was called Suratha.

" 'When my father died, our people crowned me king and I ruled to the best of my lights and ability. A thousand years passed, O Muni, in peace and plenty. For I remained within the bounds of dharma, as well as I possibly could. When the thousand years given me to be king passed, I came here into this forest to sit in dhyana, before death came for me. Before I took vanaprastha, I made my brother Suratha king.

" 'I lived here beside this lake—the asrama you slept in last night was mine—and for three thousand years I performed tapasya. By my long penance, I gained Brahmaloka, the highest of all the realms. But when I ascended into that lofty loka, leaving my body behind on earth, searing thirst and raging hunger afflicted me.

" 'I asked Brahma, "Pitamaha, your realm is free of hunger and thirst. Then why do I suffer like this? Tell me, Lord, what can I eat? For there is no food here."

" 'Brahma said to me, "Son of Sudeva, you have nourished your own body with a long tapasya. Yet you have never given any charity these past three thousand years. So eat your own flesh, Sweta, drink your own blood: to quench your hunger and your thirst."

" 'I stood startled before the Pitamaha's throne. This was no less than a curse. Brahma continued, "One day, Agastya Muni will deliver you from your hunger and thirst. Till then, devour your own body, Sweta. Do not worry, your flesh will be inexhaustible. Again and again you shall eat it, and it will never perish." '

"He pointed to the lake, and when I looked again at the clear water, the plump, white, and naked body floated there again, as if it had not been consumed, gristle and marrow, just a short while ago. Sweta said, 'For many years now, I have been slaking my hunger and thirst on that body every day; but it reappears each time, and once more I devour it.'

"Then he took a bright ornament he wore around his neck, and pressed it into my hand. Sweta said, 'Lord Agastya, greatest among brahmanas, I beg you, deliver me from this terrible curse. I offer you everything I own. I offer you all my wealth and my punya too. Release me from hunger and thirst. Set me free so I never have to return to this earth. I long to range through the realms of heaven, but I am cruelly bound, Muni.'

"In pity, I took the scarlet jewel from the suffering king, and at once, the white body vanished from the lake. An expression of untold relief suffused Sweta's face. He bowed deeply to me, ascended his vimana again and flitted away like a thought into the sky, never to return.

"Rama, this jewel that has Indra's power in it was given me by King Sweta, for releasing him from Brahma's curse."

36. Bhargava's curse

Rama asked, "Muni, when I was in exile, long ago, you told me something about a cursed forest where no bird or beast came, and no rishis. Was this the vana where you met King Sweta? What was the curse, Agastya?"

The rishi, whom even the Devas worshipped, said, "I did not tell you the entire tale. But listen to it now, Rama, if you have a mind to. In the krita yuga, Manu was lord of the earth, its sovereign. His son was Ikshvaku, who was a joy to all his family.

"When a great deal of time passed—and in that yuga men lived much longer than the men of today—Manu sought Brahmaloka for himself. Before he attained samadhi, he set Ikshvaku on his throne, and said to him; 'Be the sire of all the royal houses of the earth.'

"Ikshvaku said he would do as his father asked. Then Manu said, 'Be just in judging your people and punishing them if they err. Consider every crime and its punishment well, consult the Shastras and think deeply. For this is a king's first dharma, and only this can lead him to heaven.'

"Manu blessed his son, and left his mortal body. Ikshvaku fell to thinking, 'How shall I father sons?'

"In diverse and magical ways, he created a hundred sons, all of them magnificent as Devas. But the hundredth prince, Danda, was full of ignorance and darkness. He did not serve his father or his elders. Indeed, he became known as Danda because everyone felt sure that some dreadful punishment would come to such a dull being, to enliven him.

"Ikshvaku was fearful for Danda and gave him a part of the earth to be his kingdom, so perhaps he would mend. He gave him all the lands that lay between the Vindhyas and Saivala mountains. Ikshvaku sent his finest builders to make a city for his son to rule from. Danda's city was called Madhumanta, and he chose Usanas, Sukra Deva, to be his guru.

"The blessings and grace of the great Sukra seemed to guide Danda's fortunes for a while, and Madhumanta was like a city of the Gods upon the earth. Its men and women were pious and beautiful; their spirits and bodies, their very lives were lit with dharma. Danda's own nature seemed to have undergone a profound change, and it appeared that his father's decision to make him a king had transformed that prince.

"For ten thousand years Danda ruled with immaculate restraint and growing wisdom, and there was no other king or kingdom in Bharatavarsha to match his. Then, one day, in the fullness of his glory, Danda decided to visit the asrama of his guru, Sukra Bhargava, in the heart of the jungle that surrounded Madhumanta. It was spring, the month of Chaitra.

"Danda arrived at the hermitage, built on a lake's sylvan shore, which was like a bit of Brahmaloka fallen onto the earth. Under the glimmering trees, Danda saw a young woman, the very sight of whom made his heart stop still. She was another vision, she was utterly desirable; and he could see her naked body through the diaphanous garment she wore in this place where no man usually set foot.

"Danda accosted her, and said, 'Lovely one, who are you? Whose daughter? Oh, I want you!'

"As he approached her, his arms outstretched, she shrank from him and replied with dignity, 'I am Araja and I am Bhargava's eldest daughter. My father is your guru. Don't touch me, Kshatriya; I am my father's ward. If what you feel for me is more than mere lust, then ask my father for my hand in marriage and I shall be yours.'

"But she saw the look in his eyes, and said again, in some panic now, 'If you force me, Danda, Sukra Deva's anger will burn you and your kingdom to a crisp.'

"Danda folded his hands and raised them above his head. He said, 'If I cannot have you at once, I shall die anyway. I beg you, give yourself to me willingly. For no fear, of death or of any sin, will stop me from having you.'

"She stepped back from him. But he was on her in a flash, and forcing her down onto the soft grass with irresistible strength, he thrust himself into that virgin girl, like fire. She screamed in fear and pain. But he enjoyed her roughly, and even as she lay numb with shock, a crimson stain spreading under her, he rose and left that asrama.

"After a long time, Araja stumbled to her father's kutila and stood sobbing at its door. She stood waiting for her father, who was like a God. Sukra Bhargava came back to his asrama with a knot of his disciples, and heard what had happened. He saw his daughter's agony and her shame, as blood and the kshatriya's violent seed between her fair thighs. Sukra's eyes turned the color of the sunset.

"He cried, 'In seven days this king, and all his sons and his army, shall die. For a hundred yojanas around his city, all life shall be consumed by a rain of fire and death shall rule this sinner's kingdom. All of you must leave this asrama and go to the edge of these lands. No life will stir here in seven days.'

"He turned to his daughter and said, 'My child, you will live here beside this lake, and the birds and beasts who come to be near you in the night shall stay with you. The rain of flames will not fall for a yojana around this asrama, or on this lake.'

"Araja bowed her head, and murmured, 'As you will.'

"Sukra Deva left that hermitage and his daughter, and went away to a secret place to perform tapasya for expiation from whatever sin it was that had brought down such terrible punishment on him and his child. In seven days the sky grew as dark as the end of time, and a hissing, spitting deluge of flames fell out of it and devoured Danda, his clan, all his people, his wonderful city, and the land around it, for a hundred yojanas in every direction. The earth was charred; no life of any kind stirred upon it any more. Everywhere there were only ashes to be seen, stretching away interminably.

"Later, a dark and fearsome forest grew up here and only the creatures of night inhabited it: pisachas, rakshasas, and other evil beings. And you know that when the time of the curse drew near its end, I wandered down into this vana with the seeds of the sacred trees of Himavan in my hands, and I sat here in dhyana until most of the curse was removed, and the sun and the wind and the natural rain came again to the cursed jungle named Dandaka after King Danda.

"Of course, Rama, it was only when your feet touched this ground, during your exile, that the curse vanished entirely and this earth was blessed again."

Agastya said, "Rama, the waters of this lake are sacred. Bathe in our lake this evening, and then eat with us."

Rama went down to the lake, which was touched with the dying colors of the setting sun. He first took up a palmful of the precious water and drank it reverently. He entered the lake and bathed in it. He emerged feeling a new vitality and purity course through his body and his spirit.

Rama came back to Agastya's asrama and ate a frugal, tasty meal of fine, husked rice, and the most delicious vegetables, among them a redder radish than any he had ever seen, which he relished especially. Late into the night, under a sky full of fateful stars, the king and the hermit sat talking, until Agastya told Rama to sleep and retired himself.

In the morning, as the sun rose, Rama came and prostrated himself before the muni. "Give me leave, Mahamuni, I must return to Ayodhya. I will come to see you again and have your blessing once more, to make myself pure."

Laying his ageless palms on the king's head, Agastya said, "You are the purifier of this earth. Your presence in the world blesses her for a thousand generations of men. The Lord Indra worships you, Rama; you are the refuge and the savior of this world."

Rama took the padadhuli from Agastya's feet. He climbed into the pushpaka vimana and flashed away, back to Ayodhya. In his city, in his palace courtyard, he said to the magical ship, "Go back to Kubera now, my friend, and I will call you when I need you again."

Rama went into his palace, his lonely royal apartment, and said to a guard there, "Go and fetch Lakshmana and Bharata to me."

They came, and Rama hugged them. He said softly, his eyes shining with a new light, "I want to build the bridge of dharma in our land: the bridge that will never fall. My brothers, with both of you beside me, I want to perform the rajasuya yagna to purify me of the sin of killing the sudra. Tell me what you think."

Bharata folded his hands, and said, "All this earth and all fame have their source in you; you are the highest dharma. Every king of the earth looks up to you as the Devas do to Brahma. They look up to you as sons to their father. Rama, if a king like you undertakes the rajasuya, if a king like you sheds the blood of other kshatriyas and brings grief to their families, will that be dharma?

"If Rama destroys the peace of the earth, a tide of wrath will rise and sweep us all away. All the kshatriyas of the earth are already loyal to you, Rama; you must not challenge them in war."

Rama took Bharata's hand and said, "How wisely you speak, my brother! What you say is dharma, indeed. No, I will not perform the rajasuya. I will not provoke the kings of the earth, demean them, or force them to protect their honor in war. The wise never do anything that brings grief to the world. What the young say must be followed if they speak wisely. You are right, Bharata, I will do as you say."

Then Lakshmana said, "Perform the aswamedha instead, Rama. The yagna is the purifier of all the wise; let it be yours as well. You know how Indra himself was cleansed of the sin of Brahmahatya, when he performed the aswamedha yagna."

Rama said with a smile, "Remind us of it again, Lakshmana."

Lakshmana said keenly, "In the eldest days, Diti had a son called Vritra. Vritra was an Asura, a hundred yojanas tall. He ruled the earth, once, with dharma and compassion. And during his reign, Bhumi Devi yielded the most abundant flowers, fruit, and roots, ever. With dharma, Vritrasura's kingdom flourished.

"Then, that great and pious demon thought to himself, 'Only tapasya yields the highest joy. Every other pleasure is illusory.'

"He entrusted his kingdom to his eldest son, Madhureswara, and sat in a truly searing tapasya upon the mountain. While Vritra performed his penance, Indra grew afraid in Devaloka. Indra went to Vishnu and said, 'Already, I cannot subdue Vritrasura. If his tapasya continues, he will become Lord of the three worlds and of every creature in them. Precious Hari, how do you allow this Asura to flourish? It is because he has your blessing that no one can curb him. I beg you, kill this demon; only you can any more.' "

Lakshmana paused, and he was flushed with happiness at narrating the timeless legend. Rama said indulgently, "And how did Vritra die?"

"All the Devas echoed Indra's misery, and Vishnu said to them, 'It is true that once Vritra had my blessing, and that was for your own welfare, O Devas, to make you humble. But now his time has come. I will make myself three, so Indra can kill the Asura. One part of me will enter Indra himself; another shall infuse his vajra; and the third, the very earth. Vritrasura, master of the worlds, shall die.'

"The Devas bowed low before Mahavishnu and they went to have a final reckoning with the demon. They found Vritra at his tapasya, which was so intense it seemed he would drink down all creation into his spirit. His body seemed like a golden mountain, on fire. The Devas looked at him and shivered. They whispered among themselves, 'How will we kill this awesome one?'

"But, murmuring a prayer to Vishnu, Indra cast his vajra at the meditating Asura. The thunderbolt of a thousand joints, charged with Vishnu's power, struck Vritrasura's great head from its neck, and it fell upon the earth like the pralaya. Indra fled from there in terror, to the ends of the world, sobbing; for his sin of killing a brahmana pursued him in a dreadful form of flames. Indra transformed himself into a water snake and hid in the Manasarovara, in the stem of a lotus. He dared not emerge, he dared not stir, and Devaloka had no ruler.

"Now Agni and the other Devas sat in a fervid tapasya to Mahavishnu. They said again and again, 'You are the Primal Person, the First One, Un-born, omnipotent, the father of us all, the savior of us all: save our king, O Vishnu; his Brahmahatya pursues him relentlessly and even we do not know where he has hidden himself.'

"Vishnu said to the Devas, 'You must perform the aswamedha yagna. It is the only way to save the thousand-eyed one from his sin.'

"Vishnu himself performed the horse sacrifice along with the Devas. At the end of the solemn yagna, the Brahmahatya, who had been pursuing Indra so remorselessly, came before blue Vishnu, and pleaded, 'I beg you, Lord of Gods, give me sanctuary. Your yagna scathes me and I fear for my life.'

"Vishnu said to the spirit of the Brahmahatya, 'Divide yourself in four, O Spirit, and live in four places.'

"And one amsa of the hatya dwelt in the world, for four months of the year, the monsoon, to break the pride of sinners. Its second part dwelt in the earth. Its third possessed young women, who were arrogant of their beauty, for three nights. And its last and fourth part possessed and tormented murderers, especially the killers of brahmanas.

"Indra was rid of that scorching, ineluctable spirit, and returned to assume his throne that the worlds worship, in Amravati, the deathless city. Swarga, Bhumi, and Patala grew calm again; the spirit of chaos that had verged on creation disappeared."

Lakshmana paused and slowly drew in a deep breath. He was a self-conscious storyteller, and, blushing slightly, concluded with some solemnity, "Rama, that is how powerful the aswamedha yagna is. It took his dreadful sin from Indra, who had killed Vritrasura when he sat in dhyana. It will certainly wash the sin of killing Sambuka from you. Perform the sacrifice of the horse, my lord: all our salvations depend on it."

37. The tale of Ila

Rama laughed softly when Lakshmana finished his earnestly told tale. The king ruffled his brother's hair like a boy's, and said, "Have you heard the story of Ila?"

Lakshmana said eagerly, "No, Rama. Who was she?"

Rama began, "In the eldest days, the Prajapati Kardama was king of Bahlika. He had conquered all the earth and ruled his people as if they were his own children. Kardama had honor among both Devas and Daityas, and the nagas, rakshasas, gandharvas, and even the secretive yakshas revered that king of dharma.

"Once, Kardama went hunting in the forest. Drunk with bloodlust, he killed thousands of innocent creatures in the jungle he had entered, without favor for species, age, sex, or size. Their screams rang under the sorrowing trees. Spraying the jungle with blood, Kardama arrived in its heart, the very place where once Siva's son Karttikeya had been born.

"It happened that Siva himself was in that jungle's heart, making love to Parvati. To please her, Siva had assumed a woman's form and had come with her sakhis. They now sat together beside a hill stream that chatted its way through the deep vana. Uma sat on Siva's lap, and she wore not a stitch upon her perfect body. And by Siva's power, so Uma would not be seen naked by any male creature, every beast, bird, and even the plants of that impenetrable forest had become female, even the trees.

"Blood on his hands, steamy from his hunt, Kardama staggered into the glade where Parvati sat in her lord's lap, her arms twined

640

around his neck like vines. Instantly, the king, all his soldiers, and the horses they rode were transformed: they became women and mares. Kardama felt the change come over him. He knew Siva had done this, and he trembled.

"Kardama and his men petitioned the Lord, the blue-throated, serpent-adorned Mahadeva. They came and fell at his feet. Siva said to the son of the Prajapati, 'Arise, Rajarishi, and ask me for any boon, except your manhood.'

"Kardama remained mute; he asked for nothing. Then he remembered Uma always bestowed one half of every boon that Siva granted. Kardama came sobbing, as a woman, before the mountain's daughter, and begged her, 'Mother of worlds, bless me. Make me a man again.'

"Parvati laid her palm on Kardama's head in blessing. The Devi said, 'Only half of every boon is mine to bestow. So be a man for half your life.'

"Kardama cried in delight, 'Anuttamaa, Peerless One, let me be a man for one month and a woman for the next.'

"Uma said, 'So be it. And when you are a man, you shall not remember your womanhood; as, when you are a woman, you shall have no memory that you were a man. When you are a woman, Kardama, you will be known as Ila.'

"And Siva and Uma vanished from there."

Lakshmana asked breathlessly, "And how did Kardama live, Rama? When he was a king, and then when he was a woman? How did he live his life?"

"One day, Ila, the beautiful, seductive woman, came to a mountain in the midst of the forest of femininity. She saw a clear pool there, sparkling like a diamond. As she approached it, she saw the water shone strangely, with some other light than that of the sun above. It seemed as if the lotuses and water birds on the pool were also lit with this inner lambency.

"As Ila came nearer, she saw there was someone submerged in the pool. She gasped when she saw it was a Deva, surely, who sat in the water, obviously at tapasya. His body shone like a full moon. She did not know this, but that was Budha, Soma Deva's son by Brihaspati's wife Tara.

"Ila felt a fluid warmth fill her body. She turned away in shyness; but already the God in the pool had sensed the presence of the women. Budha opened his eyes and they fell on Ila. The Deva quivered; he had never seen anyone so exquisite in all his life. He had been with apsaras and naginas, with ethereal gandharvis; but the woman he saw now on the banks of the pool in which he sat in dhyana touched him as no other had before. There was a certain quality about her that no woman he had ever seen possessed.

"Just one thought filled his mind: 'If she isn't already given, I must make her mine.'

"Like the moon rising from the sea, he climbed out from the pool and came up to Ila's companions. He said in his irresistible Deva's voice, 'Who is your friend? I have never seen anyone so beautiful. What is she doing here, in the heart of this vana? What are you doing here?'

"They replied, tittering, 'She is our mistress, brilliant one. And we all live in this vana and roam through it together.'

"Budha, the intelligent, was puzzled: something about their story seemed strange and incomplete. The Deva softly chanted the avartani vidya, in his mind, and the occult stotra informed him about Kardama and his soldiers, and how Siva's power had turned them into women. When he learned the fate of Kardama's men, who had turned into women forever, Budha Deva was moved to pity.

"Budha blessed those women, saying, 'Let your lives be fruitful and full of joy. Become kimpurushis from now. Live on fruit, roots, and herbs, and let the kinnaras of the mountain be your mates.'

"Instantly, the women were turned into female fauns and they vanished into the forest, to find the magical kimpurushas, who are masters of riddles. When the shimmering fauns had gone, Budha turned with a smile to Ila. 'Lovely one, I am Soma's son Budha. Look on me with love in your eyes. I know all about you and I am determined to make you mine.'

"She flushed, she quivered with wanting him, and said softly, 'I am yours, my lord, do what you will with me.'

"Soma took her in his glowing arms. He peeled away her single garment, and they lay together on the thick satin moss that grew beside the pool. Great Budha made love to his strange beloved for a month, without pause, and the month passed like a few delirious hours. Then, suddenly, Kardama awoke one morning, in the bed in the asrama, as if from a long sleep. He went out and found himself beside a clear pool, and he saw Budha Deva at dhyana, seated in the posture of the lotus upon the water, with no other support.

"Kardama did not remember how he came to be here; he remembered nothing of the curse of Siva, or of Ila. He asked Budha, 'My lord Brahmana, I came into this jungle with my army. But I do not see any of my men. Do you know what happened to them?'

"Budha replied serenely, 'Your men were all killed by a shower of rocks from heaven. But you fled into the asrama and fell asleep within. Take courage, O King, live here in this hermitage. There are roots, fruit, and game aplenty for you to feed yourself.'

"Kardama grew thoughtful for a moment, then said, 'I will do as you say. But ah, I hardly want to live any more, when all my soldiers have perished. I have a noble son called Sasabindu; he will rule my kingdom.'

"And so it was. Whenever he was a man for a month, Kardama performed rigorous tapasya beside the forest pool, and served the meditating Budha; and when he was Ila, he made love with Soma Deva's son. Soon enough, Ila conceived and gave birth to a splendid boy, who resembled his unearthly father and whom they named Pururava. By Budha's power and Siva's, even at the end of a year Kardama knew nothing about Ila.

"When Pururava was a year old, Budha called some of the world's holiest rishis to the asrama. He called Samvarta, Bhrigu's son Chyvana, Arishtanemi, the blithe and merry Pramodana, Modakara, and the awesome Durvasa. Pulastya, Kratu, and Vasatkara arrived in that secret hermitage, as well. Budha told them all who Ila really was. He showed them their son, and said, 'My lords, you decide what Kardama must do next.'

"The rishis spoke among themselves briefly, then they said, 'We will undertake an aswamedha for the sake of Kardama; no yagna pleases the Lord Siva as the horse sacrifice does.'

"Samvarta, who was Brihaspati's brother, reminded them, 'Once, when my sishya, the king Marutta, performed the aswamedha, all his sins were washed from him, and he and his kingdom prospered.'

"So those munis undertook an aswamedha yagna in Kardama's name. They sent a white horse across the lands, and finally sacrificed it in the vana, in Siva's name. Siva appeared in a mass of light before those rishis and Ila. Laying his hand on her head, he gave Ila her manhood back, for good, and vanished from there. The aswamedha yagna completed, the rishis also left.

"Now Kardama was himself again, always, and he founded the city of Pratishtana in the heart of that forest and ruled from there for many years. Meanwhile, his son Sasabindu ruled over the old kingdom of Bahlika. Soon, Budha's son Pururava grew into manhood, and Kardama gave his kingdom to the wonderful youth. Kardama himself sat in tapasya for some years and then gained Brahmaloka.

"This, my brothers, is another story that tells how powerful the aswamedha yagna is. Indeed, it is said to be the most auspicious and potent sacrifice in the world," said Rama, his eyes alight at the thought of performing the noble yagna himself.

"Lakshmana, we must gather the greatest rishis of the world here in this sabha: Vasishta, Vamadeva, Jabali, Kashyapa, and the rest, from all the Pravaras. And with their blessings and guidance, I mean to loose a horse of the noblest pedigree across the land of Bharata."

Lakshmana's face shone at the prospect. He would not wait a moment, and cried, "Shall I fetch the brahmanas immediately?"

Smiling, Rama nodded that he might.

Very soon, those holy men of the earth were gathered like a constellation of stars in the ancient sabha of Ayodhya. Rama received each of them, washing their feet himself and offering them madhurparka. When they were all seated at the head of the sabha, Rama said simply, "My lords, I mean to perform an aswamedha yagna. I need your blessings."

Each of those profound munis spoke in that sabha, turn by turn, and they were all delighted at what Rama planned. When they had finished, Rama turned in joy to Lakshmana. "My brother, send word to Sugriva in Kishkinda. Tell him what we mean to do, and tell him he must come to Ayodhya for the yagna, with his vanaras.

"Send word to Lanka, also; the sacrifice cannot begin until Vibheeshana is here with me. Let word be taken across all the kingdoms and let every king who calls himself my friend be at my side. Let every brahmana be invited, and let this aswamedha be not just for us but for the whole world's sanctity. Let singers and dancers from all over the earth come to us now, and take part in our yagna."

Lakshmana asked, "Where will we perform the yagna, Rama?"

His brother had already decided. "In the Naimisa vana, so all this earth may be blessed. Let any man, woman, or child who wants to be there come to my aswamedha. Every one shall find honor at our yagna; let no effort or expense be spared."

Rama asked for royal dwellings to be built at the site of the yagna, for the kings and their entourages who would attend the aswamedha. It is told a hundred thousand men carried the unbroken rice that would be used at the sacrifice. Another hundred thousand carried sesame seeds and beans, other grains, pulses, salt, oil, and spices.

Bharata led the party from Ayodhya that was dispatched to make the preparations. He took many millions of gold and silver coins from the treasury with him, by elephant, horse, and chariot, and in litters. Moving marketplaces, with their colorful stalls, went with Bharata, and throngs of cooks, actors, singers, dancers, and, inevitably, harems of lovely young women.

In time, all Ayodhya came streaming forth from the city gates, and flowed like a vivid river toward the Naimisa vana. Brahmanas walked in the interminable crowd and countless day laborers, carpenters, masons, tinkers, joiners, and men from every imaginable trade. Most went with their families. Kausalya, Sumitra, and Kaikeyi were borne to the sacred forest in golden litters. And in the most exquisite palanquin of all, another strange figure journeyed to Rama's aswamedha: it was the kanchana Sita, the golden image of his wife fashioned for Rama by the world's finest sculptors: the image he kept near him at all times and took with him wherever he went.

38. The aswamedha yagna

Rama, Lakshmana, Bharata, and Shatrughna entered the Naimisa vana. Sugriva's vanaras arrived in their merry troops, and Vibheeshana and his rakshasas came with their legions and Jambavan with his great bears. They came with their women, exotic and striking. When the rishis who sat over the yagna had been worshipped, Rama sent a black horse of the finest bloodlines to run through the kingdoms of Bharatavarsha, challenging any king to stop its careen. Lakshmana rode behind that horse, with an army.

The kshatriyas of the earth heard about the aswamedha, and they began to arrive in the jungle with gifts and tribute, pledging their allegiance to Rama. He received them with honor, and their comfort was seen to by his brothers and ministers, and by the vanaras and rakshasas. The poor came in droves to Rama's yagna, and his generosity was like a river in spate. Beggars who came to the Naimisa went away as rich men.

And, of course, the brahmanas who came to the sacrifice of sacrifices were rewarded with gold, silver, precious jewels, and fine silks that surpassed their every expectation. Some munis, old as the very earth, said approvingly that they had never seen such an aswamedha, since the time when Indra, Soma, Yama, and Varuna performed the auspicious sacrifice.

Into the midst of all that charity, there arrived a dark, tall rishi with two splendid sishyas at his side. Rama and the other munis at the aswamedha yagna received Valmiki with deep reverence. Valmiki did not enter the enclosures of the yagna.

He accepted the homage and the fruit and savory roots offered him at the entrance. Then he said to the strapping young men who had come with him, and who were obviously twins, "My sons, tomorrow you must go and sing the Ramayana I taught you: sing it in the streets of the yagnashala, sing it before the kings' dwellings; most of all, sing it before Rama of Ayodhya. And if he asks whose sons you are, only say you are Valmiki's sishyas.

"Sing the Ramayana for the great rishis who are performing the aswamedha; play on your vinas and sing twenty cantos every day. Have no care for the wealth the king may offer you; for you are hermits, my pupils living in an asrama, and what will the likes of us do with gold or jewels?"

Then with the queerest look on his face, he continued very softly, "But honor the king, my children, because it is said he is the father of all who dwell in his kingdom."

So said the son of Prachetas, the great Valmiki, and the twins he spoke to were surprised that he repeated every detail many times, especially with regard to how soft or loud their vinas and their voices should be, and what taala they should keep, and where they should look as they sang.

Those pupils of his were Sita's sons Lava and Kusa. Valmiki said to them, "Tomorrow is the most important day of your lives. Come now, we will return to our asrama. You must sleep well, because tomorrow you must be fresh and strong." He laid his hands on their handsome heads, "Yes, tomorrow is the greatest day of your lives."

But when they asked why, he would not say. Lava and Kusa slept that night as blissfully as the Aswini Kumaras did when they had Sukra Deva's blessing. The night passed, and in its last yaama before the sun rose, the twins awoke, bathed, and offered worship to Agni. They arrived at the great hall of the aswamedha, and began singing the Adi Kavya.

Rama and his brothers, the visiting kings, and the holy rishis heard their inspired song, and they came and sat before the youths as handsome as two gandharvas; they were enraptured by their perfect playing and singing. In that audience were experts of the Puranas and others who knew music, every raga in the world. None of them had heard anything like the Ramayana before. They marveled at its resonance, its lyric beauty, its seamless construction and flow.

There were noted astrologers in the gathering, and they murmured among themselves that Valmiki had woven the threads of destiny into his poem, adroitly and without flaw. He knew exactly which planets had ruled Rama's life, when he was born, when Viswamitra arrived in Ayodhya, when Rama broke Siva's bow and married Sita, and when he was exiled.

There were famous poets in the sabha, who wondered at the perfection of the Ramayana. It was a poem, it was a song, and it was a treatise on dharma and tapasya. It was a Purana, it was a great epic; it was a love story and a story of war; it was a work of bhakti. Why, it was hardly mortal, and the most perceptive among them already whispered that only Brahma himself could have inspired such an immaculate kavya.

The rishis were in transport, the people were rapt, as were all the kings: absorbed in the Ramayana they heard and thrilled by the sight of the two singers, who were like beings of a higher world fallen to the earth.

Only some of the keen-eyed kshatriyas present said to each other, "Look, don't these youths look familiar?"

"Don't they resemble a king we know well?"

"Why, they are like images of Rama twenty years ago!"

But Lava and Kusa were clad in valkala and they wore their hair long, in matted jata. The twins sang without pause, and soon all the whispering in the yagnashala died down. The Ramayana was spellbinding. Lava and Kusa sang twenty cantos.

It was evening when they stopped, and a delighted Rama said to

Lakshmana, "Give these two noble young men eighteen thousand gold coins. Give them anything else they need."

Lakshmana called Lava and Kusa aside, and offered them the gold. But they refused in some alarm, laughing, "What will we do with all this gold? We live in the forest and eat only roots and fruit."

Lakshmana brought the youths back into the yagnashala, and told Rama they had refused the gold. The gathering at the sacrifice fell hushed. Rama was surprised; he had never known a brahmana to refuse gold, wherever he lived.

Rama asked mildly, "How long is this poem? And where is Valmiki? Why did he compose it, if not for gold?"

Lava and Kusa replied, "The Ramayana is twenty-four thousand slokas long. It contains a hundred legends. It has six kandas, and it will be sung as long as there are men in the world."

For twenty-five days, Lava and Kusa sang the Ramayana for Rama and all the others who had come to his aswamedha yagna. When the singing was over, Rama called for some messengers and said to them, "Go to the Muni Valmiki's asrama, and if Sita is found to be pure, let her come here to our yagna. Let her take an oath in this yagnashala that she is untainted and that Lava and Kusa are my sons."

The messengers came to the muni's asrama and saw him there, a flame. When they delivered the amazing message from their king, Valmiki said to them quietly, "Rama is Sita's God. She will come to the yagnashala tomorrow and swear her oath there."

The messengers returned with Valmiki's message. The night passed as slowly as an age, and Rama rose with the sun and entered the yagnashala with his brothers. The brahmanas who were conducting the aswamedha had already gathered around the agni-kunda, the pit where the sacred fire burned: Vasishta, Vamadeva, Jabali, Kashyapa, Viswamitra, Dirghatama, the awesome Durvasa, Pulastya, Shakti, Bhargava, Vamana, Markandeya, Maudgalya, Garga, Chyvana, Sadananda, Bharadvaja, Narada, the ancient Parvata, the peerless Gautama.

Also present were Sugriva and his vanaras, and Vibheeshana and his rakshasas. A hundred kshatriya kings from all over Bharatavarsha were there, as were thousands of vaisyas and sudras. Indeed, word had flown forth at night that Sita would come to the yagna, and the yagnashala was filled to bursting.

Finally, when they were seated, they saw the gaunt figure of Valmiki at the entrance to the yagnashala, and behind him was another slight, exquisite figure, and a murmur went up from those present. It was Sita, and she was as beautiful as ever: pure as a smokeless fire. She followed Valmiki even as Sruti does the Lord Brahma. Spontaneously, the sabha raised its voice and called her name, and then hers and Rama's together, warmly.

Valmiki came to a halt facing the august crowd at Rama's aswamedha yagna. A hush fell on the people when they saw he would speak to them. The rishi began, "Rama, you abandoned this Sita, who is purity itself, near my asrama. You were afraid of what the world thought of her and said of her. Why, it seems to me you doubt her yourself, that you ask her to come here and swear an oath.

"I am Prachetas's tenth son and I have no memory of ever having told a lie. I say to you, these twins are your sons. I have done tapasya for thousands of years; if what I say now is a lie, may all my punya be taken from me. If Janaka's daughter Maithili has sinned let my very soul perish within me.

"But why do I speak for her? Sita can speak for herself."

Rama sat as still as stone and his eyes never left Sita's face, not even to blink. He folded his hands to Valmiki and said, "Muni, I never doubted Sita's purity. I beg you, do not accuse me of a sin I never committed, to add to the one that I did. Indeed, I did banish my queen for fear of what the people were saying about her. But then, my lord, I am a king, and my first and final dharma is toward my people. It would never have done for them to have doubted their king, for even a moment: that he was weak and took back a tainted woman.

"Valmiki, I have no doubt Lava and Kusa are my sons. I knew it as soon as I saw them. Let all those gathered here for the aswamedha have no doubt about my love not only for my sons, but for my wife as well, this precious Sita. I beg her to forgive me for the anguish I have caused her, and now, for the sake of our sons' future, to swear her oath before this sabha of rishis and kings and also the people who doubted her."

Sita wore a brown garment of valkala, and she stood before that sabha of the greatest men in the world with folded hands. She stood perfectly still and hers was a resonant stillness. Suddenly Vayu blew a towering gust through that place, a supernatural wind, such as he used to in the krita yuga. His airs were bright with flecks of light and he seemed to enfold Sita in his grace.

Never raising her face in the presence of all those kings and sages,

Sita began to speak. She spoke softly, but her voice was as strong as the timeless wind.

"If I have never loved any man but Rama, even in my mind, if I have worshipped him as my only God, in my heart, my words, and my deeds, may my mother Bhumi Devi, who brought me into this world, now receive me back into herself. For all my life's purposes are accomplished and I do not want to live in this world any more."

A perfect silence had fallen; no one stirred. Even the wind had grown still. Then a crack of thunder erupted in that sabha. The earth at Sita's feet parted and a golden, unearthly throne rose from it, borne on the heads of five awesome nagas with blinding jewels in their hoods. On that throne sat a Goddess, and she was Madhavi, Medha: incomparable Bhumi Devi, the Earth herself. The green of the world's forests was in her hair and hands, the blue of the seven seas was upon her breasts. Her skin was the soft smooth brown of the sacred earth.

She, the mother, took her daughter's hands and drew Sita up to sit beside her on her fabulous throne. A petal rain of flowers of light, bearing heaven's scents, fell from the sky. Slowly, as the sabha watched, not a man moving, the wonderful throne sank into the earth again, and the ground closed over it, as if none of this had happened, as if the perfect Sita had never lived in this tainted world of men, ever.

Peal after peal of thunder echoed on high and it seemed the very sky would break in a thousand pieces. All the earth was still, dazed. Then silence, a complete silence, held the Naimisa vana. Just a single sound broke the deep silence, the sound of Rama sobbing.

At last he grew very still and his eyes turned red. The gentle Rama roared, "Bhumi Devi, give my Sita back to me, or I will break you open with my astras. Or open yourself to me, let me go down into Patala and live beside my love."

The Earth made no reply. Rama was furious. "I will level your mountains and dry up your seas. Your forest shall burn and all your creatures perish!"

Rama reached for his bow, the Kodanda, and the Earth shuddered in fear. He was a God again, just as he had been in the Dandaka vana, when he found Sita missing from their asrama. Then Lakshmana had calmed his brother, but now he was implacable. Rama was about to summon a great astra in his rage, when suddenly light filled that yagnashala, dazzling, unearthly light.

Brahma spoke out of that light to Rama: "Calm yourself, Rama.

Sita is in Nagaloka, with her mother. You will find her again, after this life. If you want to know the future, listen to the rest of the Ramayana, its Uttara Kanda. I gave the Adi Kavya to Valmiki. The Uttara Kanda is prescient, and no one but you must hear, yet, what it contains."

The light vanished and Brahma with it. Rama sat like a great fire put out. Slowly, as if heavier age than he could bear was upon him, he rose, and said to Valmiki, "Tomorrow I will hear the rest of the Uttara Kanda of your kavya. Give me leave until then, Muni, I feel tired."

He took Lava and Kusa by the hand and led them to his apartment. The father and his sons sat all that night in silence. Even the sacred forest around them seemed eerily quiet and absorbed in just one thought: of her who had left the world this day, she, the perfect one.

39. The Uttara Kanda

The next morning, at dawn, Rama broke his silence, and said to Lava and Kusa, "Now sing the Uttara Kanda to me. I want to know what the future holds."

Plucking on their vinas, their voices matched perfectly, the twins sang the Uttara Kanda. They sang with the grief of losing their mother, and their song was more beautiful than ever. They sang the Northern Kanda, and they came to the part of the Ramayana where Sita went down into Nagaloka on her mother, Bhumi Devi's, throne. As Rama listened absorbed, they sang on, now of the future.

Lava and Kusa sang that after Sita left the world, Rama completed the aswamedha yagna and gave lavish gifts to those who came to attend his horse sacrifice. Then he returned to Ayodhya. He kept his kanchana Sita, her golden image, with him. Never did he so much as look at another woman. In his time, to expiate what he saw as his unforgivable sin, he performed ten thousand aswamedha yagnas, one for every year of his kingship, and he felt these were too few. Always Sita's golden image was beside him, on his throne, as if she sat in her rightful place again at those ten thousand sacrifices, and blessed the earth and her husband at every one.

The reign of Dasaratha's son Rama was a perfect one. Truly, Vishnu Narayana, the Blue One himself, had come down into the world as a man, to sit upon the ancient throne of the Sun in Ayodhya. He was Lord of the earth, and all the races of men and beasts obeyed him. His grace flowed through the land of Bharatavarsha like a river, and the hearts of all creatures flowed pure.

Kaale varshatu parjannyam: the rains came on time, the harvest was always good, and the four quarters shone clear. The people in villages, in towns, and in cities had plenty and more to eat. No disease came among them and they never died before the ripeness of age was upon them. No war or other natural calamity, no flood, earthquake, or drought, visited the holy land.

When some blessed years had passed after the first aswamedha in the Naimisa vana, the queen Kausalya passed on from the world. After a very short lapse of time, even as if they could not live on without her, Sumitra and Kaikeyi followed. And all three were with Dasaratha again, in Swarga.

Rama, with his brothers and his sons at his side, ruled on, and dharma flowered in Bharatavarsha, as it never had before, at least in that yuga. One day, the king of Kekaya, old Asvapati's son Yudhajit, sent his guru, Angiras's son Gargya, to Rama's court. Yudhajit sent ten thousand horses and many caskets of gold and jewels. Rama went out of his city to meet Gargya.

When the gifts had been received and the brahmana honored, they sat together in the sabha of the Ikshvakus. Rama asked Gargya, "Holy one, why has my uncle sent you now? Is there some special reason?"

Gargya said, "Rama, King Yudhajit, your uncle, sends you word of the most beautiful land that borders his own kingdom. But gandharvas rule the unequaled country and they will not let any man enter it. Yudhajit asks if you would care to take that land from the three million sons of Sailusa, and make the city at its heart your own."

Rama said, "Brahmana, my brother Bharata will go and vanquish Sailusa and his sons. Bharata's sons, Taksha and Pushkala, will found their own cities in that country, and rule as kings. Once his task is accomplished, Bharata will return to me."

Soon, Rama had Taksha and Pushkala consecrated as kings in his sabha and drenched in the waters of abhisheka. Then, setting Angiras's son Gargya at the head of his army, and with his own sons at his sides, Bharata set out for Kekaya. It is told that there were flesh eaters in that army, thirsty for gandharva blood, and rakshasas and bhutas, lions, tigers, great reekshas, and teeming flocks of birds of prey and carrion flying above these.

For a month and a half, Bharata marched with his dreadful aksauhinis and finally arrived in Yudhajit's capital. Yudhajit joined his own legions to the forces of Ayodhya, and they marched together to the gandharva city hidden in the heart of the jungle. It was a peerless country, with great and ancient trees growing thickly, laden with incomparable flowers and luscious fruit.

Arriving at the city of the elves, Yudhajit and Bharata raised their war conches and blew a resounding blast of challenge. Like an army out of a dream, the gandharvas issued from their gates. They were taller than any men of the earth by a head, slender and altogether marvelous. They carried silver bows and were quicksilver archers. A pitched battle ensued and lasted seven days. Blood flowed in rivulets, floating bows and swords that had fallen from nerveless hands, and limbs and heads severed from their owners' bodies, and corpses.

Finally, Bharata saw his soldiers die on every side, and in fury loosed the astra called the samvarta at the gandharva host. Three million gandharvas perished in a moment, burned to ashes by that missile. Asvapati's son, Kaikeyi's brother Yudhajit, founded two cities in that beautiful wilderness. He made Bharata's son Taksha the king of Takshasila, and his other son, Pushkala, king of Pushkalavati.

When the cities had been built, with great avenues flanked by trees, with resplendent palaces and mansions and sprawling gardens, and when Bharata saw his sons had settled to the task of being rulers, he returned to Rama in Ayodhya.

Rama said to Lakshmana, "Saumitra, your sons Angada and Chandraketu are grown men now. Find them also kingdoms to rule, where they can live in peace and fulfill the four asramas."

It was Bharata who answered him, "The land of Karupatha is an auspicious country. Let Angada found a city there. And for our wrestler, Chandraketu, let us found another city and call it Chandrakanta."

So it came to pass; and those princes also had fine kingdoms to rule: Angada the archer in the north and Chandraketu in the west. Both were crowned in Ayodhya. Lakshmana went with Angada to help him establish his kingdom, and Bharata went with Chandraketu. In a year, Lakshmana returned to Ayodhya, and Bharata came home some months later.

Rama ruled the earth for ten thousand years and it was an age of plenty, an age of grace and perfection. But after Sita left the world, he himself was always lonely, and pined for her. One day, Yama arrived at his gates, in the guise of a rishi. The mendicant said to Lakshmana, who went out to receive him, "The Muni Atibala sent me to see your brother. Tell Rama I have come with a message from Atibala, to fulfill a great mission."

Lakshmana came in haste to Rama, and said, "A muni who shines like the sun has come to see you. He says he is on a great mission and the Maharishi Atibala sent him."

Rama said, "Show him in to me."

The rishi entered, and cried in the sweetest voice, "Hail to thee, O God upon the earth!"

Rama received him with honor. He offered him arghya, madhurparka, and a golden chair to sit upon. The king said, "Tell me why you have come to Ayodhya, my lord. Is there anything we can do for you? What is the message you have brought for me?"

The muni glanced around him, then said, "Rama, the message I bring is only for you. You must swear that while I give you the message, if any man hears us or sees us, you will kill him yourself."

He spoke almost casually, but it was plain he meant what he said. Rama said gravely, "So be it." He turned to Lakshmana. "Stand guard outside the door, and if anyone enters, or sees the muni and me, or hears what we are saying, he shall die."

The chamber was cleared, and Lakshmana shut the door and stood outside. Rama turned again to the hermit. "Now tell me what you have come for."

That rishi said to Rama, "Listen, then, to the message I bring, for he who sends the message is the Lord Brahma. Brahma says to you, 'Narayana, in the beginning of creation, I was born from the lotus that sprouted from your navel as you lay upon the ekarnava, the single and undivided sea.

" 'Rama, you are the God Vishnu; and you have said that you will come down into the world, from age to age, to protect it from evil. You came as Matsya, Kurma, Varaha, Narasimha, Vamana, and Parasurama, and established dharma. Now you have incarnated yourself as a kshatriya and broken the bonds of darkness again.

" 'But your mission is over and it is time for you to leave the earth. He who brings this message to you is Yama Deva, Death himself. But if you want to remain in the world for some more time, you may, with my blessing.'

"So says the Lord Brahma to you, Rama," Death said.

Rama began to laugh, gently and in joy. He answered the messenger, "Why, I am delighted you have come, my lord. I am ready to return to where I came from. I came because the Devas asked me to, and all my tasks have been accomplished. There is nothing to keep me back on earth."

Now it happened that while Rama sat speaking to Yama, the Rishi Durvasa, who is said to be an amsa of the Lord Siva, appeared in the palace of Ayodhya. He strode up to Lakshmana and said, "I must see Rama at once; I have come for a great purpose."

Lakshmana bowed to the muni, and said with folded hands, "My lord, my brother is not to be disturbed. I beg you, wait for just a while and he will see you."

But Durvasa's temper was a legend across the three worlds, and his eyes turned red as wild roses, his face grew dark. He said in a tone that brooked no refusal, "Go and announce me to Rama, or I will curse you, your brothers, your sons, and all this land of Bharatavarsha."

Poor Lakshmana thought quickly, "If I go in now, only I will die; the others will not be cursed."

Lakshmana entered the chamber where Rama sat with Yama and mumbled, "My lord, the Rishi Durvasa is here and he insists on seeing you immediately."

With that he retreated, in some fear. Rama jumped up, and, leaving Yama, he hurried out to see Atri's son.

Rama folded his hands and said to Durvasa, "I am blessed that you have come to my city. Tell me, holy one, what I can do for you."

His brows bristling, Durvasa replied, "Today I wish to end my fast of a thousand years and I have come to your home to eat my first meal. Give me food, Rama."

Rama had the finest, most auspicious food fetched for Durvasa. He served the rishi with his own hands and watched him eat as if it were amrita he was having. Durvasa washed his hands; he blessed Rama and left Ayodhya. Rama saw him off at his gates and then stood as if he had been struck by lightning. Though he had shown nothing of what he felt, as long as Durvasa was with him, Rama knew what Death had said should be the fate of anyone who entered the chamber where they sat talking. Lakshmana's life was forfeit, and he, Rama, must make sure his brother died.

Lakshmana said calmly, "Rama, as you love me, you must not break your word. You must take my life; that is your dharma."

Yama had vanished from Ayodhya. Rama called his sabha, all his rishis and ministers, and told them what had happened. Silence fell in his court. Then Vasishta said sadly, "I fear you must keep your word to Yama. You are the perfect one, and if you break your word, dharma will perish on earth. And then everything will be lost, on all the worlds."

Rama said softly, in anguish, "Lakshmana, leave me. I cannot bear to kill you, but go away from me this instant. Let me never see you again."

Lakshmana stood before him with tears streaming down his face. He touched his brother's feet, folded his hands to him, and, without a word, turned and walked out of the sabha. Never looking back, Lakshmana walked out of the city of his fathers and walked on, blindly, until he came to the banks of the Sarayu.

He knew he could not live without seeing his brother, and when Rama had sent him away, Rama had killed Lakshmana as surely as if he had cut him down with a sword. Lakshmana bathed in the Sarayu; he chanted the mantras for dying. Then he stood in the water and held his breath, meaning to die thus.

It is then that Indra, Lord of the Devas, and the apsaras of Deva-loka flung down a storm of unearthly petals on Lakshmana. Indra himself came down in a vimana, and, taking the kshatriya's hand, drew him out of his body and took him back into Swarga. Thus he who is called the fourth amsa of Vishnu returned to his primeval home.

40. Rama prepares to leave the world

After he sent Lakshmana from him, Rama was like a man who had lost his own heart. He was more stricken, even, than when he had sent Sita away from Ayodhya. Gathering his last strength, Rama announced, "I will crown my brother Bharata king of the Kosalas today. I must leave as quickly as I can. I must tread the path my Lakshmana went on."

A lament filled the sabha he had ruled from for ten thousand glorious years. Many of his ministers swooned. Bharata was numb for a while. But then, finding his voice, Kaikeyi's son cried, "No, Rama, I will not be king in Ayodhya after you leave. I beg you, crown Kusa

656

king of southern Kosala, and Lava lord of the northern territories. I mean to come to the vana with you, Rama. Let messengers ride at once to Shatrughna and tell him what we mean to do."

Outside, a great wailing filled the city of Ayodhya, as the news spread like fire through the homes and the people came thronging into the streets. Finally, they all prostrated themselves, men, women, and children, before Rama's palace, from a grief they could neither bear nor express in any other way.

Vasishta said to Rama, "The people have prostrated themselves in the streets. You must ask them what they intend. They, too, are your children, Rama."

Rama came out and the people rose before him like a tide of love. They said to him, "Rama, we will follow you out of Ayodhya and out of the world, if that is where you mean to go. We will follow you with our women and children. This is what we want; you are our refuge."

With tears in his eyes, Rama said to them, "So be it."

The same day, Rama had Lava and Kusa crowned kings of northern and southern Kosala. He gave each son a thousand chariots and ten thousand elephants and horses. He gave them vast gold and jewels, and sent his own gurus to be their counselors.

Meanwhile, messengers had already ridden to Shatrughna in his Madhura. These men rode without pausing for three days and nights to arrive in that city. They told Shatrughna about all that had transpired. They told him how Yama had come to Ayodhya, and Durvasa; how Lakshmana had left the city, and how Lava and Kusa had been crowned. They told him that Lava had been given the northern city called Saraswati, and Kusa another city in the south, which had been named Kusavati.

The messengers told Shatrughna how the people of Ayodhya had decided they would leave the city of their fathers, and follow Rama and Bharata into the next world. They told Shatrughna all this, and he sat as if he had been turned to stone. Then those men cried, "Shatrughna, hurry. You have not a moment to lose."

Shatrughna summoned his priest, Kanchana, and said, "We must have my sons crowned at once. I cannot live in this world after my brothers have gone."

His son Subahu was made master of Madhura, and his other prince, Shatrughati, the lord of Vidisa, which is also called Bhelsa. Shatrughna divided his army and the contents of his treasury and granary, and gave each of his sons an equal portion. Then, riding alone in his chariot, he journeyed to Ayodhya.

Shatrughna found Rama, clad in white silk, sitting among the great rishis of the earth. Shatrughna folded his hands and said to his brother, "I mean to follow you out of Ayodhya and out of this world, if that is where you are going. I beg you, don't say you will not take me with you. For your word must never be broken, especially by me."

Rama smiled, "You may come with me, Shatrughna."

Meanwhile, they heard a noise at the gates, and saw that an army of vanaras, rakshasas, and reekshas had arrived in the city of the Sun. Sugriva, like a flame, was at their head. Somehow they also had heard the news.

Sugriva said to Rama, "We, too, have come to follow you out of the world. I have made Angada king in Kishkinda. You know all these loyal vanaras, rakshasas, and reekshas, Rama. We will not live this life any more, when you are gone."

Rama seemed mildly dazed. His eyes and heart were full. He said, in some helplessness, "So be it." But then he turned to Vibheeshana and said, "But you, my friend, will not come with me. You must remain in the world and be king in Lanka for an age more. No, don't protest, Vibheeshana, my brother. There is deep reason for what I am saying. You must continue to rule from Lanka and you must worship Vishnu in your city."

Vibheeshana hung his head and replied sadly, "So be it, my lord. I will do as you say."

Rama turned next to Hanuman. "You always told me you meant to live in the world for a long time. Let there be no change in that, for the world has dire need of the likes of Vibheeshana and yourself."

The always serene Hanuman said, "You are alive in my heart, wherever you may be. I will live in this world for as long as the Ramayana is told in it."

Rama said, "Five of you loyal ones shall live in the world at least until the end of the dwapara yuga. Vibheeshana, Hanuman, Jambavan, Mainda, and Dwividha. Some may remain longer, in subtle bodies and guises, to ensure that dharma never perishes entirely on earth."

They sat together, those friends, through the long night. And when night's final, darkest, most silent yaama ended, Rama said to Vasishta, "My lord, let the fire of agnihotra, which I lit myself, go before us all as we leave Ayodhya. Let the vajapeya serve as the royal parasol.

Let every ritual be performed, my guru, so our departure is auspicious."

Vasishta began to perform those rites for the final journey, as they are set down in the Shastras. Rama went into his apartment and bathed. He donned his finest silks, and, having prayed at his family altar, emerged like a soft dark sun. He took up the kusa grasses from near the agni, and walked out of his palace and the city he had ruled without blemish for ten thousand years.

Never had his people seen him so radiant. Without a backward glance, Rama walked toward the Sarayu, and it is told that the agnihotra, embodied, went before him in a form of flames. A hundred great astras, also in manlike forms, walked before Rama, as did his bow, the Kodanda. Lakshmana's spirit walked beside his brother, on his right, and Bhumi Devi materialized to walk at his left.

The Vedas all followed Rama, embodied as pristine brahmanas, the Gayatri as a Goddess, the Omkara, and Vasatkara. The great rishis and the Devas of the earth walked behind Rama, and above and below the gates of heaven opened wide to receive them. The women of Ayodhya, the old men, the servants, and the eunuchs followed him. Bharata, Shatrughna, and their families walked with him. All the kshatriyas of Kosala went with him, with their wives, sons, and daughters. The ministers of Rama's sabha followed him, in the crowd; even the cows and bulls of Ayodhya walked in that throng. Every man, woman, and child he had ruled went with Rama, as he came out under a cobalt sky and walked serenely toward the Sarayu.

The birds of Kosala, the deer, and every other creature, butterflies and fireflies, all followed Rama, knowing that he was leading them toward death. Rich and poor walked side by side, no difference between them, and a tide of bliss swept over that great and motley crowd of men and vanaras, rakshasas and reekshas. Why, even the dark bhutas of the land followed blessed Rama, in bhakti, and without a shred of doubt that he would lead them to salvation.

Rama walked for a yojana and a half due west, and saw the Sarayu sparkling before him like a river of blue jewels. All the world was hushed as Rama followed the river upstream. Today, a thousand whirlpools marked the currents of the Sarayu. The river knew what a day of moment this was. The immense crowd followed Rama in absolute silence.

The sky was brighter than it had ever been, since the sky was made above the earth. It was alive today; it pulsed with divine energy. Now the Devas of the air, Indra's people, crowded the firmament in their vimanas. They and a million others, all immortal ones, were golden shadows above. The wind that blew across the world was full of light and bore the scents of Devaloka, richly.

Brahma was there, above the place along the Sarayu from where an invisible path led directly to his loftiest realm and beyond. The Devas let fall a sweet rain of flowers on Rama. The sky seemed to open and the music of gandharvas filled it. Apsaras danced on the air on immaterial feet. The earth welled in great springs of grace, gushing forth everywhere, filling Rama and those who followed him with bliss.

Rama arrived at the place by the river from where the pathway of light led up into the realms beyond. Now Brahma spoke in his voice deeper than the sky, deep as the ages: "Narayana, return to us. Come again into your immortal form, O Sleeper upon the waters of eternity. Refuge of the worlds, set aside your human body, incomprehensible, deathless, Unborn One. O Vishnu, be again as you have always been."

Brahma stood four-faced above the river. Slowly, Rama approached the water. In the west, the setting sun had turned the color of blood. Brahma held his arms open. His body growing more brilliant with each moment, Rama waded into the Sarayu. The river seemed to erupt in fire. Great columns of light rose from it and pierced the sky. Towering flames rose from it, and Rama walked into these flames.

The others on the bank of the river could not look at the water or at him who had entered her currents. Both were blinding. Then there was light everywhere, a single light, a light of lights from which all this world had come. Rama melted into that light; he was that light.

Slowly, the light faded and a gasp went up from those who still stood ashore: Rama had four arms now, he was Someone Else, someone he had always been. He was Mahavishnu, the God of Gods. He bore the Kaumodaki, the dazzling Sudarshana chakra, the Panchajanya, and the Saringa, in four hands that were the hue of the deepest blue lotus. His presence was greater than Brahma's above; his refulgence filled heaven and earth.

When Rama became Vishnu again, Bharata and Shatrughna also entered into the Blue God; they were also absorbed into the Infinite One. Then the Devas worshipped that Vision, as did the Sadhyas, the Marut hosts, with Indra and Agni at their head. All the munis of the three worlds worshipped Him, the gandharvas and apsaras, the suparnas, the nagas and yakshas, the Daityas and Danavas, and the great rakshasas.

Mahavishnu's voice said to Brahma, "These men and their families have followed me in love. They have abandoned their very lives to be with me. They are like my own self. Let them be blessed. Let all the birds and beasts who have followed me be blessed."

Brahma said, "They shall all come to Santanaka, where there is every joy, and no death. And those of them that were once born of the Devas shall be Devas again."

The vanaras, who were Devas in amsa, whose sires were the ones of light, assumed their fathers' illustrious, immortal forms again; the reekshas did as well. Sugriva entered the blazing disk of the sun; he was one with his father Surya. Great Vishnu stood at the mouth of the golden path that led out of this world, the Gopratara. He opened his arms wide to them.

In waves, like a river flowing into the sea, that throng of Rama-bhaktas walked into the Sarayu. As soon as the holy water touched them, their mortal bodies dissolved and they rose up in resplendent forms of light. Man and beast were like Gods. Why, even the rocks in the Sarayu that day were saved, and rose with shining spirit-bodies.

When the last of his bhaktas had ascended, Rama himself rose out of this world. He left his grace upon the earth for an age, and the undying memory of a perfect life and a perfect reign: Ramarajya. Narayana was in Vaikunta again. And there, Sita, who is the Devi Lakshmi, waited for him.

AUM. SHANTI SHANTI SHANTIHI AUM.

Phalasruti

This is the Ramayana and its Uttara Kanda, which are worshipped by the brahmanas and the holiest rishis. When Rama returned to Vaikunta, the Ramayana of his life and his deeds on earth was sung in the transcendent realms as well, from the Patalas to the highest lokas of Brahma, Vishnu, and Siva.

It has been said that he who hears the Ramayana lives a long life; for this Adi Kavya is such a holy poem it dispels the sins that cling to a man. It is equal to the Vedas, and should be read at funerals for the peace of the soul of the departed.

The man who has no child and reads the Ramayana is blessed with sons and daughters. The poor man who listens to it with faith becomes wealthy. The man who reads even a fourth of this holiest of poems is freed from all his sins. Why, even a sloka of the Ramayana cleanses a man of his daily sins. The man who reads the Ramayana to others is a blessed one indeed; he has honor even in heaven.

He who reads the Ramayana regularly never becomes disheartened, but is always serene and cheerful. It must not be forgotten that Brahma inspired the Rishi Valmiki to compose the Ramayana. He who hears this sacred epic, with bhakti, receives the punya of one who performs a thousand aswamedhas and ten thousand vajapeyas. He who has heard the Ramayana has bathed at all the holy tirthas. He has purified himself in the Ganga, the Yamuna, and the other great rivers. He has worshipped at Prayaga and the Naimisaranya. He has offered two thousand palas of gold at Kurukshetra during the eclipse of the sun.

Surely, he who listens to the Ramayana has all his sins exorcised and attains Vishnuloka. This is the first and the greatest epic of all: the Adi Kavya, composed by the great Valmiki. He who listens to it every day attains the very form of Vishnu and prospers beyond all belief, in this world and in the world of the spirit. The Ramayana is the Gayatri; it heals the body and the soul.

Even the ancestors of a man who reads the Ramayana every day attain Vishnuloka, when that man leaves his body. The life of Rama bestows artha, kama, dharma, and moksha; let there never be any doubt about this. So read or listen to the Ramayana with a pure heart, with no mockery, as if your very life depended on it. Even Brahma reveres the man who knows this pristine legend.

For the sleeper on Ananta, who rests upon the sea of eternity, Blue Mahavishnu, pervades this ancestral poem of the earth, this epic of the perfect man.

AUM SHANTI SHANTI SHANTIHI
AUM SHANTIHI AUM.

APPENDIX

RAVANA'S DAUGHTER: A SOUTHERN TALE

The Ramayana is the Adi Kavya, the first epic poem of the world, and it is sacred. It was after I had written my version of the Ramayana that I heard the following story in Kerala, where it is quite common. It is never told in the northern versions of the Ramayana, and may well be considered profane. Because of the antiquity of the Ramayana, it is hard to say if this tale was in fact part of the original epic and later suppressed.

She was a great queen and the most beautiful woman in the world. Her father was once the Lord of all the Asuras, until Siva torched his triune sky-cities out of the air. Now Mayaa's daughter, Mandodari, was Ravana's queen. Her husband held the three realms, Swarga, Bhumi, and Patala, in the palm of his hand. He was a king of kings, Emperor of Lanka and of all the rakshasas, invincible, apparently immortal. Mandodari's son Indrajit had tamed the king of the Devas himself, and brought him bound in coils of fire to Lanka. Indrajit was Lanka's yuvaraja, Ravana's firstborn son and his heir.

What more could any woman want?

But Mandodari was the unhappiest woman in the world. Night after night, she lay in her bed alone, yearning for her husband. She thirsted for his lean, battle-scarred body, his searing kisses, and his awesome virility. When she thought of him with the silver moon flowing in through the window over her naked body, she could hardly bear the pang she felt. She lay all night listening to the waves far below, and sobbing, sobbing.

It was three months since he had come to her apartment. It was yet another rakshasi he had brought home from his most recent war who kept him away. Her name was Dhanyamalini. Mandodari had lost count of the women he kept. She had long ago learned to accept that he was insatiable. She had known him to come raging into her room an hour before dawn, after he had been with three or four other women through the night. She could smell them on his dark skin; sometimes he was still damp with their fluids. And he would still make her cries echo against the rising sun, before falling asleep in her arms.

She herself had shared other women, of every race, with him, and felt nothing but pleasure. Now she hated him. She did not know why this had happened, suddenly. More than anything, she wanted revenge. She wanted to inflict a torment on him that he would die from. And now she knew she had the means to do just that.

Ravana had a hundred sons, powerful princes. But he did not have a daughter. Mandodari was pregnant again; she was certain the child, growing a month in her womb, was a girl. She knew how much her husband wanted a daughter. At last, here was something she could give him, or deny him.

Mandodari did not tell Ravana she was pregnant. She sent a message to him, saying she wanted to visit her father, Mayaa, in his palace in a forest of Bharatavarsha. Ravana did not find the time to come to see her before she left. He merely sent a message back, that she could go in the pushpaka vimana; and send for it again when she was ready to return. She hardened her heart for what she wanted to do. She left without seeing him.

In her father's house, she kept much to herself. Mayaa was troubled for his child. He sensed how unhappy she was. But she would say nothing to him about Ravana, or about her life in Lanka. She stayed with him for a month, and no message came from her husband asking her to return home. Mandodari's pregnancy grew day by day and she was afraid Mayaa would discover it. She said she wanted to go on a pilgrimage to all the holy tirthas of Bharatavarsha, to pray for Ravana.

Mayaa sent a trusted escort of Asuras with her, and she set out. First she went north, to the river fords of the Ganga and the Himalaya, and worshipped at all the most auspicious tirthas of grace on earth. She spent four months in Badarikasrama, where Nara Narayana once sat in tapasya. Mandodari was filled with a peace she had never known before. She felt purified, both by her prayers and by the child in her womb. She knew it was no ordinary child growing inside her. She was briefly tempted to return to Lanka and give Ravana the daughter he wanted so desperately. But then, she steeled herself to do what she had decided.

In her ninth month, she left sacred Badari and went down again into the plains of Bharatavarsha. One night, she cut the throats of her escort while they slept, and rode away by herself. They knew her secret; Ravana and Mayaa must never learn of her pregnancy. She rode numbly through the world. Her time drew nearer, and never knowing it, she journeyed into the heart of a great and ancient kingdom.

One morning, when she awoke at dawn, after a night full of the most illumined and terrifying dreams, she saw she had fallen asleep at the very hem of the jungle. She saw the turrets and ramparts of a magnificent city silhouetted against the rising sun.

Even as she roused herself, she felt the first sharp pain of her labor. She staggered toward the city, hoping to give birth there. But she could manage only a few steps before her water broke and she had to squat down in a field, because her child was surging out of her. In a few moments, Mandodari cradled a golden baby girl in her arms, and never had she seen anything so absolutely beautiful. A shower of barely substantial petals fell out of the sky over her; she heard ethereal music fill the earth, music she had only heard in her dreams. She also saw her baby was swathed in a pulsing halo.

Mandodari felt wracked with guilt at what she was about to do. But this was the revenge that would make the rest of her life in Lanka bearable. She cut her baby's umbilical cord with the silver dagger she carried at her waist. With a last, lingering kiss on the little eyes, her tears falling freely onto the tiny, perfect face, Mandodari laid her baby down on the earth. Tearing herself away and mounting her black horse, she turned its sleek face toward her father's palace.

The same day, near noon, King Janaka of Mithila went out of his city to a field south of it. He brought his rishis, and a golden plow to turn the earth for a sacrifice he was planning. Janaka had no children and he meant to perform a putrakama yagna . . .

Years later, when Hanuman first leaped into Lanka and saw Mandodari asleep in Ravana's apartment, he mistook her for the princess he had come in search of. Rama's description of Sita seemed to fit the sleeping queen so well, until Hanuman reminded himself Sita would be younger than the woman he saw. Besides, she would kill herself before she slept in Ravana's bed.

Then there is the fatal attraction Sita held for Ravana. He was the wisest king of his time, perhaps of all time. Yet he sacrificed everything he had—his people, his brothers, his sons, his precious Lanka, and at last his very life—for Sita. In the most ancient Indian tradition, it is said that at times, one's worst enemies from previous lives are born as one's children, to fulfill fate's most mysterious, most savage designs.*

THE STORY OF VISWAMITRA

This is the story Sadananda told in Mithila.

Vijaya was the youngest son of Pururavas, who was the ancestor of the race of Soma on earth. The Moon was Pururavas's father. Vijaya's son was Bheema; Bheema's son was Kanchana and Kanchana's son was Jahnu, who once swallowed the Ganga as she rushed after Bhagiratha's chariot. And she was called Jahnavi. Jahnu's son was Pooru, and Pooru's son was Ajaka, whose son was Kusa.

Kusa had four sons, and the youngest was Kusanabha. Gadhi, the great, was Kusanaba's son, and Kaushika was Gadhi's son.

King Kaushika was an able ruler of his father's kingdom. Once he went on a yatra through his country, to all its towns and villages, meeting the common people and sharing their joys and sorrows. Through cities and jungles he went, fording rivers, crossing wooded hills and remote valleys, blessing Nature's bounty and grateful that he was born such a fortunate king.

In the forests he passed through, he visited every asrama he came upon. He was a devout man, and believed that his kingdom thrived because of the holy rishis who lived in tapasya within its frontiers. One day, Kaushika came to a forest and saw a beautiful hermitage set in an orchard overgrown with fruit and flowering trees and a profusion of wild plants. A lively stream flowed past, and all the place had an air of deep sanctity: there was more than just nature at work here.

As Kaushika entered the tapovana, he was astonished to see little golden deer, no higher than his knee and obviously quite tame. Then from the jungle's silence, he heard soft music being played on reeds and fine lutes, which were so sweet he knew they were not of the world of men. Behind the trees the king caught fleeting glimpses of exotic folk he had only heard of in stories before: beings clad in leaves

---

*Another version of this story in Tamil folklore is that Sita is Vedavati's daughter by Ravana, born after he ravishes Vedavati.

and flowers, shining ones who sang and danced. They sang in tongues that had passed out of the use of men long ago, for they were not made to describe human affairs.

Reining in his horse, warning his army to stay back, Kaushika saw the elusive gandharvas, as they chose to reveal themselves to him, in a shifting dream of sight and sound, teasing and playful. His gaze was pulled this way and that, as the elfin folk appeared and vanished in different places.

Kaushika saw that many rishis sat in dhyana in that asrama, rapt, seemingly unaware of the bit of heaven on earth they sat amidst. Kshatriya custom demanded the king pay homage to the guru who was master here. He went into the hermitage and prostrated himself at the feet of the great seer within, who was called Vasishta. Excitedly, the rishi rose to welcome Kaushika. He embraced him and sent for a darbhasana for him to sit on.

Vasishta offered the king fruit from his trees and sweet water from the jungle stream. Graciously, Kaushika accepted whatever he was offered, and the two of them sat talking. Little did the kshatriya know his destiny stood nearer him than he would have cared to have her. Vasishta, who was Brahma's own son, was delighted that Kaushika had come to visit him.

"Is your kingdom at peace? Are your enemies subdued? Is your treasury full, and your granary? Is your army powerful, are your people happy?"

And so on, as is proper to ask a king when he visits. Kaushika answered directly and elegantly, and Vasishta quickly grew fond of him, even as he might a gifted disciple! The conversation wandered into more private matters, and Vasishta confirmed his intuition that this king was a remarkable man, a very unusual kshatriya.

Suddenly, the sage leaned forward and, taking Kaushika's hand, cried, "I am so happy you have come here with your army. I want to entertain you all in my asrama."

Certain that he would inconvenience the muni, Kaushika said, "Muni, I am already overwhelmed by your kindness. But it is time I left you to your more sacred pursuits."

Lest he bring shame to the rishi's hospitality—for his army was large—he rose to leave. But Vasishta restrained him, laying a hand on his arm, insisting, "You must eat with us, my son."

He would not hear of Kaushika leaving without first having eaten in the asrama, and all his men with him. Kaushika sighed inwardly and said, "You leave me no choice! Very well, we will share anything you are pleased to offer us. Though nothing can be as satisfying as your kindness."

Laughing, they rose together, their arms linked. Vasishta called softly, "Surabhi, come here, my child."

A supernaturally lovely cow came at his call. Her eyes were like long lotuses. Her skin shimmered, dappled white and black. To the king's amazement, the rishi spoke to her as if she were really a human child. "Shabale, this is the king of this country, the noble Kaushika, who has come to visit us with his army. They must eat with us, my daughter. Let nothing be lacking in the feast, for they are used to royal fare."

The king did not know Surabhi was Kamadhenu herself, the cow of wishes. She had once been churned up from the Kshirasagara with the amrita, and given to the rishis as the Gods' gift to them. Kaushika stared at her; in all his life he had never seen such an exquisite creature. And when the king saw the feast she created in a moment for himself and his army, he was astounded.

Surabhi created every kind of delicacy for Kaushika's men, and there was an endless amount of it all. Those soldiers ate and ate, because they could scarcely have enough of the unearthly food. They marveled and they ate, and their king with them. Not he, nor any of them, had ever tasted anything to remotely rival the feast Surabhi laid on for them.

At last, when he tore himself away from the table, Kaushika went to Vasishta and bowed to the muni. The king said humbly, "Never in my life have I tasted food like what we had today."

But then he was a king, and used to possessing whatever took his fancy. Looking away from the rishi, Kaushika went on, "But Vasishta, this cow of yours should not be kept hidden away in an asrama. She belongs with me, so her bounty can be shared by everyone in the kingdom. Let me take her, Muni, and I will give you a thousand cows for her. What are your needs that a thousand ordinary cows cannot meet? After all, you are sworn to austerity. This cow is a treasure, and any treasure in the kingdom belongs with me."

Vasishta was startled. He did not realize how earnest Kaushika was, and said quietly, "Shabale is not just a cow; she is my daughter.

Not for a thousand cows, not for a hundred thousand, why, not for all the gold in your coffers, would I part with her." Vasishta laid an affectionate hand on Kaushika's arm. He added with a smile, "Taking her from me would be like parting a famous man from his fame: it cannot be done."

All this was still said in the friendliest tone. And smiling, Kaushika replied, "I will give you a thousand elephants, all caparisoned in silk and gold. I will give you eight hundred chariots with horse. I will give you a crore of kapila cows. If you want, I will give you jewels such as kings of the earth are envious of: heirlooms handed down in our line from Soma Deva himself. But let me have your Surabhi."

Vasishta saw Kaushika would go to any length to get what he wanted. The son of Brahma said firmly, "Much as it saddens me to refuse you, Surabhi is the jewel of my tapasya and nothing will induce me to part with her."

Kaushika stared hard at the muni who thwarted his will. He thought Vasishta was being unreasonable, and the king's face grew dark. He turned abruptly and stalked out from the asrama. But he said to his men, "This old man will not give the cow reasonably. Take her by force."

Kaushika's soldiers dragged Surabhi from her shelter. Tears streamed from her eyes because she thought Vasishta had given her away. They dragged her to the edge of the asrama, where she tossed her horns at them and bolted back to the muni. She cried in a human voice, "Father, why have you abandoned me? What have I done?"

Vasishta saw through time as clearly as other men see what is before their eyes. He said gently, "This sorrow of yours isn't meaningless, child. That kshatriya—"

But he had no time to finish. With ringing cries, Kaushika's sons were upon him, weapons flashing under the serene trees. Great Vasishta, feared in the three worlds, drew a deep breath. With a single "HUMmmmm!," terrible humkara, he made ashes of those princes and their army.

It was as if Kaushika had been struck by lightning. He bent his head and walked away in rout from that asrama. The shock of his sons' death all but deranged that king: his fate called him, inexorably, with formidable grief. From then on, he sat absently on his throne, brooding on the rishi and his cow, and the syllable that had made ashes of his legion. He brooded that his own kingship was as dust under the feet of the brahmarishi.

Kaushika left his kingdom to a young son, who had not been out with him during the debacle in the forest. He went to the Himalaya, where kimpurusha fauns dwell, and began a fervent tapasya to Siva.

In some years Siva appeared, crystal-bodied, before Kaushika, and said, "Why such a tapasya, O King? Ask for what you want and I will give it to you."

Kaushika lay at the feet of the vision. "Lord, make me a master of the devastras."

Smiling, because he saw the deep future clearly, while Kaushika knew just his immediate ambition, Sankara said, "They are yours, Kaushika. Return to your kingdom with the astras, O master of archery."

Kaushika returned to his capital, his pride healed by the boon of astras. He told himself, "I have the weapons of the Gods. Vasishta is as good as dead."

When he was armed with the devastras Siva had given him, Kaushika's fury was rekindled. The memory of the death of his sons and the obliteration of his army burned again in his heart. Kaushika went straight to the forest where Vasishta's asrama was. With no warning, he loosed his weapons at the hermitage.

In gale and fire, the astras spumed forth. Even Kaushika stood stunned by their raw power. But he could not call them back even if he wanted: such is the nature of the devastras. Screaming, the birds and beasts of the forest fled from the apocalypse. The secret gandharvas vanished from there. The trees in Vasishta's orchard shriveled and perished in the flames.

All the asrama blazed for a moment, like a dying sun. When the flash subsided, Kaushika saw the hermitage was razed. No fruit or flowering tree, no shrub, no blade of grass grew any more on the charred ground. Just dark smoke rose from the earth, as if to mock the beauty that had been there only moments ago. But revenge has no eyes for beauty, and Kaushika exulted at what he had done. Even the little jungle stream was dry beside the asrama: the astras had turned the chatty waters into steam.

An awful silence had fallen. Then, his robes burned, his hair disheveled, and shock upon his face, Vasishta came out of the smoking ruin of his hermitage. He went quietly to Kaushika, who was surprised that anyone could have survived the inferno he had loosed. Vasishta's was a frightening quietness as he stood there with his staff in his hand. At last he said, "Kshatriya, you have destroyed my peace. You are a fool and I am going to kill you."

Vasishta raised his danda and it blazed like the fires that end time. It shone with scarlet, blue, green, and then white, smokeless flames. Kaushika stood unflinching before the ancient brahmana, his bowstring drawn to his ear, his arrow livid with an agneyastra. He laughed aloud, mocking the muni. With a howl, he shot that missile at Vasishta. The arrow flared at the hermit, burning up earth and sky, and time of which both are made.

Vasishta planted his staff in front of him like a pillar of light. All this was done in a moment. In a moment, long as a life, Kaushika saw his storm of fire, which could have consumed a city, turn to soft rain when it encountered Vasishta's bright danda and fall like a blessing around the rishi.

Roaring, Kaushika fitted his bow with five astras, one after the other. Each of them could consume the four dimensions. But he saw vaaruna, raudra, aindra, paasupata, and aishika all extinguished by the plain brahmadanda Vasishta had planted in the earth. His staff stood before the rishi like a cosmic sentinel.

Kaushika shot a manavastra at the seer, a gaandharva, a deep jrumbhana, and a swaapana of sleep and dreams that last an age. But those weapons, which could contend with the hosts of heaven and hell, were put out like children's fireworks. Not even Indra's vajra could overcome Vasishta's staff. In tears, in disbelief, Kaushika turned to the paasas, the serpentine nooses that bind body and soul in umbilical sorceries. The kaala of time and death he invoked, vaaruna of the primal waters on which all the worlds rest, and braahma of the light which shines on those waters: weapons that could undo stars. They fell by the way, to the power of the brahmadanda, burning like an eye of the universe. In despair, Kaushika summoned the whirling chakras; but Vasishta's staff was proof against these also.

The Devas gathered in the sky in their vimanas, fleet as thoughts. Armadas of crystal ships hovered above to witness the duel in the forest. Kaushika invoked the greatest weapon of all, the one that could uncurl a galaxy with its wrath. The Devas cleared the sky in panic, crying to the kshatriya to desist from such madness. But his eyes crimson, the veins standing out like serpents on his arms, Kaushika invoked the brahmastra, which could devour all of creation. He loosed the dreadful ayudha at Brahma's son, who stood mocking him with a smile.

The brahmastra rose with a million fires of spirit and flames, and briefly two suns lit the sky, the astra brighter than the other. Then it fell screaming at Vasishta's staff to put out the splendor of that danda, to consume the earth if need be. Now the muni's staff was just a blinding light; as if from its depths it salvaged a sliver of the first flare that lit the darkness of the void. Though the staff from which it shone was not even as tall as Vasishta, that light was larger than the world. It was greater than all the light and darkness in all the mandalas.

Vasishta's danda stood quivering with vast ire, as the brahmastra plunged down on it like a comet. Beside his staff Vasishta stood, blazing like Agni Deva: his body was golden, his skin seemed molten. He raised his hands skyward, with a ringing mantra to his Father. The danda yawned open like the void, and the brahmastra fell into that chasm like a water drop into a sea, a spark into a star. And it vanished as if it had never been.

The Devas rained down flowers out of the sky on Vasishta. But the muni was afire. Flames spewed from his body, from his hair, in wrath at the vanquished king before him. He cried at Kaushika, "Vain and foolish Kshatriya, you would have burned up the three worlds for your petty revenge; while the greed and the arrogance were yours in the first place. I have conquered all your weapons. Now let us see you quell my single one."

Seizing up the brahmadanda, Vasishta strode toward Kaushika. But the rishis of heaven, who sat with the Devas in their vimanas, cried down to their brother, "Stay your hand, Vasishta! Not even the Gods with their armies can match your power. What will you prove by killing a puny kshatriya? You have humbled him. Why consume the earth with your anger?"

Vasishta lowered the arm he had raised to strike Kaushika down. He grew calm in a moment; his body blazed no more. The brahmadanda in his hand, which had swallowed a skyful of astras, was a common branch of wood again, an old man's walking stick. That muni laughed softly at Kaushika, twirled his staff, and went back into his asrama, where the worship had not paused for a moment. The fruit trees and flowering plants had sprung up again, miraculously, and the little golden deer frolicked with Surabhi once more.

Kaushika stood trembling with defeat. His sighs came from him like a serpent's hisses. With a long howl, he flung his bow and arrows down. He screamed at himself, or at anyone who cared to hear, "Fie on the weapons of a kshatriya! They are toys before a brahmana's bala. I shall have the strength of a brahmana and then we will see how Vasishta faces an equal. Then we will test the timbre of his heart. I, too, will become a brahmarishi!"

Sobbing in royal shame, he stalked away toward the Himalaya for the second time. For a thousand years, Kaushika sat in tapasya, naked under the blazing sun in summer, and frozen among ice floes in white mountain streams in winter. He sat unflinching, while even the Gods above marveled. For, after all, here was a kshatriya, a spoiled king of the earth, who sat petitioning Brahma: for brahmatva, the power of the Creator, no less!

At the end of a thousand years, Brahma appeared four-headed and refulgent before Kaushika. Kaushika was sure he had achieved what he wanted, and prostrated himself at the Pitama's feet. Brahma said, "You have accomplished what I was certain a king like you never could. I name you rajarishi, Kaushika."

And Brahma vanished. Kaushika's roar of disappointment echoed through valleys of ice, between looming peaks, setting avalanches adrift around him. A thousand years just to be called a rajarishi! He had not imagined the path he had chosen would be so severe: he had asked for the world and Brahma had given him a fistful of sand.

In the race of the sun, whose ancestor is the glorious Surya Deva, who gives life to all creatures that live on earth, there was another king of dharma called Trishanku. One day an urgent desire possessed Trishanku: that he must rise up to Devaloka in his human body! Vasishta was his guru, and the king asked him to perform a yagna that would satisfy his strange craving. Vasishta would not hear of it.

He said, "An ungodly lust has seized your heart. I cannot help you; you must overcome this madness."

But easier said than done: Trishanku had neither sleep nor waking in any peace; his bizarre obsession tormented him by night and day. He relinquished his throne and wandered to the south. Vasishta had a hundred sons, each one a master of tapasya, his store of karma rich with austerity. Together they were a continent, an age, of punya.

Trishanku came to them and, with folded hands, said, "I was your father's sishya, but now I will be yours. Perform a yagna that will take me into heaven in this body of mine."

But Vasishta's sons said, "Why didn't you ask our father to perform the yagna?" Trishanku hung his head. "I asked him, but he refused. He said what I craved was unholy. But my desire feeds relentlessly on me."

Vasishta's sons said with some emotion, "Our father, who has always been the kulaguru of the House of Ikshvaku, has refused to pander to your whim. How can his sons transgress his will?"

But Trishanku was a slave to his obsession. He cried, "If your father and you won't help me, I must find another guru who will."

As he turned to leave, Vasishta's sons cursed him, "Vain Kshatriya, be a chandala from this moment!"

Trishanku headed wearily back to his city, his unnatural desire still torturing him. Day dawned after a long and sleepless night during which, again and again, he saw himself rise sweetly up into Devaloka. He thought that if the Gods had not meant his dream to be realized, they would not have planted it so deeply in his heart. Trishanku found the curse of Vasishta's sons had come to pass. His royal finery had vanished in the night, and he was wearing rags. His skin had turned coarse and black. He had a garland of wildflowers round his neck like any forester, and his golden ornaments had turned to base iron.

He entered his city, and the people in the streets did not know their king any more. They mocked the chandala who had lost his way here. Trishanku cried to them, "I am your king, don't you know me? It is I, Trishanku!"

But not even his ministers knew him, and the people jeered at him, calling him mad that he thought he was the king. They abused him, beat him, and had him flung out of the city gates. Trishanku lay bruised and despairing in a jungle, wondering himself if he was a king who had lost his identity or a chandala who had lost his mind. Then, in his agony, it occurred to him that there was one rishi in the world who might help him. He had heard of Kaushika, the rajarishi, who was Vasishta's sworn enemy.

Trishanku found Kaushika at dhyana. He sat in padmasana, the lotus posture, with his eyes shut, perfectly quiet. Trishanku stood at a respectful distance from the muni, in silence. Kaushika felt a presence near him. Opening his eyes, he saw a black and ugly chandala who was a picture of misery. Kaushika felt sorry for the forester, who was obviously in some agony. He beckoned to the wild man to come closer. When he did, Kaushika gave a start.

He cried, "But you are Trishanku of Ayodhya! Who cursed you, mighty Kshatriya?"

Hearing the concern in Kaushika's voice, Trishanku began to cry. He said, "I begged my guru Vasishta and his sons to help me reach Devaloka with my body, for the desire was upon me as if the Gods had put it in my heart. But they said my ambition was unholy. I performed a hundred yagnas, but in vain. Muni, never in my life have I told a lie and I never will. I have ruled my people with love, and I have never broken kshatriya dharma. I have always honored my elders and been a just king.

"But now I see dharma has no value and blind destiny rules men's lives. Why else, Kaushika, shouldn't I have this small desire of mine fulfilled? I am sure it is well within the power of a rishi like Vasishta to grant what I ask. I have come to you hoping you will help me."

Trishanku fell silent, and stood before Kaushika with his head bowed. Kaushika was moved by compassion for the king; perhaps since what he wanted was so extraordinary, he reminded the rajarishi of himself. Kaushika grew thoughtful for a moment, then he said gently, "Be welcome here, Trishanku. All the world knows what a noble kshatriya you are, and no foolish curse can change that. I will help you. I will perform a yagna with the rishis of the world and you will gain Devaloka in your body. Why, I will send you up among the stars in this chandala's body to mock Vasishta's bigoted sons."

Kaushika called his own sons and told them to prepare for a yagna. He called his disciples and sent them out to the other rishis of the earth, asking them to attend. They all came, except Vasishta and his sons.

"A strange and comical sight it must be," laughed Vasishta's sons. "A yagna with a kshatriya as the ritvik and a chandala the sacrificer! We wonder how the Devas will take havis from the hands of a kshatriya, and the offerings of food from a chandala."

When Kaushika heard this, his eyes blazed with old enmity. He cursed Vasishta's sons so they became nishadas. The rishis at Kaushika's sacrifice were already frightened of him. They had heard of his fiery kshatriya temper, and now they had seen proof of it. Those brahmanas sat quiet and pliant, while Kaushika addressed them in his reverberant voice.

He brought Trishanku before them and cried, "This is King Tri-shanku of the Ikshvaku line. Vasishta's idiot sons cursed him to be as you see him now, only because he had a small desire that seemed un-natural to them. Trishanku doubts that even the rishis of the world can send him up into Devaloka. Munis, with your help, I mean to have him achieve what he wants."

The rishis knew there would be grave consequences if they did not help him. This wild man was no brahmana, but a kshatriya turned a rishi. Of course, they did not for a moment believe he would succeed in sending Trishanku up to Devaloka in his untouchable's body. The Devas would hardly countenance such an insane enterprise; why, they would never take havis from a kshatriya, especially on a chandala's be-half. But those sages felt threatened by Kaushika. They had seen how his eyes burned under his great brows when he cursed Vasishta's sons. They agreed at once to participate in his yagna. After all, how could it harm them?

Kaushika sat at the holy fire, like any brahmana yajaka. The other rishis sat around him, feeling uncomfortable because of who he was. But soon they marveled at how immaculately he conducted himself: enough to make any brahmana proud.

At the end of the yagna, Kaushika invoked the Devas to come down and partake of the havis, their share of the sacrifice. But silence answered his call, and no Deva appeared. The other rishis saw Kau-shika begin to quiver with anger.

Raising the sruva, the ladle with which he had poured ghee onto the flames, he cried, "Behold the power of my tapasya! Trishanku, I sacrifice all my punya to raise you into Devaloka."

A peal of thunder rent the sky. His face twitching with painful ef-fort, Kaushika cried, "Rise, O King, rise into heaven!"

As the congregation of rishis watched breathlessly, his hands folded to Kaushika, a smile of sheer rapture lighting his black face, Trishanku rose straight up from the ground and disappeared into the clouds.

But Indra was not pleased. He cried to the levitating kshatriya, "You are no Deva and your guru has cursed you. Trishanku begone, back to the earth where you belong!"

Trishanku plunged back to the earth, screaming to Kaushika, "Save me, Lord!"

Kaushika raised a hand over his head. Lightning sprang from it, and he cried to Trishanku in a tremendous voice, "Stay where you are!"

Trishanku fell no more, but hung suspended between heaven and earth. Then, like Brahma himself, Kaushika began to create another universe for that king. He made galaxies of suns, swirling nebulae in the southern sky. He created the seven rishis of the firmament, the planets. In the north, he made Dhruva, the fixed star; he made the Milky Way, the river of stars. He made other Devas and worlds of men, time, and every other creature. There was a commotion in heaven. The rishis of the sky and the Devas themselves appeared before Kaushika. With folded hands, they begged him to stop.

Indra cried, "We meant no slur to your greatness, Muni. Only, it is written that no man cursed by his guru may enter Swarga."

Kaushika roared, "Envious Deva, you lie! He is a righteous king and deserves heaven, not punishment. Hear me well, you Gods. A thousand Indras may come and go in the yawning ages, but Trishanku will stay where he is. And his universe shall remain around him."

Indra bowed. "So be it. Let the mandalas of Kaushika and his creatures live forever. Let Trishanku be a king of Devas among them, just as I am. Let his power and his fame be immortal."

The rishis and Devas went back to their domain, by skyways of light along which subtle travelers fly swifter than time. Kaushika, who had made Trishanku eternally happy, was left alone. Now he was broken in body, drained in spirit; for he had used up all his tapasya for Trishanku's sake.

Kaushika went west and sat beside a holy lake in a place called Pushkarakshetra: to earn once more all the virtue he had spent. He sat in tapasya in that lonely place, far from the presences of men.

Trishanku had a son called Harishchandra. Harishchandra had no sons and worshipped Varuna, Lord of the ocean. In streams of spectral light Varuna appeared before Harishchandra and said in his sea voice, "You shall have a son. But do you swear you will give him to me when he is born?"

Desperate as he was, Harishchandra swore he would. Within the year, with the ocean's blessing, the king's wife bore a son. Harishchandra called the boy Rohita, and he was as dear to him as his life. But he had not enjoyed his Rohita for a day when Varuna came to him and said in his voice full of the soft thunder of waves, "I have come for your son, Kshatriya. He was the offering of your sacrifice."

Harishchandra said quickly to the Deva of the deeps, "O Varuna, a newborn child is unclean. Come for him in ten days."

Ten days later, Varuna came to the king again, and said in his voice of moon tides, "I have come for your son."

Harishchandra said, "Lord of waves, a yagnapasu must have teeth. Let Rohita cut his teeth before I offer him to you in dignity."

When Varuna came again, Harishchandra said milk teeth were not enough, and let them fall; next, that the child's new teeth should grow; and later, that the Sovereign of the seas should wait until Rohita wore armor, because a kshatriya is pure only when he dons mail. And so on, making great Varuna seem like a collector who came, again, for a bad debt.

Meanwhile, Rohita grew up. One day, in anguish, his father told him about his pledge to Varuna. He said he could not put the Deva off forever. Rohita was terrified. Taking just his bow and arrows, he ran away from his father's palace, into the forest.

When Varuna heard, he cursed Harishchandra. He visited him with mahodara, an imbalance in the bodily fluids, and the king wasted from the terrible disease. Rohita heard about this in the jungle and started back to offer himself to the Sea God. But Indra accosted him on his way, appearing suddenly before the boy, effulgent. The Deva king said to Rohita, "Go on a yatra to all the tirthas, and your father will recover."

Rohita went to the sacred rivers. He bathed in them and worshipped their divine waters. Word reached him that Harishchandra was well again. Rohita returned to his hideaway in the forest. But in a year, Varuna's affliction returned to Harishchandra. Again, Rohita set out on his pilgrimage to the tirthas. His father got better once more. But after a year, the mahodara returned to Harishchandra more virulently than before.

Five times this happened. Then, one day, when Rohita was on his tirtha yatra, he met an impoverished brahmana traveling with his wife and three grown sons, who were about the same age as the prince himself. A bizarre idea struck Harishchandra's prince. He said to the brahmana, whose name was Ajigartha, "My lord Brahmana, I will give you a thousand cows if you let me have one of your sons."

Ajigartha wanted to know a little more. Rohita told him all about himself and his father and the offering to Varuna. The brahmana and his wife stood listening carefully on that path in the wilderness. Ajigartha said, "I cannot part with my eldest son; he is like my life to me."

At once his wife cried, "I will not give you my youngest, he is like my very breath. It is always thus, prince. The oldest is the father's favorite, and the youngest the mother's."

Now they both looked at their second son, whose name was Sunashepa. That boy stared in disbelief at his parents. In a stricken voice Sunashepa said, "Rohita, take me with you. My mother and father have sold me for a thousand cows."

It was high noon, one day, when Sunashepa and Rohita arrived at Pushkara. Rohita fell asleep at the foot of a tree. Sunashepa sat numb with grief that his own parents had sold him for some cows. He was thirsty and hungry, and he knew he was to be sacrificed to Varuna. Suddenly, the brahmana's son saw Kaushika sitting under another tree in dhyana. Sunashepa ran to the rishi and flung himself at his feet.

Startled out of his samadhi, Kaushika saw that a fine young brahmana lay before him, crying. At once his soft heart was full of pity. Stroking the boy's head, he said, "Tell me, child, what grieves you? I will set it right."

Sunashepa sobbed out his story. He said, "I do not want the yagna for which my father sold me to be spoiled, Kaushika. Nor do I want to die. I want to live long, so I can do enough tapasya to reach Swarga. Help me, Muni; I have no one else to turn to."

Kaushika summoned his own sons. He said to them, "Which of you will go to his death in place of this unfortunate child? You are rich in punya by your very birth. One of you can easily be the yagnapasu at Harishchandra's sacrifice."

But his eldest son, Madhuchandas, thought his father was joking and began to laugh. Kaushika's other sons laughed with him. Madhuchandas said, "Father, how can you sacrifice one of your own sons because an orphan comes and cries at your feet? Next, you will tell us to eat the flesh of a dog."

His old enemy, rage, sprang up hotly in Kaushika. His eyes flashed and he cried, "A son who disobeys his father is not worthy of being called a son. Be you all chandalas like Vasishta's sons. And you shall indeed eat the flesh of dogs for a thousand years!"

His boys fled howling from there. Kaushika was lost in thought for a while. He turned to Sunashepa and said, "Go with Rohita to the sacrificial stamba. They will tie you to the post with ropes purified with mantras. They will smear your body with red sandalwood paste and drape wildflower garlands around your neck. I will teach you two slokas. You must sing them at the yagna, and no harm will come to you. And the yagna shall be complete as well."

Sunashepa learned the secret hymns from Kaushika. He went back to Rohita, who still lay asleep, and shook him awake. "Come, my prince, let us hurry to your father's sacrifice. I am prepared for what befalls me."

Rohita embraced him. The prince was glad the wonderful brahmana boy had accepted his fate with such serenity. They went to Harishchandra's palace. The king lay on his sickbed in a dark room, because no light should touch him. Five men carried Harishchandra to the yagnashala.

They tied Sunashepa to the yupastamba. They smeared him with the red paste of sandalwood and adorned him with garlands of gay flowers, as an offering fit for a God. Suddenly, the boy began to sing in his unbroken voice. He sang so sweetly: the magical slokas Kaushika had taught him. At first the singing was greeted with silence; it was so unexpected. But when the people realized the meaning of the songs, they began to cheer the brave child.

Two unearthly flashes of light lit the yagnashala, and Indra and Varuna himself appeared before Sunashepa to bless him. Because of Kaushika's brilliant songs, Harishchandra was forgiven by the Lord of oceans. But the king had learned a lesson from his long illness: that excessive putrasneha is a curse to any father. Now he wanted to go himself to Kaushika and learn the profound brahmavidya from that rishi.

Meanwhile, Kaushika's hundred natural sons agreed to accept Sunashepa as their eldest brother, and their father took back his curse. From that day, all the descendants of those hundred and one were known as Kaushika, and that was also their gotra.

For a thousand years, Kaushika sat in tapasya beside Brahma's sacred lake in Pushkara. One day, Brahma came to him, glorious, and said, "Be known as rishi from today, Kaushika. For you are more than a rajarishi now."

Kaushika, the rishi, allowed himself a smile. But he was determined to be Vasishta's equal, a brahmarishi yet. He went north to the Himalaya to continue his penance.

Indra was worried. So powerful was Kaushika's tapasya upon the Himalaya, Indra was anxious he would lose his place as the Lord of heaven. Also, it was the Deva's very dharma to test the penance of the rishi who had once been a king: to upset its fervent solitude with sweet temptation.

Indra called Menaka and said to the apsara, "Kaushika shines like a sun by his tapasya. He will have my throne if he continues. Go and tempt him with your charms. Make him forsake his dhyana and you will please me."

But she demurred. "This is a kshatriya who became a rishi. He cursed Vasishta's sons to be chandalas. This is Kaushika who created another universe for Trishanku that you are asking me to seduce. He is quick to anger, Indra, and I fear him. Surely, he is beyond temptation such as mine."

But the Deva king coaxed her; he threatened her. He promised he would be at hand to rescue her from the rishi's wrath, if it was roused. With Kama, the God of love, and Vasantha, the spring, and Mandanila, the breeze who unsettles men's minds with desire, all going before her, Menaka went reluctantly to Kaushika's tapovana, where he sat in padmasana with his eyes shut and his spirit yoked.

She waited patiently, that apsara whose beauty and lovemaking were a legend in Devaloka. One day, Kaushika, who had sat motionless for a month, opened his eyes. He rose for a bath in the nearby mountain stream. He came to the sparkling water, overhung with wildflowers blooming madly on the trees with the untimely spring. His mind was pleasantly stirred by the crisp mountain breeze that blew around him. The unsuspecting Kaushika saw there was a woman already in the stream: a woman of such incredible beauty that before her his own queens of old were less than plain. He saw her bathing naked in the rushing current, giving little cries as the icy water stung her golden skin.

Kaushika saw she was not of humankind. He waded into the freezing flow and found her too willing to yield to him. They lay entwined on the vivid moss, half in and half out of the water, and now Menaka's cries rang among pale ridges.

His tapasya forgotten in the apsara's arms, Kaushika took her to be his new devotion in that permanent spring. Ever watchful at the wings of their sometimes torrid, sometimes languorous lovemaking, Indra was delighted. Five years went by, and another five. Then one morning, when a great deal of his punya was exhausted, Kaushika awoke with the thought burning him that he had been tricked by Indra. Who else could have sent Menaka to him?

In rage, he confronted his apsara. She confessed everything, and stood shaking before him. But he knew that, though she had once come to cheat him, she loved him now. In as much sorrow as anger, he cursed her to be parted from him forever. He left her sobbing while he went north again, higher up the mountain, to resume his broken tapasya.

Kaushika went to the banks of the river now called the Kaushiki. She was his own sister, flowing through the world as a blessing. He sat on her banks and sunk himself in dhyana for another thousand years. Brahma came before Kaushika again, with the Devas in train, and he said, "Kaushika, I name you maharishi, O greatest among the sages of the earth."

Kaushika was unmoved, either to joy or disappointment. Bowing to the Pitama, he asked quietly, "Tell me, my Lord, have I perfect control over my senses?"

Brahma smiled and shook his head. "No, you are not yet a jitendriya."

Kaushika looked downcast, and Brahma said kindly, "But you must become that also."

Kaushika sat amidst five fires now, in summer: four he stoked around him on burning rock, and the fifth was the sun above. He ate nothing and held his arms stiffly above his head. In winter, he sat naked in the frozen river. The flame of his penance swirled up into the spiritual dimensions as a burning mist. Indra called another apsara, Rambha, and said to her, "Go and seduce Kaushika from his tapasya. He who has fallen once, can be tempted again."

But Rambha was terrified. "He won't be deceived twice," she cried. "And he will curse me to some dreadful fate, for he doesn't love me as he did Menaka."

But Indra said, "I will be on the mango tree beside Kaushika, with Kama beside me. In the tree from which the koyal will sing."

Kaushika was startled out of his tapasya by the sweet warbling of the cuckoo. He smelled spring flowers on the autumn air. Already suspicious, he opened his eyes and saw lovely Rambha standing before him, wide-eyed and fluttering long lashes. It was in the heart of a deep jungle that Kaushika now sat. He knew at once the woman who stood before him could not have come to this place unless she had been brought here. Besides, this was familiar, and he knew whom she reminded him of.

He cursed her, "Indra sent you to steal my punya from me. Be a stone and live on earth for a thousand years. So no one will be tempted for so long by your beauty."

Instantly, Rambha was turned to stone. But no sooner had the curse flown from his lips than Kaushika regretted it. He cried in anguish, "Brahma was right. I have not mastered my anger yet!"

He went away from there, to perform an even more severe tapasya. So he could quell not only the passions of his body, but the rage of his mind as well. Kaushika sat for another thousand years on the highest Himalaya. He was thin as a twig; his hair hung lankly to his waist. The spirit fire of his tapasya issued from his attenuated body, and began to scathe Devaloka. And though the Devas often put provocation in his way to incite him, he seemed immune now, beyond anger.

One day, after he had starved for years, he broke his fast and cooked himself some rice. Just as he was about to eat the first mouthful, an emaciated brahmana came begging for food. It was Indra, come to test the tapasvin. Without a thought, Kaushika gave him all he had cooked and went back to his dhyana.

By the hour, Kaushika's tapasya grew fiercer. He had mastered even his breathing and respired no more than twice or thrice in a day. Powerful emanations billowed from his head, plumed through the higher realms, and the Devas had no peace in their heaven.

They went to Brahma and said, "Kaushika blazes in tapasya. Even the sun is lusterless beside him. Oceans rise in fury and mountains spew lava from their crowns. The earth spins out of her orbit and cosmic storms rage through the mandalas. If you do not give him what he wants, his dhyana will consume the three worlds."

Brahma came shimmering before Kaushika, who sat utterly absorbed. In some haste the Creator cried, "Welcome, welcome to the highest fold, O Brahmarishi!"

A wan smile cracked the gaunt face of the hermit on the mountain.

He said to Brahma, "Let the Vedas recognize me as a brahmarishi. Most of all, let your son Vasishta, who began my journey, acknowledge that I am his equal."

They brought Vasishta to Kaushika. Brahma's son embraced the muni who had once been a king, and cried, "You are a brahmarishi, Kaushika; there is no doubt about it!"

At last the storm in Kaushika's heart subsided. Because he was so full of compassion that he could never refuse anyone who came to him in need, regardless of the cost to himself, they named him Viswamitra.

GLOSSARY

abhichara Sorcery; also, a spirit raised by an occult ritual.

abhichari A sorcerer.

abhisheka An investiture.

achamana The ritual sipping of holy water from the palm of one's hand.

acharya A brahmana master.

adharma Evil.

adharmi A sinner.

Adi Kavya The First Poem; the Ramayana.

Adisehsa Great Serpent; also, Vishnu's rest, his serpent bed.

Aditi Mother of the Devas.

Aditya The Sun God; also, twelve demigods associated with the Sun God.

Adityahridaya An ancient prayer; "heart of the sun."

agneyastra A fire weapon or missile.

agneyi Self-immolation by invoking inner fire.

agni Fire.

Agni The Fire God.

agnihotra The fire ritual.

agnihotrashala A place where sacred fire burns, where the agni lotra is performed.

agni pariksha Trial by fire.

aindastra Indra's astra.

aindra Indra's astra.

Airavata Indra's four-tusked, white, flying elephant.

akasa The fifth element, cosmic ether.

aksauhini An army or legion of 21,870 chariots, as many elephants, 65,610 horses, and 109,350 foot soldiers.

Alakananda The Ganga (Ganges).

alidha The archer's stance.

amavasya The new moon.

Amravati Indra's heavenly city.

amrita The nectar of immortality.

amsa Essence; part.

Anantasesha The cosmic serpent; also, Vishnu's rest, the bed upon which he lies.

anarya An ignoble person.

Angaraka The planet Mars; he is also a God.

anjali An offering.

antapura A harem.

apradakshina Counterclockwise, or inauspicious, circumnavigation; the opposite of pradakshina.

apsara A nymph.

aranya A jungle.

arghya An offering of welcome.

artha Wealth, possessions. Artha is one of the four goals in life (the others are dharma, kama, and moksha).

Aryaman The first man; ancestor.

asariri A disembodied voice.

asokavana A grove or thicket of asoka trees.

asrama A hermitage. The four asramas of life are brahmachari (celibate), grihasta (householder), vanaprastha (renunciate), and sannyasi (hermit).

astra A supernatural weapon.

Asura Any of a class of demons.

aswamedha yagna A horse sacrifice.

aswattha A pipal tree.

Aswins Heavenly twins, known for their beauty.

Atharva The fourth Veda, concerned with sorcery.

atibala Extreme strength.

atman The individual soul.

AUM, OM A holy syllable that represents the ultimate reality.

Avatara An incarnation of a God, especially Vishnu.

ayana A journey.

ayudha A weapon.

bala Strength.

bhakta A devotee.

bhakti Devotion; worship.

Bharatavarsha The land of Bharata; India.

bhasma Holy ashes.

Bhumi The earth.

Bhumi Devi The Earth Goddess.

bhuta Spirit; ghost.

bindu Point; mystic singularity.

braahma A weapon of Brahma.

Brahma A God of the Hindu Trinity; the Creator.

brahmachari A celibate.

brahmahatya The murder of a brahmana.

Brahmaloka Brahma's realm.

Brahman Ultimate Godhead.

brahmana A member of the priestly caste; also, "Brahma's people."

Brahmarishi A sage of Brahman.

brahmashakti Brahma's feminine power or weapon.

brahmastra Brahma's astra, known for its protective powers.

Brahmavadi A knower of Brahman.

Brahmavidya Knowledge of Brahman.

Bramadatta A bow Rama used against Khara.

Brighu An ancient rishi.

Brihaspati The guru of the Devas; also, the planet Jupiter.

Budha The planet Mercury; he is also a God.

Chaitra An auspicious lunar month; also, Kubera's garden.

chakra A wheel: in the body, a subtle center of energy along the spinal column and in the brain. See also *Sudarshana chakra*.

chakravaka A mythical bird, a symbol of despairing love.

chamara A whisk made of silk threads.

chandala An untouchable.

chandana The sandalwood tree.

Chandra The Moon God.

charana An unearthly being.

Chiranjivi A long-lived, almost immortal person.

chital A kind of deer.

Chitraratha The king of the gandharvas.

choodamani A hair ornament.

Daitya Any of a group of demons, sons of Diti.

Daksha A Prajapati who was Brahma's son and Sati's father.

Danava Any of a group of demons, sons of Danu.

danda A staff; also, punishment.

darbha A kind of grass.

darbhasana A seat made of darbha grass.

Deva Any of a class of celestial, elemental beings; God; also, "Being of Light."

devadaru The Himalayan cedar.

Devaloka The heavenly realm of the Devas.

devastra The astra of the Devas.

Devi Goddess.

Dhanu The constellation Sagittarius; also, a God.

dhanusha A bow.

Dhanvantari The original physician, who rose from the sea of milk with the amrita.

dharma Truth; justice; duty.

Dhruva The North Star.

dhyana Meditation.

diggaja One of the elephants that support the world. There are four diggajas.

Dikpala The lord of a direction.

diksha A gift or offering for a brahmana.

dumarus A two-sided hand drum beaten by stones attached to it by string.

dundubhi A percussion instrument of the Gods.

durdina An evil day.

dwapara yuga The third great age.

dwarapalaka A gatekeeper or sentinel.

Dwividha A powerful vanara chieftain.

ekarnava The original sea of life.

gaandharva An astra of the gandharvas.

gana A servitor of Siva.

gandarvastra An astra of the gandharvas.

gandharva Any of a race of heavenly minstrels.

Garuda Vishnu's Eagle.

Gayatri The mother of all mantras.

ghee Clarified butter.

gochara A planetary transit.

gotra Subcaste, clan.

guna An essence of nature. There are three gunas: sattva, rajas, and tamas.

guru A spiritual teacher or guide; master.

gyana Knowledge, wisdom.

Halahala The original poison, which Siva drank.

Hari Vishnu.

hatya Murder.

havis The offering from a sacrifice.

Himavan The Himalaya.

Hiranyagarbha Pregnant with the Golden Egg.

homa Ritual worship.

Ikshvaku A king, founder of Rama's royal House of Ikshvaku. A race of the Sun is named after him.

Indra A God, the king of the Devas.

Indradhanush A rainbow.

Jambavan The king of the bears.

Janaki Janaka's daughter, Sita.

Janardhana Vishnu.

janma nakshatra A lunar birth star.

jata Dreadlocks of the kind rishis wear.

jatakarma A caste ritual.

jaya Victory.

Jaya vijayi bhava! "Be victorious!"

jitendriya One who has conquered his senses.

jivatma An embodied soul.

jrumbhana An astra.

kaala Time.

Kaali The black Goddess.

kadamba A tree.

kali yuga The fourth and the most evil of the ages.

Kama, Kamadeva The God of love.

Kamadhenu The first, sacred, cow of wishes.

kamandalu A brahmana's water pot.

Kama shastra The sacred arts of loving.

kanchana Golden.

kankana A bracelet.

kanya A virgin; maiden; young woman.

kanyadana A gift given by a bride or young maiden.

kanya sulka Bride-price.

karma Action; duty; also, the fruit of past deeds.

Karttikeya Siva's son.

Kaumodaki, Kaumodiki Vishnu's mace.

kavacha Armor.

kavya Poem.

kinnara Faunlike being, known to ask riddles.

kinnari Female kinnara.

kirtana A devotional song.

Kodanda Rama's bow.

koyal A cuckoo.

krita yuga The first of the four ages; the purest, most pristine yuga.

krodhagraha A room reserved for being angry in; "chamber of anger."

krosa A measurement of distance.

kshatriya A member of the caste of royal warriors.

Kshirasagara A mythical sea of milk.

Kubera A Deva who is Lord of treasures.

kula A clan.

kulaguru The teacher of a royal family.

kulapati The head of a clan.

kundala Earrings; studs.

Kurma The Tortoise: Vishnu's second Avatara.

kutila A hut.

lagna An ascendant, rising sign.

Lakshmi The Goddess of fortune; Vishnu's consort.

linga Siva's phallic emblem; phallus.

loka World; realm; dimension.

Lokapala The Gods; the guardians of the four quarters; also, the world.

Madhuvana A vineyard.

magadhi A bard, singer.

maharathika A great warrior.

Mahavishnu Vishnu.

mahima siddhi The occult power to grow big and small.

mahodadi A great sea.

mahodara Consumption.

malaya Of a mountain.

Manasa sarovara A holy lake in the Himalaya that Brahma made from his mind.

manavastra An astra.

mandala Dimension; galaxy.

Mangala The planet Mars.

mantapa A pavilion.

mantra A sacred incantation.

Manu An ancient king and lawgiver.

Margasirsa, Mrigasirsa An auspicious Hindu lunar month.

Marut A companion of Vayu, the Wind God. There are forty-nine Maruts.

matrihatya Matricide.

Matsya The Fish; Vishnu's first Avatara.

maya Illusion; cosmic illusion.

Maya The Goddess of illusion.

Mayaa A great demon builder and king.

mayavi A sorcerer.

Mohini The Enchantress; Vishnu as a woman.

moksha Liberation; salvation; enlightenment.

moolabala Ravana's crack legion, the principal source of his power.

mowna Silence.

mridanga A two-sided percussion instrument.

mudgara A weapon.

mudra A hand sign of occult power.

muhurta A small measure of time; especially, an auspicious moment.

muni A seer; rishi; also, silent one, knower of minds.

musth A male elephant's season of rut.

naga A great serpent; also, a magical, serpentine being.

nagapasa An occult serpent noose.

nagina A female naga.

nairrita A race of otherworldly beings.

nakshatra Any of the twenty-seven asterisms in lunar Hindu astrology, considered stellar Goddesses and wives of the Moon.

nalika An astra.

Nandana Indra's garden.

naracha A fiery missile.

Narada An ancient sage, the son of Brahma. He was said to have been born immaculately from Brahma's thought.

naraka Hell.

Narasimha The Manticore; an incarnation of Vishnu.

Narayana The Sleeper on eternity's waters, which are called the Naara; Vishnu.

Nilakanta The Blue-throated One; Siva.

nilgai A species of deer.

nirvana Moksha; liberation.

nishada An untouchable.

nyagrodha The pipal tree.

OM The primal, holy syllable; AUM.

oshadhi A healing herb.

paapa A sin.

paasa A noose.

paativratya Fidelity.

padadhuli Dust—or a spiritual emanation—from an honored person's feet.

padma A lotus.

padmaka A variety of tree.

Padmanabha Vishnu; "lotus-naveled." Brahma is born in the lotus that sprouts from Vishnu's navel.

padmasana The lotus posture.

paduka Sandals.

padya Water for washing the feet.

pala A variety of tree often inhabited by spirits.

palasa A variety of tree.

panchabhuta The five elements: earth, water, fire, air, and ether.

Panchajanya Vishnu's conch shell.

Parabrahman Brahman The ultimate, undifferentiated Godhead.

Paramatman Supreme Soul; God.

Parasurama Bhargava The Ax-bearer; an incarnation of Vishnu.

parivrajaka A mendicant holy man.

Parvati Siva's wife; "Mountain-daughter."

Patala The underworld; netherworld.

pativrata A devoted wife.

paurnima, purnima The full moon.

payasa A liquid sweet.

pinda An offering to the dead, usually consisting of rice balls.

pipal A holy tree.

pisacha An evil spirit.

Pitama, Pitamaha Grandsire. Often used for Brahma.

pitr An ancestor; "father."

Pitriloka The realm of the manes.

pradakshina A walking around a person or thing in reverence.

pragvamsa In this case, one end of a cross-beam.

Prajapati A lord of the first races of men.

pralaya The deluge.

prana Life breath.

Pranava AUM.

prayaschitta Penance.

prayatna A difficult endeavor.

prayopavesha A fasting for a cause or boon.

preta A spirit.

puja Ritual worship.

Punarvasu The asterism under which Rama was born.

punnaga A tree.

punya Virtue; merit.

Purushottama Vishnu; "best among men."

Pushkara A lake sacred to Brahma.

pushpaka vimana Kubera's sky chariot, used by Ravana and later Rama.

Pushyami The asterism under which Bharata was born.

putrakama yagna A sacrifice for the birth of a son.

putrasneha Attachment or love for one's children.

raga A traditional musical scale of at least five notes.

Raghuvamsa The clan of Raghu, an ancient king.

Rahu A demon; "dragon's head."

Rajarishi A royal seer; a king who is a sage.

rajasuya A great sacrifice of emperors.

raksha Protection; protective amulet.

rakshasa A demon.

rakshasi A demoness.

Ramarajya Rama's rule.

ratha A chariot.

raudastra Rudra's astra.

reeksha A bear.

rekha A line of power.

Rik Veda, Rig Veda The first Veda.

rishi A sage.

ritvik A priest.

Rohini An asterism and a Goddess, the Moon's favorite wife.

Rudra Siva; also any of eleven fierce beings associated with Siva.

rudraksha Holy beads; "Siva's tears/eyes."

sabha Court; hall.

Sachi Indra's consort.

Sadhya A minor divine being; a lesser God.

sakhi A female companion.

Sama A Veda.

samadhi Absorption in the Soul/God; mystical trance.

sambur A species of deer.

samsara The world of illusion.

sanatana dharma Eternal righteousness, justice.

Sanatkumara One of four original sages, born from Brahma's mind.

sandhi Conjunction; cusp.

sandhya Twilight.

Sankara Siva.

sannyasa The condition of being a hermit.

sannyasi A hermit.

sannyasini A female sannyasi.

Saptarishi Seven sages born from Brahma's mind.

sarabha A great mythical bird.

saras A lake.

sarasa A water bird.

Saraswati Goddess of learning; Brahma's consort.

sarathy A charioteer.

Saringa Krishna's bow.

satsangha Sacred, auspicious company.

Senapati General; "lord of the army."

shakti Feminine power or weapon.

Shantam paapam "Evil, be still!"

Sharada Autumn.

Shastra Scripture.

shimshupa A kind of tree.

Shravana A lunar month between mid-July and mid-August.

siddha A self-realized being.

siddhi An occult power.

sirasasana A headstand as a yogic posture.

sishya A pupil; disciple.

Siva A God of the Hindu Trinity; the Destroyer.

sivalinga A phallic emblem of Siva.

sloka A sacred verse.

Soma The Moon God; also, lunar nectar.

srarddha A death ceremony.

sruti A tone or octave.

sruva A ladle.

stamba A post or pole.

sthula Gross; corporeal.

stotra Hymn.

Sudarshana chakra Vishnu's weapon, a blazing wheel.

sudra A member of the fourth Hindu caste.

Sukra Venus, guru to the Asuras.

sukshma Subtle; incorporeal.

sumangali A fortunate wife.

Surya The Sun God.

Suryanamaskara A yogic ritual for worshipping the sun at dawn.

suta A bard.

swaapana A weapon of sleep and dreams.

swamini A woman swami or saint.

swapna A dream.

Swarga Heaven.

swayamvara The ceremony at which a princess chooses her own husband.

taala A rhythm; beat.

tamas The third and grossest guna, or essence, in nature.

tandava Siva's dance of dissolution.

tantra vidya Black or occult arts.

tapasvin One who sits in tapasya.

tapasya A long period of penance, meditation, or austerity.

tapovana A grove of worship.

tarpana An offering of water for the dead.

tilaka An auspicious mark placed on the forehead.

timmingala A mythical whale-eating beast, possibly the giant squid.

tirtha Sacred place.

treta yuga The second great age.

trikalagyani One who sees the three times.

Trimurti The Hindu Trinity; Brahma, Vishnu, and Siva.

tripathaga Of three paths.

Tripura Three sky cities, built by Mayaa, which Siva brought down with a missile of fire.

trisula A trident.

Usanas The planet Venus; also, a male God, guru to the Asuras.

Uttara Phalguni One of the nakshatras or lunar asterisms.

vaastu shanti A rite for peace in a new dwelling.

vabdhi A singer, bard.

vabdya magadha Songs in praise of a king, with which he is awakened each morning.

vaidurya Lapis lazuli.

Vaikunta Vishnu's celestial city.

vairagya Detachment.

vaisya A member of the third Hindu caste, the traders.

vajapeya A sacrifice.

vajra Indra's thunderbolt.

valkala A fabric made of tree bark, worn by hermits.

Vamana The Dwarf; Vishnu's fifth Avatara.

vana Jungle; forest.

vana devata A forest God.

vanara A member of an ancient, magical race of monkeys; "dweller in the vana."

vandhi A singer, bard.

vanika Wood.

Varaha A boar; Vishnu's third incarnation.

Varuna The God of the oceans.

vasantha Spring.

Vasu A class of Gods.

vayavyastra A wind weapon.

Veda Any of the four ancient collections of sacred Hindu prayers and hymns. There was originally only one Veda, which became four.

vedi, vedika An altar.

vetala A hunter.

vetali A huntress.

vidyadhara A magical being.

vikarni An astra.

vimana A sky ship.

vina An Indian stringed instrument, similar to a lute.

vina nadam The song of the vina.

vishalyakarani A potent herb of healing.

Vishnu A God of the Hindu Trinity; the Preserver.

Viswakarman The divine artisan.

vrata A vow

vyuha A battle formation.

yaama Yama's astra.

yaga, yagna A sacrifice.

yagnapashu A sacrificial beast.

yagnashala An enclosure for a sacrifice.

yajaka One who undertakes a yagna.

Yajus Veda, Yajur Veda A Veda.

yaksha A forest spirit.

Yama The God of death.

yamala A tree.

yantra An occult symbol.

yatra A journey, often with religious significance.

yatudana A demonic being.

yoga "Union"; union with the Self, with God.

yogi, yogin One who, through yoga, is united with his higher Self or with God.

yogini A female yogi.

yojana A measure of distance; "league."

yoni A vagina or vaginal emblem.

yuddha A war.

yuga An age.

yuganta, yugantara A conjunction of two ages; time of change.

yuga sandhi The cusp between two yugas.

yuvaraja A crown prince; heir apparent.